SCARS

{ONE CHILD'S PAINFUL CRY FOR LOVE}

Mam,

Always know that you are loved and remembered!

Love,

By: CANDACE YVETTE COLE

Published & Distributed by:
Milligan Books
an imprint of Professional Business Consultants
1425 West Manchester, Suite B
Los Angeles, California 90047
(323) 750-3592

Cover Design by Hubert Sam

Formatting by
Precious Opal Johnson

First Printing: July 2001
ISBN:1-881524-98-1

COMMENTARY

"SCARS" is a raw, deeply felt testament to God's transforming power at work in broken lives. Candace Cole writes as one who's been there and has lived to tell about it — in all its grit and glory.

> Dr. Ron Elmore, Bestselling Author,
> "How to Love a Black Man" and
> "How to Love a Black Woman"

"SCARS" is a powerfully written story of survival and ultimately, deliverance from multiple traumas. It paints a poignant picture of the suffering and misfortune of a young african american woman as she struggles through the pain of misery and abandonment. Candace Cole fearlessly takes us through her own aching story, detailing the seamy undersign of neglect and mistreatment and the accumulative impact on a precocious young child. Discarded and exploited by both adults and children in her search for love and meaning, this effectively written account concludes by indicating that redemption is always possible through the power of faith. Thus, we see that even a gnarled tree can bring forth beautiful fruit, and an amazing flower can bloom in the most desolate of surroundings.

A compelling saga, Scars is "must read" for any young woman who wonders whether she can rise above the disturbing complications of her own life. Many young women wonder whether they will survive the horrors of their own childhood. Candace Cole demonstrates not only can they survive, they can be "reborn".

> Darryl M. Rowe, Ph.D.
> Psychologist, Nubiant Psychological Group

"SCARS" is a journey to find God.

Contrella Patrick-Henry, Theatrical Producer, Psalmist

SCARS. "A mark that remains after an injury has healed." After reading this book, a mark was left on my heart. A mark of compassion and admiration for the author.

Shelia Miller, Designer

"SCARS" is a unique depiction of one child's incredible journey from resilience to triumph. In the proceeding pages readers will be touched by a non-stereotypical, bright little girl's desperate cry for help.

If you've ever doubted the reality and lasting effects of child abuse, then this book will be a definite eye-opener. It will strategically walk one through the necessary stages that precede healing, despite the victim's inability to make sense of the abuse.   However, the unfortunate reality is, victims aren't the only ones struggling with the complexities and ramifications of such hideous acts. Society as a whole has become stuck in a state of confusion and denial. Though such acts are no longer considered taboo, they're still uncomfortable. As a result, silence and non-responsiveness have become the antidote. In the interim, our youth are falling victims to such acts at an alarming rate, with too few avenues to turn to for healing and restoration. That's why this book is so enlightening. It takes you beyond the surface of the abuse, to the core of the victim's suffering. This book is therefore a must read for anyone who has a true compassion for the brokenhearted.

Opal E. Johnson, School Counselor
Long Beach Unified School District

In Loving Memory

This book is in memory of my mother, Doris Mosachan-Woods.
How I wish that I could tell her
"Momma be at peace because God turns scars into stars."

You are forever and ever treasured in my heart,
for the timely love, laughter and tears that
we were finally able to experience.

 Dedication

*To all the hurting children in the world that have not
been able to speak or tell of the unbearable
secret pains that you have
to live with.*

*Trust in God at all times
and he will bring you through.*

*"When Father or Mother abandons you,
God promised to be your parent."
Psalms 27:10*

To My Brothers & Sisters

Earnie Mae Johnson
Gary Burton
Stephanie Liggins
Ted Liggins, Jr.
Tisinc Liggins
Charles Woods
Eric Woods
Charolotte Woods
Bernice Woods
Alvin Brewer, Jr.

To My Extended Brothers & Sisters

Melody Stephens
Cynthia Forrest
Lisa Smith
Ray Smith
Nikki Alexander

Influential Women

STRONG AFRICAN AMERICAN WOMEN WHO HAVE INSPIRED & STRENGTHENED MY LIFE!

Dr. Maya Angelo

Dr. Beverly Bam Crawford

Dr. Mary Alice Haye

Pastor Joyce Johnson

Dr. Ann Lightner

Ms. Estella Liggins

Dr. Rosie Milligan

Bishop Vashti Mckenzie-Murphy

Pastor Diane Collins

Pastor Jewell Turner

Ms. Wendy Wise

Ms. Oprah Winfrey

Doris Woods {My Mother}

Special Thanks

To my friends, colleagues and family members who have read and given input on the formation of Scars. I want to thank you for the tireless hours spent reading this voluminous manuscript, which is now a book. I so appreciate your friendship, love, support, and the sacrifice of time spent away from your families to have occasional meetings regarding Scars. Such outpouring of love allowed me the opportunity to birth this very long overdue baby into the earth realm. Only God knows the depth of appreciation and gratitude I have towards each of you.

To the following persons, thank you so much:

Maureen Anderson
Pastor Charles Brooks
Alvin Brewer
Marla Chusac
Rusty & Ann Coleman
Hurley & Carstella Cook
Dr. Ron Elmore
Teresa Francis
Maura Gayle
Earline Gentry
Pastor Mary Alice Haye
Contrella Patrick-Henry
Pastor L.A. Kessee
Opal Johnson
Linda Jones
Pastor Anthony & Michelle Johnson

Tracy Leggins
Ted Liggins
Cheryl May
Sheila Miller
Sultan Muhamed
Dr. Clyde Oden
Emily Owens
Danita Patterson
Wendy Readus
Pastor Gwen Rollins
Dr. Darryl Rowe
C-Von "Drummer Man"
James & DeEtta West
Wendy Wise
Kasey Whitney
Pastor Betty Hanna-Witherspoon

Acknowledgements

To God, who literally gave me the power, strength and charge to write SCARS, and loved me through each page.

Thank You Heavenly Father!

- Anna Alves, I thank you for bringing Scars from mere diary entries to manuscript with your skilled directions and wisdom. May God continue to bless your incredible editing gift. You have been more than a blessing to me. Thank you for being on the editing team of Scars and making such great contributions.
- Alvin Brewer, my daddy and prayer partner. I thank God it's never to late for true restoration, forgiveness and love.
- Dorothy Brewer (Mommy), I thank God for our breakthrough and for your willingness to share my dad. For allowing truth to be our only foundation. I love you!!!
- Sydney Butler, you have been an incredible inspiration and truly a guiding light. Lets do coffee and apple pie when you get time, now that Scars is finished.
- Ann Colemon, your patient ear in 1992 helped me get to the next phase of Scars. Thank you so much for hanging in there with me.
- Georgia Mae Cole, a mother for life. I love you.
- Carstella Cook, the best God-Send and God-Mother an adult child could ever wish for. You mean so much to me.
- Aunt Doris, thank you for buying my first journal, when I was just a young child. You started this writer to writing. Little did you know why.
- Rev. Kevin Dotson, my friend and mentor. What a charge you had. Thank you for your obedience.

- Dr. Ron Elmore, I am grateful for your words of courage during my journey through Scars.
- Cynthia Forrest, my big sister. Thank you for telling me how much you cared for me, at a time when I thought nobody cared.
- Teresa Francis, it's refreshing to know we can always "be real" with one another. Thanks sis.
- Pastor Mary Alice Haye, your ministry of encouragement has truly been a blessing.
- Mercy Henderson, your love, support and encouragement means the world to me. Thank you for always being there.
- Pastor Alvin Isaac, thanks for being my big brother during my times of transitions and being there when I needed "moving forward assistance" (smile).
- Pastor Freddie Johns, thank you for confirming that I had a story to tell way back in 1989.
- Anthony Johnson, your friendship throughout the years has been like gaining another brother added from God to my many siblings.
- Earnie Mae-Johnson, thank you for coming to Fresno in 1975. You will forever be my hero!
- Pastor Joyce Johnson, I am indebted to you for introducing me to the concept of counseling. Sister-to-sister, you are the best.
- Michelle Johnson, thank you for your professional input during the last editing sessions of Scars. And thank you for allowing me to cry on your shoulders when the editing got to be a bit too much.
- Opal "Precious" Johnson, you will think twice from now on before volunteering your sweet, benevolent, editing assistance to a "crazy" preacher. You took my dream book to the final line, with excellence. I'm so glad you survived. I didn't think it was possible to gain another sister, so precious and loving, that would bring such joy to my life. I love you and thanks a million!
- Sujey Chavez-McCowen, my lovable god-child. Thank you for compiling the index of names for Scars. Now, finish writing your own book!

- Daphney McQuarter, I love you baby. You are a special daughter.
- Sultan Muhamed, my love. You will always be treasured in my heart.
- Dr. Clyde Oden, your years of friendship and mentoring has been priceless.
- Albert and Betty Seay, my third set of parents. Your unconditional love will always be special to me.
- Melody Stephens, Superwoman, Bat Girl and my Shero. Thanks for always being there when I needed you most.
- Vickie Strogin, thanks for the years of friendship and pushing me forward.
- Jewell Turner, a sister beloved. I will never find another quite like you. When I was afraid to love you taught me that love doesn't always hurt.
- Ted and Estella Liggins, my second parents in Phoenix, Arizona. Thank you for accepting me, with love, as part of your family. And thank you for telling me the truth, even when it hurt you too. God knew I needed more than one set of parents and I'm so glad he chose the two of you.
- Dr. Darryl Rowe, your wisdom, knowledge and hours of investing your sound truths have been a major encouragement in my life. Thank you.
- Dr. Karen Williams, thank you for sharing healing moments. I am forever grateful.
- Wendy Wise, can you believe it, we both survived Scars. I treasure the times that we have cried, laughed and healed together, and I'm so glad that we can rejoice in the midst of it all. Always know I love you and you are very special in my heart.
- Kevin Yourman, words will never be adequate to express my appreciation of knowing you. You have a heart of gold and thank you so very, very much for sharing it with me.

STEPHANE GIBU

Your presence in my life has been a breath of fresh air.
Your unique wisdom and vast knowledge, I respect.
If angels really do exist in human bodies
I've met my first angel, in you!

Contents

Introduction

"You're only as sick as your secrets!", My counselor screamed in frustration. I had skated around the details of my issues for three weeks, only giving partial facts. I figured, she could fill in the blanks of what I didn't say. She wanted me to say it, but I didn't want to. She kept prying, as if trying to uncork a wine bottle. I thought to myself, how could she be so insensitive to make me explain repeated traumas that I had suffered while growing up. I just wanted the pain and confusion to go away. I wanted the fake smiles that I wore faithfully everyday to finally be real. That's all. I didn't want to relive anything.

Over the past thirty nine years I have experienced how secrets can truly make you sick; physically, emotionally, mentally and spiritually. It was the side affects of these deep hidden secrets that compelled me to write Scars. Further, I was advised and encouraged by a friend and counselor, Mr. Sydney Butler, that writing Scars was a must for my life and for so many others in the world. He once said, "By the time you finish this book God will have truly healed you and those around you." That statement was spoken in 1989. I agreed to do so.

Twelve years later, Scars is a reality. Scars was not a joy ride, but a rough journey back to scary, obscure places that I thought I had escaped, to never return again. I estimated that it would only take me a few years to complete it. Little did I know I was in for a decade plus assignment. I soon found myself hitting emotional roadblocks that threatened my continuation. There were times when I would place my manuscript back on the shelf and say "the hell with it. I'm not doing this book. it's too painful. I don't want to deal with it." One of the factors I had not realized, was the fact that I was no longer drunk off of hennessy or high off of marijuana or PCP, but at this point in my life I was an excited Born Again Christian, who no longer used substances. So, I was now looking at Scars with sober eyes. I was now writing it in first person and finally telling it, with my own voice, that was once threatened to silence and secrecy, and undergirded by shame and guilt.

Year after year I would take it off the complacency shelf and make a bold attempt to began again. Ironically, I would run into Mr. Sydney Bulter, who would always greet me with a gracious smile. After his greeting, with lots of zeal, as if he was waiting on the first copy, he would inquire of the status of Scars. Often times, ashamed and feeling guilty for abandoning my assignment, I would tell him it's coming along.

The pain of reflecting and walking back through those dark years of my life, at times the pain was crippling and unbearable, but it had to come out. There was no more room on the inside of me to keep it all in. Yet it seemed like not enough paper to print it all down either. But I knew I had to keep going. I knew at the end of the story victory was eminent, because I was still alive.

I found myself getting into a very distractive mode when it came to Scars. Something else would always come up and even if nothing did, I would create something else. I would write many things, as long as it wasn't Scars, I was fine. And so, two books and several stage plays later, Scars yet screamed out of the womb "complete me, it's my time."

When running from completing Scars was over and the voice of God made it apparent that I had neglected my first assignment, I began to work in haste, trusting that God would keep my mind and heart during the painful reflections that I would have to face, and He did.

ii

I made a decision to enter back into counseling for a short period of time for support, while going to the finish line. One of my counselors, Dr. Rowe, was so pleased that I was finalizing Scars. He said it was a courageous act. I told him how hard it was to still talk about it today. He smiled and said, "you've already done the hardest part." I asked in confusion, "What part was that?" "The hard part was living through it and you are here today, which means you survived it."

I must admit, I had many concerns and fears about writing Scars. My first concern was with the *Institution of Psychology*. Throughout the years, I knew I needed counseling, but I was afraid to be stereotyped and judged. I was also afraid that the counselors could not relate to what I was saying. Even if they did, would they believe me as so many did not. One of the most significant lessons learned through my experience with counseling was accepting the reality that God gave counseling, and it is healthy and helpful. If I can take my tooth ache to the dentist and my hurting body to the doctor, I can certainly take my confused mind and shattered heart to a counselor and obtain help. I learned that emotional pain is sometimes more devastating than physical pain, because scars underneath the skin are often underestimated. Where I was once afraid and ashamed to admit I was hurting, I soon learned it was natural to say "ouch".

My second concern was the *Institution of Religion*. Upon committing my life to the Lord, I was bombarded with wonderful, positive affirmations of who I was in the Lord. I was erroneously taught that everything painful that happened in my life is over and to leave the past in the past. Though it sounded good the fact was, it was my pain which drew me to the altar, seeking a God that could heal me.

To my demise, my type of pain was not discussed. Nor was a platform in place to deal specially with the areas of hurt, which existed in me. Instead, the affirmations of who I was in the Lord kept being reemphasized.

Many years later, I learned that I was living a superficial and pseudo religious life. I was not serving God in spirit and in truth, because I could not walk in the truth of who I was and where I was emotionally. I was led to believe that saved people don't suffer from the past, if they are really saved. Frankly speaking, the reality was that this particular church, like so many others, was not equipped to handle abuse such as mine. In addition, they were not able to compassionately and scripturally walk me through a process of healing. I was tired of going to church shouting and clapping, then going home still filled with emotional pain. I knew there was more to God than just sweeping my issues under a carpet of shame and denial, as if He could not handle my stuff or didn't want to be bothered with it.

I had many concerns and my thoughts were saying "You cannot tell this story. What will people think of you now?" On the other hand, after ministering to hurting women, abused children, and damaged men, my calling transcended any personal fears that tried to stop and silence me again. I have been purchased with a price far above this worlds worth of silver and gold. Consequently, liberation and healing has finally come.

Mr. Sydney Butler, thank you so much for seeing what I could not even imagine or phantom to conceive in my mind.

"They overcame by the blood
and the words of their testimonies."
Revelations 12:11

This book is in no wise intended to judge or offend anyone, but to expose the perverted, vicious and damaging truth of abuse and the realities of their transgenerational side affects.

SCARS

CHAPTER 1

THE FIGHT

We all jumped at the same time! We had never heard a noise like that. It sounded just like a big firecracker. Then we heard loud screams. My brothers and sisters ran to the window to see. They were pressed against it trying to look out. Gable told Tyrone it was coming from Roy's house across the way. I squeezed between my sisters Sadie and Tarah's because I was the shortest, but I could still see from the bottom of the window where the little ants crawled in and out. I was scared. I didn't like screams. The screams were getting louder and louder. Then the wooden screen door to Roy's house flung open. We saw a lady backing up out of the house across the way crying reaching her hands out, screaming.

"Please Roy, Please Roy, I'm sorry."

I heard Gable tell Tyrone, that's Gladis, Roy's wife. Her red see through pajama top was torn off her shoulders and that man Roy was crying and yelling at her. He grabbed her hands and then he grabbed her neck. "Woman I dun takin care of you with everything I got, and you do me like this." He was a big man and Gladis was a little woman. He hit her in her face and it look like her head almost turned all around. I covered my eyes, it hurt to see. Sadie and Tarah were jumping and saying ouch. When I took my hands off my eyes, Gladis' mouth was full of blood and it was coming out as she was still screaming that she was sorry. He was still hitting her. I guess he didn't hear her say she was sorry. Now her eyes was almost closed because he beat her in her eyes too. Grown people from next door were coming outside and yelling stop to Roy, but he didn't. One of them was Ruthie Armstrong, my mother's friend. Then there was more loud screaming sounds. Tyrone said "here comes the police". Just when he said that a tall man came out of Roy's house with blood all over his shirt and hands. Tyrone said he mustav been shot. He had a knife in his hand. I covered my eyes again. Then Sadie said "here comes the police". Two police cars drove up and they jumped out. The police men ran over and grabbed Roy off of Gladis because she was laying on the ground. They put Roy in the back of the police car. Then a lot of ambulances came and picked Gladis up and put her on the bed. The big man was put in another ambulance and they drove off.

Some of the police stayed and talked with the neighbors. That's when Gable told us to get out of the window before they see us. We went back to watch cartoons. I kept on thinking about that lady, hoping she would be okay because of all that blood and stuff. I wondered what she did to Roy that made him so mad to hurt her like that. When we sat back down, we missed all of Road Runner cause it was going off.

Over the loud TV, we heard grown people talking as if it was right outside our front door. One of the voices sounded like Momma's friend, Ruthie Armstrong who lived next door to Roy and Gladis. We heard her talking, telling someone all kinds of stuff about our Momma being gone.

"Mister, there are five kids in that apartment. They're hungry, dirty, and they Momma don't care for them. I saw the oldest boy in the garbage can looking for food to feed the rest of his sisters and brother," she said.

It sounded like Ruthie was telling off on Momma to somebody and we didn't know who. She even said that our mother didn't come home sometimes for days and nights at a time. It was all true, but Momma would eventually come home and sometimes, she would even bring us something.

"Mister, they live right there." We heard her say.

Suddenly, there was a loud knock at our door. Gable jumped. He looked at us and put his finger over his mouth. Shhhhh. Gable got up and went to answer it.

"Who is it?"

"Is your mother home?" a man asked.

"She just went to the store and will be back later,"

Gable told him.
"My name is Dean Smith and I am from the
Fresno Child Protective Services." Gable's face
changed when he heard those words.
"Could you please open the door, son?"
I could tell Gable didn't want to open it by the way he looked back
at us, as if we were trapped. He slowly opened the door, standing
very close to it, as if he was hiding us. A tall white man and a
equally tall black woman stood there. Though they were smiling, I
felt they were not nice people. The white man wore a dark suit.
The woman wore a red suit with red shoes. The man, said he was
Dean, and asked Gable where our mother was one more time.
Momma had not been home in a couple of days, but I wasn't going
to tell on her. I jumped up off the couch and ran over to Gable,
clinging to his knees.

I don't remember how we got there, but the next thing I do
remember is a tall building The lady in the red suit walked slightly
in front of us leading the way. She was talking to the white man.
I squeezed Gable's hand tightly as we walked toward this big
building. I kept looking up at Gable, wondering where we were
going, but he stayed quiet.

Once we were in the building, there were more voices but we
couldn't see them. The voices got louder as we came near the
rooms, one on each side of the hallway. Men and women were
passing us, smiling. We heard sounds of children playing and babies
crying. I saw children laying in beds asleep, some looking at TV
and others just looking up at the ceiling. I wished for my Momma.
I wondered if my brothers and sisters were wishing for her too. I
grabbed Sadie's hand. Why wasn't anyone saying anything?

We finally came to a white woman sitting behind a desk. I could
tell she knew the lady in red by the way she talked to her and called
her Helen. The white woman explained to Helen that they were
taking my sister Sadie and my brother Tyrone to one place and that
they were taking Gable to a different place. I cried as they took

my hand out of his. Gable cried too. That was the first time I saw him cry. Helen told my sister, Tarah, that she and I would stay in this building, together. I was getting more scared by the minute. Gable was the only one that made all of us feel safe when Momma was gone. Now they were taking him away from us. We went to a room with two beds in it, but I slept with Tarah.

Sometimes when Tarah had to leave for a long time, a tall dark man would come in the room. He was real big and fat. He had a big stomach. He scared me. He looked so mean at me when he made ugly faces and grabbed me real hard. I started crying, hoping Tarah would come back and catch him scaring me. He put his finger on his mouth and said shushushu, don't say anything. Soon as he grabbed me, the door would open and somebody called him.

After that day, I jumped off the bed and ran to the other side of the room every time the door opened and it was him. He told me he was going to get me. I wished someone would hear him and get him in trouble. I started crying. Someone would call him each time he started coming to get me. I tried to hide from him in the closet one time after Tarah left. I wished my Gable was here, because Gable would get him for scaring me.

One night, I asked Sadie when were we going home. Tarah said the woman in the red dress told her that our daddy is coming to get us. I didn't remember my daddy too good. I missed Momma. I hoped Momma would come back too.

Then one day our Daddy came to get us with a beautiful lady named Ms. Estee. They put us all in their big car. I was so happy, because that's when I saw Gable, Tyrone and Sadie again. We hugged each other real tight. When Gable, Tyrone, Sadie and Tarah saw Daddy they were real happy too. They remembered him. On the same day we all got back together, Daddy told us that we were going to live with him and his wife, Ms. Estee in Phoenix. We were excited but I was sad because Momma wasn't going with us.

CHAPTER 2

November 1966 – Living In Phoenix

Daddy and Ms. Estee had a big pretty house that was clean inside.
Living with Daddy and Ms. Estee was different than with Momma.
Daddy and Ms. Estee were home every night. And when Ms. Estee
left the house, she came back like she said. Daddy was funny. He
was so tall, like a giant. He always wore baggy, dirty jeans and
liked to drink scotch and milk. He was real nice though. Ms. Estee
was tall too like Daddy, and looked like a Barbie doll. She smiled
all the time and hugged me a lot.

Me and my sisters slept in one bed together in our own room. The
boys had their own room too. We also had breakfast, lunch, and
dinner every day. Daddy and Ms. Estee never left us alone. We
had a set time to wake up and a set time to go to sleep. Just like a
family suppose to be. Ms. Estee was not my mother, but you
could tell she was a real mom, because she was always there for us
whenever we needed her. Sadie and Tarah started to call Ms. Estee,
"Momma" but I could not. I still wanted my real Momma and
dreamed that she would come back to get us one day.

Daddy was the best mechanic in Phoenix, Ms. Estee told us. He
worked on cars in the back yard everyday. Sometimes, Ms. Estee
would take me to her job when day care was closed. She always
made me feel special, always kissing and holding me.

Living with Daddy and Ms. Estee was not boring and sad. They
did a lot of fun things with us. We went to the parks and to fun
places like Splash Mountain, where we played in the water and
raced down the slides.

We lived in Arizona almost a whole year and then my dream
finally came true. One day when Ms. Estee and I came in the
house from day care, my real Momma was sitting in the living

room with a man I had never seen before. I ran over to her so fast
and Momma hugged me in her arms real tight. She told me how
much she missed me while she was crying, and then told me her
man friend's name. His name was Willie McBride. He nodded at
me and said hi. He was a very dark man with white hair. Momma
said his hair was premature gray. Momma told everybody, his
nickname was the Grey Ghost because his hair was as white as his
teeth. Momma held me tight again, and I began to cry too, hoping
she would not leave us again. I didn't want her to ever let me go. I
was beginning to think she had forgotten about us. As my brothers
and sisters came into the house, they hugged Momma too.

"So what brings you to Phoenix, Doris?" Daddy
asked.
Momma lit up a cigarette and took a long puff.
"My children Tyrone. What the hell you think
brought me here, not yo ugly ass."
"Doris, what do you want," Daddy asked Momma
again. Ms. Estee looked like she was getting scared,
because she started walking back and forward in the
living room, not sitting down.
"Doris, have you forgotten what the judge told yo
ass ?"
"What are you talking about, Tyrone ?"
"The judge declared you to be an unfit mother. You
don't know how to take care of kids because you leave
them all by their damn selves."
"Fuck you, you left too. Plus you don't know what
the hell you're talking about. That damn Rosie
lied on me, I was only gone for a few hours."
Momma was talking back to Daddy real fast.
"Bullshit, Doris, you were gone for days. The
boys already told me what yo ass do."

Gable and Tyrone put their heads down when Daddy said that.
They didn't know that daddy was going to tell on them. I didn't
know what an unfit mother was, but I knew it wasn't nice the way
Daddy said it.

Momma asked Daddy again if she could take her kids back home. Daddy walked over to momma and told her to read his lips. "Hell naw," he said, standing over her. Her man friend just looked at Daddy and smiled. Momma started crying. Momma told him that she learned her lesson and would never leave us like that again.

Gable, Tyrone, Sadie and Tarah went to their rooms. I stayed next to Momma. Then she asked if she could at least have me. Daddy told her that he had to sleep on it and told her to come back tomorrow.

That night, I wondered to myself if Daddy was going to give us back to Momma for keeps. I loved Ms. Estee because she was a really nice Momma, but I wanted to be with my real Momma. When Momma said she would be back in the morning, I was scared to let her go. I was hoping she would come back.

The next morning, I was waiting for Momma to come back. After we ate our cereal, we went into the living room to watch Saturday morning cartoons. Momma didn't come back that morning, but she came over later that night. We were in the bathroom taking our bath when we heard Momma's voice. Tarah was already in the bed and only Sadie and I was left to take our baths. After we dried ourselves off, Sadie and I went into the living room to say hi to Momma. Momma and Daddy were talking about us going home with Momma. Daddy told Momma again, he had to think about it.

It seemed like Daddy had to think about letting us go home with Momma for almost a year. Momma had to get a job and a place to live while she was waiting for Daddy to think about letting us go with her. Her man friend stayed in Phoenix too, waiting for Daddy's answer.

One morning, Momma came to the house and said it was time for her to go back to Fresno.

"Look Doris, I'm not giving you all these kids
back. You can have Carla."
Momma smiled so big.
"When can I have the rest of my, kids, Tyrone?"
"You take care of Carla first. Lets see how that
goes."

Momma was happy and mad at the same time.   Then Daddy told
her to take care of me, and she better not ever leave me alone.
Saying good-bye to my sisters and brothers was so sad. I wondered
why we had to be separated again. I didn't understand why grown
people kept us apart. Why did I get to go with Momma and not
my other brothers and sisters?   I was happy to be with Momma,
but I was sad that I was leaving them. Ms. Estee held me, crying.
She told me to be good and to stay cute.

Momma had bought some furniture, so her man friend rented a U-
Haul truck. He hooked it up to his blue and white, 1964 Buick.
I climbed into the back seat and laid down. I was thinking about
Momma's boyfriend Willie McBride and if he would be my Daddy
now.
"Momma, what should I call your boyfriend?"
"Call him, Mister Willie," she said.
"Okay."   I slept all the way back to Fresno.

CHAPTER 3

February 1967 – Return To Fresno

Momma and Mister Willie found a little shack house off of a street called Clara. Momma said we live in a shot gun house. The first room was a living room, very small with wood floors. Mister Willie put Momma's dark green couch against the wall. He also set a little TV in the corner on top of a TV stand. Then he put Momma's old coffee table, the one that had the cigarette burns on it, out. There was one window in the living room with a wooden green baseball bat so no one could get in. The second room was the kitchen, and as you entered the floor made a funny squeaking sound. To the left was a white refrigerator and stove. To the right there was a sink with a small window above it. The last room was my mother's bedroom where Mr. Willie put Momma's secondhand dresser drawer and her queen size bed. It almost filled the entire room. She put her multicolored quilt on her bed. Momma told me why her quilt was so special.

"My mother made me this quilt when I was at
home." My eyes got big.
"It's pretty, Momma," I told her.

It was beautiful. Lots of colors. I liked Momma's quilt too because I could trace the squares and match the colors like a game. I asked Momma if we were sharing rooms and she told me my bedroom was in the first room on the couch. I didn't care long as I was with Momma.

Then I noticed something weird. The bathroom was missing. I asked Momma about it, and she laughed, taking me by the hand and leading me outside. There was a wooden room, about as big as the shack we lived in and it was green too. Inside was a wall between the shower and the toilet. A shower curtain was hung on a clothes wire. There was a light and a long string to pull when you needed to turn the light on and off. Because I was so short, I didn't know how I would ever reach it. I had to grow some more. Momma explained to me that this bathroom was called an outside toilet and that we would have to be really careful when using it at night. I remembered thinking, how did they forget to put the bathroom in the house?

Later that night, before I fell asleep, I remembered thinking about my sisters and brothers. I wondered what they were doing. But I was so glad to be with Momma. She came in to cut off the lights and kissed my forehead.

"Good night, Momma, I love you."
"Momma loves you too, baby."

The next day, Momma told me that we were going to meet our neighbors. So we walked around visiting everyone. In the first shack, we met a couple named Jean and Buddy who did not have children. Jean was a short, dark woman with a fat face and a little bitty mouth, with a scarf on her head, tied in the front. She looked just like an Aunt Jamima bulldog. Buddy was short and brown with slicked back red hair. I had never seen a man with red hair. Momma said his hair was conked. He had red skin too, and looked like an Indian man. Jean hugged me and told Momma she thought I was cute. They asked me my age. I told them I was 4 years old because I had just turned four when I lived with my Daddy and Ms. Estee. Momma forgot, but I didn't.

The next shack belonged to a little lady named Donna who lived alone. She was old with a lot of white hair and moles on her face. It looked like little bugs all over her face. I tried not to stare, but couldn't help it. She was also thin and humped over. Donna didn't invite us in. So we said hi and left. I noticed there were no kids in her place either. So far, I was the only kid on the block. "Who would I play with," I wondered. On our way back to our own shack, Mr. Oliver came toward us. He was real tall, fat and jolly with a big cigar in his mouth and a tall hat on his head that matched his tan pants. He reminded me of a black snowman with deep dimples in his jaws. Momma introduced him as the security guard, gardener, and landlord. Mr. Oliver thought that was funny and laughed. He had the funniest laugh you ever wanted to hear and when he laughed, it came from his toes all the way up and out through his mouth. He said, "Welcome, little princess!" I said "hi." That was the end of our day. Momma and I watched TV together the rest of the day.

I was happy now because I was with my Momma. Momma didn't leave me like Daddy told her. We went everywhere together on the bus visiting Momma's friends, shopping at the store, down to the county office to get our stamps. Momma and I ate hot dogs and pork-n-beans all the time. Though when we had dinner with Jean and Buddy, Jean cooked good food like greens, beans, pot roast, and chicken. When we went over to their house, Buddy would tell me to jump in the bed and look at TV with him while Momma and Jean were in the kitchen. It felt like I had two Momma's and one Daddy. Buddy liked to watch Gunsmoke, and he especially liked "Ms. Kitty," who was the prettiest woman in town.

As the weeks went by, I didn't see Mister Willie very much. I didn't know where he was or what he was doing, but Momma stuck to her word about never leaving me alone. She didn't let me out of her sight, even taking me with her to night clubs.

Going to clubs with Momma was weird and scary sometimes. Once we got to the clubs, she would hide me in a place where grown ups couldn't see me. She told me not to come out until she came to get me. These places had funny names like Juicy Pigs, Sugar Hills, Jericho, and Hunts. Her favorite place was called "Under the Trees." It had green palm trees and a wooden hut like on Gilligans Island, but bigger.

The club also had pool tables, a juke box, and two bars (one at each end of the hut). It was scary to me, but for grown-ups I guess it was okay. It was always crowded. Loud music could be heard miles and miles away. When Momma went to the clubs, she would put on one of her hot dresses. She had this black shingle dress that came above her knees and a black feather head piece with sequins, that tied in the back. I loved to watch Momma get dressed, especially when she put on her red lipstick. She was so pretty. Momma looked like that woman name Tina Turner who she like to watch dance on late TV. She reminded me of Tina Turner because when she danced, she always did the fast shaking dance.

The first time she took me to "Under the Trees," she hid me in a corner under one of the pool tables. She told me to be real quiet and stay out of sight. Then she partied the rest of the night. I looked around to see if other parents brought their children, but I was the only one there.

Going out with Momma always felt like a secret game where no one was supposed to know I was around, especially the owners. She taught me the "my shadow" game. I was suppose to follow closely behind her, like her shadow, so that it looked like she was alone. Once we got passed the front door, she would take me to my usual hiding place. Once I was there, I kept her black high heel shoes in my view. I would listen for her fast talking voice because I could hear her most of the time cursing over all the other voices. Momma would go from man to man, bar to bar, drink to drink, cigarette to cigarette, laughing, talking, flirting, and sometimes fussing and fighting with people. All the men called her that "crazy Indian woman" with a quick temper, who drank too much whiskey. Momma never waited to tell someone to go to hell. If that didn't satisfy her, she would fight them.

One night, a man made Momma real mad. The next thing I knew, the man was flying across the pool table, head first. Momma had picked him up and threw him. She was very strong. I wanted to run to my mother so bad, because I just knew after that man got up, I would have no more Momma (but the man was knocked out). I saw so much at those clubs; ladies throwing up on themselves and falling out, men hitting women and knocking them down, and men stealing out of womens' purses. I didn't like it so when I thought I was about to see something bad I would close my eyes real tight, or put my head down between my knees.

The mornings after Momma went out, she would wake up mad with what she called a "hangover." But Momma always knew how to get rid of it. She would drink a can of V8 juice and by noon time, she would feel a lot better. The first year with Momma was just like this all the time.

On Fridays and Saturdays, we would go over to Jean and Buddy's. More friends of Jean and Buddy's would come by and play cards. They played a game called Bid Whiz. They would start off having fun and would always end up yelling and shouting. They would drink and play cards real late. Then after they finished playing cards, off to the clubs we would go.

I will never forget this night that Momma got put out of a club. We walked in as usual. Momma took me to my hiding corner and went to the bar to sit down. I saw this tall fat woman go over to Momma after she sat down. The lady did not look happy at all. While she was talking to Momma she was pointing in different areas of the club. It looked like she was looking for something. I finally figured it out - she was looking for me! She turned right and looked right at me, in my little corner clear across the room. She told Momma that she had to leave. Momma kept trying to talk her out of it, but the lady didn't budge. When I saw Momma rise from the bar and start walking in my direction, I knew something was wrong. "Let's go," Momma said. She was so mad. I could tell because her eyebrows came together, and she started biting the bottom left side of her lip. People were looking at us as we left.

As Momma and I walked down the dirt road, a man in a black truck drove up along side of us and asked Momma if she wanted a ride. I was glad, because it was dark and cold. Momma got smart with him and asked the man, "What the hell do you think?" I figured to myself, maybe we won't get a ride after all. The man pulled over so we could get in. This man knew Momma from the club. He told Momma he overheard the woman telling her to get her kid and go home and that's why he came out to drive us home. It was not a good night for Momma, and I felt bad for her. I felt it was my fault that she could not stay and party with her friends. I wondered if she regretted coming to get me from Phoenix now. "Momma, I'm really sorry we had to go home," I whispered in her ear. "That bitch don't know who she's fucking with," Momma said, ignoring me.

The next morning Mr. Oliver came for the rent. Momma didn't have a job, but she got a welfare check and food stamps for our hot dogs and pork-n-beans. After Mr. Oliver collected the rent and left, Jean knocked at the door. Jean always came over in the mornings to ask Momma how the night before went. Momma told her about last night. Jean told Momma if she wanted to go out to the club tonight, she would baby-sit. I smiled because I liked Jean and Buddy. Plus, I wouldn't have to listen to that loud music, cursing, fighting and have that nasty smoke in my face. Momma was happy and took her up on her offer right away. Jean reached her arms out to me for a hug then told me that we would watch TV until we fell asleep. Momma didn't mind, so I was there every weekend.

Living with Momma felt lonely sometimes. Though I was with her a lot, I still felt alone without my sisters and brothers and friends my age. I would often think about how my sisters and brothers were doing in Phoenix. I missed them so much. I knew they were having fun because when I was there, Daddy and Ms. Estee took us to fun places. Then I thought I shouldn't complain, because Daddy did tell Momma not to leave me. I guess Momma was just keeping her promise by taking me everywhere. Yet, I still felt lonely. I couldn't help but think and feel I was in her way.

Head Start School

Weeks later, I heard Jean and Buddy telling Momma about a school called Lincoln Elementary which had a Head Start program. They were trying to get Momma to enroll me. They told me that I would like it because there were kids there my age and I could make some friends. I was excited about that, because I had not been able to play with anybody in a long time. My first day in school I tried to be a big girl, but I cried when Momma and Mr. Willie dropped me off. Though she kept telling me she would be back right after school, I was scared that she would forget I was there.

The teacher came to the center of the room. She introduced herself to the class as Ms. Richards. She was a white woman with long golden hair wearing a blue and white uniform. I also had to wear a uniform. I was happy about that, because it was like buying new clothes. Jean and Buddy helped Momma pay for my uniforms. I saw Buddy and Jean give Momma money and tell her she better not buy any drinks with it.

After school was over, Momma came and got me. She had told the truth about coming back. I was bouncing off the walls when I saw her. I couldn't wait to tell her what a great day I had with all the kids my age and the things that we learned. Momma talked with my teacher for a few minutes. We walked down the school halls toward the car where Mr. Willie was waiting for us. Momma told me that my teacher said I was a good little girl today. I was glad.

"So how was your day, Carla?" Momma opened the back door for me to get into the car, Mr. Willie waved.
"I had fun, Momma. We had to tell each other our names, where we lived and how old we were. Then we had a snack, and they taught us how to bless our food."
"Oh you did."
"Yes, we put both hands together like this. Then we closed our eyes and thanked God for the food. Ms. Richards said it is God who gave it to us and we ought to thank Him for it."

As I was talking, I showed Momma how we did it.
"What else did you learn today?"

"I learned that God made everybody and that He
loves us a whole lot. And that He protects us
from evil people."
"That's true," Momma agreed.

After some time went by, Mr. Willie couldn't give us a ride
anymore because he got a job working in the mornings.   Walking
to school was fun because there were days when dogs would try to
chase us, and Momma would curse them out and throw rocks at
them.   I would be running and laughing along with Momma.   It
was so funny! We passed by lots of houses that had dogs.

One night Momma asked me if I knew the way to school by heart.
I told her I thought I did, and that I would show her. I could not
wait to get up to take Momma by the hand and guide her to my
school.

The next morning, it was time for show and tell.   Momma didn't
have a clue how I knew, but I knew the way because of the houses
and people I remembered seeing on the way. Like the old couple
we nicknamed Momma Emily and Poppa Ernest, because we would
speak to them every morning.   Then there was the tall pink
neighborhood grocery store, named "Everybody's Market," right
across the street.   They used to tell Momma every morning that
they were going to "steal me" from her. Before long, I led Momma
right to the front of the school gate, not only that day, but a lot
more.

Momma started calling me the smartest little girl in the world.
Those were happy days for me. I made Momma proud of me
every morning that I showed her the way to school. Some days, I
introduced Momma to the kids on the way so she could know my
new friend's names.

After school Momma and I would walk home real fast. She   said
she had important business to take care of. As soon as we would
walk in the door, I would pull off my school clothes, change and

Momma would rush me over to Buddyand Jeans's for the night.
Buddy was like a daddy not only to me, but to Momma too. One
day I overheard him fussing at her when she took me over there
from school.

> "Doris, when are you going to slow yo ass down
> and do something with yo life and yo child?"
> "Ah Buddy, all you doing is laying on yo ass
> everyday watching TV, claiming disability while
> yo woman go to work! So you don't say shit to
> me. I don't know what you're talking about!"
> "I'm talkin bout yo damn daughter, Doris."
> Buddy stood up from the couch.
> "Look, Buddy, I'm here everyday and every
> morning she wakes up," Momma told him.
> "Doris, this is your child and she needs a
> Momma, not someone who just picks her up and
> drops her off. You need to talk with her, go over
> homework, teach her something and spend some
> time with her!"
> "I don't want to hear that shit, Buddy." Momma
> grabbed the knob to the screen door ready to
> leave.
> "Well you goin hear it today, because we ain't
> baby-sitting for yo fass ass anymore."

I started crying. I felt bad for Momma. It felt like I was making a
lot of problems for Momma again. It also felt like nobody wanted
me around, including Momma. After Buddy had his last say,
Momma told him she would find another baby-sitter and we went
back home. Momma was mad again. I wanted to tell Momma
that she could let me stay home by myself and I would take care of
myself real good and then she could go out.

One Saturday morning, I woke up and Momma was playing her
blues. She was sitting in the kitchen with her friend Olivia drinking
on some Schlitz Malt Liquor Beer and smoking her Winston
regulars. Olivia was a tall, thin, dark skinned woman. She was

pretty too, with short nappy hair. I remember seeing Olivia at the clubs. She cursed a lot too, just like Momma. Momma told me that I would be spending the night over at her place from now on. I was happy because she told me she had kids my age. That same evening I met Olivia's five kids; Meely, Phyllis, Phil, Karen, and Gino. Meely was tall and light.   Phyllis and Phil were dark skinned. I guess they took after their Momma. Then there was the older brother, Gino, and Karen, who was the youngest. Meely was a teenager and Phyllis and Phil were twins. When I saw them, I remembered seeing them walking to school. That night, Meely cooked us some homemade sugar cookies, and we sat up and looked at TV. I stayed over Olivia's every weekend. We played card games, like old maid and concentration.

Later that night something bad happened.   After Olivia and Momma came back from the club, we heard a lot of noise coming from the living room. We ran to the edge of the hallway, peeking around the corner to watch what was happening. Olivia and her cousin Catherine were in the living room.   I saw Olivia go to the door and tell Momma, "No, Doris, you ain't fighting in my house! Take yo ass home!" Momma was trying to get at Catherine. They called her "Cat" for short. Momma said, "Well give me my baby!" Olivia told Momma to wait until the morning because it was too late to wake me up. Momma insisted that she wanted me out now. Olivia told her not to start any trouble. Catherine was sitting in the den at the wooden dining table. They were all   drunk. Momma asked Cat, to tell her again what she had told her at the club. Cat crossed her legs, folded her arms and told Momma that she made her man (Willie McBride) holler and cry in bed last night. Olivia, who was on her way to the kitchen, turned around real quick to go stop Momma.   Momma had reached across the table with one hand, taking Cat by her throat, bringing her over the table choking her. Olivia started hollering, "Doris, stop that shit! Stop it! Let her go!"   Cat started choking and turning different colors. She was a light skinned woman so you could see the changes in her face quickly. Olivia couldn't take Momma's hand from around Cat's neck.

Suddenly, there was a loud knock at the door and then Mr. Willie walked in. He hollered at Momma as he was walked toward her and told her to let the woman go. Momma let Cat go and Cat fell to the floor choking and gagging still. He told Momma to get her ass home and wait until he got there. I came out from the hallway. Olivia's kids said goodbye to me as Momma took me by the hand, and we walked out. It was so dark and cold outside. It had to have been about three o'clock in the morning. We walked the whole four blocks home. Momma was crying and I just held on to her hand. She was mad too, but she marched home just like Mr. Willie told her. I wondered why Momma was crying. Was it what Cat said to her about making Mr. Willie cry last night in bed? Maybe Cat hurt Mr. Willie in bed, making him cry?

After we got home, Mr. Willie came in. He was real mad at Momma. I saw it in his face and I got scared. He went right over to where Momma was standing in the kitchen. She jumped back and he grabbed her by the neck. He started hollering at her. "What the hell is wrong with yo stupid ass? What the hell are you trying to prove?" Momma couldn't answer him because now he was choking her. He rammed her head against the refrigerator door, banging it, over and over again, real hard. I stood there crying feeling so helpless. I ran over to Momma and grabbed her leg. Mr. Willie screamed at me to go to bed. "Please, Mr. Willie, stop! You're hurting my Momma!" He stopped just long enough to shove me a few feet away from them. I fell on the raggedy wood floor and it felt like I got splinters in my knees. Momma was crying. I got so mad, looked around for something to hit him with and I remembered the green wooden bat in our window. But I was too short to reach it. I wished so bad that I could bang Mr. Willie's head in with it! I wished I could kill him for beating my mother.

Finally, he stopped banging her head and hollering at her. Then he went into the bedroom. Momma went to the other side of the kitchen where I couldn't see her, but I still heard her crying. I wanted to go in there and hug her but I was scared Mr. Willie would come out and push me away again. I lay there wondering to myself why they were fighting each other. Momma hurt that woman named Catherine and Mr. Willie hurt Momma. Mr. Willie called out to Momma to come into the bedroom. I got scared again. I was hoping Momma didn't go in the room, but she did and closed the door behind her. I prayed to God that Mr. Willie wouldn't hurt her anymore. A few moments later, I heard the bed banging against the wall and Momma sounded like she was hurting even worse. I was hoping it wasn't my Momma's head, but then I heard Mr. Willie saying things like "yeah baby, come on and give it to me like I like it. Yeh baby, yeh baby." I covered my head with the covers so I wouldn't hear them do their private stuff.

The next morning Mr. Willie was gone by the time I got up, as usual. When I saw Momma, her face was bruised on the left side. She was light like that woman named Catherine. I hated Mr. Willie for making my mother's face look bad with those blue and black shades on it. I used to think he was a nice man. I promised myself that when I got bigger, I would hurt him like he hurt my mother. Later that day, Buddy and Jean came by and saw Momma's face. When Momma told them what happened they shook their heads. Buddy told Momma that she needed to leave niggas like that alone.

> "He go cheat on yo ass and then turn around and
> kick yo ass for kicking his woman's ass who was
> talking shit. Doris, you crazy if you keep taking
> that kind of shit off of a nigga and his woman."
> Momma laughed, "Don't worry, I ain't finished
> with that hoe yet."

I didn't like to see my Momma fight or be mad. I hoped real hard that she would never see that woman again. After Momma's fight at Olivia's, I couldn't go over there anymore. At least, not until Olivia cooled off and her and Momma became friends again. So, Momma had to find me yet another baby-sitter. Then she remembered the old couple down the street, Momma Emily and Poppa Ernest. Ernest reminded me of Humpty Dumpty. He was a little red skinned man who was always dressed up. He always wore a little brown derby hat that matched whatever he had on. He also wore "Stacy Adams" shoes. He smoked a pipe that smelled really bad. Emily, his wife, was dark and round. But she was quiet. They adopted me as their little girl, just like Buddy and Jean had done when they first met me. Momma would take me over to their house for a visit after school. Their house was different from Jean and Buddy's. It smelled different, like medicine. That little one bedroom apartment was cluttered with clothes and papers. Poppa Ernest had a favorite chair which sat right in front of the TV. It was big and made out of brown leather fabric and felt real soft. When you sat on it, it sunk down because Poppa Ernest's butt print was still in it.

One Saturday morning, Momma Emily wasn't there when I was dropped off. Poppa Ernest was looking at cartoons. Momma dropped me off at the door and said she would be back later. Poppa Ernest closed the door. I was happy that Poppa Ernest liked cartoons too. He asked me to come sit down on his lap, and watch with him. I walked over and he picked me up and sat me on his knee because I couldn't reach him. While we were looking at the Flintstones, Poppa Ernest started rocking his leg and laughing. I loved the Flintstones too and I laughed with him. Poppa Ernest whispered in my ear, "Poppa loves you, Carla." I told Poppa that I loved him too. "How old are you?" I told him **four almost five years old.**" He told me that I was a big girl. Then he raised up my dress and opened my panties. He stuck his fat fingers in my privates. I didn't like that. I didn't know why Poppa Ernest was doing this. Then, Poppa Ernest put his finger inside my privates. I remember looking at Poppa Ernest and saying to myself, shaking my head, "Stop, Poppa Ernest, stop. It hurts me, Poppa Ernest." The words wouldn't come out of my mouth. He continued to rock back and forth with a great big smile on his fat face, his fingers playing inside me. He was hurting my privates real bad, so I started crying. He asked me to stop crying. He then asked, "Do you love Poppa?" "I do, Poppa, but you're hurting my privates," I was finally able to say. He ignored what I said and kept doing it with a smile on his face. He told me not to tell Emily or Momma about our secret little game. He played in my privates until I was sore. I was glad that Emily came home because Poppa stopped doing that to me and told me to go sit on the couch, way at the other end, closer to the TV. It hurt to walk.

I didn't like Poppa Ernest after that day. He was a bad man. I remember not wanting to go over there when Momma needed to take me to a baby-sitter. I started crying. Momma would get mad at me and tell me to stop acting like a spoiled child. I would tell Momma, please don't take me over there, I don't like it, Momma. She never asked me why. She would dress me quickly and tell me I was going over there and stop acting stupid like a cry baby. In Head Start, we learned that God sits real high in heaven and could see us down on earth. He could see everything that people do. He can protect you from evil. Poppa was doing evil to me, so I prayed. I didn't want to be there when Emily wasn't there, because Poppa might do that to me again. Each time she wasn't there, he did.

Buddy and Jean heard me crying and screaming real bad one time when Momma was about to take me over to Poppa Ernest. I screamed loud as I could, begging Momma "Please don't take me back over there." As we were coming out of our front door, Buddy was standing outside waiting on us.

> "Doris, why are you making that girl go over
> there if she doesn't want to stay with those
> people?"

Momma rolled her eyes and told him she needed to take care of some business for a while, so mind his own business.

> "Got damit! I'll keep her today. Just have yo ass
> back home tonight," Buddy said.

Oh I was crying, even more now, but for joy! God answered my prayers! I was so happy. I ran to Buddy. Buddy was a nice man and kept to himself. He didn't do bad things to me like Poppa.

He loved me as if I was a daughter. He loved me like a real daddy should, I suppose. I never told Momma what Poppa was doing to me. I kept it a secret. In fact, I forgot all about it, and pushed it far back in my mind so it wouldn't come up any more.

Momma knew Buddy and Jean were not going to keep me, so she had to find another baby-sitter. But she also knew I didn't want to go over to Momma and Poppa's house. So the next baby-sitter was a woman named Margaret, who lived up the street in a big white house.

Margaret's house looked like a big mansion with a upstairs and downstairs. It was the most beautiful house I had ever seen in my life. It had three bathrooms inside. One room alone was larger than our entire shack. They were rich people. You could tell by just looking at the furniture. It still had the plastic on it and they had carpet on all the floors except for the kitchen. Margaret had a son named Robert. Robert went to my school. I remembered seeing him there, a fat bald-headed boy. He liked to play baseball. That's all he wanted to do. When I would ask him if there were other games he liked to play, he would say "*no*", real mean to me. He never liked to do anything I wanted to do. It was always his way or no way. He would take the bat and make me the pitcher. After he hit the ball, I would have to go fetch it. I wanted to hit the ball sometimes too, but Robert always said no.

One day Robert grabbed the baseball bat, gave me the ball and said, "Come on, let's play." I told him, I didn't want to run after the ball today. Let me hit this time or I won't play. He got so mad, he started coming at me, swinging that bat in the air. As he got closer, I covered my head with my arms but he still hit me. Then he ran into the house. It hurt so bad, I couldn't breathe. I fell on the ground. As soon as I caught my breath, I got up and stumbled into the house. His mother asked me what was wrong. I told her what happened and all she said to Robert was, "Now you know better than that, Robert. Say you're sorry." He muttered under his breath that he was sorry. She pointed upstairs in the direction of his room, and Robert marched. I thought to myself, if that's all she was going to do, I would have done better by hitting him back up side his head with the bat too! I don't know what his problem was, but from then on I played whatever he wanted to play. I ran after every ball he hit. I did this until the day they moved away. I thanked God so hard. I got tired of walking on egg shells with that crazy boy.

The week after Margaret and Robert moved, Olivia came to the house. She told Momma her church was having a revival. Momma laughed.

"When do yo ass ever go to church, Olivia?"
"Doris, I go to church more than you!"
"You ain't lying about that. I had enough
 church when I was a child back in Bastroupe,
 Louisiana where I was baptized by my brother
 June Bug in a river with snakes in it."
"Damn, we did too girl." They laughed.

The next evening, Olivia came by to get us and we went to a church called St. Rest Baptist Church, where Rev. Riggins was the pastor. Olivia said it was in walking distance. We walked up the street and Momma and Olivia went into their purses and took a quick drink before going in. I didn't understand that. Didn't they know that God would smell their breath with that alcohol on it?

When we walked inside, everyone turned around to look at us. We sat in the last row. There was a man standing on the stage talking to the people. He looked back where we were sitting and smiled at Olivia. Olivia smiled back and nodded. Momma whispered in Olivia's ear, "You gave him some too." Olivia told Momma to shut up. I didn't know what Olivia gave him. A big gold cross hung behind him.

The church was real big inside with lots of people. The choir got up to sing about something called "Amazing Grace." They all had on red robes. The woman in the front sang mostly by herself. As she

sang tears rolled down her face.   Her right arm was up high and
her head shook side to side. I felt the song all the way to my tippy
toes. It gave me chills. I saw an old man in a dark suit jump up and
start walking, waving one of his hands in the air. He had a white
handkerchief in his hand. He was wiping his forehead, and then he
wiped his eyes. I never saw a man cry before. I looked around the
whole church and everybody looked happy. Some were fanning
themselves, others just nodding their heads smiling, and then there
were those that threw their heads back and waved their hands up at
the ceiling. I didn't know what "Amazing Grace" was, but I knew
it was good for you and that it came from God. From this song, I
learned that when you are lost that God will find you, and if you
ever lose your sight, He will give it back to you and you can see
again.

Out of the corner of my eye, I saw Momma crying but she didn't
seem sad. So why was she crying, I wondered. Maybe for the same
reason the girl singing the song was crying.   I looked at Olivia to
see what she was doing. She had a distant look on her face. Her
arms were crossed, and she rocked back and forward. Her purse
was still underneath her armpit as if she was about to run out of the
church. I didn't know why, because this place called church was
nice. I didn't want them to stop singing that song and I didn't want
to leave. I wished there was some way I could take that song home
with me to hear it over and over again. It was better than listening
to Momma's blues all day and night. Momma cried during those
songs too, but this was different. God's house made you feel so
good inside. I wished that we could come here more often.

After that song the preacher came back to the stage.   Momma
nudged me. I was at the end of the row, so I was the first one out.
I didn't want to leave, but Momma and Olivia were ready to go.

CHAPTER 4

February 1968 — 5th Birthday

My 5th birthday finally came around, and Momma threw me a party. I didn't have lots of friends, except for Olivia's kids. The rest were Momma's old friends. I don't know why they all came. I thought only kids should come to kids' parties. Momma made me a white cake with chocolate icing on it. This was the first birthday party I had with Momma. Buddy and Jean gave me a card with $5 in it and other people bought me things. I got some socks, a book, a jack set, and sweater cap for the cold weather. They also bought Momma some alcohol. Before I knew it, my party had turned into Momma's party. Momma told me to go home with Olivia's kids and she would come get me the next morning. So we left and went over Olivia's house. We didn't care, because we didn't want to be around those drunk grown-ups anyway.

When I woke up the next morning, the first thing Momma asked me was, where was my birthday money?
"Why, Momma?"
"Because I need to borrow it. Momma will pay
you back on the first."

I reached into my jeans, pulled out my five dollar bill and handed it over. I never saw it again. Later on that evening while Momma was cooking hot dogs, she told me that she met a nice little lady who I was going to go spend the weekend with. My heart jumped. I got scared.

Later that night, before I went to sleep, I prayed to God for my new baby-sitter to be somebody who likes little girls in the right way and not hurt their privates.

Friday came and she had already packed my things before I got home from school. I hated going to another baby-sitter, but there was nothing I could do about it. Momma saw me pouting and told me to straighten up my face.   "You're going to have a nice time this evening, watch and see."   We got in the car and Mr. Willie's perfume was smelling so loud. He drove us over to my new baby-sitter's house. She lived by herself in the projects near us. I felt better when I learned she didn't have a husband. Her house was pretty. The carpet and all of her furniture was white. I was scared to sit down   She even had white curtains, and white tables to match.   She had a big white Bible right on the coffee table. Momma told me her name was Georgia Lee, but Grandma Georgia to me. I never had a Grandma so that was neat. Momma told me to sit still on the couch while she talked to Grandma Georgia in the kitchen.

The smell of the house reminded me of Buddy and Jean's.   It was soul food. I heard Grandma Georgia tell Momma she was cooking chicken dinners for church tonight. When I heard she went to church, that made me feel even better. Momma came out of the kitchen, kissed me goodbye and told me to be good.   Mr. Willie was blowing the horn, so she had to hurry up.   Grandma Georgia pointed to a room down the hallway. "Your room is directly at the end of that hallway with the Teddy Bear on the bed. You may take your things back there and get comfortable."   "I get my own room," I whispered to myself.   So I took my bag and put it on the bed.

On my way back to the kitchen I could hear Grandma Georgia humming to herself while she was packing the chicken dinners in a box.
   "Do you like to go to church?"
   "Yes!" My eyes lit up.

I knew right off that Grandma Georgia was nice because she liked going to God's house.   She told me that we would be going to church all weekend.   I asked her if they sung a song called "Amazing Grace" at her church.
   "Of course! You might even hear it tonight."
   "For real, Grandma Georgia?"

"For real, baby."

She kept packing and humming. She asked me if I wanted to look at her youth Sunday School book. She taught Sunday School at her church. I sat down at the table to look at the book. On one page I saw a picture of a man with little boys and girls sitting all around him. The kids were looking at him and smiling. I asked Grandma Georgia, who was this man? She said, he was Jesus. The next page Jesus was walking in the grass and holding a little lamb in his arms. He was taking the little lamb back to his other little lamb friends. I could tell Jesus loved little lambs just as he loved the little children because he was smiling the same way. Grandma Georgia said she was going to go get ready for church. "K." "Just keep looking at that book until I'm finished."

After a few minutes, Grandma Georgia came out ready for church. She had on a little white hat and a purple dress which had a waist coat to match. She had a white purse with matching shoes and handkerchief. "Let's hit the road, Jack," she said, reaching out her hand to me. When she got in the car, she put on these real thick glasses that sat at the bottom of her nose. We pulled off real quick and I fell back in the seat. She drove faster than any old person I knew. Mr. Willie didn't even drive as fast as Grandma Georgia. But I guess he wasn't going anywhere exciting like Grandma Georgia was.

The church seemed to be a far distance from the projects. I fell asleep before we got there. Grandma Georgia woke me up once we got there. She pulled up behind a small white building. Other cars were parked there too. This church was much smaller than St. Rest Baptist Church where Olivia went. We stood in the doorway before we took our seats because Grandma Georgia was talking to one of the women ushers. The music was so loud. I looked around and saw women running. I didn't see anybody chasing after them, but they were just running and shouting all over the place. It was so loud. There were kids there too. They had tambourines in their hands, while others were just clapping their hands. All the people were happy. The preacher sat in the pulpit in his black robe, patting his foot. He was just as excited as everyone else was. People finally sat down when the drums stopped. That's when the Rev. got up and made his way to the pulpit. He started preaching on the last words of the song. They had been singing a song called "My Name Is Written In The Book Of Life." After a while, I started nodding off. Grandma Georgia pinched me on my arm and told me to listen to the preacher. I couldn't help it. I told Grandma Georgia that I was tired.

       "It's rude to go to sleep on God," Grandma Georgia
       whispered.

I looked around at the other children that had fallen asleep, and without saying anything, I looked back at Grandma Georgia.
       "You still ain't gonna sit up here and nod off,"
       she whispered through her teeth. I sat up.

When church was over, everybody went into the kitchen and sat at a long table with long white table cloths on it. The sisters of the church served everybody as they sat down and waited. I had real food that night. There was fried chicken, collard greens, yams, beans, peas, corn, cakes, pies and some red punch. This was better than the usual hot dogs and pork'n beans that Momma faithfully fixed for me.

The next morning, Grandma Georgia was up earlier than I was, humming to herself. She heard me getting up and yelled out that there was oatmeal in the kitchen. I went to the bathroom first and then came out to have breakfast with her. Grandma Georgia was so nice, she reminded me of an older version of Ms. Estee back in Phoenix. She cared for me. Afterwards, she asked me if I would help her pick some greens. I told her yes. She put some newspaper on the floor and brought a big old plastic bowl filled with wet green leaves over, then dropped it onto the newspaper. She asked me to watch her do a couple first and then follow. I watched her tear the greens and put the stems in the trash can. Then I did a few. I tore them up real good and fast, but she quickly stopped me and said I was doing it the wrong way. I had to go much slower. When we were finished, Grandma Georgia let me put on one of her aprons, and put the greens in a pot of water. I had to sit up on a chair and kneel next to the sink to pour the water in the pot.

During the rest of the day, I helped Grandma Georgia clean her white house. Afterwards, we watched TV until night time came. Then it was time to go back to church. They never sang "Amazing Grace" but I still enjoyed myself. I loved going to church instead of to those clubs with Momma. On the way home that night, I told Grandma Georgia that they forgot to sing my song again.
"Okay baby, Grandma Georgia will sing it to you."
"You know the song?"
"I sure do."

When Grandma Georgia started singing, goose bumps came over my arms. I could feel them. Her voice was beautiful. I wanted to cry as she was singing in the car, but I didn't. I just smiled at her and cried inside.

After we got home, I went into Grandma Georgia's room to watch her comb her long hair and put it up in pins. Her room was white and yellow. She had a beautiful dresser with a mirror cabinet which sat on top. It was trimmed in yellow. I loved it. It had all types of perfumes on the left side and then a large open case jewelry collection on the right side. I finally got enough nerve to ask Grandma Georgia why those people were running and hollering in church. She smiled at me.
"The Lord has done something in their life."
"Was it good or bad?"
"Baby, it's a blessing just knowing Him. Sometimes that's enough to make you shout."
"But they were crying, Grandma Georgia. Real hard."
"I know, baby." She held me closer to her and continued to talk. The presence of the Lord will make you cry sometimes. It will make you shout,

and sometimes you just sit still and moan
because you don't know what to say."

I guess I was feeling the presence of the Lord when Grandma Georgia was singing "Amazing Grace" because I had wanted to cry. When the weekend was over, Momma came to get me as she promised. I couldn't wait to tell her of the fun I had with Grandma Georgia. She walked in telling me to hurry up because Mr. Willie was waiting outside. Momma's hair was combed back. The pretty curls from Friday were tight and nappy. As Grandma Georgia untied her apron, I hugged her around her big soft waist.
"I had lots of fun, Grandma Georgia. Thank you
for letting me stay here with you." She
looked down to me and hugged me with a
nice smile, whispering, "I love you," in my ears.

Later on that night, while Momma was folding my clean clothes I began to tell her how much I liked Grandma Georgia. I told her that she can always take me over to her house when she has to leave me with somebody. She had a strange smile on her face as if only her mouth was smiling and not her eyes.
"Oh you like Grandma Georgia, hah?"
"Yes, I sure do and she likes me back."

Momma's face changed to being sad. She told me that Grandma Georgia reminded her of her mother which would be my grandmother.
"My real grandmother?" I asked.
"Yes. Your real grandmother, Mary Jane Carr."
"When will I meet her, Momma," I asked.

She got up off the couch and took the clothes to her room to put in the drawers. I could tell she wasn't feeling to happy about talking about her mother or Grandma Georgia for some reason. Momma was wiping her eyes when she came out of her room.
"Maybe one day you will meet your grandmother,
but I don't know when," Momma said.

"Don't you want to see her, Momma?" I asked.
"Sure, but I haven't been home in so many years."
She started looking up at the ceiling.
"When was the last time you saw her?" I asked.
"Maybe ten, fifteen years ago. Just once since I
left home at thirteen."
I couldn't believe Momma had been so young.
"Why you leave yo Momma so young?"
"Baby, you're too young too understand".
"Sometimes you have to leave places that you
don't want to leave for reasons that push you out
before your time."

I guess Momma got pushed out of her Momma's house too soon.
She grabbed for her Winston's cigarettes on the coffee table.
"I was ready to go after I had my first daughter."
"Which daughter, Sadie or Tarah?" I asked.
"AlmaFaye."
"I have another sister?"
"Yep, you sure do". Alma Faye was the first girl."
"Where is she, Momma?"

She whispered in a quiet voice.
"Your grandmother is keeping her for now."
"Why? Why isn't she with you, Momma?"
"One day, I will have her again and you will finally
meet your oldest sister."

Momma was right, I was too young to understand what she was
saying. Did her own Momma make her leave? I hope Momma
would never make me leave home that young. I felt sad for
Momma. Then I wondered, why did she leave her daughter with
her Momma? When Momma went back into the kitchen, I saw
tears in her eyes. She was feeling bad. I could see it. I tried to
make up another subject by telling Momma I really missed Sadie,
Tarah, Tyrone and Gable.
"Maybe we can go visit them, Momma."

"They ain't concerned about us."

Momma got really mad.

"I'm going to be bored without children around,"
I pouted.

"No you won't, because when school is out in a
few weeks you will be in the grape fields all
summer."

"Grape fields? Is that where grapes are made?" I
asked.

"You'll see." Momma started laughing to herself,
wiping her face.

CHAPTER 5

AUGUST – SEPTEMBER 1968

Three thirty a.m., the alarm clock rang. Momma yelled from her bedroom, "Carla, get up. Get up! It's time to go to the fields!" Trying to wipe the sleep away from my eyes, I couldn't believe it was time to get up because it was still black outside. I didn't want to get up to go to the fields, but it wasn't my choice. After fifteen minutes passed, I heard a loud horn blowing outside. Momma said, "That's Ersha!" "Who was Ersha" I wondered. Momma ran to the door and yelled out, "Five minutes more! Come on Carla, don't just sit there on that couch! We got to get out of here!" I felt like I was still asleep. Momma had on a rusty tan cap, blue jeans, a buttoned up shirt and some tennis shoes. I put on my regular jeans, sweater and tennis shoes. Momma suggested that I also grab my brown jacket. "It's going to be a little frosty outside this morning, but it's going to warm up by day break," she told me.

Waiting outside was a pretty lady in a big red long car. It was the longest car I had ever seen. Ersha was the woman behind the wheel. She wore a green straw hat which was tilted to the right so that only the left side of her face was showing.
> "And how are you this morning, angel?" she
> asked as we got into the car. Her voice was nice.
> "Are we ready to go?" she asked Momma.
> "Let's go make some money," Momma said.

I sat between the both of them. The front seat looked larger than our living room at home.
> "Doris, who is this pretty little girl?" she asked.
> "That's Carla, my baby girl. I told you I was going
> to Phoenix to get my kids, but that nigga only
> gave me my littlest baby back."

Ersha asked how old I was and Momma almost stuttered because she was trying to figure it out. She didn't remember at first. Then she said five.

"Well, Doris, I think him not giving you all the
kids back is a blessing in disguise." Momma
rolled her eyes at Ersha as she kept talking.
"I know you haven't slowed down enough to
handle all those kids. In fact, I think you ought
to give this little pretty girl to me and let me and
Earl raise her."
"Ain't nobody gettin my baby."
"Come on, Doris, we can give her a better life with
better things. And when you're ready, you can
have her back."
"Look, Ersha, have your own babies. Leave mine alone."
"Now, Doris, you know we can't have children."

Momma looked at Ersha and rolled her eyes again. I wondered
why they couldn't have children. Momma looked at me and told
me that this was the woman we were going to be working with for
the rest of the summer. I didn't know anything about picking
grapes. The only thing that came across my mind was eating
grapes. Maybe that's what she was talking about. When we arrived
an hour later, people were standing outside their cars. There were
different types of people. Even kids and dogs were waiting when
we pulled up.

After Ersha got out of the car and walked over to the people, she
told them how much they would get paid to work. She said it's 7
to 10 cents a tray. Momma taught me how to pick grapes. She
said, "Everybody out here must pick as many as they could before
the heat of the day scorched their backs."

Then Ersha told Momma to come here. They talked for a minute.
Momma said we were going over to our row. Momma picked up a
big bowl. She said it was her grape bowl. I would try from time to
time to help Momma, but for the most part, I just got in the way.
So I served as the "gopher." I would go and get her water, more
paper, sharper knives and whatever else. I ate more grapes than I

picked, and I would always be scared off by the bumble bees.

A couple of weeks later when the alarm clock buzzed at 3:30 a.m.,
Ersha honked her Cadillac horn for us. When we walked to the car
Ersha was telling Momma that she had a lot of new workers coming
in today. Even some Momma wouldn't recognize from past years.
I guess Momma had been working for Ersha for a while. After we
arrived at the fields, Momma and I walked back to the field that
she didn't finish out the day before. There was a black man picking
grapes on the row next to Momma's row. He asked her what her
name was.
>"Good morning, young lady," he said to Momma.
>"Hi, how are you?" Momma spoke back, getting
>her grape knife together and her tray.
>"My name is Calvin Williams. What's yours?"
>"Doris Hicks." Momma started blushing when she
>stood up to shake his hand.

He told Momma he just got out of the Army about a week ago.
He then asked Momma if he could help her cut her row out.
Momma started laughing and told him, "Sure if you like."   He
came over to our row. He saw me under one of the vines and asked
Momma, "Who's that?"   She   said, "That's my little baby girl,
Carla.   Carla, this man is Mr. Calvin."

I think he really liked Momma because I saw him looking at her a
couple of times, smiling. When the day was finished, he asked
Momma if he could give her the pay for both rows, his and hers.
Momma was smiling real hard.   He said, "It's a gift for letting me
cut with you." Throughout the entire summer, he and Momma
would cut rows together until it was all finished.   In the mornings
when Ersha would pick us up, she teased Momma about her new
man friend.

At the end of summer, Mr. Calvin and Momma started seeing each
other in the city.   Momma was so happy.   She started telling her
friends that she had met this handsome Army man.   She told them
how nice he was and how she loved the way he spoke so softly.   She

especially loved his dark skin. Momma said to Jean that she loved her some dark meat.

On the last day in the fields, Momma asked Mr. Calvin if he would take her to the supermarket after they finished. He told her he would be delighted to, if she gave him the address for pick up. Mr. Calvin came to our house to pick Momma up.

Later on that evening Mr. Calvin came knocking at the door smelling good, with clean clothes on. He didn't look anything like he did in the fields. When Momma saw him she started acting so nervous. Mr. Calvin spoke to us and we spoke back, and Momma gave Mr. Calvin a kiss on his lips. I never saw Momma kiss a man before. I laughed real quiet.

We pulled up in the parking lot of the super market.
            "Oh shit" Momma said.
            "What's wrong?" Mr. Calvin asked her.

Momma told him that her ex-boyfriend who she had told him about was sitting in the car right in front of us. He told her to not be afraid and that he would handle everything. Mr. Calvin got out of the car and walked to Mr. Willie's car. I was so happy. I didn't know what was about to happen. But I felt that Mr. Calvin was a strong man and could handle Mr. Willie. Momma kept saying, "Oh shit," to herself over and over again. I was smiling, holding on to the back of Mr. Calvin's seat, watching him. We could hear them talking. Mr. Calvin introduced himself. They shook hands and then Mr. Calvin told him to look at us in his car. Mr. Willie looked and Mr. Calvin said, "That's my woman and her little girl. I don't want to see or hear of you around her ever again. Do I make myself clear?" Mr. Willie just nodded his head up and down. I was so happy he was willing to beat Mr. Willie up for Momma!

Mr. Calvin and Momma saw each other every weekend. Then he started coming over every night. Momma would take me over to Jean and Buddy's to watch television until Mr. Calvin left. He treated Momma nice. He also took me to the store with him every time Momma would need something. None of Momma's friends ever did that or wanted to spend time with me, except for Jean and Buddy, of course.

It was good to be back at school with my friends and teachers. I met new friends and new teachers. When the teacher asked us to raise our hands and tell what we did for the summer, I told them I worked in the grape fields and everybody laughed at me. I was glad to get back to school because those grape fields were dirty and boring.

I found out that Momma could cook "real food" when Thanksgiving came around. The day before Thanksgiving, Momma started cooking all this food. I asked her how come she's cooking so much food and she told me that Mr. Calvin was spending Thanksgiving with us. I had never seen her cook like that before. We really never had a Thanksgiving dinner. I was happy to see she could cook like that. The next day, Mr. Calvin ate a lot of food. He had seconds. Momma even cooked a sweet potato pie for him. Mr. Calvin told Momma that she had to come to his family's house for Christmas so that he could introduce her to everyone. Momma said okay. I sat in the living room with my food and looked at TV while they ate in the kitchen. And Momma's food tasted good, just like Grandma Georgia's. It was good! The next thing I remember is that they were going to the back room where Momma slept. I turned the TV up real loud and watched it until I went to sleep.

Christmas came fast, right after Thanksgiving was over. Mr. Calvin came and got me and Momma and took us to his sister's house like he said on Thanksgiving night. It took us a long time to get there. They lived far away. When we walked in the door, the house was filled with kids and older people. They were playing Christmas songs and it was noisy. Mr. Calvin introduced us to his sisters and brothers. I met their children and we began to play. Mr. Calvin had bought me and Momma a gift. Mine was a Barbie Doll. I wanted a Barbie Doll for Christmas but didn't think I would ever get one, because Momma never had any money left over from her county check and food stamps. Momma opened hers too. Mr. Calvin bought Momma some slippers and night gowns. Everybody seemed to be pretty nice and they liked Momma too. We ate a lot of food and desserts. They cooked turkey and dressing, cakes, pies, and banana pudding. It was so good I thought my stomach was going to bust open.

That night, I went to sleep wondering what the new year was going to bring. Things were better for me and Momma since Mr. Calvin came around. She was spending a lot of time with him and not me. But at least she wasn't going to those clubs at night anymore. Momma told Buddy and Jean that her New Year's resolution was to not party as much anymore, and settle down with one man. Buddy told her, "It's about damn time."

When my sixth birthday came around that February, it was different. It fell on a Tuesday instead of the weekend and my whole class sang Happy Birthday to me. My teacher knew my birthday. Momma kind of forgot about it when I asked her what today was. She didn't guess and I told her it was my birthday. She said she knew, but was planning something for me over the weekend. I didn't believe her. Buddy and Jean didn't forget because they gave me another card with a $5 bill in it. I waited until the weekend and Momma still didn't do anything for my birthday. I forgot all about it after that and didn't bother Momma anymore. Buddy and Jean explained to me that Momma was so busy with Mr. Calvin she forgot, but she still loved me and was probably going to do a surprise for me later. They were probably just trying to make me feel good.

I was happy for Momma, but kind of sad for me because I wanted to spend more time with her. I wanted her to be happy with me like she was with Mr. Calvin. I did my homework and got all gold stars and A's so that she would be real proud of me. When Momma got my report card all she would say was "keep it up."

CHAPTER 6

JUNE 1969 — WEDDING BELLS

One day, I came home from school and Momma told me that she was getting married to Mr. Calvin in a few months. The date was set for June 21, 1969. I guess that was good news, but I didn't know why I felt so funny. Maybe because I would not have Momma all to myself. Maybe because now Mr. Calvin would be there every day and night with Momma. The wedding date came fast. As soon as school was over it was time for Momma to get married.

All of Mr. Calvin's sisters helped Momma with her wedding plans. One of Mr. Calvin's sisters' names was almost like Momma's. Her name was Aunt Dora. Aunt Dora had a big house and in the back was where Mr. Calvin kept his greyhound dogs that he loved. Momma told me that Mr. Calvin has to go feed his damn dogs everyday before he sees her.

Mr. Calvin's other sister helped with the wedding too. Aunt Ellen was real excited about the wedding. They decided that the wedding would be at Aunt Ellen's house.

The night before Momma's wedding, Olivia stopped by. Momma was telling her how in love she still was with her new black piece. She told Olivia that Mr. Calvin was changing her name from Hicks to Williams. Olivia said she was going to find her a piece of black meat that would change her name too. She asked Momma if he had any brothers. Momma told her he did, but they were all married. Olivia asked if they were happy. I didn't understand what difference it made if they were happy or not, they were married. I asked Momma if I could be in her wedding and she told me I couldn't because I didn't have any new shoes. I was sad. I wanted to be in her wedding so bad. I thought it just would be, new shoes or not. Then I asked Momma what Mr. Calvin would be to me when they got married. She told me that he would be her husband and he would be my step-daddy. I thought that was great for her.

The next morning, Aunt Doris came to take me to her house until it was time for the wedding. Momma stayed so that she could get herself together for that evening. When we arrived at Aunt Ellen's house, everything was set. Mr. Calvin's sisters had decorated the living room with flowers of all colors. Since I wasn't in the wedding I had to watch from the bedroom door. Momma wouldn't let me come out with all the other people. I could see Mr. Calvin and the preacher standing together, and Momma was in the room next to me with Ruthie Armstrong. This was the same woman that called the authorities on us to have us put in that foster home. I couldn't understand how she was still Momma's friend. Momma's wedding dress was beautiful like a queens dress! She had on a soft dress that looked like see-through curtain fabric. The neck was trimmed in white lace. Her face was pretty with a little make up. When Momma dressed up, she always looked good, but today she looked better than I had ever seen her. Mr. Calvin looked good too. When he smiled, he showed his dimples. He had only one man with him, Vernon, one of Momma's partying buddies.

So that day, Mr. Calvin became Momma's husband, and I became his daughter. The wedding ceremony was short and simple, about twenty minutes. The reception followed right after and was at the house too. They had cooked all night. Mr. Calvin came from a big family. His sisters and brothers were there with all of their children. Everyone in his family seemed to be very nice and friendly. Momma started putting on her music after the ceremony and started partying. Mr. Calvin's family were church people and didn't like the drinking and music. I could tell by their faces. They didn't look happy and they weren't dancing, just sat there. I overheard Momma telling Ruthie, "These are the church in-laws."

After the wedding, life was different for Momma and me. It was a good different. It was good having a man in the house all the time, not tiptoeing out before the morning. It changed a lot of things.

For once, Momma was home every day and every night and cooked a different meal each day. I would stand at the kitchen doorway to watch Momma cook.

One day while I was watching her cook, she told me
>"When you get old enough to be married, always
>remember to make sure your husband is well
>taken care of first." Especially if he's a good man."
>"Why should they go first, Momma?" I asked.
>"Because when a good man is working hard and
>providing for his family that's the right thing to
>do, plus that's the way God set it up to be."
>"So they go first when they have a job, hah?"

Momma tickled me under my arms to make me laugh. Mr. Calvin had a real job too. He was a service man for Chevron Station, and wore a uniform. Mr. Willie didn't have a job I don't think. I guess that's why Momma didn't cook for him first.

I finally had two parents, full time, like other kids I knew. I guess it wasn't so bad after all. I especially loved the fact that I had a full time Momma now.

A Different Summer -- 1969

This summer was not like the others that Momma and I had. I spent the summer with my two new cousins, Lenny and Stanton, at Aunt Dora's house. Her sons were nice and lots of fun. They let me play with their games and we played together. They weren't mean and selfish like Robert, Margaret's son.

They had a lot of boy toys, but they still let me play with their cars and army men. Aunt Dora had a big house with a lot of rooms. Lenny and Stanton had their own rooms with their toys in them.

On the Friday nights when Momma and Mr. Calvin would drop me off over to Aunt Dora's house, we would sit up and watch TV

together and have hot dogs or hamburgers and french fries. It was
a treat Aunt Dora said. Then on Saturday mornings Aunt Dora
would cook us a neat breakfast with pancakes, grits, eggs, and
bacon. Lenny would always want more pancakes than anyone else.
Aunt Dora always had to tell him to save some for other people in
case they wanted seconds. I could never have seconds because I
would get full on my first two. They were so big. So Stanton and
Lenny fought over who would get the last one. Aunt Dora would
just cut it in half and split it with them.

One day after breakfast Lenny taught me how to put a puzzle
together. He had a barnhouse puzzle. When we finished it was
beautiful. It had animals, gates, trees and the sky. The barn was
big. Lenny was real smart. He always put things together like his
train set. Stanton liked to play with his guns and shoot all the time.
I didn't like guns too much because they would scare me when they
made that loud "pop" sound. I would sit on the bed when Lenny
and Stanton played cowboys and indians. One time, I pretended
to be Ms. Kitty in the movie called "Gunsmoke." I would break up
their fights and tell them to come to the bar and get along with
each other. Then I made them shake hands and make up.

The summer was almost over when Momma told me that she had
some good news.
> "We are moving out of these shacks, Carla. The
> Redevelopment Department of Fresno offered
> every tenant a $10,000 settlement to move out."

I didn't understand everything, but I was glad we were moving to a
better place.
> "Momma, does this mean the next place we go to
> will have a bathroom inside the house like
> everybody else's?" Momma and Mr. Calvin
> laughed.
> "Yes baby, and you will probably have your own
> room this time."
> "Wow, are you serious?" That made me really

happy.
"When are we moving out?"
"Early part of next year probably," Momma said.

All evening I thought about us moving to the next place. I could have my own room like Lenny and Stanton. I could put my toys and stuff in it too.

September 1969

Summer was over and it was time to go back to school. This year I had to go to a new grade because I went from Head Start, kindergarten and now to 1st grade. I just hoped that this new class had nice teachers and nice kids. I had to get new uniforms for this class. Plus I had grown a lot too. Momma said I was growing tall like weeds out of my clothes. Instead of the blue uniforms, we had to wear green ones with blue checks in them.

On the first day of school I showed Momma I was a big girl and didn't cry. Momma said she would be back and I believed her. My first grade teacher was a black woman named Ms. Banks. She was pretty just like Momma. She had red hair like Buddy's. She gave everybody a lolly pop and said we couldn't eat it until our parents came to get us. I liked her, she was nice. We went over our alphabets and numbers that day. Momma came back just like she said she would after school.
     "Momma, guess what I have?"
     "What, baby?"
     "Ms. Banks gave us some candy, but we can't eat it
      until our parents get here."
     "Fine, go ahead," Momma said.
     "So how do you like your new class?"
     "It's great. I'm going to have a lot of fun."

Now we lived the same way every day at home. I went to school, Momma stayed home and cleaned up and cooked for her new husband first and talked with Jean and Buddy. Mr. Calvin went to his good job and to feed his dogs after work. Then he would come home and we would eat dinner together.

With Momma not partying and going a lot of places anymore I saw her all the time. I saw Mr. Calvin everyday too. I liked that.

I didn't see my cousins that much now because we were in school, but sometimes on the weekend I would see them if Mr. Calvin took me by their house when he went to feed his greyhounds.

On one weekend, I hurt myself real bad in Lenny's room. Me, Lenny and Stanton had a contest of who could jump the highest on Lenny's bed. Lenny had a big bed. We were jumping and jumping so high. Stanton had fallen off the bed a couple of times but not me and Lenny. He was trying to reach the ceiling with his hands when he jumped up. Me too. Aunt Dora was hollering at us from the kitchen to stop that jumping but we didn't. I fell too, but onto the bed, and jumped back up jumping again. Then, all of a sudden my leg twisted some how and I fell back. As I was going back a spring had popped out of the mattress pointing at an angle and it scraped the back of my thigh. It hurt so bad. I screamed. I looked at the back of my leg and I had a scrape from the back of my knees up to my thighs. It was white and then it filled in red with blood. Aunt Dora ran in screaming.
"I told you kids to stop that jumping."
I was crying hard now.

Lenny and Stanton were standing in the corner while Aunt Dora looked at the back of my thighs.
"Yawl are just so hard headed and you won't stop
until something bad happens to ya hah."

I couldn't talk, because it hurt and stung so much, I just cried. The boys stayed quiet too. Aunt Dora put about four band-aids on me. It looked like a long train track on the back of my leg.
When I got home, Mr. Calvin told Momma what happened and she whooped me. I couldn't understand why when I was already

hurt from my fall. I didn't go over to Aunt Dora's house for a long time after that because Momma said I don't know how to act right.

Christmas 1969

This year I had another good Christmas. Mr. Calvin bought Momma a silver Christmas tree with bulbs, lights and the works. I even had gifts under the tree! Momma had gifts too. She got a beautiful pink robe with matching house shoes. Mr. Calvin bought me two dolls and a complete dish set. I also got gifts from his family too. I got a one year diary, more dolls and dolly clothes. I liked the diary the most, because my Aunt Dora who gave it to me told me that I could talk to God in it and write my feelings down. I really loved my new aunts, uncles and cousins. I felt like they loved me too. Every time they would see me, they would hug me.

After the New Year my seventh birthday came around fast. This birthday Momma let me go over to Aunt Dora's and she had cake, ice cream, and clothes for me. I also had some money in my birthday cards. I had a party with all my new cousins on Mr. Calvin's side. Aunt Ellen's kids were there: Glenn, Rita and Stephanie. They started singing "happy birthday" to me when I came into the kitchen. They were waiting for me to walk in to surprise me. I was surprised because I never had a surprise birthday party before.

It was so nice and Momma didn't steal my birthday party or my birthday money from me this time. We had so much fun playing pin the tail on the donkey and other games, I didn't want to go home. Momma said I could stay the night and come home the next day as long as I minded.

The next day, Mr. Calvin came to pick me up to take me home. Momma was in the kitchen cooking and humming to herself like Grandma Georgia use to do when she was cooking too.
"Did you have a good time?"

"Yep, I had a big surprise birthday party and I
   got lots of toys and gifts."
"What else did you get?"
"I also got some cards."

I didn't want to tell her I got some money because I knew Momma
would take it. I sat at the table watching her cook. She didn't ask
about money. Momma told me that she had a good surprise for
me and that she was going to tell me after she finished cooking. I
couldn't wait. I asked Momma to tell me now. I thought it was
another birthday gift for me.

"I'm pregnant." A frown came over my face.
"Huh, Momma?" I asked.
"I'm going to have another baby, Carla."
"Why?" I asked without thinking. "I mean,
   when?"
"This year. Probably in early December."
"Ain't I enough, Momma?"

She could tell that I wasn't happy so she came over and hugged me.
"Carla, you are going to have a little sister or
   brother to play with. Aren't you glad about
   that?"

I was so mad inside. How could she, I thought to myself. She is
barely spending time with me now. How could she crowd our time
with a new child?

The next afternoon, when I got home from school I was still mad. I
took a pair of scissors, went through Momma's closet and cut slits in
all of her dresses and pants. That fixed her for being pregnant!
When she finally found out what I had done to her clothes, she
called out to me. She had a switch in her hand.

"I'm going to ask this question only once. Who
   cut up my clothes?"
"I did," I screamed. "I don't want you to have a
   baby! I thought I was your baby!" Tears were

running down from my eyes.

I had been wanting to be her baby for so long. I wanted her to see
that I just wanted to be her little girl. Now she was spoiling it with
another child.
"Girl, bring yo ass here right now," she yelled. I
was brave. I went to her so she could get me.

She whooped my butt something terrible. I had to deal with the
fact that another child was on the way whether I wanted it or not.
She didn't understand my feelings and my fears. She didn't
understand, but I knew God could look in my heart and know what
I was feeling. So I talked to him about it in my diary. Momma
and Mr. Calvin went to the grocery store after she whooped me and
said they would be back a little later. "Don't go outside," Momma
hollered. I grabbed my diary and talked to God until I fell asleep.

Dear God,
I know you heard what just happened. I know I was
probably wrong for cutting up her clothes. I'm sorry
Lord, but I was so mad at her. I know you
understand because all I wanted was her love for me.
It seems like we may not be tight like I wished we
could be. You know, God, like I see other
Momma's and their children. When they come to
school to get them, they be playing with their
children, and talking with them about everything.
They even go places together and go to the parks. I
know because they tell me what they do sometimes.
I don't have a lot of things to tell them that me and
my Momma do because we have not done a lot of
fun stuff together. I don't know, maybe I should
just grow up and not be a cry baby like Momma
says. I'll just be strong. Good bye God, I'm going
to go to sleep and take a nap until Momma come
back home.

Momma seemed like she was mad at me forever. She wouldn't talk to me at all. I came from school and looked at t.v. and she wouldn't say to much to me other than change your clothes, get ready to eat and take your shower. I wished Momma would talk to me at least a little. She would talk to Mr. Calvin.

She was getting fatter with that baby coming and she seemed like she was getting meaner and meaner every day. I just tried to stay away from her because every time she said something she would holler at me.

I tried to make her feel better by showing her my good stars and my happy faces that I got in school, but she didn't want to see them. She told me to just put them on the table and she would look at them later. She never did. I guess Momma was real mad at me still for cutting up her clothes. How long would she be mad at me forever, I wondered. I wished so much I could buy her some new ones and then she would love me again.

Summer School 1970

School was coming to a close and summer time was here. Momma said I was going to summer school. I was glad. I loved school. I could play with kids my age and Momma could have more time by herself and with Mr. Calvin, I guess.

After summer school, I went to the second grade. I went to a new school called Franklin Elementary. Momma said she was going to buy me some new clothes. We went to the used stores and the Salvation Army the next day. Momma bought me two pairs of pants and found some blouses to match. She said, "All you need now is a pair of tennis shoes and a pair of church shoes." My clothes didn't look like the other kids clothes. I could tell they went to the real stores. But Momma said, "We don't have money to go to the real stores and just be satisfied because there are kids in other countries that can't even afford shoes and clothes. Like in Africa."

I didn't like the way I looked when I went to school, but I still loved school,   I loved my teachers and I loved learning. Mostly, I enjoyed getting good grades and gold stars on my papers. My classmates were a lot of fun too. I didn't like when school was out because I had no one to play with once I got home. So each year, I would ask if I could go to summer school and Momma would say yes. This allowed her to be around her new husband more. And it allowed me to be with other kids more.

Momma and Mr. Calvin had their first argument. I had never heard them argue before. I felt scared. I was hoping Mr. Calvin wouldn't hit Momma the way Mr. Willie used to hit her. I put my ear up to the bedroom door and heard them arguing about me. I had asked Momma the day before if Mr. Calvin liked me because he was taking his nieces and nephews places and not me anymore. He took them to the movies and to the park on Sundays. So when Momma asked him, he didn't have a good enough answer, other than, "I have always taken them to those places, and I just didn't think to ask her." Momma said, "Well, begin to think to ask her!" I still didn't feel he wanted to, deep down inside. I was beginning to feel real bad, so that night before I went to bed I grabbed my Mickey Mouse pencil to tell God.

Dear God:
I was real happy at first because Momma got married. It made her so happy too. Mr. Calvin seemed real nice for her and he even acted like he liked me. But now I see something is different between us. He is not as friendly toward me like before and he don't even play with me like before. You know how he used to pass by me and grab my hair when I wasn't looking and pretend it wasn't him? Then he used to take me over to his family's house to play with my cousins. Not no more. Maybe he was just treating me nice to get next to my Momma. Or maybe since he is going to get his own child by Momma now, he don't need to be nice

to me anymore. I don't know why. Maybe because
I cut up Momma's dresses when I found out they
were having a baby. Maybe that's why. I don't
know, but maybe you can tell me God. I don't
want to be the cause of them not being happy with
each other, but I am feeling kind of left out and
alone again. I know I am not because you are my
friend and you are always with me. Thank you for
being my friend forever.

I noticed that things started to change after that talk. Whenever
Mr. Calvin would go places, he would now ask me if I wanted to
go with him. Even if it was only to go pick up his pay check or to
the market to get groceries. I really liked when he would ask about
going over to his sister's (Aunt Dora) house, who first gave me the
diary to write to God. Plus, Lenny and Stanton were my favorite
cousins. I liked them. Aunt Dora would sometimes ask if I
wanted to go to church with them on Sundays. I would say yes, if
Momma let me. I found out everyone in Mr. Calvin's family went
to the same church. In fact, almost all the members of that church
were his family. Everybody went to church except for Mr. Calvin.
Mr. Calvin's brother, Uncle Kyle, was one of the preachers there and
he had a wife named Maura. Then there was my cousin, Falona,
who was the granddaughter to Pastor Rice, and Uncle Kyle was his
assistant. Falona liked to hang out with Uncle Kyle and Aunt
Maura as if she were their daughter. She and I became close
because of our ages. I would always sit with Falona when we went
to church.

I loved church, but this church was nothing like the church
Grandma Georgia took me to when she used to baby-sit me.
Grandma Georgia's church had a real choir with shouting and
praising God. This church was very quiet and boring as if they
didn't know the same God that Grandma Georgia's church people
did. Maybe because Pastor Rice was so old. But it was still
boring even when Uncle Kyle preached. And he wasn't old like
Pastor Rice!

Every Sunday after church, we stopped by Aunt Doris' house to eat the dinner that she prepared the night before. Aunt Doris made delicious banana pudding. I always promised her if she let me have dessert first, I would eat all my food. She did and I would keep my word and eat all my food. But even though I had such a nice day, that night when I came home, I wanted to write God. I wanted to tell him about all the good things and bad things in my mind.

Dear God:
So many things have happened in the past year and a half. Seems like everything happened so fast. Some good and some bad. I was skipped to the second grade. Momma didn't act to excited about it. I guess she was mad at me at the time and then forgot. I met some nice people. One was Emily and Ernest. Some were bad people, at least Poppa Ernest was. I didn't like him and you know why God. Then Robert Jr. and Margaret. Margaret was nice but her son was bad. He had evil all in him. You remember he hit me in the head with that bat and made me fall out. But then I met a real special lady, Grandma Georgia who was so beautiful and nice to me. She loved me in a real way. I think she was a angel God. Only you know if she was or not. Thank you for letting me meet her. People seem to come in and out of my life God. That's the way it always seems. They come into my life only to leave. When will I have someone for keeps? Is this the way it is supposed to be? My other sisters and brothers stay in the same place with Daddy and their new mother. I guess with Momma meeting Mr. Calvin, getting married and having a baby from him was exciting. After I see what the rest of the year is going to bring, then I will write you again. I'll try not to wait so long next time. I'm going to sleep now God.

CHAPTER 7

New Home

Every Saturday morning, Mr. Calvin took his greyhound dogs hunting for jack rabbits and cotton tails. I never heard him leave in the morning. I slept real hard. Momma used to tease me and say I can sleep through an earthquake.

This certain Saturday Momma woke me up with her screaming and shouting. She was saying it was time, it was time. She was waving this paper in her hand. I could barely see because sleep was still in my eyes. She told me that she would be right back. She was going to go see if Buddy and Jean got their letters too. Momma sounded like a little girl for the first time. I wasn't talking too much because I didn't know what she was talking about. I could hear her calling out to Jean and Buddy as the screen door closed behind her.

The next month, we moved into a two story, two bedroom, two bath apartment. It was great! We had a downstairs kitchen, a front room, and two bathrooms inside the house with a shower and bathtub in it. I had my own room, which was upstairs next to Momma's bedroom. I had good wood floors in my room and a large walk in closet. I had two windows. I never thought I would have so much space all to myself! I loved my room! The only clothes I had were about four dresses, three pairs of pants, some blouses (to fold up and place in my dresser drawer) and two pairs of shoes. I had my own room not a couch in the living room. It was a real room that I could put my own stuff and my own clothes in. Momma and I used to share closet space, but not anymore. After we moved into our new place, Momma and Mr. Calvin started doing a lot of shopping, buying new furniture from second hand stores. They also bought a new car, and new clothes for Momma and me.

The Atchison Courts were beautiful and had many kids around. The buildings looked almost like mansions to me, just like Margaret's house. No more shotgun house with the toilet outside.

I loved it, our new home. We even had a phone. Momma told me that she was going to write home to her mother and AlmaFaye in Louisiana and give them our phone number. I was hoping my big sister would call and then I could talk to her. Momma said I would get a chance to talk with my grandmother too. She told me that they didn't have phones at her mother's house, but she was hoping she could go somewhere to call us. So Momma sent the letter and we waited. Everyday when I got home from school, I ask Momma, " did they call yet." She would say, "Not yet."

Our new neighborhood was filled with lots of children. I couldn't wait to meet and play with them. One morning, I ran down the stairs real fast because I heard lot of children outside. I went to the kitchen to eat cereal real quick. Momma was in the kitchen drinking coffee and smoking her cigarettes. After my cereal, I asked Momma if I could go outside to play. Momma looked up at me real mean and said, "you just stay on the porch and be satisfied." I told her that there were a lot of kids outside. "I don't care, just stay on the damn porch."

Momma didn't want me to play with the kids. That was all right with me. I was just glad to be able to live where other kids were. I could just talk with them and speak to them as they passed by. That was good enough for me.

A few months later, in December, Aunt Dora was taking me home after church. She found out that Momma had been taken to the hospital because she went into labor. I had to stay over to Aunt Dora's for three days until Momma came out of the hospital. I didn't care. I was happy that I got to stay at Aunt Dora's house. December 5, 1970, Momma had a baby boy named Calvin Jr. After that, I began to feel neglected again, because Momma and Mr. Calvin gave him all of the attention. I guess now, Mr. Calvin had a real child of his own and Momma finally had a baby by a man that married her. I was just a jealous little brat.
The new baby didn't make me feel too good. Momma started showing me how to change his diaper, fix his bottle, hold him, and

really treat him like he was my own baby. The first time I changed his diaper, Momma was standing right there. Calvin Jr. had on a plastic pair of pants and a cloth diaper underneath. Bushy curly hair was all over his head. Momma said I had to be careful with the safety pins and not to stick him. I took out the safety pins on each side and the diaper was real wet. I was nervous to see what was in the diaper. Nothing was in there, thank God. All he had done was pee. Momma laughed and said, "You lucked out this time, but you won't next time." I laughed too. I loved laughing times with Momma. She could be so funny.

Later that evening, Momma called me into the kitchen with her.
"It's time that you learn how to cook" Momma told me reaching to the top cabinet pulling out a bowl.
She told me she learned how to cook at seven years old and I should too.

The first lesson was how to make homemade cornbread. I ran and got some paper and pencil to write everything down. There were seven things Momma said went into cornbread. Corn meal, flour, baking powder, sugar, salt, two eggs and milk. She even showed me how to grease the glass pan, and how to set the temperature on the oven to heat the pan before pouring the corn bread mix in it. The next lesson was the collard greens. She told me that she boiled the salt pork and hammock to get the seasoning for her greens. While the water was boiling, she and I went into the living room. She asked me to bring her the newspapers off the kitchen table so that we could lay the greens on top of it. Then she showed me how to pick the greens and throw away the stems into a brown paper bag. I dared not bust her bubble and tell her that Grandma Georgia taught me already, because I could tell she was proud of herself in teaching me this. After we picked them, we soaked the greens a few times in the sink filled with water. Momma used a little soap detergent to clean the greens. She washed them several times then added them to the pot with the salt pork meat and put a lid on the pot.
"Now you can start your own cookbook."

"I can Momma?"
"Yep, you sure can. And you can call it Carla's
cookbook." I was so proud of myself!

That evening was great cooking and talking cook-talk to Momma.
Momma was watching the clock and looking at the door for Mr.
Calvin to come home from hunting. Momma said she was about
to make some calls and if I wanted to go outside and sit on the
porch, I could. I was so glad Mr. Calvin bought Momma a phone,
because when she was ready to get on the phone she would send me
outside to play on the porch. The phone rang before she could get
on it. I ran outside.
        "Don't go off that porch, girl" Momma hollered.
        "I won't. Momma, I'm staying right here" I hollered
        back.

She didn't want me to get lost I guess. Then, I heard Momma
hollering at whoever called her.
        "When in the hell did that happen?" Momma
        asked.
        "That's a damn lie, somebody could have found
        me within a damn year and a half. I sent the
        damn letter months ago, why you just now
        calling me with this shit?"

Who could she be talking to about a letter? I was trying to
remember. Then I remembered Momma wrote home to her
Momma and to my big sister AlmaFaye. I don't think Momma
was talking to her Momma like that. I was hoping she wasn't
talking to AlmaFaye like that either. Then I heard the phone hang
up. The phone ranged again. It was her friend, Alice. I heard
Momma telling Alice that her brother J-Hue had just told her that
her mother had died over a year and a half ago. Momma was
crying now. She told Alice that her mother had cancer, but
nobody told her about it. She told Alice her brother said the
family couldn't find her anywhere and nobody knew where she was
in Fresno. I got up from the porch to go back inside, while

Momma was hanging up the phone.
"Carla, your grandmother, Mary Jane, died. I'm
sorry you didn't get a chance to meet her."

Momma started crying again. But you couldn't hear it, you just
saw the tears rolling down her face. I put my arms around her neck
and she hugged my waist. I could feel Momma was hurting bad. I
was real sad too. But she would not cry out loud. The phone rang
again. Momma wiped off her face.
"Hello?" Momma started frowning a little.
"Who is this?" Who ever it was Momma didn't
know at first. Then she said, "Hey my baby.
How are you doing?" I guess she found out who
it was.
"Carla, its your big sister, AlmaFaye." I was so
glad, but I didn't move. I just stood up right
where I was sitting.
"Can I speak to her" I asked Momma.

Momma kept right on talking. Momma talked to her for a long
time so I went and sat down until she was finished and then she
called me to the phone.

I was able to speak with my sister for just a moment because the bill
was going up. It was weird, and all I could say was,
"I can't wait to meet you one day."
"I always think about my babysister in
California" she said. That made me feel so special to be
called a babysister.
"When will I see you?"
"Hopefully real soon." I could hear her t.v. in the
background. Before hanging up, she told me to
remember how much she loved me.

After that day, I didn't hear Momma talk about her family in
Louisiana anymore. Momma changed that day. She was different.
Momma began to stay mean all the time. She was also drinking

more alcohol. Since that day, when they told her that her mother had died, seem like something inside of Momma died too. She just wasn't the same anymore. She started really drinking a lot.

Christmas and New Years were real sad like and quiet. We still had a tree and some gifts, but it was sad. Momma played her blues all day long, and had her drinking friends come by the house.

Momma didn't comb her hair like she use to everyday either. She let it get real nappy and just pulled it back in a ponytail. Momma and Mr. Calvin starting fussing more these days. Mr. Calvin mainly was fussing at Momma because he said all she do now is drink and party to much with her old friends. Mr. Calvin did not know Momma's friends too good. These were her friends she used to be with all the time. He was arguing with her about burning his food too. Momma would cuss at Mr. Calvin. I never heard her cuss at him before. Mr. Calvin only knew the hard working Momma in the field. He didn't know this side of Momma, but I did. Mr. Calvin told Momma he didn't want his house to be a night club around his child. Mr. Calvin started hunting more. I heard Momma tell Mr. Calvin,
"I might as well keep partying everyday since my husband is never home now!" Mr. Calvin told Momma, "that's why I'm never home, I can't get with your wild life."

I was in charge of watching little Calvin Jr., and staying in the front room while Momma partied with her friends. Momma was real strict, and she didn't want me to ever go outside and play with the other kids. I would just look out of the screen door at the kids that were in the streets playing ball and different games. I wished so many times that I didn't have to baby-sit, and that I could go out too. She said, "Those kids are fast and you don't need to be out there." I asked myself, when is it my turn to start having my own friends and fun?

FEBRUARY 1971

The phone rang. Momma called upstairs for me to get the phone.
It was Aunt Dora.
>"Hey Carla, Happy Birthday."
>"Thank you Aunt Dora."
>"What are you doing today on your Birthday?"
>"I don't know, probably nothing."
>"I'm sure Doris is fixing you something isn't she?"
>"Well, she may have forgotten, she hasn't said
>anything yet."
>"Some people want to say something to you".
>Aunt Dora put Staton and Lenny on the phone."
>"Happy Birthday Carla", Lenny and Staton yelled.
>I got a new puzzle Carla" Lenny said.
>"Hey how old are you Carla" Staton asked.
>"Eight years old". I'm getting so old hah" we
>laughed. Lenny said I was the same age as he
>was.
>"I'm gonna help you put it together, okay Lenny"
>I told him.

I knew he wanted me to help him put it together. Aunt Dora took
the phone back.
>"Well I have a gift for you and I can send it by
>Mr. Calvin when he comes by to feed the dogs,
>okay?"
>"Okay Aunt Dora, thank you."

I wondered what Aunt Dora got me for my birthday. Was it
another diary to talk to God or something else, I wondered. I
went downstairs and Momma told me Happy Birthday.
>"You want one of my vanilla cakes with chocolate
>frosting on it for your birthday?"
>"Yes, you didn't forget?"
>"Of course not, I remembered."

"We will have cake and ice cream later today,
okay?"

Momma hugged me. I don't know if Momma forgot or not, but I
was happy to be getting a cake. I did my chores and watched my
brother the rest of the afternoon, while Momma talked on the
phone in the kitchen and cooked.

Later that evening, Momma's friends started coming by. Each of
them told me Happy Birthday as they came in the house. I guess
Momma told them it was my birthday. They came to celebrate
my birthday, said Momma's friend Eunice. She was so pretty.

That night, I couldn't hear the t.v too good, because Momma and
Eunice were arguing so loud.
      "Bitch, I will kick yo yellow ass, you pull that
      shit again."
      "Fuck you Doris, you don't know what the hell
      you're talking about."

Eunice got up and was walking out of the front door. She was
going to Joe's car since he was taking her home that night. Momma
was still calling her all kinds of names. I don't know what they were
fighting about. Maybe the bid whiz game. Momma followed her
outside.   I ran to the door and saw Eunice lying on the cement
next to the curb. Then I saw Momma raising her foot over Eunice's
head and stomping her face into the sidewalk. She stomped on
Eunice face until it was bloody.

Joe ran to grab Momma away from Eunice, but not in time for
Momma to do the last stomp. When Momma picked up her foot
to stomp Eunice, she turned her head away and Momma's foot hit
the curb instead of Eunice's face. Momma's ankle bone came out of
her skin from the impact of her stomp on the cement. I don't know
who called the police, but they were coming around the corner.
They took Eunice and Momma to the hospital.   Buddy and Jean
stayed with us until Mr. Calvin came home from work. They told

him Momma was at Valley Medical Center and he went to go see about her.

We stayed over to Aunt Dora's until Momma came home from the hospital. I was glad. I was sad about Momma's foot, but I was glad to be with Lenny and Staton. When she came home, it was a few days later. They had to do surgery on her foot to reset the bone back in its place. Eunice and Momma stopped being friends for a while.

After this Mr. Calvin told Momma, "This partying is going to have to stop. I can't live like this." After that, I learned that Momma was pregnant again with her second baby that Mr. Calvin gave her. It was coming home in December again. I really wasn't happy about that either because all it meant was more baby-sitting time. But I didn't cut up any more of her clothes.

Not only did I have to look after my little brother, now I had to look after Momma too, because her leg was in a cast and she couldn't go to the bathroom. She had a bed pan. I hated it. I had to dump her bed pan on top of changing my little brother diapers too. I wished Momma would have given me to Erha now for real.

The end of the school year was close and Momma told me I could not go to summer school this year because I had to watch my brother and help her out because her foot was still healing. That summer was so boring and I was so mad every day.

CHAPTER 8

Skipped From 2nd Grade to 4th Grade

This was a special year, because I was skipped from 2nd grade to 4th grade. I didn't have to do my 3rd grade year. I was so glad, but Momma didn't make a big deal out of it. So I stopped jumping up and down in excitement when she didn't act excited like I thought she should. I was so glad that school was back. It felt so good to go to school and not be at home with all the chores and watching my brother and Momma. Plus, my cousins went to the same school I did. I was able to see Lenny and Staton more now and play with them on recess.

Momma was getting back to herself nowadays. She started having her card parties again. One day while one of Mr. Calvin's friends (Mr. Tucker) was waiting on him to come home, he told Momma about he and Mr. Calvin growing up. He told her that Mr. Calvin used to drink Peppermint Snap and play dominos back in his day. Momma started laughing real loud.
"So all I need to do is get him some Peppermint Snap and get a domino game started and everything will be all right."
"Yep" Mr. Tucker said.
"You have to include him Doris. He feels left out."
"Shit I can do that." Momma puffed on her cigarette.

So the next week, when Mr. Calvin was coming home from hunting, Momma told everybody that they were switching to dominos as soon as Mr. Calvin came in the door. They all agreed. They were so funny! Like little puppets, I thought. Sure enough it worked. Momma had bought him a bottle of Peppermint Schnapps and invited Mr. Calvin to a game of dominos. Momma called him in the kitchen soon as he came in the front door.
"Hey baby, come here".

"What is it Doris?" Mr. Calvin was tired and still
had his work clothes on.
"The guys want to know if you know how to play
dominos?" He started laughing. Then
everybody else in the kitchen invited him to sit
down and play.
"I used to play a little back in the day. Don't have
much time for it now."
"Ah man, sit down and lets just play one game. I
know you just got off of work, but let's just play
one game."

Momma had already finished dinner and was up fixing Mr. Calvin
a plate while he played dominos with the guys. Momma gave the
Peppermint Snap to Joe to offer to Mr. Calvin at the right time.
Mr. Calvin sat there playing and eating his dinner. I turned around
after I saw that he lost the fight, and finished looking at TV.

Now that Mr. Calvin was a part of partying with Momma every
now and then, the arguments were less. Sometimes when he came
home, he went straight to the kitchen where everybody else was.
He would also always have his Peppermint Schnapps that Momma
made sure was there. He was changing a little too now.

DECEMBER 13, 1971

Momma was screaming one morning and I ran to her room. She
wasn't there.
"It's time."
"Oh shit it's really time."

Her and Mr. Calvin were downstairs. Momma was sitting on the
couch with her legs open. It was time for Momma to have the
baby. Mr. Calvin had to go faster.
"Carla call Aunt Dora to come get you guys."
He and Momma were going out of the front door.

Aunt Dora came to get us. The school Christmas vacation started the same day Momma had to go in the hospital. As soon as Aunt Dora pulled up in her driveway, I ran into Lenny's room. He was laying down real quiet.

> "Hi Lenny. We going to be over here for a few days while Momma is in the hospital to get her other baby."
> "That's good." Lenny didn't seem happy.
> "Lenny are you okay?"
> "I'm sick Carla, I don't feel too good."

Aunt Dora came to the room and told me that Lenny needs to rest for now. I went into the kitchen with her.

> "Carla he can't play the way he used to. He has to get his rest." You can go play with Stanton if you like."
> "What's wrong with Lenny, he has a cold?"
> "No honey, he doesn't have a cold" he has Leukemia.
> "What's that Aunt Dora?"
> "Baby it's hard to explain, but it's a disease that they have not found a cure for and he is going to start having to go to the hospital for treatments."

Aunt Dora seemed like she was about to cry, so I gave her a hug around her waist real tight.

> "Lenny is going to feel better" I told her.

Later on that day, I asked Lenny if I could put his puzzle together and he told me if I could figure it out I could. I wanted to show him I could so he could be happy again. Staton helped me and we both finished. It was beautiful. It was a picture of an ocean and a big eagle flying across the ocean. The sky was blue and beautiful with clouds. Lenny said we did good. Lenny still didn't get out of bed to play with us that whole week. He just ate and then went back to bed.

Momma came home, but she didn't have her baby with her.
> "Momma where is your baby?"
> "The baby needs to stay in the hospital a little
> longer because she was premature and only
> weighed 3 pounds."
> "What is premature ?" When the baby comes
> before her due time, momma said. She was searching
> for words to explain it to me.
> "She came too early."
> "When does she come home?"
> "When she gains some more weight, which will
> probably be next week sometime."

Momma didn't take long to get back started with her partying gang. She rested from the hospital for a week and then was back partying and drinking. My baby sister, Brenda, finally came home. She was so tiny. I never saw a baby that tiny. I guess that was the premature stuff Momma was talking about. I wondered why she was so little. I was so afraid to hold her at first.

Things were back to normal in no time. Everything was the same except for now, I had two babies to baby-sit from the time I came home from school and after doing my chores. Christmas was the same this year. Same tree, same bulbs, same partying company for Momma. Same t.v. programs to look at on t.v.

JANUARY 1972

When we came back from the Christmas vacation, I didn't see Lenny at recess anymore. I only saw Staton. I wondered where was Lenny. Stanton told me that Lenny still wasn't feeling to well.

I came home and asked Momma what leukemia was and she told me that it was a bad disease that they can't cure. I told her that Lenny had it.
> "Lenny is going to be fine Carla ."

"He hasn't been feeling good since Christmas
time. Is he going to ever feel better?"
"I'm sure he is, he just has to get help". Momma
changed subjects and said she had something to
tell me. I grieved. Oh how I wish it wasn't what I
thought it was.
"Guess what Carla?"
"What Momma?"
"You are going to have you another sister or
brother."

I started counting the months for the due date to come again. I
wish she would stop this. I went upstairs to my room. I wanted to
write to God.

Dear God:
I know you see everything that is happening. I wish things
were so different. You know Lenny is sick and I wish you
would make him better so that he could be a kid again.
Find the cure for him God, please. Also you know
Momma is going to have another child. Why she keep
doing that? Can't you stop her from having children? She
doesn't take care of them, she just leave them with me all
the time and I'm tired. Please help me.

After Easter Break I saw Lenny at school in the hallway. I was so
happy. He looked different. His face seemed fatter. He was
darker and he had on a curly wig. The kids in the hallway were
laughing at Lenny. I felt so bad.
"Lenny, why do you have that wig on your head?"
"I have to, the radiation treatment took all my
hair out."

I got so scared for Lenny. I wished he didn't have to go through
this evil stuff. One of the boys that was laughing was tall and
talking about Lenny being a girl now. He walked up to Lenny and
knocked his wig off of his head. Everybody in the hallway started

laughing. I saw Lenny's head. He had hardly no hair, just in patches. Lenny reached down in the dirt and picked up his wig and dusting it off. He had tears in his eyes. God how I wished I could beat those boys up for Lenny.

"It's okay Carla, I can handle it. They don't understand what I'm going through."

Lenny didn't even sound like himself anymore. He sounded like an old man. I didn't know what I could do. I wished I could make it all go away. I prayed to God for him. When I went home that day, I was so sad. I cried for Lenny. I didn't understand.

The card and domino games went on month after month. I became even more quiet. Even when I went to school, where I loved to be the most, I found myself being quiet. Mainly because I didn't feel like I fit in with my schoolmates. They always seemed to be much happier than I was. I just pretended and went through the motions. They didn't know I had child after child to take care of while my mother partied every night and her husband hunted most weekends.

JUNE -- SEPTEMBER 1972

After summer time, Lenny spent a lot of time in and out of the hospital. He changed a lot. He started really getting big and fat. Aunt Dora said the medicine was blowing him up. It hurt to see him because now he was getting mad. He wasn't nice and he didn't smile too much anymore. Aunt Dora would tell me to just over look him because he is going through a lot by not being able to be a kid anymore. Aunt Dora loved him so much. I could tell by the way she took care of him and looked after him every minute she could.

Momma was going into the hospital with her third child that Mr. Calvin gave her. She was in the hospital the same amount of time. Me and my brother and sister stayed over to Aunt Dora's house until she came home.

Momma did her usual 1 week recovery and was back on her feet with her normal everyday life again. This time the baby didn't have to stay in the hospital any extra time. She brought home another little girl, named Catherine.

OCTOBER 1972

One night, Momma and her friends were downstairs partying. I was rocking my baby sister Brenda to sleep. After I went to sleep Momma and her friends must have partied until early in the morning. Something strange happened. I was in my bed asleep when I woke up suddenly. I looked toward my closet, and there stood Mr. Calvin. It looked like he was hiding from something, or maybe he was scared. He was black as the darkness, but I saw him in the glow of the night light. He had yellow eyes just glowing in the dark. I was between sleep and being half awake, so I fell back asleep.

The next day, he didn't say anything to me, I didn't say anything to him either. So I was convinced that it was a bad dream about him being in my room. How stupid of me, I thought to myself. From that moment on, I never felt comfortable around him.

A few weeks later, on Halloween Night, Momma and her friends were playing cards and drinking as usual. Mr. Calvin joined them after he got in from work. After 11:00 p.m., Calvin Jr. was sleep and I had to rock Brenda to sleep then make sure Cathy was taken care of too. I took my bath and told everybody goodnight.

It must have been many hours when I awoke, feeling suffocated. This heavy thing was on top of me, breathing hard. At first I could not see what it was. Was I dreaming, or was it real? I was about to say something, and then I heard him whisper "Shhhhhh". He was on my chest, the little bit I had, sucking on me and feeling on my private area. I tried to push him off me, but he wouldn't stop. He was biting me so hard, it felt like it was tearing me apart. I began to cry, "Stop!" Finally, He got up and told me,

>"You better not tell your mother, or she will kill you." As he was walking toward the door, he turned around and said,
>"She won't believe you anyway."

I cried wondering why my step daddy did this to me. I dared not tell Momma. I had seen my mother fight men. I knew she could kill my little self. I hated Mr. Calvin now. He reminded me of Poppa Ernest who stuck his finger in my privates too. I didn't say anything then either.

That next week, I tried not to remember what Mr. Calvin did to me. Yet, the more I tried, the more it kept coming to my mind. I didn't feel like Carla anymore. I don't know what or who I felt like. I wanted the dirty feelings to just go away. I dreaded the mornings when I ran into him while going to the bathroom, next to my room. When I would pass him in the hallway, or see his face at the breakfast table, I would want to throw up. I asked myself, how do I live with this? How do I act normal?

Mr. Calvin went from day to day as if he never came into my room. I needed to talk to someone, but there was no one, except my diary and God. I wrote in it for hours, so it seemed like. I took my diary to school with me so that no one would catch me writing. At lunch time, I stayed in the gym area by the bleachers and just wrote.

>Dear God:
>I need to talk to you so bad. I am so mad. I hate his ass, I hate his ass so much! I know what I'm about to tell you is no surprise to you. Please help me. I can't go through this by myself. I am tired of it. You know I have no one to talk to and you know he hurt me. I shake while I write these words, I have to stop so I can wipe my tears to keep them

from falling and go on. Help me write to you and tell you what's on my mind. Please God tell me what to do. He said if I tell my Momma she will kill my ass. She can do that, you know, because she is a mean ass woman. All she want me for is to baby-sit anyway. Why he come into my room God? He is suppose to do that stuff with grown ups not kids. Did he drink too much and came to the wrong room? Please keep him out of my room from now on. I hurt each time I think about it. I can't make it go away. I don't want it in my mind and in my nose. I don't know how I feel sometimes. Sometimes I just don't want to be here. I just want to die and you know that. Maybe you're keeping me here for a reason. Please help me. I get so sad. As I look out at the playground, the kids are running and happy. I don't know what that feels like. I want to be like them. I'm not. I know it. Life changes too much for me. I don't like myself, God, and I don't like my family. If I had another family maybe this would not be happening to me. If I had another Momma and Daddy, this wouldn't be happening. The bell is ringing, God. I have to go to class now. I know my secret is safe with you. Please be there later on when I have to write again.

Even though God wasn't there in person, something in me knew God could hear me and take care of me. I knew there were lots of people in the world, but I believed that God would soon come to my house and change this mess for me. Aunt Dora said I could always talk to Him. I hoped He heard everything I wrote. I knew I used some bad language, but I knew He understood that I was angry. I told Him to take it away from me; my memory, my sore feelings.

After that, I found myself thinking about what happened. I would try to replace the thoughts with anything else that could come into my mind. I wished to myself that I had a mother that I could talk to and would be sober long enough to listen. Instead, I had a mother that only gave orders for me to do her work and take care of her responsibilities. Do the dishes. Change the baby diapers. Feed the babies. Prepare the similac milk. Vacuum the floors. Take out the trash.

These were my secret conversations with my mother. Why the hell didn't she want to know how my day was? If I needed to talk about anything? I would yearn and ache for her affection. I wanted her to tell me that I was pretty or that she loved me every now and then. Even give me an occasional hug like Grandma Georgia gave me when I was at her house. I had seen other mothers do that for their daughters when they came to pick them up from school.

It often bothered me that my mother didn't know simple things about me, like my favorite color, my favorite subject in school, or my fears and doubts. She never asked me about my dreams or what I wanted to do or be when I grew up. I wanted my mother to know me and find out what was inside of me. All that she knew was that I went to school every morning, and I better be back from school by 3:30 p.m. I had to be back so that I could take care of the kids and do my chores.

Some mornings, I found myself waking up crying because I was having nightmares about Mr. Calvin. Some of the dreams I knew were not dreams but it was really Mr. Calvin in my room on top of me. Each time it would happen, I would put it way in the back of my mind. I would just pray to God, "Please take the nightmare away from me." But it still kept happening.

A few weeks later, one Saturday evening, Aunt Ellen came to get the kids for dinner. I didn't care as long as I didn't have to watch the kids. I felt like it was a break for me. She kept them that entire weekend. Later on that night, when Momma's company arrived, Momma saw me looking out of the screen door at the kids in the neighborhood. She yelled out from the kitchen "Go on outside." I stood there frozen, wanting to ask her if she was sure she was talking to me. I didn't want to do the wrong thing and be embarrassed. Then she said, "You better go before I change my mind." I flew outside that screen door without looking back.

The first person I saw was this girl named Glundy. Glundy was my age and went to my school. I had some classes with her, and we spoke sometimes in passing. But the word was out that I was a sheltered home kid. So the kids never tried to be friends with me. Glundy had two other sisters, Lois and Pam, who also went to my school. They were in different grades, one behind the other. They were the life of the projects. When Glundy saw me come out of my door and off my porch, she yelled at me.
    "Hey, can you play?" I smiled,
    "Yep, I sure can! What are we playing?"
    One of the boys hollered out, "Hide and go get
    it."

We were supposed to hide from the person that was "It" and if he found you and tagged you, you were "It." It was so much fun to hear everybody moving about, whispering, hiding, and trying to help each other get to safe grounds. I was actually out there playing. I couldn't believe it! We played for hours and had a ball.

A little later, I saw a great opportunity to get to safe ground. The person that was "it," was clear across the other side of the street. I just knew I could beat him to the tree, the base that we were to touch. I broke out and started running at a high speed, looking back to see if anyone was chasing me. When I turned my head to the front, I met up with a tall wooden telephone pole. Next thing I remember, the ambulance was coming to take me to the hospital. Blood was running from my forehead and I could hear the voices around me saying "She just ran into the pole. I guess she wasn't looking where she was going." Momma was furious and acting so dramatic. She was screaming at the top of her lungs, "My child, my child! Oh my poor baby!" I was thinking, I guess I'll never get another chance to go outside again. So off to the hospital we went.

In the ambulance, they tried to calm Momma down. I guess they knew she was a little drunk, because even I could smell the liquor fumes on her breath. We got to the hospital, and after the doctors examined me further, they informed Momma I would be blind, but only for a few hours. They told Momma that I had suffered a minor concussion, but I would be all right. They kept me in the hospital that night for observation and told Momma she could come and get me in the morning. Before Momma could leave, Mr. Calvin walked into the room at the tail end of the doctor's instructions to Momma. My stomach turned when I saw him, and I gritted my teeth.

"How are you doing, Carla?" he asked.

I wanted to say none of your damn business and what do you really care, but instead I mumbled, "fine." The doctor was saying, "See you in the morning," to Momma and assured her they would take good care of me. Momma showed signs of relief when the doctors told her I would be okay. That was the most concern I had ever seen from her. Then Mr. Calvin said, "Good night and we will see you in the morning." When they left, I wished I had my diary so bad. I talked to God about it until I fell asleep. "I hate the fact that he came up here, God, but I guess he had to pick up Momma. I wish I could stay in this hospital." All the attention, concern, and care felt so good. Throughout that evening, and into the next morning, nurses were coming in and out checking on me. It was a nice change from diaper changing, fixing plates, and rocking babies to sleep. Now, I was the one being brought food.

The next day, Momma and Mr. Calvin arrived bright and early to check me out. I didn't like the fact that they came so early, because I wanted to eat lunch there. I especially didn't like seeing Mr. Calvin. How dare he come to my bedside again! He could have stayed outside in the car. I didn't ever want him near me while I was in any kind of bed. I didn't care if it was my death bed. I still didn't want him near me. I returned home that afternoon to unfinished chores in the kitchen. There were dishes in the kitchen sink that needed to be washed. There was trash that needed to be taken out. Cinderella was back home.

CHAPTER 9

November 1972
Visit Daddy & Ms. Estee

A few weeks after I got out of the hospital, I had the surprise of my life. I was washing dishes in the kitchen when there was a knock at the door, and I heard Momma say, "Well looka here! Jesus must be coming back." Then I heard laughter and voices. When I heard a male's voice say, "Doris, do you have some milk?" a big smile crossed my face. It was so good to hear their voices. I dropped the dish towel and ran into the front room. It was Daddy and Ms. Estee. Ms. Estee stood there with a pretty blue jean outfit on. I was so happy to see her. Her hair was beautifully pinned up. She looked like a movie star. Daddy had on his baggy jeans with a plaid buttoned up shirt that showed a little hair on his chest because he missed the first button. He was asking for milk for his scotch.

"Hey, girl," he said. "How are you doing?"

"I'm all right I guess." I was as honest as I could be.

I wanted to scream and say, please take me away from this place, please rescue me, but I missed my chance a long time ago. My little sister Brenda walked up to Ms. Estee and said "hi." Ms. Estee smiled and picked her up. I was instantly jealous. Mr. Calvin came into the house, and Momma introduced them to him. They had small talk, and then Mr. Calvin was on his way to go hunting.

"So Doris, you're about to have another baby?"
Daddy asked.

Momma was six months pregnant with yet another child. Momma didn't answer and went to the refrigerator to grab a beer. She asked Ms. Estee if she could get her anything and Ms. Estee refused. When Ms. Estee spoke it was class and grace. She didn't drink that crap that Momma was drinking. She was a lady.

"So, what brings you to Fresno?" Momma asked
my Daddy.

"I came out here to see my relatives as we were

passing through. We've been all over the place."
"Is that right?" Momma smirked like she really
didn't care.
"How's my girls and my son?"
Daddy said, " They are fine."
Ms. Estee interrupted, saying "They ask about
you and Carla all the time."

That made me feel good because I thought they had forgotten all
about me. Momma was still angry at Daddy, I could tell it in her
eyes and the way she looked at him. She didn't try to hide it.
Momma could never come to the full truth or confess that she
could not be responsible for her kids. I began to think that Tyrone
Jr., Sadie, and Tarah were lucky after I saw how my life was going
with Momma. I wouldn't have been as miserable. If only Daddy
had not given me back to Momma.

Momma invited them to stay for dinner, but they had to keep
going. Ms. Estee asked if we could all take pictures outside so that
she had something to show the kids when they got back to Phoenix.
Momma said "Okay." I grabbed Little Calvin and Brenda and
went to the backyard where it was sunny and nice outside. Ms.
Estee gave the camera to Daddy to take the pictures.

When we got back into the house, Daddy asked Momma since I
was on school break, could I go back to Phoenix to visit. They said
they would see to it that I got back to Fresno in time for school.
When I heard him ask her that, I began to pray inside. Please God,
let me go. Please let her say yes, I whispered in my heart.
Momma crossed her leg and grabbed a cigarette, looking at his
head.
She said, "I have to think about it. When yawl
going back?"
"First thing in the morning," Ms. Estee said.
Daddy looked at Momma and said, "Hell, Doris,
just let her go be with her other sisters and
brothers. What is it that you have to think

about? Just let the girl go."
Uncrossing her legs, leaning forward, she said,
"And whose damn fault is that, hah?" Momma
snapped.
"Look, Doris, I'll make sure she's back here in time
for school." He avoided answering Momma's
question all together.
"I need somebody here to watch these kids with
me," she said.
"Fine," he said and stood up, motioning with his
head to Ms. Estee, "Let's go."

So they left. I stormed upstairs to my room in tears, cursing my
mother and her children out. I went directly to my diary.

Dear God:
It's not fair, why isn't she letting me go? It's not fair
God! It's not fair! Why does she have to make me
miserable because her ass is miserable? All I want to
do is see my sisters and brothers again. She just
wants me here to watch her damn kids. I hate her
ass. I'm tired of it. How come she can't watch her
own damn kids? She had them, not me!

It took me a while to stop cursing Momma under my breath about
denying me to see my sisters and brothers. It seemed like my
feelings were never important to her. She only cared about herself.
I hated Daddy gave me back to her.

During the Thanksgiving Holiday Momma and Mr. Calvin were
talking about moving into Aunt Ellen's house. He was telling
Momma he wanted to rent it because she had a backyard. His
greyhound dogs were kept at Aunt Dora's house. He was tired of
going over there to feed and take care of them after work. Momma
was happy. She wanted her own house. She lived in the projects
most of her life.

Soon as Mr. Calvin left, Momma grabbed the phone and called Eunice to tell her that her husband bought her a house. Eunice and Momma never got back close like they were before Momma stomped her face in the ground, but they were still talking and hanging out, every now and then. Momma jokingly said to Eunice, "I'm leaving all you no good niggas in these projects and going to a house with a gate around it." Eunice must have asked Momma when was she moving, because the next thing Momma said was, "In a few months." Eunice told Momma, "Good, get your ass away from here!" They were weird friends. Fight, curse each other out, and then the next day they laugh and talk some more. Momma asked her if she had anything to drink over there. Eunice told her no. Momma said she had some money to get something if she could get a ride. Eunice was over in the next couple of hours.

When Eunice came over this time, she had her daughter Satrina Wilson with her. I had never met her before. She wasn't tall but looked strong. She wore a red natural hair style and was in the ninth grade at Irwin Jr. High School. I was in the 5th grade at Mary McCloud Bethune. I idolized her after hearing Momma and Eunice talk about what kind of girl she was. She was tough and could fight. Eunice had an old man that would beat her when he got drunk. Satrina would come home and find out what happened to her Momma and kick his butt. I wished I could kick Mr. Calvin's ass and Momma's too for a different reason.

From that point on, when Eunice would come over, Satrina would come with her and make small talk with me. Satrina knew I didn't have any older sisters. I was much younger than her, but not too young. She asked me once,

> "What do you do from day to day and on the
> weekends?"
> "Nothing, I am my Momma's baby-sitter when I
> leave school."
> "Well we have to change that and get you out of
> the house."

"Yep, we need to do that," I agreed.

I thought about her all evening. Could she be my big sister? I hoped so. Maybe God was answering my prayer through her. That night, Uncle Kyle, Mr. Calvin's brother, came by with all his nephews and nieces except for Lenny. Uncle Kyle wanted to see if Momma would let me go to the movies with them. She actually said yes and I was so happy. We went to see a Bruce Lee karate film. I loved Bruce Lee! Uncle Kyle had a station wagon, and his niece Falona asked me if I wanted to get on top of the roof with her to watch the movie. As we were looking at the movie, I noticed Falona lay real close to the driver's side where Uncle Kyle was sitting. I saw his arm reach up to the roof of the station wagon as if he was feeling for something. Falona scooted toward the edge even more. Then I saw what they were doing. It was dark, but I saw him feeling on Falona's titties. I could not believe my eyes. I wanted to throw up. She wasn't jumping or scared. In fact, she moved closer. They knew what they were doing. Then it all made sense to me. I felt so bad for his wife, Aunt Maura, because I was sure she didn't know about this. I never looked at Uncle Kyle the same after that. When he would invite me to his church, I would always say I felt too sick to go. From that point on, I never wanted to go out with them again. I put it far in the back of my mind, so I wouldn't have to think about it anymore.

A week later, Satrina came back over to our apartment to ask Momma if I could go to the football game with her. Momma gave her a bit of a hassle. Satrina quickly added, "Doris, she will be with me and you have nothing to worry about. She's damn near ten years old so she will be fine." I was crossing my fingers while they were talking. Momma said, "Okay now, I don't want no stuff." We left and went over to Satrina's house.

Satrina took me into her bedroom where there were really cool posters of all the latest albums. Earth Wind and Fire, Ohio Players, and the Spinners. She even had the Jackson Five on her wall. She was hip. She had a nice bedroom set, that had a bed with matching

dresser. It was really cool.
"Hey, you want to wear your hair out like mine?"

She had a pretty red Afro. Satrina dyed her hair, but it was still pretty. I had long hair, but Momma always kept it in ponytails.
"My Momma would kill me if I took my hair
down."
"Don't worry about it. We will put it back up
when I take you home."

She got her natural comb out and hooked me up until I had a big Afro. She sprayed Afro-Sheen in it, and it got so big! Then she said, "Let's go do your face now. Just a little lip gloss to give a little life, okay?"

I laughed and nodded. That was the most I had done with make up. She told me that her boyfriend Ricky and his friend Michael were coming to pick us up. I said, "Cool," trying to sound cool.
"We also need to change that old fashion blouse
of yours. I think I have something that would
make those jeans look much better."
Satrina went into their drawer and pulled out a
white sweater.
"Where did you get that blouse, the salvation
army?"

She handed me the sweater to put on. It was nice. It fit real tight too. She didn't know that she guessed where I got my clothes from on the dot.
"Now there you go. It makes you look like you
are in Jr. High. Your titties look big too. What
you been doing, girl?" I felt ashamed.
"Nothing." I put my head down. Satrina started
laughing.
"I know yo ass ain't been doing nothing with a
strict mother like yours."
Eunice yelled from the kitchen at Satrina,

"Ricky's here!"
She said, "Are you ready, Carla?"
I said, "Yep."

I grabbed my second-hand store coat, and off we went. I sat in the back and Satrina sat in the front. While we were driving, Satrina was introducing everybody to me. I was so shy and scared. I didn't know how to sit, so I just sat still. Boy, I thought I was hip. I had my hair down, last years jeans, and one of Satrina's white sweaters that she told me to put on at the last minute before she combed my hair out.

When we got there, the guys went to buy us something to drink and eat while we reserved some seats.
"Momma didn't know boys were going," I told
Satrina.
"Good" She said.
"Neither did I."
"You will be fine, baby girl." Satrina pulled me to
her.

Fresno High was playing Sacramento High. We were rooting for Fresno High. I learned that Ricky played for the team, but he hurt his left leg. He just came to support his team. After each play, the audience was filled with screaming and hollering cheers. Fresno High won by one touch down -- twenty-one to fourteen. He picked Satrina up right off the ground, he was so happy! It was a fun game, although I didn't understand the plays. Michael kept trying to explain them to me. I didn't know what a touchdown, a tackle or a field goal was. I ended up smarter than I was when I started off. As we were leaving the stadium, there were thousands of people moving at the same time. We finally got to the car and started out of the parking lot. Ricky was still screaming to Michael about the last play when his team mate made a touch down in the last forty seconds. They were high fiving and saying all kinds of things. Satrina was in the front seat looking for another tape to play. Michael looked at me and asked me if I enjoyed myself. I

said, "It was fine. I really liked it." I felt stupid with that answer.
He smiled, almost to say, it's okay, you did fine.
"How old are you?" he asked next.

Oh no, I said to myself, what do I say? Do I tell him the truth?
I said, "Nine and a half."
"When will you be ten?"
"In a couple of months, on February 3rd."

He had this surprised look on his face as his eyes centered in on my
breasts.
"Boy, you look at least fourteen or fifteen."
I asked how old he was.
He said, "Sixteen going on seventeen."

He looked like a grown man as far as I was concerned.   I guess
because he was 5'11" and I was 4'11".   He told me he was in the
11th grade and would be graduating next year.   Boy, was that
scary to me!
He asked, "Why do you look so mature?"
"Maybe because I have been through some
mature things," I replied.
"Oh, yeh? Is that right? Like what?"
I said, "Nothing that I would like to talk about
right now."
He then said, "When can we talk about it, later?"

I think he got the wrong impression. I meant I had been through
things that I was too embarrassed to talk about. Like why I
believed my breasts were the size they were. It was Mr. Calvin's
fault. If he wasn't on my breasts, maybe they would have never
grown this fast.

We soon arrived back at Satrina's house. Before I knew it, Michael
had reached over and kissed me right on top of my lips. Oh God!
I didn't know whether to laugh or cry! Satrina didn't see it because
she was all necked up in the front seat with Ricky. I really didn't

think we would see them again anytime soon. Michael cleared his throat as a hint to Ricky to "Let's go." They stopped kissing and started laughing at us. We got out of the car.

As we walked in the house, Satrina asked, "So how did you like the game?"
>"The game, I survived. But what that boy did I don't know if I will ever recover from."
>"Why, what happened?"
>"I got nervous, well you couldn't see because you were all necked up."
>"Did he kiss you girl?"
>"Yeh, real quick."

Satrina laughed. "Probably because he saw those real healthy breasts in that tight white sweater." She grabbed a brush and rubber band so that she could put my hair back up like it was when I left home. Satrina didn't know I hated my breasts that were growing bigger and bigger. I didn't think a 5th grader should have a size 34B cup. But I did and couldn't do anything about it. I wished I could cut them off or something. I was the only girl in my class with titties that big.
>"I better get you home," Satrina said.

So we walked around the corner to my house. Momma and Mr. Calvin were up in the living room, looking at TV. Satrina made small talk with Momma and then left. Momma asked if I had fun.
>"Yep, thank you so much for letting me go."

I couldn't believe it. I actually got to go out, and with almost grown people at that!

DECEMBER 1972

Christmas was different this year. Momma told me that Aunt Dora wanted the family to go to the hospital to see Lenny. I really wished Lenny didn't have to spend Christmas in the hospital.

Later that afternoon when we arrived at the hospital, all of the family was there. Uncle Kyle and his wife. Aunt Ellen and her daughters. Even Aunt Brenda and her son Gary, plus us. Lenny had a big room and all of us fit in it.

Aunt Dora was placing gifts under a tree in his room. Lenny was looking at the ceiling. He didn't look too happy. He laid there with a needle hooked up to a pole in his arm. A machine was by his bed with numbers on it.

Lenny had lots of gifts. Aunt Dora was trying to make Lenny cheer up. "Smile Lenny, all of your family is here." Lenny didn't say anything. Mr. Calvin walked over to Aunt Dora and gave her our gift. I don't know what he bought him, but it was from the whole family. Everyone, except for the children, seemed so sad. The adults were not saying too much. Aunt Dora asked Lenny should we start opening the gifts.
> "I don't understand why all the gifts when you
> know I won't be able to play with them," Lenny
> whispered in his scratchy voice.

He turned his head away from us, looking toward the window where the cars were passing by and sounds were loud. The sun was shining through the white curtains on Lenny's face, that had gotten larger.
> "Yes, you will, Lenny. Don't say that baby. You
> will be able to play with them."
> "Momma, take the gifts out of here when you
> leave because they ain't mine."

Lenny knew something nobody else knew. It didn't sound like Lenny. The day after New Years, Momma got a call from Aunt Dora and she sounded real sad.
> "Oh no, Dora, baby, when? I am so sorry."

I didn't know what was happening but Momma had to sit down in the kitchen. Then I heard Momma say, "When will the services be held? Okay, now whatever you need us to do, please let us know." Momma put down the phone and just shook her head, grabbing her cigarettes.

I was afraid. I was scared inside. I thought something bad happened to Lenny.
> "Momma, are you okay?" I walked in the kitchen
> and sat next to Momma at the dinner table.
> "Baby, your cousin Lenny died this morning.
> That was Aunt Dora calling the family to let
> them know."

I felt like I didn't know what to feel like. Momma reached out her hand for me to come get a hug from her.
> "I know how you loved your cousin Lenny. He is
> in a better place now. He doesn't have to hurt
> anymore. He is with God, baby."

It felt so good, Momma holding me in her arms. She let me cry. I felt so bad for Aunt Dora and Stanton. Stanton doesn't have a brother now and Aunt Dora only has one son. I never knew anybody that died before.

The next week we went to the funeral service at the Funeral Home. The family was there waiting outside for everyone else to arrive so that we could walk in together. Once we all were together, we got in line. As we walked in the Funeral Home, the organ began to play and Uncle Kyle read the bible out loud.

Up ahead of us was a coffin like the one I saw on television that Dracula sleeps in during the day. Lenny was in this casket looking like he was sleeping, but he was dead.

As we sat down, Aunt Ellen's two daughters covered their aces under her arms, while Glenda (the oldest) sat with her head down.

Aunt Dora was shaking her leg. Stanton was just looking at the casket where Lenny lay. A lady got up to sing a song called "The Last Mile" and seem like everybody in the place started hollering and crying. I cried too. It hurt so much that Lenny died. I sat there and thought about him and how we use to have fun together. I thought about putting the puzzles together with him and how he taught me the way to do it. I then thought about the kids at the school and started hating them because they were so damn stupid. Then I thought about Lenny's last words about Christmas, "These gifts are not mine. You know I won't get a chance to play with them." Momma put her arms around me when she saw the tears rolling down my face.

JANUARY 1973

After Christmas Break, I made a friend my age from my class. Mavis Fordington was her name. She was a beautiful girl. She was in all of my classes. She had real long brown sandy hair with hazel brown eyes, and was always dressed well. You could tell that her mother didn't take her to the Salvation Army, or any other second-hand stores. I learned that her mother didn't raise her, but her grandmother did. She knew all the "in" people at our school. Yet, she was still willing to be friends with me, no matter what kind of clothes I wore.

For the next year or so, Mavis gave me her hand me-downs so that it looked like I had new clothes. She took good care of her stuff. She was the first real friend I ever had. She accepted me the way I was.

One day it was raining, so her grandmother picked us up from school. Mavis' grandmother was real old and bent over. She was about six feet, even when she was bent over. She must have been a giant when she was young. She wore big glasses and drove a big navy blue car. She offered to drop me off at home. As we were driving, her grandmother asked me if I wanted to go to church with them next Sunday. I said, "Yes, of course." She said, "Good, I will ask your mother once we get to your house."

Mavis' grandmother got out of the car and came to meet my mother just like she said she would. Momma was in the kitchen cooking dinner. The kids were playing in the living room with their Christmas toys. After Mavis' grandma met my mother, they left. I said goodbye to Mavis and told her I would see her tomorrow at school. I was grateful to Mavis' grandmother for giving me a ride, and I told her that. I would have had to walk home in that bad rain.

Momma agreed to let me go to church that coming Sunday. I was so glad that I didn't have to go hear Uncle Kyle preach and be around him. Every time I saw him I couldn't concentrate, I would just see his hands reaching up to Falona's titties.

The next day, it didn't rain, so Mavis and I walked home together. I learned that her mother was on drugs and in jail. That's why Mavis was with her grandmother. Then I told her some things about me and my life. Our stories brought us closer. The only difference was that Mavis ended up with a real spiritual grandmother who had money and loved her. Unlike my mother, who was still not ready for kids.

After school one day, we saw some kids smoking in the bungalows (which were buildings separated from the main campus). We looked at them and frowned. "My mother smokes like a train," I said. Mavis' eyes lit up.
    "She does?"
    I said, "Yeh, why?"
    "Do you want to try some cigarettes?"
    I said, "How?"
    "Just get some from your mother."

We plotted and plotted. It was my job to sneak two cigarettes from my mother's pack and bring them to school before Friday. Later that week, when I came home, Momma was sleeping on the couch, snoring. Her cigarette pack was in the kitchen on the counter. I looked around to see where the kids were. They were sleeping too. I sneaked in quickly and grabbed two of them. It only left her with two in the pack. I was worried that she would remember that she had four originally. She woke up after hearing me drop a glass off the shelf, and I damn near messed in my pants. Momma got right up, went to the kitchen and said, "Pass me my cigarettes." My heart started beating so fast! I saw her feeling on her pack and then she called me. I just knew I was busted.

"Yeh?" My heart was beating fast.

"Find me some paper and a pen. I need you to go to the store and get me some more cigarettes."

I went upstairs, put my books down, hid my own cigarettes, and came downstairs with paper and pencil for Momma to write a note. I went to the store and came back so fast, she didn't even know I had left yet.

The next day, when I brought those two cigarettes to Mavis, we started laughing. She said, "Okay, at my house after school, right?" I said, "Right!" I kept the cigarettes in my coat pocket and kept my coat on all day. It was hot that day, but I didn't want to take any chances. Mavis grandmother was gone to work, and we went to the backyard to sit on the porch. The backyard was filled with so many fruit trees, it looked like we were in the middle of a jungle.

"Here's the matches, let's go!" Mavis pulled me by the hands.

"I hope your grandmother doesn't come home early."

"She won't, she's gone for hours."

I brought out the cigarettes and she struck the match. I put the cigarette in my mouth, and she put hers in her mouth. We lit both cigarettes at the same time. We didn't know how to inhale or exhale. So we puffed and puffed without blowing it out properly, gagging on the smoke like fools. It was so funny! I had to hit her on her back, and she had to hit me on mine too.

Then we stopped and decided to take our time and talk grown
while we were smoking.
    "Hey Mavis, let's pretend that we are our mothers
    and talk like they do."
    "Cool, because my mother be talking so much
    stuff."

I crossed my leg just like I saw Momma cross hers every time she
got ready to go off on somebody.
    "Yeh bitch, if you keep talking that shit, I'm go
    stomp yo ass in the ground."
    "Fuck you hoe, I don't think so. You got to bring
    some to get some." We laughed.

So we puffed real light and held the cigarette in our mouths with
one eye kinda closed like grown ups do. Boy, this was so cool! I
think we finally got the hang of it right before the cigarette burned
all the way out. We agreed, we would do it some more whenever I
could steal the cigarettes from Momma. Afterwards, we sprayed
ourselves with Mavis' grandmother's perfume, did mouthwash, and
I went home.

CHAPTER 10

FEBRUARY 1973 - 10TH YEAR
(5th - 6th GRADE)

That year, in February of 1973, Momma gave me a tenth year birthday party and told me I could invite my friends. It started off great. I invited my cousins and neighbors I knew from the Atchison Courts: Glundy, Pam, Lois, Norma, Larry, and whoever else. I couldn't believe she let me invite some of the kids from the neighborhood. Momma prepared the usual - her white cake and chocolate icing. This time we also had potato chips, ice cream, and cold cuts. The only fear I had was if she got drunk. She was on her way, because they were drinking a lot already. I was just hoping she would stay in the kitchen. I opened all of my gifts. My cousin Gary bought me the Ohio Players album "Fire", and Momma even let us play it. Aunt Dora bought me a another five year diary. I appreciated it so much, because I had just about filled up the one she gave me for Christmas a few years ago. Even though I had my friends and cousins there, I missed Lenny.

Of course Momma's friends were there too. They were in the kitchen, playing cards, while we were in the front room dancing and having fun. Then it happened. Momma staggered into the living room.

"Alright, the party is just beginning, we got to
change this damn music."

She ripped the needle off, scratching my new album. She put on her Bobbie Blue Band. I was so pissed at her! I could have hit her. The party was over then. Why did I have to go through this same thing?

Momma had her fourth child on March 7, 1973 by Mr. Calvin and I was fit to be tired by now. Momma said she tied her tubes and that she could not have anymore children. I was so glad I didn't know what to do. I wondered why she waited so long.

Now I had two sisters and two brothers. Edwin, the last baby, was also premature like Brenda was. Not only was he premature, he also had health defects. He had a bad nerve in his eyes that would cause the lids to not open all the way. I felt so sorry for him. He was only a baby and by the time he was one years old, the doctors were talking about operating on his eyes to lift up his eyelids.

I didn't mind watching Edwin at all. He was like my own little baby. He kind of reminded me of my cousin Lenny because Lenny got sick real young and had medical problems too.

SPRING -- APRIL 1973

Spring came and we were getting out of school for two weeks for the Easter Break. I wouldn't see Mavis until it was time to go to church on Sunday.

A couple of days before Easter I received a surprise visit from two people I love so much. Daddy and Ms. Estee had come through Fresno again on their way back home, and asked Momma if I could go with them. Momma said yes this time. I ran up the stairs and grabbed a few things. They were leaving within thirty minutes. I only needed five. What got into Momma? Was she drunk? I knew she had been drinking, but I wanted to get out of there before she sobered up and came to her senses. Momma and I were at home alone, which was rare. The kids had just left to spend the weekend over to Aunt Doris house. I was so glad, because that gave me an out, and Momma would have no excuse not to let me go. Ms. Estee whispered to me that I didn't have to pack too many clothes, because she was going to take me shopping. We got on the freeway and started for Arizona. The drive was long but fun.
    "Wake up, Carla," I heard Ms. Estee say.

We were in Arizona. Ms. Estee told me to put my hand outside the window. I felt the Indian summer, very hot and humid as Daddy called it. When I finally saw my sisters and brothers again,

I hugged them and it felt so good. But so many years had passed by. We didn't know each other like when we were real small. I noticed an immediate distance.

But everyday, my sisters babied me, taking me all over Phoenix. My brothers spoiled me at night, taking me for drives around their friends and showing me mountain views. We went up to this really cool place called "South Mountain," and looked over the entire Phoenix region. It was beautiful! My sister Sadie worked at Jack in the Box, so Tarah and I would go up there all the time. They would treat me everyday to lunch. My regular meal was a small hamburger and orange soda.

One weekend, we went to Splash Mountain. It was a recreational park that had this large slide that ended up in water. We kept getting on it over and over again. At the end of the two weeks, we had bonded. I was so happy about that because I didn't think they loved me anymore.

The last night before we left for Fresno, Daddy called me into the den and sat me down. I didn't know what he wanted to talk to me about. He carefully said he had something important that he needed to tell me, and he felt that being ten years old was old enough to know.

"Has your Momma ever told you anything about
me?"
"No."
"Got Dammit, then I need to tell you something."

My heart started beating so fast. I thought I did something wrong.
"Carla, I am not your real Daddy. Travis Bynum
is your Daddy, not me."
I was silent, and confused. He said,
"Look, when you were born, your Daddy did not
own up to you, and so I told Doris to give you my
name."
I just looked at him. I still couldn't say a word. I was hurt, sad,

and felt stupid. My eyes watered, but I tried to fight the tears. I wasn't going to let them show.

"Listen, I will be your Daddy if you want me to be, but you have a right to know the damn truth." Finally I was able to say, "Thank you for telling me."

Though I felt better off if I had never known the truth. I really didn't want anymore bad news. I wanted to go lay down now and sleep for awhile or go far away.

Who in the hell is Travis Bynum, I thought to myself. I never heard Momma talk about a Travis Bynum. I reflected on the time we got out of the foster home and when Momma came to Phoenix to get all her kids, but he only gave up me. No wonder, I wasn't his real child. He wanted to protect his own. No wonder Momma had to settle for me. That night, when everyone was asleep, I cried out to God with all the "whys" I could think of.

The next morning was time to say good-bye. I cried and didn't want to go back home to Fresno. They had no idea what life was like for me and I didn't waste my precious moments with them telling them. I wanted to enjoy every waking hour. They were now only my half sisters and brothers, but I loved them just the same anyway. When I packed, I had two more bags filled with things that they had bought for me. Pretty clothes and shoes that would last me an entire school year.

When I returned to Fresno, I didn't tell Momma anything. I didn't trust Momma's words too much after that. How could she let me believe such a stupid lie? I put it far behind in my mind and forgot about it. I walked in the door and Momma was there with her friends in the kitchen as usual, drinking and partying.

"I'm back, Momma."

"Good. I sure missed you."

"You did?" I was shocked.

"Hell yeh! Those kids almost ran me crazy!"

Daddy and Ms. Estee didn't stay over ten minutes. They only came in to drop me off and get right back on the freeway back to Phoenix.

The next day after I got up, Momma told me that we were moving the next week to Mr. Calvin's sisters' house. I hoped where we were moving to was better and not worse. I didn't want to move, because I was finally feeling secure with the people around me. People like Glundy and her sisters, Mavis who lived up the street, and the neighborhood regulars that would pass by daily. I had a close friendship with them. The closeness was about to end.

MAY 1973 -- NEW HOME

We moved into Aunt Ellen's house the beginning of May. It was the same house my mother got married in. It had a beautiful front yard with two rose bushes and a gated fence all around. It also had a living room, dining room, kitchen, and back washroom. Momma's bedroom was right at the front of the house, and my bedroom was separated from theirs by the bathroom. Catherine was a baby at the time, and she slept in the living room in a large baby bed. Little Calvin and Edwin slept in the den. Brenda and I slept in my room together. The house came with a dog named Blacky who used to belong to Aunt Ellen. They couldn't take him where they were moving, because they weren't allowed to have pets. He was so adorable! Blacky was a little black dog, like a midget German Shepherd, very friendly too. I don't know what breed he was, but he became my own personal pet.

The neighborhood seemed to be full of old folks. Momma told me that across the street lived a woman named Mrs. Harrison. She was paralyzed from the waist down. On our immediate left was Mrs. Sullivan who was a widow and lived in a big house all to herself. Then to our right was a couple who were uppity black people. They did not like to talk too much. Right next to them was a man named RL and his wife, who worked all the time.

Momma got real close with RL, because he was always home during the day while his wife was away. Of course, after awhile, RL and Momma became drinking buddies. Then my final question came. Where are the children in the damn neighborhood? Well at least our backyard had a swing in it. I would go back there and swing all evening and sometimes play with my brothers and sisters. My house was far from my school, and the best thing about it was that it took longer to get home. This meant more time after school to play with my friend Mavis.

After we had gotten all moved in, Mr. Calvin tried to tell Momma again to stop the partying.

> "Now Doris, all this partying everyday needs to
> stop. These children don't need to be around all
> this drinking and crap." Mr. Calvin didn't like to
> curse like Momma.
> "Bullshit, I ain't stopping shit. You can leave and
> go be with your damn greyhounds in the
> backyard if you want to."

Mr. Calvin just looked at her and shook his head. I just stayed on the floor in front of the television and pretended I didn't hear a thing.

JUNE 1973

On the last day of school all the kids in my grade were excited about going to Jr. High School in September. All the kids were hyped. Mavis and her other friends were giving high fives. Going from grade to grade was never a big deal in my home, but I still faked like it was a big deal with the kids. Momma never got excited like other kid's parents. I learned that lesson when I was skipped from the 2nd grade to the 4th grade and it didn't seem to be a big deal to Momma. Momma never really knew what I got on my report cards. She didn't even care as long as I was going from one grade to the next.

This school year I was going to the seventh grade at Irwin Jr. High. It started off awesome! Mavis and I thought we were so bad now. We were going to the big kids' school. Satrina Wilson was in her last year of high school.

As the school year got on, it began to get real interesting. I met a young boy named Kendon Starr. He was so fine, dark skinned, tall, and the word around school was that he was a black belt in karate. He was also a gang banger. I didn't care. He had white teeth and thick eyebrows. I would see him only from time to time, but he was polite and would speak to me. I thought I would die each time I saw him in the hallways. Mavis tried to hip me to him with bad news. She told me that he went to juvenile hall a lot, at least six times a year. I didn't want to believe her. One day, I was walking up the street to school and here comes Mr. Kendon Starr walking up along side of me. He asked me my name. I told him. He, in turn, introduced himself. He told me he had seen me around quite a bit, and told me I was a real nice girl. I thanked him for his compliment.

"I'm serious, you're not like other girls," he repeated.

I thought to myself, you ain't lying, I ain't like a lot of things. Instead, I said, " thank you again." I didn't fully understand what he meant. He wanted to know what grade I was in, and he wanted to know if he could have my telephone number. I had never given a boy my telephone number. I didn't even know it at first! I had to really think about it. I had never called myself and nobody has ever called me, unless it was Mavis.

So I asked him, "Can I have yours first?"

He said, "Of course."

From that day on, we talked on the phone at least three times a week. Our initial conversations were centered around our families. He lived with both of his parents. He had a small brother named Jimmy and an older sister named Michelle. He also loved music. His favorite groups were the Commodores and the Isley Brothers. He would always play the Commodores in the background while he was talking to me.

One night I asked him if he had a girlfriend, and he said, "Well, I guess something like that." But he quickly asked if we could still just talk as friends. I said, "Oh yeh, sure," but deep down inside, I was so disappointed. I had never had a boy that was a friend. I soon felt I was falling head over heels in love. He was so nice to me. Not once did he ever talk about my body, sex, or anything like that. He was a gentleman, no matter what Mavis was saying about him. And he was honest too. Momma started noticing me on the phone for long lengths of time.

One day Momma asked me who I was talking with. I had just hung up the phone with Kendon. I told her, "A young boy I met at school."
　　　　"Alright now, don't start smelling your piss
　　　　around here just because you in Jr. High School."
　　　　"I'm not smelling nothing, Momma," I said.
　　　　"Don't be talking back, just listen. Shit, you're
　　　　starting already."

The next couple of years seemed to be the most boring and lonely years of my life. I found out how much Momma didn't know when I started Jr. High. When I started having problems with Algebra she told me that she could not help me. In fact that's when I learned that she only had a 5th grade education. I thought it was so sad that she didn't get a chance to finish school. Maybe that's why she doesn't get too excited about school for me. So I received extra help from my teacher's aid when I got stuck.

NIGHTMARE NIGHT

I don't know how long he was on top of me. First the smell of that soap! Then the suffocating feeling. He was biting on me as the sleep tried to linger. I jumped up with a muffled yell. "STOP! MOVE! DON'T DO THIS TO ME, PLEASE DON'T DO THIS TO ME!" I quickly lowered my voice because my sister, Brenda,

was in bed with me. Her back was turned to the wall. I was so afraid that any moment she would turn over, and she would have to live with this nightmare too. He wrestled me back down on the bed as I was pushing at him. I was trying to knock him off. He still held my tittie in his mouth real tight and his finger deep in me. I was hitting him harder and harder, but he covered my whole body.
"I hate you!" I gritted my teeth.
"I hate you for this!"

He stopped and looked at me. Then he got up and tiptoed back to my mother's room. I was scared, but I got up and followed him. He was not going to leave me in that room this time feeling like a piece of torn up meat. He went and lay under my mother as if he had been there all night. I was shaking as I walked through their bedroom door. Crying still, I shook my mother, "Momma, Momma, please wake up! I got to tell you something. Momma, please I need you now." He interrupted me and said, "Girl, you better go back to your room and leave your Momma alone. You see she's sleeping."

I knelt down by the bedside next to her, placing my head in her right hand as it lay lifeless next to her side. I was on my knees crying for my mother that could not wake up out of her drunken sleep. She had been drinking all day and night. She was dead to this world and all its happenings. I couldn't stand up, I was so weak. I couldn't walk out of that room. I crawled to the end of the door, and when I knew I was out of his sight, I pulled myself up with all my might and walked over to my bed to rock and cry myself to sleep. I promised myself before I went to sleep to tell my mother tomorrow. "You watch, I'm telling no matter what. She can kill me if she wants to. At least, I won't have to live with this shit happening to me anymore."

The next morning the sun shone through my bedroom window. I awoke, squinting my eyes from the glare. I pulled the covers over my eyes and then snatched them right off as the memory of last night surfaced. My mother was sitting in the front room as usual gazing out of the windows. As always, she had her cup of coffee, puffing on her cigarettes. I came into the front room, after I finished in the bathroom, without saying good morning.

"Momma, I have something to tell you."
She turned around. "What?" she asked.
"Tell Mr. Calvin to stay out of my room," I said.

Tears were starting to come, but I was fighting them back. I had to get this out!

She said, "What are you talking about, girl?"
"He was in my room last night."
"What was he doing in your room, Carla?"
"He was messing with my chest and stuff."
"Messing with your chest and stuff?"

She was repeating everything I said to her. She then looked at my little brother Calvin, who was sitting on the floor in front of the TV. She told him, "Go into the backyard and tell your Daddy to come here." Momma stayed looking toward the window, just looking out without looking at me until Mr. Calvin came in the living room. When Momma knew he was there, she started talking without turning around.

"What is this girl talking about you were in her room last night on her chest and stuff?"

He looked at me for a second with a grim, crazy looking smile on his face and said to me,

"Girl, what are you talking about?"
I snapped at him, "You know what I'm talking about."
Momma finally turned around, looking at him.
"The girl said you were messing with her chest and stuff last night, Calvin."
He started backing up, looking nervous.
"That girl must be crazy or dreaming, and I ain't got time to hear all this bull mess. I'll be in the back. That girl is crazy." He quickly left.

Momma turned her back on me and started looking out the window again, just staring out. I waited for her to say something else, but she never turned around again. I wondered what she was thinking. I sat there asking myself, how could he lie to my face? He had looked right at me and called me crazy. I must have been dreaming. For a quick second, I asked myself "Were you dreaming last night, were you dreaming the other nights?" I felt so confused and lost, I began to weep. I cried out to my mother talking through my teeth, "I wasn't dreaming, Momma! I wasn't! He did it and he knows it!" I got up off the couch, ran into my room and closed the door.

I went to my closet and sat on the floor in the back with my head in my knees rocking back and forth crying, not knowing what to do, or what to say. My closet door was open, so I fixed my eyes to the corner of my room and stared at the crease in the wall which led up to the ceiling. It led up into a cross shape. I just stared at it. I never noticed it like that before. It gave me comfort. I held myself real tight and didn't want to let myself go. I wished they were the arms of my mother holding me, but she didn't even come near me. I was frozen. All I could do was to rock my stiff body back and forth and just let the tears fall, until God turned off the faucet. I grabbed my diary and wrote to God about all my feelings, talking out loud at the same time. I didn't come out of my closet for a couple of hours and nobody missed me.

Dear Lord:
You saw it last night, Lord! You know I'm not crazy, and you know I'm not dreaming. My breast is still hurt from him and I still smell the damn Irish Spring Soap scent that was on his body. I hate that soap! I thought he could be my Daddy. Why can't he treat me like a real daughter and love me the right way? I wish I had my real Daddy, whoever he is. I know he would probably love me right. Am I that horrible?

When I was able to pull myself together, I came out of the closet. Though I wanted to stay in there forever because it felt so safe and peaceful. I sat at the edge of my bed and looked toward the corner of my walls where the four corners came together to form the cross. That said to me that Jesus was in my room, and that God was always in my corner. I knew He was with me. I knew He saw the truth, no matter what Mr. Calvin said. God wouldn't let me lose my mind, but from that moment I noticed something changed inside of me. I felt hard.

From that day on, my life was just going through the motions. I did not come out of my room unless I knew Mr. Calvin was at work, in the back yard, or gone away somewhere. I would come out to do my chores and to eat, in that order. I would go directly back to my room. My room began to feel like a prison cell. I was sentenced there and then let out to clean, eat, and every now and then go to the recreational room to watch TV. My favorite shows were I Dream of Jeannie, Get Smart, Lost in Space and Sanford and Son. After those four shows, I knew it was time to go back into my cell. This silence went on for a few weeks. They were the loneliest and longest weeks of my life.

I noticed Momma's routine changed drastically too. Momma was now drinking in the mornings also. I noticed one morning on my way to school, Momma had a half pint of Canadian Mist on her desk where the coffee used to sit each morning. She used to be home every evening when we came home from school, but she would now be over to her friend's houses getting drunk and playing cards. Momma started going out more and more. Not only on the weekends, but nightly too. I hated that she did that to me, because she was leaving me there alone with Mr. Calvin more often. When he would come home, he would speak abruptly and keep going on with his business.

I became closer and closer to my dog Blacky. I would do my chores, and go out and stay on the front porch with him until Momma came home. She would walk right by me without saying anything, not even hi. I didn't care if she would have said hi in a mad tone, I just wanted to hear her voice notice me or just speak to me.

We lived right across the street from Kearney Airport. Blacky would sit up under me while I patted his back. I would talk to Blacky like he was my only friend. I knew he didn't understand a lot, but maybe God gave him a special liking for me. "Look at the planes fly away, Blacky. I wish I could fly away too." Every now and then Blacky would lick my hands, and I would hug him around his neck. It felt peaceful watching the planes land and take off, sitting there with Blacky.

Going to school that first week was so hard for me. I ached inside when I heard the happy sounds from my schoolmates. The echoes gripped at my broken heart. They were happy kids and I longed to feel that way for real and not just fake it, but I learned to fake happiness real good. I wished I had someone to talk to about my home, but there was no one I could confide in. I often wished that one of my counselor's or teachers could read my mind or feel me in some way. My best friend, Mavis, or my other new friend, Cheryl, wouldn't understand, I thought to myself. They wouldn't understand, and plus they would probably not want to be friends with a girl that came from a crazy family like mine. So, I smiled and pretended that everything was all right until I reached about four blocks from home. Then my heart would start pounding, and the butterflies would start. I didn't want to go home. Anywhere else but home. I always made myself smile when I got to the porch, because Blacky would be right there wagging that little tail, running up to me, to lick my hands.

CHAPTER 11

Silence Broken

Momma's silence broke one Friday evening, six weeks later. I came home from school, going toward my room to change my school clothes. She called me into the front room and asked me to tell her again what had happened. So I did. I wasn't as scared and nervous as before, because the hardest part was getting it out. I looked her right in the face while I talked. "He came into my room and started messing with me while I was asleep, and I didn't wake up until I felt like I couldn't breathe." I paused, because my voice began to quiver, but I continued on. "Then I felt him on top of me. He was on my breast and trying to do things down there. I came into your room and tried to wake you up. But you wouldn't wake up. Momma, this isn't the first time he did this. When we lived in the Atchison Courts, he came into my room at different times too. He told me you would kill me if I told. He told me that you wouldn't believe me so I was too scared to tell you."

She grabbed my hand, pulled me to her and held me around my waist real tight with her head resting on my stomach. "I am going to do something about this, baby, don't worry. I don't know what, but something will happen," she whispered, her voice stern and steady. As she held me, the tears wouldn't stop. The hardness I felt melted away as she embraced me in her arms. My yearnings for my mother were all fulfilled in this moment. I never remembered my mother holding me like that except for the time when she came to Phoenix to see us after we were all broken up. I felt like her little girl again. Not a far away stranger. When I went back to my room, I had a smile on my face. I looked toward the ceiling at the cross in the crack of the crease in the corners and said, "Thank you, Jesus. My mother loves me." I wondered if we were going to move away from Mr. Calvin and go live by ourselves. I wondered if Momma was going to kill him, or call the cops, so he could go to jail. I hoped that we would not have to see him anymore.

My comfort was soon snatched away as I noticed my mother's daily drinking. She was now drinking for breakfast, lunch, and dinner. She was, at the same time, becoming more and more quiet toward me again. Maybe Momma was plotting how we would leave here, so I didn't bother her. I came home, did my chores, fixed plates for the kids to eat, went to my room, or sat outside on the porch and watched the planes fly away with Blacky. Everything still felt uncomfortable, even though Momma said she was going to take care of things.

Soon after, Momma would get sloppy drunk and start acting strange. She started telling me that what Mr. Calvin did to me was all my fault. She began to turn the truth around and blame me for it. I couldn't believe my ears when she began to curse and threaten me. She started calling me bad names and threatened to kill me. I thought to myself, Mr. Calvin was right. She told me, "If you were not flouncing or throwing yourself around him all the time, he would not have done what he did." I couldn't understand. Momma now believed him and not me. Yet, I had no reason to lie.

As time went on, she got worse and worse. She moved from calling me a little whore and slut to even worse. I would go to my room, climb into my closet and be real still so I could cry. I dreaded coming out to even eat. Especially when Mr. Calvin was in the kitchen eating too. I knew Momma would start blaming me again. I didn't want to be around her. But just as suddenly she would go to the opposite extreme, she would apologize and tell me she knew it wasn't my fault. Then she would say, "I am going to kill his ass and it's only going to be me, you and the kids." But then she would pull a Dr. Jekyll and Mr. Hyde on me. She would suddenly say, "Girl, you think you're slick, huh?" I hated her behavior, because my sisters and brothers would hear her drunken outbursts too. I was hoping inside that they ignored her and kept watching TV. I didn't know what they thought of me, or even if they were old enough to form an opinion one way or the other.
Momma's house parties grew louder and louder and started earlier and earlier in the day. Soon as I would come home from school, there was always somebody in the house. They would stay later

now, and more would come over and start a card game. Things continued to get worse.

One night, while I was going to the kitchen for some water, my mother and all of her friends were packed there playing cards. Momma said, "Yeh, there she is. She wants my husband. That's her little ass." I just looked at her and turned back around, forgetting about the water. I couldn't believe it. I hoped in my heart those people knew better.

The next day, I thought Momma would wake up and explain it to me and then apologize. But she did the opposite. I came home from school, and she was sitting there in the window waiting for me. I spoke to her and kept going, keeping my head down.
"You know, I got to thinking about it more closely."

I had hoped that she was going to get Mr. Calvin. Her voice sounded like she was angry. She continued to talk. I turned to her standing up behind me.
"You said it wasn't the first time, yet it took you until you got ready to tell me it was happening. Why it take you so long, hah?"
"Momma, I told you why! I told you I was scared. He said you would kill me."
"Yeh, he was right. What would you do if your daughter was fucking yo old man?"

Her words made me feel as if I was going to throw-up at that very moment. She continued to scream at me. "Hah. Just ignore it? I think it took so long because yo ass liked what he was doing to you." I was shaking my head no.
"Didn't you like it?" she screamed.
I couldn't hold back the tears as much as I didn't want to cry now.
"No, Momma. I hated it. I hate him."
I felt so confused standing there.
"Momma, I wasn't flouncing myself around him.

I promise. I told you the truth, Momma."
"Yeh when you got good and damn ready."

She took the cap off her Canadian Mist and drank it from the bottle. Momma was still in her house coat. She hadn't gotten dressed all day.

"I'm going to tell you one thing, Carla. You better
stay your ass out of my way. You hear me? Just
stay out of my damn way."

I couldn't say nothing else, so I turned around, went to my room and went right to my closet. I went all the way to the back and just rocked back and forward. The tears could fall now and they did.

Momma continued to curse me out and call me the most horrible names I ever heard her say to anybody. She would also threaten to kill me at least twice a day when either passing me or walking from one room to the next.

"I'm just laying dead for your ass. You're going to
slip up, and I'm going to catch you, and when I
do, my foot is going to be all in your ass," she
would tell me.

My stomach would quiver and the butterflies would swim up to my throat every time she threatened to kill me. The other children in the neighborhood eventually found out through my mother. Then everybody at my school found out. But they all knew Momma's version, not mine. Not the truth. I was so ashamed. Though the kids never said anything to me, it was obvious by the way they acted. The crowd would soon break up and go their own way, leaving me standing there. There was no peace. The only peace I got was being away from home or in my silent closet at home talking to God. God knew I didn't mind talking with Him, but I also needed someone on this earth to listen to me, to talk to me, and to believe me. In the meantime, I leaned on my diary to talk to God, and my dog Blacky who loved me.

Dear God:
Please send me someone to talk to. I don't know
how much longer I can live like this...Lord I am so
weak in my mind. I feel like it's about to explode
because I can't release the pain I have so deep inside
me. I can't understand all that I am feeling. My
heart has been broken in a thousand pieces. I am
trying to hold on but it is not easy. I can't handle
much more of this stuff that my mother is giving
me. You know I don't deserve this kind of
treatment. I really think I'd rather be dead than to
go through this until I'm 18 and on my own. I
thought I could last, but seven years is too long for
me. I want to die. I don't want to go through
anymore pain. Can't I just go to sleep and never
wake up again? Can you please at least do that for
me?

I looked forward to leaving the house. The only good part about
coming home was right before I got to my front door. I was
always faithfully greeted by Blacky. I had learned to lean on him
too. Sometimes, I would test him and call him two blocks away
real loud. I wasn't even in sight, but you best be sure that Blacky
would come running down the street, hitting those corners as if he
was in a race. I would laugh so hard, because he filled my heart in
a special way. I loved that dog so much. I believed somehow,
someway, God let him understand my pain, and he loved me back
even more.

Momma continued with her cycle, and Mr. Calvin continued to
walk around me and talk every morning as if he never touched me.
Sometimes, he looked like he wanted to say he was sorry, but he
never did. I couldn't understand why I felt sorry for him
sometimes when I should have been hating him. I often fought the
feelings of forgiveness that tried to surface. These mixed emotions
were wearing me out. I tried to be strong. I kept telling myself,
you can handle it, don't give up, please Carla just hold on.

Momma's crazy cycle of Dr. Jekyll, and Mr. Hyde repeated itself
through the next year. I felt like a walking dart board. I had many
holes where my mother's words pierced me and hurt me all over.
The only positive thing was she stopped having children and she did
tie her tubes as she said.

CHAPTER 12

Happy New Year's
JANUARY - FEBRUARY 1976

Mrs. Harrison, the elderly lady who lived across the street, had a nephew named Darnell who stayed with her. Momma would wave at Mrs. Harrison every day when she went to the store. Like Momma she loved to sit in the window of her living room. She could see everyone else's yard from there. Anyway, Darnell was starting a night job, leaving Mrs. Harrison at home alone at night. This was a problem, because she was paralyzed on her left side and couldn't walk very well. Mrs. Harrison asked Momma if she would let me work for her at night, putting her to bed and staying until early morning when Darnell got off work. Momma asked me if I would be interested. It was a job paying $15 a week for four days a week (Monday, Wednesday, Friday and Saturday). I immediately said, "Yes!" I'd do anything so that I won't have to be home anymore, especially at night. I believed this was a miracle from God. I had asked Him for help and peace, and He gave it to me.

I asked Momma, "When do I start?"

She said, "Next Monday night."

Mrs. Harrison's house was a tiny, blue, two-bedroom house. When you walked through the front door, you were in the middle of the front room. On your immediate left, there was the kitchen that was always filled with everything but kitchen stuff, thanks to her nephew Darnell. In one corner, he had his mechanics tool box sitting on top of two stacked tires, and a pile of stereo equipment in another corner. Straight ahead, there was a small hallway leading to the bathroom and the two bedrooms. Standing in the small hall area, on your immediate right, you could see the first bedroom where Mrs. Harrison slept. Her room was a typical elderly woman's room. Wall to wall clothes that she never wore and a closet full of shoes never used since the accident. All types of costume jewelry were draped over her dresser. Different colors, shapes, complete sets, and some mismatches that had been lost through the years. A pair of beautiful emerald earrings with large emerald stones was a standout. I could tell her favorite color was blue by looking at all that jewelry and all her clothes in the closet. A mirror stand on top of the dresser had a permanent stained reflection that would not come out, even with the most improved Windex cleaner. It was ancient, right along with everything else in that room, Mrs. Harrison included.

Her bed was a queen size, bordered by metal bars so she wouldn't fall out of bed at night while sleeping. It let up and down. Her phone was right inside of her bed for easy access in case of an emergency. Facing the door within her room, you could look right into the bathroom. To the immediate right of that was the second bedroom where I was to sleep. It was also Darnell's room.

On the Monday night I was to begin, I gathered my overnight things and yelled out to Momma that I was going across the street to Mrs. Harrison's. I left around 7:30 p.m. I wasn't due there until 9:00 p.m., but I wanted to leave early. I was escorted personally by Blacky. As I ran across the street I felt so free. He ran with me, lying in front of the door as I went in. Mrs. Harrison sat there with a smile.

"Hello, Carla," she said, greeting me.
"Hi Mrs. Harrison," I said.
I sat my things on the couch, and she told me
"Put those in the bedroom and get comfortable."
I did so quickly, and then came back into the
front room.

The first conversation we had, Mrs. Harrison expressed her gratitude and appreciation to my mother for letting me stay and take care of her at night. She said it was a blessing from God. Also, she commended me for having such care in my heart that I wanted to do the job. She said "Most young girls wouldn't be interested in something like this, and they are usually too busy chasing little boys, or just doing kid stuff." I realized she was right, but what she didn't know was that I never had a chance to do that kind of stuff anyway. Though I had ulterior motives of getting out of my house, I cared for Mrs. Harrison instantly.

"How old are you, sweetie?" Mrs. Harrison asked.

"I just turned twelve," I said with my head down, hoping she wouldn't say anything about my mature breasts.

I was also too embarrassed to tell her I just had a birthday, since it was just another day that Momma partied away like all the rest of them.

"What grade are you in?"

"The seventh grade. I go to Irwin Jr. High."

"Well good for you. You seem pretty bright."

"Thank you," I responded.

Mrs. Harrison had a big face. Her jaws slumped over her mouth, and she had a wide nose. She also had very thick dark hairy eyebrows over dark eyes, and a meaty neck, all piled on top of her big body. As for my job, Mrs. Harrison explained all she needed. The main thing was having someone present with her at night in case of an emergency, as well as answering the phone and taking messages for Darnell.

After a week on the job, I was fine with everything except for those trips to the bathroom. More specifically, when she had to do what they call the "number two." I would have to stand there waiting and then help her up off the toilet and into the wheel chair. Then I would flush the toilet, because she didn't like for me to flush it while she was still on it. Boy, did I hate that. I would then hurry her off to bed and tuck her in so that I could have some TV time to myself.

Each morning before I left, Darnell would walk in the door and thank me for staying over hugging me real tight. He was tall like Tyrone Sr., who I thought was my daddy. Darnell reminded me of the Pink Panther, because he was also skinny and fair. He had a perm in his hair, like a press and curl. He was nice.

"Any calls, Carla?" he would ask.

"Not last night, Darnell."
And off to school, I would go.

Momma continued with her nasty abusive words. So I would quickly do my chores, feed my sisters and brothers and run across the street to Mrs. Harrison's house.   When Momma picked up on what I was doing, she demanded that I wait until 9:00 p.m and sometimes 9:30 p.m., making me late for my job.

One night after cleaning the kitchen, washing the dishes and grabbing my overnight bag to go over to Mrs. Harrison, Momma surprised me.   When I came out of my room, Momma stood in the doorway, swaying back and forth drunk. She had to hold on to the door knob of the front door. My heart started pounding and the butterflies started swimming up to my throat.

> "Look got damit, remember that your first job is
> here with me and these kids, don't you ever
> forget it," she yelled.
> "I don't know why you got to go over there so
> damn early. Your damn conscience is probably
> getting to ya, hah?"
> "No," I said softly, with my head down.

Then I made my way past her and went across the street.   I hated how I was beginning to feel about my mother.   The only time she would be halfway decent was when she was "borrowing" the money I made with Mrs. Harrison each week. I knew I would not see it again.   But that was my only way of trying to show my mother I loved her. And I would give her anything I had. That still was not enough. She would just go and get liquor with it. As I walked across the street that night, I wished that Mrs. Harrison needed me every night. Then I wouldn't have to face my Momma anymore. But I was grateful to God for the four nights a week that I did have. After a month I could tell Momma was getting jealous of our relationship, because Mrs. Harrison would brag to Momma about how well I was doing for her.

One Wednesday evening, when Momma was sitting at her desk in front of the window, she told me that I could not work for Mrs. Harrison on Saturdays anymore. She said I could work on Sundays instead. She wanted me home to watch the kids so that she could go visit and party all night on Saturdays.

"I got a life too, you know. I need you here helping me with my kids."

She grabbed her Canadian Mist off the desk, turned it up to her mouth and then took a long draw off her Winston regular. My sisters and brothers were in the backyard with their Daddy feeding the dogs. Momma was such a pitiful sight to see. She had started to let herself go. She no longer went to the hair dresser. She didn't dress decent, the way she used to. It seemed like she would wake up and just throw anything on her body.

Mrs. Harrison was sitting in her normal chair right in front of the window, rubbing her right shoulder when I came in the door. She would tell me that God was going to put the feelings back on her right side. I tried to make her feel better by trying to massage her shoulders. Her face lit up when she saw me. She had become so fond of me and I was fond of her. I dreaded what I had to tell her about Momma wanting me to work all day and night on Saturdays. It broke my heart, because she didn't deserve to be treated like this. How Momma could treat an old woman like this, I could not understand.

After I told her, she asked me why was Momma doing this. I told her, Momma just wants me to be her baby-sitter while she parties and that's all that matters to her. I told her nobody and nothing else matters to her.

On Sunday nights Darnell was home, which meant she was covered but I decided to go anyway and not tell Momma. I would have to sleep in the front room on the couch because Darnell would be home in his room, but that was fine too.

Mrs. Harrison told me to try not to worry about her because she was going to ask her maid (that came in the mornings) to come on Saturday evenings. I didn't know she had a maid during the day, but I was glad.

By now, Mrs. Harrison got to know Momma and her crazy ways pretty well. I found out that Momma came over to Mrs. Harrison's house while I was at school trying to borrow money. Momma knew that Mrs. Harrison only received disability checks.   Needless to say, Momma told Mrs. Harrison her version of the disgusting daughter who screwed her husband. Mrs. Harrison didn't believe her and just encouraged me to trust God.

One morning after leaving Mrs. Harrison's, I went home to pick up my books and I overheard Momma talking on the phone.
          "You want to move to California, AlmaFaye?"   I
          couldn't believe my ears!

She was talking to my sister in Louisiana. I began to pray to God to let her come.
          "Please, Lord, I need my big sister, let her come."
          I prayed out loud.   Then Momma saw me and
          called me to the phone.
          "Your sister AlmaFaye wants to talk to you."

I got on the phone.   She sounded like a breath of fresh air. I told her how much I always think about her and wished I could meet her one day.   She said "Well, we may be granting that wish soon." I said, "For real?"

She and Momma had talked about her coming and staying with us until she got on her feet.   I was jumping for joy inside.   After Momma hung up the phone, I asked when was she going to ask Mr. Calvin about it.
          "As soon as he gets home," she told me.

When I came home from school that day, I made sure I wrote in my diary to thank God for answering another prayer. Mr. Calvin told Momma that night in the kitchen that he didn't care if AlmaFaye came out to California to live with them.

Momma said, "Well, she wants to come soon as possible."

He said, "Fine."

My sister was on her way! This felt like a late birthday present.

APRIL 1976

For the next year or so Momma found new clubs to go to. Juicy Pigs, Jericho, and Sugar Hills had closed. I heard her talking about going to places like Hunts and the Elks Club. These were new places and Momma met new friends that followed her home at times.

One day I came home from school and found a new set of friends that I had never seen before. The older woman named Leona was real fair skinned and looked almost red in the face also. Her hair was black and white, but it was long, bushy and soft. It looked like Chaka Khan's hair. The other girl was her daughter, Gabriel. She was chubby too. Her hair was real black, but soft and bushy like her Momma's. And Gabriel had real big titties.

I noticed that not only were Momma and Leona drinking Vodka, but also Leona's daughter. I thought it was so weird for her Momma to let her drink. I politely said hello and then went on to do my daily chores.

The kids were in the backyard as usual. Probably pushed out there by Momma because she needed to open her revolving party door for her new friends. Leona was getting bored because she was asking Momma about the people and more drinks.

"When are the people going to get here?"

She was loud just like Momma. Seemed crazy like her too.

"Shit Leona, they got to get off of work, change

clothes and then come by. Yo ass the one early, shit."

Momma got up and went over to the stereo. I cringed at the thought of what I knew I was about to hear, that damn B.B. King's the Thrill is Gone. My predictions were right again. I knew every guitar string by now and all the words. They rang inside as I cleaned from one room to the next.

Mr. Calvin had started disappearing throughout the day and nights too. I guess he didn't feel strong enough to enforce his laws anymore. Momma would curse him out on the spot every time he looked like he wanted to say something, even in front of her new friends. The old friends were used to Momma's telling Mr. Calvin to go to hell.

One night, Mr. Calvin was telling Momma that he wanted peace in his house and that this time he ain't going to stand for people to come in his house. The next thing I heard was the back door slamming. Mr. Calvin went to the backyard to be with his greyhounds, I guess. He didn't say anything to Momma anymore that night, or much after. The kids were in the front room trying to hear the TV, but couldn't because of the music, the loud talking, and the drinking. Momma stood up from the table where they were right in the middle of a Bid Wiz game, and screamed right in front of her friends, "Here's the son-of-a-bitch that's been fucking my daughter since she was a baby." I heard it all the way in the living room.

On Sunday mornings Momma would sleep until almost 12 noon because the party didn't stop until 6:00 that morning. I couldn't go to church with Mavis, because someone had to be here when the kids got up Momma said. Sure enough the kids got up early to have their cereal and watch television.

After feeding them I would get my diary and pencil, put the stereo speakers by the front door and set on the porch with Blacky, watching the planes take off. From 8:00 a.m.- 12:00 noon the radio stations would play church music. This particular Sunday, I heard a powerful song by a woman named Tramaine Hawkins. She was singing a song called "I'm Going upa Yonda." Just when I thought it was over, the DJ said, "the long version," and it came back on. It sounded like the words of the song said, "I can take the pain, the heartaches they bring, the comfort is in knowing, I'll soon be gone." Well, that song did something to me. When the song went off, what kept playing over in my head was the part when she said on the long version: "One of these old days, one of these old days, I'll soon, I'll soon be gone, I've got to run, I've got to run, run on and run on and run, and ruuuuuuuun wooooooooo, until I see Jesus, until I see Jesus, until I see my Savior Face! Face! Face! Face! To Faaaace!" Then it would finish with the chorus, "I'm going upa yonda, I'm going upa yonda to be with my Lord!"

The planes were going upa yonda too. The words of that song brought tears to my eyes. I could feel God on my porch. I fixed my eyes on the skies and watched the white clouds. God knew I was having church on my porch, and I knew He was there with me while I was happy like they were at Grandma Georgia's church. But I wasn't running, though I kinda felt like doing something more than crying. I was telling God, I wish I could see your face too one day. Heaven seemed to be a place where you get your reward or diploma from making it through the stuff that you deal with on this earth. I wanted to go to that place.

My younger sisters and brothers spent lots of time with Aunt Ellen's kids when Momma would let them. Just like Momma, Aunt Ellen kept having kids year after year. I never was really able to develop a close relationship with Aunt Ellen's kids.

I often felt so sorry for my sisters and brothers because of Momma's ways and her drinking. I prayed what they saw and heard Momma do wouldn't affect them and that they wouldn't remember as they grew older. Edwin (the youngest) was two years old now, Charlotte was four years old, Brenda five years old and Calvin Jr. was six. One thing they did have that I didn't have was both of their parents at home with them. Their real Daddy and their real Momma. They belonged to their Momma and Daddy. I always felt like I didn't belong to nobody and I didn't feel loved and wanted like they did from their Daddy and half sober Momma.

Momma's favorite out of the four kids was Calvin Jr., her first baby that she had by Mr. Calvin. She treated him like he could do no wrong. When Momma was sober, I would even hear her play with the kids while I was doing my chores. I hated those sounds. How come she could never play like that with me, I would think. Even though I was jealous of them, I didn't want them to have a sad life at home like me. At least they had each other to play and talk with.

As time went on, Momma began to grow meaner and meaner toward Mrs. Harrison. There were days Momma would tell me that she was going somewhere and to watch the kids. I would have to remind her that it was one of the nights I put Mrs. Harrison to bed. She would merely say, "That got damn woman don't need you all the time. She's just across the street, and she got the number. Just put her ass to sleep and then come back over here. She can call you if anything happens." That would make me so mad.

One Monday, Leona, Gabby and Momma wanted to go over to the Hunts club. Momma called over to Mrs. Harrison while I was there and said, "I need Carla to come home to watch the kids." I tucked Mrs. Harrison in and assured her that I would be over from time to time in the middle of the night to check on her. I was sad. Mrs. Harrison wasn't happy with this, but what could she do? Momma really didn't care if she liked it or not.

MY FIRST DRINK 1976

On April Fool's Day, Gabby and her mother were over for drinks again. I went out of the house to go sit on the porch when I saw Gabby in her mother's car listening to Stevie Wonders "Isn't She Lovely." She yelled out for me to come over and kick it with her.

I didn't want to be bothered. I was trying to find a quiet space. Gabby asked me if I needed a drink. Momma was in rare form and Gabby thought a drink might mellow me out. She knew how Momma went off on me when she would get drunk and I guess she was preparing me for the inevitable. I asked her what was she drinking and she told me vodka and orange juice. I was nervous, but I decided to try it. Boy, was it strong! It was real tangy tasting. After a sip or two, I felt a rush to my head and dizziness. She smiled and said, "Boy, that went right to your little young blood stream, didn't it?" I looked up with my eyes buck wide, not knowing what would happen next.

Later that evening other new people started showing up. I noticed that the regulars and some younger folks had come by too. After the partying got started, I began to smell a funny smell in the house. I had never smelled this before. I asked Gabby what was it and she told me marijuana. She said I should try it, because it would mellow me out. I told her, no thank you. I made my sisters and brothers go to Momma's room to look at TV. Momma came in the bedroom and told me to stay with the kids.

Some of Momma's new friends had brought their teenagers with them. They also partied with their parents. I became acquainted with all of them. I even noticed that Momma allowed them to play their own music which they brought. They played all the popular singers like The Commodores, Ojays, and smooth singer Barry White. I stayed in the room that night but Gabriel found me and made sure I had enough to drink. I felt myself getting light headed. It felt good and Gabby was right, it did mellow me out.

After that night, I found myself sneaking a drink of my mother's whiskey when she would leave it out. It was a good pain killer. When I was "high" with that stuff, she could say whatever she wanted and I didn't feel it like before. I began to need it more and more just to be in the same house with her. I had to be careful because I couldn't sneak it like I could sneak a cigarette and Momma not miss it.

CHAPTER 13

ALMAFAYE MOVES TO FRESNO

April 10, 1976 was the best year of my life. This was the day my big sister was finally coming to California to live. Mr. Calvin and Momma had gone to the bus station to get AlmaFaye and her two children, Steve and Rochelle. I had to stay home with the kids. I sat in Momma's chair and waited, looking out of the window for them to come back. Steve would sleep on one of the couches because Little Calvin and Edwin slept in the den on the other couch that let out into a bed.

Momma had Mr. Calvin go and buy an extra bed to put in my room for AlmaFaye and her daughter Rochelle to sleep on. Brenda, Catherine and I usually slept in my bed.

AlmaFaye was very fair skinned, about 5'1", thin but shapely with high cheekbones and tight eyes like Momma. She was almost the spitting image of Momma. As she walked toward the gate, my heart leaped. "That's her," I said, not letting my eyes off her until she walked into the door. I ran and hugged her.

"You must be Carla."
"Hi AlmaFaye!" I held on her so tight.
"Let everybody in the house first Carla," Momma said, with a fake smile on her face.

Steve and Rochelle followed right behind her. AlmaFaye introduced them to the rest of us. Rochelle was about the same age of Little Calvin (who was six at the time) and Steve was the same age as Catherine (who was four). Mr. Calvin brought in all the bags. There were a lot. He also took another trip to the bus stop to get the remaining things that could not fit in the car the first time. Momma showed AlmaFaye where everything was and let her know where she would be sleeping. She told her to help herself to anything she saw, and that this was her home. This hospitable side of Momma must have been hiding somewhere between her toes. I stayed sitting on the floor right in front of the TV while she gave AlmaFaye the grand five room tour.

AlmaFaye was tired and wanted to take a bath. Her children went outside with the other kids and played on the swings. Momma went into the kitchen to finish cooking dinner. All she had left to cook was the cornbread. Everything else was done. Momma was so proud that her oldest daughter was home with her. I could see it. I even overheard her on the phone telling one of her friends. I guess in a way, she felt a sense of fulfilling her responsibilities. About twenty-seven years late, but so what. It must have seemed like her second chance. AlmaFaye came out of the bathroom and sat on the couch facing the TV.

"So, we have a lot to catch up with, hah?"

Her voice was gentle and she was lotioning her legs from her knees down. She had the cutest red, blue, and white short set, with white sandals on.

"Yep," I said.

Momma walked in suddenly, saying, "Dinner will be ready shortly."

"You want a beer, Momma?" asked AlmaFaye.

"Don't mind if I do."

"Come back here in the kitchen with me, and tell Momma what you've been up to all these years," Momma said.

AlmaFaye got up to follow Momma to the back.

"We'll talk later, okay?" she assured me.

I was so damn mad Momma took her away from me. Momma and AlmaFaye went for a drive that evening. The kids were already in the living room watching TV. Mr. Calvin was in the back yard with his dogs. So I started preparing to go over to Mrs. Harrison's for the night. Darnell was leaving, since he knew I was coming. " Hey Carla, fix me up with your sister," he said. "She has a pretty nice body." I looked at him and rolled my eyes. I was very quiet that evening. Mrs. Harrison and I didn't talk as much as usual because I was thinking about my sister, and where she could be with Momma. I didn't want Momma to say anything to her that would make her regret coming out to California.

The next morning I jetted back across the street quickly, saying good-bye to Mrs. Harrison and Darnell. I rushed into my front door and found AlmaFaye and the kids in the kitchen, already up and eating cereal. When the kids left the kitchen, we sat there, and she had coffee while I ate a bowl of Total. She told me how she longed for that moment to just hug her baby sister Carla. She just held me. We sat up all morning talking before Momma got out of bed with her usual hangover. It was Sunday, so I put on my church music and AlmaFaye liked it. She even knew some of the songs that came on, because she started singing them.

"How are you doing in school?" she asked.

"I'm doing fine." I replied.

"What is your grade point average?

"I get all A's."

"You do?"

"Yeh," I repeated.

"That's great!" She looked real pleased with me.

"And what grade are you in?"

"Eighth."

"Woo! What do you want to be when you grow up?"

I wasn't sure how to answer this question. "I don't know - maybe a policeman, maybe a lawyer."

"I wanted to be a nurse," AlmaFaye said. "But I started having kids, and got married. One thing led to the next, and here I am. But I do want to go back to college to get my degree."

Momma was making her way into the living room. "Good morning," she said, buttoning her cotton blue housecoat Mr. Calvin bought her several Christmas ago.

"Why didn't you tell me I had a straight "A" sister"

AlmaFaye asked her.
I said to myself, because she didn't even know or
care.
"Yeh, she's pretty smart, I guess," Momma said.
"I want to go Downtown today. Will you show me
where it is Carla" AlmaFaye asked me.
I looked at Momma, "Can I?"
"Yeh, what you looking at me for?" she said.
"I sure ain't dealing with all those folks down
there."

I remembered how to get down there because the salvation army
and the second hand stores were there. That's where we always got
my school clothes. Momma had not cursed at me, or threatened
me in the three days since AlmaFaye arrived. Was Momma staying
on good behavior to impress AlmaFaye? I was just glad it stopped.
AlmaFaye was my protector. We talked so much, it seemed like
she had been there for a year already. We were on the bus by noon
and loving it. At least I was. It was hot and around eighty
degrees. The spring weather was scorching through the bus
windows. The crowded bus was filled with colorful faces, Hispanic
families, young people on their way to weekend games, and the
people on their way downtown for after Easter sales. We bought
something in every store we went to. She bought me a pair of pants
and some summer tops. They were brand new, not used!

We went to a hot dog shop called Coney Island for lunch and had
chili cheese dogs and french fries. My sister had a giving heart. She
had already decided to spoil me and would not let anything come
between us. She started asking me about life at home. I had to
tell her about what happened with Mr. Calvin and me. She didn't
like that and she couldn't understand why Momma would be so
mean to me.

She told me if I was back in Louisiana with our Grandmother, Mr.
Calvin would be somewhere in a tree. His head would be off and
his body drifting somewhere in the Mississippi River.

"That's how your grandmother was," she chuckled
to herself.
"Grandma would fight a lot?"
"She sure did. She didn't mind telling a nigga or
anybody for that matter where to go."

Maybe that's where Momma gets her fighting from, I thought. She
told me not to worry, that she was here now. She asked me how
long was I taking care of Mrs. Harrison, and how I started doing
that. I let her know that it was an answered prayer until she got to
Fresno.
"I am getting tired of it now, because things are
changing and all, but she genuinely needs
someone," I said.
"Listen, I don't plan on being with Momma long,"
AlmaFaye said.
"I have been around her long enough to know
that we clash, and that Momma is a bit wild. If
you ever need a place to stay, you can always
come live with me when I move away from here."

We cried together on that patio and didn't care who saw us, because
it felt like we were in our own world. A better world.

Later that night, Momma told AlmaFaye they were going out to a
club called Hunts, out on Fig Street. AlmaFaye really didn't want
to go, but she went with Momma's wishes. It was amazing looking
at my sister and my mother together. They were almost twins.
They looked so much alike. AlmaFaye put on a dressy black
blouse with tight fitting blue jeans that really showed her size seven
curves. Momma just grabbed her normal polyester pants and
matching blouse that buttons up.

Two o'clock that morning, I was awakened by AlmaFaye getting in
the bed.
"Hey sis, how did you like it?" I whispered.
She said, "Girl, it was horrible! All those stinky

drinking men breathing all over you. Old as
your daddy's daddy, trying to touch and feel on
you! Girl, yo Momma is crazy! I think she got
so drunk that she forgot she was married."
"Naw sis, she didn't forget she was married. She
was just being herself," I said laughing.

We snickered together while the kids were snoring in their sleep.
"Hey sis, you better look out for Mrs. Harrison's
nephew, Darnell. He has his eyes on you," I
whispered.
"I know. He came over here the night you went to
take care of Mrs. Harrison, smiling and licking
his tongue out at me. He made up some excuse
about he needed a cup of milk."

We laughed. I never heard that one before!
"You know that Momma gave him a rough time
and told him exactly why he came over!"
"Girl, I know she did."
"Well, what do you think about him, AlmaFaye?"
"I think he's tall and cute. He asked me to go out
with him this week."
"Shut up! He did? That fast boy! What did you
say? Are you going?"
"Slow down, let me answer one at a time. I'm
going, but I'm certainly going to play real hard
to get. Because he knows he's cute."

We laughed again. AlmaFaye made herself real comfortable
pulling the covers closer to her chin.
"Good night, baby girl."
"AlmaFaye, I'm so glad you are here with me.
Thank you for coming."
She threw me a kiss and we went to sleep.
The next day, the telephone rang. It was Mrs. Harrison. Her
nephew from the Navy (Officer Knowlton Morris) had come home.

His grandmother called him "Knowlton," but he insisted that we call him "Tim." Mrs. Harrison asked Momma to come over and meet him. She told me to come with her, and she'd introduce us to him as part of the family. She told Tim how I had been taking care of her throughout the week. He really appreciated that. He was twenty-one years old, brown-skinned and handsome. He had perfect, shapely lips. A slender, neat man, with a nice voice too. He had on his uniform, shining black patent leather shoes, clean cut, low hair, and a fresh shave for the day. When he stood up to greet us, he looked strong, firm and straight. He didn't slouch over and drag like Momma's friends. You could tell he really cared for his grandmother, because this was the first stop he made off the bus. Before we left, Momma told him that we were having a party over at the house later on, and that he was welcome to come by. He said, "Okay I think I will do just that," looking at me out of the corner of his eye, winking. I felt weird inside, but oh was he the cutest man I had ever seen in my life! And his uniform made him even more handsome!

The party started at 8:00 p.m. The music was loud, as usual. Momma and her card friends were at the Bid Wiz table in the kitchen talking crazy and laughing loud, while B.B. King played in the background. I was in the front room watching the kids as usual. Tim came over to me. I could tell he liked me a little bit. I felt nervous and twitchy. He began to ask me real personal questions. The guy was not shy, nor did he waste time.
        "Hey cutie, how old are you?"
        "Thirteen, going on fourteen."

He told me that he was twenty one. I could smell he had been drinking before he got to the party.
        "So do you think that I am too old for you?"
        I didn't know what to say.
        "I don't know. Why would you ask me something like that?"
He was swaying back and forward. I was hoping he didn't fall.
        "Well, just in case we thought we wanted to get

next to one another, I just wanted to make sure
we were mature enough. Your breasts are very
large for your age which tells me some things,"
he said.

He told me that I looked older than thirteen years old (as he was
looking right at my chest). God knows I hated them. They were
like womens' breasts. I wanted to know what he meant about my
breast size tells him some things. I wanted to know but I didn't at
the same time. I was hoping he couldn't tell what Mr. Calvin did.

I couldn't believe my ears. The nerve of this man! Hops off a bus,
comes right over here and makes a bold play for me! Who does he
think he is? But he sure was handsome and no matter how bold he
got, I was flattered. So I tried to act grown for a few seconds as we
talked.

Momma walked through the den to change the music and saw Tim
sitting there talking to me.
     "Tim, do you play Bid Wiz?"
     Tim just shook his head no, not taking his eyes
     off of me.
     "We got some real good Bid Wiz going on in the
     kitchen."
     "Doris, I don't know how to play cards, I play
     dominos."
     "Well, hell! We can play that too! Go in the
     kitchen and grab you a beer or something."

I could tell she wanted him to just get away from me. I could read
it all over her face. She was looking at me while she was talking to
him.

Showing Momma that he don't jump when she speaks (like Mr.
Calvin), he took his sweet time before actually going into the
kitchen. Momma put on Bobby Blue Band's "Woman in a Red
Cadillac," then Johnny Taylor's, "It's Cheaper to Keep Her," then

back to B.B. Kings "The Thrill is Gone." Boy, were those records depressing. How could they party to this type of music? But that's what they listened to all night long. Tim finally made his way back to me to finish our conversation.

"Do you drink?" I was shocked he asked because my mother was in the next room.
"Yeh a little, but my mother don't know about it."
He smiled. "Cool, look we can have our own little secrets, you know."

I nodded, blushing. I wanted a drink so bad I could taste it. It didn't matter what, just a strong drink. He continued to make small talk.

"So you look after my grandmother at night, hah?"
"Yes, during the week nights."
"Well, that's real good. I remember her talking about you when she wrote me last."

He told me that his grandmother was the only positive person in his life. He looked sad talking about his family. Then I found out that he had a wife and a child somewhere. They were separated. He suggested that some nights when I was staying over at his grandmother's, maybe he could stop by and visit me. I could call him. I said, "I don't know about that. My mother would probably not approve."

Darnell walked in the front door without knocking. He came to see AlmaFaye. He went straight to the kitchen where she was. While passing he looked at Tim and smiled, with a little smirk. Later that evening, AlmaFaye came out of the kitchen and we went into the bathroom together.

"I see how that Navy boy is bothering you, Carla. So just watch yourself, because he means to get him some of your draws!"
I laughed, waving my hand at her to say "Shut up."

"He's too damn old for you and he knows it. So
watch out, okay?"
I changed the subject to tease her.
"I see Darnell is over here tonight."

Momma looked at us real crazy as we entered the kitchen together.
Momma hated when we talked about something that she didn't
have a hand in.   She wanted to control everything within the
environment.   Tim had come into the kitchen.   Momma was
looking over her cards at me.   I was standing right behind
AlmaFaye, looking at her play cards.   Momma saw Tim looking at
my breasts.
          She said, "You better watch out for that one.
          She's not as young as you think she is."
          He said, "Who, Carla?"
          "Oh yeh, she's more woman than you probably
          could handle."

Tim smiled, but I didn't.   She was about to start on me.   It had
been a week, and I guess she was coming back to her old self.
          She looked at me and said, "Isn't it really past
          your bed time, Carla?"
          Darnell jumped to my defense, "Let her stay up,
          Doris. She ain't bothering nobody."
          "Good night, everybody." I gladly went to bed.

I didn't want her to get started.   AlmaFaye had not seen that side
of her.   She couldn't embarrass AlmaFaye, but she could embarrass
the hell out of me.

The next day, when I came home from school, I could hear the
Bobbie Blue Band music playing high and Momma was at the
window with a can of Schlitz Malt Liquor in her hand.   Momma
stood up as soon as I hit the door.   AlmaFaye was coming out of
the kitchen.   Momma came toward me and grabbed my chest.
          "I am tired of all this sneaking around on me!"
          AlmaFaye jumped right in between us and

grabbed Momma's hands.
"I am going to be the fucking death of you, do
you hear me, bitch?" Momma spouted out.
"You ain't going to get away with the shit you
doing with my husband forever."
My english and math books fell to the floor.
She continued, "Pay day is a mother fucker!"

At first, I was scared as usual. My heart was beating fast and
butterflies were swimming in my throat. But this time I felt
different. I wanted to strangle her to death. The anger was
building in me so much that I began to shake all over.
"Yawl must think I am a damn fool, hah," Momma
yelled.
AlmaFaye was getting angry. She hollered at Momma.
"Momma, let her go! Let her go, Momma, please!"
I starred back at Momma as she looked at me so
mean.

I interrupted AlmaFaye because I really didn't care anymore what
would happen to me or to Momma at this point.
"Go on and kill me, Momma. It would be so much
damn better than living here through all of this
hell."
"All of what hell? You ain't going through no
damn hell! Your problem is that your shit has
just caught up with you."
"Momma, you need to stop it. You really need to
stop it now. Don't you see how much you are
hurting Carla? Can't you even see what you are
doing to her?"

AlmaFaye began to cry, looking at both of us. Tears slowly ran
down my face too. I didn't want to cry anymore. I didn't want her
to see the hurt she kept causing me. I didn't want to give her the
satisfaction anymore. Momma held my collar in her hands. My
heart was beating fast. She stood there and looked at me with no

reaction.

"How come you just can't love me? How come
you hate me so damn much, Momma, it's not my
fault," I whispered.

She slowly let me go. I didn't know what to do. I wanted to leave
the house so bad, but I had nowhere to run. With the exception of
my closet, that I was getting tired of. But it was the safest place I
could go. I felt like I was about to explode and lose my mind. As
I went to sit down in my usual corner of my closet, my heart was
still beating fast.

I wanted to cry to God so bad. I grabbed for my diary from out of
my bottom drawer, but instead I grabbed the Bible that I received a
long time ago from Mavis' grandmother. When I looked at the
pages, it opened to Psalms 13. So, I read it to myself:

"How long wilt thou forget me, O Lord?
Forever? How long wilt thou hide thy face
from me? How long shall I take counsel in my
soul, having sorrow in my heart daily? How
long shall mine enemy be exalted over me?
Consider and hear me, O Lord my God; lighten
mine eyes, lest I sleep the sleep of death. Lest
mine enemy say, I have prevailed against him;
and those that trouble me rejoice when I am
moved; But I have trusted in thy mercy; my
heart shall rejoice in thy salvation. I will sing
unto the Lord, because He hath dealt
bountifully with me."

After I finished, it made me think. That's exactly how I felt. My
life felt as if there was an enemy, who happened to be my Momma
who was tearing me apart. Whoever wrote this had a life just like
mine.

AlmaFaye walked in the door and saw me reading. She walked
over and held me. As I layed on her shoulders, I wished she could

hold me forever and never let me go.
"I am with you, baby, and I believe you.Okay?"
The tears rolled down my face.
"Thank you, AlmaFaye."

She told me she was going across the street to visit Darnell for a minute, to get out of Momma's face. She asked if I wanted to go. I told her I wanted to sleep. I was so glad that she was there. After she left, I grabbed my diary.

Why Lord? Why do I even have to go there with my mother? Why is she driving me to hate her? I have never wanted to kill my mother. It almost feels like she is trying to run me out of my mind. Yet, I see more and more each day she seems to be going out of her own mind. I don't think she really knows what to do, so I have to do something, God. I must get away from here now. I need to leave this place. No child should have to live like this. I don't know if I can survive this stuff any longer. God, I feel trapped and it seems like no one understands but you. Because you can see all the way inside of me. There must be something you can do for me. Please help me leave here. Please help my sister get her a place, and maybe I can go live with her. God, thank you for my sister. I'm going to sign off now. Next time something happens, I will let you know. Thank you for being there.

When I heard Momma walk out of the front door to get into her car to leave, I came out of my closet. I went to bed early that night without eating.

The next day I went over to Mrs. Harrison's a little early, since Momma wasn't home anyway. Mrs. Harrison had her maid bring out all of her old photos to show me. Helen came over on Sunday and Monday mornings only. She was a nice short, tiny-built Hispanic woman. She had a lot of moles on her face. She brought

the picture albums for Mrs. Harrison.
>"Now, Carla, these pictures cover the time when I
>first met my husband Louis in 1940 up to the
>70's."

The memories sounded so fresh in her head, you'd think he was still here. I could tell she treasured them, as the tears rolled down her cheek. She reminisced on the anniversary pictures. She joyfully explained the various surprise birthday events and the Christmas out in the snow of Washington.
>"Ah, this is when you were a size 5, hah?"

I saw a picture of her sweet husband holding her at a park. He stood next to Mrs. Harrison holding her around her tiny waist. He had on a white cap, striped shirt (that had 3 buttons in the front), short sleeves and beige pants. Mrs. Harrison had on this blue and white polka dot dress that was real tight in the waist, and flared out at the bottom. It also had a v-neck which showed the top of her breasts. She was so pretty in her young days.
>"Yeh, that dress is in that closet in the room
>there."
>She pointed toward her bedroom.
>"I promised myself for years that I would get back
>into it."
>"Did you?" I teased her.

We laughed and kept turning the dusty pages. I loved to hear her raspy voice turn into uncontrollable laughter. Mrs. Harrison had lived a full happy life with her husband. She told me how they were constantly on the go. They had one daughter named Lisa, Tim's mother.
>"Carla, fix me a bowl of Rocky Road while I pull
>this other photo album out."

Mrs. Harrison's favorite ice cream was Rocky Road. Sometimes at night, she would have me serve her a bowl before beddy-bye. I would have some too, with chocolate chip cookies. She was becoming more and more like the grandmother that I never knew. She was pleasant and filled with wisdom. She always knew when I was sad. I guess it was all over me. She would tell me,

"You are too young to not smile. You have too much life to be lifeless. Keep your head up child, the storm is passing over."

I don't know what storm she was talking about, but my storm had five more years before I was eighteen. And then it would pass over, as far as I was concerned. In the meantime, I just needed to learn how to swim and keep my head above the waters.

After I put her to bed that night Darnell came into the door, leaving it open. His car was still running and you could hear the loud music playing by Natalie Cole, "I'm Catching Hell." The lyrics were ringing loud.

"I'm catching hell, yeh livin living livin here alone alone I tell you the truth, I tell you the truth I'm going out of my mind...yeh, do you hear me tonight." The words echoed in my heart.

Darnell made small talk with me, as he went to the refrigerator to get his stash of marijuana. He asked me what Momma was talking about the other night.

"What did she mean you're more woman than he can handle?"

I felt so embarrassed. I guess it showed on my face, because Darnell apologized for my mother's behavior and said it wasn't fair. He walked over to me and placed his hands on my shoulder. "I'm sorry, Faye told me all about what your stepdaddy did." I started crying. Darnell sighed to himself with regret for me.

"Hey, just chill out. Pretty soon you will be grown and on your own."
I looked up at him, "Darnell, I don't know if I can stay here much longer."
"Yeh, I hear you. But hey, my cousin Tim really digs

you, ya know."
"Yeh, but he's too damn old for me, don't you think?"
I cursed with Darnell because I felt cool doing it.
"Well, Doris did say you were a lot of woman - just
kidding!" I cut my eyes up at him.
"Listen, do you want a joint?" Darnell offered.
"I don't smoke that stuff."

He grabbed his Cool Long cigarette packs out of his shirt pocket,
and a joint fell out. He threw me the joint as he was walking out
the door. "Try it, you'll love it." When Darnell drove out of the
driveway, the music faded. I said to myself, "I'm catching hell too,
Natalie, I know what you mean." I locked the top latch of the
front door and placed the joint in my front jean pocket. I grabbed
my diary and kicked back on the couch.

Dear God:
Thank you for my sister AlmaFaye. She has been a
real friend to me. She makes me feel real special and
wanted. When Momma tries to say something bad
about me, she comes right behind her and says
something good to me. Thank you so much again.
Now Lord, about this man, Tim. I must confess he
is so fine to me! He is so good looking! I know I
want to save myself until I get married, but he is
making it very hard! He makes me so curious. I
know I shouldn't be thinking like this but I am.
Please help me do the right thing. Good night,
Lord. I'll see you in the morning.

CHAPTER 14

Alma Faye Moves Away From Me

AlmaFaye informed me that she had finally signed up with the welfare system and placed herself on the waiting list for housing placement. She went downtown while I was at school one day to do it. They told her it would take anywhere from thirty days to six months for housing placement, depending on availability. I knew AlmaFaye was ready to leave when I began to hear her and Momma arguing all the time.

One night Momma told her that there were too many grown women in her house. She started treating AlmaFaye as if she was only eighteen years old. She was jealous of us. She would interrupt us every time we were having a good conversation. Even when AlmaFaye was helping me with my homework, she would get annoyed.

I came home from school one day and AlmaFaye was so happy. She told me that she received a call from her social worker letting her know they had availability.

"It came through," AlmaFaye yelled.
"What came through," I asked.
"My housing!"
"Oh, that's great," I mumbled.
"That means I can start moving this weekend!"

She had no idea how sad I felt inside. I knew she was happy to be leaving Momma's house. But this meant she was not going to be home with me anymore to shield me from Momma's vicious attacks. She had already begun to place things in boxes and store them in the corners of our room. I walked in the bedroom, and all of her clothes were taken out of the closet and folded away in sacks. Boy, was she ever ready, I thought!
As they say, when it rains, it pours. Later that night, when I went to work for Mrs. Harrison, she told me that Darnell had lost his job.

She would only be needing me two nights out of the week, Sundays and Mondays.   Mrs. Harrison was worried for Darnell, because of his misfortune.   She said, "It's hard for a black man to be without work." Mrs. Harrison didn't realize that he was selling dope out of her house once she was put to bed in the back. He was making lots of money, from what I could see.   I would be on the couch watching television, and I would hear people come by asking for nickels and dimes.   I found out quickly that "nickels" and "dimes" meant $5 and $10 worth of dope, not real silver nickels and dimes.

Darnell came over Saturday morning to help AlmaFaye move all of her things.   The only great thing about it was that they placed her about fifteen minutes away in a housing project up the street.   I asked Momma if I could go on the last trip to help AlmaFaye unpack and set up, and she approved.

AlmaFaye had a big three-bedroom place.   I helped her place cabinet shelving paper inside the cabinets.   Then as we unpacked the kitchen boxes with canned foods in it, I placed them on the shelves.   I told her how much I was going to miss her. It was going to be crazy with her gone.
> "Girl, you know you are always welcome here.
> Especially when you want to get away from
> Momma's."

I grabbed a chair to sit down for a minute, while I unpacked another box. Changing the subject, I asked her how her relationship with Darnell was coming along.
> "I think I love him." She shrugged her shoulders,
> placing her hands inside her red and white dress.
> "Love? That's a Big word," I joked.
> "The only thing I don't like is that damn dope
> business he's in," she said.

I knew AlmaFaye didn't like that, but he didn't like what she did either -- dipping snuff and spitting it out. I would even watch her open her mouth real wide, moving her tongue to the left so she could pour that powdery black stuff in it. It would sit up under her tongue and the juice would mix with saliva, and then she would spit it out. So AlmaFaye always had black stuff between her teeth, making her look like she had been eating mud. I guess it didn't bother her love life with Darnell. I saw another side of my sister with Darnell. She was caring, attentive and loved her man. Though she tried to play "Miss Hard to Get" on the surface, Darnell knew he had her heart and she wasn't afraid to give it to him. He got along well with her kids too. They seemed to like him. AlmaFaye's phone rang and she asked me to get it.

"Carla, I need you to come home. I need to go somewhere."

"Right now?"

"Yes, and hurry."

Why did I answer the damn phone.

"Was that Momma, Carla?"

"Yeh and she said I have to come home right now, she has somewhere to go."

I hugged my sister and walked home. I got a call from my sister an hour after I had gotten home and she was whispering.

"Guess who's here?"

"Who?"

"Yo damn Momma and some woman name Leona."

"Oh, so that's where she was on her way to, hah?"

AlmaFaye was mad. I could tell by her voice. We hung up the phone. On Sunday morning (that next day) after I got out of the bathroom, I turned on my favorite radio station to the gospel music again. I sat on the porch with Blacky, hoping to hear our favorite song, "I'm Going Upa Yonda" by Tramaine. It came on the last hour of the show. I was disappointed though, because I was waiting for them to go back into the bridge and bring in the long version. But they did not. My brothers and sisters were over to Aunt Dora's for church. Momma was snoring in her bedroom, but you could still hear her outside because her window was right there. It was kind of quiet for a change. AlmaFaye wasn't there, and I was so lonesome. I truly missed her.

The next day was Monday and I ran to school. We only had another week before the summer break. School kids were running from class to class, bumping into each other down the aisle, before the last and final bell. Nowadays, going to school was a big fog for me mostly.

As I sat in English Composition class, I stared at the chalkboard while my tall Swedish, gold-haired school teacher gave the requirements and expectations for the final which was the following week. My other classes were just as exciting to me. Yet the end of a school year was so depressing, because it would leave me with too much time on my hands. Too much time in a home filled with despair. I never looked forward to June like most kids. Most of my school life was pretty much the same with the exception of different teachers year after year. Not only did teachers come in and out of my life, it seemed to be that way on a personal level too. The only regrets I had about the end of the school year were not being able to see my few friends. I would miss laughing with Mavis and Cheryl and running across Kendon every other week. I had not seen Kendon in a long time. I wondered where he was. Had he ever called? Did I not get the message from Momma? I called a couple of times and left messages with his baby brother Jimmy. After no return call, I stopped calling him.

One week before school was out, Kendon Starr shows up at my doorstep. I almost collapsed when I saw him standing there. I was so head over heels. He stood there with this black jersey top on with holes in it. You could see his well-developed chest. He had on blue jeans that fit just right. I couldn't believe he was there. I came outside and talked with him on the porch. He saw me in school today, and watched me as I left campus.
          "So how come you didn't speak?"
          "I was so far away, and I didn't want to yell at a
          princess."
          "Are you sure it wasn't your girlfriend that held you

from calling out?"
I teased, but was real serious.
"I'm real sure of that because we broke up."
"I'm sorry to hear that," I lied, an insincere look on
my face. He smiled.
"Thank you anyway, for faking to care."

I asked him what he had been up to and where had he been. He
told me that he had business to take care of. Finally I said, "You're
too young to be handling so much business. What kind of business
are you talking about?"
"You don't want to know."
I said, "Trust me, I do want to know."
"I was in Juvenile Hall," he admitted and put his
head down, looking into the dirt beneath his feet.

I didn't act shocked, because Mavis had already told me about his
track record.
"What was the reason you went there?"
"I had some friends who got caught stealing a stereo
out of a Radio Shack."
"Why do you do this kind of stuff?
"No real reason, just be doing some risky crazy stuff."

Blacky came around the corner and scooted his way between
Kendon and I. Kendon looked down at him and laughed.
"He's jealous," I told Kendon.

We had a full blooming red rosebush on each side of our sidewalk
that led up to the front steps of our house, where Kendon and I sat.
Right then Kendon got up, picked a rose and gave it to me. He
said, "A rose for a rose." I blushed and couldn't stop. I asked about
his family. His smile disappeared.
"I am tired of my daddy beating on my mother. I am
tired of seeing them fight so much. That's why I get
in so much trouble, I guess. I feel like I'm mad at the
world."

I felt sad and hurt with him. He got real quiet and looked to his left toward the airport. His voice was faint. "I tried to hurt my Daddy one night while he was hitting my mother. So I had to leave." He was shaking his head.

I thought to myself, why was he telling me this stuff? I guess he trusted me and that's what friends do with each other. I was not used to being open with anybody but my sister and God. I wished I could see into his heart and say all the right things to him. We watched a plane landing. I reached over and took a rose off the bush and said "Hey, you deserve one too."

I didn't know how to respond to his pain other than by giving him a rose too. At that point, I heard my mother walking near the screen door. I froze inside. It was silent. I didn't know what to do, or what to expect, since this was the first time a boy had ever come to my house.

I whispered, "That's my mother." Kendon smiled in her direction. Peeking through the screen door, Momma said,
> "Hello there,"
> "Hello, mama," Kendon said.
> "How are you?" she asked.
> "I'm doing fine, Mama."
> "Mama," I said to myself.
> Momma continued to talk. "You know my
> daughter?"
> "Yeh, we go to the same school."

She opened the screen door and stepped out on the porch looking from his shoes up to the last strand on his head.
> "Would you like to come in the house, young man?"
> "Okay, thank you."

I guess Kendon understood that was not really a polite request, but a demand. We went inside, and Kendon sat on the couch while

Momma sat in her usual chair in front of the window. I offered
Kendon a glass of water. He refused. As I was walking back into
the living room, Momma was still asking Kendon questions.
"Do you drink?"
"Yeh, a little."
"What do you drink?"
"Mainly beer," he responded.
"So can you go around the corner to the store and
pick us up a six pack of Schlitz Malt Liquor?"
"I can try." I couldn't believe my ears, I was so
embarrassed.

She looked at me after Kendon left to go to the store. "He seems
like a nice boy," she said. Kendon returned within fifteen minutes
with the six pack in his arms. Momma took it from him and gave
him one. She popped the top and began to drink her own.
"So you like my daughter?" I hadn't heard her call me
daughter twice in one day, ever.
"Yeh. She is real special."

Apparently, Kendon could handle himself, and I was relieved. I still
didn't know what this guy saw in me and what he meant by this
"special" thing.
"Oh, she's special, hah," Momma mocked at him.

After he and Momma had a beer together, Kendon said he had to
go. He said goodbye and I walked him out to the gate. He was so
handsome. He had the prettiest, dark, smooth skin. The deepest
dimples you wanted to see, and piercing beautiful eyes. I had a
mad crush on him. He was so cool! He hugged me and kissed me
on my forehead. God, I hoped my mother didn't see him do that!
When I came back into the door, Momma said, "You
know he's a thug."
I said, "No, Momma, I don't know he's a thug."
"Well, he has manners, but he's a street nigga. I can
tell them a mile away." She sounded as if she had
been talking to my friend, Mavis.

I went to my room and mumbled underneath my breath, "He's my kinda street nigga."

SUMMER TIME
GUEST FROM OUT OF TOWN

There seemed to never be a dull moment at my house that summer. I heard that Mr. Calvin's family was coming to town but Momma didn't know exactly when. A week later his family just showed up. I overheard Momma laughing and talking with two strange voices. I walked in the kitchen where they were all seated and said hello. Momma turned around from the stove and said,
        "Carla, meet Mr. Calvin's brother and sister-in-law. This is your Uncle Daniel and his wife, Mary."
        They both nodded politely and greeted me.
        "Good morning." I said.

Uncle Daniel stood up to shake my hand.   He was the tallest man in the world. He must have been about 6'3". He had sandy red hair, just like Buddy's back at the shacks. His wife was chubby and dark. She had on teacher glasses that sat on her nose. I excused myself to go change and begin my chores.

I found out that Mr. Calvin's relatives would be here for two weeks. Later that afternoon I overheard Momma talking on the phone to her friends telling them how handsome Daniel was. I heard Momma say, "Girl, the hell with his wife, he's still handsome." Apparently, Momma and Uncle Daniel really hit it off. Every day Uncle Daniel would start driving over to our house in the late mornings to sit and drink beer with Momma while Mr. Calvin was at work. I guess the rest of his family was too spiritual. I thought that was kinda strange.

One day, I saw something that made me take a double take. Momma and Uncle Daniel were kissing each other when I came in the house from going to the store for Momma. After Uncle Daniel left, Momma looked at me and smiled. I thought to myself, how can a man carry on with his own brother's wife? How can a wife kiss her husband's brother? I couldn't understand for the life of me how they could do it and feel good about the situation. Momma seemed like she didn't care that I caught her. In fact, Uncle Daniel prolonged the visit to three weeks, but his wife had to go back because she had to go to work.

One night, Momma got drunk and when Mr. Calvin came in the front door she was waiting for him. Uncle Daniel had just left. Momma started talking crap to him. I was sitting on the couch looking at TV, watching Sanford and Son. Momma was real drunk. She and Uncle Daniel had been drinking since morning. Uncle Daniel kept going back to the store for more drinks. As fast as they drank them up Momma would send him back for more. Mr. Calvin walked in the door and looked at her real mean. Momma stood up from the desk.

"Now how does it feel for your own wife to fuck your brother? How does it feel, Mr. Child Lover? You fuck my daughter, and I fuck your big brother. Now we're even." Momma was wobbly and holding on to the table. "And let me say another thing, at least mine wasn't no damn baby! He's a got damn grown ass man."
Then she turned to me and said, looking at me, "Y'all better just leave me the fuck alone."
God, her words hurt me so much my heart ached.

I knew Mr. Calvin was wrong for what he did to me, but I knew Momma hurt him real bad that day. She tore his insides out. Now I understood the saying that my teacher taught one time, "two wrongs don't make a right."

Momma had a way of sticking a knife in you, turning it, and looking you dead in the eye when she did it. So I guess they were even. I was ashamed my mother would stoop so low. That's not the way I wanted her to handle what her husband did to me. I guess by not knowing the right thing to do, she did only what she knew how to do. Do back to others what they have done to you, no matter how low you will have to go. Uncle Daniel and his wife left town that next day and Momma went back to her usual. Going about to her old hang outs and partying all day, at home. She would leave when Mr. Calvin came home, to go and hang out over to her friends house and get home later at night. When he came in, she went out.

"See y'all. I can't stay here with you two." And then she was gone for the rest of the night.

I felt so horrible. I wished so badly I had somewhere to go too, but there was nowhere for me to go.

MOMMA GOES TO JAIL -- JULY 4, 1976

On the 4th of July, I was awakened around midnight by lots of hollering coming through the front door. AlmaFaye and Momma came in the house with a man named L.C. He was the new man Momma was supposed to be screwing. I shook my head and took a second look to make sure I wasn't dreaming. It was him. Momma brought this man to her husband's house. They had to have been sloppy drunk. As soon as Momma got in the house, L.C. left. AlmaFaye screamed, "Call an ambulance, I've been shot!"

"What?" I asked.

"Momma shot me in the arm, but she didn't mean to."

AlmaFaye said.

Mr. Calvin came out of the bedroom to see what all the hollering was about. Momma explained to Mr. Calvin that she accidentally shot AlmaFaye.

"Hell, you know I didn't mean to shoot my own Goddamn daughter. It was an accident. She got in the damn way."

Mr. Calvin's mouth was open in shock. I ran to call the ambulance for AlmaFaye.

"Where did you get a gun, Doris?" I heart Mr.
Calvin ask Momma.
"Shit, it's your gun. I don't go nowhere without
packing me something."
"Who in the hell told you that you can take my
gun?"
"Look, I don't have to ask for a damn thing that's in
this house."
Mr. Calvin was speechless, not knowing what to say
next.
"AlmaFaye got in the way, I was shooting at
somebody else."
"Doris, who were you shooting at?"
"Some hussy trying to flaunt her shit around me.
She won't do that shit again."

Momma lost her balance, and fell in the chair that she was
staggering in front of, continuing cursing and talking loud.
"Hell, that bitch was trying to stab me," Momma
told Mr. Calvin.

Suddenly we heard sirens. The sirens were getting closer and
closer. I thought it was the ambulance that I called, but instead it
was the police. I looked out the window and the lights were
flashing and going around and around. Then the officers got out
of the car walking toward our house. My heart starting beating so
fast because I didn't know what to expect next. A knock came at
the door. Our front door was open and the screen door latched. A
white officer looked through the door asking for Momma by
name.
"Is there a Doris Williams here?"
"Yes, I'm Doris, can I help you?"
"Mam', we would like to ask you a few questions."

Momma tried to get up, but fell back into her chair. Mr. Calvin let
the officers in the house. The only time I was this close to a police
officer was at school when I was in the fifth grade and it was Career

Day.

They were asking Momma questions about what happened tonight with her and Leona at the club.   Then I heard them tell Momma that they needed to talk further downtown.

Momma was leaving. Momma was going downtown to the police station to answer more questions. I wondered why they had to take her way downtown to answer questions. She was doing fine in the house, I thought.   She looked at me and said, "I'll be back later, just go to bed."   I know she could see the worry in my eyes.   By this time the ambulance had arrived to get AlmaFaye, and the cops were escorting Momma to their car. Mr. Calvin was right behind them.   I stood in the middle of the yard wondering what was going on.   All the kids were still sleeping.   I waited and waited for someone to come back, but I couldn't keep my eyes open.

AlmaFaye came over bright and early the next morning to check on me. I had just woke up and was coming out of the bathroom when I heard her coming through the front door.
        "Sis, what happened last night, and are you alright?"
        I could see her arm all bandaged up.
        "First, I must get a cup of coffee then I'll tell you
        about it."
        AlmaFaye went directly to the sink to run water into
        the pot to boil.
        "Well Carla, I should have listened to my first mind.
        You know I didn't want to go out with Momma."
        I nodded yes.
        "Well, after Momma saw her boyfriend L.C. talking
        with her friend Leona, Momma got an attitude."
        "But, she's married, AlmaFaye!"
        I joked in disbelief because Momma was tripping
        like this.
        "Girl, hush up and just let me finish telling you the
        story."

Then, Leona started talking shit to Momma. She told Momma that she needed to learn how to share since she already had a husband at home. AlmaFaye got up to pour the hot water into her cup and she continued talking. Momma told her to kiss her ass and leave her old man alone. She told her that she could have as many men as the law allowed. Leona pulled a knife out of her jeans, pointing it at Momma, and told her, don't let me have to cut your ass, Doris. When Momma saw the knife, Momma told her , if you ever pull a knife on somebody, you better mean to use it. Then Momma went in her purse to get her gun, cocked it and shot her in the chest. That's when I started running across the bar, trying to stop Momma from shooting the second bullet. I got there just in time to throw my arm. That's when I got the bullet."

I grabbed for the sugar because AlmaFaye was frowning as she sipped her coffee. She forgot to put the sugar in it. She smiled when she saw me getting it for her.

"So Momma's in jail for that stupid shit?"
"I suspect they will do a quick trial and sentence her on Monday, next week, " AlmaFaye added.
"Monday," I said. Momma's in jail!" I panicked.
Checking the refrigerator for cream, AlmaFaye continued to talk.
"Yeh, she's in jail. She's not in her room."

Momma's door was closed when AlmaFaye and I went into the kitchen. I thought Mama was in her bedroom. I never thought she was in jail. I thought she had come back in the middle of the night like she said she would

"Momma is in jail." I played her words over in my head.
"I'm sure you can feel relief for a while now that her ass will be locked up, hah?" AlmaFaye said.
She grabbed the milk carton instead.
"You don't have to deal with that shit you been dealing with all these damn years," AlmaFaye said
"Hell yeh. Thank God."

After AlmaFaye finished telling me what happened, I had a lot of mixed emotions. AlmaFaye was joking, but she was so right. I did feel a sense of relief, and immediately I felt guilty. I missed my mother, but at the same time I didn't want her to come back. A spark of hope popped into my mind. Maybe she would come back different and find that she loved me. Maybe she would come back and want to be my mother and believe me about Mr. Calvin. Maybe she would have time to think about everything that happened. I wondered and I thought nervously. Then the scary thoughts came. I wondered how it would be here with Mr. Calvin without my mother. Though my mother didn't believe me, I just knew deep down inside he would never touch me again with my mother around. But would he try it again while Momma was in jail? I prayed and hoped not.

"Hey Carla, I'm going across the street for a minute and wake up Darnell's ass," AlmaFaye said. She couldn't reach him the night before. She was pissed when she was talking about him.

Before she left, I asked her how her arm was. She told me that it was fine. The bullet scaled her skin. She held it up and pointed to the place where the bullet scaled it. She said, "I will never forget what Momma did as long as I live."

On the following day, there was an article in The Fresno Bee titled "Mother Shoots Daughter." AlmaFaye was so mad, because the media made it look like they were fighting over the same man. As soon as she got the newspaper, she called me to bitch about it. It also talked about another woman involved (which was Leona) and said she was in stable but serious condition.

The following Thursday morning, Momma was charged with attempted manslaughter. She was sentenced to do a minimum of one year to five years in a woman's prison camp. They sentenced her to a camp instead of prison, because she was a first time offender. Now it was just my little sisters and brothers, Mr. Calvin

and I left in that house while Momma was in jail. I knew I would
be doing even more cooking and cleaning.

That next couple of weeks I kept busy with cleaning the house,
washing clothes and cooking everyday. No one complained, so I
guess it tasted good. My sisters and brothers really didn't ask about
Momma. Their Daddy told them she had to go away for a while
and would be back later. I guess he thought they wouldn't
understand. He was probably right.

Since I didn't have summer school, I sat on the floor of the living
room everyday in front of the radio listening to the hits. I had
learned the words in full for "I'm Catching Hell" by Natalie Cole,
and other songs that I really liked. Music helped me to escape from
feelings of fear and loneliness.   I guess that's why people like
music. Sometimes you can luck up on a song and the words will
say exactly what you feel.

Of course, I had to let my job with Mrs. Harrison go entirely now.
She understood and was very sorry Momma was in jail. Momma's
friends didn't know, or maybe they were not at the party that night.
They started calling and asking about her. I had to tell them one
by one where Momma was.

After a couple of weeks, AlmaFaye called and asked me if I wanted
to go to a house party. She told me that Darnell's cousin Barbara
and her husband Bobby were giving a party.
>   "I would love to, and I will ask Mr. Calvin as soon as
>   he gets home from work," she said.
>   "That asshole better not tell you that you can't go.
>   He has no right to tell you nothing! He ain't your
>   damn Daddy!"
>   "AlmaFaye, I know. But I still have to ask him," I
>   said.

Personally, I did hate the fact that I had to look to him as someone
"taking care of me", but I couldn't help it. I waited for him to

come home from work. He came through the back door as always, because he would check on his dogs before even coming into the house to check on his children. As he walked into the living room, I said, "Mr. Calvin, AlmaFaye called, and wants to know if I could go to a house party with her." My voice was quivering. He tried to get that parental posture, clearing his throat.

>"Is this the kind of party that a 13 year old is
>suppose to go to?"
>"Yes, and my 27 year old sister will be looking out
>for me, Asshole," I said silently. I wanted to call
>him an Asshole so bad, but I just said it under my
>breath.
>"Yeh, you can go," he replied looking offended.
>"Thank you," I said, and walked to the kitchen.

I guess I didn't know how much I hated this until I was in the middle of it. I called AlmaFaye back and told her I could go. She had bought me some jeans and halter tops from downtown the week before (spending about fifty dollars on me for some summer clothes). I was so happy!

AlmaFaye came by the house about 8:30 p.m. I had on the blue jeans and put on my red and white halter top she bought me. AlmaFaye had on her favorite Levi's and a white blouse. She looked cute. AlmaFaye was a natural. She didn't believe in a lot of makeup and eye shadow shit (as she called it).

>"How are we getting there?" I asked.
>"We go pick em'up and put'em down."
>"What?" I asked.
>"Hey, we're walking. It's right up the street." We
>laughed and were on our way.

We talked all the way there. She wanted to know how the kids were doing and was Mr. Calvin acting right?

>"Yes, he better." I was so glad that my sister was so
>concerned and keeping track of me.
>"I miss you, sis."

"I miss you too, Carla, but hey, you can visit anytime
you want. You know that, don't you?"

Our relationship was so neat. My sister was so much older than
me, yet she had a desire to be with me so we could hang out
together. I felt grown and so loved being around her.
      "Momma's gone now, and ain't nobody gonna tell
      you that you can't come visit me."

The night was hot. It had just gotten dark. It was 80 degrees at
8:30 in the evening. As we approached the main street of Fresno
Blvd., ongoing traffic was coming both ways. As we waited to cross
the street, horns were blowing by cars filled with men. I thought it
was the coolest thing. We finally arrived at the party and the house
was jumping with music and people. We walked in the door and
there was a blue light in the living room where everyone was
dancing. I had never seen a blue light bulb. The room had to have
had about fifty people in it. They were blasting the Ohio Players
cut "Fire." I remembered getting that album for my tenth
birthday. That's about all that was worth remembering from my
tenth birthday. There were all kinds of odors in the room. I found
out later that it was a combination of Columbia Weed and PCP
(better known as Angel Dust). People were dancing all over the
place having a ball. You heard yells and people saying "Party over
here!" "Party right here!" I noticed these people were old people
like my sister. Or shall I say "older people." They were not the age
of Momma's party friends. They were not my age. They were all
in their mid to late twenties.

AlmaFaye nudged me and said, "let me introduce you to Darnell's
cousin and her husband." We walked over to the bar and there
stood the two sharpest people in the entire place. They were the
bartenders. AlmaFaye got their attention by clearing her throat.
      "Barbara and Bobby, I would like you to meet my
      little sister, Carla."
      "I didn't know you had a younger sister,
      AlmaFaye," Bobby replied.

"I have four more," she told him.

Barbara just looked, smiled, and said, "Nice to meet you, Carla."

Barbara was a pretty, fair skinned woman with red hair. She was beautiful and wore a bad black mini-skirt outfit. Bobby was a small boned man with a perm. It looked like a press and curl. His hair looked better than some of the girls at the party. AlmaFaye asked for a beer. I just stood there smiling and watching her.

"Would you like a drink also?" Bobby asked.

Not wanting to feel too young, or out of place, I asked for my mother's usual drink. "I'll have a Schlitz Malt Liquor beer." I was hoping he didn't ask if I was old enough, because then I would have been busted. AlmaFaye laughed and said, "Okay little Doris, let's go get a seat."

On our way through the crowd and the trip lights, we ran into Darnell. "Hey, baby, "he said to AlmaFaye with a big old smile on his face. I could tell he was high as a kite, because his eyes were so tiny. They danced a couple of dances, and I sat back and secretly giggled over my sister. She wasn't a dancer. She moved from side to side with one step and would snap her head side to side shrugging her shoulders to the music. She never moved her feet. I guess that was the country side of her. I wanted to dance so bad. Each week when I would watch Soul Train, I would dance with them when Momma wasn't watching. I learned all the new dances that way. I finally got asked to dance . I didn't think that Marvin Gaye's "You Got To Give It Up," would ever go off. But I was having fun trying to keep up. After that, other guys came up to me asking me to dance. I danced most of the night. It was so great! Before I knew it, someone had hit my shoulder and shoved a joint in my face. As if to say, it's your turn now. I took a couple of hits and passed it on. I will never forget that night. It was great. Darnell took AlmaFaye and me home. They dropped me off first then Darnell went home with AlmaFaye.

The next afternoon, Kendon Starr came over to my house again. I had not seen him since that day on the porch. I heard he was back in juvenile hall. I was so happy to see him again. I told him my mother was in jail for shooting a woman. He said "Damn, I'm sorry to hear that." We sat outside on the porch and began to talk about our home lives. He told me how sad he was with his parents. His Daddy's abuse toward his mother was still going on. For some reason I also felt I could talk with him about my own unhappiness. I told him about what Mr. Calvin had been doing to me and why my home is so screwed up.

"Carla, do you want me to kill him for you?"
"What! Kill him! Are you crazy?"
"No, I care about you. And no one is going to be
   doing that kind of stuff and getting away with it!"
"No, Kendon," I said
"Why not?" he asked.
"I don't know, but you can't just take somebody's
   life."
I had never seen Kendon this upset.
"I will kill his ass for you. You don't deserve that,
   Carla. I don't want anyone to ever hurt you or
   disrespect you."

From the look on his face and the rage in his voice, I knew without a shadow of a doubt that he was serious about killing Mr. Calvin. I made him promise me that he would not. Reluctantly, he agreed. He asked one final question.

"Do you feel safe alone with him while your
   Momma's in camp?"
"Yeh, I'm sure I will be alright," I said.

He held me in his arms, and just comforted me. I felt so safe. I felt the way I used to feel when my oldest brother Gable took care of me when I was a little girl. This time I felt a love embracing me that I could understand. After that day Kendon and I grew so much closer. I trusted him like I had never trusted anyone in my life.

He told me to call him if I needed anything. He kissed me on my forehead and left. When he would leave me, I always had a built in fear that I would not see him again. I use to hate to see him go, because I never knew how long it would be before his return. How come he couldn't be in my life everyday, I asked God (as I watched him walk down the street and out of my view once again).

AlmaFaye finally let Darnell move in with her. He had already began to move in a little bit at a time, until one day all he needed was the key. Certainly, she was not complaining, because she loved her Darnell.

Not too long after Darnell moved in, AlmaFaye started hearing rumors of Darnell having women on the other side of town. She told me about this girl called "Little Bit." She said that Little Bit had a baby by him. AlmaFaye was hurt. She didn't show it all the way, but I knew she was. By the way she would start talking about the rumors, I could tell she believed them.

Even though AlmaFaye had her own life with her children and Darnell, she still made time for me. We started going to pool halls on Whites Bridge Avenue. We didn't know how to play, but we went in anyway. We played the juke box, racked up a game and taught ourselves. The place was a hole in the wall. It was kind of dingy, but there were a couple of brothers hanging outside and inside at various pool tables drinking beer. They were talking loud and looking at us. I would drink beer with AlmaFaye, while we played our version of pool. I loved playing the juke box, because they had great songs that I had heard on the radio. Gladys Knight & the Pips, Midnight Train, Marilyn McCoo and Billie Davis, Jr., and so many more hits that we liked. One of AlmaFaye's favorites was a song called "Don't Leave Me This Way" by Thelma Houston, one of mine was "Distant Lover" by Marvin Gaye. I thought about Kendon when I sang mine, and AlmaFaye thought about Darnell when she sang.

When we were not shooting pool, we were at her house drinking and playing word rhyme games. I would start off saying, "Hey fool," and AlmaFaye would respond, "Go to school." I would continue, "I want to shout," she would say, "If you don't you'll become a drop out." We would go on and on until we got stuck and neither of us could find a word that rhymed. The game would usually leave us laughing till our sides were in pain.

Although many of my mother's friends had stopped coming by, Tim, Mrs. Harrison's nephew, still came lurking around every now and then. He told me that he was coming by to check on me and make sure I was alright. He had heard Momma was in jail. However, each time he would come by, he would always make a point to tell me how much he digged me and wanted to get next to my body. I would laugh and just tell him I thought it was time for him to go. It became a kind of game. I must admit he was someone who thought about me and thought I was something special. I knew it was only physical. For a boy his age to think I was pretty made me feel wanted and good. I certainly had my mind made up that this grown boy would do nothing with me. I was going to be Mrs. Kendon Starr one day.

Coincidentally, each time Tim would stop by Mr. Calvin was always home. In fact, Mr. Calvin would just be getting home from work. Tim would stumble across the street with a beer in his hand, and was always high or drunk. Sometimes he would speak to Mr. Calvin and come on in our front door looking for me to mess with.

One day, Tim came by a little earlier. I was sitting in the living room listening to my Earth Wind and Fire tape singing "Devotion." This day the kids were playing ball up and down the driveway. When I saw Tim coming toward the house I immediately got up off the floor and sat in Momma's chair. He walked in the door without knocking, sat on the couch next to the chair where I sat, leaned back reclining on his elbow and said,

> "Hey, sweet girl."
> "Hey, Tim."

"You know Carla, I don't care how old you say you
are. I know you can handle me."
"Excuse me, Tim?" I crossed my leg, rolled my eyes
and looked out of the window like I had seen my
mother do.
"That's a nice white skirt you have on there."

I had on my white summer skirt and a red tube top that AlmaFaye
bought for me downtown. Tim got up and came over to me trying
to kiss me on my neck. I jumped.
"What's wrong with a little kiss?" he asked.
"I don't do that."
"What you mean you don't do that?"

Tim sure was not the one I wanted to have my first kiss with. I
knew and had already decided that when the time was right
Kendon Starr would be the man I kiss for the first time. Before I
knew it, Tim grabbed my face with both of his hands and kissed
me real hard ramming his nasty tongue down my mouth. I almost
choked with disgust. I tried to grab both of his hands off my face,
but he held my face too tight.
"Listen, I have been wanting you too damn long,
little girl, and you know that." His voice sounded
mean.
"You better go back home!"

I began to feel really scared inside. Tim was acting real strange and
almost evil. I didn't know this Tim. I didn't like this Tim either.
Tim was real heavy handed and looked real crazy by the eyes. I
could smell the beer on his breath as he struggled, trying to keep
control of my face. I hated his breath.
"I can't wait any longer, Carla," he yelled.
"Wait for what?" I asked.
"Hell I ain't had no pussy in a long time and I'm bout
to get some. You know you want it too."
"No please, I don't."
"Quit bullshiting me. Even yo Momma said you

were more woman than a man could handle."

Tim grabbed me, pulling me out of the seat, trying to take me to the couch next to the chair I sat in. I kept looking out the window to make sure my sisters and brothers were not near by. I could still hear then playing along side of the house. He stumbled and I continued to get loose from him. I kicked him in his leg hoping he would weaken and I could run. Instead, he fell back (still holding on to me) and we both fell on the couch.

He fell and quickly jumped on top of me, pinning me down. He quickly unzipped his pants. I kept trying to pull my skirt down that had come up from the fall. He could see my red and white polka dot panties and I felt so embarrassed and mad.

Tim was breathing hard and telling me to come on and stop fighting him (spitting in my face from his drunkenness). I scratched at him, telling him to let me go. He seemed to not feel it. He also acted as if he didn't hear me begging. He just ignored me. I was praying to God to not let the children come in.

I started feeling like I was suffocating. It was a hundred degrees that day and I felt like fainting in the midst of this battle that I was losing. I could see the clock on the wall reading 1:55 p.m., and Mr. Calvin got off work at 2:00 p.m.. He didn't work far from the house, so he would be coming home very soon.

Then Tim reached down and grabbed my panties, pulling them to the side of my leg. That's when he pulled his thing out trying to stick it in me. It couldn't go in me at first but he was ramming it at me. He was getting so mad.
"Shit, relax. Just relax, Got dammit!"

I couldn't relax. I started crying. He was hurting me. It felt like he was trying to tear my body apart. My heart felt like it was beating a hundred miles an hour.

Then he busted in me. I screamed so loud from the pain. Then he started cursing again. "Oh shit, not now. Dammit." Then he started going fast. Almost as fast as my heart was beating. The next thing I knew, he was laying slumped over on me breathing hard and loud. He was finished. I felt like I was in shock and almost numb. All I could do was cry, pushing his drunk smelly ass off me. I could feel his wet stuff all over my legs when he rolled over off me. I hated it.

I went to the bathroom to wash his stuff off of me, crying. I looked out of the bathroom window to the driveway where the kids were still playing outside of the window. I felt so dirty. No matter how hard I scrubbed myself, I still felt dirty. I hated Tim. I also hated myself for being there. Kendon's vision of me as special is all gone now. Wasted in a matter of seconds to some drunk son-of-a-bitch.

After a few days passed by and AlmaFaye didn't hear from me she called to see how I was doing. I was to afraid and ashamed to call AlmaFaye. I didn't know what I would say to her. I felt like a dirty little sister. When she asked me how I was doing tears just rolled out my eyes. She could hear it in my voice. She knew something was wrong.

  "Carla, what's wrong, honey?"
  "Tim came over here and made me..."
  "Made you what?"
  "Tim made me do it with him."
  "Are you saying he raped you?"
  "I don't know. I guess, I think. All I know is I didn't
   want him to do it."

AlmaFaye was silent for a minute. It reminded me of when Momma got quiet after I told her what Mr. Calvin did to me. I was scared AlmaFaye was going to stop talking to me.

  "Well, did you tell him that you didn't want him like
   that?"
  "Yeh I did but he kept on doing it."
  "Well I'm going to kick that motherfucker's ass. You

hear me." She sounded so mad.

"AlmaFaye that's okay. Please don't say anything to him."

"Look, if his ass raped you than he can't get away with that shit. Unless you wanted him to do it."

"No, I didn't. I told you that. Just drop it."

"His ass go pay, you just wait and see."

"AlmaFaye, I'm not a virgin anymore."

My insides still ached with pain and feelings of shame.

"I know, baby," I'm so sorry. He needs his ass killed.

"No Faye, don't worry about that. God will get him."

"I know, but you have to worry about something more important now." Her voice sounded real serious.

"What?"

"Did he come inside you?"

"Yuk, why you have to say it like that?" I asked her.

"Because, shit, if he did now we have to be worried about if you are pregnant or not."

"Oh no, can it happen just like that? I didn't even like it."

"Shit you ain't got to like it, that's what's so fucked up about a bad fuck or rape."

"Oh God, please Lord, don't let me be pregnant. Please God please." I prayed out loud without realizing it.

"You better pray."

"AlmaFaye, Kendon can't find out, okay. He thinks I'm a virgin and I was until that asshole...."

"Oh shit, that's who I was going to get to kick Tim's ass for me."

"Promise me, AlmaFaye, that you won't tell him. Please." I begged her.

"Alright, fine."

We got off the phone. AlmaFaye knew how much I loved Kendon and how I wanted to save myself for him. She also knew how ashamed I felt. I knew she would protect me, because she always did.

Every time I would see Tim, he would just wave at me and not stay around too long. It almost felt like he was ashamed too. This summer was like no other. There were parties every weekend. One night while Tim was over to AlmaFaye's house he overheard her talking about going to a party that night. Tim asked her if he could hang out with her. AlmaFaye told him yes so that we could have a ride. Tim didn't know that Kendon and I were going also, but after he found out he still offered to drive all of us.

The party was in a big house in the country. It was a big beautiful house. We had to walk down a narrow pathway at the side in order to get to where the party was. The party was packed with everybody in town. The music was playing good and loud. They had the trip lights rolling and the people were jamming hard. I saw lots of school friends that were amazed to see me there. I saw Phyllis (Olivia's daughter), who I knew from my early childhood. I heard through my friend Mavis that Phyllis liked Kendon Starr a lot, but I wasn't worried because she was definitely not his type. Kendon excused himself and told me that he would be right back. He walked off with some of his home boys. AlmaFaye and I went further into the party and started dancing. Tim made his way to the bar. Kendon soon returned and put his arms around me. We slow danced to his favorite song by the Commodores named "Easy like Sunday Morning." As I held on to him, I realized I loved him so much. I felt so secure being in his arms.

When we left the party, we were all drunk and Tim drove us home. Only God could tell you how we got to the house in the state of mind that we were in. He parked the car in front of the house. He turned off the car and tilted his head back. It had to have been around one thirty in the morning. I was in the back seat with Kendon and AlmaFaye was up in the front with Tim. In seconds,

Tim was snoring, and AlmaFaye had fallen asleep also. I pretended to be asleep, because I didn't want to get out of Kendon's arms so soon. I felt Kendon trying to feel on my titties. It almost felt as if he was feeling a girl's body for the first time. Not knowing how to touch them, but with driven curiosity going on any how. Then he put his hand in my blouse, unbuttoning the front and pulling up my bra so that he could kiss my breast with his lips. His lips were so soft, and he was so gentle. I melted inside. After that he leaned his head back on the car's head rest, as if to say "I did it!" Then he fell asleep too. We stayed in that car until 3:00 a.m. I couldn't believe I was with Kendon all this time. It felt like we spent the night with each other. All I could keep thinking about was this could never happen if Momma was home. I felt so safe with Kendon. I didn't want the night to ever end. Then AlmaFaye woke and told Tim to take her home. Kendon woke up and told Tim to drop him off at a house up the street where his cousin Carl lived. I said my goodbyes and went into the house.

Mr. Calvin was awake and saw me come in. He was peeking out of his door. I know I was drunk, and the fumes of alcohol and marijuana probably came through my clothes and skin. I smelled just like Momma when she used to come home from partying all night, except for the marijuana smell. I went straight to bed, and Mr. Calvin didn't say anything or ask me why was I so late.

The next morning I was suddenly awakened by heavy weight and heavy breathing. I felt someone trying to penetrate me. At first I thought I was dreaming. Then I wished to God that I was dreaming but discovered that I wasn't. It was Mr. Calvin! I could smell that stupid soap he wears. He had his mouth on my titties, and he was between my legs. I immediately felt moisture down there. I didn't know if it was from me or him. I remember fighting to wake up before he was able to do anything inside of me. I broke through my sleep and got up using all the strength I could. I screamed at him.
          "Get the hell up! Stop!" I screamed.
          I spoke with more force than ever.

"Why are you doing this to me? Why are you
messing with a child?"

I begged him for an answer, staring right into his eyes. He just
stood there looking at me sadly, speechless. He did not say
anything.

"Don't you know I hate this? Don't you know it
hurts me!"
I was screaming at the top of my voice, like never
before.
"I'm a kid, and you are suppose to be like a Daddy!"

My voice was trembling. Pulling my pajama top together,
buttoning it up, I stood up.

"Why, Mr. Calvin, Why?" I cried. I just want to
know why?"

The whole thing was so different this time. It was daylight instead
of night time when he usually lurked in the dark, creeping, sneaking
around my bed, and leaving once I woke up. He replied in a
hushed voice,

"I am sorry, Carla. I really am sorry. I don't know
what's wrong with me, but I will pray to God and
ask him for forgiveness."
I looked at him in disbelief, surprised that he even
mentioned God's name.
"Then I will go visit your mother in camp and tell her
what happened and ask her for forgiveness," he
continued.

I just stood there, crying, not saying anything. I felt stronger
because I had never talked to him like this before. I walked past
him to go to the bathroom and clean his smell off me. I scrubbed
harder-as hard as I could. I could still smell that damn Irish Spring
soap that I hated. I wouldn't use it for myself! I'd rather use the
Ajax that sat in the corner next to the toilet.   When I finally came
out of the bathroom he was gone, but I noticed a note and seven

dollars on the television. The money was to buy socks for school.
School would be starting in a few weeks. Lord knows I didn't want
to take it, but I had to. I was angry and humiliated, so I left and
went over to my sister's house.

It was around eleven o'clock a.m. when I walked into AlmaFaye's
back door. She could tell I had been crying. In fact, I cried all the
way over there. I told her, he did it again. She got furious and
yelled, "Hell naw this is it!" She grabbed her butcher knife out of
her chef collection and stormed out of the door. I ran after her.
She said, "Momma won't slash that nigga's throat, but I damn sure
will!"
> "No, AlmaFaye! You can't! You can't! Please don't.
> It's not worth it."
> "You are worth it, Carla, you are!" She was crying.
> "But your children, Faye! They need a Momma!"

She dropped her head. We both stood there in tears in the middle
of the backyard looking at each other, crying. She grabbed me and
held me in her arms. We went back into the house and I asked her
for a joint and a beer. We decided that I would stay over at her
house until Momma got out of prison camp. AlmaFaye told me
that we were going to go get my clothes and that she would be cool
as long as Mr. Calvin didn't say a word to her.

Mr. Calvin was in the back tending to his dogs. Once he knew I
had returned, he came into the house. AlmaFaye quickly spoke up
and told him I would be staying the nights at her house until
Momma came home. He nodded okay, with no questions or
resistance. I continued to get my things together. I hated so much
to leave my little sisters and brothers with him. I wished I could
take them with me, but I knew I couldn't. I promised myself that I
would pray for them all the time. I didn't know what Mr. Calvin
would do to them, especially my little sisters. But I felt like I had to
save my own life at this point. I was tired of this house and
everything that went on in it. Before I left I told Mr. Calvin that I
would come over each day and cook dinner for the kids. He said

he appreciated that.   He couldn't even look me in the face as he
said, "Thank you."

CHAPTER 15

LIVING WITH ALMAFAYE

Staying with AlmaFaye was different, yet familiar. Her house was known on her block as the dope house. She had her friends and party people as well. The only difference was that they were not old and depressing like Momma's friends and didn't listen to blues all day. They listened to all the upbeat rhythms. I went through her stack of albums laying on the floor next to her stereo. She had all the cool music: like the O'Jays, Commodores, Peabo Bryson, the Emotions, Maze, Rolls Royce, S.O.S., Earth, Wind and Fire, and one of my favorites, Natalie Cole. Her friends were not there every night, but every week-end.

Living with AlmaFaye, I was able to smoke all the dope that I wanted. In fact, when Darnell would bring his shipment down, AlmaFaye would help Darnell pack the bags. Then she would drop some in another bag for my own private stash. We didn't tell him because he would've been pissed off. I was so glad I was able to smoke so much because it kept me feeling so good inside. Then I didn't have to think about the shit that happened at my house with Mr. Calvin.

One Saturday, while I was washing dishes, Bobby came over to my sister's house looking for Darnell. I remembered him being the same guy who gave the first house party I went to with AlmaFaye. His wife Barbara was with him.   He was dressed to kill, in dark slacks with a silk bronze shirt. His shoes were nice, casual dress shoes that matched his tie. AlmaFaye walked into the kitchen from the bathroom.
    "Hey, Bobby, how's it going?"
    "Fi-Fi- Fine, Faye. How are you?"
     Bobby stuttered a little bit. I wanted to laugh, but
     he was so cute.
    "You remember my baby sister, Carla, don't you?"
    "Oh yes, I remember that cutie pi-pie."
    "Nice to meet you again," I smiled and laughed

inside.
"Is Darnell here?"
"No, he isn't. He went to pick up something real
quick."

I realized from AlmaFaye's tone that they were talking about dope.
Bobby was getting ready to leave, and he looked and winked.
"Take care of yourself. I hope to see you again."
"I hope so too." I felt so embarrassed after I said it.

AlmaFaye teased me from that day on about Bobby's words. Off
and on he would come over for Darnell and would always have
something cute to say. He really made me feel like he liked me.

The summer was ending and I had done more partying, smoking
and drinking than probably all the kids in my school put together.

SEPTEMBER 1976 - (13 yrs - 9th Grade)

School was beginning. I was enrolling into my last year at Irwin Jr.
High. I called Kendon's house to see what was going on. I was
hoping he would be returning this school year. I had not heard
from him since the night we all went out to the party.
Unfortunately, when I spoke with his mother she told me that he
had gotten into some trouble and was in juvenile at the Waco
facility. Surprisingly she told me that he had mailed some letters
addressed to me to her house. She said she called me at the house
but I was never there. I guess Mr. Calvin didn't tell her I was
staying with AlmaFaye. I gave her AlmaFaye's address and told
her I was living there for a little while, and she could send his letters
there. She told me she would mail them.

This school year was different for me in many ways. I had met so
many different people at the parties that AlmaFaye and I went to
during the summer break. When the kids saw me at school, they
treated me real cool and thought I was part of the hip crowd now.

They didn't know I lucked out because my mother was in jail. My transition into the ninth grade seemed to take a hundred degree spin, as far as what I had been through and exposed to that summer. I had gotten into marijuana and was drinking more than ever. Now, I was carrying more than my books to school. I also had my bag of marijuana to smoke or sell.

The following Saturday, Bobby came over again around four thirty. I was alone in the house. AlmaFaye, Darnell and her kids went down town. I had been playing music all day, smoking a little weed, and drinking beer. He asked me if I wanted to go for a ride with him. It was almost dark, so I asked where.
"Just around town. I would like to get to know you a little bit. If you can't go, I understand."
"Yeh, I can go. No one says I can't go." Bobby drove a long yellow Cadillac.

When we walked to his car, he opened my door and let me in. I had never had this type of treatment shown to me from a boy or man before. After we drove off, he turned on his tape player to listen to some music. I was a little nervous because I didn't really know him other than through Darnell and AlmaFaye. I also knew he was married. He started up a conversation by asking me if I had a boyfriend. I told him I didn't have one. I was unsure of how to label Kendon since he was in and out of juvenile hall.
"A cute little girl like you don't have a boyfriend?"
"Nope," I said.
He then reached inside his shirt pocket and pulled out a joint.
"Here. Fire this up."

I pushed in the cigarette lighter and lit it for him. I passed it to him once it was smoking, and he said, "Go ahead and taste it."

He turned up the music. He put in another tape, Frankie Beverly and Maze. The joint was real strong. I choked real hard on the first puff, and then I smelled a mint odor and it filled the car. Because I choked he asked if I was okay. I asked him what was I smoking. He smiled and said, real softly, "The best Columbian with a touch of Angel Dust."

I swallowed hard from fear of that word "Angel Dust" because I heard people talk about that at school and of how you can trip out on it. "Oh, okay" pretending I was cool with it.

Then a song came on called "Happy Feelings." It was perfect, and smooth, because I started feeling real happy and strange inside. I had never felt that way before. Then I passed the joint back to him, hoping it wasn't too soon, because then he would think I was a punk. He drove to Rodeo Park, circling it a couple of times, and stopped. We were near the zoo entrance. The music was still going when he turned to me.

"You are very sweet, I can tell."
"Thank you," I said.

He scooted over a little bit, lifting up his middle arm rest. He took another hit off the joint and passed it to me. I hit it again and rested my head back on the car seat. I had never been this high before. Everything felt like I was in a tunnel. I could hear him beginning to breathe hard.

"How old are you?" he asked me,
"I'm thirteen," I said, feeling my voice slurring.
"You sure don't look it."

My heart started beating real fast. He raised up my blouse and began kissing on my breast. It felt so good. His tongue was moving slowly from one to the other one.

"Let's get into the back seat," he whispered.
"Okay," I nodded.

It began to rain outside. When we got into the back, he started taking my clothes off. I sighed heavily to myself, knowing what was about to happen. I was feeling so far away, but cool at the same time.

"I want you to relax."
I guess he could tell I was a little tense.
"I will be very gentle, just let me love you."
"Okay, I am." His words made me feel real
comfortable.
"You need to be loved, don't you?"
"Yeh, I guess so." I didn't know what else to say, I
hunched my shoulders.

He laid me back on the seat and began taking my clothes off. I started breathing hard. My heart would not stop beating fast. He raised up to unzip his pants. He put my hand down there so I could feel him. It was so big. I could feel me getting wet.
"Don't worry, I'm going to go nice and slow."

I smiled at him. He knew exactly what to say to calm me down. After taking his pants off, he took off all of my clothes, kissing my body while he took off each piece. When he took off my pants, he began to kiss me where I didn't know people kissed at. He went up and down my thighs and then he kissed me inside of my privates. I screamed so loud. Whatever he was doing down there felt so damn good to me. He moaned and spoke to me while he was down there.
"Baby, don't this feel good to ya?"
"Yes!"

He grabbed my ass at the same time. It felt so good, I felt like I almost couldn't breathe. I could feel my body raising up off the seat. I had nowhere else to run or go but right in his mouth.
"Tell me how good it is to you. Tell me!"

He kept licking me and raising up to say things to me. I repeated everything he asked me. It was true, it did feel good. After awhile, he slowly made his way up, kissing my stomach until he got to my breast again. Then he was directly on top of me and then he kissed me so deep. Everything he did to me felt good. I could feel his thing inside my legs. I was so wet.

He was gentle and took his time like he promised me. It was so good once he got inside. The feeling made me feel like crying, but it was a good cry that I couldn't explain. All I could do was moan and hold him tight.

When he was finished, my heart was still beating fast. It had to have been at least two hours of him on top, giving me love as he kept repeating in my ear. He kept going back down between my legs to eat me and then back up to love me inside again. I felt like I was loosing my mind with all the different good feelings I kept feeling, but I still felt like I was in heaven. I could not believe what had just happened. It felt different from Tim.
  "How do you feel, Carla?" he asked.
  "I can't explain how I feel, but it's not bad, it's
  different."
  "You make me feel like I've never felt before, you
  know that, little girl?" he asked.
  "For real?" I was surprised.
  "You know, I could fall in love with you."
  I shrugged my shoulders. I didn't know what to say
  to these words. Nobody ever said that before.
  "I better get you back to Faye's house." He quickly
  put his pants on.

Then he helped me get my clothes back on because I was too high and drained to do it myself. On the way home, I felt so many different feelings. I could feel me coming down from the high. I felt the good queasy feelings from what he did to me. Then I thought about his wife and began to feel real bad. I was still wet between my legs with his stuff. Then I began to feel like dirt. I began to ask myself, how could I do what I did to this man who was married. I thought about Momma screwing Mr. Calvin's brother and how low that was of her.

As Bobby was driving he asked me what school I attended and what time I got out of school. I told him, not knowing why he wanted to know. Then he told me some days he might be in the area after school and give me a ride home. A few moments later we were pulling up near AlmaFaye's house. Bobby dropped me off at the corner, so that nobody would see him. The fact that he couldn't take me right home, made me feel even more guilty. I walked in the back door and AlmaFaye was sitting there watching TV.

"Where the hell have you been?"

"Out, and I am going to take a shower and go to bed early."

I felt like she could see everything I had just done.

"Why are you going to bed now? What did you do out there, screw somebody?"

My heart dropped. "Hell naw! You crazy," I replied defensively.

"I'm just kidding," she said. "Calm down and good night!"

I didn't know what time it was and how long I had been gone. I had lost all track and sense of time. I could still feel myself high on that PCP. As the water hit my body, I was hoping the shower could take it all away. I knew it wouldn't. I was feeling like I was getting deeper and deeper into being such a slut and a dog like my mother always called me. It was too late. I wasn't special anymore like I was before. "Damn it!" I hit the wall with the palm of my hand to let some frustration and pain out. I started crying. I felt like I was getting dirtier, and dirtier. Not able to get back clean. Not able to be the little girl that I once was. I went to bed with mixed emotions. On one hand, I couldn't deny the good feelings I felt with all that stuff that Bobby was doing to me. On the other hand, I couldn't deny the wrong of what I did with a married man and feeling dirty.

The following Monday evening Darnell walked in the door with groceries, and AlmaFaye told him that Bobby was looking for him earlier. I was so glad I was at school when he came by. I didn't want to see him anymore. I was having problems concentrating, because I was thinking about him all the time. Then I heard

AlmaFaye giving Darnell hell, because he had been gone all all day and week-end. Darnell told AlmaFaye he had to make just one more run over to Bobby's, and he would be back.

"I be got damn! I'm going with you," AlmaFaye said.
"Fine, pack up the kids, and we can all go over there." He was laughing, thinking AlmaFaye wouldn't take him up on it. She did. We all had to go with her.

I began to get nervous as we drove over to Bobby and Barbara's to get another shipment of dope. AlmaFaye and I sat in the den at the bar. Bobby was behind the bar fixing up the dope. I could feel someone's eyes on me. I looked up, and it was Bobby. As soon as I looked at him he winked at me. I cracked a half smile at him. After that I looked down embarrassed. As I sat there, the music was playing. We were listening to Side Affect's new album, and "SOS" "Take your time do it right." That brought back memories of that night we were in the back seat of the car. Then Bobby put on Frankie Beverly's song "Happy Feeling." I thought, why did he do that? He knew the whole 8-track was playing while we were in the back seat of his car. I began to reflect back to the night I was with him. I couldn't stand it. I wished that Darnell would hurry up and come on. I thought the whole incident might have been reflected on my face. I felt so guilty sitting in Barbara's house thinking about what I did with her husband. We finally left, and I was so relieved. But for the next few days, I couldn't stop thinking about him. Everyday, I would think about him. I didn't want to, and I tried to stop, but it wouldn't happen.

One day, after I came home from school, Bobby was sitting in AlmaFaye's house. I got so nervous. I was happy to see him and scared at the same time. AlmaFaye and Darnell were in the back room.

"Hey, there she is," he said.
"How are you doing, cutie?"
"I'm fi-fi fine, I guess. I started stuttering like he did sometimes.

"I've been thinking a lot about you and wanting to
see you real bad."
I smiled and said "me too" before I could stop
myself from saying it..
"Maybe I can pick you up from school sometimes
and give you a ride home."
"Yeh, maybe," I said going toward the back room.

AlmaFaye and Darnell were coming out, arguing. I guess Faye had
to give him some more county money so he could get his dope.
When I came from the back room Bobby and Darnell were gone.
AlmaFaye was sitting on the couch steaming. I asked her for a joint
and a beer.
"There's a beer in the refrigerator. I only have a little
dope left, but you know Darnell and Bobby are
about to go get some more then I'll give you some."
"Cool, sis."
"How are those kids doing today?" she asked.
"They seem to be doing alright."

I noticed at least three times out of the week, Bobby would find his
way to my school after I got out. One day I was coming down the
street from school and saw his yellow Cadilac coming my way
slowly, as he looked at each student. As soon as he saw me he
yelled out if I needed a lift. There were days he took me straight
home, and then there were days we found ourselves on the back of a
dirt road in his back seat. I felt so bad, but it kept happening and I
didn't know how to tell him to stop it.

I was torn between loving to see him but hating what he ended up
doing. I often wondered if he felt the guilty dirty feelings like me.
Bobby always had dope with him. So the first thing he did when I
would get in the car is hand me a joint of PCP or Columbian mix.
Then off we would go and do our thing.

After weeks of Bobby picking me up, I tried to tell him that I knew
I was doing bad things with a married man. I even told him, doing

this in the car was horrible too. He responded by telling me that it's not so bad when two people really love each other.

"I'm so in love with you, Carla, I can't help myself.
Don't you love me too?"
I was quiet at first, not knowing what to say.
"I love you too, but it's wrong. How can it be right?"
"It's in the heart. That's all that matters."
"Why do I feel so bad then?"
"Baby, you have to stop feeling bad. Stop fighting
the truth and then you will feel better. Watch, try
it."

He started kissing me on my neck. He took me home that evening without doing anything and told me how much he loved me. I felt so confused, but I felt good too. No one has ever been in love with me before. I kept saying that to myself.

The next week after Bobby picked me up from school, I told him I must go right over to AlmaFaye's house. He started in her direction, but then turned down a side street. I looked at him, and he knew why.

"Why you miss the street?"
"Baby, I just need to spend more time with you. I
miss you so much. I just wish we can just go
somewhere for a little while and be with each other."

I thought that was special, but what did he mean and where could we go? He pulled up into a motel and told me to stay in the car.

He returned shortly and said, "Let's go." We got out of the car and we went to a room. When we got there, I stood, and Bobby sat on the bed.

"Come on over here, I'm not going to bite you."

He started laughing. I did too. I sat down on the bed next to him.

"Now tell me you haven't been thinking of me," he

said.
I knew I had, and I guess he knew too.
"Yeh, I've been thinking about you."
He started feeling on my back and around my
waist. He started kissing on my neck.
"I can't stop thinking about you. I think I'm in love
with you."

I didn't know what to do or say. I was enjoying the feeling of his affection. He made me feel good telling me that. He started to undress.
"Can I make love to you, Carla? I got to have you."
I said, "I guess so."

This second time, a sadness came over me again. Yet I couldn't resist the feelings. Needless to say, on the way home, those feelings I had before repeated. Feelings of good, bad and feeling dirty all at the same time. I got to AlmaFaye's house when it was dark. I could feel she was wondering where I was, and if I was still cooking at Momma's house. The fact is, I didn't make it. Bobby dropped me off around the corner again. I think that's where the dirty feelings really hit. AlmaFaye was in the bathroom when I walked through the back door which was good. Darnell was sitting there smoking a joint and kicking back in front of the TV.
"Hey girl, where your ass been?"
"None of your business," I said.
"Oh, you're grown now, hah?"
"Yeh, I'm grown now."
"Yeh, I heard something about yo ass that you don't
know I know."
I got scared. "What!"
"Ah, you wanna talk now, do you?"
"What?" I asked again.
"I'll just sit on it."
AlmaFaye came from the back.
"Hey girl, where you been?" she asked as she stood
there with her hands on her hips, waiting for my

answer.
"Oh, tripping with a friend up the street after I
finished cooking for the kids," I lied.

What could I say, I was with Darnell's cousin's husband at a motel?
The thought made me feel so ashamed and sick.   I felt like a bad
habit and I was in too deep to quit.   Not only was I getting dope
from AlmaFaye, but I was also getting some from Bobby as well.
My getting high was all the time now.   Not only when I came home
at night, but sometimes before I got to class.   My thoughts were
filled with guilt and loneliness. I guess desperation could find its
way in there too.

Eventually, my sister caught on to what Bobby and I were doing.
She started telling me that his wife was going to find out and come
over and kill my ass. I couldn't explain to her how it happened, and
I couldn't explain to her how much he loved me. That's what he
said.   Most of all, I couldn't explain to her, or myself, about feeling
addicted to him and loving him out of my mind.   I knew she was
right, and she made it very clear I was in danger. From that day on
I found myself walking in fear looking over my shoulder everyday
for his wife.

Once again, the year was coming to an end. I hated this time of the
year.   1976 was the craziest year for my life so far.   I had nothing
to be thankful for as far as I was concerned. This year was different.
I thanked God that my mother wasn't around to curse me out.
My sisters and brothers spent Thanksgiving and Christmas holiday
over to Aunt Dora's house. I was so glad that I didn't have to cook
for them.

In February I finally received the letters from Kendon that his
mother said she was going to mail to me. His letters were so
beautiful. He addressed me as queen and sometimes as his little
princess. I didn't fit those shoes anymore and I would ache in my
heart as I read his words.   I felt I wasn't worthy to be called them
anymore. I was nothing now and he didn't know it. Kendon

always told me how special I was and how he couldn't wait to see me when he got out of jail. I tried to write him back in the most truthful way I could without telling him that I had been so bad. When I wrote him, I told him how much I missed him and that I was waiting for that special day to see his face. I assured him I was doing alright, because he would always ask if Mr. Calvin was behaving himself, or did he need to come out of there to kick his ass. As much as I felt so unworthy of Kendon's love for me, I looked forward to his letters and finally for him to come home to me. My attitude had changed since I last saw him. He didn't know I did drugs now and drank as much as I did.

14 YEARS OLD -- 1977

On the night of my 14th birthday, AlmaFaye gave me a birthday party. It was packed with a lot of young grown people. This was the first birthday that Momma could not turn into her own personal old folks party. It was the greatest party I ever had. Everybody got higher than a kite. The night ended with one last guest showing up, Mr. Bobby himself. I tried to stay near my sister most of the night, because they had already warned me to stay clear of him. He tried to ask me what I had been up to and how come he didn't see me anymore walking home. He didn't know that I had changed my route. I told him I missed him, but couldn't keep seeing him. I told me I was feeling uncomfortable and that what we were doing was bad.

"But can I see you one last time?" he asked

"Please, no, I really have to stop." I told him.

"I won't bother you anymore." He dropped his head, looking real sad.

Then I began to feel guilty. I told him my mother was in jail for this kind of stuff. She shot a woman for messing with her old man.

"I don't want your wife shooting me in my chest," I told him.

"You don't ever have to worry about no one hurting

you, Carla. That will never happen."

He promised me that he would leave me alone forever if I would just see him one last time. AlmaFaye saw me talking to him and got mad. She called me a fass ass. I thought to myself how dare her. She gives me dope, beer, wine, and my own room to screw in if I wanted to. Yet, now I'm too hot. Then she started accusing me of flirting and maybe screwing her man, Darnell. She said she accused me of that because one day her old man looked at me kinda strange. Yeh, he had been trying to, but I never told AlmaFaye. In fact, she would tell me, "I know that you are screwing Darnell. I know you are, if you're screwing a married man." Darnell flirted with everything and everybody. I soon suspected my sister was getting jealous of me. I felt it. I didn't understand it, but I could tell. I tried to make sure she didn't observe anything questionable when Darnell was around us. She was acting just like my mother. How weird, and my mother didn't even raise her. But she was acting as if she had been around my mother all her life.

A few months later, while AlmaFaye was cooking dinner one night, I came out of my room to the kitchen. I grabbed an Old English 800. I sat down at the kitchen table, cluttered with bags of groceries that needed to be put away. I volunteered to put the food away, and started talking about life in general.

"Why did certain things have to happen to me?" I
asked AlmaFaye. I told her how I missed my
mother in spite of her constant badgering and abuse.
asked her again,
"Why did Mr. Calvin have to start doing that stuff
to me when I was a little girl?"
"Why, AlmaFaye? Why he screw up my life? Why
he turn my Momma on me? Why do I have to go
through this? How come I can't be like the kids I
see at school? They look like they are so happy and
normal. But not me. They go places with their
parents and have so much fun. They sit around and

watch TV together, and they talk to one another
like family. Whatever the hell that is."

AlmaFaye just listened without interrupting me. I continued to
talk aimlessly. "Their mother and daddy are regular parents. They
don't leave and not come back, nor do they change and treat you
like they never knew you or wanted you. AlmaFaye, why do I have
to have two freak parents that's trying to make me out to be a
freak?"

AlmaFaye kept on cooking and placing individual pieces of chicken
in the hot scorching frying pan. She must have figured I was
getting things off my chest, and it was long overdue.
    "You know what, AlmaFaye? My school friends
    don't treat me as if I am like them. Now they don't
    want to be around me, because now I have a
    reputation. They leave me by myself when I have
    nothing else to offer, like drugs or something.
    Mavis, who was my best friend, shines me off
    sometimes in public depending on who's around
    when I come around. Sometimes I feel like I don't
    even know who I am. It's as if something in me has
    changed."

AlmaFaye finally broke her silence.
    "Look, do you want a joint? I put away some stuff
    for you after Darnell broke his shipment down," she
    said, avoiding the questions.
    "Sure, let me make a big fat one," I told her as I tried
    to gulp up the entire Old English 800 in one sitting.
    "Maybe I can just O.D. off the biggest joint I can
    roll."

The next evening, after cooking the kids dinner, I walked over to
AlmaFaye's around seven. She was sitting in the living room
watching Sanford and Son on TV. I made myself comfortable

right next to her. Suddenly, there was a knock at the door and it
was Barbara, Bobby's wife. She had on a black and white pin-striped
suit with a broke down brim hat. Boy, did my heart drop to my
ankles!
            "She finally caught up with me," I thought.
            "What in the world do I do now?"
            "Hello, Faye," she said.
            AlmaFaye was a little shocked at her visit too.
            "What's happening Barbara?"
            "Nothing much! Wanted to talk with your
            babysister for a moment, if you don't mind."
            I looked at her and didn't know what to say.
            "I don't mind you talking to her if she don't mind,"
            AlmaFaye said.
            "Carla, can we talk privately in the bathroom?" Her
            voice was soft.
            "Uh, sure," I stuttered.

My heart was pounding so hard now, I didn't know if I would
make it there without fainting. We walked into the bathroom and
she closed the door.   I thought I was going to mess on myself.
What better place to be, right in the bathroom. So when she is
finished killing me she can just flush my little ass down the toilet,
I thought. My sister watched us go, saying nothing. Was she in
shock? I couldn't understand that either. Barbara locked the door
behind us. She started smiling while talking to me.
            "So, I've heard a lot of things about you."

I didn't know whether to close my eyes or duck, in case she hit me.
I was feeling weak and dizzy at the same time. I didn't' say
anything.
            "I also heard about what happened to you at home
            with your step daddy and your crazy ass mother."
            I ate this part up, because maybe I could win on her
            sympathy level.
            She continued, "I understand you know my
            husband, Bobby, pretty well." My eyes bucked.

"That's okay with me," she said.
Boy did she lose me there! I started stuttering
again.
"Yeehh, yehhhh yehhh I dddoodoo."
She finally saved me from total embarrassment and
fainting by saying "Personally, I like you for
myself."
At this point, I was so confused I could not think
straight.

What the hell was she talking about? I knew I was high, but I wasn't
that high. I was wondering how come she wasn't beating me up.
Then, she walked up to me and placed her hands on my shoulders.
I pressed into the wall behind me. I got so nervous, I couldn't talk.
She was talking to me steady, in a nice, soft, and sexy voice. Was
this woman feeling on me like a man does? Was this woman
touching my body the way I thought she was? Then she asked me,
"Have you ever been with a woman?" I still couldn't talk, but I
shook my head "no". What did she mean? Questions kept coming
to my mind. She said "Well, I won't hurt you. I just want to love
you. You've been hurt enough in your life. It's time that you
receive real love." That was the same thing her husband said to me.
"Are you scared?"

I still couldn't open my mouth so I shook my head "no," lying. She
began kissing me on my face, then my lips, then my neck. She was
so soft. With her hands on my waiste she started rubbing my
thighs. I couldn't believe what she was doing to me. She wasn't
killing me, she was kissing me. She unbuttoned my dress. I began
to get weaker in my knees. I wished I could sit down. She acted
just like her husband by the things she began to do to me. After
unsnapping my dress she talked about how beautiful my body was.
Then, all I could hear her do was kiss and moan as she touched my
body with her tongue all over me. I wanted to scream. I couldn't
because AlmaFaye would have ran in there and seen her. She asked
me to spread my legs open a little bit and got down on her knees to
kiss my thighs. I leaned back on the bathroom door feeling for the

door knob so that I could squeeze something. I knew I would fall any minute. The feelings were too good to stand up with. I couldn't reach the door knob so I had to hold her head. I tried not to squeeze it too hard, or pull her hair out, but I couldn't help it. When she started getting up, she kissed me all the way up to my neck and then in my mouth. She kissed just like her husband. At times it felt just like him, except for she didn't put anything in me. She whispered in my ear.

"You are so special. I want you to know that."

"Thank you." After I said it I felt so stupid.

"Just know that anything you need you can come to us."

I shook my head okay.

When we walked out of that bathroom, I felt so different. "Shit," I kept saying on the inside of me. I didn't know what to say to my sister. I couldn't speak. Barbara was holding my hand as if we were school buddies. Barbara asked AlmaFaye if she needed anything from the liquor store?

"Yeh, a six back of Slitz Malt Liquor." She looked mad.

"Carla, would you like anything?" Barbara asked. I just shook my head "no."

She walked out the door and said she would be right back. I watched her walk out the back door.

AlmaFaye looked at me and said, "What the fuck just went on in there?" I still couldn't talk too well. I just looked and shook my head for about two minutes.

"AlmaFaye, you really wouldn't believe me if I told you."

"Try me, nigga."

"Let's just say, she ain't mad at me."

"Well, why the hell not?"

I didn't want to tell AlmaFaye at first. I didn't know what she would think. I really didn't know why she wasn't mad at me. She already thought I was getting too fast. So I decided she would have to figure that one out herself.

Barbara returned with two six packs and we sat around and drank beer after beer. Barbara drank Hennesy and asked if I wanted to try it. We cut off the TV and started playing music. Not long after, AlmaFaye wanted to go to bed. She said it was getting too late for her to keep sitting up and she was sleepy. So she said good night and went to bed. Barbara moved toward me and started kissing on me again. This time, I kissed her back and held on to her. She asked me if I would mind if she spent the night with me. I didn't know what to say.

"I guess it's alright," I told her stuttering again.

"Come on, let's go to bed," she said.

I took her to my room. She continued where we left off in the bathroom. I was hoping AlmaFaye didn't wake up or come inside the room.

The next morning, she was up and gone before AlmaFaye woke up. I still couldn't believe what had happened. I didn't know how to explain it and what else to expect. One thing I was certain of was I didn't have to fear for my life anymore.

The next week when I came from school, Mr. Calvin handed me a letter from Momma. She finally wrote home. It was general small talk. She mentioned how lonely she was without us and how much she missed us. She also mentioned that they were treating her well. She asked us to come visit her. I guess Momma had some private things for Mr. Calvin's ears only, because one page was missing at the end that I didn't see attached. The other kids were too young, so the letter didn't have as great an impact on them. I was fourteen years old, little Charles was six, Brenda was five, Catherine was four and Edwin was three. When I finished reading the letter to the kids, I went into the kitchen and poured a glass of water, looking out of the kitchen window. I reflected on the words in Momma's letter. Her words were sober. She sounded like a lady who missed her family and her husband. I began to miss her so much. I hung on to every word she wrote about missing us and wished she was home. I really wanted that deep down inside. I wanted to be with that Momma who said she wanted her children. I finished my glass of water then said good-bye to my sisters and brothers, who were watching tv on the floor. Mr. Calvin was outside in the front watering the lawn. He said good bye too. I walked over to AlmaFaye's before it got dark. I hated to leave my home because of these circumstances. Why did I have to be away from what's supposed to be a child's home?

The following week-end, Mr. Calvin called me at AlmaFaye's house to see if I wanted to go see Momma on Sunday with the kids. I said "yes" and we went the next day. We passed many vegetable fields and fruit trees. Mr. Calvin tried to make small talk with me.
        "How are things over at AlmaFaye's?" he asked.
        "They are great" I said,
        "Good," he said.
         After a moment of silence, he asked "Are you going
         to tell your mother what happened and where you're
         staying?"
        "No, Mr. Calvin. I will not do that to my mother."
        "Okay," he said relieved. "I still plan on telling her
         how sorry I am for what has happened."
         I thought to myself, "Yeh, right. When hell becomes
         the North Pole you will."

The day was hot and the sun was beaming down on Momma's blue Ford. The air-conditioning had gone out and Mr. Calvin had not fixed it yet. All the windows were open and little Calvin and Brenda stole bits of breeze as they held their heads outside the window. It took us about forty-five minutes to drive there. We finally arrived at the women's camp. It was a plain gray building with no sign of life anywhere. Bars were around the windows at the top of the two story building. We got out of the car and walked up a long pathway towards two metal doors. As we entered, there was a window with bars in front of it and a white lady sitting behind the desk. She instructed Mr. Calvin to fill out some papers and have a seat in the waiting room. There were chairs all around. Twenty minutes later, we were called. No one else was in the waiting room. We walked through more metal doors, down a hallway which led into an open room with tables. They looked like picnic tables and chairs. Momma came through the doors on the opposite side. She had on a blue and gray, two piece pants outfit. She looked so good and clean. She hadn't been drinking and you could tell. I missed her so much! I saw that she missed me too by her smile. Her face looked so clear and her skin was so bright! Her hair was healthy and shiny. It was in a pony tail, pretty and neat. She looked beautiful. I was so used to seeing her sloppy drunk. But this was the total sober Mom. The kids were just as happy to see Momma. They hugged her a lot and asked when she was coming home. It almost looked like they didn't miss her, until they saw her. Something ignited, making them realize that she hadn't been around. She told them, "Real soon. Momma will be home real soon."

Mr. Calvin didn't talk too much. He asked Momma if she was eating well. I had to be real careful not to let it slip out that I wasn't staying at the house. I concentrated on that so hard, I missed hearing a couple of times when Momma was talking to me. I had to snap out of my deep thoughts of hoping she couldn't tell that Mr. Calvin had done something to me. For the most part, we spent the one hour just going back and forth talking about the summer, my cooking, and washing. She also asked how AlmaFaye, Darnell, and her kids were doing. I filled her in and told her I would tell them she said hi.

It was finally time to go and I wasn't prepared. For the first time, I felt like I was leaving my mother in a place that she didn't want to be. Kind of like she used to do with me and the baby-sitters, when I was a little girl. I could see in her eyes that she longed to be away from that place, but again there was nothing I could do. We each hugged and kissed Momma and walked toward the large metal doors. Mr. Calvin had a few last moments with Momma, to say their private stuff, I guess.

Afterward, we returned to Fresno. Mr. Calvin drove straight to AlmaFaye's house. I was getting out of the car, saying goodbye to the kids and Mr. Calvin. Then Mr. Calvin got out of the car and walked toward me. I didn't know what he was going to do. He asked me with his head down, not being able to look at me,
"Can you come back home to take care of the kids?"
I looked at him, not knowing what to say. I guess
he read that on my face.
"Well," I started to talk.
He interrupted and said, "I am sorry and promise it
won't happen anymore," his head still looking down
to the ground.

I felt so sorry for him. I hated the fact that I felt sorry for him too. I told him I would think about it and left quickly. I walked in the back door right over to AlmaFaye and told her what Mr. Calvin had just asked me.
"So, do you believe him, Carla?"
"I don't know, AlmaFaye. He seemed real sincere."
"Plus, I don't want Momma to find out while she is
in there what happened."

I appreciated being with AlmaFaye, but I always felt like a visitor there. So I decided to accept Mr. Calvin's request. Being back home was kind of scary, because I wanted to believe that Mr. Calvin would keep his word. I could only pray that he would. I hadn't written in my diary since I left home, and since Momma went to the camp. I drank, smoked, and escaped more through everything else I found myself doing while I was away from home. But, I was back home now, and it was okay. My Blacky was waiting for me as if he missed me so bad. I missed him too.

Later that evening, Kendon Starr showed up at my doorstep. He was acting as if nothing was wrong, with that pretty smile on his face showing all those white teeth. I was so happy! I couldn't believe it!

"How have you been?" he asked.

"Fine."

"Are you going to the party at the West Gates?"

"I am now, if you're going to be there," I said.

Then, he held me.

"Have you been good?" he asked.

Was that a trick question I thought, or is my conscience just wearing on me? I had to swallow. I had been through so much since the last time we saw each other, his head would spin if I told him.

"Yeh, I've been good," I said, hoping the word "Lies" didn't appear branded on my forehead in neon lights for him to read! Then he asked about Mr. Calvin.

"Has he tried to do anything to you?"

"No, Kendon," again, hoping "Lies, Lies" didn't appear on my forehead. I couldn't bring myself to say anything about it. I just couldn't. I knew if I did, Mr. Calvin would be a dead man and his kids would be orphans.

Later on that night, after I fixed all the kid's plates, put them to bed, and washed the dishes, I let Mr. Calvin know that I was going to a party at the West Gates. I walked by myself. It was about a thirty-minute walk. I wasn't scared. I was too excited to be scared. I knew I was going to be with my baby, Kendon Starr.

After I got there, I looked around and didn't see Kendon. Everybody was partying hard. The music was loud, the smoke strong, and they were truly getting it on. I saw Phyllis and sat down beside her.

"Hey, Phyllis, what's been happening?"

"Nothing much, just partying and thangs, you know?" Phyllis had an old english in her hand.

"Yeh, I hear you."
"Who you come up here with?" she asked.
"Oh, by myself. I'm meeting Kendon Starr here."

I looked around the room, trying to find him. Her eyes got big. I
knew why, but I didn't let on to the fact that I knew she liked him.
I asked her who she was with.
    She said, "Gino." Gino was her older brother who I
    hadn't seen in a long time. Then a guy came up
    and asked me to dance.
"Yeh, I guess so." I hesitated at first.

We danced and danced, song after song. I was still keeping my
eyes on the door to see when Kendon walked in, but he didn't. It
was now going on 12:00 a.m., and Kendon still hadn't showed up
yet. I told Phyllis I was getting worried about him, but I had to
leave and go home.
    "How are you getting home?" she asked
    "Well, I thought Kendon was going to get me
    home, I said, but now I 'll have to walk back."
    "Hell no", she said.
    "I'll get Gino and his friend to take you home."

Gino was happy to see me. We hugged and he told me to sit tight.
He was going to ask his friend Brown to give me a ride. His friend
said, "Cool" and we started to leave the party. While we were
driving, I noticed that this brother was not going toward my house.
He was headed toward the country fields, and I said to Gino,
"What's up with your friend, and where is he going?" he said.
    "Man, what's up? Where are you going?"
    "Chill. Just chill out and shut up," his friend
    responded.
    He stopped the car and told Gino to let me out. I
    was sitting between them.
    "What's happening, man? What do you mean, let
    her out?" Gino said.
    "Look if you don't want to keep your ass out here,

just do what I say," Brown responded.
Gino said, "Man, you must be really tripping!"
"Why are you letting me out here? This is not my
house," I said.
"If you want to get home in this car, you will get
your ass out and ride in the trunk, like I say."
"The trunk?" I was shocked and scared at the same
time.
"Why?" He smiled and looked at Gino.
"Gino, open the damn door, and let her out!" This
time he hollered at Gino.

Gino opened the door and let me out.   There was nothing but
woods around me. Echoing in my ears were howling sounds like
wild dogs on a mission for their prey, and other types of barking
animals. It was pitch black, and you could hardly see anything in
front of you. I stood there, shaking in fear. It was dark and it was
scary. Brown got out on his side and opened the trunk. He turned
around and said "There is your seat and ticket back home."

I had no where else to go, and I knew this drunk fool wasn't playing
with me. I didn't know why he was doing this, but I thought I'd
better go along. Gino was watching and shaking his head. I put my
purse in first and then got in. I thought he was about to close the
trunk on me, but he jumped in the trunk and put down the hood.
I grew even more scared, not knowing what the hell was happening.
He reached in his pocket and took out his lighter. He flicked it on
so he could see. I watched him as he smiled at me. He reached
into his shirt top pocket and pulled out a knife. I think it was a
switchblade.
        "Now, I want you to take off your draws for me."
        I started shaking my head, "I am not."
        "Oh yes, you are, or else," he said.

I tried to be bold as long as I could.   He scooted up on me, put
the blade inside my blouse between each button causing them to
pop open. Then my chest was exposed, showing my bra and breast.

"Man what's happening?" Gino hollered.

I could hear Gino's trembling voice. He didn't know what was going on.
        "Why are you doing this," I started crying and
        asking.
        "Just take off your damn clothes and shut up," he
        said.

I refused to. He took the knife, barely touching the top of my breast and drew it down, penetrating me enough to cut the surface of my skin. Not once, not twice, but three times he cut my skin on the top of my breast to show me that he could cut me even deeper if I didn't cooperate. I could feel the cut. After the third time, I started taking off my clothes. He unzipped his pants and put himself inside of me. The knife felt like nothing when it tore my skin compared to the sickening penetration of this evil boy. I hated him as he continued to take out his perverted pleasures on me. I cried bitterly and bit my bottom lip. He stunk and smelled like a dog. After his nut, he lay there for a second, breathing hard. Then he rolled off me. He hollered for Gino to pop the trunk.

He said, "Man, let me out of here with this bitch." He told Gino where the knob was in his car to open the trunk. As Gino was looking for it, he told me "You better not tell Gino nothing, or your ass is mine."

I was frozen and didn't say a word all the way home. Gino went crazy.
        "What the hell was going on in there, Carla?"

I kept quiet, but he could feel me shaking and could see the tears flowing out of my eyes. We finally pulled up to Gino's house.
        "Alright, Gino man, I'll check you tomorrow," Brown
        said, smiling.
        "Later, man" Gino mumbled.

I got out as soon as Gino got out of the car. I went into Gino's house and called Mr. Calvin to come and get me. He was there in no time. He could hear that there was something wrong in my voice. On the way home, he asked me if I was okay. I told him what I had gone through, and he was real quiet. I thought to myself, what could he possibly say to you, Carla? He's no better than that boy Brown. Mr. Calvin just looked straight ahead with his head turned slightly away from me. When we got home, I felt so alone. I wanted someone to hold me but no one was there. I wished I had Kendon to tell me it was going to be alright. After I washed and scrubbed myself, I cried myself to sleep.

The next day, Kendon came by to apologize for not showing up. He asked me how the party was.
    "It was fine, until I got a ride home with Gino and
    his friend."

After I told Kendon, he got real mad. He told me not to worry about Brown anymore. Kendon immediately said he had to go and take care of some business, and he would be over tomorrow. He kissed me on my forehead and walked out the door.

I didn't want to see him go, but I knew I couldn't hold a boy back who had so many things on his mind and so many things to do. I was so grateful when I did see him. He was the best guy I had ever known in my life and he loved me, and I knew it. He didn't know how dirty I had become, but he loved what he knew on the surface.

Not long after Brown's attack on me, I heard through the grapevine that he was almost beaten to death, with broken bones and left for dead, but he miraculously survived. The word was out that Kendon had something to do with it. A pack of boys jumped Brown one night at a party, and Kendon made sure that he let him know it was for me. I thought about that Brown boy everyday until it just went away. I didn't go to any more parties after that incident. It was okay because school was starting back in just a couple of weeks.

Sure enough, two weeks later, the school halls were filled with first day greetings and students laughing, talking, comparing classes and teachers. I ran into my faithful friends Cheryl and Mavis, who I had spent hardly no time with over the summer. We all greeted each other with a high five, and hugged.

All of my classes were with Mavis and Cheryl, which was cool. We could help each other with homework as usual. The first day back felt a little weird. It felt like I was misplaced, and I didn't fit in, because of what happened to me during the summer. Around lunch time when we sat out by the bleachers like we always did shooting the breeze, Mavis and Cheryl were talking about basketball games that were played during the summer, while I was smoking dope, drinking, being turned out and raped. I couldn't really talk about kids' stuff, because I did none of those things.

On the first day of school during gym period, I was watching Mavis get ready for gym and as I watched her undress for gym, I began to look at her body in a different way. I looked at her the same way Barbara looked at my body. I shook my head and told myself to snap out of it and to not look at her like that. I didn't tell Mavis about my shameful experiences and I was hoping she didn't hear about them either.

After a week in school Bobby was cruising the streets looking to give me a lift home. When I saw him coming, something inside me was so happy, but then I felt the guilties coming on me. Then I thought about his wife and both of them loving me. I didn't know how to feel.

Bobby pulled over to the side of the street so that I could get in.
          "Hey, come on, Barbara prepared some lunch for us."
          I was especially hungry too, because lunch at school
          only lasted until the bell rang.
          "Cool." I got in and he placed his hand on my thigh
          as soon as the door closed.

"How's my baby been doing?" He kept rubbing my leg.

"I've been alright." I hadn't seen them in awhile.

We arrived at Bobby and Barbara's home. I had never been over there before. It was five minutes from my mother's house. I couldn't believe they only lived up the street from me all this time. Once we got to the house Barbara opened the door and grabbed me. She gave me a big hug and a kiss. Bobby was standing right there and he didn't even mind. Barbara had hamburgers, french fries and chili prepared. It was really cool.

After we ate lunch at the bar, she fixed us a drink of Hennessy. Bobby took our glasses to the bean bag chairs. We fell onto the floor on top of each other from being a little tipsy after the first few shots of Hennessy. I lost track of all time. Before I knew it, we were taking our clothes off and doing things to one another. After having both of them loving me, I was so drained and tired. Then they loved each other. I just laid back, watched and heard all the sounds of moans and groans they both were doing. Around seven o'clock that evening Bobby drove me home. I knew Mr. Calvin was probably wondering where in the world was I. I walked in the door kind of tipsy. I know marijuana and Hennessy were smelling on me. I could smell and taste my own breath. He didn't say anything to me. I kept going to my room.

That was the weirdest thing that had ever happened to me. Things just seemed to be getting more weird. Later that night, after I got out of the tub and went to get me something to eat from the kitchen, Mr. Calvin was drinking some water.

"Your mother will be coming home in a few weeks."

"Oh, that's good."

"Yeh, it will be real nice to have her back home."

"Yep. Sure will."

There was nothing else to eat other than a drum stick from Kentucky Fried Chicken. All the corn and mashed potatoes were gone. That day over to Bobby and Barbara's really threw me off guard. I was feeling so funny. Too many mixed emotions. I wasn't feeling guilty anymore for sleeping with a married man or woman. I was just feeling guilty about the whole grown up stuff that I felt I should not have been doing.

Again, I found myself at a place of needing to talk to somebody but not having anybody around. I knew I could tell God, but I was embarrassed to go to him because of all the dirty stuff I had been doing lately. I thought about Momma coming home again and felt nervous in my stomach at the thought. At first I was happy, and then I got scared. I wondered how would she act when she got out. So much had happened. It felt like it had been three years, because things happened so fast. I sat down in my room for the first time since I left. I decided I needed to write God and get some things off my chest.

Dear God:
I know I haven't talked to you or wrote to you in such a long time. I think it's time now. You know Momma has been in jail over a year and I have been with AlmaFaye. So much has happened to me, God. I don't know who I am. You know I was saving myself for Kendon Starr, but that damn Tim took my virginity. I still hate him for doing that. He spoiled my plans with Kendon. Then Mr. Calvin's lying ass did that shit again, and I know You saw him do that too. Then I know I was wrong with being with Bobby and Barbara, I know I was. God, they seem to be the only ones who really love me. All they tell me is how much they love me. I don't know how I got into that. I do believe they love me from their hearts. I don't know how to stop the sex stuff. I really don't, Lord, but please don't leave me. Stuff keeps happening to me. I try not to let things happen but I don't know when they are going to happen next, God. Then that damn Brown. It took almost two weeks for those knife marks to leave. I don't know

what will happen to the rest of my life, God. Only You know what's going to happen to me. I am so tired of the pain and shame I live with everyday. When will it stop? You remember I was so glad when AlmaFaye came out here. Well she started treating me like Momma a little bit. I didn't like that. If she can't trust me then I am doomed, God. Also, when Momma comes home in a few weeks. I don't know what that will bring. Will she be different? Or will she just pick up where she left off? Every time I think about her coming home my stomach quivers. I'm going to go cook now, God. I will try and write much sooner, okay? Okay. I love You and thank You for still loving me.

A week before Momma came home, AlmaFaye gave a party at her house. She invited all of her friends, including Bobby and Barbara. As always, Bobby and Barbara were the sharpest dressers in the house. They had on matching white and silver pin striped suits. Barbara had on a hat that matched her outfit. Barbara and Bobby sat on each side of me on the couch in the living room.

AlmaFaye was in the kitchen talking to some friends, but she saw Bobby and Barbara sit next to me. They asked how I was doing?
> "So we haven't seen you in a couple of days. What's up?" Barbara asked.
> "Nothing much."
> "Well listen, if you ever need a place to stay, you know where home is, right up the street. Don't you?"
> "Yeh." I was shocked that they wanted me to come and live with them.

Bobby leaned over and reaffirmed what Barbara said. Bobby added, "When you are ready to leave that hell house, you can come live in heaven with us. We will love you like real family."
By now, AlmaFaye had discovered what had happened between the three of us. When everybody left for the night, AlmaFaye and I

cleaned up the house together.

> "Carla, I may not agree with a lot of what you do or
> have done. Because you have been so abused. I can't
> judge you, or deny anything you want that makes
> you happy baby.
>
> "You're not mad at me?" I asked.
>
> "As long as it doesn't hurt you, Carla, I support you
> one hundred percent."
>
> I looked at AlmaFaye to see if she was really serious
> and she was.
>
> "Baby, I mean it from the bottom of my heart."
>
> "Thank you, AlmaFaye. I thought you would hate
> me and think I was so horrible and weird."

AlmaFaye made me feel so special.   She gave me a big hug before I
went to take a shower before going to bed. I thanked her for being
my big sister and my shero.

CHAPTER 16

MOMMA COMES HOME

Momma came home on a Friday. We were all at school when she got home. After walking in the door and seeing Momma at the window like old times, I ran faster into the front door. I went right over to hug Momma and she stood up to hug me back. It felt so good.

"Hey girl."

"Momma, how are you doing?"

"Baby, I'm great. Just glad to be out and at home with my babies."

The kids had already seen Momma. They got out of school earlier than I did. Momma had already started dinner and the house was smelling like it used to. Momma wasn't drunk and she was beautiful. Her hair had grown so long and thick. Her face was bright and clear. She showed the most lovely dimples and white teeth when she smiled. That place really made Momma look good in a strange way. She hugged me. It felt so good.

I went into my bedroom to put up my books and change my clothes. I was so happy. I hoped everything would be fine. No more cursing out, no more making me feel like I was not important. I hoped that life would be better, since my mother had to think and sort things out.

The first couple of days were great. I would come home and Momma would be right there faithfully in front of the window with her Winston regulars and a cup of coffee. Momma spent her time during the day getting readjusted to being out of jail. She was bored, so she cleaned the house over and over again, prepared big meals, and re-arranged her bedroom. When I came home from school, she would even make small talk.

"So, what did you do while I was away?"

"Well, not too much. Just watch the kids, cooked, cleaned up and visited AlmaFaye every now and

then."
"Are you alright?"
I didn't understand where that question came from.
"Yeh, Momma, I'm fine" I said.

I wondered why she asked that way. I didn't want her to ask me any questions about any particular time that she was gone. It was good to taste Momma's cooking again. She was keeping a low profile. It was like I had a new Momma. Then one day, I came home from school, and she was playing Johnny Taylor "It's Cheaper To Keep Her." I could hear the music playing loud before I got inside the house. I heard voices, but didn't know who they were at first. I walked toward the kitchen and overheard Alice, Tim and Momma talking. I thought to myself, oh shit, not them. I guess people began to hear that Momma was back home.
"Yeh, Doris, every time I wanted to spend some time
with her, Mr. Calvin would be hanging around
making sure I was never alone with her." Tim lied.
I couldn't believe my ears.
"Yeh, and when I would call, she was never available.
I just always wondered what was she doing that she
couldn't come to the phone." I heard Momma
saying "uum ummm han hah, yeh, aha. "
I walked to the door. They looked and were
shocked.
"Well, there she is, Ms. Busy Woman," Tim spouted
off.
"Yeh, it seems like she's been busier than I thought,"
Momma replied.

I rolled my eyes at Tim's drunk ass. I was so angry with him I could have kicked him in his face. He didn't bother to tell her that he raped me. I turned around and went to my room. Things were about to get real ugly and I knew it. I stayed in my room until they left and it was time to come out to eat dinner and clean up.

A few days later, Momma and AlmaFaye were sitting in the front room discussing what happened with me and Mr. Calvin. I went straight to my room to do my homework before Momma said anything crazy. She and AlmaFaye were drinking that Slitz Malt Liquor beer. A few hours later right before night fell, Momma called me to the living room. Butterflies started swimming in my stomach. I heard her pick up the phone to call someone. I didn't know who. I didn't have a good feeling about it. I walked in the door and AlmaFaye smiled at me and told me everything is going to be alright now.

"I just want you to tell Momma what really happened while I was locked up," Momma said.AlmaFaye nodded as to say go on.
"What are you talking about, Momma?"
"The police are on their way, Carla, and I am going to have that nigga locked up once and for all.
My eyes bucked out and my mouth flew open.
"Just tell me, baby, AlmaFaye already let me know some things."

I couldn't open my mouth. I was so scared. I couldn't say anything. I don't know why I couldn't say. I began to cry and shake my head no. My hands were getting sweaty and my head felt like I was going to faint.

Mr. Calvin was in the backyard feeding his dogs. I immediately got scared and nervous. Before I knew it, the police arrived and Momma got up to stand in the door. AlmaFaye tried to make me feel comfortable by telling me that there was nothing to be afraid of. She told me to tell the police everything that happened. I was scared, but finally said, "Okay, I will tell them what happened."

We stepped outside where Momma was standing. Night was falling now. The two white police men approached me to ask questions. I didn't open my mouth. By this time, Mr. Calvin had come to the front from the backyard. Seeing him made me more nervous. Momma was telling the police that he had raped me.

The police were telling Momma about the legal process.

> "Ma'am, we can't do anything until your daughter
> says so. She has to open her mouth and speak for
> herself." The officer seemed to be getting very
> agitated. Momma was forcing him to arrest Mr.
> Calvin.
> "Shit, my word ought to be enough, I'm her damn
> Momma."
> Mr. Calvin spoke up.
> "That girl ain't going to say nothing, because she's
> just lying out of her teeth. You can't believe
> nothing she says."
> I began to shake.
> AlmaFaye yelled at me, "Just tell the police now,
> got damnit, Carla! Say it, shit!"

I looked around at all of them and the only thing that kept coming into my mind was to run. I broke and ran as fast as I could down the street. Night had fallen and I remembered where Bobby and Barbara lived, up on Snow Street. Mr. Calvin started laughing and talking loud,

> "See! I told you that girl was crazy! And she didn't
> know what she was talking about."

I could hear his voice fading and his laughter. It made me sick to my stomach. I almost couldn't see my way from the tears running down my face. I ran all the way up the street to Barbara and Bobby's. I felt like I was running from everybody in my life. I wished that I could run forever and never have to return. It was warm and I was sweating and crying.

As I got to the last block before their house, I saw their yellow Cadillac parked out front. I knocked on the door and Barbara let me in. I was out of breath.

> "Hey, Carla, what the fuck is wrong, baby?" I fell in
> her arms.
> At first I couldn't say anything for trying to catch

my breath.

"Yo crazy ass Momma fucking with you again?"
Bobby asked. He was sitting in front of the TV on
the bean bag.

"She called the police to put Mr. Calvin in jail for
what he did to me," I finally was able to say.

"She's a little late, isn't she? She should have done
that shit long time ago."

"See youuu yuuu ought to juussst paack your shit up
and come home" Bobby said. He got up and cut
off the TV and sat next to me at the bar.

"I don't know how you can live in that place
everyday Carla. Bobby and I are waiting for you."

Barbara was rubbing my back. It felt so good. She loved me and I
could feel it. Bobby passed me a joint to calm me down. We sat
at the bar, drinking Hennessy and smoking joint after joint.
Bedtime came, and we went to the bedroom drunk and high. We
all slept in one bed. On one hand, I felt like I was in bed with
Mommy and Daddy. Then I felt like I was in bed with my
boyfriend and my girlfriend. No one touched me and I was so
glad. I didn't want them to. I just wanted to be safe.

The next morning Barbara and Bobby reminded me that whenever
I was ready to come to their house, the door will always be open. I
thanked them and left.

As I walked home, I felt so weird. I didn't want to go home, but I
didn't think I was ready to go and stay with my grown-up friends
yet. I felt stuck somewhere in between, which was a real sad and
lonely place. I didn't feel I belonged at home nor did I feel
anybody wanted me at that place called home. I didn't feel ready
to go to Barbara and Bobby's because it was so strange. I just
wanted to die and go be with God.

As I walked in the door Momma was by the window, looking out as
always with her cigarette and coffee on the table. She didn't say

anything at first. No good morning or anything. I went in and changed clothes. I came out to take out the trash and Momma stopped me on the way back.

    "Where have you, been?" she asked.

    "Over my friends house."

    "What friends?"

    "Bobby and Barbara."

    "Do you think I am a damn fool?" she screamed at me.

    I said, "No," my heart beating fast as I spoke.

    Momma continued. "So, are both of them fucking you now? What's going on?"

I couldn't speak. Her words hurt too much. I thought to myself, AlmaFaye must have told her everything that happened while she was gone.

    "Last night, why didn't you tell the police what happened? Well, I did what I was suppose to do. Then you make me look like a damn fool as if I don't know what I'm talking about!"

I felt a sudden satisfaction given the fact she has made me feel like a damn fool most of my life. Tears began to slowly roll out of my eyes. Momma had a way of making you feel like a cheap and low down dirty person. But this time she didn't succeed with me. Bobby and Barbara loved me. I believed that. They knew I was hurting inside, and cared about me. They expressed love, not hate for me. They loved me for who I was in spite of what had happened to me. I don't know why my mouth was numb, when I could not speak or tell the police what Mr. Calvin had done to me. I stood there reflecting on the night before when I was running down the street to Bobby and Barbara's house. I was thinking about Mr. Calvin telling the police, "See, I told you that girl is lying, and she's crazy too!" The words made me sick.

    "Are you listening to me, girl?" Momma yelled.

    "Yeh."

    "Go do your chores."

Oh, how I ached! I wanted her to hold me, or tell me to "come here, everything will be alright." I wanted her to give me a hug and tell me that she understood and loved me. She didn't.

Momma was back to her usual self. I felt myself going deeper and deeper into depression. I had headaches almost every day. I even felt too weak to stare into my cross corners. I couldn't even pick up my diary and write to God, as bad as I wanted to. I was so tired and weak. I didn't feel human anymore. I felt like a tether ball that was constantly being beat on and thrown around the same old pole. Thoughts of death at the hands of my mother would come in my mind. I became sad and bitter. I needed something to keep me going. I needed something to help me out in the face of this hopelessness. But what? Where can a 14 year old go? I kept questioning and wondering in my mind. I never came up with a real definite answer. I did know the answer wasn't at this house.

I thought about leaving home and wondered what would it be like to be gone from this place. Just the thought of it put a smile on my face. But where would I go? "Bobby and Barbara's," I thought. Didn't they say I could always go home to them if I needed to? I figured it would be better with them than at home.

A week later, Momma and AlmaFaye were in the front room listening to Bobby Blue Bland, drinking their Schlitz Malt Liquor mixed with a little whiskey. At first, they were laughing and talking to each other. Then, it seemed like someone invisible walked in the room, tapped Momma on her shoulder and told her, "It's time to switch courses now, curse your daughter Carla out because she's fucking your husband behind your back." This particular night, Momma was talking about Uncle Kyle, who had been cheating on Aunt Maura with his niece, Falona. I remembered that night at the drive in when Uncle Kyle was feeling on her breast on top of the car. Even though Momma was talking about Uncle Kyle, I could feel that the conversation would eventually turn to me. Momma was telling AlmaFaye about her conversation with

Kyle's wife, and how hurt she was. Momma said "if she was Kyle's wife she would have strangled that little bitch to death." Then she looked at me. The butterflies started swimming in my stomach. I quickly got up and went to the bathroom. Not because I had to go, but to avoid another verbal dagger soon to be headed my way.

> "Yeh, she don't want to hear that, does she" Momma
> said laughing to herself.
> "But your day is coming," she yelled out to me.

While I was sitting on the bathroom tub, I started talking to myself and God:

> "God why was I even born?" I took my blue towel
> off the rack so I could hold on to something. "Why
> am I even here? God, I need you. How I wish you
> could talk back to me just this one time." I cried
> into my towel.

That night, I decided that I was fed up and could not take anymore from Momma or Mr. Calvin. I came out of the bathroom, sat in my closet and finished listening to her talk about me.

> "All she is ever going to be is a damn whore fucking
> everybody's man or woman."
> "No I am not!" I couldn't hold in the words.
> "Don't talk back to me, who in the fuck do you think
> you're talking to?" I could not sit there any longer. I
> wanted to tell her to shut up and stop talking about
> me.
> "Momma, why?" I asked.
> She stood up.
> "Why do you hate me so much? Why do I have to
> be your whores and bitches every gotdamn fucking
> day?"

I felt insane, not knowing where this boldness was coming from. But I felt like I had nothing to lose. She didn't love me anyway. At least I could get some damn answers out of her.

> "Well, you brought this shit on your own damn self.

Shit, you made your bed, now you got to lay in it,
baby"!
She had her hands on her hips wavering from her
drunkenness.
"You don't like it? You want to try to whoop my ass
or something?"
Momma started walking toward me, raising her
voice. I came toward her too.
"Momma, come on and leave Carla alone,"
AlmaFaye jumped up, yelling.
"I ought to choke her to death."
"Go ahead, Momma."

When I said that, her right hand quickly grabbed me by the neck.
She kept the grip and her hand grabbed my collar. Momma and I
were eye to eye, nose to nose, and toe to toe. I stood looking at her
straight in the eyes, wanting to kill her ass with my bare hands too.
I could smell the liquor and cigarette smoke on her breath.
AlmaFaye finally got Momma's hand off from around my collar,
and Momma staggered back as she released it.

I stood there, looking at her hard and breathing loud. This was
going to be her last time grabbing me, I made up in my mind. I
was shaking, not from butterflies this time, but from wanting so
badly to kill her and stop the madness.
    "I am going to call me a cab and go home, Carla,
    you can come over and spend the night" AlmaFaye
    said.
    "Yeh, take her crazy ass with you," Momma said as
    she sat slumped in the chair.

My insides cried and ached. I didn't know what was going on with
me and my Momma. It was getting worse. Would she really have
killed me with her bare hands if AlmaFaye wasn't there? The
thoughts scared me. I went into the bedroom to get some clothes
to spend the night.

The cab driver was there in less than five minutes. AlmaFaye asked the cab driver to stop at the liquor store before we reached her house. She asked me if I wanted anything. I said, "gin and orange juice." She was in and out of the store in no time. We arrived at the house and there were people all around the back door. I guess they were really anxious since AlmaFaye was over at Momma's all day long. She got rid of the crowd and we were alone. I fixed me a drink and lit a joint. I wanted to get high as a kite, so I wouldn't feel any more pain. AlmaFaye began to talk.

"Carla, you know Momma doesn't mean all those things that she says to you. I don't know what's wrong with her, but I do know that she can't possibly mean it. I just can't figure her out. Just when I think we are going to have a good time, Momma always goes off. I didn't know I was coming home to this craziness again."

"AlmaFaye, she does mean it. She knows what she is saying and she is serious about it. She never apologizes, or takes it back. It only gets worse and worse. I am sick and tired of being her daily bitch. There is not a day that passes that I don't hear that. Why?"

AlmaFaye walked over to me and gave me a hug.

"I don't know, baby, but I love you, Carla. I will always love you, no matter what."

"I know AlmaFaye, and I love you too, but I want Momma to love me. Is that asking for too much?"

"Carla, just block out all that stuff. I don't know how you go through it everyday, I really don't. You are stronger than I am, for sure. You are stronger than you know."

"That's bullshit, AlmaFaye, I am not strong. I don't want to be strong! I want to be loved. I want a normal damn life. Is that so wrong to want? I just want a Momma that loves me."

I couldn't stop the tears. My stomach ached, pain coming from the depths of my inner being. I realized in that moment how much I wanted love and how distant I was from the one I wanted it from. It felt like an impossible dream that would never come true and I could not bare the reality of it.   How could that be? To have a Mother that didn't or couldn't love her child.   We sat up and talked for hours. AlmaFaye let me lay on her shoulders (like a little baby sister) and rest.

"AlmaFaye, please tell me the truth about how you
feel about my relationship with Bobby and Barbara?"
"Whatever makes you happy. I am all for it. You
have been hurt too many damn times. I just want
you to be happy, baby. I love you, no matter what."

Her kids came in from the back door and sat down with us to watch television. We watched TV until it was time for everybody to go to bed. The next morning was interrupted by a telephone call from Momma. AlmaFaye was in the kitchen when she hollered out that Momma wanted me to come home right away.

"Damn," I hollered.
"AlmaFaye what the hell does she   want this early
in the morning?"
"I don't know," she said.
There was a knock at the door, as I made my way to
the bathroom.   I heard muffled voices through the
door.
"Hey Faye, is Darnell here?"
"No Bobby, he isn't." I walked out and there Bobby
stood. He looked over at me.
"Hi, Carla. What are you up to?"
"I was about to go home," I told him.
Bobby offered to take me home.
He reached over and placed his hand on my thigh,
rubbing it gently.
"So, are you ready to go straight home?"
"Well, if you have something else to do, I guess we
can have a slight detour."
"Barbara is at work so we can stop by the house if you
want to," he said.

"That's fine, we can do that," I said.

We went to his house, which was five minutes away. As soon as we stepped foot into the house, we were undressing. He was telling me how much he missed and wanted me, and how I had been holding out by not coming over enough. We did not make it to the bedroom because we were falling on the bean bags and throwing pillows all over the floor. We started kissing and hugging. I was wondering if Barbara came home from work for lunch, how would she feel about this?

On the way home, Bobby asked when was I coming home.
        "It feels like sooner than later."
        "We are waiting for you, and I want you there
        badly."

He dropped me off a block before my house, and Momma was in the window looking out as I walked in the door. Momma's friend, Mr. Reed, was sitting in the front room talking to her.
        "Good morning," both of them said.
        "Good morning," I responded quietly and went to
        my bedroom to put my things up.

The kids were in the backyard playing. Momma yelled out to me, "Carla I need you to go and get me some cigarettes."

I went to the store real quick and came back so she couldn't say anything to me about being too late. When I got back, Momma's friend Alice was there. She was drinking a beer. Wiping her mouth from a little drip, she smiled at me.
        "Hey, pumpkin." Alice was swaying in her seat as she
        talked to me. I could tell she was drunk already.
        "Hi, Alice," I said.

I gave Momma her cigarettes and went to the back to pull out the vacuum cleaner. I heard Momma say to Alice, "Let's go in the kitchen because she got to clean up in here."

I finished my chores and went to my room. I sat against the bed with my back against the wall. I thought about leaving. Questions started forming in my mind one after another. "Do I want to continue staying here where I can't stand to be in the same room with my step daddy and I can't stand to be in my mother's presence?" I asked myself.

"Momma, how come you can't love me right? Why
do you have to torture me?"

I believed it was really time for me to go. So I decided to call Bobby. I called Bobby and told him I would be calling later tonight after everybody went to bed.

That night, I sat down on the edge of my bed and began to write Momma a good bye letter. I had made up my mind to leave. I could not spend one more night in this hell house. Just like Natalie Cole says in her song, "I'm Catching Hell, Living Here Alone." That's exactly how I felt.

Dear Momma:
I know that you weren't expecting this. You always tell me to pick up the pieces, and that's what I'm trying to do. I am trying to pick up the pieces left in my life. Momma, I'm tired. All you do is embarrass me around your friends. I love you. What you are putting me through, I just can't take it any more. Whatever goes down, I still love you. Momma, I didn't want my life to start like this. Do you know how I feel? I feel like I was born and nobody knew or cared. But you know I'm the one who has to live with this. Not you, not nobody. Just me, myself and I. You see, I don't want your husband but you throw that against me no matter what I say. Momma, every word I write hurts me deep down inside. Some nights when we are all up looking at TV, you make the kids go to bed and only the three of us are up. I will get up and go to bed too. I don't be sleepy,

Momma. I go to bed because someone makes me feel
like I am worth nothing. You don't be drunk all the
time. When you and Mr. Calvin argue, I overhear you
say, "At least I'm not fucking your Daddy." You know
how I feel then? I feel just like a damn dog. I am 14
years old and have a mind like a grown woman.
Everything that happens in this house, I'm to blame for
it. I'm tired of it.

When I look at my little brothers and sisters, I wonder
to myself what will become of them? I wonder if the
same things will happen to the girls that happened to
me. The day you told me that you would be the death
of me, I died. At night when I lie in bed, I cry a lot
because of what I am, what I've become, and what you
are always making me. When I go to school, I hear kids
talk about all the fun that they have with their parents.
Here I am, scared to be in the kitchen with my own
mother and step daddy.   Want to know something,
Momma? When I went to Phoenix, my so-called
Daddy (as you have told me all these damn years) told
me a whole different story. He told me why he picked
us up from the foster home. Why when you came to get
the kids, he only gave you me. He told me why. He
said he wasn't my damn Daddy. He just gave me his
name because my Daddy wouldn't claim me. He also
told me that if I let him and want him to be, he would
be my Daddy.

Momma, you have told me so many lies. Now I guess I
understand what you meant when I was a tiny girl and I
would ask you about my seeing my Daddy, sisters and
brothers in Phoenix. You would sometimes say, that
ain't your Daddy, Mr. Willie is your Daddy. Then you
would sometimes say you were just kidding. I thought
you were just mad at Tyrone. But then you would
sometimes say, other men were my Daddy (men I had

never heard of). But you never told me who my real daddy was, if it really wasn't Tyrone. Momma, I love you more than anything in this world, but you are wrong. You don't treat me right. You embarrass me in front of people all the time. Deep down inside, Momma, I feel like you have broken my heart. Good-bye Momma.

I folded the letter up and placed it in my pocket until it was time to leave. That night after dinner, I cleaned up the kitchen one last time. I felt so free. I smiled for the first time in a long time. I knew I was leaving and no one was going to stop me. Everyone went to bed at the usual time. The kids were sleeping by 9:30 p.m. and Momma was turning in about 10:00 p.m. I called Barbara and told her that I was ready to come and live with her and Bobby.

She said, "Good. It's about time. I didn't know how much more I could take. We will wait for your call." At 10:30 p.m., I was finished cleaning the kitchen, and I went to my bed to lay down until I knew for sure everyone was fast asleep. Around 1:00 a.m., I tip-toed toward the kitchen, passing my brothers who were sleeping in the den. I took the letter I wrote Momma and placed it on top of the desk in front of the window. I put it right next to Momma's phone, where I knew she would see it. I called Bobby. He said he would leave right away and meet me in the back alley behind my house. By the time I dragged my bag of clothes to the alley, he would be out there. I had to pass Mr. Calvin's greyhounds and coonhounds. They must have been very sleepy, because not one of them barked. Blacky came up growling behind me, and I identified myself. I said, "Blacky this is Carla. Go back, boy!" I didn't want him to come out of the gate and try to follow me. Leaving Blacky behind was one of the most painful parts of leaving home that night. I was sad for my sisters and brothers too, but I knew I couldn't do anything other than pray for them.

Bobby was there and got out of the car and opened up the trunk. He put my bag in. I got in the front seat. Then we pulled off.

"Hey, what's happening?" he asked.

"Nothing much," I said.

"Well, I am glad you are coming over," he said.

"You will be fine now."

I said to myself, I sure hope so.

Barbara was in the bedroom. When she saw me she rolled over on the bed and said, hey girl!

"How ya doing?"

"Pretty good, I guess," I said, almost embarrassed.

I didn't know what to do or how to act. I just stood there in the doorway of her bedroom. It was dark.

"Hop in the bed. Ain't nobody about to get up,"
Barbara said.

"Okay," I said.

"But everything is packed up."

"Look in that drawer right there and grab a
gown."

So I did. I got into bed on one side and Bobby got
on the other side, and then we all just went to sleep.

CHAPTER 17

Move In With Bobby & Barbara
(END OF OCTOBER 1977)

The next morning came quickly, and I was the only one not leaving the house. I learned that morning that Barbara had two young daughters (Sheila, 7 and Tessie, 8). Bobby and Barbara were going to work and their two girls were going to school. Before leaving, Barbara showed me where certain things were and gave me a closet right next to hers. I wondered what my mother was thinking. By now, she had read my letter. Will she call the police? Then I thought about AlmaFaye. I knew she was probably worried about me. I knew I needed to call her eventually, so that she would know that I was alright. Maybe she could tell Momma that everything was alright and not to worry? I sat on the edge of the bed looking up at the ceilings. The ceilings were not boxed ceilings. Therefore I didn't see the shape of the cross in their room, but I knew God was with me. I walked around the house to look in every room. Barbara told me that her Daddy lived with them also and stayed in the back room. He would come home in the morning so that he could sleep all day and party at night. He had a drinking problem.

There was another room next to his, which was the girls' room. Their room was very messy. It was like two girls who didn't listen to their mother when she told them to clean up. There were shoes in the middle of the floor, clothes thrown in piles at each corner, drawers pulled out and beds not made up. Barbara and Bobby's bathroom was very spacious with lots of room to walk around. It had a shower/tub and a large sink with a mirror above it. The toilet was at the back next to the shower/tub. Barbara and Bobby's room was very large and decorated in mostly red. The bedspread was crushed red velvet and the pillows were black velvet. There was also a red throw rug. They had a kitchen, den, bar, and living room. They kept drinks behind the bar and I could help myself if I wanted. After my self tour, I unpacked my things. Barbara had made room for me in some of the dresser drawers. I straightened up the bedroom and cleaned up the house after that. Cutting on the TV, I watched some of the daytime soaps. I wasn't used to this at all. I wasn't used to being home this time of day or being in a strange house with no kids to holler at and no real assigned chores. So I picked up my diary and talked to God.

Dear God:
I am now out of the house and really don't know exactly what I am doing. Please guide me and stay with me. I know this is a totally different world and perhaps it's not right, but I can say it's a whole lot more peaceful. I believe these people love and care for me. I have not been called a dog, a whore today, nor have I been accused of anything. I just want a little peace, God. I will talk with you again soon, okay?

Before I knew it time was winding down, and soon everyone would be coming home from the work day. What would happen then, I wondered? Have I cleaned up enough? Am I doing the right thing? Will they be pleased that they asked me to live here? Barbara and Bobby came in finally, and they had food in their hands - cheeseburgers and fish burgers with french fries. They had shrimp dinners too. Barbara came over and hit me on my butt, saying, "Hey girl!" I smirked. They were looking at the mail while taking off their work clothes. Barbara worked at a pre-school as an assistant teacher, and Bobby worked for the Del Monte Raisin Factory.

"Where are Sheila and Tessie?" I asked Barbara.
"They're over to Bobby's mother's house. We'll pick them up later."

So we all sat down at the bar, eating and talking. They asked if I had heard anything from my Momma.
"No, and I haven't called," I said.
"What about AlmaFaye?" Bobby asked.
"I haven't called her yet either. It's been quiet."
There was a knock at the door. It was Darnell. He noticed me at the bar right away.

"Hey, Carla! What's happening? I heard that you
ran away from home."

I thought to myself, you only lived across the street from me I am
sure it didn't take long to find out. Barbara interrupted and said,
"Don't be talking to her. I'm surprised it took her this long to run
away. Her damn Momma is crazy." "Hey, I am just saying, you
know the word is out and Doris is around talking lots of shit.
Anyway, what y'all got going? I need some."

Barbara asked if I wanted a drink and I asked for a strong one. She
gave me a glass of Hennesy straight. It was very strong. She fired
up a joint and we talked while Darnell and Bobby tightened things
up. Barbara began to tell me what they sold out of the house. It
ranged from marijuana, to angel dust, to cocaine.
    "Wow! That's a lot!" I said.
    "Yeh, it's a lot of money too. We have to be very
    careful. We don't just open the door to any and
    everybody. The pigs are slick, and we have already
    been busted once before."

After the transaction, Darnell left and Bobby asked Barbara to fix
him a drink. So we all stood around the bar and continued to talk
and get high.

One conversation led to another and before it was over, we were
discussing dreams. Barbara said she wanted a lot of money, clothes,
and a fine car. Bobby said almost the same, I did too, with the
addition of traveling. I was really too young to know exactly what
I wanted out of life. Anyway, we kept on talking. We decided to
work toward, getting those things for one another in our own little
time. Bobby suggested a toast to our new beginnings. Each of us
hit our glasses. Bobby talked about how the drugs could give back
returns doubly if we were careful. Bobby and Barbara drove a
yellow Toyota Celica now. I don't know what happened to their
yellow Cadillac.

There was another knock at the door and it was another dope sale. I watched how Barbara acted with the women who came and bought drugs . I saw she had no affection toward them, other than as a buddy type. I guess I thought maybe she liked all the women just like she liked me, but not these. All types of people came over all through the night. There were people with no money, and people wanting a hand out. Some were saying, "Aw man! Y'awl know we good for it. Let us try it first. I want to make sure it's good." You can tell he didn't have any intentions on buying anything. Barbara said, "Look! If your ass gonna buy something, buy it! If not, get the hell out of here. We ain't got time for that." Barbara was really rough. I wanted to be strong just like her.

Later on, Barbara and I talked about some of the people that had come by that night. She mentioned who was a regular, who could be trusted and who could not. She also mentioned the women that came by, letting me know that one of them wanted the same set up that we have (meaning all three of us).
   "Did you see the jealousy in their eyes when they saw
   all three of us kicking it together? Yeh, home girl
   wants to be my woman. But she ain't my type,"
   Barbara boasted.

I guess I was supposed to feel lucky and I did. We had music playing in the background as always. A song by Cameo called "Lost and Turned Out" just happened to be playing and from that moment on, every time I heard that particular song, I personalized it. I would think to myself this is what "turned out" means. In a shameful way, I began to listen to the lyrics and felt just like that girl.

The night was soon over, and it was time for bed. We were all high and feeling good. Barbara and I went to the bathroom and took a bath. Bobby could not fit, so he rushed us because we seemed to be having a lot of fun and he wasn't.
   "Hurry up in there," Bobby hollered.

We laughed. We came out, and Barbara passed me a red sheer chiffon gown. She put on the black one that was identical. I felt grown . I guess my raggedy pajamas were not worthy. Barbara had a beautiful wardrobe full of lingerie. We went into the bedroom, and Bobby went into the bathroom to take a quick shower. It was real quick too. We all got in the bed, and Lord knows I didn't know what to do, but they did. I couldn't believe what two people were doing to me at the same time.

The days and nights during the week repeated themselves. We would lose ourselves in sex. We would only stop for the dope traffic. There were times when we didn't eat. We would start off with a joint of sherman or marijuana, whatever was available in the house stash. I noticed that Barbara did this more often than I did. I noticed her getting so freaked and spaced out, that I would not smoke as much. I just pretended too so that I could be sober enough to watch over her crazy ass.

I recall times when people would come over to the house and sometimes get high, start crying and talking about their "no good" life. I would try to tell them to trust God because He will help them. I don't know why I thought they would listen to me, but that was the only solution I could offer as I seemed to be the only one sober enough to give advice.

The week-ends would come around fast and there was always somewhere to go and something to do. One night, we decided to go to a club called Disco 2000. You needed to be 21 to get in, and I didn't fit that by a long shot. The best we could do was dress me up like a grown up and slap a wig on my head. Barbara did something with the owner and before we knew it, we were in. Knowing Barbara, she probably promised to give him some. All three of us were partying together! We did everything together. When they played a slow dance, people were waiting to see which one of us would dance with Bobby. Barbara said, "Let's all dance." We broke faces, because we both slow danced with him; one in the front and the other in the back, alternating positions very slowly. I could not believe it myself. I was embarrassed at first, and I knew people knew us. After a couple more drinks, I didn't care what they thought. If I was not so high on Hennessy and weed, I know I would have never had the nerve to do that.

I was now hanging with a crowd that was much older so I pretended that I was grown. I was learning the street life, how to handle myself, and how to handle anybody else. Barbara put that mentality in me, because she was tough and no one bothered her, including Bobby.

    "Let no body control you. You always be in control
    of your situation, understand?"
    "Yeh," I would tell her.
    She held her weight, and she got her way all the
    time, or it didn't go at all.

Every now and then, I would run into Darnell at a club or house party. Each time he saw me, he would tell me to take my little young ass home. He'd say, "You know you don't need to be out here in these streets." I would laugh at him, because home was prison to me, torture day and night. I was sentenced to a life of judgment at home, so I guess I chose the lesser of the two evils. I told him I had no other home than where I was.

It wasn't party all the time, because Barbara had two daughters who came home during the week when they were not at her mother-in law's house. Those nights would be very calm and low key. But they still saw all three of us in bed together often. I didn't like that, because I was afraid they would grow up and think this is the way life was supposed to go. Even though I knew better than that.

After one month passed I finally called AlmaFaye, only to get cursed out. I expected it, because I had not talked to her in some time. It had only been a few weeks but it felt like it had been longer. She asked me how was I doing and how were they treating me. I told her they were treating me fine, and I was very happy. "They love me, AlmaFaye," I told her. She told me that Darnell

told her where I was. Then she asked me how come I didn't come
to live with her?

      "That would be the first place Momma would look
      for me," I told her
      I begged her not to tell anybody, especially
      Momma.
      "I hear they are using you," her tone growing louder.
      "They are not," I snapped.
      "Look, I don't want them using my baby sister."
      "AlmaFaye, we are a family. No one is using
      anybody.
      You are hearing lies, probably from Darnell."
      "It don't matter who it's from." She was pissed, I
      could hear it in her voice. Is it true that you are
      whoring for them?"
      "Hell, naw, AlmaFaye. Are you crazy?"

Her words pierced me. I felt ashamed at what she thought I was
doing and how she made Bobby and Barbara sound. On Saturday
mornings, Barbara and I would always go to a little thrift store up
the street. It had antique jewelry. The owner knew Barbara very
good and would put clothes on the side for her. She bought me
some pretty interesting items, like men's hats and blazers.

      "You want to be in charge don't you?" she looked at
      me and said.
      I laughed. But she was serious.
      I said, "Yeh."
      "Okay. I'll teach you. You will be the aggressor."

She picked out this man's suit and a brim hat to match.   The
pants were smooth navy blue pin stripe pants. They fit me a little
baggy. She told me that's the way they should look. We went to
the mirror and there I stood in a white button up shirt, navy blue
pin-stripped suit and a tie with a matching hat.   I felt like a little
man in that suit. She took my arms and began to play with me.
      "Hey baby, you sure look good. Can I be your

woman?"
"You sure can." I played the game back with her.

The people in the store thought we were joking, but I knew Barbara was for real. She bought me a few outfits like that along with some girly looking clothes, like blouses and jeans.

We also went to yard sales throughout the city. She the kids and myself always had fun on Saturdays when it was just us. When we got back home, Bobby would always be there doing business with the clients. Barbara would give him a kiss and walk away. I would give him a kiss too. The guys always did a double take.   Barbara told me to do that (kiss each other) when we came home.

When the guys left, Bobby came in the bedroom where Barbara and I were changing clothes and putting up the new rags she bought.
     "Hey, we have to have a family meeting."
     "After we take a bath, we will be in there" Barbara
     told him. Barbara washed my back and cleaned all
     over my body.

She kissed me throughout the whole time we were in the tub. At first it felt like a Momma washing her daughter, but then it changed when she started kissing and touching me. Being with her made me feel so good and safe. I never wanted to leave her side. In a weird way, she felt like the man of the house.

Barbara and I sat down at the bar, while Bobby fixed our regular drinks, Hennesy on ice.
     "The subject is about money" Bobby said.
     "What about money?" Barbara said.
     "Our drugs are running low, and the pigs are
     watching our house. We need to keep making
     money but we have to lay ow on the drugs for now."
     That was not good because Barbara had just got laid
     off her teachers' assistant job.
     "So what's the game plan Bobby?" Barbara sounded

impatient.
"Look, we may have to go back to the camps" Bobby
said.
"Oh shit no. Not them again." It sounded familiar
to Barbara, but very unfamiliar to me.
"Shit, how long got dammit?" Barbara asked.
"Just until the pigs lay off and we can get another
shipment."
"How much help do we have?"
"I haven't gotten any calls back from the others."

I didn't know what the hell they were talking about. Then Bobby
said it's just us this time.
"Well, we just got to do what the hell we got to do
to reach our dreams. Right?" She looked at me.
"Yeh, what's happening?" I said nervously.
"We used to run these camps outside of town. A
camp with Mexican men. Friday evenings, they get
paid and come down to this little saloon outside of
Fresno, to get drunk and wasted."
I still didn't know what she was talking about. She
continued.
"We use to go out there and turn tricks with them
for fifteen to twenty five dollars a wop for five to ten
minutes each. It's fast money. We could make
anywhere from two hundred to three hundred
dollars a night if we play it right."
"What's a trick?"
"Fucking assholes and getting paid for it."
My stomach started getting butterflies and I felt
sick.
"Bobby will look out for us, and all we do when we
get in is ask for the money up front." She continued
to explain.

I stayed quiet. I didn't know what to say or what I could say. I
tried to sound grown and at least ask more questions.

"How will they know that we are there?"
"Well first, we go into the bar and circle it once.
Then go outside. They follow us out. Trust me
they will be hot on our trails."
"Where do we turn the tricks?"
"In the back seat of the car. It's easy."

I didn't know what to say about it. I was at a loss for words. I knew one thing I wasn't going to do, and that was to tell them "no" after all they had done for me. I thought about all the things they had bought me, and how much they loved me. I was scared, but I thought this was the least I could do to help them if I was to be a part of the family plan. After all, it was for the family and our dreams. It's not like they were using me. We would all be doing it together. Barbara would be the main one, and I would be the trainee.

"So when does all this happen?" I asked.

Barbara picked up a magazine on the bar and was flipping through the pages. I guess she was finished with the conversation.

"A few weeks," Bobby responded.
"We can sell the dope we have left until we are totally
out."
Barbara lifted her glass up. We lifted our glasses for
a toast.
"To Plan B." She smiled and licked her lips at me.

CHAPTER 18

THE CAMPS

I was nervous for weeks waiting on the camp days. I prayed that something would come up and we wouldn't have to do it. But, the time finally came. It was Friday night. The kids had gone over to Madea's, who was Bobby's mother, house and Barbara and I were in the bedroom dressing up. Barbara gave me a long black wig to wear along with a real tight red mini-dress. She wore a gold wig with a red, orange, and green tight fitting dress. She helped me make my face up so that I would look much older than I was, and we both sprayed one another with Estee Lauder perfume. Bobby's favorite tape, by a group called "Maze" was playing while we were getting dressed. He was walking around the house whistling the lyrics to himself, while he served us drinks in the bedroom. I told him to roll me up a fat joint, so that I could be totally bummed out and numb. Barbara put towels in each of our purses, so that we would not drip all the way back home. I thought to myself I might use my towel to vomit and cry on all the way back home.

On the way there, we continued to drink and smoke joint after joint. It was about a thirty-minute drive outside of Fresno. We finally reached this tiny little saloon. You could hear the band playing loud and clear. Bobby stayed outside in the car while we went in. Barbara said, "Follow me and do what I do." We walked in the door, and it seemed like everybody in there turned around as soon as the door opened. Clouds of smoke hit our faces and nostrils as we walked in.

"Smile and wink at every man you see," Barbara whispered.

I tried to wink and smile. It was difficult.

"Now lick your lips," she whispered.

They were smiling back and looking so hungry, as if they were going to eat us alive. We circled the room once. To me, the walk felt like it lasted ten days because it was so intense. We couldn't walk too fast or too slow. Barbara told me that they had to see the merchandise from all angles. They were undressing us with their eyes and teeth, as they grinned to each other. You knew they were hungry and you were their upcoming meal. I said to myself, for the sake of making a joke, "damn, I hope we ain't got to fuck every Amigo in this place. If so, we could be here until next Friday!" There were men who could not speak any English, and spoke to us in their own language. Then there were those that could speak English and you understood everything they were saying to you. We finally came back to the door we came in. I was ready to go home after that ordeal.

Barbara said, whatever you do, say Vente Cinco (which means twenty-five dollars). I kept repeating that phrase to myself, so I didn't forget it. We stood by the car where Bobby was standing, and sure enough within minutes there were guys lined up at the door. Barbara with her bold self whistled to signal them over toward the side of the saloon. I stood there and looked at Bobby. Without saying anything, he gave me a reassuring look, as if to say don't worry it will be over very soon. Barbara lined up her tricks one after another. The windows were down on each side of the car so we could pass the money to him once they gave it to us. The first man who got in the car had his pants already unzipped. He got on top of Barbara, and within seconds he was gone, and it was over. They were up and out in no time. I was next.
    "Oh, shit, I said to myself." Here it goes."

I took a deep breath. My guy was waiting. He had been standing next to me feeling on my arms and back. He was moaning in his language that I couldn't understand. I looked at him and said, "Vente." He said, "si, si," nodding his head yes. I opened my hand.

Then, I climbed in the back seat and with the other hand, I passed the money out of the window to Bobby. I pulled up my dress, and he was ready. Boy, was it strange! This man who didn't even know me, was on top of me. Thoughts were running through my head, but I kept a smile on my face and a moan and groan on my lips as

Barbara taught me.

After Barbara saw that I could do it, she said we were going to cut time by doing it at the same time. She opened both back doors and the men could choose which door they wanted to go into. Everything was happening so fast. Every now and then, I would grab the Hennessy bottle on the floor and take a big drink during transition time. I can't even remember how many men came through that night. I stopped counting. I didn't want to anymore. It was too shameful and too painful. Finally, Barbara raised up and said, "We better head out." She had noticed a Mexican woman at the door pointing to us. After we turned the other men away and closed the door to the car, Bobby drove off fast. Barbara started explaining to me how that woman was probably going to be calling the police pretty soon, because we were taking the men away from the Mexican women.

"They don't like that," she said.

I said to myself, how come she didn't miss those damn men earlier?

"Hey girl, you did real good tonight. You shocked me," Barbara said.

Bobby looked in his rear view mirror and agreed by nodding his head. We reached the house, and Barbara ran to the bathroom to run hot bath water. She took out two douche bags for both of us. She called me in the bathroom and said, "Fill yours up with water and a tablespoon of vinegar." I didn't know what she was going to do with that. I saw one in the bathroom at home that Momma hung on the back door of the bathroom. I asked Barbara what was I suppose to do with mine. She told me that I was going to clean all the shit that those men put inside of me. We douched and then soaked in the tub for about thirty minutes. As we were soaking, somehow I still felt dirty and like some of those men were still inside me somewhere. Bobby brought us both joints and drinks. He turned on the music. Barbara reached over and started washing my back as she was holding me in her arms. I laid on her shoulder and just rested there for a while.

"How long have you been doing this?" I asked her,
referring to the camps and turning tricks.
"Off and on, ever since my mother taught me as a
young teenager."

My mouth opened wide. She dropped her head slightly and the
expression on her face looked very sorry and sad. I felt so bad for
her. How could her own mother teach her to do something like
that? I thought it had been Bobby. I then saw a side of her that I
didn't know was there. She could get sad too.   I didn't say
anything more about the night, and neither did she. The water was
good, bubbly, and soapy. We decided to go out that night to
celebrate. Bobby's brother, Pete, was giving a party and Bobby said
we ought to check it out. After we got out of the tub, I decided I
wanted to keep my wig on. I thought it was a good cover up, in
case somebody saw me. We went from the outskirts of the city
into some Mexican camp that nobody knew about, to a bathtub at
home, to going across town on the white side for a party.

The next day was Sunday, and I woke up about 10:00 a.m. Wiping
the sleep out of my eyes, my mind immediately replayed last
night's events with all those Mexicans at the camp saloon.
Suddenly, a deep sadness came over me. I felt dirty and ashamed.
I never imagined doing something so horrible. Even though I was
drunk, it didn't take the pain or memory away. I wished to myself
that I hadn't done it, but it was too late now, and there were too
many more weekends that would require the same thing. As I
looked in the mirror, I didn't like who I saw and what she was
becoming. I held my head down and began to pray to God to
somehow, someway, bring money to Bobby and Barbara so that we
didn't have to keep doing this.

That following Monday Barbara woke up and said, "we have to get
ready to go to the clinic."
          "Who's sick?" I asked.
She said the V.D. clinic, as if I knew what that meant. She said one
of those ass holes probably gave us something Friday night and we

want to go get medicine in case they did. I was scared and hoping and praying to God that they didn't give us anything. As we approached the doors to the clinic, I began to feel butterflies. I had never been in a place like this, and what if I saw somebody that knew me? What if the word gets back to my Momma that I was here? Oh man, what a bummer! We walked in the door and there were people leaning around, just waiting. All three of us had a seat after signing in and waited for our individual turns. People were looking at us and I tried not to make eye contact with anybody. Some people were real old and some were real young. I sat there wishing it was over and that we didn't have to do this stuff. I wondered if any of the people in the room had to go to the camps. Our tests and results came up clean. We had a celebration drink for every time the tests were clean. I prayed all the time to not get the V.D. disease that Barbara always talked about as soon as we left the camps.

One Friday, after we came from the campsites, we went home and got real high on some Sherman and Hennessy. We had our own little party, just Barbara, Bobby and myself. When it was time to go to bed, Barbara kept looking for her lighter and couldn't find it. Bobby told her to forget about it and let's go have fun in the bedroom. After our fun, we went to sleep.

About two hours later, I was awakened by a voice which told me to slowly scoot my way off the bed onto the floor, right now. Without thinking, I obeyed the voice and began sliding to the edge of the bed onto the floor. I laid on the floor wondering to myself why I was awakened and who woke me out of my sleep. Just as the questions were coming, I heard a "WHAM!" I raised up only to see Barbara's hand holding a keen spiked high heel shoe. There was an imprint in the pillow where my head was moments before the voice told me to get off the bed. If I had stayed, my skull would have been cracked wide open by that heel. Bobby immediately grabbed Barbara's arms, shaking and jerking her.

"What the hell is wrong with you?" he asked her.
"I know I had my lighter and one of yaw'l asses have

it."

I yelled out in my defense, "I don't have it,
Barbara!"

I quickly got up and cut on the bedroom light only to see the high
heel shoe laying on the pillow as Bobby still held Barbara's arms up.
Bobby was so angry, he kept talking to Barbara, "Listen, damn it!
Get out of the bed." He asked Barbara to go get her robe. Her robe
was on the floor. She picked up her robe and handed it to Bobby
and there was her lighter inside the robe pocket. I was very nervous
and she was only slightly sorry. Bobby was mad and pissed off
still. He yelled at us. "Let's go to bed!"

I personally wasn't too sleepy after that incident. I laid there
repeating over and over in my mind, she could have put a hole in
my head or in one of my eyes. That voice that woke me up and
told me to get out of the bed was bothering me. That was God.
That was God, I started saying to myself. Thank you God for
watching over me. I was still shaken up, because there was no sign
before going to bed that she was even pissed off about anything.
The next morning was normal, as if nothing had ever happened. I
never heard Barbara talk about that night, so I guess we were all still
friends.

A few weeks after that incident, Barbara came home and said we
were going to Los Angeles to visit her sister, Viola, for the week.
She said her mother, Antoinette, would drive us up there. I asked
why were we going and she told me that her mother liked to play in
the bingo tournament in Los Angeles. Bobby could not go with us
because the Del Monte company had just rehired him back to his
part-time position.

We traveled through the prettiest mountains I had ever seen in my
life through, which was called the grapevine. It wasn't like the
grapes that my mother use to pick. It was just a weird name given
to this certain area filled with beautiful green mountains and waters
between the mountains. It felt so peaceful as we were driving

through them. I couldn't take my eyes off of the scenery because it was so beautiful. As I sat in the back seat I thought about my life and wondered where it was going. While Barbara and her mother Antoinette talked I could tell they had a weird Momma-and-daughter relationship. They almost sounded like sisters, talking and cursing with one another. I slept most of the way after we got through the beautiful mountains.

Four hours later we pulled up to a beige two-story apartment complex. There were kids out front and music playing loud. After we walked in the door, Barbara introduced me to her sister, Viola. Viola looked at me strangely. Viola asked Barbara right out who in the hell was I. Barbara told her I was her little lady. Viola shook her head and walked in the kitchen, mumbling.
"You motherfuckers are still doing crazy shit."
"Oh baby, just showing some love." Barbara threw
her a kiss since she was a smart aleck.
She grabbed my hand.
"Let's go take a nap, baby."

We had driven to Los Angeles non-stop all the way and I was a little tired too. We went to one of the bedrooms in the back. I don't know whose room we went to, but I guess it was okay since no one said anything.

After we rested a few hours, Barbara and I went back to the kitchen where Viola and Antoinette were sitting. Barbara wanted to go driving and wanted to use Viola's car. She asked Viola if she had heard from their mutual friend named Eddie. Eddie was the man Barbara usually tricked with for extra money when she came to L.A. She told me that he was still working at the gas station up the street off of Century Boulevard. Barbara finally asked Viola if she could borrow her car. You could tell that Viola and Barbara had previous fights about using her car by the way Viola looked at her when Barbara asked.
"Look, Barbara, I don't want you fucking up my car.
I want your ass back here in a few minutes because I

remember what your stupid ass did last time you
were down here."
Barbara went over to massage the back of Viola's
back.
"Vi, don't trip, I'll be back."

Barbara got the keys, we jumped in a maroon Cutlus Supreme and
drove off. The weather was nice in Los Angeles. It had to be
about eighty degrees. Barbara knew where she was going and sure
enough, she pulled up into this Shell station. There was a short
black man walking toward the car with a big smile on his face.
    "That's Eddie," Barbara whispered.
    "Barbara! "Is that you?"

I said to myself, she must have given him some at some point. You
could see his horny thoughts coming out of his ears as he looked at
her. I didn't like it. Barbara got out of the car and motioned for
me to get out too so she could introduce me. We walked inside the
station where Eddie's office was. I had a seat while he and Barbara
went into another room and closed the door. Shortly after we got
back into the car and Barbara told me that he gave her a hundred
dollars and she promised to pay him later, in a more tangible way.
She gave me fifty dollars for spending change.

On the way back from the station, Barbara told me that we were
going downtown to the Alley where all the inexpensive clothes were.
We hopped on the freeway and before we knew it we had
transferred to three different freeways. Still, no Alley downtown
was to be found. We were soon on this narrow dark road. Night
had fallen. We had been driving a long time. Barbara was getting
worried about Viola cursing her out. We kept on going, trying to
find our way back to Viola's house since it was getting real dark.
But we were lost and couldn't find our way. We stopped by a
liquor store before getting on the freeway to get a pint of Hennessy.
Maybe if we wouldn't have drank so much and smoked so many
joints, we could have found our way home. Finally we were on a
road that was going downhill. Once we reached the bottom, we

saw a Chevron gas station. Barbara pulled up into it and staggered to go call Viola to get instructions on how to get back home.

When Barbara got back into the car, she was laughing. I asked her what was going on, and she told me that Viola was pissed and we were only twenty minutes away from the house. The directions that Viola gave were real good, because we got home within fifteen minutes. As soon as we walked in the door Viola asked for her keys. We ran to the bathroom because we had been holding our pee for hours. We raced there and Barbara beat me, but I still got in before her. Then the funniest thing that I had ever seen happened. Barbara yelled out, "Oh, shit."

I looked and couldn't believe my eyes. The toilet seat was all the way down, including the top seat. Barbara was pissing on top of the toilet and not into it! She was peeing on herself! I cracked up and couldn't stop. I almost peed on myself, it was so funny. Then, we had a weird moment after that. We sat in the corner of the bathroom and just started talking to each other. Barbara began to sing a song to herself. I was listening because she had a sexy voice. She asked me if I liked singing. I told her yes. She said we ought to write music together. Then we started putting lyrics together and words started coming out. Before long, her head was leaning on mine, with our backs against the bathroom tub. We were exhausted, and still pretty high. Barbara was so cool at times, seeming like a big sister.

After cleaning up the bathroom, we went to the bedroom to smoke a joint and plan our night. Barbara's mother and Viola were getting ready to go play bingo. After they left, Barbara found out where Viola put her keys. Barbara said we would have to be back before the break of day so they would never know that we used the car. We got dressed and started cruising again. We went to "Zody's," on the corner of Century and Crenshaw. Barbara suggested we find us something cute to go in. We ended up buying some satin pants and accessories. We went back to Vi's house and put on our new clothes. Afterward, we went back to the gas station where her friend Eddie worked. They went in the back again and this time it took about thirty minutes for her to come out. Maybe she was paying the debt she owed him.

Later that night, we went out to party and had a wonderful time at a club not far from Crenshaw and Century Boulevard. The Club had glass all around it. You could see the dance floor from the streets as you pulled up in the parking lot. The lights were going on and off. People were standing outside and on the ramps as we walked in the front door. Men were making all kinds of remarks toward us and we ignored them. I was hoping they didn't ask for any I.D. because I didn't have any. All I had was my handy long black wig, with red lipstick and high heels to make me taller. No one was at the door. We got a seat at the bar and ordered a drink. Two guys approached us to dance after about fifteen minutes. They were tall and cool looking. Barbara looked at me and said, "Let's show these people how to party." I smiled and took her by the hands. The men didn't know what to make of us, I'm sure. We danced with them, and then turned to each other and danced together. The two men came up behind us and sandwiched us in. We were having a good time. After the dance, the older guy took Barbara to the side to talk with her. When Barbara came back to the seat, she told me that she had a trick for the night that could bring us about three hundred dollars. My stomach started turning. Why did we have to do that, I wondered. I told her, cool, whatever she wanted to do, I was game. The plan was to follow them after the club closed. We were to trail them back to their house in Marina Del Rey. We followed closely behind these guys who were driving a bad ass Mercedes Benz. The traffic was crowded. They were driving real fast and so was Barbara. Then a light separated us and as we tried to catch up with them, we lost them. Barbara hit the steering wheel. Got Dammit! Where did they go? I shrugged my shoulders. Oh well, so much for that. We went home and went to bed. Barbara was so pissed. She cursed all the way home, about how much money we missed. The next morning Barbara's mother knocked on the door, telling us to get up because we were headed back to Fresno. After saying good bye, we went to the gas station to gas up. Three and a half hours later, we were exiting the freeway. Barbara's mother drove real fast. I remember a depression coming over me as we passed certain streets in Fresno. Especially when we passed Toulomne Street (my mother's street). I wondered what my mother was doing now. Did she miss me at all? I certainly missed her. We finally reached the front door of our house and went in. I grabbed a joint and a beer. I started feeling real sad all of a sudden. I guess the thoughts of wanting my mother, but knowing she didn't want me, were flooding my mind. I drank until I fell out that night.

The next day, Bobby called another family meeting. He explained that money was running low again. He also added that his part-time position at Del Monte's would be up in another week. Barbara was rehired at her old school as a teacher's assistant. It was decided that night that we would have to go to the camps more often, if need be. I felt sick. I hated the thought of having to go back to the damn camps.

As the days went by Barbara got tired of me being at home, because I wasn't going to school. She told me I was too young to not be in school. I guess that was the mother side of her coming out.
  "We will enroll you tomorrow," she said.
  "Cool," I said. I was really glad about that.

The next day, Barbara and I went up to the school. She pretended to be my older sister. I was re-enrolling in the tenth grade at Edison High School, even though I had missed quite a bit of the semester. I was glad Barbara cared enough to get me back in school.

The first day, I was dressed to a "T". I wore Barbara's suede fitted jacket with fur trim, and matching boots. I had on a sweater and blue jeans tucked inside of some suede boots. That's how the "hip" kids wore their clothes. I was in style for once in my life. As I went to the classes that the advisor assigned me, I began to see familiar faces. I saw Cheryl Harrison, and my friend Cheryl Dickson, who

I met the previous year in school. I had always loved school, because it was a great escape for me from home life. Many people were asking where I had been all this time. I told them to Los Angeles and back. They were impressed. They saw that I wasn't the little timid girl they knew in Elementary and Jr. High School.

After I came home Barbara and Bobby were looking at TV on the couch. Barbara asked me about my first day back. I told her it was fine but it really wasn't, because I was questioned all day about where I had been and what I had been doing. Most of the things I couldn't share because of the shame. So I just told the kids the cool things, like getting high and selling drugs. I told Barbara it was an interesting day and walked to the bedroom to change into something comfortable. She yelled to me, asking if anybody asked about me running away from home. I told her no, it never came up.

After I got out of the bathroom, I couldn't wait to go to the bar to fix me a drink. Barbara told me that we needed another person to work Friday nights with us out at the camps. I felt better because that would take some responsibilities off of me. Or, putting it real blunt, it would take a few Amigos off of me. She said we were going over to a friend's named Darlene and Fred for dinner to start up an orgy. Barbara told me that once that girl got a piece of Bobby's dick, she would be hooked and would do anything they asked her to do. I started wondering if that had been their original plan for me. I got sad inside, because something told me that's exactly what happened. I swallowed my whole drink and went to the bathroom to cry. I prayed to God to get me out of this game. I told God they really didn't love me like I thought they did.

Later that evening, we got really dressed up and drove over to Darlene's house. I was quiet the whole time we were driving because the truth of what I realized was so painful.

Darlene answered the door with a big smile. Darlene was about 5'3", shapely, green eyed, long blond haired white woman. Her

husband Fred was tall (6"3), medium build, black Jheri- curl
wearing man. He was very macho, with his t-shirt on and bulging
muscles. They had prepared a nice chicken and pasta dinner. It was
tasty. After dinner, Barbara poured everybody a drink and lit up a
joint. Barbara broke the casual silence and suggested that we play
cards. Barbara kept looking at Fred and smiling in that way that
she does which turns anybody on. I was thinking to myself, damn
doesn't she know that Darlene can see her? I guess it was all in the
plans. Barbara ran her tongue across her lips and asked him if we
could play strip poker.
     "Yes," Fred said without blinking.
     Darlene quickly cleared her throat. "Well, I don't
     know."
     "Oh, baby," Barbara said, grabbing her hand.
     "It's going to be a lot of fun." Barbara looked at me
     as to say, now add your little two cents.
     "Yeh, Darlene, it's going to be lots of fun," I muffled
     out.

So we picked up from the dining room table and went into the
living room, sat on the floor and began to play strip poker. Bobby
began to win more and more, and each of us had to take something
off. Before the night was over, there we sat, Darlene in her panties
and bra, me and Barbara in just our panties, and Fred with his Fruit
of the Looms. Bobby was the only one with everything on, except
his shoes, socks, and shirt. We were also getting high, from lighting
up joint after joint and passing the Hennessy bottle around.
Barbara scooted over by Darlene and put her arm around her waist.
She started massaging her shoulders. Darlene was not sure how to
respond. She was real high and feeling good by now. She had this
smile on her face that she couldn't wipe off if she wanted to.
Barbara got my attention and motioned for me to come over next
to her. I started massaging Darlene's legs, just the way I had been
taught to massage Bobby's legs. Before long, Darlene was on her
back and we were giving her a massage from top to bottom. Bobby
and Fred sat by themselves, watching us girls have fun. Then we
motioned for Fred to come join us. He jumped up. The orgy

began.

Barbara started kissing and feeling on Fred. She laid him on his back and got on top of him. Bobby unzipped his pants and took off his clothes. It was time for him to fuck Darlene. He took my hand and made me pinch her nipples while he fucked her. She started moaning louder and louder. It was feeling so good that she started calling her husband's name, who wasn't even fucking her. I saw the whole act right in front of my eyes. Bobby kept asking her if it was good to her. She kept telling him yes. I was getting madder and madder. I saw myself laying down like Darlene, being fooled and set up. She was loving it. She was scratching and holding him so tight. Hours later, all of us were all over the floor. Everybody fucked everybody. Now it was time to go home. Darlene and Fred walked us to the door and saw to it that we got in the car.

This was the plan. I was kind of quiet on the way home, because in a weird way I felt like I was being cheated on. I guess I didn't like all this sharing, because it felt like we were no longer special to one another. I didn't tell them what I was feeling, because I didn't understand it all myself and didn't want to sound like a big baby.

The next day, I came home from school but Bobby and Barbara weren't home yet. I went in and sat at the bar to fix me a drink. It was hard to have quiet moments at Barbara and Bobby's, because we were always doing something. I hadn't written in my diary since I left home. I was really feeling too ashamed these days. I had done so many bad things. I knew God was probably real mad at me about them.

GO VISIT ALMAFAYE/HOMESICK
NOVEMBER 1977

I was so depressed the day after the big orgy.   I got to thinking about AlmaFaye and my mother.   I couldn't believe I was getting homesick, but I was and had been for sometime.   Each time the thought of my family came to mind, I would get something to drink or smoke so it would go away.

The next day when I got home from school, Bobby and Barbara were not there.   I went to the bar and drank as much as I could. Barbara and Bobby finally came home hours later.
    "Hey baby," Barbara said, kissing me on my lips.
    "Guess what?"
    "What?"
    "Fred and Darlene called today and told us what a
     great time they had so I invited them over here
     tonight for dinner."

I felt that sickness in my stomach that I was so familiar with when I felt out of control. Barbara and Bobby had grocery bags and food in their hands. When I asked where her daughters were, she said they had taken them over to Madea's for the night.
    "We are going to have another exciting night, Carla,
     and after tonight her ass will be ours to work those
     camps."

I smiled and pretended that I was cool with it, but Barbara could see through my smile.   She immediately asked me what was wrong.   My eyes started tearing and I told her I missed my family. I told her I wasn't trying to, but the feelings kept coming back and I couldn't make them go away. I told her I needed to go visit my sister for a few minutes just to see her face.   Barbara was understanding. She came over and held me for a while.
    "Are you sure you want to go over there now? You

know your Momma probably reported you missing
to the police and they may be looking for you"
Barbara whispered.
"I know, but I will be real careful to watch my back."
"Okay, I hope to see you later tonight."
By Bobby's expression I could tell he didn't agree,
but he kept quiet.

Out that door I went. I skipped those streets all the way to my
sister's house, like I was Dorothy in the Wizard of Oz going home
to a familiar place. I began to feel better as I got closer and closer
to AlmaFaye's house.

The back door was not locked so I walked into the kitchen.
AlmaFaye was standing at the sink washing dishes.
"Where in the hell have you been?" she yelled.
"You know where I have been, baby!" I was trying to
be smart.

It was real nice to see her. We sat down at the kitchen table and she
passed me a beer and a joint. My regular menu as she recalled it.
We sat at the table and just talked. About one hour later Darnell
walked in the door. As soon as he spotted me, he started talking
shit. AlmaFaye told him to leave me alone. He asked me how it
felt having a pimp and a woman pimp for a living. I told him to
kiss my ass. I tried to be tough and deny everything he said, but
deep down inside I knew it was true and it hurt me so much. I then
started thinking about the orgy and Barbara and Bobby plotting to
get Darlene hooked. AlmaFaye stood up and told Darnell to get
the hell out of the house if he didn't shut up his mouth. He started
laughing, walking toward the back rooms. As AlmaFaye was going
to the bathroom, she overheard him talking with Momma and
telling her that I was there if she wanted to catch me. AlmaFaye
turned around and told me about it. I flew out of there. I could
hear AlmaFaye cursing him out when I was going out of the back
door.
"Nigga, you ought to mind your own dam business

and leave my family's business alone."

Barbara and Bobby were watching TV, when I walked in the door.
Barbara asked how was the visit? I told them it was okay, but
Darnell called my mother on me.
"See, we told your ass that it wasn't a good idea,
didn't we?" Bobby snapped at me.

The phone rang and I ran to get it, to avoid more "I told you so"
from Bobby. It was Darlene from last night.
"How are you doing, Carla?" she asked.
"Oh, fine. One moment. Let me call Barbara."
I passed the phone to Barbara and whispered,
"Darlene is on the phone."

Barbara took the phone to the pillow with her. I went to fix a drink
and go find something to eat in the kitchen. I sat at the bar as
Barbara was finishing up her conversation with Darlene.
"Bobby," Barbara said, looking at him, "you have
hooked that little bitch! She don't know what to
do! I told her we changed our minds about tonight
and let's get together tomorrow night. She almost
started crying."

Barbara and Bobby started laughing. I laughed a little bit too. She
also said that Fred had an attitude when we left, because she was
feeling too damn good.
"Give her another week, and she will have Fred doing
whatever she wants him to do," Barbara said.

The phone rang again and Barbara picked it up. It was AlmaFaye.
AlmaFaye told her that the police were on their way to get me. She
told them if they had any drugs over there, they better get rid of
them. When Barbara hung up the phone, she turned to me and
said, "Your damn Momma has lost her mind. We have to take you
to a Got damn motel for the night. Get some of your belongings
together because we can't afford for them to come here and find

you." My heart jumped and I began to get butterflies. Barbara stayed at the house while Bobby took me to find a motel.

It was cold outside. The streets were jet black, as we approached the truck stops. There was a motel on the right side of the street that looked fairly dark and vacant, except for a little light burning in the office. Bobby got out of the car and said he would be right back. There were no cars in the parking lot. I sat, nervously waiting for him, looking around at everything that moved. I thought to myself, how did I get here? I am on the outskirts of the city about to check into this cheap sleazy motel. Where will this lead, I wondered. It was so dark and scary. Truck drivers were looking into the car as they passed by. They could see how young I was and I'm sure wondered what I was doing out here this late. I don't know where the melody came from, but I began to hum these lyrics:

> It's dark and scary,
> so dark and scary,
> it's dark and scary
> So dark and skareeey
> I don't want to be alone,
> I just want to be free,
> But it seems like someone's always
> putting chains on me...

Tears began to roll down my cheeks, as I felt loneliness all around me. I didn't know what I was about to face tonight.

Bobby came back to the car. "Okay, Carla, let's go in. Everything is ready." Bobby opened the door to a little bedroom about the size of a standard living room with a TV, phone, and bathroom. Bobby closed the door behind us and I put down my little bag. Bobby brought in the bag from the store with some drinks and snack foods that we picked up along the way.

"I'm sorry you have to go through this shit, you
know?
I wish your Momma would just leave you alone.

She knows that you are not happy there."

Bobby came near me. He could see that I was shaking. I was not shaking from the cold, but from fear and nervousness. He held me in his arms and told me not to worry. He sat me down on the bed and started kissing me, whispering, "I want to be with you." He had sex with me so long that all I could do when he finished, was roll over and fall asleep. As I was drifting off , I could hear Bobby tiptoeing out of the door.

The next morning the sun was shining through the dingy beige drapes, and there was a loud noise outside the window. Trucks were pulling in and going out to their destinations. I wondered what time it was. I went to the mirror to look at myself.
"Oh well, so much for beginning school," I thought
to myself.
I called AlmaFaye to see what was happening.
"AlmaFaye?"
"Hey, girl, you better get your ass out of there. The
police are looking for you," she screamed.
"I'm not at the house anymore," I said.
"Where are you?" she asked.
"I'm at a motel on the outskirts of the city near the
truck stops." I felt so weird to be in this place alone.
"A got damn motel! That's dangerous! I know they
didn't put your ass up at the Holiday Inn, did
they?"
"Hell naw. We don't have that kind of money!"
"What the hell you mean yawl don't have that kind
of money? You don't have a job!"
I tried to clean it up real quick. "I just mean that I
know what type of money they have."
AlmaFaye didn't buy it.
"It must be true what they are saying about you,
Carla. You have been prostituting for Barbara and
Bobby." .
"I got to go. I just called to say hi!" I could hear her

say "wait."
I hung up the phone before AlmaFaye could say
goodbye.

I still needed to talk to somebody, somebody that loved me,
understood me and would not judge me. Kendon Starr! I called
his house, but his baby brother told me that he was not there and
would not be back. Then Mrs. Starr got on the phone and told me
that Kendon was in a lot of trouble and wouldn't be back for a long
time, maybe a couple of years. I broke. I couldn't stand it. I
broke down crying.
　　"Are you okay, Carla?" Mrs. Starr asked.
　　"Yes, I'm fine. I will call you later."

I got off the phone, so angry at Kendon! How come he couldn't be
there for me? Kendon, why the hell you are never around when I
really need you, I screamed aloud. I need you now! I need you
right now, Kendon! I started crying real hard. Then I got scared
that I would not be able to stop. So I made myself stop. "You can
handle this, Carla, just relax," I coached myself. I looked to the
corners of the walls where I knew the cross could be seen in the
crease of the joining walls. I grabbed a piece of paper and a pen. I
began to write to God. I didn't have my diary, but I had a pen and
used the hotel's notepad. I felt bad going to God because I had
been so far away from Him. I hadn't kept in touch, but I couldn't
help it now. I felt I would lose my mind if I didn't talk to Him.

　　Dear God:
　　Well I guess you see this mess I am in now. I don't
　　know what to do. I don't know where I'm going
　　next. I wish You could speak back to me so I could
　　hear Your voice. My life is a real sad picture to
　　watch and I'm tired. I am so tired of it all. How
　　come it just doesn't stop? God, I wish I had
　　somebody to talk to. Maybe You can somehow let
　　me know You hear me.

Before I could finish, I heard the keys turning at the door, so I put the paper in my pocket. It was Bobby.

"Oh, you scared me," I told him.

"How come you didn't knock or yell who you were?"

"I'm sorry, baby. Let's get you ready," he said.

We went back to the house. I guess during the day, it was safe to hang out, but at night I had to go to the motel. We did this until we figured the cops were not looking for me anymore.

Since I only saw Bobby and Barbara in the day time, I wondered to myself, what had been going on during the nights when I was away. I felt out of order and misplaced. The night life was still the same at the house. The drug traffic picked up some more. I noticed a few new girls coming over at night. They must have been addicts. Barbara took one girl in the back and I wondered what they were up to. I felt like I lost my special place. I asked Barbara after the last lady left, "who are these ladies to her?"

"Why? Are you jealous?" she said, with a little smile on her face.

"No! I just want to know."

Barbara told me they were some of the girls that they were trying to get lined up for the Friday camp nights. I thought to myself, "Oh no, it's that time again."

I tried to go back to school, but it just wasn't working out. My mind was busy thinking and my heart was bleeding because I missed my Momma. I missed my younger sisters and brothers too. No matter how much of a woman they tried to turn me out to be, there was still a little girl inside, yearning and aching for her family. I missed my dog Blacky.

Time went on and fast money kept rolling through the drug traffic. We kept shopping and buying a lot of clothes and jewelry. Wherever we wanted to go, we went. Whatever we wanted to do, we did, but something was still missing in my life. I still felt trapped. One day, Barbara and Bobby went somewhere and told me they would be back in a few hours. I stayed home and found myself pacing the floors, throwing questions at God. I needed answers and direction.

"How can I get out, Lord? How can I get out of this situation? Isn't there somewhere I could go to find some peace and normal living? Or, maybe I will never be happy and would just be better off dead. That way, I wouldn't have to figure a way out of this. Lord, I need You! I need to talk to somebody!"

I began to cry so hard, I would lose my breath and gasp for air. I cried for God to rescue me. The room was just silent and nothing could be heard. So I began to hum that melody I sang to myself at the motel that first night, adding even more words as they came to me.

"It's dark and scary, oh it's dark and scary...Dark and scary, so dark and scary...
I don't want to be alone, I just want to be free, but the chains of darkness won't let go of me,
The streets are dark, long and far
Never really ending, from pains to scars,
It's dark and scary, so dark and scary, it's dark and scary yes, it's dark and scary.
I want to be released, I want to find the keys that.. would unlock these doors and set me freeee
It's dark and scary, oh it's dark and scary."

A few hours later, I heard a car door slam. I turned the lights on and ran to the bathroom to clean my face. Barbara came in and yelled for me.

DECEMBER 1977

I walked out and Barbara could tell right off that I had been crying. She came over and wrapped her arms around me without saying a word. I began to cry even harder.

"Hey, baby, what's wrong? You can talk to me."

I tried to pull myself together.

"I don't know, Barbara. I was just going over my life and thinking about everything, and I just don't feel right. I am miserable here but I don't know what to do. I miss my family, but I don't want to go back to them. I love you and Bobby, but I want to finish school. I want to do the right thing in life and be somebody special for God, but it seems like I am not going to make it. Nothing is working out for me. I am so confused!"

Barbara said, "Hey, you don't have to be confused! You know what's at home, and you know what's at AlmaFaye's, and you know what's here. You have to choose for yourself what you want to do. Can't nobody tell you what to do in life. You must make those decisions for yourself, and you can. You know your mother is weird and is going to give you hell, until you leave there for good. You have lots of potential. I just don't want to see you hurt. Whatever makes you happy, that's what I want for you. I will handle whatever you decide to do."

"Thanks," I said.

"I do want to go see my sister, but I don't want to go see Momma, because I know she will start talking crazy to me."

"I don't know if that is a good idea, Carla. You know the police were looking for you."

"Yeh, but ..."

"Okay, baby, do what you want. Just be careful."

I held her and she kissed me on my forehead. For the first time, she treated me like the little girl that I was. AlmaFaye always kept her back door open. I walked in, and there she was with a beer in her hand playing "Stairway to Heaven," by the O'Jays.

"Hey sis!"

"Hey sucker! Bring your ass over here and give me a hug. What's going on?" She was drunk.

"Nothing much. How's Momma doing?"

"Oh, do you have to ask? She's getting on my damn nerves."

AlmaFaye was so frustrated with Momma, it made her mad to just talk about her. Then she changed the conversation to me. She asked me how come I never called Momma just to let her know how I was doing. I tried to tell her I couldn't bring myself to it. I was afraid of being cursed out or rejected. She told me that Momma really cared about me and missed me. I found that hard to believe. She told me how miserable and depressed Momma had become since I left. I didn't want to hear anymore about Momma.

The back door opened and it was Darnell. I jumped to my feet. He laughed as soon as he saw me. He told me to sit down and relax. That was too hard to do, seeing that Darnell called Momma on me the last time I was there. He apologized and said he would never do it again. AlmaFaye threatened that if he did it again, he would have to move. Darnell got an attitude and left.

A few moments later, there was a knock at the door and AlmaFaye said, "Now, who in the hell is this?" AlmaFaye went to the door and there they were, two white cops. They asked for Carla Lee. They were already looking into the living room at me as they looked over her shoulder. I wasn't scared. I started thinking about juvenile hall and how peaceful life might be. I would be off the streets, away from Bobby and Barbara. Away from the drugs and having to go to the camps when money was low and most of all away from Momma.

The officer asked, "Are you Carla?"

I said, "I am."

One of the officers let me know that I was going to have to come downtown with them. The cops took me by the hand and escorted me to the Fresno Police Car. I looked at AlmaFaye and she told me not to worry, she would call Momma's ass and see what she's up to. I told her to also call Barbara and Bobby and let them know what's happening. She nodded. They placed me in the backseat. The neighborhood people were looking and wondering what was going on. A crowd gathered. I had never been in the backseat of a police car. There was a glass divider that separated me from the officers. The officers were talking about something, I don't know what. Then one asked me, "So how are you doing back there?" I said, "I am fine." I began to wonder how Momma knew I was there. Then I remembered Darnell's ass. He probably went and told Momma.

We pulled into the back of the police station. One of the cops opened the back door and escorted me inside. He asked me to have a seat in the lobby. He seemed so nice. Not like the mean cops I had heard about. The walls were beige, and there was one table and two chairs in the room. The room had no windows. I thought about what had happened over the past months. I thought about how much I had to change quickly into a woman's lifestyle yet still in a child's body. I didn't even sound like myself anymore. I took on Barbara's voice, ways, and manipulation skills. I wanted my slow ways back. I wanted my youth back, but it was gone. Every time I thought about the things I had done, I would feel so ashamed. Time passed slowly while I was waiting in that silent room. I could hear noises from the outside. I heard a girl's voice screaming, "let me go." Later I heard a guy say, "Man, you wait until my attorney take care of yo ass. You won't hit another black nigga again." Then I heard men laughing and talking,"Yeh they got to find yo dumb ass first."

Suddenly, the doors opened. There were the police officers, with AlmaFaye and Momma. I looked and couldn't believe my eyes. Momma said, "Come on girl, we are going home." She didn't hug me or anything. The officers started smiling at me, as if this

warning was really effective and their little plan worked out .
AlmaFaye hugged me and said
　　　"Don't worry, baby, I wasn't going to let them take
　　　　my sister nowhere."
　　　"Thanks," I said disappointed at the rescue. One of
　　　the cops told me to keep my nose clean and stay out
　　　of trouble.

We went out of the back door and there was Momma's car. I
wanted to hug Momma so bad, but I just couldn't. I guess I was
scared of her rejection and maybe she was too. We went home, and
AlmaFaye came with us to our house. I got out the car and started
up the walkway. The kids came out with kisses and hugs. I never
realized how much they loved me. Blacky came licking and
jumping on me.

BACK HOME WITH MOMMA

It was about 9:00 p.m. when we got home. It was time for the
kids to go to sleep and the adults to stay up. Momma was going to
the kitchen, so she asked if I wanted a beer.
　　　I said, " yeh."
　　　"You do everything else out there, you might as well
　　　do it in here too. It ain't no secret," she said.

AlmaFaye shook her head as to say, "just ignore her." I didn't have
the energy anyway. I drank one beer and then another. I had to
listen to Momma's sad ass blues. I guess Momma and I would be
drinking buddies just like Gabby and her Momma. I never wanted
that type of relationship with my mother. I guess it was bound to
happen to be this way at the rate of disrespect and hatred that we
were feeling toward each other. Later that night, I crawled into my
old bed with my two baby sisters. I was happy not to be in bed
with a married man and woman. I noticed that the two twin size
beds were gone and replaced with one king size bed, big enough for
four people. I laid there, gazing through the darkness at the ceiling
wondering where my life was going from here.

CHAPTER 19

LOOKING FOR DADDY

It seemed like Momma had thought about some things while I was gone. She had a game plan. When I asked Momma, she told me that she was going to track my Daddy down. That shocked me.

The next morning was interesting. The kids had already gone to school, and Momma was in her usual place at the window, but not in her terry cloth white housecoat. She was fully dressed as if she was going somewhere. Soon as she heard me moving around, she hollered out, "We are going to visit your Uncle Randy and Aunt Ladonna." Why in the hell are we going to see them I wondered to myself, as I pulled the quilt over the sheets, making the bed up.

"Okay, Momma, I will be out of the bathroom in about thirty minutes."

"How are you going to find him, through Uncle Randy?" I asked her.

"Oh they will find him. That's you Uncle Randy's brother," she smirked with that half smile sitting on her face as she always did when she knew what she was talking about.

I had remembered Randy and Ladonna from growing up. I was introduced to them as Aunt and Uncle, but everybody was my aunt and uncle, or grandma or grandpa.

I wondered what would really come out of this. We pulled up to this yellow house trimmed in brown. We walked through the door and went inside. I wasn't up to any more disappointments and let downs. Momma yelled out to Randy, "You got any beer?"

"Yeh, in the refrigerator."

"Sit down, girl."

I hugged both my aunt and uncle. Ladonna was a dark-skinned woman who wore a press and curl hairstyle with a part on the left side and the curls going back. She also had lots of hair on the side of her face. She had sideburns and a little hair underneath her chin too. I thought that was so weird. Uncle Randy was dark too, with lots of hair on his face also. But that was normal, because he was a man, I thought to myself. Ladonna said, "Now, Doris, what is this that you were telling us over the phone about Carla?"

"Well, that's what she is here for. She can tell you
herself," Momma said.
"Carla, what did your step daddy do to you?" Aunt
Ladonna asked.

Randy walked through the living room door from the kitchen, handing Momma a beer. I thought to myself, here I go explaining this same story for the hundreth time. Why am I telling this over and over again, nobody is ever going to believe me! So I started telling her everything that I had told Momma before. After I finished telling the story, Momma asked Randy if he could reach a Travis Bynum. I heard him tell Momma, he's right up the street in Los Angeles.

"I'll call him this evening."
"Let me know when you have reached him. Tell him
it's his turn now," Momma said.

Momma finished her beer and was ready to go. On the way home, Momma and I had a conversation about my daddy. She told me that she thought I would be better off living with him.

"But, Momma, I ain't never seen my Daddy. What
makes you think he would want me after all these
years?"
"The damn nigga better want you. He ain't never did
nothing for your ass all these years. He better do
something now. Hell, you almost grown," she
hollered out.

I began to ask Momma questions.
"Momma, if this man is really my father, how come I
don't have his last name?"

"Listen, when you were born your father didn't
believe you were his and so he denied you. At the
time Tyrone Lee who is your other sisters' and
brother's father, told me I could give you his name."
Momma started laughing real loud.
"I had too many damn boyfriends, I guess."

Then she told me that she slowed all the way down because she
really liked my Daddy, but it was too late. She told me that she
almost lost her life with him one night.
"Girl, one night we were all drunk. It was your
Uncle Randy, Uncle Curtis, Aunt Ladonna, your
father Travis and me on our way to find this party in
Madera."

While Momma was telling the story she almost seemed like she was
right there reliving it again. She smiled, showing those dimples as
she talked.
"I was arguing with your Uncle Randy about being
lost. I told him that I knew his ass couldn't find shit
if you put it in his face. He kept telling me to shut
up."
Momma seemed to be enjoying her story.
"He kept telling me that I probably had the got
damn name wrong. He said he had never heard of a
club like that before. Shit I done forgot the name
now, but anyway. Curtis, another one of your
uncles, was in the back snoring and Travis was in the
front seat next to me talking shit in my ears.
"Was he my Daddy then?"
"Hell naw. You weren't even born yet. In fact, it's a
damn miracle that you are here at all."
"Why, Momma?"
"Because that was the same night that we were in an

almost fatal accident. Your Uncle Randy was drunk
and driving too fast. He hit a center divider in the

middle of the freeway and the car jumped the other
side of the freeway down a cliff. "
"Oh no. Momma was scaring me.
"I am lucky to be alive today.
"What happened?"
"They said I was thrown ten feet from the car. Your
father was hanging out of the car. Your Uncle
Curtis was still in the back snoring and Uncle Randy
was thrown a few feet from the car."
"Everyone was able to go home that night except for
me. They said I broke my hip bone and my entire
pelvic bone was cracked in two. The doctors told
me that I would never have another child again."
"But that tall, fine, black man Travis made a liar out
of those doctors. Because shortly after a year of
rehabilitation, I was pregnant with you. You came
through a broken pelvic bone trying to heal.
According to my doctors you were not going to be
born." I smiled.
"They told me that I would never have another child
in my life."
"But what happened to you and my Daddy after t
hat?"
"Well, I think he was scared or something, because I
was still kind of with your older sisters and brothers
father."
"Who, Tyrone Lee?"
"Yeh, that crazy nigga. And Travis wasn't believing
you were his."

As I listened to Momma, I didn't know whether to feel like a
miracle baby or a big mistake.   I was glad to hear Momma talk
about my Daddy, because for the first time I believed that this man
Travis Bynum was my real father.

It had been days and Momma still had not heard back from Randy
and Ladonna regarding finding my Daddy. Some nights before

going to sleep, I would sit up and think about him. What did he look like? What was he doing? Did he ever think about me? Did he have other children? Why didn't he want to own me as a baby? Why didn't he give me his name? From the time we left Randy and Ladonna's house I thought about my Daddy constantly. I had not thought about him before this because it had been so confusing trying to figure out who he was. Momma had told me over the course of time that my Daddy was four different men.   It was depending on who she hated that day. She would say, "it was that loser, or that one." But now, it was final. She couldn't change the story. Now it became a fairy tale and a dream. I was waiting for the day it would come true.

I continued to drink and smoke weed as much as I could. I would see Barbara and Bobby also, between leaving home for school and getting home that evening. Sometimes I would ditch school. I couldn't hang out with them like before and they knew it. We saw each other mostly on the weekends. When Momma thought I was going over to AlmaFaye's, I would slip over to their house every now and then to hang out and get high. I wasn't part of the family so much now, other than a buddy and partner. That was cool with me because I hated a lot of things we used to do, especially those camps.

Time went on and I had another boring Thanksgiving . This was the most depressing time of the year for me.   The three dynamic holidays: Thanksgiving, Christmas and New Year's. They brought me no joy, only pain and emptiness. Momma invited her regulars over. Before you could breathe again, Christmas was knocking at the door. The same old boring silver Christmas tree was put up with its half-cracked ornaments and tired gifts. I didn't get anything special. All I got was some house shoes. During the holidays I found myself depressed as always, because holidays never reflected their true meaning in our house. It was supposed to be love and family togetherness.   But it was only another opportunity for Momma to call her gang of friends over to party.

The end of the holidays came and went fast. Thanksgiving was over and Christmas was right around the corner. All I could think about as time seemed to drift away, was what would this New Year's have in store for me.

The latter part of the year was like none other. It almost felt like Momma and I were on even level. She treated me as if I was already about to move with my father and therefore she was at peace with me. Mr. Calvin kept his physical distance.

A few weeks after New Year's Aunt Ladonna called. She told me that she had somebody who wanted to talk with me. My heart started beating fast. Then I heard this real strong, yet gentle voice on the other line calling my name.

    "Carla?"

    "Yes," I replied, with tears forming in my eyes.

    "Hi, how are you?" he said.

    "I am fine, thank you."

    "Do you know who you are talking with?"

    I said, "Yes, I think so. Are you my daddy?"

    He said, "Yes, this is Travis. I came down to see about you. Where is your mother?"

    By this time, Momma had entered the room. I gave the phone to her and they began to talk.

    "When did you arrive? When do you want to see her?"

My heart felt like it was going a hundred miles an hour. Momma hung up the phone and looked at me with an approving smile.

    "So you are going to finally meet your real Daddy."

    "Yep. I sure am."

    "Well, go in there and get ready. They'll be here to pick you up in a few moments."

I stopped cleaning and went to find the best thing I had in my closet. I found a brown blouse, that I made in homemaking course in the seven grade, and some beige pants that I got from Barbara.

I hope my Daddy likes me. I hope I am not too ugly. I hope I favor him at least a little bit, so I can know he is my Daddy and that I am his child. My mind was racing with all kinds of thoughts as I hurried to get dressed.

About fifteen minutes later, I heard a horn blowing outside. They were here! I looked out the bathroom window, but only Aunt Ladonna and Uncle Randy came. They came in and talked with Momma until I got out of the bathroom. I heard them telling Momma that my Daddy had decided to wait at their house. I walked out.

"Are you ready?" Ladonna asked.

I said "yep" standing in the doorway.

"Doris, you ain't coming?" Ladonna asked her.

Momma said, "No. I know what that nigga looks like."

She took a drink of Canadian Mist.

"I will be over later to pick her up."

As we were walking to the car, Aunt Ladonna put herarms around me.

"Are you nervous?" Ladonna asked, as she opened my door.

"Yep, a little bit," I said. "What does my Daddy look like?"

"Aw girl! I don't know, look at your Uncle Randy. He looks like his brother."

We soon pulled up to their house and my heart began to beat faster. There he stood, my real Daddy! God, I thought I would faint in that instant. I made sure I stayed in control though. I walked in the house. There he stood in the window. He was tall, dark and very handsome. My Daddy was fine! I had an instant pride, because he wasn't a drunk or anything like that. He was a great man as far as I could see. His voice was soothing. He sounded proper, almost like white people. He looked at me and started to smile. Oh, I was so happy when he smiled. Did that mean he approved of me? Words cannot explain how I felt. I immediately thought to myself, "He came down here just for me!"

He held me and I held him. I didn't ever want to let him go. It felt awkward hugging him. He pulled away and said, "Boy you are pretty!" I said "Thank you!" and blushed, looking down at my shoes. Then he said, "I want you to meet somebody." He turned toward a lady sitting on the couch.
　　　"This is my wife, Denise."

She stood up, a tall black woman, with very beautiful soft skin and a kind smile. She gave me a hug too. She reminded me of Tyrone Sr's wife in Phoenix, Miss Estee. They had the same height and beauty. I went back to my Daddy, and we sat down on the couch and talked. He asked me about school. I finally felt like the little girl I so longed to be. I didn't feel like the whore or the freak my mother called me so often. All her names lost their evil powers in the face of my Daddy's hugs. I felt finally I had someone who really loved me. He then said, "I heard what was going on down here, and I had to come and see about you." I said, "Oh?" I was embarrassed, not knowing what to say, or not knowing how to feel about how he felt. He expressed his disgust and told me that's why he couldn't come to my house to get me. He didn't want to see the man that did this to me because he wouldn't be responsible from that point on.

Uncle Randy eventually came in the living room with the camera and said, "Hey, let's take some pictures!"

After a few snapshots, we continued to talk on the couch and discussed his family in Los Angeles. Before long they ran out of beer, and Randy came in the living room asking Daddy to go to the store with him. Daddy asked me if I wanted anything from the store. I said, "Just an orange soda." I really wanted a drink deep down inside. Maybe a shot of Hennessy to calm my nerves.

I really didn't want my Daddy to leave me for one second, but I told myself to grow up, he's only going to the store. As soon as they left, I immediately went to the bathroom. I didn't have to use it, but I had to go somewhere because I had so many emotions that needed to come out. I cried and thanked God in that bathroom for sending my real Daddy to come see about me.

When my Daddy returned, I sat right next to him on the couch again. We took a walk outside and he asked me what I thought about living in Los Angeles.
"L.A." I said.
"Yes," he said.
I said, "Whoa. I don't know, I am sure I would love it!"
"Well, me and your mother are going to talk about it."

A few hours passed and sure enough, Momma pulled up to come and get me. My Daddy and his wife were leaving that evening to go back to L.A. I didn't want him to go back home. When Momma came into the house, they started discussing things privately. I went outside to play with my cousins and the next thing I knew, the announcement came. I was going to live with my daddy in about three to four weeks. I felt so good inside! They were coming back again just for me! Afterwards, Momma said, "Well, I have to get back home. Let's go, girl." I hugged my Daddy tight.
"This is good-bye for a few weeks," he said.
"Okay," I said, not knowing if I could trust that.
He nodded and said "Okay. I'm coming back."
Maybe he saw the doubt in my eyes.
"Nice meeting you, Ms. Denise."
"You too sweetie."

It was something about her that made me believe she was not that happy about meeting me.

On the way home, my face was lit up with a big smile.

"Are you happy now?" Momma asked.

"Of course I am!" I said.

"You finally got a chance to meet that ugly man. Hah?"

"Excuse me, my Daddy's fine, Momma!" We both laughed.

"You're going to be living with him soon." Momma had a sadness about her now.

"I hope you will be happy, Carla."

"I am sure that I will be, Momma."

As Momma drove, she became silent. I thought to myself, why did Momma call my Daddy now? Was it because she really believed my side of the story, or was it that she didn't trust me with her husband? The daughter in me wanted to believe my mother was truly coming to my rescue in the best way she knew how.

Every morning after I woke up, it was the count down for my Daddy to return for me. The weeks seemed to go by so slowly. I occupied myself with school, and sitting on the porch some days with Blacky. I said good bye to everyone but Bobby and Barbara. That was the scariest thing, for some reason. I wasn't hanging with them, but I felt this tie to their lives. I guess I felt chained to people. I also felt obligated to them, like I still owed them for taking me in and buying me so many things. I didn't want to look ungrateful but I didn't want to call them either. I wanted a clean start.

Surprisingly, my days at home with Momma were much nicer. She had less critical comments about me and her husband. I guess she was fine with the fact that I was going away. I would overhear Momma on the phone with her friends telling them that she had to find my Daddy and tell his ass to own up to his responsibilities once and for all. I guess Momma was feeling proud, like she did when Alma Faye wanted to come to California. While I was washing dishes one day, in the kitchen, Mr. Calvin came through the back door. He stopped and spoke to me.

> "So I hear that you are going to live in Los Angeles
> with your Daddy."
> "Yes, I am."
> "I hope you have a good time, Carla. I really do, and
> I am sorry for all the hell I put you through."

All of a sudden I began to feel sorry for him. I felt myself wanting to hug him and say thank you. But my insides reminded me that I was supposed to hate him, not love or forgive him. So I just stood there, looking very hard, as he walked away. I fought the feelings of compassion for him.

I finally talked with Barbara and Bobby about me leaving. I told Barbara and she said, "Well, I guess you can go. It's better than going to juvenile hall. I don't want you in there." I kept saying to myself what does she mean, she guess it's okay that I can go. She ain't got nothing to say about it. Then I thought, or does she?

Later on that night, my Aunt called to tell us that my Daddy would be here the next morning between 9:00 and 10:00 a.m. When Momma got off the phone she called me in the front room to tell me. I didn't want to sleep that night at all.

CHAPTER 20

DADDY COMES BACK – FEBRUARY 1978

The next morning I was so anxious to see my Daddy again. 9:00 a.m. and 10:00 a.m. had passed. Every now and then I would anxiously look out the window. Momma would tell me to go somewhere and sit my ass down. Then the phone rang, it was Daddy. First, he talked to Momma and told her that they had just arrived in Fresno and suggested that she bring me over to Aunt Ladonna and Uncle Randy's. Momma said, "Well, can't you come and get her?" He told Momma that he didn't want to come to Mr. Calvin's home. Momma told him fine, she would bring me over.

Momma got off the phone and said "Well, girl, put your things in the car and get ready to go." Momma packed up the kids and we were on our way. As we got closer, I started getting nervous. Butterflies began to flutter inside my stomach and all my emotions were surfacing. I was looking at my little sisters and brothers. I realized that I might not see them for a long time and, maybe forever. I then looked at my mother, who I loved yet hated at the same time. Thoughts of leaving her hurt me, but it hurt more to stay with her. I realized that I had not really been that close to my sisters and brothers. Because of my resentment of having to take care of them I was mad at my sisters and brothers.

When we arrived at Aunt Ladonna and Uncle Randy's house, I saw my Daddy's green station wagon parked out front. We walked in the door and there stood my tall handsome daddy, his wife, Aunt Ladonna and Uncle Randy. But there was somebody else too that I had never seen. My stepmother introduced her daughter to me. Her name was Sharon. Sharon looked at me, and I looked at her. We smiled and said "Hello." I said "Nice to meet you" and she said, "Nice to meet you too." She was black, but she was the prettiest, blackest thing I'd ever seen. She was also tall like her mother. I had never seen such tall folks. I thought, maybe everybody in L.A. was tall. Momma was talking with my Daddy privately in the kitchen. I wondered what she was telling him about me. I am sure his wife did too. I caught his wife looking at them every now and then. I saw jealousy in her eyes. But she didn't have to worry about my mother. Shit, they were in the corner in the same house and we would be leaving very soon. Now if they were staying in town for a few days, wouldn't know what to expect.

Momma came out of the kitchen with Daddy.
>"Now look, be good, girl," she said. She came over and gave me a hug and a kiss. She whispered, "I love you."

I felt like I was going to faint and start crying uncontrollably. Her words were the words I had longed to hear. How I wished in that moment that Momma never had to let me go. That her love for me would last forever. Then I began to cry, but not Momma. Momma was as hard as a rock on the surface.
>"Alright yaw'l, get your hugs now, because your sister is going away and you don't know when will be the next time you'll see her."

Momma walked out of the house. The kids hugged me one by one. I could tell they were a little confused and had questions but didn't know how to ask them.

I hugged each of the kids for the last time and they were crying too. This was even harder than I thought it would be. Momma sat in the car waiting for the kids to come out. Her eyes were fixed straight ahead, never looking my way again. I followed them out as far as the porch and watched them get in one by one. One by one. What was she thinking, I wondered. What was she feeling inside as she sat there? Could she be hurting like me? It felt like a bitter sweet moment... Did she have any regrets? The tears were still running down my face. I wanted my tears to stop, because I was scared my Daddy would suggest that I stay here with my mother if I really didn't want to go but they kept coming. The car was finally pulling off. Soon I would have no excuse to stand on the porch. The weather was chilly and cloudy. I closed the door behind me and turned around to face my new family.

We got in the car, Sharon and I in the back seat and my step-mother and real Daddy in the front seat. As we drove off, I tried to relax. I began to think about how I would get to know my daddy, and how I hoped we could do fun things that daughters and Daddies do together. I thought about us walking in the park holding hands, going for drives around town and just talking. I wanted to talk and put all the pieces back together that were so scattered in my mind. I couldn't wait. I didn't know his middle name, his favorite color, or even where he was born. I didn't know his Daddy or his people which were my family too. Daddy interrupted my thoughts by asking me if I had ever been to Los Angeles. I had to lie and say no. I couldn't tell him that Barbara and I had been down to L.A. partying and visiting her family. I don't think he would have liked that.

Five hours later, we pulled up to this beautiful, yellow brick, trimmed house, with two palm trees in the yard. It was very dark, but the porch lights lit up the house like a Christmas tree. Inside was the rest of the family -- Clarissa, Cecilia, Travis Jr. and Dave. Only Travis Jr. was my father's blood son by his wife Denise. I learned I would be sharing a room with him. When we walked in everybody was asleep. It was very late.

Daddy brought my bags in the room in the back and showed me where I would be sleeping. Someone was already in there sleeping. It was my brother, Travis Jr., Daddy told me.

FEBRUARY 1978 - 10TH GRADE

The next morning when I woke up I felt kind of weird, not knowing what to expect. I stumbled going to the bathroom. When I came out, Ms. Denise was coming out of the bedroom.
"Good morning, precious," I was greeted
"Good morning, Ms. Denise."
"As soon as you get ready, I'm taking you shopping

for some school clothes, okay?"
She had the sweetest voice you ever wanted to hear.
"Sure, thank you." I wondered if it was real.

When I came in the kitchen, I looked at the house I would be living in now. Boy was it beautiful in comparison to where I used to live. They had a beautiful brown furniture. Everything was beautiful compared to my mother's thrift shop mix-match furniture.

I was looking for my Daddy to be up by now.
       "Is my Daddy up yet?"
       "Your dad works late, so he sleeps late. We must be
       at work no later than 3:30 p.m."
       "OK," I said.
       "But you will see him before we go to work today."

Ms. Denise told me that I was scheduled to start Crenshaw High School the next morning.
       "We are going to buy you some pretty things," she
       said again.

I was happy to get all the new stuff she was buying me. Until I met AlmaFaye, Barbara and Bobby I never had this kind of treatment. Now my new family was buying me things too. That was so cool, I thought.

Driving down Crenshaw Avenue and Manchester Boulevard, things began to look familiar to me, but I didn't say anything about it. Los Angeles streets were so wild to me. It just seemed like a fast-paced place with a lot of people out on the streets, unlike Fresno.

Ms. Denise used the time we were driving around to fill me in on some of the ins and outs of the house and what every body does.
       "Your father is a Deputy Sherrif for the County of
       Los Angeles." Wow, that made me feel proud.
       "And I am a Registered Nurse for County General
       Hospital.". Your Daddy and I work the same

shifts -- 3:30 p.m. to 12:00 midnight.
"That's late at night."
"Yeh, you children will be asleep each night when we
get home except for weekends."

After she talked about their jobs and the hours, she went on to talk
about the bus I would be catching. After all that information, I was
tired of talking. I didn't want to tell her that though. She was so
nice, plus she was buying me things too. Then finally, she talked
about the rotating chores that I would be apart of. I didn't want to
know anything about any more house cleaning and chores. I had
done enough to last me my whole life. But I smiled and listened.
Then she said, "I know that I am not your mother. So you can keep
calling me Ms. Denise or Mommy which ever makes you feel
comfortable."
        "Mommy feels comfortable to me," I said.
        I thanked her and starting from that moment I
        always called her Mommy.

After a full day of shopping we came home to a long-faced girl.
Sharon had heard we were out shopping. I don't quite know what
was wrong with her but it didn't feel too comfortable being around
her. Daddy spoke to me as I was on my way back to my bedroom.
        "Hey, how was your day?"
        "It was good." I had butterflies speaking to him.
        "You're getting ready for school tomorrow right,"
        Daddy hollered from the other room.
        "Yep," I answered.

Before long Mommy and Daddy were headed for the front door to
leave for work. The only people home were Travis Jr. and Sharon.
Travis Jr. was in the living room watching television with Sharon.
After I put everything away, Mommy and Daddy introduced me
to Travis Jr. He was short with me, not taking his eyes off of the
television really.
        "Alright kids, we will see yaw'l tomorrow," Mommy
        said as they were going out of the front door .

They were in their work uniforms. My father had a gun on his side and she was in her all white nurse uniform. They looked good.

The evening was very quiet after Mommy and Daddy left. Both Sharon and Travis Jr. were quiet and did not talk with me. I felt so misplaced, as if I didn't belong or nobody wanted me there. They would laugh with each other about things that were on the television, but would never invite me to laugh with them. The television show "Good Times" was on. I still laughed. I laughed to myself. I went to bed right after it went off. I didn't want to stay up with Sharon or Travis Jr. because I knew they didn't want me there. I could feel it. Why are they treating me like this, I wondered. Sharon was so nice when I met her in Fresno, but now she has changed. I laid in my bed and just talked to God.

The next morning, Mommy was knocking on my door.
> "Carla. Wake up. It's time to get ready for school."
> "Okay, Mommy, I'm getting up."

I couldn't sleep most of the night. I didn't fall asleep until I heard my Mommy and Daddy come home and closed their bedroom door.

We pulled up to Crenshaw High School. Boy it was huge compared to most of the schools in Fresno. Once we arrived we ran into one minor problem. Daddy didn't have papers showing he had legal custody of me and my last name was different than his.
> "Your mother is going to have to come down here
> and register you, Carla."

I felt so bummed out. I didn't want my Mother coming to LosAngeles. Daddy called Momma as soon as we got home and told her what happened. Momma told him that she would be there in the morning.

The next morning, Momma and AlmaFaye came down on the

Greyhound Bus and registered me in school. It was nice to see them for that brief moment. As soon as Momma signed her name, I was rushed to my classes. Before I left, Momma told me that she would not be in town after I got out of school. She was going right back to the bus station. I hugged her and AlmaFaye and thanked them for coming. It made me feel real important.

I had a lot of catching up and proving myself to do. Starting a new school in the last part of the year with a new curriculum was going to be a challenge. The school was so big. It was three times the size of Edison High in Fresno, and there were so many students. Too many damn kids if you ask me. I heard cursing and grown-up conversations, as I passed them in the hallways. It was so different than country Fresno. You could tell the difference between the hard core group and the proper group. Their style of dressing was very fashionable and hip. They even looked like grown-ups. Maybe it's something in the L.A. food and water that made them look so mature and developed. I could tell that it was going to be pretty interesting going to a L.A. school. That first day, I collected all my books and assignments. I stayed to myself for the most part and went straight home after school.

After getting home, I noticed Daddy and Mommy were gone to work. This would happen everyday. I would already miss Daddy by the time I would come home from school.

When I walked in the door from school, Cecilia and Clarissa were in the living room watching TV, and Sharon and Travis Jr. were in the kitchen fussing about something. I guess Dave was still gone. I spoke to everyone and they spoke back politely, except for Sharon and Travis, Jr. Their hello was kind of weak. Cecilia asked how was my first day. I said, "it was pretty interesting." I went on down the hallway to put up my books and change clothes.

When I finished changing, I didn't know whether to stay in my room, or go out and continue to mingle. I chose to go mingle. I first went to the kitchen to get some water and try to break the ice with Sharon. "Where's the drinking cups?" "They're over there," she pointed. "Thanks," I said. I used the faucet and got some ice out of the crowded freezer. I had never seen so much food in a refrigerator in my life. I sat in the living room and watched TV with Cecilia and Clarissa. They asked me questions about Fresno. I told them the boring sides of Fresno, which consisted of the schools, the limited shopping areas, and the out-datedness compared to L.A. I liked Cecilia and Clarissa. They were older and real nice to me. Cecilia asked if I left a boyfriend back in Fresno. I smiled and I thought to myself, "Not only a boyfriend, a girlfriend, a married couple, and a dog friend too." I just said, "A boyfriend kind of, nothing serious." By this time, Sharon came in the room with Travis. They sat on the floor to the left, kind of staring at me from a distance. They were not being friendly at all. Most of the evenings were quiet between Sharon and Travis Jr. On the other hand, Cecilia and Clarissa were nice. They were out of the doors once they knew Mommy and Daddy were long gone, flying to their boyfriend's houses for the rest of the evening. I kept wanting the weekend to come so I could see and talk to my Daddy.

The first weekend came and I understood we were going over to Momma Johnnie and Big Momma's house. These were relatives of Ms. Denise. Her Grandmother and her Mother lived together. In fact, they had a four generation family. Anyway, we went to this house that had lots of people everywhere. They were standing outside in the front yard, on the side of the yard, and in the back of the house. Kids were running around, laughter was in the air, and music was playing loud. Sharon and Travis immediately started hugging and kissing on all the relatives. There were young people, middle aged people, and a few senior citizens there. I stayed by Mommy's and Daddy's sides. Then the introducing began. Mommy took me by the hand and introduced me to her grandmother and her mother as Travis' daughter, Carla. I politely spoke and shook their hands.

We went to person after person for introductions. The more

Mommy said, "This is Travis' daughter," the more I saw shock on
their faces. How come my Daddy wasn't introducing me, I kept
wondering. Shouldn't he be introducing me? Maybe, he was too
embarrassed, or was it the fact that it was her family and not his?
Whatever the excuse, I wished my Daddy was proud enough of me
to want to introduce me to the world. Soon, I began to feel like the
forgotten daughter. Then we got to some younger people, cousins
and nieces.

All of a sudden, I had cousins in this family. Sharon was standing
by a girl named Sandy when Mommy introduced me to her.
Sandy was polite and spoke to me.
    "Hi, Carla. Nice to meet you, cuz."
    "Nice to meet you, too."
    "I'm sure Sharon probably told you that I go to
    Crenshaw too. Maybe we can meet up for lunch."
    "Yeh, that would be cool," I said.

I didn't want to look at Sharon because I could feel her anger
oozing out of her eyes at me. Sharon turned her head away from
our conversation. That day was long and odd. I could not wait to
leave. I didn't know anybody, and didn't want to know anybody at
that time. I was glad when Daddy said he was tired and ready to
go home.

The next day was Sunday, and Daddy and Mommy had to go to
work by 3:30, but again Daddy didn't get up until 11:00. He
stayed almost an hour in the bathroom showering and shaving, only
to rush out to eat lunch that Mommy had prepared. Then off to
work they went. He said hello to me as I was coming out of my
bedroom and kept going.

After a few months, I would watch Sharon and Travis go into
Daddy and Mommy's bedroom to talk with them when they
would get home late at night. They would run in their room and
play until Mommy would tell them to leave and go to their own
rooms. I didn't feel comfortable enough to just go in and jump on

the bed, nor was I ever invited. I would just sit in my room and listen to their playful conversations. I noticed that my new Mommy wasn't as friendly and sweet anymore, at least not to me. I would come out of the room every now and then and stick my head in their door to say hello to each of them. Daddy would say, "How are you doing, girl?" I said, "fine." "How is school coming along?" he asked. "It's good". The answers would be quick and short. I felt after I answered the questions, it was time to keep going. I didn't know what else to say. Then after a certain time, their door would shut. I wished so many times that my Daddy would come home and sit at the table with me and talk. But instead, we were like two ships passing in the night. I started getting discouraged and lonely. Even though Sharon and I went to the same school, she never once asked me to meet for lunch or anything. I would see her with our cousin Sandy and other friends, but she didn't even want to claim the fact that she knew me. It was making sense to me. Sharon was the baby girl before I came and I guess I walked in on her parade. Her quiet, distant treatment became bold and verbal. She started telling Travis Jr. to not be friends with me. That made things more difficult. At least when he and I were in our room he would talk briefly to me.

One afternoon while I was in the kitchen, I over heard Sharon say, "She ought to stay in the back room, because nobody likes to be around stray dogs." Travis started laughing. I placed the cup in the sink and went directly to my room. Her words hurt me and I began to fear her. From that moment on, I would stay in the bedroom unless Mommy and Daddy, or Clarissa and Cecilia, were home. I knew Sharon wouldn't pull that stuff then, because she was always portrayed as "Little Miss Nice Girl" around the rest of the family. Travis Jr. and Sharon started calling me names every day.

After two months of their evil stuff, I began to get tired of it. I started taking my time coming home from school. I found a nearby liquor store where young men stood outside. I paid one guy a dollar of my allowance to buy me an Old English 800. He was grateful and came right back out with my tall can. I drank it on

the way home so that I could be a little high.   I repeated this for
the next few weeks.

Sharon and Travis Jr.'s name calling and teasing continued. In fact,
it felt like she hated me more and more every day. I decided
within myself that I could not take anymore and that the next day I
would tell my parents.

The next evening after Mommy and Daddy got home from work,
I knocked on their door. Mommy said, "Come in."   Daddy was
taking off his gun belt.
     "Well, come on in and sit down," Daddy said.
     "Baby, what's on your mind so late, shouldn't you be
     asleep?"
     "Yeh, but I can't sleep. I need to talk to both of you
     about something."

I told them how Sharon and Little Travis had been treating me.
The only response came from my Daddy. In fact, he could have
kept his damn mouth closed.
     "Carla, you have to get along with everybody because
     they have to get used to you. It's an adjustment that
     we all have to try and make."
     "I have tried, Daddy."
     "Well, you are just going to have to try harder and
     give it some time. Furthermore, I understand that
     you haven't been coming straight home from school.
     What's going on with that?"   I looked up, shocked.
     "Who told you that?"
     "Sharon told me that, and she should have. You are
     new out here and you have to obey the rules of this
     house. Everybody comes straight home from
     school, unless permission has been given."

I couldn't even argue. He said what he had to say and that was
that. I left and went to my room. I couldn't believe how the tables
were now turning on me. So Sharon had been telling them lies

about me all along. They were not saying a thing to me until now. I lied and told him, "I had to sit with some of my teachers from time to time to get extra help on my homework." I wished I could have told him that I was getting high to numb myself before coming home to his evil children.

I went back to my room and thought about my life again. I began to see that I was really not in a better place, just a different place. The shit was happening here too. The same feelings were present in this house too. I still felt like I didn't really belong to anyone. I felt like my mother was jealous of me. I felt I didn't have a father who was there for me and loved me. I needed so bad to talk with somebody who could understand me. I didn't have a diary. The two that I did have were full. I talked to God that night, looking up at the ceiling in the crevices of the corner of the room.

The next day I took a chance and tried to confide in one of the older sisters, Cecilia, about how I was feeling. Cecilia told me that "It's an adjustment and everybody don't make adjustments well." I said, "But why doesn't Sharon or Travis Jr. like me?" She explained that they were the babies of the family and I was a threat to that.
>"How could I be a threat, I never get a chance to talk
>to my Daddy. I never get a chance to be close to
>him like them."
>"It might get easier with time. Just give it some
>time, Carla."

Cecilia was trying to leave so that she could go visit her boyfriend Juan. She didn't have time to stand there and talk with me.
>"It's already been four months! How much more
>damn time?" I asked?
>Cecilia shrugged her shoulders.
>"I got to run honey, just give it a little more time.
>Remember, nobody knew anything about you and
>it's still kind of a shock."

Right in that moment, I didn't want to live anymore and the only person I could tell that to was God. I told God I was tired of being so alone and unloved. I wished I had some drugs, liquor, or anything that could make this painful reality go away. After two more months of Sharon's shit, I decided that I would go out and find me some friends to be with.

One day at school during break I noticed a crowded area where most of the kids stood. You could tell there were a lot of things going on in that crowd. I found out that there was a hangout place called the "tunnel" on the other side of the crowd. Drugs were sold there. The tunnel was located in the center of the school. It was like an underground pathway that connected the school to the outside street area. Then I saw a girl that was in my first period class named Sheila. Sheila always had a cheerful face on. She looked like Chaka Khan by the way her natural looked. It was big, curly and covered most of her cute dimpled face. She was a little on the chubby side too, like Chaka. She was talking with a guy standing near the tunnel. I decided she would be the one that I would make my friend.

"Hey, what's happening, aren't you in my first period class?"
"Yeh, I am. I remember seeing you in there. You always so quiet though.
"Yeh, because I'm new out here to the LA area."
"Cool, where ya from?"
"A little country place called Fresno."
"I ain't even never heard of that place."
We laughed.
"What's happening out here?" I asked her.
"Nothing much, just trying to get a buzz before s second period."
"I heard that. Where can I get turned on to some?"
She said, "This is the man here." She was pointing to a guy that had was handing another girl a bag. I saw it was marijuana.
"Alright, let me get a joint."
"That will be one dollar."

"Is it good?" I asked reaching in my back pocket."
"Yeh, it's homegrown, but it's bad."
"Damn man, in Fresno homegrown usually goes for
fifty cents."

After I got the joint, Sheila and I went around the corner to smoke
it. It was good. I knew I would get a good buzz off of it.

We started talking about one another's families and found out that
we had so much in common. Sheila had two kids already. She had
her daughter at the age of 14 by her stepfather. I damn near threw
up. She says her mother still doesn't know that it's by her husband.
Damn I felt so sorry for her. I couldn't imagine what I would do if
Mr. Calvin made me pregnant. I would probably have to kill
myself and the baby. We made a pact that day that we would be
each other's play sisters and would be there for each other.

Before we went to class, she introduced me to some of her home
boys and home girls. Now, instead of standing by myself looking
like some kind of stupid lost nerd, I was hanging with the "in
crowd." Sheila and I hit it off great. We spent all of our lunch
breaks together getting high.

A week later, I noticed Sharon and my cousin Sandy hanging out in
the tunnel. Her back was turned toward me. She turned around
and didn't see me coming. Before she knew it, she said hello to me.
She was taking a bag from the same contact I found with Sheila. I
was so happy, she couldn't say shit to me. I thought to myself, now
let her ass go and tell Daddy this shit.
        "Hey Carla, how are you doing?" Sandy said.
        "Girl, I'm cool, just trying to get high." Sharon
        looked and smiled.
        "See you later on at home," Sharon rushed off.

I noticed that the homegrown wasn't getting me high enough and I
wasn't buzzing like I wanted to. I asked Michael the dope man if
he knew where I could get something a little stronger. Sheila was

worried.

"What the fuck do you want, Carla?"

"Just something I can feel, shit! This is elementary
shit!"

"Look, what you need is further down the tunnel.
They got that lovely shit, if you can handle it.
Ask for Damon."

Michael pointed to the end of the tunnel. Sheila was shaking her
head no. I was shaking my head yes.

"You don't understand girl, I need something
that's going to take some pain away right now."

"Well, it may take more than you want it to take
away. People that fuck with that shit be tripping
out girl."

"It's cool girl, I have had some pretty weird shit
before I came to L.A. so don't worry."

I walked up to a brother with long pressed hair, glasses and gold
rims. He was smooth. His clothes were tough, kind of like Bobby's
back home. He was matching from head to toe. He even had
gold rings on every finger.

"Yeh, baby, what cha aimon from Damon?"

He had his own little riddle too.

"I just want something better than some
homegrown."

"Well, I got some volumes, speed..."

"What you got to smoke?"

"We got the best lovely on this side of town. Can
you handle it? You only need two hits of the shit
and then you're tight."

"Fine, give me a few volumes and a couple sticks
of your lovely."

He handed me the lovely stick and gave me a bag of volumes. As
everybody was going back to their classrooms I went to the ladies'
room. The final bell would be ringing in five minutes for those

that were still out trying to get to class on time.

I went into an empty stall and lit the lovely. I hit it twice and choked so bad I thought I would die. I sat there for a moment and nothing seemed to be happening. I thought the brother may have bullshitted me out of my five dollars. I hit it about four more times and wrapped it back up in the foil paper. As soon as I tried to reach back to put it in my pocket, I felt myself falling back into the wall behind me.

I saw the room in a daze. The wall had separated and the floor seemed to be coming up. I slid down on the floor because I felt so unbalanced I just knew I was going to fall over. It hit me so hard. The guy's voice came to me when he said don't hit it more than two times. It was too late for that shit. I had hit it six times. I felt sick, but I couldn't feel my mouth to throw up and began to feel numb all over. I wasn't able to move because I couldn't feel my feet, so all I could do was sit against the wall. The noises from the outside sounded as if they were echoing far far away. It felt so spooky. I felt like I was out of the realm of earth but still slightly attached to it. It was so spooky.

The next thing I knew, Sharon came in the bathroom and saw me leaning up against the wall. She came up to me and asked me if I was alright. I muttered that I kinda got messed up with some bad shit. I couldn't even feel my throat moving. I was hoping she could hear me. She told me don't go to my class, just wait there and chill out until you come down. I wanted to tell her so bad, "Shit, I can't even move let alone go to some damn class." She returned with a carton of milk and told me to drink it all.

I fell asleep on that floor and the time I came to people were around me trying to wake me up. I lied and said I had cramps so bad I took pain reliever medicine that put me to sleep. I don't know where Sharon went. I even questioned myself if I really saw Sharon or was I so high that I thought it was her.

As I rode the bus home, I was wondering if it was my sister and if she was going to tell on me, but she didn't. After that Sharon and I began to talk to each other little by little.

MAY 1978

I'll never forget the night after Mother's Day. I asked Mommy if I could call my Momma long distance to wish her happy Mother's Day. I could tell it didn't sit well with her because she told me that we have to be mindful about the phone bill.

Later that night I overheard Mommy and Daddy arguing. She was still talking about the phone bill and other things that I couldn't make out too well. I didn't call my mother that often, so the bill should not have been that high. Plus, my mother called me most of the time. Then I heard her scream at my daddy that he should have told her about me.

"Travis, you should have told me."

Daddy kept silent, I couldn't hear him at all. I know she was referring to me, because Daddy told me that he didn't tell her that he had a daughter until the day he exited off the freeway in Fresno to come get me. He told her at that very moment that he was there to see about his 14 year old daughter. Then I heard her scream again.

"Ever since she's been here things have not been
the same, Travis! I am sick of this shit."
"Well, Denise, what do you want me to do?"

I finally heard my Daddy say something. He sounded so damn weak. How come he couldn't have said, "Shut the fuck up and let me be with my daughter?" How come he sounded like a wimp? Plus, I didn't know what things had not been the same, seeing that she never complained to me about anything. As far as I was concerned she kept my Daddy locked up in that back room, or he hid from me and acted like I didn't exist.

The more she hollered the more I felt like a misfit. I wanted to talk to somebody, but who? There was nobody around. I dare not call my mother and listen to her laughing in my face. I wished I could leave out the door and get high. I thought about that lovely and changed my mind about that. I finished my hair, rolled over and placed the covers over my head to drown her voice out. I whispered a prayer to God.

> "God I just wish I had one somebody that loved and cared for me. It's been a hard 15 years and you already know it has. I don't know what else to do. I wish I could come be with you and just be there. Please don't make me stay down here too long. I don't know how much I can take."

The next morning I woke up feeling so depressed from the night before. I thought about the volumes in my pocket. I laid there in my bed, not wanting to get up for another day of "All In The Family." All kinds of thoughts started coming to my head about taking my life. People don't care if I died, I found myself saying out loud.

> "I thought there was hope for me when I met my Daddy."

That was a joke. I started rocking back and forth like I used to see my baby brother Edwin do. My heart was in so much pain. I felt I had my answer and felt nothing else really mattered at this point. Ending it all would take care of everything and I wouldn't be everybody's problem.

Later that evening, after Mommy and Daddy left, I was waiting on everyone to go out and play. Now Sharon had a boyfriend next door too, Juan's brother. Travis Jr. was away somewhere, I wasn't sure where. No one else was left in the house but Cecilia, and I knew she would soon be leaving too. I began to write in my note book.

> "I'm so tired, God. I am so tired. Please let me come

home to live with you. I want to take these pills, fall asleep and wake up in Your arms. You always love me and You never make me feel bad. I just want to be in your arms where the evil people are not. Please let me come home to you. Nobody cares Lord, but you and Blacky. Blacky is too far right now. Nobody seems to care about me on this earth. I know You do. I just want the pain to stop."

I went to the bathroom, and Cecilia was in the hallway. She spoke to me on her way out of the house. Then she turned around again and said, "Hey how's it going?"

"It's alright, you know."

"What have you been crying about?"

I didn't want her to know. I tried to hide my tears.

"I'm just not happy Cecilia. I'm just not happy."

"I know that feeling, Carla."

She took a deep breath. "I just have to wait until I get on my own, you know?"

I nodded my head, not knowing what her frustration could have been.

"Look, I know you haven't been the happiest here, and I'm sorry about that, but I'm happy to know that you are a cool person. You just need to be given a chance, you know?"

Her words made me feel like she cared and understood. But maybe it was a little bit too late.

"Just give Dad a chance to find his way to you, okay? He's new to this thing. When we met him, he had no kids and adopted us as his own, until he and Mommy had Travis Jr."

I kept hearing "He had no kids when they met him."

"But he had me. He did have a kid," I told her.

"You know what I mean. Please give him a chance."

"Cecilia, I just want to die. I don't have any more
chances to give."
I started crying and the tears would not stop.

Cecilia grabbed me and held me. That was the first hug I received
since I had been in that house.
"Carla, I'm so sorry it's been so hard for you.
Hold on, please, honey. It's going to change. You
just have to be strong and not let them make you
give up!"
"I already did."
"No, you can't, baby girl. You have to be strong."

She let me cry in her arms. As I wept in her arms I felt so good but
guilty at the same time because I knew I was holding her up from
seeing her boyfriend. I tried to stop so she could go and be with
him. She held me tighter.
"I was going to kill myself, Cecilia, because nobody
cares for me."
"How were you going to do that?" she yelled and
sounded like she was panicking.

I pulled the pills out of my pocket and showed her the volumes.
She made me flush them down the toilet.
"Listen, you have to live for me. I care for you.
Forget everybody else. You are important to
me. You hear me."

She was yelling and shaking me at the same time.   I smiled and
laughed at the same time.
"Yes, okay. I understand." We both started
laughing together.

My tears turned into joy. I felt like I had the one person in the
world that cared about me. After I flushed the pills down the toilet,
I promised her that I would not commit suicide without letting her
know. She made me promise her I would let her know.

After I calmed down she went on next door to visit with her boyfriend. I finished my chores because it was my turn to clear the kitchen that night.

CHAPTER 21

GOING HOME FOR THE SUMMER – 11TH GRADE

June finally came and I was so happy that the school year was over. I couldn't believe I had been with my Daddy for only four months. It felt like ten years of hell. When I came home from school that day he asked if I wanted to go to Fresno for the summer. I was so happy. Daddy made sure I knew I would be returning after the summer was over. I went into my room and started packing immediately. I couldn't wait to go. I was leaving the next morning.

The bus ride was beautiful as always. I loved seeing the mountains in the grapevine. It was sunny and clear. I pulled out a sheet of paper and began to write. I didn't know it at the time, but I wrote a poem about my best friend "Blacky."

He's My Best Friend

I have a best friend that I love
I know he was sent to me from above
and he loves me back, that's a fact
Can you understand
He's my best friend
He can hear me when I laugh and when I cry
he lays next to my feet
and never leaves my side
because he's my best friend
I know he's not a boy
and no he's not a girl,
but he's the only friend I ever had
in the whole wide world
When I'm sad and when I'm ill
he holds his head down
I know, my pain he can feel,
because he's my best friend,

you understand.
My best friend can hear, he doesn't mind to listen
he stands at attention, with his panting breath and his
eyes that glisten
because he's my best friend
He stands near me always to protect
when he doesn't trust
you will know the mark
because he will make a circle around you and
then begin to bark
because he's my best friend you understand?

I laughed to myself while I was writing because it sounded so cute. I pictured Blacky and the thoughts tickled and brought me so much joy.

When the bus pulled into the Fresno depot, I could see Mr. Calvin waiting. I wondered to myself why didn't Momma come and get me. Why would she make me ride with this child molester? Maybe that was her way of punishing me.

"How are you doing down there in L.A.?" he asked.
"Oh, it's cool." I tried to avoid any details.
"Sorry, it didn't work out for you."
"What do you mean it didn't work out for me?" I
asked.
"Doris told me you had to come back here because
you were having..."
I interrupted before he could finish his sentence.
"She's lying, she asked me to come home to help her
with the kids."
"Oh maybe, I got the story wrong!"

I told Mr. Calvin, he didn't have the story wrong, we both had a piece of Momma's stories. It was silent after I said that. I was so happy that the house was only five minutes away.

Momma was sitting in her faithful place. As soon as I put one foot on the ground, Blacky was right there wagging his little tail. "Hey boy, hey boy," I patted him with the one hand I had available, holding my bag with the other.

"I'll be back as soon as I get these things out of my hands Blackie," I said.

I walked in the door. Momma stood up and hugged me.

"Sorry," she said.

"How are you doing, Momma?"

"I am fine, I guess" looking away, shrugging her shoulders.

Momma was sitting there in her robe as if she had just woke up. AlmaFaye was sitting there too, I hugged her next.

"Hey girl, good to see you back down here where you belong. I told Momma I missed my sister, and we got our heads together and came up with a good one, huh?"

I looked at her and both of them started laughing.

"I should have known that you two were up to something. But it's cool, it was probably good timing anyway" I admitted.

"Why? Were you tired of them, or were they getting tired of you?"

"I think both. That wife of his was tired of me. Her kids were tired of me and Daddy wasn't saying nothing."

"Girl, go take your bags in the room," Momma said.

When I walked to my old room to drop my things on the bed. I could feel all my emotional trauma. It almost felt like a spirit was there. I couldn't explain it. When I came out of the room Momma handed me a beer.

"So did you terrorize their home down there?" Momma asked.

"No I didn't."

"What was it like living with Travis?"

"At first it was nice, but then it got real quiet."
"What do you mean quiet?"
"That woman of his is so possessive, she don't let you
get close to him."
"Well, how close do you want to get to him?"
"I just wanted to know my real Daddy. That's all. Is
that so terrible?"

I decided to go sit on the porch and talk with Blacky. I grabbed
my tablet and called Blake. He came running.
"Hey boy, I wrote something about you. You want
to hear it?"
Blacky kept jumping up and down, rubbing his head
up against my hands.

Before AlmaFaye went home she said she wanted to tell me
something privately. Momma was in the bathroom.
"We're having a party tonight," she whispered.
"Oh yeh? Cool."
"Don't say anything to Momma."
"Trust me, my lips are sealed."

That night I went home with AlmaFaye and told Momma that I
would be back in the morning.
"Now the reason I didn't want Momma knowing
about the party over here tonight is because she has
gotten so controlling and crazy. She would try to
run the whole damn thing" AlmaFaye said.
"So Momma hasn't changed."
"Hell naw, I wished she had. Listen, I got some
Columbia, you want some?"
"Hell yeh. I hope it's good, because L.A. has some
good shit down there."
"Ah nigga please."
"I'm serious. L.A. shit make Fresno shit taste like
sunflower seeds.

A few hours later, people started coming to the party. I saw some familiar faces and a few strange faces. One of the faces was Tim, and as soon as he spotted me he ran over to me.
"Hey baby, what's happening city girl?"
"Nothing much, Tim." I tried to ignore him.
"Oh yeh, you must be hip now."
"I was hip when I was here, Tim, now get out of my
face."

He was stinking. He came to the party drunk as usual. I felt them come through the doors and it made my heart jump. It was Barbara and Bobby. I was real happy on one hand and scared on the other. We talked, got high and planned on seeing each other before I went back to L.A.
"I know you're going to spend some time with us
at the house, ain't you?" Barbara said.
I said, "Sure, of course."

I missed Barbara. I missed the closeness that I had with her. I missed Bobby too, but not as much. I wanted to go with Barbara and Bobby that same night, but I knew AlmaFaye would have been through with me. I felt starved for love and attention. I knew they would give it to me.

The next day I had a hangover from drinking and smoking too much. I hadn't had one of those things in months. The entire time I was in Fresno Barbara and Bobby kept me quite entertained and AlmaFaye gave me whatever I thought I wanted. I tried to stay away from Momma as much as possible, but I had to come home to babysit and cook for her.

The summer was coming to a quick end. The night before I had to leave, I made sure I got good and high. I drank enough to last me the entire year. I laid in my bed thinking and talking to God as I reflected on all that I had done that summer. I thought about AlmaFaye and saying good-bye to her again. It felt like a bitter sweet moment. I always felt so secure with her and being around her, but knew there would always be a time I'd get into it with her about something. Even though we had our crazy fights and arguments, one thing I did know and that was that she loved me. I thought about Barbara and Bobby too. I laughed to myself hearing Bobby say, "You know you can always come back home to us if things don't get any better." I laughed because I knew now that wasn't home at all. It was just another place to stop off at through life. I felt I could never ever go back there to live.

The next morning I was scheduled to get on the 7:00 a.m. bus. When I woke up Momma was already at her window. I tiptoed behind her and snuck a hug from the back. She jumped in my arms. I laughed.

"Alright girl, if you don't want a cigarette in your
eyes, you better watch who you try to sneak up
behind."
I laughed so hard, because she couldn't go anywhere.
I had her.
"Ah Momma, you wouldn't burn your baby girl
would you?"
"Hell, my baby girl brought it on her own self." She
laughed and pushed my arms away from her.

I grabbed the phone and called for a cab to come and take me to the bus station.

"You all ready to go back to your sweet stepmother's
house?"
"Funny, Momma. Real funny."
"I really hope things get better for you and your
father.
He can be a nice man, he just too damn quiet."

Talking to Momma like this was so emotional for me. I wished I could hold on to her sober conversation forever. That's the Momma I wanted to get to know. The one I would sometimes see early in the wee wee mornings before the mid-to-late morning booze would roll around.

Before I left I went back into the room and kissed my sisters on their foreheads. They were still sleep. I went in the den and kissed the boys too.

"Tell them I love them, Momma, when they wake
up."
"Alright baby, and you take care of yourself."
"I love you, Momma".
"Yeh, me too."

I hated when Momma said "me too," but I accepted it for now. The cab driver blew the horn.   Blacky was out front waiting, wagging his tail. I patted him and told him I loved him.

CHAPTER 22

RETURN TO LOS ANGELES – NEW HOUSE

I didn't realize I would be so nervous and scared to return to L.A., but I was. I was praying that my Daddy's family had changed a little bit when I got back, especially Sharon. I prayed that she and Travis Jr. would like me. I also prayed that my Daddy's wife would change her feelings about me. I just hoped things were better.

Daddy was there on time to pick me up from the bus station. I gave him a big hug. He was by himself. I was so glad.
> "Where's everybody at?"
> "Well, some are at home, and some are not at home anymore."
> The crowded lobby separated Daddy and I while we walked back to the car.
> "Since you left, we have moved to another house. We live on Hobart now." He yelled over a Mexican man's head who had walked between us.
> "Sharon and Travis are the only ones left at the house. Cecilia moved in with Juan, and Clarissa is with her boyfriend in West Covina. Dave is in jail."
> "Boy, what a change," I said.
> "Yep, it sure is."

Daddy filled me in but didn't tell me everything. Sharon was pregnant. She hugged me real tight when I walked in. I thought I would faint. Then Mommy came out of the bedroom and said, "Hello baby, did you have fun in Fresno?"
> "I sure did. Thank you."
> "Your room is in the back with Sharon."
> "Okay." I felt like I had just walked out of a dream.
> "I'll take you back there," Sharon offered.

Mommy and Daddy were getting ready to go to work. After they left, Sharon told me she was going to give me the run down on what happened while I was gone. She told me how she and Patrick, the baby's daddy, had plans on being together in Vegas. She also told me that Mommy didn't like Patrick.

"Why not, Sharon? What did he do to her?"
"He hasn't done a thing. She just don't like him.
That's Mommy, though. She don't like nothing I
do! I never get her approval."

I thought to myself, I guess I'm not alone. I never thought I would hear anybody else say those type of things about their mother, but me.

After my return to L.A. I noticed Mommy did speak to me, but there was still something uneasy about her. I couldn't put my finger on it, but it was still there. Daddy and Mommy still stayed in their room, while Sharon and I were constantly talking and spending more time together now. She finally told me all about their life and her real Daddy. She told me how her mother used to be abused by her Daddy, and I told her about my life, from foster home to meeting my real Daddy. We both agreed that we had been through some pretty rough stuff.

My first week home was not a great one. I found myself in the doghouse with my parents. On that following Monday while walking to the neighborhood Boys Supermarket, a man in a blue decked out van honked at me. The van was real cool and he was looking fine too. He had a tank top on with no sleeves which showed his muscles and chest. He made small talk with me while driving slowly along my side of the street. I told him he would get a ticket and he told me I was worth it. He asked me if he could take me where I was going and I accepted the ride. While we sat there in the parking lot talking, he spent most of the time looking at me, telling me how cute and sexy I was (while he played with himself). He lit up a joint and gave it to me. I don't know what was in the joint, but I smoked it. Then one thing led to another and we became horny. He had a camera and wanted me to take pictures of him posing naked on the back seat of the van. He had the longest thang I ever seen in my life. It was so long it scared me to death. I didn't let him do anything real close, just kissing and feeling. He asked me to keep the Polaroid picture with me at all times and gave me his number in case I ever needed another ride. I told him I would and left. I put that picture in my pocket and went in the store to shop. After I got home, I hid that picture in my top drawer.

Sunday evening, Mommy's sister, Aunt Drena, dropped by. From the time I met her, she would always ask me to go to church with her. I would put her off each time. She would always talk to me about Jesus. Why this woman kept bugging me, I could never figure out. But she kept asking until I said yes. We went to a church called Academy Cathedral. The church was big inside and it's name was written in bright glittery lights, like in Las Vegas. It looked like a large theater with balcony seating. On the stage was a mass choir. I felt good as I sat there. Every now and then, Aunt Drena would take a look at me and smile. She was checking out my reactions. Then a fair skinned woman in the choir came to the microphone. She had red hair. The piano began to play. At first, it sounded familiar. I was trying to catch the beat, but it kept slipping away. Then her first words came out of her mouth.

> If any body asks you...
> Where I am going...
> Where I am going, soon.
> If you want to know
> Where I am going
> Where I am going soon
> I'm goin up a yonder.

I sat up in my seat. She was singing my favorite childhood song. The first song that made tears come to my eyes, while I hoped to leave the place where I lived to go up a yonder place. Those memories flooded my mind. I couldn't believe this woman was singing my song. The people were shouting and clapping their hands. The long version started to play and I stood up and started waving my hands. I knew I was out of control. I had never expressed myself in church like this. I couldn't help it though. I just couldn't help it. The tears ran down my face again, just like they did the first time I heard the song. I began to shout and before I knew it, I was "out in the spirit." The next thing I knew, women in white dresses were fanning me.

I was coming to while people were still shouting. I didn't know what happened, but it felt good to me. The lady was still singing. I could still hear the words.

> I've got to run
> I've got to run
> Run on and run on and
> runnnnnnnnnnnnnwhoooo!

The preacher got up next and preached about the song. He preached about going up a yonder to be with the Lord, but having to go through some things down here first. Then he gave the invitation for salvation for anybody who was not sure if they were going up a yonda. I went down to the altar and the pastor asked me to kneel. The ladies in white came up to me and started asking me if I received the Holy Ghost. I said, "no." Then each one got on both sides of my ears and told me to kneel at the altar. I did. One was saying, "hallelujah," and the other was saying, "thank you, Jesus." They said repeat after me as fast as you can. I started saying, "hallelujah, thank you, Jesus," real fast and before I knew it, I was speaking in another language. They said it was the Holy Ghost. I started saying things that I didn't understand. It felt good but, but I didn't understand it.

Afterwards, Aunt Drena came to get me from the altar. She said I got saved and received the Holy Ghost. When we got home that evening, Aunt Drena told Mommy and Daddy what had happened to me. They just nodded and kind of casually acknowledged it. Aunt Drena said, "I'll see you next Sunday. Remember read your

Bible everyday so the Lord can talk to you." I hugged her and thanked her.

I went to the back room where Sharon was and she said, "She finally got you in church hah?"
"Yeh. It was good, sis. I got saved today."
"Good," she said.

While laying quietly in bed I wondered what all of this meant to me. I felt it was time to do the right thing by God. Stop smoking, getting high, and doing bad things. Read my Bible and go to church. I felt really good about my new life with the Lord and going to Academy Cathedral Church.

On Monday when I got home from school, I had two angry parents waiting for me. Daddy said he needed to see me. I was still on my spiritual high from Sunday. Mommy was sitting in the living room looking evil. I took my books to my room and returned to the living room.

Mommy started talking first.
"Carla we found something very disturbing in your room".
"What?"
Mommy handed me the picture of that man in the van that I caught a ride with to the supermarket. I almost swallowed my tongue.
"Where did you get that" I yelled without thinking.
"It was in your dresser drawer." I went to put something in your drawer and found it right there."
Daddy interrupted, "who is that damn man, Carla?"

I wanted to say it really didn't matter because we didn't do sex and plus I just got saved so can we just forget it. They were so angry. Mommy said, "see Travis, I told you she was going to be trouble!" She got up and walked out of the room. I didn't know what she meant by that statement, but I did know I was finished. My daddy put me on punishment for a whole month. Not to use the phone, not to go anywhere but to school. I was angry but I obeyed. I knew it was no use trying to explain anything, because I was guilty. I knew this would draw my Daddy away from me now. I knew he must have thought I was a horrible person. Only a few weeks after that incident, my relationship with my Daddy and Mommy grew more distant. Sharon and I shared our war stories relating to home and that brought us closer. Sharon and Mommy were growing apart. There was a lot of tension in that house and I needed relief.

My school had also changed because we had moved from our last house. The school district changed also. I was tired of moving around to different schools. It was just frustrating. I didn't make many friends at L.A. High either. I just went to school, did my work, and came home. I did my chores, watched tv and started shooting the breeze with Sharon.

ULTIMATUM GIVEN TO DADDY
(DECEMBER 31, 1978)

Just when I thought I was getting comfortable in my new home, Daddy and Mommy had this real bad argument. She told him, "Well, you better choose tonight, me or her." Then she told him that he was going to have to get the hell out of the house if he chose me. Not long after I heard those words Daddy came to the back and said, "We have to go. Get all of your things."
I said, "What? I just got back here."
"I know, baby, but we have to leave" he said,
"You too, Daddy?"
"Yeh, she gave me an ultimatum, and I took it.
So get your things together now."

He sounded so calm. I don't think I ever saw my Daddy too upset, or his voice raise too much. Even when he was angry, he was cool.

Daddy and I got in the car and started driving around, looking for an apartment. An hour went by and no luck. Daddy had worked all night, so he was tired. He wanted to get a hotel room and get some rest. I got so nervous. I didn't feel comfortable at all going to a hotel with my Daddy. It felt so nasty. I felt ashamed of what people would think when they saw me with this old man. We checked in a place, and Daddy slept. Afterwards, we were back looking for an apartment all day. Finally, Daddy told me that he might have to send me back to Fresno until he got situated and then he would call me back so we would be together.

"Carla, how does that sound to you?"
"Well, it sounds fine if that's the only thing we can
  do right now."
"We really don't have a choice."
"Yeh, as long as you call me as soon as you find our
  apartment."
"I will, I promise."

Daddy took me right to the Greyhound bus station. He bought my tickets and then went to a phone booth to let Momma know I was on my way back to Fresno for awhile.

Daddy and I sat on the outside of the bus station where we could wait on the bus. The smell was strong. I could smell the fumes from the buses that had come and gone. Many people sat waiting on their bus too. I wished it was quiet, but the noises from the people talking got louder and louder. Kids were running up and down the sidewalks.

"Carla, I never meant for you to go through all these
  changes. As far as I'm concerned, you have been
  through enough in your life."
"It's not your fault, Daddy."
"Yeh, it is. But I want you to have a happy life, and
  I'm going to make it right."
"I wanted it to work out so much for everyone to be
  happy. I guess it wasn't meant to be."
"What a way to spend a New Year's Eve."

The bus pulled up and it was time to tell Daddy good-bye again.

"I love you, Daddy. Please call me as soon as you
find the apartment for us. Okay?"
"I told you that I would," he assured. I got on the
bus and watched my Daddy wave me off.

I thought I would just sit back and fall asleep, but suddenly my
mind was flooded with that very familiar song that I wrote.

So dark and scary.
It's dark and scary
So dark and scary
It's dark and scary yes
It's dark and scary.
I don't want to be alone
I just want to be free
Seems like someone is always rejecting me
I just want to be loved and I want to be ....
I fell asleep and five hours later the bus driver was
announcing the Fresno arrival.

It was late when the bus arrived, so I caught a cab to Momma's
house. Everyone was asleep except for Momma. She knew I was
coming, so she waited up for me. She had her lamp on next to the
window. When the cab pulled up I could see her body reflection
behind the curtain. She had the curtain cracked so that she could
see me when I arrived. When I came in the house, I noticed the
empty cans and bottles from where she had been sitting up drinking
by herself.
"So how have you been, Carla?"
"Okay, I guess. Thank you for staying up for me."
"How's your Daddy?"
"He's okay."
"Now why did this woman put both of you out?"
"She's crazy, I guess. I don't know."
"Was it anything that you and your daddy did that
made her want to put you out?" Momma said in her
accusing tone.

"What do you mean by that statement?"

"Just answer the question, girl."

"No, Momma. We didn't do anything to make her want to put both of us out. She gave him an ultimatum between choosing me or her, and he chose me! She didn't accept me from the beginning, and she still don't.

That's it."

"Okay, fine. Time will tell."

"Thanks a lot, Momma. I appreciate your confidence," I said sarcastically.

I took my bags into my old room and got ready for bed. I was thinking, why did I have to keep coming back to a place that I was trying so hard to never return to. Too many shameful memories and losses in this place. Momma went to bed, and I decided to go to the kitchen to write. I hadn't written in a while.

Dear God:

I am very unsure of what's going on with my life. It is unpredictable. Just when I think I have a home, I have to get up and go somewhere else. When I think about it, that is really how it's been most of my life. It has been too much for me, God. I just want to settle somewhere and stop feeling misplaced. I just want to belong somewhere, to somebody where I am loved and wanted. I'm trying to do better with my life, but I keep getting back into this old life. I want out of here, once and for all. Please God, help me. Please get me out of this place for good. I'm sorry every time I talk to you it's complaining, but you are the only one I can confide in and talk to.

Thank you, God.

CHAPTER 23

NEW YEAR'S DAY 1979

I woke up to two smiling faces on New Year's Day. Brenda and Catherine were tickling the bottom of my feet. I threw the pillow at them. They were laughing. Whenever I came down to Fresno, our relationship got closer and closer. I appreciated and loved them after moving away. I guess because I could really see them as my sisters and brothers, not just as a baby-sitter. Calvin Jr. and Edwin came into the room and gave me a big hug. They had a million questions for me. They wanted to know what L.A. looked like. They wanted to know if I had been to Magic Mountain or Disneyland and so on. It was hard getting them out of the room, because they missed me so much and I missed them too. I promised them we would play and talk later, but I had to get out of bed now.

I took a long shower. As I was getting dressed, I could smell the food all the way in the bathroom. The greens were smelling good and the black-eyed peas were steaming. The turkey was roasting and the dressing was on its way. Momma really knew how to bring in the New Year with some good old fashioned cooking. I knew that this day would be very busy as far as company was concerned, because Momma's friends knew that she had some money and would probably be buying all the drinks. They would bring the dominos, the cards were out, and we would be partying from twelve noon to twelve midnight. This was their tradition. I went in the kitchen and there Momma stood looking out the window. She didn't look happy at all. When she turned to say good morning she had tears in her eyes.

"Momma, what's wrong?" I said.

"Nothing," she said.

"Sometimes, if you live long enough, it will make you cry."

"Ah, Momma it's going to be alright. This is a New Year and things are going to be much better."

"Mr. Calvin didn't come home last night" Momma

whispered, without looking my way.
"We have never missed a New Year's Eve together."

I didn't know what to say. My mother was hurt and expressed it. I couldn't handle her like this, because it was the first time that I could put my hands on her pain. Real pain she was expressing to me. It must have been even worse then what she was saying, because my mother was a very prideful woman. That I knew about her. Later on that day, the house was full as usual. The New Year's party got started about 11:45 a.m. Mr. Calvin had come home around 4:00 o'clock that day. He stayed in the backyard with his dogs and never came in. He left as soon as he fed them. I know Momma saw him, but she continued to entertain her company. AlmaFaye came over with her kids. Darnell and Tim stopped by also. All of a sudden an argument broke out. One of Momma's friends accused Momma of cheating.

"What did she do that for?" the woman asked.
Momma told her to get her tall ass out of her house.
The woman said, "I came here with my man."
And Momma said, "You ain't' leaving with him, get your ass out of here now!"
The woman left, without her man. Tim asked if we could talk.
"You know, Carla, I am very sorry about what has happened in the past, ya know. I hope we can still be cool.
"Tim that's behind me, it's cool." I still didn't care for Tim. It made me sick just looking at him.
"Hey Carla, I wanted to ask you something personal though."
"What, Tim?"
"Well, is it true that you like women now?"
"Why, what the hell is it to you?"

He started stuttering, he couldn't speak clearly.
"Well, I just wanted to know."
"Well you satisfied now, yeh it's true and a whole lot

of other shit you ain't heard yet too. When you hear
it just know that it's probably true too."

He was so late. Even though Barbara was the only woman I had
been with at that time, I still didn't mind making him feel like it
was still happening. He stumbled his ass back into the kitchen after
that talk.

Three weeks went by without me hearing from Daddy.   Then I
decided to call him myself.
          "Hello, security, may I help you?"
          "Yes, is Travis Bynum in?"
          "I'm sorry, he is off today."
          "When will he be back at work?"
          "One week from today. He is on vacation."

I hung up the phone, disgusted. What a time to start a vacation!
          "I need you, Daddy, " I screamed, surprising myself
          at the outburst.

The next week went by like a turtle in a snail race, but I managed to
get through it.

HAPPY BIRTHDAY - FEBRUARY 1979, 16 Years Old

My sixteenth birthday came while I was in Fresno.   Nothing was
different, other than another year added.   I remember being
depressed, like previous birthdays, so I went over to AlmaFaye's to
get high. Before the night was over, Barbara and Bobby celebrated
my birthday with me at their house all night long.

The next morning when I woke up, I realized how much influence
they still had on me. I knew I was doing wrong, but I just couldn't
resist them. A big part of me didn't want to because they were the
only ones who ever really made me feel somewhat important and
needed.

When I got home Momma was on the phone while looking out of the window.

"Hey girl, your Daddy's on the phone."

"Give me the phone, I need to talk to him."

"He put me on hold," she told me.

I was so happy. I just knew Daddy was about to tell me when he would be sending for me. Momma was hanging the phone up as I walked in.

"Hey Momma, what happened? I wanted to talk to him."

"He got a call, Carla. He said he was calling back."

"Did he say he had found an apartment?"

"I don't know, hell, I didn't ask him all that! What makes you think he wants your ass back there anyway?"

"Because he told me he did."

"Yeh, right" Momma said, as she sipped her drink.

"I'm calling him back." I picked up the phone and dialed the number. A man answered the phone.

"Hello, Officer Bynum speaking, may I help you?"

"Hey Daddy, this is Carla. How are you doing?"

"Fine baby."

"Well, did you find a place? When can I come out there? This week-end?"

"Yes, I found a place, but now I have to prepare it for you with some essential things."

"Daddy, I don't need anything."

"Carla, slow down, you need a bed to sleep on."

"No, I don't Daddy. Get me a sleeping bag. I can sleep on the floor. Just get me out of this town. I am sick of this place."

"Listen, I promised you that I would and I am, just give me a few more weeks. It will be over with before you know it."

I reluctantly said okay and hung up the phone. I didn't realize how upset I had become. I was anxious to get out of Fresno. I had a fear of slipping back into all the crap I had been in before. I knew if I had to stay there much longer, I would probably be back at Barbara's and Bobby's permanently. I didn't have the strength to tell them "no" when they wanted me over there.

"He don't want you back down there."

"He does! He has to make things comfortable for me."

"You believed that! You can't trust men as far as you can see them. You done broke up his home, his marriage and now he's trying to give you back to me."

"I'm going back, Momma. I don't care what you say."

"When did he tell you that he would be ready?"

"He said give him a couple of weeks."

"Okay, I'll tell you about these Daddys, they get amnesia in a minute, they forget they even have kids."

I was exhausted by now and wanted to lie down. I took a nap.

During the two months of waiting, I grew more and more depressed. I needed to call my Daddy one last time to ask him if he was ready for me to come. If he said no, I would tell him to never worry about me again, and that I would do the best that I could in this hellish city.

"Hi Daddy, it's Carla. Can I come now?"

"Yep, you sure can," he replied.

"What?" I couldn't believe it.

"Of course."

"This week-end?"

"Yep."

"Oh Daddy, thank you so much."

"Call me and let me know what time your bus is arriving, and I will pick you up."

"Okay Daddy, I'll call you right back."

I hung up the phone and started crying and laughing at the same time. Momma was coming out of the kitchen.

"What's wrong?"

"Daddy, just said he's ready for me. I'm going back to Los Angeles."

"When?"

"Right now. As soon as I can. Momma, you have some bus money for me?"

"Hell no! Mr. Calvin don't get paid until Friday night."

"Oh no. It's Monday. I don't want to wait until Friday night."

"Well, find your own money or tell your Daddy to send it to you."

I didn't want to call my Daddy back and bother him about sending for me. He might change his mind. I decided to just wait until Friday night. I called my Daddy to let him know that I was coming home on the 8:00 a.m., bus which would arrive around 1:00 p.m. on Saturday.

The night before I was to leave, as always, I ran into Barbara and Bobby over to AlmaFaye's. I was almost out of the city. AlmaFaye told them tonight was my last night. Barbara asked me for my Daddy's number. I froze inside. How do I say no? I told her that I didn't know it yet, but as soon as I got there I would make sure she got it. She informed me that she was going to be there in a couple of weeks and wanted to hook up with me. Then she asked me to spend the night. I couldn't say no for some reason. I wanted to say no, but I couldn't do it.

I noticed later that night, when we started partying, Barbara had really started smoking the Sherm more than the Hennessy drink. I was really worried about her because she was becoming wilder. I couldn't do anything, but try to watch her every time I was around. Barbara was wild like my mother when she got drunk. She'd say anything and do anything to anybody.

The next morning I came home extra early to get ready for the Greyhound bus ride. My sisters and brothers were already up watching cartoons. Momma was up too with her coffee and puffing on her Winston cigarettes. I went into the room and finished packing. They came in and talked with me while I finished packing.

"Are you coming back to visit soon?" Catherine asked?

"I don't know, baby, maybe."

"We are going to miss you again," Brenda said.

The boys just watched and stayed quiet.

"Well, are you guys going to miss me too?" They nodded yes.

"Well, give me a hug." I hugged all of them at the same time.

Each time I would leave, I would feel sorry for them. I would only hope and pray to God that Momma or Mr. Calvin would never send them through the hell they sent me through. I felt they were old enough to now understand that God was always there for them, so I began to tell them to make sure they pray to God everyday. They said they would. "Make sure you guys always love each other and tell each other you love each other okay?" They assured me that they would. I was so happy to be leaving. This trip to Fresno was no different than any other, because Momma's relationship and mine didn't get any better. Momma was the same. Maybe the next time I will have a positive impact on Momma and she will see something different in me, I hoped. Riding back on the bus, I grabbed a sheet of paper out of my notebook to write to God.

> Dear God:
> I am too excited about this day. I am going to live with my Daddy, just me and him! No stepmother, no hollering and jealousy around me, coming between me and my Daddy. No sibling rivalry to

face or anything. God, please help me and my Daddy get to know one another. I know so many years have passed by, but please let us have a good future together. Thank you for letting him want me back and letting me come live with him. Thank you. I also have to thank you for getting me out of Fresno in the nick of time. You saw what was there and what I would have been involved with. I didn't want to be trapped again, God. Thank you for loving me. God please watch over my sisters and brothers and don't let bad things happen to them. And God, please watch over my mother. I wish she would stop drinking and stuff. Until next time, God. I'll talk to you then.

CHAPTER 24

ARRIVAL IN LOS ANGELES

Five hours later I was clearing the sleep out of my eyes from the long bus ride and the bus driver was announcing Los Angeles. I jumped in my seat, because I had slept all the way. I looked out of the window and saw my Daddy standing near the glass waiting in his Deputy Sheriff uniform. My heart was filled with joy.

"Hey, Daddy!"

"How's my baby doing?"

"Great, now."

"Well, let's get your bag and start our life together."

On the way to the apartment I kept sneezing and coughing. Daddy asked me if I was doing alright. I told him I had a little cold, but nothing serious. He told me that we were going to nip it in the bud with his home remedy of a hot toddy.

"A what!"

"A hot toddy."

"What's that, Daddy?"

"Whiskey, honey, lemons and hot tea."

"Yuk! Are you serious."

"I sure am. I know it sounds nasty, but it's good for
you.

However, you will have to stay wrapped up and in bed all night and when you wake up, you will be all better."

"How does it take the cold away?"

"It sweats it out of you. I know you may not like the
liquor, but it's only for your cold."

"Alright, I'm going to trust you, Daddy."

I laughed to myself because I knew my father didn't have any idea of how much liquor I had consumed in my short life. I was glad my Daddy didn't know all the bad things I had done.

As we drove through the crowded intersections of downtown L.A., we talked.   Daddy asked me how was Fresno.   I made up some innocent teenager stories for him, so that I wouldn't be judged before our relationship had a chance.   I would show him the good side of me.   He didn't ever have to know anything that I had ever been through.   Life was fresh and new from this point on and that's the way I wanted to keep it.   I switched conversations and started asking Daddy questions.

"How is your wife, Daddy?"

"Well she is still the same, still tripping."

"And how are Sharon and Travis?"

"Fine, I see them every now and then. On Monday we are going to enroll you back in school."

"Okay. I can't wait to see Sharon."

Then Daddy quickly changed the subject and began telling me about the apartment. His voice was happy now.

"You will like the apartment. It's cute and the right size for both of us. You will also like the apartment complex we're in. There are young people your age."

My age huh.   I thought about that. I wasn't interested in kids my age, but I was certainly open to adjustments. We arrived at this three-story, yellow and brown apartment building. I was impressed, but deep down inside I didn't care what it looked like as long as I was away from Fresno and with my real Daddy.   As we were getting out of the car, there were two guys hanging over the rail of the second floor talking and looking. One of the guys was kinda middle aged with a Jheri Curl, and the other guy was an older man. Daddy grabbed my suitcases and we went up the stairs. The younger of the two said, "Hello, Travis." Daddy said, "Hi Lonnie. Let me introduce you to my daughter. Carla, this is Lonnie and Mr. Jones. Lonnie lives right next to us and Mr. Jones lives up on the third floor."

I looked at Lonnie. He had a hungry smile with a little smirk on the end of it. I could tell, because I was looking at his eyes. I shook their hands politely and said, "Nice to meet you both."

We went into our apartment. I walked in and smiled. It was a cute one bedroom apartment just like Daddy said. To the immediate left was a living room with a brown plaid love seat set, and brown matching coffee table. The kitchen had a little dining table set. It was all standard and small, but large enough for Daddy and me.

Daddy said, "The couch is yours. It lets out into a bed."

"That's fine with me, Daddy," I smiled.

"And your closet is right next to the bathroom in the hallway."

"Good, I don't have a lot of clothes anyway."

Daddy went in his room and got on the phone. I quickly unpacked my things and used the linen closet to store my folded-up items. It was perfect and compact. After Daddy got off the phone he asked me if I was hungry. I told him I really didn't have an appetite, but Daddy was persistent.

"Well you have to eat something before I give you this hot toddy. I can go and get you something if you like. I need to run some errands anyway before I go off to work."

"Okay, Daddy." I said.

"Get acquainted with the place and I will be back in a little while."

It felt so good to be there. I felt like I was finally reaching peace at the end of troubling days. I heard the roar from his motorcycle as he zoomed down the street. Daddy had a Volkswagen and a motorcycle. I turned on the television and made myself comfortable.

When Daddy returned several hours later, he handed me a Kentucky Fried Chicken bag that had chicken, mashed potatoes, and corn in it. I had been watching television all afternoon while he was gone. I ate, and when I finished he gave me that hot toddy he promised me. He was right, it was strong, but he was wrong on the part about liking the liquor. I could handle the liquor. In fact, I wished that he had given me more than the cup he did give me. I woke up the next morning and my sinuses were clear as a summer breeze.

The next day was Sunday and I was awakened by the next door neighbors' kids running up and down the steps. I got up and went to the bathroom. The door to Daddy's bedroom was open, and he was long gone. The phone rang.
    "Hello."
    "Hey girl, what's up?"
    "Nothing much, who is this?"
    "This is your sister Sharon, turkey. So you done
    forgot about me, huh?"
    "Naw, what's up with you?"
    "I'm coming over there in a couple of hours, okay?"
    "Yeh, come on."

I was so happy that Sharon was on her way. I really looked forward to seeing her. I remembered our relationship had just started on a good foot, then was interrupted when Mommy put us out. I cleaned up the living room and bathroom. There were a few dishes in the sink from Daddy fixing something to eat. Daddy had shown me the wash room downstairs, and I needed to wash a load that I brought with me from Fresno.

Daddy drove up as I was bringing my clothes upstairs. I waited for him to get off his bike and we walked up the stairs together. At the top of the stairs stood a fair skinned woman with a beautiful smile. Daddy whispered to me, "That's Mrs. Martin." As we approached her, Daddy introduced me to her. She suggested that I come over and introduce myself to her kids, who were my age. I told her I would. She was so pretty and sexy to me, but she was the age of my mother. She had on blue short pants and a t-shirt with flower prints.

When we entered the apartment, Daddy noticed that I had cleaned up. He thanked me for doing a good job. I was happy that I pleased him. I guess it felt more important now than when we were living with his wife and family, because now I got my due compliments and attention that I couldn't get around them. Then he told me he was getting ready to go to work and his hours were not too convenient for a single dad and daughter. He worked from 3:00 to 11:00 at night. His off days were Sundays and Mondays. I told him not to worry and that I understood his schedule, but we would have to make up on Sundays and Monday evenings. He nodded, with a warm smile on his face. "That's my Daddy," I said to myself. As Daddy was leaving for work I told him that Sharon was coming over to visit. He was so happy that I wouldn't be by myself. "Tell her I said hello." He closed the door to the bathroom and hurried to get showered, shaved and dressed for work.

An hour later, Sharon was at the door. We hugged and greeted each other joyfully as if we hadn't seen each other in years. She asked about Daddy.

"You just missed Daddy about twenty minutes."
"Oh yeh, well I guess it's cool to get high. Did you
   bring some from Fresno?"
"You know it, fresh and potent."

I opened the curtains to our window which gave an all around view of the front complex and everybody passing by. As soon as I opened them, Lonnie the guy that lived next door, was walking by. He looked in the window, saw Sharon and me and smiled. He had nice dimples. Sharon asked who he was. I said, "Probably somebody that wants some panties." We laughed.

I will never forget this day because for the first time Sharon apologized to me for how she treated me when we first met. She said, "I was so jealous of you. I was the baby before you came. Then you came and took all that away from me. Then I saw my mother treating you (at first) nicer than she even treated us and that pissed me off too.   I guess my jealousy got in the way of ever accepting and knowing you. I'm sorry."

> "Thank you, sis, I forgive you. I admit, it's some
> pretty hard things to accept and get adjusted to,
> but I'm glad yo mean ass has changed." We
> laughed.
> "Maybe your mother may change how she feels,
> hah?"
> Sharon looked at me, raising one eyebrow, "One
> miracle at a time."

Changing the subject, she started talking about what I should expect from L.A. High School. I didn't care one way or the other. School was never a "die for experience" as I got older. We decided to walk across the street to the little shopping mall to check it out and see what the neighborhood had to offer. There was a McDonalds, Winchells' Doughnut, some clothing shops and a check cashing place on one corner. There was a Boy's Market facing the apartment building. Everything was in close proximity. We decided to get a couple of wine coolers and go back to the apartment to just kick it. Sharon and I shot the breeze all evening, playing music and getting high. Sharon put on her favorite tapes which were Smokey Robinson, and Earth Wind & Fire. "Reasons," "Heatwave," and "Always and Forever," were her favorite songs. We jammed on Daddy's little stereo. Before she left, I told her to tell Travis Jr. and her mother I said hello. I walked Sharon down to the end of the hallway, and Mrs. Morris' door was open. I stuck my head in, and she was at her kitchen stove cooking some chitterlings and greens. Boy, did they smell good!
> "Hello, Mrs. Morris."
> "Hey baby, how are you? Come on in here."
> "Let me lock my door, and I will be right back."

When I got back, her two daughters, Sheila and Monika, were in the kitchen. Mrs. Morris introduced them to me. Sheila was older than me and Monika was a couple of years younger. Those girls were so pretty. I was hoping they didn't catch me staring at them. I felt myself really attracted to the older one. Miss Morris told me that her son Joseph, who also attended L.A. High, was gone and would be back later. Her daughters asked me questions about Fresno and made small talk. They were genuinely friendly and country as they wanted to be. Monika went over to their stereo and started jamming some sounds. Then someone else walked in the door. Her name was Joy, Mrs. Morris' sister, who happened to be the landlord. I met her and her two children that were eight and two years old. I found out that they were all from New Orleans. Joy popped open a beer from Mrs. Morris's refrigerator and took a seat at the dining room table. Mrs. Morris had a pretty nice layout. Her apartment was much larger than ours, because she lived in a three bedroom. They had a goldenrod colored couch set with white drapes, nice matching carpet, and a wooden dining room set where we sat and talked.

"I heard about you from the others in the building," was his first words to me as he reached out his hand for a handshake. Hi, I'm Carla. Pleased to meet you and I hope you heard good things." We exchanged polite smiles.

It seemed everybody in the apartment building knew each other. Before long, Mr. Jones stopped by and took a seat. They began to talk about cards, and I interrupted and said,

"Are there any Boston Bound people in the house?"
They looked surprised.
Mr. Jones said, "Are you referring to Bid Wisk?"
I said, "if you have to ask the question, I don't want you as partner. Give me somebody that knows the game and the language." They laughed.

Then it was on. I partnered with Joy, and Mrs. Morris and Mr. Jones were partners. All of a sudden it felt like back home in Fresno, except for the music and the crazy cursing everybody out. I fit right in with the older crowd as always, because I knew the cards, the dominos, and anything else they thought they wanted to play.

So I found my home away from home.

When Daddy would go to work, I found myself going next door and hanging out with the Morris'. It was fun. Soon, I was drinking beer with them too. Mrs. Morris asked me if my Daddy knew, I said, "no mam' and he mustn't find out."

Finally, it was time to enroll into the School system once again. L.A. High was located in a four-story building. It looked like a penitentiary on the outside because of all the iron. I had a fresh start. No one knew me, or my past. The girls there also looked so much older than those in Fresno. The first day of school was cool and on the quiet side.

Each morning Mrs. Morris's son, Joseph, and I would walk to school together. He would light up a joint every morning. I asked, "How in the hell do you learn anything when you are high?" He said, "that's when I could concentrate the best." Every now and then I would take a hit with him. Joseph and I soon developed a sister/brother relationship.

The relationship was so good, I felt that I could tell him about my sexual preference. He thought it was so cool. At first he didn't believe me, but after we talked about it more, he knew I was serious. He said, "I am cool with it. Is that why I could not get any further with you?" he asked. "Yeh, buddy, that's why, I wanted your fine sister, not you." We laughed.

One day after school, before Daddy left for work, we had a conversation about my future. He said "Carla, you need to start thinking about your life." I had one more year in high school. I politely listened. He talked about bills, savings accounts, and civil service jobs that I could prepare myself for. I appreciated the talk, but as far as I was concerned it was too soon to talk about my future.

CALL BARBARA

After a couple of months, I started thinking about Barbara. Just out of nowhere, there she was in my mind pulling on me. I tried to talk myself out of calling her. I even warned myself that it was dangerous. I told myself that she was like a bad drug addiction that you can't say no to. I than felt so indebted to her for all they had done for me and I had not called to see if they were alright. It felt like what they describe as withdrawal. I convinced myself, I could just call to say hello and that would be it. Once I was fully convinced, I rushed to the phone to call her.

Barbara answered the phone. She was so glad to hear from me. That made me feel good. She told me that she was coming down the next weekend and was hoping that she could somehow find me. I began to really get nervous. I didn't realize all this was about to happen, otherwise I would not have called her. I didn't know how to react to her suggestion.
"Do you think we can hang out together, baby?" she
asked, really sexy.
"I don't know Barbara, let me see."
"Well, give me the number before you hang up so
that I can call you when I get in town."

I hesitated and gave her the number. I hung up the phone as soon as we were finished. I thought to myself. you just had to call her hah? Now you are about to get into some crazy shit. I felt bad all day for opening that can of worms again.

The next weekend came so fast. I started getting butterflies on Thursday night. I didn't want Friday to come at all. But, Friday came and went and no word from Barbara. Saturday morning about 10 a.m. the phone rang. It was Barbara.
"I'm here baby girl."
"Oh, good. How are you doing?" I pretended to be
excited.
"Can I come get you now?"

"I don't know, Barbara, give me the number where
you are and when my Daddy gets up I'll ask him
and call you back."
"Okay baby, don't keep me waiting." She sounded
anxious.

Daddy was getting out of bed as I was hanging up with Barbara. I
asked him if I could go hang out with an old friend that was here
visiting her relatives in L.A. He said, "Of course." I called Barbara
back, and she was on her way to get me. I had totally forgotten the
fact that Barbara didn't look like a little teeny bopper.

An hour later the doorbell rang. Daddy was in the shower. I
answered the door. She looked so good. Her hair was nicely cut
and curled in layers. She was wearing this tight black and red dress
with a red bag and red high heels. Daddy was coming out from the
bathroom going into his bedroom. Her legs were so pretty. Her
dress was short enough to see her beautiful brown thighs. I was
trying to get out of the house fast so he didn't see her. He came out
with his T-shirt and trousers on. He looked at her kind of strange.
Oh shit, I said to myself. I better get her out of here before she
begins to flirt with Daddy. I quickly introduced them and Barbara
took his hand him and said, "very nice to meet you Mr. Bynum."
"See you later, Daddy."
"Alright Carla, be back here before I go to work."
"I will." My heart was beating so fast. As soon as we
got to the bottom of the stairs I couldn't wait to jam
Barbara up.
"What the hell were you trying to do coming over
here dressed like that?"
"Baby I was trying to look good for you" taking her
tongue and running it over her bottom lip side to
side. I turned away from her and walked faster to
the car.
"Hey baby, I hope Daddy is taking good care of
you."
"He is," I said without turning around. I just wanted

to get her inside the car before anybody else saw her.
"I know you know where to get some shit from, don't
you?"
"What kind of shit?"
"Some Sherm."
"What you want some of that shit for? What about
Hennessy?"
Her hands started rubbing my arms that rested on
the arm rest.
"Baby don't you want to freak off with me?" I
couldn't deny to myself wanting to feel and kiss her
all over like we used to do to each other in Fresno,
when Bobby wasn't around.
"Of course I do, but I don't know, my daddy is
waiting for me," I told her.
"Well let's hurry up and find some shit before you
have to go back home to Daddy," she teased.

We drove around in the Pico area where I knew one of Joseph's
friends sold that shit. After hours of driving around and not
finding anything, she said fuck it! Thank God, I thought to
myself. So we pulled up to a liquor store and got a pint of
Hennessy. I lit up a joint that I had bought from school. I told her
I had to get back to my daddy. She was mad because she wanted
to spend all day together. She told me that she was leaving out the
next morning because she had to be at work. I wanted to be with
her so bad, but I was glad I had restrictions that kept me from her.
We pulled up to a park near Olympic and laid in each other's arms
and drank. We talked. Barbara expressed her love and missing me
like never before. I didn't know quite how to take it. I asked how
Bobby was and she disgustedly said, "He is fine, doing the same old
dumb shit." I asked about her daughters and she told me that they
were staying over to her mother-in-law's more these days.

I felt a loneliness and emptiness in Barbara. I felt sad that I could
not return the same sadness to make her feel she wasn't alone. She
kissed me over and over again, as if she was trying to store up

enough to take back with her.   It felt good being loved by her that way.

Daddy was getting ready to leave for work. I stayed home the rest of the day and didn't even answer the phone, in case it was Barbara again.

The next morning, I was on my way out to school and so was Joseph. We walked together. I asked him what was Lonnie's story. Joseph told me about the many women that went in and out of Lonnie's apartment.
     "What are they doing, orgies?" I asked.
     "I don't know, but whatever it is they like it and
     come back for more," Joseph said.

That same day, I finally met a girl I could hang out with at school. Her name was Phyllis and she was from Alabama. She was a freak momma to her heart wearing her high pumps and showing cleavage for everybody to see. She always wore deep red lipstick and tight clothing. She was hot and had a nice body, and she knew it. She didn't know about my lifestyle just yet, because I didn't know how she would take to me. We began to hang really tight. We were in a few classes together. She lived with her sister who had a violent boyfriend. Phyllis' sister was jealous of her, according to Phyllis. Phyllis was very unhappy, and she always said she could not wait until graduation to move back to Alabama.

MEET GREGORY
APRIL 1979

I needed to buy new shoes and had saved up enough allowance to get some. I noticed a shoe store across the street. It was owned by a man and only men worked in the store.

As soon as I stepped foot in the place, a cute salesman came to my side and asked if he could help me. He was brown skinned and wore a blue walking outfit. He was bow-legged. He looked just like a young boy I knew back in Fresno named Danny Graves - St. Patrick.

> "Hey, cutie. Can I help you find those Cinderella
> slippers you lost?"
> "Oh, that's a good one. Never heard that one I can
> truly."
> "You must be a princess, as cute as you are."
> "Well don't tell me you are my prince that's going to
> fit my perfect shoe." We joked with each other as if
> we knew each other for years.

I let him show me several pairs of shoes. But the minute I saw the prices on them, I knew in my mind that I would be walking out with no shoes. His company was amusing though. He kept trying to talk to me, and I wanted to ask him if he had a sister his age that looked kind of like him, but I knew he would have thought I was crazy.

> "Thank you for showing me all these shoes, I just
> don't see anything that I like yet."
> "Well, listen, maybe I can take you to lunch one
> day." He handed me his card.
> "Maybe, let's see. I'll let you know."
> "Can I have your number?"
> "I will call you, don't worry. See ya later."

When I came back from window shopping, Daddy said he wanted to ask me something. I tried to think real quick what I had done now. I couldn't think of anything that I had done since I got back from Fresno, unless he wanted to talk about Barbara. I started getting butterflies. But I played it off by smiling.

> "What's up Daddy?"
> "Carla, why don't boys ever call here?"
> "What do you mean?"
> "You know what I mean!"
> I started stuttering.
> "Joseph calls here for me all the time Daddy."

"Carla, outside of your walking buddy, Joseph, no
other boys call here. Your mother called me last
night to tell me that you like girls."

I looked at him in disbelief and before I could catch myself, I
blurted out, "Momma did what!"
"Yes, Carla, she told me! I should have figured it out
for myself. I was thinking you just didn't have time
for boys because you were so busy with your school
work. But you're some kind of freak."

His words pierced me. Then he began to ask me a series of
questions without letting me answer any of them.
"What's wrong with you, Carla? Do you actually get
satisfied?" He kept asking questions.
"Aren't you ashamed? How long have you been like
this?"

I wanted to tell him, ever since I've left home looking for love, but
instead I was frozen as he continued to ask question after question.
I felt like my back was against the wall. My insides were boiling
with mixed emotions. The nerve of my mother telling my dad!
The nerve of my dad going off on me and not trying to
understand! I began to feel like this was the last straw. My mother
just couldn't let me and my Daddy be happy with each other. I
finally spoke up.
"Daddy just let me be me!"
"What the hell you mean, just let you be you? Don't
you know that isn't normal, only freaks do that kind
of stupid stuff."
"I am not a freak Daddy! I am normal," I yelled
out.
"You consider that behavior normal? Don't you like
guys?"
"No I don't and I don't have to" I snapped.
"Why not?"
"Because I just don't, Daddy!"

"Well, you better do something because I ain't gonna
tolerate that shit in my house. I don't want any of
those freaks coming over here, calling my house, and
I don't want you calling them on my phone!"

He walked out to get ready to go to the race track. After he left I
cried and paced the floors. I was so mad and hurt. The last chance I
had for a real chance to know my Daddy was blown now. He will
never love me, I thought. Not as long as he thinks I'm sick and a
freak.

From that night on, I tried to think of ways that I could make
Daddy love me again. I made sure girls didn't call the house. No
one was calling, but Sharon, Barbara, and Phyllis. I told them I was
on punishment and would let them know when it was safe to call.
My Daddy was very cold toward me for a long time. He barely
said anything to me. This kind of treatment tormented me.

I came home every day from school and cleaned the house and
cooked when needed. I made small talk with Daddy when our
paths crossed. I never mentioned a woman. I only talked about the
male teachers in my school. I began to spend a lot of time with my
sister, Sharon. He would see her at the house on the weekends
before he would leave, hoping it would leave a positive image of me
in his mind. Daddy didn't know that Sharon smoked weed. They
always saw her as so pure.

One day, I was thinking about Greg, that guy across the street in
the shoe store. He had asked me out for lunch and gave me his
number. I thought, "Maybe this is an opportunity to impress
Daddy with a boy in my life." I went across the street to shoot the
breeze and say hello to Greg. He wasn't there, so I left my
telephone number for him to call me when he returned. Daddy was
in his bedroom. The phone rang. Daddy answered it. It was for
me. He yelled out for me to pick up the phone. It was Greg.
    "Hey, Carla, I heard you came by."
    "Yeh, I did. I wanted to take you up on that lunch

offer."
"Cool, can you come now? I just came back from
making a bank drop for the store."
"Sure, I'm on my way."
"Daddy, I am going to lunch with my friend Greg
from across the street. And oh yeah, Greg wants to
meet you." He gave me a half-way crack smile of
hope.
"I would love to meet this Greg whenever he wants to
come by." He sounded skeptical.

I went across the street and got Greg. I told him that my Daddy
wanted to meet him before he took me out to lunch. Greg laughed
and said he could respect my Daddy for being old fashioned.

Greg and I walked in the door and Daddy was sitting at the table
eating some spaghetti that I cooked the day before. Daddy and
Greg exchanged casual greetings. Daddy offered Greg a seat and I
excused myself to go to the bathroom and pray that this hook up
would work to turn my Daddy's love back to me. I don't know all
that they were talking about, but I heard them laughing as I was
coming out of the bathroom. Daddy was getting up from the table
shaking Greg's hand, because he had to get ready for work.
"Nice to meet you, Mr. Bynum."
"Same here Greg, hope to see more of you."
"Me too, Mr. Bynum."

Greg asked me if I could go out with him that night. I asked him
if he had asked my Daddy. After he said no, I told him that he
better do it right now before the opportunity leaves.
"Mr. Bynum, I almost forgot the most important
reason I came over. Can I take Carla out to dinner
this evening?"
"Yes, you may. She must be at home before twelve
o'clock."
"No problem, sir. We won't be far."

I said to myself "Damn, midnight, that's when the party gets started real good." I walked Greg to the door and said, "Where are we going Greg?"

"It's a surprise, but I think you will just love it. I think I know where you will have the time of your life, my little girl."

"Oh yeh?"

"Oh yeh!"

CHAPTER 25

RUBY'S CLUB

Gregory picked me up at 8:30 in a burgundy Lincoln Town car.

"Carla, you are going to have a nice time tonight."

"I believe it. I don't go out with a prince every day
you know."

We laughed together, remembering our conversation
when we first met.

"Where are we going?"

"It's a surprise, but trust me, I believe you will love
my surprise."

He told me that we had to make some stops before getting to the party. I told him I was there for the ride. He pulled up to this big beautiful home in Gardena. We went in and women were getting ready to go out. Greg introduced me to them.

"Sparkle, this is Carla. Carla, meet Sparkle."

Sparkle was cute, her name fit her. Her smile was pleasant and nice.

"Nice to meet you, Carla. Greg you got yourself a
cutie pie!"

Greg whispered in my ear that she was the owner of the home and she was also Greg's roommate. She stood about 5'2" or 5'3". She looked very masculine, but sexy as well. I wondered to myself if she was like me and Barbara

"You have a beautiful home," I told her.

"Thank you very much. Make yourself comfortable."

She was graced with a classy aura. Her clothes were sharp. You could tell she had some money. Even her fragrance smelled good. I envied her smoothness and thought to myself, that's a cool ass woman there, whoever she is.

The woman at the table doing her nails never looked up. She looked like her sister maybe, but I didn't ask. After a few moments,

Greg yelled out, "Let's go, Carla." I said good-bye to Sparkle and she told me that she would see me at the party.

"For real?"

Greg said, "For real, let's go."

Off we were to the next spot to pick up a friend of Greg's, named Roger. I kept thinking about that woman Sparkle.

Fifteen minutes later, we pulled up to another large house. Greg blew the horn once. Roger came to the car and said, "okay, get in the back, I'm chauffeuring you guys." Greg jumped in the back and opened my door to usher me to the back with him. Whoa, this was fun. I just kicked back and watched with a smile on my face.

As we drove down Crenshaw Blvd., Greg held my hand. He smiled at me every now and then and shook his head up and down, saying yes.

"Carla, this party is going to be the bomb!"

"Oh yeh?"

"Watch what I tell you, you will never forget it."

"You don't get out much," I teased. We laughed.

Roger lit a joint and passed it back. It was some smooth Columbia.

We finally pulled up into this parking lot where the club was. The music was blasting loud. We entered what seemed like an underground tunnel. They didn't ask for I.D. at the door. I wondered how I was going to get in here.

The lights in the club were freaking out. The people were jamming to the sounds. The smoke was rising to the top and the bartenders were swooping by every second delivering drinks. It was awesome! I had never been to anything like it! There were hundreds of people. It was jammed packed. The club had an upstairs and downstairs. People were hanging on the stairwells. Greg offered to buy me a drink. I told him that I would like a straight shot of Hennessy. He stopped one of the waiters and ordered our drinks.

Then Greg said "Let's go on the dance floor while we wait for our drinks." We had to squeeze through people just to get to the dance floor. You could feel the music in your heart beat. It was thumping so loud, and the bass was so awesome. As we danced, I saw something that almost made me have a heart attack. There were several women dancing with women. Then I saw men dancing with men.

Were we in the wrong club? Did Greg see what I saw? As I turned toward him he was looking at me with this big smile on his face, pointing at me.

He winked his eye and said, "Did I do good?"
"Ah man, you did better than good. You are a miracle man."
"This is one of the largest clubs for gay people in Los Angeles," Greg yelled out.

I was speechless, and couldn't say one word for a minute. I wondered if Greg was gay too.

As the evening went on I found certain people to be very interesting. Greg came up to me and asked how was I doing? I said, "Man, need you ask?"

He said, "I'm so glad I wasn't wrong about what I thought I felt in you."

I was too shocked. How did he know? Was it written on my forehead? Roger came by and asked Greg to dance. I didn't think I heard him correctly, but when I saw Greg go out on the dance floor I almost passed out. I wasn't prepared for that bombshell either.

Finally a cute young lady asked me to dance and it was on. I danced for at least two hours straight, from one person to the next. It was so cool.
The night was getting really late, 11p.m. to be exact. The gang wanted to go to another club called Gino's, but I knew I couldn't go

because of my stupid curfew. I made up a lie and told Gregory that I was getting sick. Though he already knew what time I was due home, I wanted him to tell that lie to the girls so they wouldn't think I couldn't stay out late. I sat up in bed that night rolling my hair and shaking my head to all that had happened. I felt like I had hit the jackpot.

The next morning, Daddy asked me how my date with Greg went.
"Daddy, I had the time of my life!"
"So you enjoyed yourself with Greg," he emphasized.
"Oh yeh, I can go out with him anytime. Greg is a
  perfect gentleman, Daddy."
"I'm glad to hear that." He was pleased and went on
  out the front door.

An hour later there was a knock at the door. It was my sister Sharon.
"Hey girl, come on in, what's up?"
"I was on my way to the park and just stopped by to
  say hello to ya and see what's happening tonight."
"Well I don't know yet, I'm trying to get into
  something."
I knew she probably wanted to go to some
  straight club, which I wasn't interested in at all.
"Well, if you want to go somewhere, you can count
  me in."

I thought about it. I figured, I better play this thing all the way so that Daddy can think I'm really turning straight.
"Cool," Sharon said. Let's go hang out at the park
  for now and get high."

I made a pit stop to the bathroom. Do you have some smoke?" Sharon asked?
"Yeh, I know you ain't got nothing" I told her.
"Let me go to the bathroom real quick and we can be
  on our way before Daddy gets back."

We could not have picked a better summer day to go to the park. It was beautiful and warm outside. Los Angeles felt great in the summer time. Everybody had on their summer shorts, halters, shades and straw hats. Cars passed by, jamming the sounds and blowing their horns. As we stood at the bus stop I reached for a joint and noticed I didn't have my bag. I looked at Sharon and my eyes got big.

"What! What's wrong, Carla?"

"Uh, I think I left my bag of weed in the bathroom."

Without saying a word, we broke out running down Western Blvd. back to the house to see if it was in the bathroom. When we turned the block, Daddy's motorcycle was parked right out front.

"Oh, shit," we said in unison!

"He's back," I said.

Well maybe he had not gone to the bathroom yet to shower for work. We crept in the house and sure enough the shower was running. Daddy was inside the shower stall. Sharon looked at me, and I looked at her. The shower went off. My heart began to beat faster. Daddy walked out of the bathroom with his robe on and spoke to Sharon. I pretended I had to use the bathroom so bad and rushed right in past Daddy, closing the door behind me. I looked all around for the weed, it was nowhere to be found. How I wished that I had accidentally flushed it down the toilet. I came out of the bathroom. Daddy and Sharon were right there. Something told me that Daddy had the weed. Something told Sharon that too, because she volunteered to leave. After she left, Daddy told me to sit down.

"I found that shit that you left in the bathroom," he said.

I didn't say a word. I froze. He started to take his belt off his Deputy Sheriff trousers and told me to stand up. I said within myself, what the hell does he think he is about to do to me with that belt?

I felt more stupid than he looked with that belt in his hand. Before I knew it, he started to whoop me. I was humiliated and pissed off at the same time. I am too damn old for this type of discipline. I am sure he felt as stupid as I did. Then it began to get harder and harder, and I could no longer stand there looking crazy at him.
"Oh you are going to be stubborn are you? I can whoop your ass all day if I have to."
Something said, "You better start crying if you want this to stop."

After the whooping, Daddy grounded me for two weeks. He got ready for work and left. So much for trying to go out to the club that night. The next two weeks were difficult. I was angry everyday I saw my Daddy. I almost hated him for whooping me. When Greg would call the house, Daddy would let me talk to him and even go out with him. Of course we would go to the gay bars that Daddy didn't know about.

The end of the school year was drawing near and Daddy asked me if I wanted to go see my mother for Mother's Day. I reminded him I was on punishment and he said that would be an exception if I wanted to go. I didn't know if he was trying to get rid of me for the weekend or if he was sensitive to the fact that I might want to see my mother for Mother's Day. I would always think about my mother on these types of holidays, with such hope of this one being the best. But each year seemed to get worse and worse, all because of her drinking. Also, I could never do anything right in her eyes. Plus, I was still mad at Momma for telling Daddy that I like women, even though I couldn't stay mad with her long for some reason.

I decided that I would go to Fresno for Mother's Day. Even though I'd hope for the best, I was always prepared for the worst. Going to Fresno was always an emotional toss, not knowing if you are going to war or peace. It almost felt like I had to take a deep breath and exhale once I entered that city.

MOTHER'S DAY IN FRESNO
May 1979

When I got off the Greyhound bus I took a cab to my mother's house. As soon as I got out of the cab, Blackie came running up to the car. I was so happy to see him.

"Hey, dog of my life. Where have you been?"

Blacky just jumped and barked, jumped and barked.

I knew he was speaking back to me.

Momma was sitting by her little window looking out as usual. When she saw me, she smiled. I loved to see her dimples. Momma was a very attractive woman when she wasn't killing herself with that alcohol. The alcohol made her look crazy. She would not comb her hair or put on decent clothes. Now I noticed her hair graying.

She was just forty three years old, and she looked like she was favoring a sixty year old woman. I put my bag down and hugged her real tight. She didn't stand up, but she did hug me around my waist.

The kids came running in the door from outside. They were glad to see me. They made me feel so good. I had missed them as well. After getting things together, Momma and I sat down for a beer together and talked. I had brought home some shoes and things for the kids, along with a gift for Momma. I always brought my sisters and brothers and Momma a gift. Momma wanted to talk about my Daddy. She started off by asking about our apartment. Then she got to the meat of the matter, our relationship.

"So how are you and your Daddy getting along these days?"

I couldn't resist bringing up her tacky move, when she called him to tell him about me being gay.

"Momma, why did you have to tell him that?"

"Because, he has a right to know, dammit."

"I have the right to tell him when I want him to
know!"
"You're just mad because all your shit is coming to
the light, Carla. You can't hide anything, can you?"

I got up, stormed out and went to sit on the porch to play with
Blacky. I was so angry with her. Momma came outside and told
me that she was leaving and to keep an eye on the kids. I thought,
a weekend of baby-sitting for "Mother's Day."

Later on, AlmaFaye came over and sat with us. It was a joy seeing
her. We laughed about old times, and the times we partied while
Momma was in prison camp. I asked AlmaFaye about her kids.
She gave me the run down of how they were trying to work her last
nerves. I also asked about her boyfriend, Darnell. She told me he
was playing on her and she was not going to stand for it. I told her
not to. After she left I sat up and watched TV with my sisters and
brothers. Momma was still out at some club partying for the
evening.

The weekend seemed so long, I couldn't wait until it was over. I
was tired of watching the kids. I called Barbara and Bobby to see
what they were doing. They said they were just kicking it and for
me to come by before I leave. I told them, I would have to come
over right away because I was leaving in the morning. I decided to
walk over to their house.

The door was unlocked and I walked in. We started talking. They
both seemed happy to see me. They immediately started joking
with me about leaving them behind. I tried to ignore those words
and asked them what they had been doing. They told me the same
old same old, drugs, partying, and just living it up.
    "Where have you been partying?" Barbara asked.
    "Ah man, I found out that there is this club in L.A.
    where a lot of gay people go, both men and
    women."
    "Gay men and women," Bobby said.

"Yeh, it's so cool.   There's even this lady that's trying
to like me."

I told them about how my Daddy leaves to go to work and I
pretend that I'm a little sweetheart, then I go out late at night.   I
just poured my heart out on how amazed I was to see so many
beautiful gay women! Barbara wasn't as overwhelmed as I thought
she would be. I thought I should shut up.

I fixed me another drink of Hennessy.   Then Bobby approached
me, trying to take off my clothes at the bar.
        I looked at him and said, "No, Bobby, I don't want
        to do that."

We got into a tug of war.   I got pissed off.   I didn't want to have
anything to do with him sexually, or any other man for that matter.
I tried to tell him that, but he got even angrier.
        "Oh, you don't want me anymore huh? Oh you just
        want women? The problem is, you haven't had no
        good dick since you left here and your young ass
        have just forgot how good it is."

I began to cry, because at this point he was ripping off my clothes. I
couldn't do anything about it.   Barbara was in the corner just
looking and saying nothing. She finally said, "Bobby leave her ass
alone. She don't want your ass, you heard what she said. She got
her own life now. Leave her the hell alone."
        "Shut up. She's going to get some whether she wants
        it or not. That's probably what's wrong with her ass,
        she ain't had this good dick."

I just laid there and stopped fighting since I was losing.   Barbara
walked out of the room.   When Bobby was finished I got up and
put on my clothes. I was hurt and felt raped. But how do you feel
raped toward someone you use to love and have sex with all the
time?   I hated Bobby immediately and didn't want to see him
again in life. Barbara came back talking about how I cheated on her,

and how I'm playing games with her. She thought I went to L.A.
and was sleeping with every woman I met. I didn't know what to
do. Bobby was mad at me because I didn't want to screw him.
Barbara was mad because I found another link in the world on gay
women. I preferred Bobby's anger over Barbara's, because she was
crazy and you never knew what she was going to do next.

I had Bobby drive me back over to my mother's house. He was
sorry and even apologized for Barbara. I was just glad to get out of
there and back home. He asked me if he could take me to the bus
station tomorrow. I said, "Sure." I didn't tell my mother, or
anybody what happened. All Momma would have said is, "Yeah
that's good for you," or maybe she wouldn't have believed me at all.
So I decided to keep it to myself. That last night I stayed real
close to the house with my family. We played cards and partied. I
didn't see much of Mr. Calvin the whole weekend.

The next morning, Bobby came over to take me to the bus station.
I said my good-byes to my family and Blacky. Bobby and I were
off. I asked, "Where's Barbara?" He told me that she was over to
her mother's house. I told him that I wanted to say good-bye to
her.

When we got there, she still didn't seem happy to see me. She just
looked at me crazy and asked what did I come by for. I tried to
tell her to not be so sensitive about the clubs and all.

     "Barbara, don't take it so serious. It ain't nothing like
     us."
     "That's not how the fuck you sounded yesterday.
     You didn't have to tell me about the little bitch that's
     trying to like you either," I tried to explain.
     "Barbara, I didn't know that you were going to get so
     upset."
     "How in the fuck did you think, I was going to feel,
     hah? Was I suppose to be happy and shit for you?"
Bobby jumped up. He saw that she was getting more upset and
told me to go get in the car. I got up like he said and started

walking to the car. Bobby went over to calm Barbara down. I saw Bobby coming to get in the car, but then I saw Barbara behind him coming to my side fast, still yelling. She had tears in her eyes. "So you're just going to leave me just like that! After all the fuck that I have done for your ass!" I didn't know what to do. I just sat there looking at her.

"I am not going to let you break my heart, little girl! Do you hear me?"

Then Barbara went into her jacket pocket and pulled a gun out, pointing it toward my head. I saw her family coming outside standing on the porch -- her mother, sisters and brother Daniel. They started screaming, trying to get her attention. I felt frozen, not knowing what to do. All I could see was that gun in my face. Bobby stayed in the car and did not move. Barbara's brother slowly came up behind her.

"Come on, Barb, please, put the gun down." I kept staring at her, thinking to myself, did she really love me that much? Have I broken her heart like she said? Was she serious all that time about running away with me like we use to say to each other?"

I started praying, God help! God, please help me now! I never meant to hurt her. I didn't know it was this serious! Eventually, her brother put his hands on the gun. Tears ran down her face. Her arm fell to her side and her brother held her in his arms as she began to cry even more. Then, Bobby burned rubber pulling off.

As we were driving to the bus station you could hear a pin drop. It was so quiet. My heart felt like it was beating a hundred miles per hour. We got to the bus station, I got out of the car, and Bobby helped me with my bag. He stood there and looked at me.

"I apologize for what I did to you because I know I was wrong. But I love you and wanted to be with you so bad."

"You know I love you guys, but I know this must stop."

"I am really sorry for what Barbara did back there. I
ain't never seen her trip like that."
"I believe it's over now, okay?" He nodded and said
okay.

We embraced and I told him I forgave him. As I was walking away
he yelled out, "Hey little girl, you just stole our hearts, what can we
say?" I laughed to myself and boarded the bus.

When we arrived in Los Angeles, Daddy was there to pick me up on
time. After all I had just been through in Fresno, I wanted to
jump off the bus and run to him and hug him. But I knew we
didn't quite have it like that. So I just said hello to him.

On the way home he asked how the weekend went. I told him that
it was the same old same old stuff, drinking, still ridiculing, still
fighting, still hollering. We were quiet for the rest of the drive.
When we got home, Daddy started getting ready to go to work. I
unpacked my bag and flopped on the couch to look at some TV.
Daddy left.

As I laid there, I began to think about Fresno. I grabbed my
notebook to journal.

> Dear God:
> I need to talk to you so bad. Thank you for being
> with me all weekend. I wished now that I did not
> go. I would not have seen or experienced all that
> crazy stuff down there. I hate to see my mother get
> worse and looking as bad as she does. Please help
> her, God. I know you can. I hope that AlmaFaye's
> boyfriend stop cheating on her and mistreating her
> like that too. Help her with her children and
> protect her, God. I see my sisters and brothers are
> growing up. Momma said Mr. Calvin was hunting
> day and night now. Then my life flashed in front of
> me in the car when Barbara was holding that gun up

to my head. What really stopped her from pulling that trigger? I never thought she would do anything like that to me. My mother yes, but not Barbara. I wish it would all go away. I don't know what all is going on with Barbara and Bobby, but I know I need to stay far away from them now. I need your power and strength to stay away. You know part of me really loves them a lot, but I know You don't like what we do with each other. I am sorry for hurting Barbara, I never meant to. I guess life is just not that simple. God, I wish all this stuff never happened. What do I do now, God?

Tears began to roll down my face. I wished so badly I could really for the first time talk to my mother like a true daughter should. I wished she could give me some direction. I knew she couldn't help me, but I just wanted to hear her voice. I signed off on my diary and went to call Momma.

I grabbed the phone and called her. She picked up.
"Hello?"
"Hi, Momma."
"Hi, baby."

I held the phone, knowing this would be the extent of our conversation.
"What's wrong, baby" she asked. She didn't sound drunk yet.
I said, "Nothing. I just called to let you know I made it home safe."
"Well, I know something is wrong because I can hear it in your voice, but you don't have to tell me if you don't want to."

Oh, how I ached to pour out my heart to her. I wanted to reach out and say, "It hurts Momma, and I am so confused, I don't know what to do anymore. I don't know if I am going or coming. Make it go away, Momma." But I was scared she would turn my pain around, making it my own fault like she always did. She couldn't make it go away anyway. She was part of the problem. But her voice was sufficient for then. Just hearing it lifted me up in spite of the confusion. She sounded so compassionate. I told her I better get off of Daddy's phone before I get in trouble. We laughed and said our good-byes. From that conversation on, I decided that I would just call Momma to hear her voice and have a brief conversation and hang up before she got crazy. I would call when I felt real lonely and sad.

Daddy was gone all the time now. If he wasn't at work, he was at the race track. If he wasn't there, he was visiting somebody. I didn't care, as long as he wasn't around to judge me.

The following Saturday night after I got back from Fresno, Greg, Sparkle, Diamond and I went to this club called Gino's. This was the weekend that Daddy went to Fresno. As we stepped out of the car, I heard this black woman saying to this white woman, "Hoe, I will stomp you to this ground! Do you understand me? Now go do what I told you to do." I looked and was shocked. Diamond looked at me and said, "Don't trip it, that's Ms. Pete's Hoe." I said, "Her what?" Then Diamond began to explain what was happening. She told me that this woman had about five women on the streets working for her, the same way a man pimp has women on the streets for him. We walked in the club. This club was nothing like Ruby's Club. The songs were more disco, instead of soul jams. I didn't like it.

DADDY'S WORK HOURS CHANGE

One day during the summer, Daddy came home and gave me the best news of the year. He told me that his work hours were changing from three to twelve midnight to the graveyard shift (eleven at night to seven o'clock in the morning. I faked like I was so sad. I even told him how scared I was going to be in that apartment all night by myself. He did as a Daddy should I guess and told me that everything will be safe, he was just a call away. I was shouting for joy inside. Now I could hang out with the gang more often all night long.

My night life became more and more active in the streets of L.A. I got hooked on the club Greg turned me on to. I even got the calendar of events from Monday through Friday and was there every night I could be. They started advertising their baseball game tournament coming up for the summer. I couldn't believe my ears. I said, "This life is so cool, man. There is everything in it. They do just like the regular people do."

Before I left the apartment each night, I would let the couch out and put a dummy in my bed. I shaped it as best as I could like a human body, in case I was running real late. Daddy had a very predictable pattern. He would come home and within twenty-five minutes, he was snoring loud. I placed the dummy under the covers as if I was there. Hoping Daddy would never need to wake me up for anything when he got home from work. So the dummy trick was cool and worked real well. I remember one time I came home about eight o'clock in the morning. When I turned the key in the door, I could hear Daddy snoring before it was fully opened. He was sleeping hard. I quickly replaced those clothes with my body in case he woke up.

Daddy's new work schedule really allowed me to get loose. Not only did I not have to come home on time, I didn't have to come home at all. My life got real busy and wild. I met all sorts of women. Young, middle-aged and even older women (up to forty-five years old), who I found myself more attracted to. The circle of people was very familiar. I got to know many people on a first name basis.

One night I came home after three o'clock in the morning. I had been partying most of the night. I couldn't sleep and so I began to write and reflect on my life.

Dear God:
Hello, I need someone to talk with for awhile. I know I
am getting away with so much freedom that my Daddy
don't know about. I find myself feeling so bad. I am
not the girl he thinks I am. All he knows about is this
young girl trying to finish school, and stay put while he
is at work at night. God, if he knew half the things I was
doing, he would probably have a heart attack. You know
he would, God.

You also know that I feel guilty and ashamed at all the
stuff I do. I know no matter how bad I want to be his
little jewel, I am not that type of daughter that he wants
and that he could be proud of at this time in my life. I
feel so lost in so many things. I'm lost in drugs,
drinking and "this lifestyle called gay" that I can't shake
right now. I know I am deceiving him.

I don't know to make him understand my life and even
how it got like this. I guess I don't quite understand
how it got like this either. I feel like one day I woke up
and shit just wouldn't stop happening to me. It was
always shit that had to be hid or hush hush. God, you
know I started playing hiding games as a little child.

I hid with my Momma hiding me under pool tables
while she partied. I hid secrets of Poppa Ernest playing
in my privates. I hid shit I saw my mother do that a
little girl was not suppose to see. Then hiding the truth
of what her stupid husband was doing while she was
sloppy drunk. Hiding in fear and confusion of her
wanting to kill me. I have always been hiding, God, I
wish life was different for me.

Now my Daddy does not know who I am nor where I
come from and perhaps that's why it's so difficult for
him to understand me. Nothing seems to satisfy me in

life. You know that I still feel so depressed deep down inside where even the drugs and alcohol can't reach and drown out.

Good night, God. I will talk with you later.

CHAPTER 26

MEET DESMUND

I went out one night with Diamond, Sparkle's girlfriend. I found out that Diamond lived about ten minutes from me so we decided, maybe we could go clubbing the nights that Sparkle had to work or was too busy. Sparkle didn't mind. She worked long hours sometimes. She owned her own Ice Cream Shop.

Diamond and I went out for a Tuesday night oldies but goodies night in the Ruby's Room. As soon as we walked in the door, we ran into Ms. Pete's standing with a woman next to her. I took a double look. Now Ms. Pete's is a stud and she was with this woman that I knew was a stud, too. I said to myself, "Okay who is in control? Has Ms. Pete's sweetened up or what?" As soon as I overheard their conversation, I knew Ms. Pete's was still in control of that relationship. She wasn't making her trick for her, but she had her selling drugs. She introduced her to everyone. Her name was Desmond. She was German. She had jet black hair and beautiful lips. Simply beautiful. Manly, but beautiful. I was turned on by her. But this was Ms. Pete's woman, so I had not better go there. We sat down at the same table. Throughout the night, I would look at her when I could, and her eyes would return to me. I saw that the attraction was very much mutual, we just couldn't do anything about it.

As we were leaving, Diamond asked me to make a run with her over to Pete's apartment to pick up a package. Come to find out, Desmond and Pete's lived together. We went to this red brick building, the fifth floor. I sat in the den area with Diamond. Apparently the package that Diamond came for was not there yet. Pete's, Desmond and Diamond went in the bedroom. "What in the hell was going on?" I wondered. There were kids sleeping in the living room. There was this one little girl who looked as if she was white. She was simply adorable. I overheard them talking in the back about picking up some drugs and making a drop. I heard Ms. Pete's tell Desmond to go take care of the drop and they would

take care of the pickup when Brenda came by. Then they came out
of the bedroom. Desmond was about to leave the house by herself.
"If I could only leave now, then I could have a chance to talk with
this fine woman," I thought to myself. Then, Diamond asked me
if I could hang a little longer. She said her roommate Brenda
should be on her way soon and they would drive me home. I said,
well I don't know because my daddy may be getting home real
soon, and I need to be at home when he gets there. By this time
Desmond was grabbing her black leather jacket to leave. Then Pete's
said, "Well, if you want to beat your Daddy home, you better get
your ass home now. I tell you what, she looked at Desmond, "take
Carla home on your way to the drop off."

I could not have timed it any better.,I said to myself.
    "Well I don't want to take her too much out of her
    way."
    "Shut up, it's cool, you only live fifthteen minutes
    away. Don't trip it." I said,
    "Okay."

The little girl laying on the couch began to cry. I turned around
and saw Desmond go over to her and assured her that she would be
back soon. I was shocked that she had a baby so young. The child
must have been about three or four years old. She looked up at me
and motioned let's go. I gave Diamond a kiss on her cheek and
shook Ms. Pete's hand.
    "I'll check yall next weekend," I said.
    "We'll see you, baby," Diamond said.

We walked down to the elevator and pushed the button. We stood
there without saying anything to each other. The elevator opened
and we got in. Immediately after the doors closed, Desmond
grabbed me in her arms and kissed me. The elevator door bell
rang again and we separated. A couple of white boys got on. We
looked at each other and smiled.
As we walked out Desmond told me that she had a driver by the
name of Jessie, who chauffeurs her everywhere. A black Cadillac

was waiting out front for her. We got in the car. She introduced me to Jessie who was black with a Jheri Curl and white teeth. We sat in the back seat together as he drove. She grabbed my hand and held it. She leaned over and whispered in my ear.

"Do you know I was looking at you all night?
I couldn't keep my eyes off of you."
"I was looking at you too," I whispered.

She told me that Pete's would kill her if she saw her looking my way for one second. I let her know that I knew all about Ms. Pete's and her temper. Desmund wanted to know about me and who I was. I told her that it wasn't much to tell other than the fact that I was sixteen years old, in the eleventh grade, and living with my Daddy. I asked her what about herself and she told me that she was twentz-seven years old and had a four year old daughter named LaKenya. She also told me that she was a hustler selling drugs for a living. When I asked her if Pete's was her woman she seemed a bit bothered. She told me that she didn't know because their personalities clash so much.

"I care for Pete's, but she dogs me out. Listen, do
you have to go home right away?"
"Hell naw, that was just my excuse to leave with
you."
Desmund decided to take me home after making
the dope drop.

We went far out to a truck stop where there were truck drivers standing around. Jessie drove the car about twenty feet away from where they were standing and Desmund got out of the car with her briefcase. The guys recognized her, did hi-five's and exchanged small talk. She handed them the briefcase and they handed her another briefcase that looked identical. Was that the drop bag and the refill bag, I thought to myself. Desmund rushed back to the car, and Jessie drove off. What kind of exchange was I just involved in? I didn't know, and I didn't ask any questions either.

"So you live with your Daddy?"
"Yeh I sure do."

"Is he at home?"
"No, actually, he won't be home for another six
hours."
"You think I can come to your pad and kick it for a
minute or so?"
"Sure."

I told her my address and she told Jessie to take us there. She was
very affectionate and attentive to my every movement. She was real
aggressive. I wasn't used to being the submissive one, but this
woman was really sexy, as well as macho, so I didn't mind. We
kissed all the way to my Daddy's house. I got out of the car and
she whispered something to Jessie, and he was gone. When I got
home, I took out my keys and opened the door. I couldn't believe I
was bringing this woman into my Daddy's house! I turned on the
lamp and left everything else dark. I knew we wouldn't need much
light. We began kissing and holding each other. Before I knew it
our clothes were coming off.

Suddenly there was a noise at the door. Keys started rattling. I
said, "shit" She asked is there a back door. I told her she was on
the second floor. We quickly started putting our clothes back on. I
jumped up and went to the door.
    "Who is it?" I yelled out.
    No one answered. I said it again. Then I looked out
    of the peek and there he was. A figure of a tall man.
    I opened the door and it was over.
    "Lonnie," I shouted.
    He said, "Hey man what's up?"
    "You're at the wrong door, that's what's up!"
    "Ah baby, forgive me."

Lonnie was drunk. I closed the door on him. She asked who was at
the door and what was he talking about. I told her nothing and
everything was okay. She didn't feel quite comfortable after that.
Within moments, she was fully dressed and ready to go. I gave her
my number and told her when to call and when not to call.

The next few weeks Desmund and I started seeing each other on a daily basis after Daddy left for work. She started bringing me gifts. Diamond earrings, scarves, clothes, and then money. She told me that she wanted to be my lady and nobody else. I wasn't sure if I was ready for a relationship with her and told her I needed to think about this. In the meantime, we kept spending time with each other. Desmund started bringing her daughter around me as time went on. I grew so attached to that pretty little girl as if she was my own child. She took to me right away.

Desmund started being affectionate toward me around her daughter and I didn't like that. It was okay while it was just she and I. Every time I told her not now, she would get so pisssed.
        "Are you ashamed of me?"
        "No, Desmund, if you didn't notice LaKenya can see
        us."
        "And, what is that suppose to mean?"
        "She shouldn't see this kind of carrying on."
        "Why the hell not? You're my woman and I love
        you."
        "Sweetheart, I can't explain it too good, but what we
        are to each other, shouldn't be so open and in the
        face of your daughter, that's all I know. We need to
        protect her."
        "Protect her! What the hell are you talking about,
        Carla?"

I was getting so mad, because I knew I was sounding contradictory and hypocritical. I couldn't explain to Desmund that I felt we were confusing the hell out of her daughter and I felt guilty about it.
        "Well, just don't kiss me in front of her. What I do
        intimately with you is between you and I not anyone
        else."
        "Look, if you are ashamed of me then say so, I can
        handle it."

She made her voice sound so sexy and masculine at the same time.
"Look, I'm not ashamed of you, I just don't want to
confuse no little child's mind."
"Shit, she might want to like women one day and if
she does, I'm all for it."
"But, Desmund, let that be her decision okay, not
ours."
She saw how mad I was getting and backed off.

The three of us would go out to dinner often and would attract so
much attention, because Desmund dressed just like a man. She had
style though. She spent good money for her clothes and they were
sharp. She looked like she walked out of a GQ magazine. Then she
had a little bop to her walk that began to really get on my nerves.
There was not a time that we didn't get bad vibes from people or
comments from men as we were leaving places. Desmund would
get so pissed off. Defending her manhood was so sickening to me.
"Baby, you just ain't had the right man. I can make
you feel like the woman that's hidden under that hat
and those baggy pants."

Desmund loved wearing her hats, which made her look like a
gangster and almost like a man if you didn't look too hard at her
beautiful womanly features. She tried to hide her curvaceous body
with her baggy pants, but that shape would slip out sometimes
through certain things that she wore like her Sasoon jeans. Her legs
were so gorgeous too. Her legs were hairy and shapely too. Men
would always comment on her when she would wear men's short
pants with a sports top.

I didn't really care about the public judgment, because I finally felt
a genuine love from Desmund. She was so real with her feelings for
me.

As weeks continued to go by, Desmund represented the first
committed relationship I had ever come close to. So the judgments
and whispers were tolerable. I became so bold, I introduced her to

the Morris' next door. They would see her and her daughter each time Daddy would leave. I began to have a private relationship with the Morris' that was totally secret. They knew my Daddy didn't have one idea what was going on. They also knew my life story, as we talked about it one night at the table. They began to love Desmund, and Ms. Morris had her say about her, "as long as you are not hurting anyone, it should be okay." They saw every gift, every time a cab came to pick me up for dinner or to take me to Desmund's hotel. Whatever else Desmund would do for me, I would run over to the Morris' to brag.

Our life was almost like an ongoing fairy tale. Desmund treated me like a princess. Desmund was still asking me if I was her only love. I finally told her that I was committed to her and I could live the rest of my life like this with her. We couldn't stop spending time together. Every free second I had, I was with Desmund.

Desmund started meeting me outside the gate after school. The kids at my school figured out what was happening between Desmund and me, especially when Desmund would get out of the cab as I walked toward it and open my door for me. I didn't care because they weren't my friends anyway.

June was here. The school year was coming to a close. Daddy was still constantly busy with work and his race track fetish. I was wonderfully involved in my relationship with Desmund that he knew nothing about. All he did was walk around every now and then and ridicule me for being the way I was. I didn't care because somebody loved me. That's all that mattered to me. After Desmund stopped messing with Ms. Pete's, she started living in hotels because Ms. Pete's kicked her out. She didn't care because she could afford to live anywhere she wanted to. Her drug sales brought her a thousand dollars a week. Her hotel ran her about a hundred seventy five dollars a week and the rest of the money we would splurge on each other and LaKenya. Daddy never questioned my new clothes because he never saw me.

SUMMER TIME - 1979 (June - September)
LIFE WITH DESMUND

I spent the summer with Desmund and we went to as many places as we could think about. Every weekend was a movie, dinner and the Dorothy Chandler pavilion. Sundays were parks, and beaches, so LaKenya could go with us. Then our night life was filled with concerts and expensive, exotic dinners in the hills of Beverly Hills and romantic hotels.

Desmund needed a black blazer and said we were going to go to the mall before going out for the night. I loved going shopping with Desmund because there was nothing that she wouldn't buy me if I wanted it. We had never shopped for her until now. After arriving at the mall, Desmund said she was going to be in the men's department while I looked for something for me in the ladies' area. At first I didn't think too much of it, other than she wanted a better jacket or a unisex look.

After a hour went by and she could not find anything, I suggested that she come look in the ladies' section.
    "Are you being funny?" she yelled.
    "Do I look like I'm cracking jokes?" I kidded back.
    "Why not!"
    "Because I don't wear girly things."
    "Desmund, there are things over there that are suitable and nice."
    "I don't care, I only wear men's clothes."

I knew right then and there things were really wrong. When people began looking at us, I got so embarrassed. I started talking through my teeth as seriously as I could.

Another time while shopping with Desmund, I discovered how crazy she was about her role as the aggressor. Desmund would not go in the ladies' section at all. In fact, she got so pissed off that we

ended up getting into an argument right there in the store. Then
she said she needed some boxers. I thought I would faint.

"Oh hell naw. You got to go buy some what?"
"You heard me, boxers."

One night I was some weird looking briefs on her. I thought she
only had one pair, but she said that was all she wears. I wanted to
ask her so bad, what are you putting inside the boxers.

That day she was quiet the rest of the evening and so was I. I
couldn't believe how adamant she was about buying only men's
clothes. I was so embarrassed, going from one men's section to the
next, especially having so many men's eyes on us.

The next evening, Desmund told me to dress up real good because
we were going to go to one of the best restaurants in town. I told
Daddy I was going out with Greg. He said cool. Desmund's driver
arrived about eleven-thirty. Desmund was waiting in the back seat
with twelve beautiful long-stemmed roses. She was the most
romantic and giving woman I had ever known. When we pulled up
in the valet area, it was first class treatment from that moment on.
Desmund whispered something to her driver and turned to me,
reaching out her hand. Desmund took me by the hand. I jumped
at first. But then I relaxed because I knew I was not going to run
into anybody I knew at this place. The valet people didn't even look
at us funny. I guess they thought Desmund was a man, she was
looking pretty handsome and manly too. Desmund had on a pair
of black baggy tuxedo pants with a white starched tuxedo shirt and
a black bow tie. She had on a black swinging blazer to match.
Damn, she looked good. Her hair was beautiful and full layered,
going back evenly on her shoulders. I loved Desmund's hair.

"You're ready to have the time of your life?" she
whispered.
"I guess so, you mean I have not had it yet?"
"No, baby, there is so much more that we are going
to experience together."

On the inside, there was beautiful soft music playing. The floors were elegant and shiny marble with a diamond pattern in each of them. I had never seen anything like it before. A spiral staircase climbed to the left. Then they had high ceilings that seemed to reach heaven with a chandelier the size of an airplane. The architecture was breathtaking. I felt like I was in another world. The world of the rich and famous. Well tailored and polite men greeted us at the entrance of the restaurant.

"Do you have a reservation, sir?" Desmund loved when people would mistake her for a man. It made her feel so proud, I would tease her and say "You're probably growing hair on your chest right now, hah."

"Two for Desmund" she said in the most manly voice she could muster up. The gentleman found her name.

"Ah hah, follow me please."

We were seated by a window with a view of the mountains and millions of lights of the city laid beneath our table, sparkling through the glass. It was so beautiful. It seemed that we were on top of the world.

"Desmund, this place is so beautiful. Oh my God."

"For a beautiful lady like yourself." She winked.

A nice woman handed us a one sheet wine menu.

"We will have your finest champagne," Desmund said.

"Whoo, I have never had champagne before," I told her.

"I love you, Carla."

"I love you, too." The woman waitress came back with two sparkling champagne glasses.

"To the most beautiful woman and lover I've ever had."

"Cheers," I said.

"To many years together of total happiness."

"Cheers. Thank you." I felt like crying. I had never
been treated like this.

A few seconds later the waitress brought us our menus. The prices
were very expensive, not that Desmund would have a problem with
them. Thirty five dollars for a chicken dinner was crazy.
"Do you like steak, sweetheart?"
"I like pork chops."
"Well, you will probably love their leg of lamb."
"Well you order for me, okay?"

The waitress returned and took our orders. Desmund ordered for
both of us. The champagne glasses were refilled immediately once
the waitress observed we were near our last sip. Dinner was
delicious. The meat was so well seasoned and tasty.
"Are you satisfied?" Desmund asked.
"Quite. Thank you."
"Well then, we can go up to our room."
"What, we have a room here?"
"Of course, the night wouldn't be complete without
wining, dining and reclining you."

Desmund already had the key. She must have planned this way
before we got here. We walked into a beautiful elegant room. The
king-size bed was draped with a nice mauve comforter with rose
patterns deeply embedded in it. The drapes matched. Then to the
left of the room was an elevated Jacuzzi bathtub which seemed to be
the size of the king-size bed. A bucket of champagne was sitting on
the marble edge of the Jacuzzi. Desmund held me from behind as I
stood there looking at this illustrious room fit for a king and queen.
"I want to make you feel so special and so loved. I
want to give you everything your heart desires."

I didn't know what to say. All the things Desmund had done for
me to this point left me speechless because it always felt like a fairy
tale that I was not use to living in. Waiting to wake up at any
moment.

"I wonder what champagne would taste like if I
   licked it off your body?"
"I don't know."
"You think we can find out?"

Desmund turned on the Jacuzzi tub and filled the room with warm
moist steam from the pool. We undressed and got in. The jets
were so soothing to my back. It was my first time for that.
Desmund opened the bottle of champagne which was waiting next
to the tub.

That night felt like a honeymoon that I had never been on.
Desmund poured champagne all over my body and made love to
me from the Jacuzzi to the bed. I didn't have a sip of champagne
on my body when Desmund finished kissing and licking my body
all over. I always knew she was a good lover, but this night was so
different and so special. I knew what pure ectasty felt like before
we left that gorgeous place.

Her driver was outside to pick us up at the break of dawn. The sun
wasn't even out yet, but he was there standing by the door waiting
to open it for us.

There was not a place that I wanted to go to in Los Angeles I had
not gone with Desmund and her daughter. When we went out at
night, Desmund had a friend that would keep her daughter. But
for the casual daytime outings, LaKenya was right there with us.

Then the unthinkable happened. One day Desmund and I got into
an argument. I brought up an issue that had been breaking my
heart ever since I noticed it. Each time her daughter would call her
Mommy, Desmund would correct her very harshly, demanding
that LaKenya call her Desmund. This day, I had to say something.
   "Sweetheart, why don't you let your daughter call
      you Mommy?"
   "Because, I don't want to be a sissy. Why?"
   "Well, Desmund, you are her mother. You are not a

sissy if you let her call you that."
"Hell naw. I'm the man." I was pissed.
"The last time I checked Desmund, men could not
have children, only women and where in the hell did
you get that crazy ass thinking from?"
"Carla, do you want to be the man now?"
"Hell naw. I don't even want a damn man nor do I
want to be a man. If I did, I would go get me one.
All I'm concerned about is confusing the hell out of
your daughter."

Desmund started walking back and forth in the room. LaKenya
was in the other room watching television. I was hoping she
couldn't hear us arguing. This was the second time I questioned
my lifestyle relating to children. The first time was with Barbara
and her girls when I lived with them. I told her how much her
daughter needed a mother.

There was silence for about three minutes. I stayed quiet. Then,
tears began rolling down her face.
"I don't know how to be a mother, Carla."
I wondered to myself how it even happened.
LaKenya was four year old. That was not that long
ago, I said to myself.
Was this an arranged situation, an accident, or rape?
I was afraid to ask, but I had to ask.
"Where is the father to your daughter?"
She looked at me as to say, I can't believe you are
asking this question.
"I don't know." Her jaws got even tighter.
"Look it wasn't suppose to happen, okay. Ms. Pete's
wanted a baby. I don't want to talk about it."
"Oh my God" I said, without thinking. I couldn't
help it, it came out before I knew it.
"You had a baby for another woman?"
"I proved my love to her. It didn't matter because
she still dogged me and treated me like shit."

She scared me because I didn't know women got that damn deep with each other. Damn, I thought to myself. This is deeper than I thought it was. She sat down on the bed next to me.
> "If I let her call me Mommy, you won't think I'm a
> punk, will you?"
> "Hell naw. I would respect and love you even more."

I felt she deeply wanted her daughter to be able to call her Mommy, but she didn't know how others or I would view her. Her whole reaction to my question shocked me. I didn't know all those fears were in her mind.
> "I just don't want to be weak. I want you to be
> strong for you. I want you to see me as the
> provider," she cried.
> "Baby I know that you are a provider, but you don't
> have to lose your womanhood to prove it. You don't
> have to confuse and deprive your daughter either."

We finally came to an agreement. She would let her daughter call her Mommy from now on. After that conversation I really felt guilty for being with Desmund. I couldn't get over her depriving her daughter from calling her Mommy because of her fear of how she would be perceived by me or other women. And I couldn't get out of the fact she had the baby for another woman to prove her love for her.

I kept saying in my mind this is some sick shit and it's really time to go. But I loved her so much and I loved her daughter too. I made up in my mind on the way home that day I would break it off with Desmund and stop contributing to the confusion of that little girl. Instead of growing apart, Desmund and I started getting closer and closer. She spoiled me more and more every time I saw her.

One day I made Desmund mad when I tried to make love to her. She pushed me out of her way.
> "What are you doing?"

"I'm trying to make love to you. Is there something
wrong?"
"Yeh, I don't let women make love to me. Do I look
like a punk?"
"Desmund, baby, what's the problem? I'm confused,
you don't let women touch you because you are the
strong one?"
"Yeh, don't I satisfy you?"
"Of course you do, but I want to be satisfied by what
I like to do to women too."

Desmund explained that she didn't let women caress her breast or
go down on her because it made her feel wimpish. She was the
man in the relationship and didn't want to feel like a fag.

"Damn girl, I know men that let women go down on
them, if you want to go there. It's called making
love to each other. Why do you have so many damn
hang ups about who do what?"

Desmund let me make love to her but I could tell she didn't want
me to get to comfortable with doing it all the time. Though she
enjoyed it, she struggled with not making sensuous noises that
showed her excitement. She would stop me before she ever reached
a climax or a place of ecstasy. One time I felt real devilish and
locked her thighs to the point she could not move and get away,
and had to experience the full feelings that were coming. And boy
did she scream.

She was so mad at me after she got her breath together. She felt so
embarrassed at the same time, but I was glad and laughing. I held
her and told her how much I loved her and she had no reason to be
ashamed of her body or her womanhood.

She cried and asked me over and over again if she was still the man
in the family. I told her she could be anything she wanted to be.
From that time on, I could tell when Desmund was in the mood to
let me make love to her. She had the most curvaceous body and

beautiful thighs on a woman. I thought it was so sad for her not to be able to be free in her womanhood and have to hide behind big clothes and manly mannerisms to affirm her role in her gayness, but all in all wishing to God she could be free and a woman. Afraid of what it would feel like or be like to not have some masculine identity attached to herself. She was so afraid of the control and vulnerability till it was depressing to watch her over compensate.

After a few months, I noticed Desmund disappearing for lengths of time. First she started off doing it when she had to check out of a hotel by Friday and into a new one in case the cops were on her trail for selling drugs.

She would somehow forget to call me and let me know the hotel she checked into. Our arrangement was that she would contact me anytime she would check into a new hotel. Weeks started going by, and I wouldn't know where she checked into. For days I would be so scared and nervous, not knowing anything and not hearing from her after being use to hearing from her every single day.

The last time Desmund did that to me, she showed up on my doorstep, not knowing if Daddy was there or not. I was so glad that he wasn't. I couldn't believe she was knocking on my door.
"Hey, baby, let me in."
"Desmund, what in the hell are you doing?" I yelled
   through the window, looking at her.
"I have to talk to you. Let me in, baby"

I was so scared Daddy was going to walk up any second. I opened the door and told her to stay right there. I grabbed my key and took Desmund over to Miss Morris' house. I told Miss Morris I needed to talk with Desmund in private. She said we could use her bedroom.
"Look baby, I know you are mad at me because I've
   been gone," Desmund started explaining before I
   could say one word.
"You damn straight, Desmund. I don't know if you

are locked up in jail for selling drugs, killed from a deal gone bad, missing or what. That's a lot of damn pressure on me. I'm worried about LaKenya and her safety."

"Well it ain't none of that, baby. I've just been working around the clock. LaKenya has been fine, she's been over to my friends. And then when I come in I sleep all day."

"Well, Desmund, since none of those bad things happened to you, then you really don't have one damn good excuse for not calling me in two damn weeks?"

"Look..."

"No you look, do I look stupid to you? That shit don't even make sense to me! Where in the hell have you been for two damn weeks?"

"Baby I told you, selling drugs and laying low. The cops were on me kind of tight and I had to just stay low. I didn't want to call you or bring you around because I didn't know how close they were on me and I didn't want to bring you into no shit."

Desmund tried to pull me to her to kiss me. I jerked my arm from her.

"Look, I'm going to give you one more chance, but if you do this shit to me one more time, don't ever call me again."

"Baby, I ain't never going to do this to you. I'm sorry, baby."

"Hey, can we go out to dinner tonight?"

"Look I have to see what my Daddy is doing, I will call you if you give me the damn number where you're staying." She smiled and shook her head at me.

"Here, baby, a couple of hundred dollars for you in case you need something."

"Don't think you are buying my madness away."

She kissed me and ran down the stairs to her driver who was waiting patiently.

Miss Morris wanted to know if everything was okay with Desmund and myself. I told her about what had me so mad. She said I needed to understand that's the type of woman I have. A woman who is a hustler but a woman that also loves me to death. That made me feel so good that Miss Morris saw how much Desmund cared about me.

Daddy came home about an hour after Desmund left. After Daddy got home that evening he said he wanted to talk with me about responsibilities. We sat at the table in the den and he asked me what did I want to do with my life. I wanted to tell him none of his damn business. What was this, some sorry ass approach to communicating with me?
"Listen, Carla, it's about time you started planning your future. Pretty soon you will be out of school and will not know what handling money is all about."

I wanted to tell him so bad, that I have handled and made more money than he has probably seen in one pay check. When he finished his lecture I told him that I would go look for a job and start a savings account up.

After a week or two, I decided to go across the street and apply for a job at McDonald's. Before the night was over, I received a call from McDonald's saying I had the job.

I learned in the first week that McDonald's was a fast paced, hard job. They made you do everything from washing the side walks to cleaning the grill. I just wanted to be a cashier. I had a fun time at work even though they made me clean up outside and around the tables after people ate. I appreciated my own little money, but I knew Desmund would be mad once she found out I was working.

When Desmund finally called, after not calling me after our last missing in action argument, I told her about the job that I had at McDonald's. She was furious!

"I give you close to two hundred dollars a week, Carla, isn't that enough?"
"Desmund, I don't think I could tell my Daddy that you support me."
"Listen, Carla, if you want more I can give you more, but baby don't work, please."
"Desmund, you haven't heard a word I have said. It was my Daddy's idea I told you, not mine! Plus you are not around every week anyway. So I can't depend on your support all the time."
"I can give you more now if you want me to. I can't wait till you graduate next year so we can get our own place."
I thought to myself, who said we were going to get our own place together? I just let her talk

LAST SCHOOL YEAR
(SEPTEMBER 1979 - 12TH GRADE)

My last year in high school. I made it. I couldn't believe it. There were so many times in life that I didn't think I would ever make it to the twelfth grade. I had to do extremely well this school year in order to graduate on time.

I didn't go out as much because of my many classes and homework. I saw Desmund on the week-ends now because of the school schedule and homework. I was trying so hard to graduate with my class, but I knew I had to make up a lot of credits.

The holidays this year went by real fast because I decided not to go back to Fresno as I did each year. I knew I wouldn't be missing anything. Nothing ever changed when I would go down there anyway. This Thanksgiving was boring. I had waited for Desmund to call me like she said she was, but she didn't. I was mad and worried at the same time again. She did me like this also for Christmas, but I made up my mind after that, it was over.

The holidays were so boring and empty. Daddy was with whoever he was with and I didn't see him for a couple of days, which was real nice. I stayed in my depression at home without any interruptions.

The day after Christmas Desmund called me. She said she wanted to see me and could send a cab for me. I told her sure, because I wanted to talk to her too. After arriving, I walked into her room where nothing but gifts were laid out on the bed and on the chair for me. I looked and she was smiling.

> "Those are for you, baby. Merry Christmas. I had to work all night."
> "I don't want your gifts, Desmund. I don't want your money."
> Desmund ignored me and took this little black box out of her pocket, walking toward me. She opened this beautiful little box and there lay a diamond ring with a wedding band.
> "Oh no. It's too late for that, Desmund, it's over this time for real.
> "Come on, baby, give me another chance. I'm working for us."
> "I am tired of waiting for you week after week, hoping you will come back and wondering if you are going to show up. Wondering if you are dead or alive. You don't understand what that does to me and I can't go through it anymore."
> "Baby, you know I can take care of myself. I have just had to lay real low from the feds. You know how it gets."
> "No, Desmund, I don't. All I know is that I can't handle this guessing worried game anymore. If I'm not worth giving a courtesy call to just to let me know you and LaKenya are fine, then you are not

worth another chance at this time."

Desmund was pleading with me to change my mind. But my mind was made up and nothing was going to change it. Desmund interrupted and began to tell me how much she loved me. She said all the sacrifices of not being able to see me was building a future for us. She said she was making money and putting it away for our future together. I thought to myself, another damn lie that she expects me to believe. I looked at her daughter who was sitting on the floor in front of the TV. I felt so bad for her. I told Desmund that her daughter needed to be in pre-school, not running from hotel to hotel with her. I told her to keep her cab money. I will take the bus home. As I was leaving, her daughter ran to the door to give me a goodbye hug. I did this child a favor by getting out of her life, I thought to myself. She will probably face so much confusion later in life. I didn't need to be adding to it. I hated to see Desmund cry. It tore me apart.

As I rode the bus home, I felt mixed emotions. I felt free on one end and still locked up inside on the other end. Free from the guilt of being around Desmund's daughter. Locked up because I still wanted her affection but I knew deep down inside she was unstable and I didn't want to deal with anymore unstable situations in my life. God, I hoped she could get her life together.

NEW YEAR'S - JANUARY 1980

I got one of the scariest calls the first of the year. My stepmother called for Daddy. I thought, "Oh no, not her again!" I knew she still didn't care for me, because she never apologized to me for how she threw me out of her house and gave my Daddy an ultimatum. She just started talking sweet again as if nothing ever happened. She was a Dr. Jekyll and Mr. Hyde, like my real mother. Overhearing their conversation, Daddy was talking real nice to her. I noticed from that day on they spoke regularly. Then the next thing I knew she was coming over to the house and spending the night on Daddy's off days. He would spend the night over to her house.

Now his son Travis Jr. was spending the night at our apartment. We were cool. In fact, we started really being sisters and brothers, since everybody saw that I wasn't going anywhere.

BIRTHDAY, FEBRUARY 1980
(17 YEARS OLD)
New Job at Winchell's

My seventeenth birthday was one of the loneliest of all. Daddy had to work and I had to study for mid-terms. I felt I was getting older but going nowhere. I just lost my job at McDonald's due to a lay-off. I was glad when it was over. I heard about Winchell's hiring next door. I decided to put in an application and was hired on the spot. The owner was a black man named Fred. He was so nice. He told me he ordinarily didn't hire on the first interview, but he loved my smile and personality. I ran home to tell Daddy the good news, but he thought it was bad. He talked about stability and not running from one job to the next. I said to myself "whatever." Winchell's started me off as a cashier, and I had lots more hours at night there.

A couple of months went by and the doughnut business proved to be more exciting than I thought. I began to meet all types of people. There were regulars that came in every morning. I noticed this older man with gray hair that came in each morning and smiled at me. One day he decided to talk to me. He told me that he had been watching me for a few weeks and wanted to get to know me. I wasted no time in telling him I didn't want to get to know men, I wanted to know only women. He chuckled to himself and gave me his card. He said, "We need to really have lunch now."

On April Fools' Day Fred came in the store with his head down. He told me that the owners were selling the business to new management and that the new management would probably hire new personnel. And it wasn't an April Fool's joke like I thought it was at first. He felt real bad for me. He told me that we had another two months. I told him don't worry about me. I thanked him for giving me a chance to work for him. I used the next month to look for a job and sure enough there was one right across the street. I applied at the Melody Shop dress store. I was hired a week later as a cashier. I was so lucky I thought to myself. My Daddy couldn't believe it, but he was pleased that I still had a desire to work. He didn't approve of not having money in a savings account.

One day I finally opened an account and shocked his socks off. The Melody Shop was a nice dress store. The girls that worked there were young and middle aged. There was this girl named Balinda who was gay. She started taking clothes home from the store. She was the lead cashier. I caught on and started doing the same thing. She and I would close the store at times, and she would say, "I need something new to wear to the club tonight." I said I wish I had something new.

"Get you something baby, no one will know. I
won't tell" she said.
"For real," I said.

She said nope, I sure won't. After that night, every week I had something new to wear to the club, courtesy of the Melody shop.

STORE INVESTIGATION
JUNE 1980

One day I came into work and everybody's face was drooping down. I asked Balinda, what's going on. She shrugged her shoulders. By this time the manager of the store came out from the back and said, "May we talk with you Carla?" I said, "Sure." I placed my lunch down behind the counter and went in the back with the owner. I sat down in this room and there were two other white guys in the room. They started off by explaining that the store was under investigation. He talked about all the merchandise that came up missing. As they were talking, my heart dropped. They knew, I thought. What was going to happen, I wondered.

The manager told me that he had asked everyone to cooperate and to take a lie detector test so as to clear their names. Then without warning he asked me if I had been stealing any of his clothes. My eyes bucked,

> "No, sir" I said real firm. "I don't know what you
> are talking about."
> "Well, I need to leave you here with Detective
> Lewis," he said,
> He left the room.
> Det. Lewis started off by saying, "Now the other
> girls have already confessed to the crimes and they
> also included you". I want to give you a chance for a
> couple of reasons.
> "One, how old are you?"
> "Sixteen," I said,
> "Okay, first of all, you are a minor. You are not
> facing serious charges like the others because they are
> over twenty-one. If you cooperate and save us court
> time in proving you are guilty, you will have the
> lesser charge, if any at all."

I didn't need time to think about anything. I told him everything he wanted to know. Then when it all came down to it, the detectives had lied to me about speaking to the other girls. The other girls had not confessed and they were off the hook. I ended up being the only one getting a court date, trial and probation. Needless to say, my daddy was furious. I was put on one year probation and was grounded for the rest of the year.

PREPARATION FOR GRADUATION
JUNE 1980

Graduation was nearing. I came home from school one day and asked my daddy if he was buying me a graduation dress. It was only a few weeks before graduation.

> "No, I don't have any money," he said.
> "Well what am I supposed to do, Daddy?"

"Ask one of your women to buy it for you. They
get you everything else."

I ached with pain from his words. I wanted to say can't you just be
my damn Daddy for one damn minute. Instead, I asked if he had
twenty dollars so that I could go buy some fabric and make my
graduation dress. He reached in his pockets and pulled out a
twenty dollar bill and gave it to me.

I went and bought some beautiful white, purple and green fabric. I
also bought a McCalls pattern of a beautiful dress. I got working
on it immediately. I was so happy that I took that homemaking
class for three years in high school. I was also glad I bought my own
sewing machine a year before with some of the money Desmund
had given me.

Things were real bleak around the house. In a matter of weeks I
would be graduating from high school. I couldn't believe it because
out of twelve children that my mother had only a few graduated
from high school. I called my mother and asked her if she was
coming. It meant so much to me. I wanted to finally let her see
that I could do something so great, since the other years were not
acknowledged as any major accomplishment. Maybe this will be the
one that would make her proud. She said she would be there with
AlmaFaye.

Graduation Day was June 14, 1980. We were leaving the house and
Momma and AlmaFaye hadn't arrived yet, but I had to be at the
Dorothy Chandler Pavilion at a certain time. Daddy told me not
to worry, they would be here. So he dropped me off and came
back to the house to wait for them.

I met up with my classmates and saw my one friend, Phyllis. She
gave me a hi-five and said, "I'm out of here!" We laughed.
Everyone had on their blue and white robes and were carrying their
hats. I felt like a fish out of water. I felt so weird and out of place
with those young people.

Three hours later the ceremony started. It went by so fast. The place was packed with thousands of people from all over the place. The class of 1980 was a large class. The bleachers were filled to the max. Everybody in the room looked like little ants. I couldn't see where my family was seated. The Principal was calling out the names of each student, and the crowd would clap while they were walking to receive their diploma. Some applause delayed the actual ceremony. They tried to make an announcement a couple of times to tell the audience to applaud once everything was over.

I was not supposed to walk the stage on this date, because I was short a semester due to my many transitions from Fresno to Los Angeles. I lost units when I ran away and stayed out of school an entire semester. I only had to make up six units.

Then it was time for the L's to be announced. Carla Lee. My name was called and the applause quickly left. That's when it hit me. No one really knew me at that school. I didn't make friends, I didn't go places with groups, I didn't know anyone. Phyllis, my family, plus some teachers, yelled for me. It was almost the most embarrassing moment in life. I couldn't wait until it was over. This was the first time I wanted to be like the other kids.

At the end of the ceremony, I was very sad. Kids were hugging each other, crying, laughing, and talking together. I waved and nodded at a couple of students that I recognized who were in my classes. They nodded back and started back talking to their friends and buddies. What a lesson to learn on the last day of school. Make friends and you will have friends. Even my only buddy Phyllis was popular. She had many friends other than myself. I couldn't tie her down to only be with me.

I knew I wouldn't see these kids anymore. When we got to the end of the tunnel, the parents were waiting there impatiently for their children. I finally spotted my small group of supporters which was my Dad, my little brother, my Daddy's wife, and that was all. I didn't see my mother or sister. My heart changed as I walked toward them. My Daddy's wife tried to be encouraging but my daddy wasn't. He didn't even hug me. He barely said congratulations. My Daddy kept walking. I wondered how come he didn't hold me. I gave him my hand and said, "Thanks Daddy." I rode in the back seat very depressed, wondering to myself why my Daddy did not hug me. It bugged the hell out of me. This wasn't an exciting day. There were no fireworks on my behalf and no real acknowledgment from my Daddy or Mother. I felt like a fool to desire anything different from what I had been getting prior to this day. Daddy took his wife and son home first and then we proceeded to our house.

Finally, it was only Daddy and I at the apartment. He asked me if I was going to the Grad Night Party. I told him I probably wasn't going anywhere. I didn't have any money.

"Daddy, can I ask you something?"
"What is it?"
"Why didn't you hug me at my graduation?" I
nervously asked.
He looked at me crazy.
"I wanted to, but I didn't think you wanted men
touching you since you like women."

After he made that remark he walked out and went to his room. I went to the bathroom and wept in my towel so that Daddy couldn't hear me. It hurt so much. I sat in the corner of the bathroom against the tub looking for God's help, answers, and comfort. I looked to the top of the ceiling, at the edge of the corner in the wall, and I focused on the cross that I was able to find in the corner of every wall.

"God, why? Why does life have to be this way? Why do I have to be here? My mother and sister didn't come and I have a Daddy that can't set his views aside long enough to love me. I really don't see any reason for my being here. I can't, Lord. I just want to leave this world right now. No one loves me like You do."

Moments later, Daddy knocked on the door and told me not to be long because he needed to get in. I told him I was coming out. Wiping my face quickly I walked out. I was glad he was leaving for work. I was very glad. I wanted to get high, drunk, and lose my mind. I went next door to the Morris's to see if Joseph was home from the graduation. He answered the door.

"Hey man, are you going to Grad Night?" I asked.
"Naw, are you," he yawned.
"I don't want to be a part of that stupid shit. It ain't me," I told him.
"I want to get into some real feel good, you know."
Joseph's eyes got big and he smiled.
"Yeah, we can do something," he responded.

I told Joseph to work on getting us something to get high on and I will work on the place that we can go and get wasted. Joseph left, but never returned that night.

> Dear God:
> What a laugh in the face. The day I thought I always waited for which was to graduate from high school. This was the day I thought I would get the maximum acceptance, love and appreciation from my parents and it just blew up in my face as everything does that I try to impress them with. It just doesn't seem to work out for me. I hope you were proud. I wished my mother and sister could have been there for me. I should have known better. What would make me think that Momma would come and be so happy for me? It was too good to be true, I should have known better. Now I don't care about none of their asses. Just leave me the fuck alone, I wish. I wish I could just disappear from there asses and they won't have to worry about me anymore. I am so mad God, you know that I am.

Please forgive me for cursing, but you know how mad I am. It hurts so bad to want love from your parents and receive nothing but rejection and abandonment all the time. I wish you could give me a big hug, God, like a father. You know I need one, don't you? Why wouldn't my Daddy hug me? He could have stabbed me in my chest and that would have felt better than the shit he told me about not wanting to hug me. I don't know, maybe I should have never met him, I'm sure he would be better off and maybe me too. Please don't ever leave me, God. You are all I seem to have for sure. Thank you for being there every time I need to talk to You. Thank You for loving me when it feels like nobody else does.

CHAPTER 27

SUMMER SCHOOL
(July - August 1980)

Summer School came and I took up an Auto Mechanic class which gave me all the credits I needed to receive my diploma. I was the only girl in the class and received all the assistance I needed from the guys to help me pass the course. The summer at home this year was kind of slow and I was growing bored. I was still getting over Desmund and wanting to fill that empty space inside. I just didn't know with what. I found a telephone number on the back of one of my old payroll check stubs. It was the number from that old man I met when I first started working at that Winchell's. I smiled to myself. I remembered the look on his face when I told him I liked women. I thought I'd give that Mr. Brown a call. I called Brown after my Daddy left. A nice warm man's voice answered.

"Hello?"

"Hey, is this Brown?"

"Yes. Who's calling?"

"It's Carla, from the doughnut shop."

"Well, little lady, long time no hear. I didn't think I would ever hear from you."

"Yeh, I know. I've been very busy."

"Oh yeh, with those women friends of yours, eh?"

"Naw, Grand Theft, being fired and finally graduating from high school."

"Wow, you had a heavy load on your shoulders."

"Yeh, in more ways then one."

"So, when are we going to get together for that lunch or dinner?"

"Well, I was calling to cash in that rain check today if it's cool."

"Well what about tomorrow evening?"

"Sounds good to me, Brown, I'll call you before I leave to get your address."

We hung up and I sat back on the couch wondering what was about to come out of this weird association.

The next day I called Brown to get his address after my Daddy left
to go to the race track. Brown lived only two blocks from us. I got
ready and went over.   I rang the doorbell and he answered with a
great big smile on his face. He was handsome, tall, and dark - a
distinctive looking old man.
    "Come right in, my dear."
    "Hi, how are you doing?"
    "Just waiting on you, my dear." He was so nice.

I walked into a contemporary earth-tone colored apartment with
beautiful furniture. He had prepared dinner and set the table for
two, with wine glasses. How quaint, I thought to myself. Soft jazzy
music was playing in the background.
    "I prepared some smothered steak, green peas,
      mashed potato and gravy, and a large apple pie for
      dessert," he bragged.
    "All this for me, man," I asked.
    "Yes, it is," he smiled.

I could tell we were going to be so cool. I went to the bathroom to
wash my hands and saw the same beautiful environment.   The
towels were evenly set on their racks and the soap dish shining and
sparkling. The carpet on the floor matched the hanging shower
curtains. His favorite colors must have been beige and gold with a
little black accent. Those were the colors throughout his apartment.

We sat down and talked while he poured a glass of white wine for
me. We talked about each other's lives. We talked about my
young, but very adventurous, life from the time I left home to live
with Bobby and Barbara. Brown said it seemed that I had been
forced to grow up too soon. Then he started asking real personal
questions.
    "So how many children do you want to have?"
    "None."
    Brown seemed real concerned about that.
    "None, why not?"

"I'm not the mother type."
"I think you would make a beautiful mother. You
    seem so caring about others."
"I help my mother raise my four brothers and sisters
    and therefore I feel that I have fulfilled my motherly
    responsibility."

What he didn't know was that I was petrified of the thought of
having children. I never wanted my child to be subject to a man or
to have their Daddy molest them. I didn't want to be a single
mother either. I didn't feel I had enough love to offer a child.
Maybe that's why I didn't get what I needed. All these thoughts hit
me as I was sitting in front of Brown answering his questions. I
didn't want to talk about that too much so I switched subjects.

"Tell me more about your life, Brown."
"Fine, where would you like me to start?"
"Start with how you ended up where you are today,
    Mr. Cool Bachelor."

Surprisingly, he was very open about the good, bad, and ugly of his
life. He was a recovering divorcee with a broken heart. He
explained how he was still going through a nasty divorce from his
twenty-five-year marriage to his high school sweetheart, who walked
out on him for another man.

He was currently working for the post office. He got high with the
guys on the weekend. They would have a casual toot of cocaine and
smoke reefer all night.

After he told me about his past and his present life, I asked him
where does he see a young woman like me possibly fitting into his
life.
"We are from two different worlds, I know, but it
    seems like we have so very much in common."
I didn't know what he was talking about at this
    point.
"How so?"

"You are wild at heart, risky, a survivor of some really
deep shit and you are still surviving it. You like to
have fun and get high. The other main thing we
have in common is that you love women and so do
I."

Brown was fifty-six years old and understood my desire for women
very clearly. He said, "After going through what you have been
through, I can really understand how you feel now." He raised his
wine glass to mine to toast.
      "To a new friendship and lots of fun."
      "Yes." I nodded my head.

We clicked our glasses. I took a sip without taking my eyes off of
Brown. He then began to tell me about a young lady that he
worked with at the post office whose fantasy was to be intimate
with another woman. I told him, maybe one day our paths would
cross and she won't have to live in a fantasy world anymore. He
smiled and said, "Maybe your paths can cross very soon."

We finished dinner and I complimented him on such a tasty dinner.
He told me that his mother taught him how to cook when he was
only eight years old. He said he had cooked for his wife 70% of
their marriage because he loved spoiling and serving her. I told him,
if I ever turn straight and get married, I pray my husband would be
able to cook just like him.

Our evening was coming to an end and I enjoyed myself a lot.
Brown played music throughout our evening. I loved listening to it
too. He played this song entitled, "Stay In My Corner" over and
over again. While I poured myself one last glass of wine I listened
hard to that song. I was feeling very tipsy and really enjoyed the
melody of the music. Brown laughed and told me that the record
was way before my time. I told him, all I have listened to most of
my life was music before my time, especially when I lived at home
with my mother. We said good night.

Two blocks later, I walked in my front door and Daddy had not returned from the race track. I went next door to kick it with the Morris family for a little while. Ms. Morris was cooking and talking to Mr. Jones from upstairs and her sister in law. I sat down at the table and joined in the conversation. I heard keys next door and I jumped up to see if it was my Daddy. It was. I stuck my head out to let him know that I was next door. "Alright, I'm about to get ready to go to work," he responded. It was almost 10 p.m., a full day for him and me.

Later on that night, I decided to go out to the club. I hadn't been out since the time I met Desmund. I went totally off the partying scene. I vowed to myself to not get involved with any more aggressive women in my life. They will not be in control of me and break my heart again. Barbara would be ashamed of me if she knew I let somebody do me like Desmund did. She taught me to always be in control of my life, and my heart.

After I arrived at the club I ran into a sweet young lady I had met one night while partying with Ms. Sparkle and Diamond. Her name was Cloe. Cloe always tried to talk with me, but I never gave her the time of day. We noticed each other and she asked if I would join her at her table. After drinking and dancing for about three hours, I called a cab to take me home. Cloe gave me her number and asked me to keep in touch with her.

When the cab dropped me off, I ran upstairs and got ready for bed because Daddy would be coming home soon.

All night, I kept telling myself not to think about Cloe. I thought to myself, "Why have I never given her any attention?" She was always so pleasant and nice. Then she kept reappearing in my mind throughout the night. I kept telling myself, but she is aggressive and you said you were not getting close with any more aggressive women because they were too damn controlling. I promised myself that I would be the aggressor from now on. I tried to go to sleep.

The next day Sharon came by to visit. I was always so happy to see her, she was cool. We made small talk and then she asked about my relationship with Daddy. I tried to change the subject.

"So tell me how are you and Daddy getting along?"

"Don't ask, it's no good."

"Why not?"

"He doesn't like or agree with who I am."

"What do you mean who you are?"

I hadn't told Sharon for fear of her rejecting me and not wanting to be cool with me. I didn't want her to act like my Daddy and reject me.

"I don't know if you are ready for this, Sharon."

"Look, you can talk to me about anything, Carla, you should know that."

She told me that she had heard some things. She overheard Mommy and Daddy talking too.

"Sharon, I wish I'd never have even met Daddy. He doesn't have time for me. Nor does he want to after finding out who I am and what I've become. He is in his own little world, no time for the "rebellious freak" as he calls me."

Sharon tried to convince me of Daddy's love, but I wasn't buying it. I was subject to his silent treatment everyday, with the exception of his communicating his whereabouts and questions of any phone calls.

"Are you going to tell me or what?"

"Sharon, I'm gay. Okay, I like women and not men."

"Damn! Since when?"

"Since, before I met my Daddy or you."

"Okay, as long as you are happy, then fine. But you fooled me."

"How come Daddy can't say that!"

"Carla, you are new to him and he is trying to do the best he can."

"Now hell, I was born a long time ago. I'm not new.
and I am tired of parents that are trying to do the
goddamn best they can. What the hell is this thing
about parents doing the best they can!"
I had to get up and walk as I went off. No, I don't
go for that shit anymore! When they were fucking
they were doing the best they could, so why not be
responsible for the after affects?"

Sharon had to calm me all the way down. I hated the fact that she
tried to defend my father. I was so glad that she didn't judge me
about my lifestyle like Daddy did.

Sharon told me that she had to leave and get back home to cook.
Sounded like old times. She said she would get together with me
later on in the week. I know she was tired of hearing from me.

Later on that day Brown called me to see if I could stop by later on
for dinner. I told him I would be over once I scooped out my
Dad's whereabouts.

Brown had another nice spread of soul food cooked for us. We sat
and talked more about possible things that we could get into
together. Brown told me about some of his hang outs. He
mentioned that he wanted to take me to a club on Florence called
"Charlie's." This was a club where topless women danced. I
laughed. I asked him how did he think I would get in being a
female. He told me that I wouldn't have a problem because I was
with him and he's taken other women. He wanted to go later after
we ate dinner, but I told him tonight was not a good night. Then
he told me about some more freaky things that he likes to do in his
spare time.

Brown told me a funny story about the time he went downtown to
the movies. He would sit in an aisle where only women were and
begin to flash and do some crazy perverted stuff for them to look at
him jack off.

I went home that night emotionally exhausted. I thought about Brown and his sick kicks. I didn't know if I really wanted to hang out with him or not. He was in a whole different world.

The next morning Sharon called and told me to prepare myself for a job interview with her at Koby's Shoe Store where she was the Assistant Manager. She told me that they would hire me, but we had to go through the motions of the interviewing process. I jumped up from the couch and began to get dressed so I could get to the interview that afternoon. The interview went great. I was hired and scheduled to start the following Monday just like Sharon said I would be.

When I got home later that morning, I couldn't wait to tell Daddy. He was already gone, but I purposed to tell him soon as I saw him. The phone rang. It was Cloe. She told me that she was going swimming over a friend's house and asked if I wanted to come. I thought it was a great idea. I told her I didn't know how to swim but she insisted that she could teach me. I caught the bus over to her friends Bridget's and everyone introduced themselves. I met the neighbors and the roommates. I asked where the restroom was so that I could change. Cloe was looking fresh and ready to swim in her white t-shirt and blue swim trunks.

When I came out of the bathroom, I noticed Cloe doing a double take when she saw me. I kept walking without responding. We went outside to the back where there was a nine foot pool. I started getting nervous and she asked me to calm down.
        "I am here, and I won't let anything happen to you,"
        she gently assured me.

After a few hours, we gave up my training lessons, dried off and went in the house to get high. Her friend Bridget passed around joints as we sat in the living room listening to music.
        "Hey, let's go shoot some pool," Bridget suggested.
        Cloe said, " Cool."

"Do you shoot pool, Carla?"
"Yeah, just a little bit, not much," I said.

I knew inside I couldn't play if they paid me, but what the hell, it would be fun. After a few games, Cloe decided to show me how to hold the stick. I caught on quickly. We ended the night about 10:30 p.m. Bridget took Cloe home first, since she lived downtown at a hotel on Main and 8th Street.

On the way back Bridget and I talked.
"Cloe has the hots for you" Bridget said.
"Oh yeah," I said, I got the hots for Cloe too."

All throughout the day Cloe reminded me of somebody, but I could not place who. Then it hit me. Cloe was smooth dark. She had pretty white teeth and a beautiful head of curly hair. I noticed a protective streak in her and that's when it hit me. Kendon Starr! I smiled at the similarities. They were both Taurus, dark as the night, and beautiful in spirit. They were very protective, and their smile knocked you out because of their pretty white teeth. I shook my head to myself and said, "I have a woman Kendon Star!" That night I showered and prepared for work the next day.

My job at Koby's was short lived. I got laid off for being late and falling asleep at the cash register. I couldn't believe it. One day I was ringing up a customer and fell asleep standing up. It was the loud opening of the cash register that woke me right back up. The customer was very upset. I laughed, but the manager, observing this, thought maybe this was not working out. She said, "Whatever you are doing in your spare time, it has you totally consumed." I agreed with her and left. I knew Sharon would be upset with me.

Later on that week I got a call from Cloe. She asked if I wanted to go to the Catch Won with her. I didn't have anything else to do I told her. I told her that I was going to go away for the weekend to Fresno, but I could spend sometime with her if she wanted me to. I met up with her later that night. She had lots of friends over who

belonged to a new women's band.   They were releasing their first
album at the beginning of the year.   I was impressed. I found out
that Cloe was dating the bass guitar player, Angelette.   I also
learned that Angelette had a bad drinking problem and was very
abusive.   She and Cloe would fight all the time. That's what Cloe's
sister, Mable, was whispering in my ear.   Mable was twenty-eight
years old and very much overweight.   She was about two hundred
thirty pounds, five foot eleven and had the cutest dimples you ever
wanted to see.   She must have lit up a dozen joints by herself that
night. Anyway, Cheryl and Angelette were lovers now and they
both played the guitar. Bridget was also there, and off we went to
the club. Everybody was talking about going to this grand opening
of the new night club, the Catch Won.

We made a stop at a house to pick up some weed on the way to the
Club. Cloe and I were in the back seat. She asked me if I did
speed. I nodded yes, knowing I hadn't.   She gave me this little
white pill. I put it in my mouth and we walked in the club. It was
so hard to believe, because the club had about two to three thousand
people in it.   It was part of the Ruby's Club, located downstairs in
the tunnel. People were partying down!   I think my speaking level
advanced to a hundred words per minute, and I danced until the
sun came up.

The next day when I came home, Daddy asked me how was
Fresno?   I almost forgot that I really didn't go, I just pretended
that I went and stayed the week-end with Cloe. He asked what
was I going to do with my life. Since I lost my job at the shoe store,
he suggested that I apply for a government job and work downtown
at the Hall of Administration building. It wasn't what I wanted, so
I just let it go in one ear and out the other.   I was definitely
convinced Daddy really didn't know who I was. To be able to pull
the stunts that I had pulled throughout the few years I had known
him, either he was deaf and dumb, or just didn't give a damn and
decided what's the use. He and his wife were officially getting back
together, and I knew he cared about that relationship more than his
and mine.

Weeks later I got a surprise visit. Aunt Drena and my stepmother came over to the apartment. Aunt Drena was smiling and excited, as always. That woman had just too much energy for me. Aunt Drena asked that I go to church with her sometimes.

"I don't know, Aunt Drena. I'll let you know, okay?"

"Okay, now if you don't have a ride I'll come and pick you up, you know that, don't you?"

"Yes, Aunt Drena, I do and thank you."

Mommy was just standing there looking around the apartment, I guess looking for Daddy, who was out as usual doing his thing. They left after I told her that Daddy wasn't home. I started thinking about church again. I convinced myself it wouldn't hurt to just go on a Sunday here and there. I could at least hear some good singing. Maybe I could hear that woman sing "I'm Going Up A Yonder," my favorite song.

The following week I went downtown to buy some fabric at the fabric mart. Before I left, I went to a corner phone booth to call Cloe. I told her I was downtown, but I wanted to check to see if she was home before I got on the bus to go home. She invited me over, and we went to eat lunch.

We went back to the hotel after lunch and played spades for about an hour. Cloe was a Michael Jackson fan. She had his album covers all over her walls and played them 24/7. I didn't mind because they all reminded me of her. I was really enjoying my friendship with her. She was so sweet. We enjoyed many weekends and evenings together talking and dancing.

Life was always so pleasant and peaceful when I was around her. She had caring ways that touched me so deeply. Cloe had a quiet touch about herself. I felt loved in her presence. I never doubted her sincerity or geniuses. She never cursed or raised her voice. She was extra affectionate, which I loved about her. Every time she would pass me she had to either touch my shoulder or my face. She was just sweet that way. She always wanted to make sure I was safe and had everything I needed.

One day after trying to connect with Cloe for about two days, I got worried. I finally spoke with the foreign lady at the front desk and she said they had not seen her, but she wasn't checked out of her room. She told me that she was paid up for the entire month. That didn't sound like Cloe. I was praying I had not gotten involved in another Desmund situation. I called Mable. I remembered that Mable gave me her number the night we all went to the club together with the all woman's band. A lady answered the phone.

"Hey, Mable, this is Carla. What's happening?"
"Nothing much," was her response. She sounded sad.
"Is there something wrong?" I asked.
"You haven't heard, I guess," she said.
"Heard what?" I got scared.

She told me to come over to her house and she would explain everything. I grabbed my bus pass and jacket and quickly went over.

When I got there, Mable opened the door real slow. The lights were out, and I felt real spooked. We sat at the table and Mable lit up a joint. I asked her why was it so dark in the house. She told me that they had cut off the lights. She didn't have the money to pay the bill. When I asked Mable what was going on she told me that Cloe and Bridget were in jail. I screamed. Mable went on to tell me that they were caught robbing a bank Tuesday morning. She told me that the cops picked them up later that night. They would have gotten away but Bridget did not remember to take the license plates off the car. She said they had been gone all day, and that night the cops traced them to her house. I was so shocked. I sat there frozen in silence. Then I thought, "Maybe Cloe and Bridget were in the back room playing a trick on me." But it was no trick, Cloe and Bridget never came out, and Mable grew sadder.

Mable asked where I lived, and I told her not far. We decided to go to the liquor store to get some beer and come back to the house. We drank Old English 800 and smoked a couple of joints. We then began to share our life stories. I found out that Mable and Cloe had a crazy mother. I thought my mother was crazy, but theirs was waco! Their mother use to not feed them and lock them up in rooms as a punishment. She would talk crazy to them and call them all sorts of names. After we exchanged our stories, we began feeling sorry for one another. I guess misery does love company. Before I left, Mable asked me if I was happy at home with my Dad. I told her I was not happy and that my Daddy really didn't care for me, or understand who I was. She told me that I could come live with her. We looked at each other and shook hands. I said, "It's a deal." I told Mable that I would be back as soon as I could pack my stuff.

I left Mable's house so happy and feeling relieved that I was moving from my Daddy's house. It was so timely. I was finished with summer school and making up that one class. Now it was my turn to live on my own. I didn't have a lot to pack, just a bag of clothes, shoes, and my handy dandy sewing machine. I needed a ride and I thought about Brown. I got home, no one was there as usual. I packed as soon as I could and called Brown to give me a ride.

As I was moving the last bag out of the house, my stepmother and a friend of hers stepped in the door. I looked at her and instructed Brown to continue to move my things to the car. She asked if I was going somewhere, and I gladly told l her I was moving. She continued to ask if my daddy knew. I told her, no! Then in a real insincere way, she asked if this was what I really wanted to do. I knew she didn't mean that. I knew she was glad his little girl was out of her way. I was too! She never apologized to me for blocking my relationship with my Daddy. She never apologized for giving my Daddy an ultimatum, and probably never will. That's how I knew she never really cared for me. She liked to hide behind that sweet-sounding voice, but it didn't fool me for long.

If I didn't leave now, I knew it was only a matter of time before he would have to choose between me and her again.   I left them standing in the door.   Brown and I made small talk on the way. Brown knew I was upset, so he gave me space.
"Are you going to still keep in touch with me man?"
"Yes, Brown, you're my old friend. I'm not going to get lost," I assured him.

In a very weird way, I was feeling as if I was still running away.

CHAPTER 28

MABLE'S PLACE

The next morning I dragged myself to the bathroom. I was so tired. Mable and I had drank the night away. As I passed the kitchen I saw Mable cooking and cleaning. It smelled so good.

Mable had prepared some eggs, sausages, and potatoes. When I came out of the bathroom she hollered, "it's time to eat."
    "Good morning. Is there any coffee in the house?"
    Boy, that was a quick change from waking up fixing my own breakfast. Now I have a roommate that cooks.
    "Sure, honey bun. I'll fix you some right away."

For the first time, I saw the house in the daylight. Mable wasn't the best housekeeper, but that was okay because I was. I thought I could bring balance to our home together. After all, it was rent free. We clicked so well, as if we had been knowing each other for years. She made closet space for me and showed me where everything was located. As I was getting the grand tour I felt right at home. After breakfast we sat down in the living room to let our food digest. Michael Jackson music was playing in the background. I thought about Cloe instantly because that was her favorite singer. Mable grabbed a joint out of her upper right pocket. She threw it at me to light up. Afterwards, we walked around the corner to get some Old English 800. Mable loved her Old English 800. She began to tell me about her work schedule. She worked in the customer service department of May Company, her hours were 7:00 a.m. to 3:30 p.m., everyday except weekends.

Later that afternoon, Mable asked if I would like to go see Cloe tomorrow. I told her that I would love to. I was scared that Cloe may be embarrassed for me to see her in such a place. Mable told me that she would not be embarrassed at all.
A few hours later there was a knock at the door. I didn't know if I should answer it or not. Mable had gone to the wash house. I fell

asleep watching television. The knock got louder and louder. I got up and went to the door. I recognized the face. It was Angelette, Cloe's ex-girlfriend. She looked a little weird. I opened the door.

"Hey, what's happening?"

"You got it. Mable isn't here right now, she went up the street to wash clothes."

"Oh okay, I remember you, you're Carla, right?"

"Yeah, we met that night when me and the band picked up Cloe to go to the club."

"Yeah, you the crazy woman that gave us some speed. Yeah, in fact, I'm on some speed right now, you want some?"

"Nah' man, thanks anyway. Do you want to come in and wait for Mable?"

We sat and made small talk about the band, about the gay life, the party scene and getting high. Nothing of any real meaning. I could tell that she was feeling me to see if I was the aggressive or passive woman in a relationship. Then I heard Mable at the front door fumbling with her keys. When she walked in she dropped the grocery bags from the market on the floor. Mable told us there was a cab out front and asked us to go out to get the rest of the clothes and food. Angelette asked what we were doing that night. We didn't have any plans other than chilling out and just waiting for the next day to go see Cloe. Angelette was trying to get into something real bad, itching for a party. Mable told Angelette if she wanted to go to the club tonight we would go with her. Angelette's eyes lit up. "Cool," she said. After that, I volunteered to cook dinner before we left for the club. I fixed some fried chicken, green beans, and mashed potatoes.

After dinner, we got dressed. I put on all black leather pants, jacket, boots, and my silver waste belt. Mable dressed in her same jeans with a clean sweater. Angelette came ready. We didn't have a car because Mable's was impounded in the bank robbery. She didn't have the money to get it out yet. We caught the bus to the club and partied all night long.

BUS RIDE TO SYBIL BRAND
1980

The alarm clock went off at nine o'clock in the morning.   It was time to get up and go see Cloe.   We all had a hangover but we were still going.   Mable had her schedule down pack.   We hopped on the bus and went all the way to the back where the so-called smokers were that weren't suppose to be smoking.   Mable started telling me what to expect at the jail.   I sat wondering to myself what would I say to Cloe.   As the bus was pulling up, I asked Mable how much time did we have with her.   She said, "twenty minutes."   We got off the bus and the lines to the visiting window were already long with people waiting.   At the window, the Sheriff asked us for our I.D., just as Mable said they would.   They told us they would be calling us as soon as Cloe was contacted.

As we stood waiting, we saw people that had been in jail and were being released.   They would come out of the gate with their little clear plastic bags of belongings.   Some came out partying and jumping.   Some came out mad and complaining that the authorities took their money.   Some had pimps waiting for them.   I couldn't believe it.   They were sitting right there in their Cadillacs ready to pick them up.

Finally, they called out visitors for Jepa C. Cooley over the loud speaker.   Mable said, "Come on, that's us."   I said to myself Jeptha! What kind of damn name is that?   No wonder she goes as "Cloe."   I would change my name too.   The iron gates opened, and we went through two double doors.   We walked down the long sidewalk leading to the next building.   Then there was another window to check into in case you were leaving money.   Mable left a lot of single dollar bills and I saw them put the money in some water.   A strong-looking woman in a sheriff's uniform told Mable to go sit by window 25.   We went through another door and there were all these windows with numbers over them and a phone receiver on each side of the window.   There was one small chair for the visitor.

I asked, "Mable, why did they wet the money?"

 "Sometimes people try to put drugs in money."

 "How in the hell can they do that?" I asked.

 "Trust me," she said, "there are ways of getting
  drugs in."

We found our window, and no one was on the other side. Finally, I saw Cloe coming from the release area. She was wearing a dingy looking blue dress. All the inmates were wearing the same blue dresses. Her hair was braided, and she had a warm smile on her face. The thick window separated us. I thought to myself, "How could something this cute and mild attempt to do something so crazy?" Mable sat down first so she would be the first to talk with her. I was glad because I still didn't know what to say and what not to say. I heard Mable telling her that she left her fifteen dollars on the books. Mable changed subjects and asked Cloe if she had heard more from her attorney. Cloe shook her head no. Mable told her that the trial was in a few weeks. She then motioned to me, and said, "It's your turn."

I sat down and took the phone. My heart was pounding. I was afraid of what to say. Her voice came over the line.

 "Hello," she said. Her voice was calm and soft as it
  always was. It made you feel like you were walking
  on clouds with her. Always so calm and peaceful.

 "How are you doing?" I asked and immediately
  felt dumb.

 "I'm alright. I am so glad to see you."

 "Thank you. I am too." I felt dumb again.

We were eye to eye. Then she changed her expression with me. She looked very sad and said she regretted being away from me the most.

 "You didn't know that you were getting involved
  with a criminal, hah?"

 She smiled, showing those beautiful white teeth and
  deep dimples.

I told her how much I missed her. She said she was glad that I was living with her sister. I was glad to hear her approval of our arrangement.

The time was up and the announcement came over the speaker "one more minute." Cloe asked if I would write her, I told her that I would write every week. She smiled and motioned a kiss with her lips. We placed our hands on the window as she stood up to leave, until Mable took me by the hand to walk me out of the room. She could tell I was about to cry.

     "Come on, Carla."

     "Mable," I didn't know what to say. I kept turning around, hoping to still see her standing there.

The metal doors and keys were ringing in my ears as we walked away. You could hear the metal doors slamming all the way down the hallways as you made your way out of the facility. I didn't realize seeing Cloe in there would hit me so hard. I didn't know what to expect really. I was a wreck. It made me think about the time when I visited my mother at camp. I remembered her leaving to go back to her room when our time was up for her too.

The bus ride home was very quiet. We sat there and didn't say a word to each other. It felt like we were in shock. Angelette had cleaned up the bed and the kitchen by the time we got back home. She was sitting in front of the television, smoking a cigarette.

     "Hey ya'll. How's Cloe?"

     "She's doing pretty good," Mable said.

I went to the bathroom. I overheard Angelette telling Mable that Dennis and the gang would be by later on to play some dominos.

Around eight o'clock that night the front door opened, without a knock. Dennis, Tom, Eddie, Butch, Leonard, and Kirk came in with bottles in their hands, talking shit. Angelette asked her brother

Tom for a joint. He threw her one. Mable said, "Hey guys, let me introduce you to my new roommate, Cloe's lover." She introduced me, and the turkeys gobbled and waddled at me, making passes. I laughed the whole time. I guess guys will be guys. What Mable said went totally over their heads.

The guy named Eddie was Mable's boyfriend, she told me later on. Leonard asked me if I played dominos. I said, "yeah." We all gathered in the kitchen, pulled out some chairs and there we stayed for the night.

Later on that night, a couple of lady friends from Mable's job came by. The night progressed and Shirley from next door came by. Mable whispered to me that she was the landlord's daughter. She acted as if she was a beauty queen stepping out of Vogue. She was so damn conceited! As she pranced around, I checked her out. I was ready to blow this joint though. I was having fun and all, because it reminded me so much of Fresno. It reminded me of when Momma would have folks coming over to the house playing dominos and cards. Everyone was related, or had been friends for years and years.

Angelette came over to see how I was doing. I said, "Fine, but I'm ready to go you know where." Angelette wanted to hang with me instead of staying with her family. We needed some wheels though. I told her to let me call my old partner. I was referring to Brown. He came by that night to get Angelette and me. He said I could keep the car and just bring it by when we were done. I knew what he was up to. He wanted us to come by and freak off in front of him when we were finished, but he didn't know that Angelette and I weren't like that together.

The night at the club was long and fun. We exchanged a few numbers between women and played with a few girls in the car, me in the front, Angelette in the back We left the club around four in the morning. I invited a couple of women to go to breakfast with us. Then, they wanted us to come over to their place in Baldwin

Hills.

Brown didn't see us or his car back until 9 a.m. the next morning. I called to let him know everything was going alright. He was ticked. By the time we returned the car, he had calmed down.

"Hey man, I'm sorry! We got kidnapped by three
freak Mommas who wouldn't let us go."
He said, "You should have told them to come
over here! My whole night was blown, because I
thought you were coming back here to party."
"Nah' man. Sorry about that." Brown dropped
us off at Mable's house.

Later that week we caught the bus to see Cloe in jail. Mable spoke first. I thanked Cloe for the letters she had written me. I had not written yet. I told her each time I sat down to do it, I would break out in tears. The truth of the matter was that I had started going out every night of the week, including weekends, since I moved out of my Daddy's apartment. I promised her, I would do better. We left her twenty dollars and some tennis shoes and jeans. She was appreciative. The court date was in a few days, and I told her that I would be there. I told her to just pray to God and He will help her. I told her I would pray for her too.

One day after Mable came home, I was feeling very depressed. After she sat down and rubbed my arms she asked me to tell her what was wrong. Mable never liked to see me sad or down. She would always say, "Fuck that! It's time to get high. We don't have time to be down and depressed."

I couldn't shake it this time, and I wasn't in the mood to get high. I told her that I felt that I was out of control. I told her I seriously needed to talk about my feelings.

"Okay, honey bun, what's going on?"
"I feel like a cheap freeloader and I don't have
much respect for myself."
"Don't say that, Carla. You are not a freeloader.

You pull your own here." Mable lit up a joint.
"Mable, I need to have a job by now. I got to start
paying some of my way so that I can be
responsible."
"Carla, you have your whole life ahead of you.
You are young and it's time to have fun."
"Mable, all I do is have fun. Surely there is
more to life than just having fun. I mean, just
getting high, fucking around with women, and
doing crazy shit." Mable tried to pass me the
joint, I refused to hit it.
"Well, I just want you to know that you being
here has helped my life so much. I don't know
what I would do without you here with me.
"Thank you."

She sounded as if she pulled out a desperate statement on that one.
"Look, I have been feeling guilty too."
"What do you mean, guilty?"
"All the women I fuck around with. Especially
the nights that I don't come home. I struggle
with not being faithful to your sister."

Mable felt that it wasn't all that bad, because I had never
experienced this level of independence. It was a fad that I must live
out until I get tired, she said. She told me that I should slow down.
"Mable, don't you feel bad that I'm cheating on
your sister?"
"My sister doesn't know, and therefore you are
not hurting her directly. Plus, my sister is in jail
with over a thousand women every night and we
don't know what the hell she's doing in her time
of need for companionship."
I was surprised at her response. I told Mable that I
genuinely cared for Cloe.
After thinking about our conversation, I realized that Mable didn't
fully understand. She didn't understand that I wanted to do

something with my life, I wanted to become someone respectable.

However, Mable did let me know that she was concerned about me burning myself out. She said, "I know the women are crazy about you, but don't let them burn you out." I told Mable that every time I slow down and be still, too much pain comes and I don't want to feel the pain that keeps surfacing in my mind.

That same night I decided that I wasn't going anywhere at all. I was just going to stay at home and watch television with Mable. Mable couldn't believe it. Before she went to bed, she joked and said, "now don't be slipping out here after midnight because you're going through withdrawals." We laughed and said goodnight. I laid there and began to think about my Daddy and his wife. I couldn't help but feel that I was out of their way, and I'm sure they were happy. That didn't make me feel good and so I started thinking about my young sisters and brothers in Fresno. I hoped they were doing fine. I drifted off to sleep, thinking about my family.

Mable came home the next day from work and said she had good news. Her job was hiring part-time temporary personnel. She said that she would get me in through her manager Eddie Coleman. I was so happy about that. I hugged and thanked her. Then she said, don't forget that Cloe's sentencing is tomorrow."

Mable, Angelette, and I sat in the back of the courtroom. I could see Cloe up front near the public defender. She turned and saw us. She nodded to Mable and Angelette, but she blew me a kiss. I was nervous and shaking in my boots. I heard the judge ask Bridget to stand. They gave her five years, plus time off with good behavior. Then the judge asked Cloe to stand. They told her she would get thirteen years and would be sentenced to the San Antonio Women's Institute for the duration of her time. Immediately, they escorted her out of the courtroom and back to the bus for downtown. I sat there dumbfounded and speechless. I could not move. Mable said, "Let's go." I just sat there. Thirteen Years. "Carla, get your ass up and let's go." I snapped out of it and got up.

On the way back, Mable explained to me how she would probably get off in two to three years with good behavior. It was another silent ride home. I guess everybody was thinking. We got home later on that evening and I was totally depressed. I didn't feel like doing much of anything. I guess I really didn't acknowledge this woman was going to get some serious time until now. We all went back home and started drinking and playing music. Mable started crying which started all of us crying. I had to get out of there. I said, "Angelette, let's go and play pool at this place I have been scoping out on Normandie and Adams." We left to catch a bus. The pool hall was crowded with men, which didn't bother us. I didn't care because I was there for one reason, and that was to get fully lost in my game. As Angelette and I started playing, we noticed guys looking and whispering about us. Angelette got pissed. I looked at one of the brothers and let him see me touch Angelette's ass. His mouth went wide open. I laughed and Angelette was shocked, but didn't say too much to me until we were on our way home. We visited that pool hall at least twice a week. The guys became very familiar with us and stopped trying to hit on us. I guess they worked up some kind of respect for us. Then some of the old men grew friendly and wanted to help sharpen our game. They taught us all kinds of moves and shots. Before long, we were able to play for money and it was so cool.

One day while we were in the pool hall drinking beer and listening to some cool music, we heard a roaring engine that kept cranking itself up. Within a few moments, a man came through the door, a man we had not seen around. I looked up and a brown skinned man that stood about 6'3" walked in. The first thing my mind said, was, "What in the hell was that?" I heard one of the guys say, "Hey, Dog is out!" I tried to not be obvious with my unshakable attraction to this guy.

He had on leather pants and a cool jean jacket. He had the prettiest smile you ever wanted to see. Pretty white teeth. I loved pretty white teeth. Then I caught myself. I had to talk to myself for a good five minutes. I convinced myself that I was being a punk looking at some nigga.

"What the hell is wrong with you, girl?"

Snap out of it, I told myself. I was also hoping Angelette didn't see me. I focused more into my game.

A few minutes later, I saw the guy looking over at our table directly at me! I got nervous and started making bad shots. I couldn't concentrate. Angelette noticed the change in my game. She didn't say anything at first, but she started to look at him looking at me and me trying not to look at him. Our game was almost over and Angelette said she was ready to go home.

"Cool, let's get the hell out of here," I said.
On the way home, Angelette said, "I saw that guy looking at you, and you looking at him."
I said, "Which guy?"
Angelette got mad and hollered, "You know what damn guy I'm talking about."

I looked at her as if to say, what the hell is wrong with you. By now, I realized that Angelette was growing closer and closer to me. She was becoming possessive over me. I went home and couldn't get that fine man out of my mind. It frustrated the hell out of me. I didn't want to be attracted to this guy, or to any guy for that matter. My mind was set on my lifestyle and I hated these feelings of wanting to know more about him, but I couldn't fight them no matter how hard I tried.

CHAPTER 29

Hot Dog - November 1980

Mable came home and told me that my application was accepted and I was to start work the next Monday at May Company. I was so happy. I said, "Let's celebrate." We went to the store and got a couple of Old English 800 and bought a bag of weed. We got high all night. She explained that I would be working in inventory department working with towels, sheets, pillow cases and rugs.

The next day I called Angelette and told her to meet me at the pool hall. I bragged about my new job. She was excited for me. She said, "Cool, I will be over as soon as I can get there." I wondered if that guy would be there today. I was hoping that I wasn't going soft or getting girly, but if I was so what, I thought to myself.

Our table was right next to the jukebox. I walked in looking for the guy, but he wasn't there. When Angelette was talking dope talk to one of the guys selling weed, I went to the owner who knew this Hot Dog guy. I asked him the story on that fella. He smiled. He asked if I was interested. I said, "Hell nah", I just wanted to know where he came from." He said, "From San Quentin. He's been doing time. He just got back on the street a couple of weeks ago."
     "Okay, cool, thanks for letting me know," I said.
     Then he said, "His real name is Carl Maxi."
     I told him, " I like that name better than 'Hot Dog'"
     He smiled.

Carl was not there the following two times we came to the pool hall. But he finally came by the same time we were there Friday evening.

Angelette and I got so good, other men were challenging us now and we were kicking ass in the game. Angelette was playing with one of the guys, when all of a sudden we heard a motorcycle engine roaring. My heart dropped. Angelette looked at me and dropped her head. Within seconds, he walked in the door. My heart started pounding. I tried to pretend I wasn't looking for him to walk in that door. He immediately saw me and smiled, nodding his head as if to say hello. I returned the greeting with a great big smile. I had to catch myself again, but I blew it. I didn't want to show I was glad to see him.

Within seconds, he made his way to the jukebox. He put his dime in and made a selection. He then passed by me and said, "This song is for you." I listened for the song to come on. It was a record called "Foxy Ladies". The song talked about a woman blowing a man's mind. Then he offered to play me a game of pool.
"How much can you afford to loose?" He smiled and looked shocked all at the same time.
"I can afford to loose it all to you, if you want it."

Damn, I bit off more than I could chew on that question. I played it off and didn't let him see me quiver.
"Cool, we can play the first game for five dollars."

He racked the balls and let me bust first. Angelette was fuming with anger and jealousy. I didn't care, I was having fun. This man was so fine to me. I couldn't fight this thing any longer. I decided, I was going to let us go as far as we wanted to.

We talked during the course of the game.
"What's a pretty girl like you doing in a hard place like this?" he asked.
"This is the best pool hall that I've come across so far."

I didn't want to tell him that I was just as hard as the place I played in.
"I guess it's the tomboy in me." We laughed.

I beat him the first two games. He told me that he let me beat all the games because he was a perfect gentleman, but now he must teach me a lesson in case I think it was all my doing. I noticed every time that song went off he was back at that jukebox replaying it.

  "How about dinner sometime?"
  I didn't know what to say. "How about it?"
  "Can I take you out?" he asked.
  "Sure," I said without thinking.

He gave me his number and I gave him mine. A couple of the guys saw him and yelled out HOOOOOT DOOOOOOOOOOG!

NOVEMBER 1980

It was time to go home.   Carl asked if he could call me tonight. I told him yes. He said, "Please be there, because when I leave here I am racing home to call you."   Boy, did that give me butterflies. He kissed me on my forehead, then Angelette and I walked off.

On the way home I came right out and told Angelette that I was attracted to this guy. Angelette was so mad at him for talking to me. I could tell just by the look on her face.
  "So you're punkin' out, hah?" Angelette said to me.
  "Look, I knew yo ass was going to say something to
  me about that."
  "Yeah, and what's up with that?"
  "I'm just talking to the man. I like the way he looks,
  that's all. He's cute to me."
  Angelette started walking faster passing me up.
  "Fine, you can do whatever the hell you want to do.
  I don't have any rights to be mad at you," she said.
  "Thank you, buddy. I really appreciate it," I said
  sarcastically.

For the next couple of weeks, Carl was picking me up and taking me to shoot pool with him. I was scared of motorcycles, until I met him. I didn't mind jumping on the back of his bike and riding anywhere he wanted to go. Over the next weeks we talked about a lot of things. He understood what lifestyle I was in, I had to come clean with him, but he didn't seem to be bothered by it. He assured me that he didn't want to rush me into anything, but he did want to spend some time with me. He asked me if Angelette was my woman. I told him that she was my partner who got a little too attached to me. He told me he could feel her vibes every time he would come around. Eventually, Carl opened up to me and discussed his jail record. He sold dope and had a couple of armed robberies on his record. Then he said they were trying to blame him for a gruesome crime he did not do. He didn't go into it and I didn't pry. I thought to myself, I am having a time attracting prison bound people. First Kendon my little juvenile crush, Cloe and now Carl. I learned that he lived with his mother and was twenty eight years old. I was always so nervous around him, but he would try and make me feel comfortable. He would hold me in his arms and I would melt. I will never forget the night he kissed me for the first time without asking. I thought I would faint. He told me he had wanted to kiss me for weeks. I got real angry afterwards and didn't want to see him for a while.

I didn't talk to Mable about Carl, because I knew she would have thought I was totally confused. Each day I would go to the warehouse to see her on my lunch break. We'd talk about everything except for my new friend. Needless to say, I wasn't keeping my word as far as writing Cloe like I said I would. I was involved and focused on Carl.

The next day was Thanksgiving. Carl came by and said "Let's take a ride along the Coast." Holding on to Carl always felt right and natural. The weather was especially nice and warm. The sun hitting the dark shades of the water was so beautiful. The water was calm and made the ride up the coast so romantic. But we would collide here and there when it came time to do the gentleman thing for women. I would always start opening the door first for him. If we were hugging, he would bend down and I would put my arms around his waist, then quickly correct myself and placed them around his neck. We pulled up near a park site overlooking the ocean. He parked the bike and took me by the hand. We walked near a vacant spot near a tree and sat down on the grass. He was so compassionate and patient with me. We looked at each other a lot and smiled, not saying anything, just looking at the ocean. He asked why was I giving him the time of day if men were not my thing. I told him I was asking myself that same question from the moment I saw him.

"Listen, whatever your reasons are, I feel like a lucky man. I think you are beautiful."
I felt so awkward hearing that kind of compliment coming from a man.
"Thank you, Carl, you are very handsome too."

Then he got real serious and said he wanted to ask me a lot of questions.

"Go for it," I said.
"Do you have any children?"
"No," I yelled, before thinking.
"Whoa, did I say something wrong?"
"No Carl, I just meant no I don't have children and I don't want children." Carl looked surprised.
"Did you have a bad upbringing or bad experience with children?" he asked.
"I'm just not the parent type."
"I'm sure that you would be a beautiful mother to any child" he said.
"I would never bring a child into this crazy, corrupt, perverted world."

He noticed that the subject was making me very upset so he decided to switch gears.

"Let's go have some dinner."

We rode to a place off the coast that served all American food. The sunset was coming out. The sky had a bright orange burning look with the sun slowly fading.

After a nice evening of pigging out we decided to go back into the city. Before we left, Carl asked if I would spend the night with him.

"What?" I couldn't believe my ears.
"Will you spend the night with me, Carla? I want to
sleep with you and hold you in my arms."

I started stuttering and my voice was cracking. I hated being put on the spot like this and he could tell.

"Look, I have been patient and understanding, but I
need you to know that I am a man, and I want all of
you. You are a woman, Carla, nothing else. A
beautiful God created woman. I want you and
believe you want me too, so let's stop playing this
confusion game."

I couldn't say anything. I was speechless. I was embarrassed and relieved at the same time.

"Can we stop by the liquor store and get something
to drink?" I asked.
"Sure we can. But I don't want you too intoxicated.
I want you to remember this night."
"I'm sure I will," I quietly said. His forwardness
turned me on so much.

He picked up some gin and coke. We drove to a motel near the beach, and checked in. Once we got in, he put the radio on. He found some smooth sounds of oldies but goodies.

"You want to take a shower with me?"
"Not right now." That was stupid to say, I told
myself.
"Well, I will be right back."
"Okay, leave me some hot water so that I can take
one too."

While he was in the shower I paced the floors not knowing what to do, how to act and what to expect. The water turned off and he yelled out, ready.

He walked out with this towel around his waist. His chest seemed to be the color of that burning sunset we just left outside. His skin was so smooth and the muscles in his chest were awesome. I could tell his body was in good shape.

"Don't take all night please," he whispered as I passed by, going to the shower."

"I won't," I chuckled.

I was so wet, it was embarrassing. I was glad I had to go to the shower first.

"Can I dry you off?" Carl said, after I had been in there fifteen minutes.

Damn, I guess I had to get out one day.

"Thanks."

He stood outside of the shower with the towel in his hands waiting for me to walk into them. He hugged me with the towel and began to dry me off. He took his time and dried me off one arm at a time. Then he laid one of the towels on the floor and got on his knees and dried my thighs.

Oh, I could have screamed. I stood there naked in front of him, nipples hard, body still being wet inside and out, feeling so hot from his touch. I felt like I would faint from the anxiety that was running through my mind wanting him so badly now.

He took me gently by the hand and walked me to the bed. The covers were already pulled back. He had our drinks already poured. He handed me my glass and then offered a toast.

"To a night to remember."

"Yes," Was all I could mutter out.

He only let me have one sip before he laid me back on the bed and began kissing me. His lips were so soft they felt like cotton candy melting in your mouth. He rolled his tongue across my lips top and bottom. Then he gently entered my mouth, sucking on my tongue.

Damn he was a good kisser. He kissed my neck and held my body so firm in his arms. I held his body, it was so hard all over. He had muscles in his back and all the way up his sides. His arms were so beautiful and muscular.

"I will be gentle with you."

"Okay."

"Relax your body, baby. I promise to be easy," he whispered.

His words made me melt inside. I could feel him and how hard he was. I could feel his penis on my legs, going up and down my thighs. He teased me and made sure I wanted him badly by the time he was ready to go inside me.

"You're ready, baby?"

"Yes."

"You're sure?"

"Yes, Carl, please come on."

"That's what I want to hear, I'm ready too baby. I've been ready for a long time."

Carl kept talking in my ears and loving me at the same time, squeezing my titties, then caressing them. I wanted to scream, "Come on." My pride wouldn't let me, so I pulled him to me. I kept pulling him inside me, hoping he would enter me. Once he did, we both moaned so loudly. It was so good and hot. He was gentle, he was easy. He was good and physically fit. He made me feel so good. It seemed perfect. He made love to me all night long.

The following morning I felt so awkward. I couldn't even face him. I wanted to just hurry up and get home. I had a nice evening, but I felt so dirty at the same time. Carl took me home immediately, like I asked him to. I had to be at work in less than two hours. We drove up to the house and I told Carl I had to get ready right now.

"You felt so good to me last night."

"You felt good to me too."

"Can we see each other again?"

"I can't talk right now, Carl, I have to go, okay."

Carl wanted to talk but I was almost late for work. I walked in the door. Mable was already at work, thank God. I couldn't face her like this. I had not only cheated on her sister, but I also stayed out again all night long without telling her. Then on top of that it was with a man. I rushed off to work. I decided within myself I couldn't see Carl anymore, he was making my life so damn hard and confusing. I didn't need to see anybody else at this point.

That night I called Carl and told him I really had to talk with him. He got real concerned. He asked me to hold the phone until he went into another room.

"Okay, baby, I'm back. What's going on?"

"Carl, I really loved being with you last night, but it was all very overwhelming for me."

"Wait a minute, I enjoyed last night too and I look forward to many more nights with you."

"Carl, just listen to me please. Look, I am totally out of control and I am not all that comfortable right now. Before this gets any deeper, I need you to know that I can't handle this feeling of wanting to be with you so badly, but also wanting my gay lifestyle too."

"Carla, can't you see, that's why you are struggling. That's not the life you should be in, baby."

"Well, I need time to think, okay? I just really need some time to clear my head. Let me call you after a week or two.

"Hey, if you need a little time that's cool."

"Carl, please don't call me until I call you, okay?"

"If that's what you want, Carla, fine. It's going to be hard, but if you are sure."

I couldn't help but feel part of me crying out for my mind to change. I grew mad at myself for stooping and falling weak to this man. I beat myself up for days. I struggled with wanting to see him, then calling him and hanging up the phone after I heard his voice on the line.

A few days later, I went up to the pool hall to see if I would run into him.   He wasn't there.   I asked Jerry, the owner, had he seen him. He told me that he had heard some bad news about Hot Dog. I was afraid to ask, but I did.   He had gotten picked up and taken back to jail.
> "He was doing so well, but I guess people can't seem to stay out," he said.

I felt so bad.   As I was walking out of the door, "Watching Ladies" came on the jukebox and it tore me apart. That was his song that he would play for me every time we were here.

I went home and tried to put everything that had happened in the last few weeks behind me.   I told myself that I needed to get back into my old lifestyle so I could forget all about this mistake. I called up Angelette and said, "Hey, I'm back."
> "I was wondering how long it was going to take your crazy ass," she said.

I asked where was the party tonight. She suggested we go to the Bowl of Cherries, a new club. I said, "Cool, let's do it."

CHRISTMAS 1980 -- NEW YEAR'S 1981

This Christmas season was going to be wild. No boring Fresno, no curfews, just hang out as long as you wanted to. Mable, Leonard, Dennis, Angelette and I went to the club and partied until sun up. The guys were talking a lot all throughout the night about the gay guys. Mable had talked the guys into coming to the gay bar and they made her regret it, but we had fun anyway.

The whole month of January passed by and I had not seen a blink of my period. I started getting nervous and scared. I had to tell someone, but who? I couldn't tell my Daddy. I couldn't tell my mother! Sharon was in Vegas again. I certainly couldn't tell Mable. Not my woman's sister! Could I be pregnant? The thought petrified me. I can't bring a child into this cold world. I kept saying to myself, "They will hurt and destroy her like they tried to do me." I began to plead to the Lord. I looked for him in the corners of the ceiling. Eventually, I had to talk to somebody human. So, I told Angelette. She told me I had to get tested immediately. We went to the doctor together just as we planned to do and the test was positive. I nearly fell into Angelette's arms when I walked out of the consultation room. When she saw my face, she knew I was pregnant.

"What are you going to do now?" she asked.

"I am not having a baby, Angelette, I can't have a kid." I started crying.

"No way! It might be a girl and then what? She'll be raped and molested all her damn life. I am not doing that to her. Angelette, help me." I was hysterical.

"Are you going to tell, Carl?"

"No! I can't, he's back in jail somewhere. Angelette, I can't have this baby. Angelette please, I got to do something."

"I have a plan, okay? You can get an abortion. I've done it before" Angelette said.

"Oh no! I'm about to kill a baby, Angelette." My eyes got so big.

"Well what the hell do you want to do? You can use my medical card."

"Go ahead, schedule the damn abortion," I mumbled feeling trapped.

That whole night I tossed and turned. I was scared. I tried to tell God how afraid I was and how it couldn't be. "I can't do it, God. Please, I can't have a child." I told him how sorry I was for falling into sin with that man. "Please have mercy on me God, please."

CHAPTER 30

THE ABORTION

I couldn't believe the abortion date had arrived so soon. Angelette came to get me and we caught a bus to Hubert Humphrey Hahn Medical Center to do the abortion. A nurse came out to the waiting room wearing a smile and holding a chart. She looked around the room and saw only three ladies left. "Angelette Williams," she called out. I jumped inside because she was referring to me. I was shaking. Angelette gave me a little pat of security and kind of pushed me on the way. "I'll be right here, baby." The young nurse walked me down this long hallway. I saw rooms where people were just lying around awake as if they were waiting for something to happen. The halls were dim and gloomy looking. Some of the girls in the rooms were curled up in a fetus position. I could hear little moans and groans here and there. I wondered if they were here for the same reason that I was.

Finally, we arrived at room 101. The nurse was very polite. She asked me to get undressed and place all my belongings in a plastic bag on top of the bed. I guess she saw the fear jumping all in my eyes because she held me for a bit. She whispered, "It's going to be alright, trust me, you will be fine." I held on to her hand tight and wondered how she knew it would be alright. Was she ever in my position, or was she just telling me this to calm me down? She began to let go of me, and I thanked her for her comfort. As she left the room, I began to wonder how it must feel for a nurse to see women come through here to throw away their mistakes day after day. I laid there in that cold and damp room thinking of my decision and wondering if this was truly the only way out.

I prayed to God asking Him for forgiveness, again. The nurse came back in to give me a shot to calm me down. I asked her if the operation would hurt. She said no, you won't even feel or remember it. I said, "Will this shot make me go to sleep right away?" She told me that I would be asleep by the time the doctor was ready for me. "Is this your first time?" she asked. I said, "Yes, and hopefully my last time." She left the room. I tried to make the shot hurry up, because I was tired of being awake. I did not want to think of anything else. As I laid there, I began to feel all sorts of mixed emotions. I felt sad, alone, and angry all at the same time.

"Angelette, are you alright?" a voice said.

I didn't answer her.

She called me again, and I jumped up. She said,
"Relax, I just wanted to tell you that it won't be
long now."

"It has not happened yet?" I asked in a paniced
voice.

She kind of laughed and said, "You haven't even
been asleep yet."

I thought I had. I guess I was daydreaming. The nurse returned and gave me another shot, and then I asked her, how much longer is it?

"Just a few more minutes. The doctor is finishing up
with another patient."

"Is my friend Carla still waiting for me?" I asked.

"Yes, she is," the nurse said. "She is a good friend,
Angelette."

"Yes I know," I said. The nurse left the room, saying
she would be back shortly.

A few moments later, two different nurses came in the door pushing a bed through the door. As they came over to my bed, I raised up.

"What are you doing?" I asked.

The little lady said, "It's time."

"Time to go?" I asked.

"Yes, the doctor is ready for you now."

"Where is my nurse?" I asked in panic.

"Mrs. Lyons will be there," the Hispanic man replied.

"Come on, you must get on this bed and we will
take you to O.R.".

They rolled me down the same long dreary hallway into this large room with all kinds of machines in it. As soon as we entered the doors I saw Nurse Lyons and a few other people. My heart jumped in my throat. I was being pushed under a machine. I wasn't asleep, so I was afraid.

Before I knew it, I said, "I am not asleep! The medicine is not working"!
The doctor said, "Calm down, Angelette. You will be fine in a minute."

I felt tears coming out of my eyes. The nurse patted my hands and said, "Believe me, you will be asleep by the time the doctor is ready for you." I said, "Isn't he ready now?" She said, "Yes, but we are still preparing for you." At that moment, a guy in an all-white suit came up to me. He started putting these needles in my arms. They were IV's. "Ouch," I said. "That hurts!" I began to get mad now, because I didn't know what was going on.

A few seconds later, another doctor came in with this long needle and said, "Now this is going to sting a little bit but it won't be long." He took my hand and laid it flat on the bed, then tapped the top of my hand searching for a vein. I had never gotten a shot on the top of my hand. He found the vein and in went the needle. It stung. I yelled "damn!" I then immediately felt something coming through that needle that felt like a ton of bricks going through my veins. It was hot and it hurt. I kept mumbling "I am not asleep!" I could see the doctors and everyone closing in on me. But I was fighting, because I could still see them. I kept saying, "it's not time yet! It's not time yet!" The doctor came over to me and said, "Angelette, I want you to start counting backwards from 100. I began, "100, 99, 98, 97." I could feel myself falling under and then I was gone. Suddenly, I was a long ways off somewhere. I heard voices way far but I wasn't there. Then I got to a point I heard nothing and it was over for me.

"Angelette, are you alright? Angelette?"
All I could do was moan and groan.
"Come on, take a little juice."
I heard a soft voice trying to get my attention. I blinked my eyes a couple of times before I could focus on anything. Then it came clear

to me. Nurse Lyons was right there. I cracked a half smile. She said, "See I told you it was going to be just fine. You don't even remember it, do you?" I shook my head, not realizing I could talk.

"How do you feel? Any pain?"

"No," I said .

"Well they are going to give you some pain pills for later," she said.

I looked down and my sheet was spotted with blood. She saw my concern.

"Well yes, you are also going to be bleeding for a few days. Just lightly though, nothing heavy" she said.

I was still dazed and not fully coherent.

"Where is Angelette?" I said.

"You are right here, my child, in the same room you started off in," she laughed.

"Oh, okay." I caught myself and said, "Where is my girlfriend, Carla?"

"She's out there in the lobby waiting for you."

"Good," I said .

"Are you ready to go home?"

"Today?"

"Yes. It's over. You can leave now. That is if you feel strong enough."

I asked her if my friend could come back and help me get ready. She said sure, but first we have to clean you up, get you some pain pills and schedule you a follow-up appointment for the clinic.

"How long will this take?" I asked.

"Well, it's in the process now, so no more than 30 minutes, okay?" she said.

"Good, I can lay here and rest. Then for sure I will be ready to go. Can you please tell my friend it won't be much longer?"

She left the room and I slowly began to talk to God.

"It is done, God. It is all over. It's gone away. It's

dead. There is no hurt, no risk, no worries, no
one walking out on you, no one touching your
little girl when you are not home. I know it was
a bad thing to do, but I just didn't know what
else to do, God. I promise you I will never do this
in my life again. I ain't touching no man and I
ain't letting no man touch me."

Tears began to roll down my face as I reflected on all the reasons for
not wanting that child. All the reasons I was scared to have a child
and God forbid it be a girl child.

The sun burned my eyes when we walked out of the hospital. It
was damp and cold. It had been raining that morning. I will never
forget Slauson and Main. That's the corner where I killed my baby,
I thought to myself as I looked at the street.

We took a bus ride home. We sat in the nearest seat available,
because I couldn't walk to far. I felt like everybody on the bus knew
what I had done. I felt so horrible and ashamed. I couldn't wait to
get home and out of the public's eye. As I sat there, I kept thinking
about what I had done.

CHAPTER 31

FEBRUARY 1982 — 18TH BIRTHDAY

I pretended I was sick so Mable wouldn't give me a party. My eighteenth birthday was too depressing to even think about celebrating. Though it was the "Big 18" everybody couldn't wait to reach, I didn't care if it came or left. I was not in the birthday mood. I knew Mable didn't understand when I told her I wasn't feeling too good. I was so depressed about the abortion which had just occurred a month before. I couldn't eat or sleep half the time. I just couldn't bring myself to celebrate my life after I ended a life.

I guess I could say that 1981 didn't start off pleasant. Now several months after the abortion, I still found myself depressed as the reality of what I had done began to sink in. The entire year was consumed with grief and depression. I continued to struggle with killing my child. I couldn't hide behind my fear. Though my reasons were real, they were not excusable to me. I felt like a murderer.

I spent every day working and coming home, watching television and writing Cloe senseless and romantic letters that I didn't mean. Mable was proud of me for not going out so much, but she really didn't understand the reasons why. I was in a hard, confused, lonely space where no one could help me, not even myself. The thoughts wouldn't go away and I wanted to kill myself. I couldn't even drink them away.

I wondered to myself what would Carl think? Would he have wanted the child? Would he have understood my fears of having a baby? I made up in my mind that he would never know about the baby.

One day I called my Daddy to see how he was doing and to give him my telephone number and address. He didn't ask me how I was doing. He didn't express his regrets of us not working out or anything. He didn't even say I love you. All he said was, "What are

you doing now?"   All Daddy was ever concerned with was if I was
working or in college. The conversation dwindled. After I hung up
with him, I called my mother.

"Hi, Momma, it's Carla."

"How's Momma's baby?"

"I'm fine." The tears began to roll because I wasn't
      fine, I was so depressed, but she couldn't help.

"When are you coming home to see us?"

"I don't know, Momma. Real soon, I guess."

I was long overdue for a visit to Fresno. I told her that I loved her
and all she said was "me too." I wanted her to say the actual words,
not just agree with me.

I told Momma I had a roommate and she thought that was good. I
asked about AlmaFaye and the kids. She told me that everybody
was doing the same. When I hung up the phone, Mable was
walking into the kitchen. I told Mable that we were going to Fresno
for Thanksgiving to be with my family. Mable was glad. All she
wanted to know was how would we get there and when were we
returning. She was game for almost anything.

After Mable left the room, I found myself wondering about my
sisters and brother who lived in Phoenix with Tyrone and Ms. Estee.
I wondered what they were doing. I had not called Phoenix to
speak with Tyrone or Ms. Estee in a long time, though I
remembered their number like the back of my hand. It was
embedded in my brain so I decided I would call Ms. Estee next.
Ms. Estee was always cheerful and loving no matter what time you
called. She picked up the phone her voice was like a breath of fresh
air. I could hear her smile through the phone when she discovered it
was me.

"Hey, Carla, how is my little precious doing?"

"I'm doing great" I told her, lying through my teeth.

"Sadie and Tarah were just here a couple of hours
      ago. You just missed them."

"Oh yeah, that's what I was calling for. I wanted to

see how they were doing."

"They both got jobs. Sadie is working for the
hospital as a candy striper and Tarah is working
Harry's Hamburgers.

"That's really good. I'm glad to hear that. What
about Tyrone Jr.?"

"Oh I'm sorry to say he's in jail for robbery."

"How long has he been in jail?"

"The real question is how many times has he been in
jail," she said.

"Well, how is big Tyrone?"

"He's fine, still working on cars."

I changed the subject entirely to take her back to my past. I
thanked her for all the love she had shown me as a little child when
they came to get us out of foster care. She was always so nice.
There were vague areas in my life that I always wondered about
surrounding the foster home and court process. She made some
things really clear and precise about the exact date when she and
Tyrone picked us up from the foster home. She even told me that
she still had the court papers and could send me a copy if I liked. I
told her I would like to have a copy if she didn't mind. After
hanging up the phone with Ms. Estee, I felt so much better.

Ms. Estee kept her word and I received the Court documents in the
mail a week later. I anxiously ripped open the envelope, only to
find some of the most depressing court documents I would ever
read. The first one was entitled "PETITION." This document
was from the Superior Court of the State of California. It gave
information that took me back so many years.

INSTRUCTIONS

(1)   Completion of hearing date Information is optional.

(2)   Verification not required on Certification from
        criminal court.

_____

_____

SUPERIOR COURT OF THE STATE OF
CALIFORNIA
FOR THE COUNTY OF FRESNO
JUVENILE COURT

In the Matter of LEE:

Tyrone	7 yr.	Dec. 26, 1958)	
Sadie	6 yr.	Jun 6, 1960)	No. 30229
Tarah	5 yr..	July 8, 1961)	Petition
Carla	3 yr..	Feb. 3, 1963)	

_____

I, the undersigned petitioner, say:

(1)   The persons names, address, and age shown
        in the above caption, are under twenty-one years
        of age.

(2)   these persons come within the provisions of
        Section 600b of the Juvenile Court of Law of
        Los Angeles, California, as follows:

That the home of said minors, Tyrone, Sadie, Tarah, Gable, Carla Lee, is an unfit place for them by reason of the neglect of their mother, in that on or about September 2, 1966, said minors were found in a filthy condition in their home and without proper provisions for their care and safety; further, said minors are frequently left in the family home without proper supervision.

(3)   The names and addresses of parents and guardians of the above named person, known to me, are as follows: Daddy, Tyrone Lee, 1144 McKinley, Phoenix, Arizona, Mother, Doris Hicks, same as minors.

(4)   The name and address of an adult relative residing within the county, or, if there is no such person known, the name and address of the adult relative known to the petitioner and living nearest to the court, is:

(5)   The above persons were detained on September 2, 1966.

THEREFORE, I request that these persons declared dependent children of the Juvenile Court.

Dated: September 7, 1966.

_____

(Petitioner)

I noticed that they had Tyrone Lee, Sr. listed as my Daddy, but he wasn't, but still let it be that way. I also noticed that Gable was not on our forms, but on a form by himself, because he had a separate Daddy. His Daddy came to Phoenix to get him right after we got there.

I sat back in my chair. I reflected back on my abortion and thought it was better I didn't bring a child into the world than to bring her into the world and neglect her as my mother neglected us. My depression came back on me again.

As I was putting the papers back in the envelope there was a knock at the door. It was my sister, Sharon. Daddy had given her my address that I gave him last week. I introduced her to Mable and they hit it off just fine. We went to the store to get something to drink and had a chance to talk a little. I told her how I ended up with Mable.

      "I know you were glad to leave Dad's place," she said.
      That wasn't good for you. You guys didn't know
      what to do with one another.
      "What's happening tonight?" she asked.
      "Well, we are going to have our usual gathering
      when Mable's friends come over and party a little.
      You want to hang?"
      "Sure."
      "I want to introduce you to somebody."
      "Who?" she said.
      "Don't worry you will find out when you meet
      him," I said.

I was referring to Mable's cousin Dennis. I thought he was cute and Sharon wasn't dating anyone. This was the first night I kind of felt myself coming back since the abortion. I had my sister with me now. I felt a connection to the outside world. That night when Dennis and the gang came over, I introduced my sister to Dennis. From that point on they were a hot number.

Thanksgiving was here and it was time to go to Fresno. Mable was so excited. We arrived Saturday morning. We paid the cab driver and grabbed our bags. Once there, I called out to my dog Blacky who I missed so much. He came running fast from the back of the house. I fell to my knees to catch him in action. He jumped up on me, licking my hand and face. I held him around his neck. I noticed that he was graying in the top of his hair. I guess Blacky was getting old like me. "Mable, this is my love away from L.A. He has never changed on me." She laughed. I told her how we used to sit on the porch together and watch the airplanes take off.

Momma had already started her Thanksgiving dinner and you could smell the food from the front door. Momma was surprised that we actually came. I had been threatening to come for the longest. I introduced Mable to Momma and all the kids. I showed Mable my old room so that she could set her bags down. That room gave me such an awkward feeling. This was the room where I was violated, but it was also the room where I hid in my little closet to cry out to God and He would comfort me. I went to the bathroom where I still saw the same damn Irish Spring soap being used. I still couldn't stand the smell of that soap. Every time I saw it, I hated it because I could smell it all over me.

After we got comfortable, I asked Momma where was AlmaFaye these days? She said that she would be over soon. I was surprisingly excited about being home. Momma seemed pretty cool, so far. Plus, she was sober since it was early in the day. The kids were growing taller. Mr. Calvin was nowhere to be found. Probably out hunting with his buddies.

I got on the phone and called a couple of people from the old school to let them know that I was in town. I called Mavis first.
"Hello," a raspy voice said.
"Hello, is Mavis there?"
"No, she isn't. This is her grandmother, can I take a message?"
"Hi, this is Carla. Remember me from the Atchison

Courts?"
"Sure, baby, I remember you. I use to pick you up
and take you to church with me and Mavis."
I was so happy that she remembered me.
"Where is Mavis?"
"Well baby, she don't live here anymore. She has her
own little family. Though she ain't do all that
well, she dating this boy that's beating on her. She
also is on dialysis machine three times a week."

Her grandmother just kept talking and talking about Mavis. I was
getting sadder and sadder. I didn't know what Dialysis was or why
she had to do it but it sounded bad. I wanted to see her so bad.

"Can I leave you the number where I am so you can
give her my number?"
"Yeh baby, because she can't keep that phone on
sometimes. That boy she was with in the army ran
the bill all the way up and so she can't keep a phone
on. Alright baby, good talking to you."
Mavis, the prettiest girl in school, was doing pretty
bad.

Later that evening Alma Faye came by. That night we partied at
Momma's house. It was packed. Folks came over to play Bid Wisk
and dominos. Mable had a ball. Momma was playing her Bobbie
Blue Bland for her friends. It's interesting how friends never change.
Mr. Calvin had come home later. He walked in the door and spoke
to me. I felt funny. I didn't know exactly how to respond to him,
so I took some time to introduce him to Mable. He was cordial
and then excused himself to take a bath. We played and partied
till the wee hours of the night.

The next morning I woke up early. Early enough to go in the front
room and find Momma staring out of the window. I came over
and gave her a hug and a kiss. I loved Momma's hair. It was always
so soft and fine like cotton candy. I started brushing it as she
stared out on the world and sipped on a can of beer.

"So how you been girl?" she asked.
"I been pretty cool, Momma."
"What are you doing for yourself these days?"
"Just working and keeping to myself. Momma,
  how are you doing?"
"I'm alright, I guess. I don't feel my time is long,
  Carla."

Momma would say this in the past in her drunken state. She would tell us, "My God knows that I am tired of this and He's going take me home." I used to wish he would take her home. But now I was trying hard to get to know her for who she was. I told her that she wasn't going anywhere.
"You're only forty-six years old."

The weekend was just about over and it was time to go home. Mable and I had a good time and I wanted my mother to come to L.A. with me. She told me that there was nothing in L.A. for her. I kept trying to persuade Momma that it would be a nice change. We had lost so many years.
"Momma, one day I will have enough money and
  I will buy you a place out there. Okay?"
"Yeah, we will see. You just get the place," she
  smirked, lighting a cigarette.

I had promised to spend the last day over to AlmaFaye's. So I left Mable at my mother's and walked over to AlmaFaye's that evening. AlmaFaye was a cook like Momma. Her food was smelling up the neighborhood. I walked in the back door and I yelled, "I'm here!"
"Come on in," she said. I wasn't sitting only there
  two minutes and my sister threw me a bag of dope.

AlmaFaye's neighbors were over so we sat around and talked and smoked weed all evening. People that knew me before I left Fresno were impressed because they thought L.A. was a hip place to live. If you could survive there, you were alright. My brother Gable finally came over and started crying about me needing to come back to

Fresno where my family was. I didn't see Darnell and had not seen
him for a few years. I wondered how he was doing but I didn't ask.

The next morning, I called Momma and told her to wake up
Mable. Momma was sad to see us go. She hugged Mable and
asked that we come back soon. I hugged the kids and gave them
some money. I hugged Momma and she held me tight.
      "I love you, Momma."
      "It was good seeing you again, girl," she whispered.

The cab blew for us and we left. Everybody came out waving
goodbye. Blacky was also out there, wagging his tail.

Leaving Fresno was always an emotional experience for me. Mable
brought my head onto her shoulders and said,
      "It was a nice weekend and I'm glad you had a
       decent time with your mother for a change."

I cried because I wanted so much more. I thanked Mable for
coming with me.

CHAPTER 32

Brown's Proposal

A week after we returned to Los Angeles, I got a call from Brown.

"Hey, what's up partner?"

"Nothing, man. Where you been? I have been calling you for a week."

"Mable and I went out of town to Fresno and you know I'm working."

Brown said he needed to talk with me. He sounded real serious. I got off the phone and Mable looked at me with questions on her face.

"So, who was that wanting to take you to dinner tonight?"

"That was Brown saying he wanted to talk with me about something."

Mable laughed and asked if he wanted me to turn another woman for him.

"You know, Mable, that's getting so tired it's not even exciting. But no, that's not what he wanted."

I told her we were only going to talk and I would be back home in a couple of hours. An hour later the horn blew. It was Brown. I grabbed my jacket and said bye to Mable.

Brown and I went to a restaurant not far from the house. We ordered sandwiches and salad.

"So what's the news Brown?"

"Carla, I'm moving to Inglewood to a two-bedroom two-bath apartment."

I told him congratulations and asked him what did that have to do with me. He went on to say he had given this subject much thought. He said he was familiar with my lifestyle and how I have been surviving.

> "Carla, I want you to be my roommate!"
> "What! Ah, man I don't know about that! A
> roommate?"

I told Brown I appreciated him thinking of me but I didn't know
what the women might think. He told me that he had a full
package for me. He told me to just shut up and listen. So, I
listened.

> "First of all, I believe in you. I know you have
> some awesome things inside you and I don't
> want them to go to waste. It's okay to be wild,
> but you must have balance. I'm offering you an
> opportunity to start your higher education and
> get involved in a career. You can have your own
> room, with your own bathroom, your own phone.
> You can keep the car and drive it to school. I get
> paid every Friday and I will share an allowance
> with you."

Damn, that sounded too good to be true, I said to myself. Then he
dropped the bombshell on me. I asked Brown what would it cost
me. He told me absolutely nothing and that everything would be
free.

> "The only thing I ask is a little entertainment
> every now and then," he smiled, taking a sip of
> coffee.
> "What the hell you mean by that?" I asked.
> "Since you will have carte blanche to have your
> own private company and come and go as you
> please, every now and then let me watch and get
> off."
> "Hell nah," I hollered, getting up from my chair.
> Brown grabbed my arm to sit me down. "Come
> on, Carla!"

I sat there thinking. Brown motioned to the waitress for a refill of
coffee. I knew Cloe was sent up the river for a long time and by the
time she got out perhaps we could get together. I had no obligation

to her sister other than I would hate to break her heart by leaving. I
was considering it real serious now. I did want to become someone
that my Mother and Daddy could be proud of.

"Brown, let me think about it for a few days."

"Man, that's cool."

"Listen, how long will it be before you move?"

"Probably after the first of the year.

Brown dropped me off back at the house.

"Remember, no strings attached."

I walked in the door and Mable was watching television. I sat on
the couch next to her. Mable was like a big sister but acted like my
mother at times.

"Hey, did you bring me something back?"

"Yeah, part of a salad and a whole sandwich."

"What did old Brown want with you? To freak off
with some girls?"

"Nah', Mable, not this time. It was something
totally different. He asked me to consider
moving in with him the first of the year."

"Moving in with him?"

"I know, it's crazy, hah?"

"Why does he want you to move in with him
honey bunch? Is he in love with you?"

"No, Mable!"

"I believe he is, Carla. Why does he want you to
move in with him then?"

"He wants to give me a hand in life. He also
wants to send me to college."

Mable asked me if I was worried about leaving and hurting her. I
looked up at her and before I could say anything she began to talk
again.

"Baby, I don't want you to go, but you must do
whatever you know will help you to the next
level."

"But what about Cloe?" I said.

"Cloe is in jail and life goes on. Don't you be in
jail mentally. She'll be alright. The most
important thing here is that you do what makes
Carla happy and complete. I would be selfish to
hold you here."

I told Mable that I appreciated how nice and loving she had been
toward me. She was a true friend and nothing would change that. I
knew in my heart that there was nothing that Mable wouldn't do for
me and likewise there was nothing I wouldn't do for her.

We sat in the living room that night and talked about everything we
experienced in the last two years together. After that evening of
reflecting, we decided that we would party every night until I left.
We talked about my birthday coming up and throwing a birthday
party that I would never forget. I agreed. She reminded me that I
would be turning the big nineteen years old.   I began to feel so old.

For the next two months all we did from sunrise to sunset was
party, drink and smoke. After work we had the evening planned.
The gang would come over and we'd play dominos and Bid Wisk
until we all fell asleep.

FEBRUARY 1982 (19 Years Old)

My birthday reminded me of my abortion. This year I received a
surprise call from my mother wishing me happy birthday.   That
made me feel so good. I didn't care what else happened that day
after that call.   My Momma remembered my birthday.

I got up and started my day with an Old English 800 and
continued on until the late evening (which in actuality was the next
morning). We went to the club and made a complete drunken
smoking mess out of ourselves.
My last night with Mable was spent over to Dennis' house for his
birthday party.   Dennis lived on the East side. When we got to
the house, it was already jumping. People were dancing and eating

barbecue all over the place. I saw my sister Sharon and she gave us a drink to get started. Dennis had about seven rooms in his house and each one was filled with a different kind of action. I went to the room with the acid in it. There was Eddie, Butch and other familiar faces standing alongside the walls. They looked bombed out! I said give me some. The girl that was cutting the paper told me this stuff came from Japan. She gave me three pieces of paper and said, "Suck on this and you will be flying quick."

"Look, you just be careful," my sister said.

I told her I was cool. I was on my way back to the other room when within minutes I found myself crawling instead of walking. I can remember someone asking me what I was doing on the floor and me telling them it's too high up there, I can't stand the height. They got me off the floor and put me on my feet. I could see my sister laughing, but she stayed close to me.

The next day Mable was laughing all day, telling me about all the craziness I had done while on acid. It was sad leaving her behind. I knew just as I was looking forward to a fresh start, Mable really needed a fresh one too. I could not see living in the fast lane like that the rest of my life. I knew there was more to life, at least more for me.

The following week May Company laid off all of their part-time temporary helpers. I guess the timing was great. I was scheduled to move to Inglewood with Brown and it would have been a long commute to downtown Los Angeles.

CHAPTER 33

Moving In With Brown – February 1982

I was all packed and ready to go. Brown picked me up early Saturday morning. We went over to the apartment and sure enough my room was ready. I had a beautiful queen-size bedroom set. The mauve comforter set was jamming. There was a six-drawer dresser with a mirror on top, two night stands with lamps on both, a cream throw rug which felt like fur and a phone on the left side of my bed. I was in love with the room. It was so clean. I had my own bathroom and it was just beautiful. Brown had decorated it in cream and gold. He said he remembered my two favorite colors were white and gold. My shower curtain was also clear white with gold streaks throughout. I felt so special. I looked at Brown and shook my head as he followed me from room to room.

"Did I do a good job, Carla?"

"Of course you did, man, you did too much," I
said.

"Never too much for you, Carla. I told you that
you were special to me."

When he said that, I thought about what Mable asked me (if he was in love with me). But I dismissed it.

"So, man, thank you very much. I didn't
expect this at all."

"What did you expect?"

"I don't know, but it wasn't this."

Brown brought all of my baggage in and I put up my things. Already, I began to feel as if I had my own place. I got settled in and Brown left to go to the supermarket to get a few things. Soon as he left, I got on the phone to call all of my ladies to give them the new number.

After Brown returned from the grocery store he put everything up and opened a bottle of Zinfandel.   I sat at the kitchen table to make small talk. The entire apartment was so beautiful. We began to discuss the do's and don'ts of the apartment pursuant to the lease. He warned me of the strict landlords.   I asked him about the tenants and he said there were two exciting tenants in the whole unit.   That was the couple across from us on the second floor. Then he told me about the gay couple on the same level as we were. He said they were quiet and not open to friendships at all.   I got concerned because I didn't want to run into my buddies or anything.   They would call me a punk or something, knowing I lived with a man. We talked about school. I told him that I had looked in the newspaper for certain trade schools and was interested in taking Legal Secretary courses. He agreed that was a good idea. I told him I would go up to the college next week to enroll because the classes were starting in two weeks. He said, "good for you."

After our official talk, we began to laugh about the past freak Mommas we had freaked off with together. Brown was telling me a couple of the women were asking about me and wanted to get back together. I ignored him.   We ate and went to our respective rooms for the night.

The next morning Brown knocked on my door around 6 a.m. to ask if I wanted to keep the car and take him to work. I told him sure. I got up and grabbed my coat, since it was so early and took him to work, then came back and got back in the bed. Brown said he would be off work at 2:30 and would wait out front for me to pick him up. That was cool with me. That day was kind of different. For one, I was in a new place with new smells, new surroundings and it was refreshing. Everything was very nice and clean. Brown was a clean man and didn't like dirt around him. I could really live with this. Around noontime, I called my Daddy.
    "Hi, Daddy!"
    "Hi, Carla. How's it been?"
    "It's been pretty good, daddy. I got very good
     news, I am living with a man."
    "You are living with a man," he repeated

cautiously.

"Yeah. We have a two bedroom apartment in Inglewood."

"Oh, a two-bedroom in Inglewood. And how old is this man?"

"Well he is a little up there."

"How old is he, Carla?" Daddy sounded real firm now.

"He's fifty-six years old."

"What!" Daddy screamed.

"Fifty-six years damn old! He's older than me!"

"I didn't know that Daddy." I didn't know how old my Daddy was.

"Well, he is. He's old enough to be your damn granddaddy. Oh, so this is good news, hah?"

"He's a man, Daddy, that's the damn good news part."

"What can you do with a fifty six year old man? And what can he do for you? He must be some kind of freak or pervert", he snapped. I really thought that Daddy would finally approve and accept me as a normal daughter again.

Well that announcement backfired. I told myself I would never call my Daddy again in life. I walked around my room in tears talking to myself! The hell with you, Daddy. Go straight to hell! I will never be your damn daughter anyway. It seemed like I kept doing all the wrong things. How come he couldn't love me anyway, in spite of me being a misfit? You don't deserve a daughter like me any damn way!

Later that morning, I had a few things that needed washing and went to the first floor to wash some clothes. And who did I run into, Ms. Landlord. I knew it was her before she opened her mouth. She saw me coming out of Brown's apartment and looked at me over her bifocals. "Good morning," I said. She said, in a curious

way, "Good morning." I kept going. I finished my wash. By this
time it was time to pick up Brown from the job. Brown worked for
the World Way Post Office off of Century Boulevard. Hundreds
of people were getting off at the same time that he was. I was
hoping people didn't think I was his woman coming to get him. He
got in the car with a big smile on his face.

    "Hey, Brown. How's it going?"

    "Great. How you doing today, cutie?"

    "Just fine." I didn't like him calling me cutie.

    "Have you eaten, Carla?"

    "No, I was going to fix me a sandwich when we
      got back home."

    "Well, let's go up here to the barbecue place and
      pick up some food."

    "I ain't got no money, Brown."

    "Did I ask you if you had any money?"

    "No."

    "Okay then, go on."

We brought the food back to the house and sat in the kitchen to
eat.

    "So how was your day?" Brown asked.

    "Well, it was great up until I called my Daddy."

    "Why? What was wrong with your Daddy?"

    "He didn't like the idea that I was living with a
      man older than he was."

    "Oh, what century is he living in?"

    "I don't know and don't give a damn. I also,
      finally met the old hag from downstairs and she
      gave me this weird look over her glasses."

    Brown started laughing.

Changing the subject Brown told me about an inquiry he had today
on his job.

    "Carla, I got these two friends, Katie and Debbie,
      that I was talking to today about you. They said
      they wanted to meet you as soon as possible."

"Oh, is that right?" I thought to myself, it's pay
day.
"Yes, and they invited us over for dinner
tomorrow night."
"Oh, is that right?" I said out loud this time.
"Yep."

Brown didn't waste any time with our little arrangement. That
night, I discovered Brown doing something that I really didn't have
a stomach for -- cocaine. I asked him how long had he been doing
it. He said only a short time. It makes freaking out more exciting
for the girls. I told him I didn't want to be around that stuff under
any circumstances. He saw that it really bothered me. I had seen
too many of my friends die and lose their souls to it. I remembered
the first time I hit that stuff. It made me feel so good I took the
pipe back to the person that had just passed it to me and told them
never again in life. They laughed at me that night, but I never hit
that shit again. Brown said if it offended me that much, he would
leave it alone. I thanked him. I went to bed early. I told Brown I
was tired. He said he had some runs to make anyway. He would
check me out tomorrow.

It felt like I had not had this type of peace ever. I was so grateful
and thankful for the living arrangements. I could lay in my bed,
lock my door and get as comfortable as I wanted and no one would
bother me or interrupt me. But then I remembered why I kept so
busy most of the time. I couldn't help but think about my family
and everybody else that was in my life. I really missed my mother
the most. I hoped that this was a real good move for me and that I
was on my way to better things. I have to be, I told myself. I told
God I wanted to be something in life. Not just an old whore, slut,
or all the other things I've been called. My mother used to tell me I
would have a thousand kids. She thought I was screwing
everybody's man. Maybe that's another reason I didn't want kids.
She had twelve kids by four different men. I knew I wasn't going to
do that. I turned on my portable radio and listened to some jazz.

The next night, Brown and I got ready to go over to Katie and
Debbie's house. On the drive over I asked him if these were cute
girls. He assured me that I would be thoroughly satisfied.

We arrived at the doorstep and rang the bell. A young lady about
5'2" with long beautiful hair, nicely built, answered the door. She
was dressed in a red dress that fit her body like a glove.
    "Come in! Hey, Brown, how are you doing?" She
    said she was excited.
    "Fine Katie. Meet Carla."
    "Nice to meet you, Katie."
    "Same here, been looking forward to it."
    She told me she had heard so much about
    me, as she escorted us to the couch.

Katie told us that her roommate, Debbie, had gone out to get some
wine and dessert and would be back shortly. I thought to myself, I
wonder what Debbie looks like because Katie was breathtaking.

Within moments, Debbie walked in the door. I knew right off that
the night would be great. She was so pretty! She was wearing a
beautiful multi-print dress, which draped her hips. Her legs were
extremely smooth like baby skin. I couldn't believe how cute she
was. I wondered how Brown got this connection. We spoke and I
was introduced as the guest for the evening.

Katie put on some jazz. We laughed and talked through dinner.
Afterwards, Brown broke the ice by asking, does everybody play
cards? Brown suggested strip poker. I could have kissed him for
that one. Debbie and Katie cleared the dinner table and we began
to play.

The rules were, whoever won the hand could make a wish for
someone to do anything they wanted them to do. The game got
more intense as the night progressed. Katie was the first to win.
Her request was for me to caress her titties and bite her nipples, real
softly as she put it. Not too hard and not too soft for five minutes.

"Can you handle that?" she asked.
"I think I can."

So for the next five minutes I sucked Katie's titties while she squirmed in her place trying to play cards.

The next hand, Debbie won. Her request was for me to keep sucking on Katie's titties and take my hand and play with her clitoris at the same time for the next five minutes. I loved their requests. They both had the most sensuous sounds and moans coming from them. That turned me on and out of my mind. I lost myself in both of them for hours.

Brown seemed like he was getting a little bothered because they were not asking him to do anything, but he enjoyed watching. I almost wondered to myself if this was their plan.

Their bodies smelled like they had soaked in strawberries for twenty-four hours. The games and requests then escalated to straight sex. I ended up in bed with both of them, while Brown was stuck in a corner jacking off.

Brown and I left around two in the morning. We got home and went to our respective rooms. I was so tired. The next morning, I told Brown to go to work. I didn't want to get up to take him. I was too tired from the wild night. After work, Brown came home with a report card that Katie and Debbie had written out for me. It was quite complimentary.

That Friday, Brown and his men friends came home from work together. I was in my room. I heard the noise and came out. Brown and his friends were getting ready to cook some cocaine. I went back into the room. A couple of hours later I came back out and they were still there. Brown introduced me to his friends and they all did the "goo goo eye thang." I looked at Brown real stern and he noticed my disappointment. After they left, he came to my door.

"Can I talk to you, for a moment?" Brown asked.

"Sure, what's up?" I said.

"I know you didn't appreciate that stuff we were
doing, but its just a thing that me and the fellas
do some Fridays after a long week's work. It's no
harm."

"Brown, you don't understand the power of
cocaine. It's a lot of harm. It will slip up on you
and bite your ass off before you know it."

"Baby girl, thank you for your concern. But trust
me, I got it under control."

"Fine! I will keep my comments to myself."

ENROLL IN SAWYER'S BUSINESS COLLEGE
1982

It was time to start school. I enrolled in classes and met a couple of
nice girls. One girl's name was Deena Trotter. She was the only
black person there. She was cute with pretty brown eyes. We
learned that we didn't live far from each other and decided to car
pool on some days. She was the first straight friend I had met in a
long time. After school that day I was so excited. I picked up
Brown and he could see it in my face. I had done it. I was now an
official full time student! We changed clothes and Brown took me
to this real nice restaurant in Marina Del Rey. We talked and
discussed school, financial aid, classes and the girls there. He
couldn't resist asking me if I had met any freak Mommas and I told
him no.

The next day I decided to call Momma. I told her that I was living
with this fifty six year old man and shared with her the proposal he
gave me. Only about school, not freaking out with other women.
She got excited.

"Momma, I'm not saying we are together or
anything like that."

"What do you mean?" she asked.

"You said, you pay no rent, you don't have to
work, you don't have to buy groceries, he does
everything, what the hell is wrong?"

"Momma, the man is too damn old for me! He is
older than Daddy."

"So what? Yo Daddy ain't taking care of your ass,
is he?"

"No, Momma."

"Okay, then the hell with your Daddy!"

"Daddy is mad at me!"

"Let Brown be your Daddy and your Sugar
Daddy."

"I don't know, Momma. I don't love this man
like that."

"Let me tell you one damn thing," she snapped.
"If you never listen to anything else that I have
told you, hear me when I say this. Fuck what you
want, baby. Get somebody that loves you and
eventually you will learn to love them.
Either you will have to get away from the love or
you will run toward it. Momma knows what
she's talking about."

"Momma, I like women!"

"You don't know what the hell you like. If you
ask me, it sounds like you are fighting something
you are already feeling for this man."

"No, I am not, Momma!"

"Look, I been in this world too damn long. I know it
don't matter what you want because that might not
be the person that's going to die for you. Where is
this man anyway?"

"He's in his bedroom."

"Put him on the phone."

"No! I don't want you talking to him."

"Girl, put his ass on the phone right got damn
now!"

I knocked on Brown's door and told him, telephone. He asked me who was it. I told him it was my mother.

He smiled and said, "Oh? What does she want to do? Cuss me out?"

"No," I said under my breath.

Brown started talking to Momma. I thought to myself, I couldn't allow someone to love me and not love them back. Momma was really out of her mind. But it was so much fun talking with her like this. This was a first. Momma would mostly be drunk when I called and I would have to be content with just hearing her voice on the line. But today she appeared to be giving motherly advice, no matter how weird it was. I wondered why Momma didn't feel toward Brown the way Daddy did. How come she was so open to it? Maybe because she was a woman and wanted me taken care of. Maybe that's all she knew and age didn't matter to her. Brown hung up the phone. I asked what did my mother say to him and he told me that she ordered him to take care of her crazy ass daughter.

After the sixth week school really started getting exciting. I was really enjoying the classes that I was taking. It was a nine- month course, five days a week, 8 a.m. to 2 p.m. That worked out well because Brown got off of work at 2:30 and by the time I got to him, he would be walking out of the post office doors. I was at another level of happiness with my life. I felt on top of the world. I didn't realize how good this was and how it affected me. I found myself wanting to do less partying and more studying and going forward.

As the weeks went by, Brown and I spent a lot of time getting to know each other. We found ourselves talking for hours sometimes, then going to bed. We would walk to our separate quarters and wave good night. Brown was becoming the male friend I never had before. We were going to movies and dinners more. He told me that I was helping him stay away from his cocaine buddies. We were helping each other because I was not going out as much either. Brown would ask me periodically how I was doing in school and was always pleased with my answer. He was happy that I was happy with what he was trying to do for me.

One day Brown got a phone call that changed his spirit. When he hung up the phone, I asked what was wrong. He told me that his mother was very ill and needed her transportation back. Apparently the last time he visited his mother he drove her car back to Los Angeles. Now his other relatives were having to take her to the doctors more frequently and they needed the transportation. I told him to give the car back. He said he had another car in his ex-wife's garage that she was not using. He was referring to a 1972 blue and white Cadillac. I told him to go get it and be through with it. He was concerned that I would be upset that the new car was leaving. I told Brown I was not into that kind of material stuff. As long as I get where I need to go, I'm fine. Brown let me know that he was going to take his three-week vacation in Texas and that's when he would take the car back to his mother.

From that night on, I noticed Brown becoming more worried about his mother. He would call her at least four times a week. I started spending more time around the house cooking dinner. Brown was very complimentary and told me that he didn't know I could cook like this. The first meal I prepared for him was smothered short ribs, yams, black eyed peas and homemade cornbread. He went out before we ate and got some sweet potato pie and ice cream for dessert. After dinner, he helped me wash the dishes and clean up the kitchen. Brown was such a neat man. He made a proposal after dinner. He offered that we would take turns cooking dinner instead of spending money eating out at restaurants so much. I told him I was cool with that.

One day, Brown caught me off guard. We were at the dinner table. He shared with me that he was aware that his behavior had changed in the last month. I interrupted and told him that I understood his mother was really worrying him. He told me that was partially true, but I was the one that was really bothering him.
    "I think I'm falling in love with you, Carla."

I jumped up and cussed him out. I told him not to start talking like that. I told him that was not part of the deal and I was not standing for it.

"I love women and that's all it is to it," I screamed.
Take your love and go freak off or something."
He looked at me in such a crazy way.
"What's wrong, Carla? I took the risk of telling you
that because I thought the feeling was mutual. I
guess I was going on what I started seeing you do
around the house.
"What things did you start seeing around the house,"
I asked.
"Well for starters, you stop going out. You cook
almost every night on the alternate night. You
even prepare my plate. You opened up to me and I
know practically everything about your life."
I told Brown that cooking and cleaning were the
least I could do.
"I got to do something! Don't mistake it for love," I
told him.

Then all of a sudden, he started laughing hysterically. I got pissed off and stormed out of the kitchen. I felt so angry. I don't know if I was angry because of what he said to me or if I was angry because I felt the same way he did. But I was determined to prove him wrong. I decided to go out to the club that night. I came out of the room and asked him what was he doing tonight. He responded, "Nothing." I said, "good, I need the car. I want to go to the club."

I went into my room to call Mable and Angelette to go out with me. I had not spoken to them in the last three months. Mable had her boyfriend Eddie over, but Angelette was ready to go. I left and went to pick her up. Angelette was so surprised to see me. Mable had not told her the details of where I went and what I was doing. We went to the Bowl of Cherries. It was entertainment night. The audience was able to participate in singing and ad-libbing competition.

As soon as we got in, I found a table close to the floor where the entertainment would be. I sat down and ordered us a drink. There was a young lady singing "Portuguese Love" by Tina Marie. She was pretty, brown skin, tall, red hair and sexy. Angelette saw me looking at her and asked if I wanted to dance. I didn't want to dance. I just wanted to lose myself in somebody's arms. I guess Angelette caught on and pursued her own private party. After the song, I turned my head for a second and the young lady was suddenly in my face asking for a light. Her name was Ronnie I searched for a match and came up and her tittie's were right in my face. I was choked up for a minute. I asked her if she was alone as I lit her cigarettes. She came with a couple of buddies that were on the dance floor.

"Maybe we can get a dance going later" I said.
She said, "Sure." Angelette came back to the
table, looking all weird.
"So what was that all about?"
"What do you mean what was that all about?
About me trying to meet that woman," I said.
"Oh, so do you want to dance now?" she asked
again.
"Nah', Angelette, I'm going to sit this out again."

They switched the music on us from fast to slow. I looked over at Ronnie and motioned, so she got up and came my way. Luther Vandross was playing. We made small talk and she said it would be nice to have my company after the club closed. After that dance the night began.

I took Angelette home and caught up with Ronnie at her place. I got to her place and it turned out to be a restaurant. I was amazed. How do I get in? I knocked on the back window and a voice yelled, "go out to the front." They had gone in and started some weird kind of freak off party. The girls were undressed and one guy was there. I was tired of this shit. I had orgies and freak out parties up to my got damn nose with Brown. I sat down and just watched, feeling angry. They asked me to join and I told them, I wasn't in the mood. Ronnie saw how I responded and urged them to take the party somewhere else. After the man got off, they left. I was highly disappointed. I asked her how often did she entertain this kind of party. She said, "Only on an as needed basis. I take it you don't care for it." I told her I had just had enough of it in my little nineteen years of life. She was surprised.

"You're only nineteen?"

"Yeah, but in age only," I started for the door.

"Whoa," she said in disbelief.

"I've got to go, maybe we can get together next week," I told her. I went home and got prepared for school the next morning.

School was really getting interesting and I was learning a lot of valuable information. I couldn't wait for my first job. I wanted my own money now. Brown and I were talking at the table one day, and I brought up getting my own job and he totally disagreed. He went on about how I needed time to study and take my time through school. I told him that I needed my own money. He recommended that we sit down after his next pay period, gather the bills, pay them and what ever was left over, we would split in half.

"Is that reasonable?" he asked.

"That's crazy! I'm not your damn woman! You can't be doing that."

"Carla, I just want you to concentrate on your career. It won't be that much longer. You only have a few months to go and you will be out of school."

I finally agreed.

One day Ronnie came over to the house to visit me. When she got there I took her right to my room. Brown was watching television and his eyes got so big. I didn't even introduce her to him. After a few hours we came out and she went home. When we came out of the room, Brown was standing in the doorway. I had to pass him, so I took that opportunity to introduce them. Brown was furious. I wasn't sure if he was mad because she was there and he wasn't invited to join us or if he was jealous of the relationship altogether. I went to bed early that night.

The next day, I walked in from school and Brown was off work. He and some woman were sitting up in the house playing records and having a drink in the living room. I couldn't believe my eyes. How dare him, I thought to myself. How could he have her out in the open? At least I took mine and closed the door behind me. I didn't rub it in his face, I thought to myself. Okay, he's going to play like that. I couldn't believe I was reacting like this. He saw the anger. I walked in, spoke and didn't give him time to introduce her, even if he was going to. I went to my room mad.   The woman left later that evening.   I came out of my room and went to fix me something to eat.

>"Are you going to fix enough for me?" Brown
>asked.
>"Your slut should have fixed you something
>before she left."
>"Carla, what's wrong with you? That's no way
>to talk about my friend." He had a cocky smile on
>his face.
>"I know Brown. I'm sorry," I said sarcastically.
>It came out before I thought about it.
>"But, no, I'm still not fixing you anything; you do it
>yourself." He started laughing.
>"What's so damn funny?"
>"You should have seen your mouth when you walked
>in the door," he said, laughing.

I told him that he should have seen his bald head when I walked in the door with Ronnie yesterday.   He started walking toward me.

>"I wish I could eat you while you are this angry. Do
>you think we can do that?" he asked.
>I could have hit him.

CHAPTER 34

Mother's Day – May 1982

It was close to Mother's Day and I told Brown that I was thinking about going to Fresno to see my mother. He thought it was a good idea. I started preparing to go that week-end.

Fresno was so hot around this time of year. Momma was playing music. I surprised her because she didn't know I was coming. I loved surprising her. I got out of the cab and rushed in the gates. I got bad news as soon as I got there. I yelled Blackeeeeeee! But I got no response. I kept yelling as Momma was coming out of the front door to greet me.

Momma told me that Blacky died a few weeks ago. I couldn't believe it. I never imagined ever coming home and Blacky not being there. Blacky was always there to greet me. My only friend. Momma told me that the kids buried him. I asked where and she said in the back yard near the gate. I never knew how much that dog meant to me. I couldn't imagine Blacky being dead. I kept shaking my head no. Momma told me it was only a dog and to calm down. She didn't understand how that dog comforted me during the hardest days of my life as a child.

I eventually got comfortable and hung out with Momma most of the day. I had called my old friend Cheryl and she told me that there was an awesome party going on that night on her block. I told Momma I wanted to go to a party later on and could I borrow her car. She said yes.

Once I got to the party, I had the shock of my life. Who stood before me, but Kendon Starr, in the flesh! My mouth dropped open. I was scared to even go up to him right away. Then I feared I would probably never see him again, if I didn't.

"Hello, stranger," I said.

He looked at me. "Carla! Baby!" We grabbed each other.

"What are you doing? Are you back out here in
Fresno?"
"No, I'm just visiting for Mother's Day."
He held me tighter. "Carla, I ain't never forgot
about you. I always hoped that I would see you
again."
"Me too, Kendon."
"Let's go outside where there is some quiet."

I was so happy I came to this party, but I still had not seen Cheryl,
who invited me.   Kendon was still so handsome and the same
feelings were there for both of us. We talked and decided to go to
his house so that I could say hi to his parents. I asked him what
had been going on in his life? He reluctantly told me that he was
pimping. He had a few women on the streets. He told me that he
had been out of jail for a good while now. The street life was
paying off and he was rolling in consistent cash. I told him about
my life style, but I didn't have any women on the streets. He
laughed and didn't seem to mind too much.

"Carla, can I ask you something?"
"Sure, Kendon, what?"
"Did what your step daddy do to you make you
start liking women and not men?"
"I don't know, Kendon, I really don't. I guess it
could be."

Kendon hadn't changed much. He was still compassionate and
concerned. All I saw was the boy I never forgot. We were driving
to his house when this car behind started blowing its horn real loud
at us. I looked in my rear-view mirror and it was a car full of
women, at least four of them. I ignored them.

"Do you know those women back there?" I asked.

He turned around and said, "Oh, shit! That's part of the girls I was
telling you about."
"What, yo hoes?"
"Yeah."

"Oh, my God!"
I stepped on the gas and so did they.

They got so crazy, they started driving on the other side of the
street to catch up with us.   Then the driver got on my side and
started cursing and calling me names.
    "Hey bitch I'm going to kill you. You hear me, I am
    going to kill you" she blurted out.

I couldn't believe my ears! I didn't know what to do. I could see
Kendon getting very angry. Kendon started yelling, "I'm going to
kick your ass when I see you. Don't be calling her no bitch. You
the bitch. Bitch!"
    "Kendon, stop it! Don't be talking like that" I told
    him.
    "Nah", Carla, she don't disrespect you like that!"

We were coming near to his house. They stopped the car and she
went into the trunk for something, I couldn't see what. Kendon
said, "That bitch is crazy. Hurry up and get home." I looked again
in my mirror and they were, coming faster. Oh no, I said. The
lights were red so I went through both lights. I wasn't stopping.
Kendon told me to go into the house as soon as we got there. I
swerved around that corner. He said, park right here and go into
the house right now. Tell my mother to come out here." I was
frozen.
    "Do what I say right now Carla!"   he yelled at
    me.

Just as I was getting to the porch, they swerved around the corner,
jumping out of their car. I ran to the door and rung the door bell.
Come on, Mrs. Starr, I was saying to myself.

Kendon was yelling now at the woman who jumped out of the car,
who was the same one that was calling me all the names. I turned
to look at them and Kendon had grabbed her by the throat. He
was shaking and hitting her with his fist. Her head turned like a

tether ball. Mrs. Starr finally came to the door. All I could do was point to Kendon, I couldn't say a word. The girl's face and mouth were so bloody. I felt terrorized just to look at her. Mrs. Starr told me to go in the house and close the door. I ran in there and went to the window to watch. I saw Mrs. Star stop Kendon. It seemed familiar to her. She told Kendon to go into the house. Then she stayed and talked with the girl. I saw him coming toward the house and his clothes were bloody. The girl started yelling, "I am going to have your ass thrown back in jail! I am going to have the cops come and get your ass!"

Kendon walked in the door, went to the couch and flopped down. I ran to him.

"Kendon, are you all right?" Kendon looked so
drained and disturbed.
"Are you all right, Carla?"
"Baby, I'm fine but that poor woman, Kendon. How
could you hit her like that?"
"Carla, you don't understand, they like that sick
shit."
"Kendon, I don't know about that. They might like a
little push or slap here and there, but I can't believe
she like her teeth being knocked out of her mouth."
"Drop it, Carla, " Kendon looked at me and said.

His mother came in the house looking for Kendon. She asked Kendon several questions.

"Kendon, what happened tonight?"
"Mama, she was calling Carla names."
"So you beat her up?"
"Yes, Momma, I beat the girl."

I sat there listening. It almost sounded as if it was a therapy session and he had been here before.

"You know you are on probation and if that girl
calls the police you are going back to jail for a long
time" she said,

"I know, Momma. I know, but she ain't gonna call
them."
"How do you know this, Kendon? She's got to go to
the hospital and get stitches. They are going to ask
how it happened and she's going to tell them."
"No she isn't, mama, trust me," Kendon said.

The phone rang an hour later. It was the girl. She was threatening
him to get me out of that house because she was going to kill me.
She said she had to go to the hospital to get stitches. She was
talking so loud I could hear her. He hung up on her. She kept
calling back every fifthteen minutes. Kendon needed to get away
from this damned place called Fresno, I thought to myself.   I
wished to myself that he could come to Los Angeles, but how and
where?   Mrs. Starr finally said, "Carla, it is so good to see you after
all these years. You look so different and mature.
    "Thank you Mrs. Starr."
    "What have you been doing in L.A.?"

Boy, was that a loaded question. I carefully chose my answers,
mainly about work and school.   She seemed to be slightly
impressed.

The longer I sat there, the more worried I was that police officers
would be knocking on the door and this would be the last time I
would see Kendon again. His mother finally went to sleep. She left
Kendon and me up in the den and brought me some covers for the
couch because Kendon told her I was spending the night.   Kendon
and I discussed the possibility of him moving to Los Angeles. We
just couldn't come up with a place where we both could live.
    "Where am I going to live, Carla?"
    "Well, I don't know right now, but give me a couple
    of weeks and I will figure something out, okay?"

The girl Kendon beat up called back one last time and apologized
to Kendon for making him mad. I couldn't believe my ears. She
was really apologizing after he knocked her teeth out. What is

wrong with her, I wondered. Then Kendon hung up the phone, held me in his arms on the couch and rocked me to sleep.

I woke up the next morning and got out of there quickly. When I got home, Momma asked about last night. I told her everything that had happened. She just nodded her head.

"You better get your ass back to Brown where you're safe."

She didn't know I had found the only love of my life and that Brown was history as soon as I could come up with a plan. I was going back to Los Angeles that evening. I talked with Kendon before I left and we talked about him coming to Los Angeles to live with me again. He said, "Cool. I would love to leave this place." We couldn't wait.

Brown was right there at the bus station ready to pick me up when I returned from Fresno. I was glad to be home but I had lots of work to do. My mind was on Kendon and how we would get together. How would I do it? On the way home, Brown asked about my trip and I gave him all the details except for the part of running into Kendon. He wanted to know how my mother was doing, since he was in her good graces.

The next evening, Brown let me know that he was leaving at the end of the week for Texas. According to his older sister, his mother was taking a turn for the worse. She told him he ought to come now if he wanted to see her. I felt very sad for Brown. I was praying that he makes it in time to spend time with his Mother. I was also immediately glad, because it meant time for me to be with Kendon. Brown was taking his three week vacation in Texas. That meant Kendon could come visit with me for those three weeks. As soon as Brown was out of the apartment, I ran to call Kendon to see if he could come to L.A. He was home and excited to say yes he would be more than happy to spend the time with me.

In the meantime, I bought the Los Angeles Times Newspaper to search the classified ads for a job. It's times to gain control of my life again.

I spent the next couple of days looking for a job. I placed applications in various places. The last place was in a podiatrist's office as a billing typist. I knew I could do it because I had learned how to type while attending secretarial school. The doctor that interviewed me hired me on the spot. I had the perfect schedule, 3:30 p.m. - 7:00 p.m.

I couldn't wait for Brown to get off of work so I could tell him about the new job. He didn't take it as I thought he would. He was so mad, but I didn't care. I had plans that he didn't know about. He started arguing that his split of his payroll check should be enough for me. I told him I wanted him to keep his money and let me do what I needed to do.

Brown was set to leave for Texas about 5:00 the next day. Kendon's bus was coming in at 3:30 that afternoon. I saw Brown off at the door. When I went into the bathroom, I found a hundred dollar bill with a note.
"Have fun, but be careful."

At school that day, I asked Debra if she could take me to pick up Kendon from the bus station at 3:00. She agreed. On the way to the bus station, I told Debra all about Kendon and our growing up in Fresno and how he was always there for me. She was impressed and thought Kendon was a Lone Ranger type guy. I also told her about my plans to leave Brown and find us a place of our own. She asked how would we survive. I told her I found a part-time job and would be starting the next day.

KENDON ARRIVES IN LOS ANGELES FOR 3 WEEKS

Kendon stepped off the bus wearing dark slacks and a designer sweater. He was always so GQ! That boy knew he looked good! We held each other so tight. Debra dropped us back at the apartment. Going up the stairs, the first person I ran into was our landlord. She looked at me and then at Kendon. I said hello to her and she ignored me. I asked Kendon if he was hungry. He said, "yes." I told him about the restaurants that were around the area so we decided to take a walk and get something to eat. Kendon was still very shy, I could tell. If it was up to me I would have torn his clothes off as soon as I saw him, but I remained cool. We went to a hamburger stand and ordered hamburgers and fries to go. After returning home, we talked about plans and our future.

"Have you thought about moving out here?" I
checked him to see where his head was.
"Yeh, I've been giving it some serious thought Carla
and I think it's time I make a change in my life. I've
been living a rough life and I know it's a miracle that
I'm still alive. This might be the change I need."
"Oh, Kendon, I hope so." I was excited.
"Where would we stay?" he asked.
"Well, I got some ideas. But we are definitely
hooking up."
"Yeah, babe. I can't let the only woman I've ever
loved slip out of my hands again."

He leaned over and kissed me. The phone rang. It was Brown. He was letting me know he stopped for gas and food. He wanted to know how I was doing? I told him everything was fine. Kendon had gone in the bathroom.

"How is the drive coming?" I asked.
"It's okay, I wish my partner was with me."

I encouraged him to be careful and make sure he calls me once he arrived.

When I got off the phone, Kendon asked if he could take a shower. I told him yes. Then, he asked if I would join him. I nodded my head, yes. I ran the water so that it would be steaming hot for us when we got in. Kendon started to take off his clothes, and so did I. I saw his body, piece by piece. He took his shirt off first. Every inch of his body was filled with muscles. He had the most smooth six-pack frame. I didn't want to appear as if I was staring. I kept taking my things off too. The steam was filling the room. He took me by the hand and escorted me in.

He still handled me as gently as he did when we were younger. The water beat down on Kendon's muscular back as he held me so close to him. The music from the living room was playing. I made sure I had some Commodores ready for his arrival on continuous play. When we finished our shower, Kendon stepped out first and grabbed a towel. He wrapped it around his waist and grabbed me out of the shower. He picked me up and walked me to the bedroom wet and all. The only man I ever loved was holding me in his arms and walking me to my bed. I knew I was dreaming. He dried me off with his towel.

Kendon's touch was so soft and firm. It reminded me of his touch that I felt years ago when we were outside my house in the back seat of Tim's car.

> "Do you know how long I have waited and hoped to make love to you, Carla?"
> I was speechless at his words. His words sent chills down my back and all over my body.
> "Baby, I use to be so scared to touch you, I thought you would melt away. That's how precious you were to me. And now I can't believe I have you here in my arms. It's a dream come true."
> "Kendon, you are my dream. You always have been and I don't ever want to wake up again."

He laid my arms flat on the bed and kissed me in the palms of my hands, burying his face in the palm of my hand. His face was as smooth as a baby's bottom. His broad shapely lips were moist and firm at the same time. Kendon kissed from the inside of the palm of my hands up my arms under my neck. He turned me over onto my stomach and held me tight by my hips. I could feel his muscular chest on my back as he grinded on top of my ass.

> "Can I feel your whole body, Carla?"

"Baby, you can do whatever you want to."
My breathing was so hard from being so turned on I
didn't think I was going to last in my calm state. It
felt like thunder and lightning was going off in my
mind he excited me so much. Kendon's touch
drove me crazy.

He touched every inch of my body, taking his time to hold me and
feel my body. At one point, it almost felt like he was examining
my body to see if it was real.

He told me that he wanted to touch every inch of me. He told me
he waited for this day and wasn't going to rush into it. He rolled
me over and moved me on top of him so that he could kiss me. He
then moved me up so that he could kiss my breast. He kissed my
breast so softly, biting my hard nipples gently with his teeth. He
then asked me to move up a little bit more so that he could kiss my
navel and embrace my ass tightly in his hands. Then he turned me
over on my back again and started slowly moving into me.
"I have dreamed about this moment, Carla, I thought
it would never happened after you left Fresno."

I was moaning too much to comment or to talk back to him. My
eyes were closed, savoring every second of a dream come true. His
words felt like they were falling off clouds from heaven.
"Now, can I make love to you like I've always wanted
to."
"Yes baby, please do. Please. Please. Please."

My words faded at his entrance. I could finally exhale from the
tension of waiting for him to come in. Watching Kendon make
love to me was almost better than him loving me. But it was so
worth the wait. It was unbelievable how his movements and
charisma overwhelmed my emotions and body. I knew I was
straight again, never ever to return.
The next day I didn't want to go to school or work. I wished I
could start next week. I got up and fixed Kendon's breakfast. I

told him I had to leave for work and would call him throughout the day. He said he would kick it and look at TV. I went to work but mentally I was not there. My mind was with Kendon and the beautiful night I just spent with him.

I finally got home. Kendon was picking his teeth looking at a Los Angeles Times newspaper. He had gone out to the liquor store and got some beer.

"So you found your way around, hah?"
"Yep, sure did. Kind of got bored.
"How was work for you?"
"Well, I should have called in sick today like I
wanted to, because I frustrated the hell out of my
boss."
We started kissing and ended up in the bed within
minutes.

Time passed with Kendon. I had not been to school since he arrived. Debra finally called me and asked what was happening? I told her what was up. She told me that I still had to go to school, because we were now entering mid-terms.

"Don't mess up at the last minute, Carla," she
warned me. I told her I was going to be fine.

The three weeks went by so fast. The count down was upon us. Kendon was leaving in another day. We were able to live in a storybook world for three weeks. We got the chance to find out more about each other and made some solid promises about our future together.

We talked and agreed that we would give ourselves a month to get everything together. We agreed to save up our money so we could get us a nice place to stay. Kendon was leaving that day at 4:00, and Brown was expected later on that night. I cried like a baby as I waited at the bus station for Kendon's bus to come to take him back to Fresno.

I knew that Brown was scheduled to return from his trip but I had not heard from him. I thought I had better check, so I called him at the number he left in Texas. I found out that the schedule was the same.

BROWN RETURNS HOME JUNE - JULY 1982

Brown came in real late that night. I was sleeping by the time he got in. He knocked on my door to let me know he was back. I turned over and whispered, "Welcome home. See you in the morning." He closed the door.

The next morning, Brown was in the kitchen moaning and humming.
"So how is your mother doing?" I asked.
"Mother is doing great. My sister exaggerated just to
get me down there. All they really wanted was for
me to give the car back."

I told Brown that we needed to talk about some things. He asked if it could wait until later. I told him sure.

I let a couple of weeks go by before talking to Brown about my plans to move. I was nervous and knew it would hurt him. I couldn't keep putting it off. I had to speak to somebody about my dilemma. So I called my sister Sharon. I explained everything that had happened.
"Look Carla, just follow your heart." I understand
the difficulty but you have to be concerned about
your own happiness."
"I feel so obligated to him, Sharon."
"Hey, he set the rules in place. Nobody told his old
ass to fall in love with you."

That didn't make me feel any better, but at least I was happy that I could follow my heart. But not just yet. It wasn't that easy to do.

In the meantime, I finished the program at Sawyer Business College and received my degree as a Executive and Legal Secretary. I finished typing a hundred words per minute and ninety words in shorthand. I was so proud of myself. So was Brown, to say the least.

He wanted to take me out to dinner to celebrate but I felt too guilty because of what I knew I had to tell him. He was so persistent, and ordered a delicious dinner to bring home to me. He begged me to come out of my room.

"Hey, girl, you going make me eat these ribs alone?
"Brown, I really don't feel like it."
"Come on now, you just had a major
accomplishment."
I knew I had to come out at some point , so I might
as well get it over with.

Brown had already set up the table for two. He had a bottle of champagne on ice and glasses ready.

"There she is, the achiever."
"Thanks, Brown. I know I really owe you for what
you have done for me. Thank you for pushing me
andbelieving in me."
"Baby, I told you I saw some potential in you. Now
you are on your way. Don't stop there, just keep on
going as far as you can."

We ate dinner and I pretended I was sick. I thanked Brown again and excused myself.

I TELL BROWN I'M MOVING
1982

The next day I had to tell Brown. Later that evening I told Brown we needed to talk. I sat down and didn't know how to start, but I had to say something.

"Brown, I am going to be moving out soon." He

looked very surprised.

"What do you mean you are going to be moving out soon?"

"It's time for me to go. I can no longer stay here with you."

"Why, baby, what's wrong?"

"Nothing's wrong. I just need to do something different."

"Where are you going? With some woman?"

"No, I'm moving in with my sister Sharon."

"Carla, baby, don't go, please. Don't leave me now. I need you!"

"Brown, don't do this to me. Don't put me on a guilt trip, it's not fair."

"What the hell you mean it's not fair, when my whole world looks like it's caving in, you up and leave. What will my friends say? My car gets taken from me and the next thing they see you leave."

"That has nothing to do with it, Brown. Remember, we are not married."

"Carla, I know that, but I love you. I am willing to do whatever it takes to keep you here with me. Just say it and we can work it out."

"No, Brown. We had fun, but it's over."

"When do you plan on moving out, Carla?"

"Tomorrow night."

Brown got up from the table and pushed the chair so hard that it fell over.

"Tomorrow!" he screamed.

I left at that moment. I had to leave for a few hours. I didn't want to further hurt Brown, but I could see that he was not taking it too well. When I got back to the house, Brown and some guys were in the kitchen cooking some cocaine. Brown knew that I hated when he did that stuff.

I was really glad I was leaving. Who wants to be around a base head, I thought. A few minutes later there was a knock at the door. It was a few women coming to join them. Brown had just got paid and his whole check was being blown in one night.

I went in my bedroom and stayed. I felt so bad. I felt like I was running Brown to smoke. His friends didn't know what I had just talked to him about, did they? They based all night long. I could hear them going in and out of the house to get more.

The next day, I came in the house and Brown was sitting in the living room.

"So you plan to leave tonight, huh?"

"Yeah. Why?"

"My landlord told me an interesting story today."

"Oh yeh." I didn't know what he was about to say.

"She told me about some son-of-a-bitch you had up here in my house while I was gone."

"Oh, shit!" I said to myself.

"When were you going to tell me we had an out-of-town guest? On your way out the door? That's probably who you are going to go be with, isn't it?"

"No, it isn't, Brown. I told you who I was moving in with."

"Carla, how could you? After all I have done for you. How could you lay up under my roof for three weeks fucking some boy when you won't even let me fuck you? We were supposed to have a goddamn arrangement and you haven't lived up to eighty percent of your half yet. How could you?"

"Look, it's not that damn serious. Brown, what's the difference whether it was a boy or a girl? You said I had my own fucking room to do whatever the fuck I wanted to do."

"You know how I feel about you. Now I feel used and made a fool out of." Brown stood up.

"Look I didn't mean to use you. You laid out the

cards, I went ahead and played what you dealt me.
I didn't ask for it, Brown. You offered everything, I
received it. I never sat and plotted how I was going
to use your ass, you just kept offering. That's why I
really have to go, because it's out of hand now."
"You damn right, it's out of hand!" he yelled.

I jumped. Brown was looking very weird around the eyes. I left the
room and said, "I need to go finish packing." He began to cry,
telling me, "no!" I called Sharon on the phone and said,"come and
get me now."

      "I'm sorry for yelling at you, Carla." Brown tried to
      apologize.

I kept packing. I felt horrible. I knew it wasn't going to be easy,
but I had never seen a grown man react like this. I felt so horrible. I
hurt Brown and it hurt me. I began to cry to myself. It was
beginning to tear at me now. Brown walked to my bedroom and
he said, "Please, any other time, but not now. I really need you to
stay."

      "Stop it, Brown. Please just stop it. I can't stand to
      see you like this." I couldn't stand to see a man beg.
      Something about it tore me apart. Brown lost it.
      He started throwing things at the walls and yelling.
      "How could you hurt me like this, little girl?"

He picked up a wooden chair and threw it at the wall near my door.
I screamed out.

      "Stop it. Stop it."

Sharon was knocking at the door. She walked in when nobody
answered. That's when Brown stopped.

      "Is my baby sister here?"

She looked at Brown as to say you better not fuck with her. Sharon
was one mean ass black girl and I knew she was crazy. I stood there
in the hallway looking at her.

"Where is your shit?"
"In the room."
"Let's load it up now," she said to me, not taking her
  eyes off of Brown.

Brown was pacing the floor in front of her, not saying anything.
Sharon moved most of the heavy stuff to the porch as I brought it
out.

On the last trip out I told Sharon to go to the car. I would be all
right, but I had to say goodbye to Brown alone. She said, "Scream
if you need me. I'll be right outside." I closed the door. Brown
stood there leaning against the bar.
        "Brown, I just want to thank you for all that you have
        done and the wisdom you have shared with me.
        You have really done a lot for me. I don't mean to
        hurt you like this, but I must continue to find Carla.
        If it means moving from place to place, person to
        person, or whatever, I've got to do that. I don't have
        the answers. I'm not right, Brown, but what is really
        right to do in this situation? I don't know. If I can't
        leave now, then when?"

The tears were coming out of both of our eyes as we stood facing
each other.
        "You are a wonderful man. But I don't deserve you
        yet. My Momma told me that day she spoke with
        you and to hell with what I wanted and who I think
        I should be with. Hold on to who wants me and
        their love would grow on me. I hope I don't live to
        be haunted by those words."
        "Come here," Brown told me. He opened his arms
        toward me.

He held me in his arms and wept on my shoulders. I tried to stop
crying and be strong, but it was time to let go of being strong and
face the reality of the moment.   We embraced for a long time.

"I must go now, Brown. Sharon is waiting."
I went to the door.
"Hey, keep in touch, you hear me?"
"Yes Brown, I will. I promise."

I closed the door and walked down the stairs. It was good- bye for
Brown and me. It was truly over now. What does life hold
tomorrow for Carla, I asked myself. I thought about my
experience with Brown, from the first night he made the
proposition to me leaving, all the way to Sharon's place.

JUNE 1982

The drive home was quiet. I didn't feel like talking much and
Sharon knew it. She didn't ask questions. She just played the radio
and sang to herself. She had the most beautiful voice.

Sharon had a one-bedroom, with a nice size living room and den
area. She gave me closet space and things that I needed to feel at
home. Sharon wasn't at home very much. That worked out for me,
to have time and space to myself.

After I settled in, Sharon walked in the living room with a basket of
clothes that she just took out of the dryer from downstairs.
        "Hey, how did the last few minutes with Brown go?"
        "Girl, it was too emotional. I couldn't handle it."
        "Like I told you, he made the rules, Carla. Shit, his
        old ass don't have a future. You have your whole
        damn life ahead of you."
        "I know, Sharon, but I still feel so damn guilty."
        "Why, shit." If he was sincere in his offer to help
        you get in school and on our feet, then he
        accomplished what he said he wanted to do."
        "Well, I hope our friendship will survive."
        "Why? Just move on. Now what are you going to
        do about all those women that are crazy about your

ass?"

"Girl, that is truly over now."

Sharon looked at me in great disbelief.

God allowed the only boy I ever loved to come back into my life. He was and is the only man I trust with my life.

"Damn, that's pretty serious."

"It is, and what we had from our childhood was
pretty serious too.   He's the only man that could
walk into my life and make me turn straight."

She smiled and was very approving, as she folded
towels.

"He was my hero during the times he wasn't in
juvenile hall."

"Damn what did he do for you?"

"He believed me and wanted to protect me as much
as I would let him."

"How much can a kid protect another kid?"

"Kendon was not just a plain kid, Sharon."

We laughed. I told her how he even wanted to kill Mr. Calvin for molesting me.

Sharon was anxious and wanted to meet this tall black handsome man I bragged about.

"As soon as I find us a place to stay, you will meet
him," I assured her. I switched subjects and asked
how was she and Dennis doing.

"We are getting married."   My mouth flew open.

"What, are you serious?" She was gleaming all over.

"I didn't realize that it got that serious."

She went on to tell me about how Mable was getting serious with her new boyfriend, Al.

"Mable is living with Al. She is still paying rent at her
old place but stays over at Al's." My mind started
thinking fast now.

"You mean that no one is staying at Mable's place?" I
asked.

"That's right."

"I think I see a miracle, Sharon."

Sharon didn't know what I was getting to at first,
then she started smiling.

"Do you know where I just went?"

"Yeah girl, you want to move over there with your
honey Kendon."

I asked her for Mable's number and ran to the phone to call her.
She picked up.

"So is this the lady of the house?" I joked with her.

"Who in the hell wants to know?" Mable responded.

"Your honey bunch do."

I could hear her cracking up laughing.

"Carla! Is that you?"

"Yep! What's happening Mable?"

"Nothing much."

"You a damn liar, I heard all about it."

She kept laughing.

"Listen, let me get right to the reason I'm calling
you."

"Run it down to me."

"Well Mable, I ran into my Jr. High School love. We
are getting together as soon as we can find a place
out here."

"Sharon told me that you are not at your place
anymore, but you are still paying rent on it."

"Slow down girl, take a deep breath." I was talking
fast.

"Well, we want to rent it from you."

"Shit, what happen to Brown?"

"Girl, shit, that's a long story. We would have to get
together for that conversation. Just know that it's
over."

"Alright."

I told her that I would pay the landlord what she pays her every month because I had a job. She was happy to hear about me working at the podiatrist's office. She said, "Cool, you can have the place anytime you need." She warned me that the place needed a lot of cleaning. She said, it's real bad.

I was so crazy in love I didn't care if the L.A. Zoo was camping out at her place. I got to work immediately. I called Kendon and told him it was on. He gave me his Uncle Walter's telephone number, who lived in L.A., so we could arrange to pick him up. We agreed on a moving date for Kendon to move on the following Friday.

KENDON'S BACK
1982

The bus station was wall to wall people. I was rushing through the crowd to get upstairs to Gate 29. Uncle Walter was telling me to slow down. I didn't want to be late, and didn't want Kendon waiting. I wanted to see his handsome face the moment he got off the bus. I was going so fast I ran past the door and had to back up. Uncle Walter was standing right by the door smiling. He was really laughing at me.

The bus hadn't arrived yet, so Uncle Walter and I started to talk. He was kind of a quiet man. He was in his early forties and seemed very cool. His style and voice reminded me of Al Green. His lips were always wet for some reason. He asked me a question that almost embarrassed me.

"What is a nice young lady like yourself doing hooking up with a wild man like Kendon?"

I didn't understand him talking about Kendon like this. This was his nephew, how could he try to down him, I thought. I knew within myself the type of person Kendon was. The fact that he decided to come live with me proved that he had changed and wanted something different in life.

Trying to stay positive, I told Uncle Walter that Kendon is changing and if I can help him change, I will. Uncle Walter told me that he just didn't want me to get hurt. Kendon's bus was pulling up. I was thinking to myself, God, I hope we are doing the right thing. I turned to Uncle Walter.
"Thank you for your concern."

I hugged him before the passengers started getting off. A man's voice saying "Bus 29, now arriving in Gate 7" came over the loud speaker.

There he was, getting off the bus looking very sharp! Kendon saw me as soon as he was off the bus. I thought I would burst with excitement!
"Hey baby, how's it going?"
"It's going good now." He shook Uncle Walter's hand, picked up his only suitcase and said, "Let's go."

I told Kendon on the way to Mable's place about the condition of the apartment. He smiled and said, "Whatever we have to do, let's do it. I'm just happy that we are together again." He held my hand tighter as we walked through the terminal.

Uncle Walter brought us right home. We said our good-byes to him because he had to go straight to work. I found the key under the doormat just as Mable said. We got to the house and my God, it looked like a tornado or something bad had hit it! We heard the little mice scrambling as we walked in the door. It smelled bad too. I was scared to put my bags down, Kendon didn't look like he wanted to put his down either.
"Yep, Carla, we have a lot to do," he said.

We rushed to the supermarket and bought up all the Ajax, Lysol, Purex and mousetraps they had. We came back. I turned on some smooth sounds from KJLH 102.3 FM radio. We both got buckets and began to scrub rooms for the next five to six hours. We were exhausted. But we were determined that we were not going to stop until we finished. I took the first room, because it was the easiest. Kendon took the second room, which was the living room. We did the kitchen together, because there were things crawling in the refrigerator and a whole family of things under the stove. I never jumped, screamed and ran so much while cleaning a house. We also did the bathroom together. There were spider webs and filth everywhere. We opened windows, swept floors and we worked our asses off. We took breaks to get food, but did not rest until every spot in the place was cleaned. We finally finished around midnight. We were exhausted and fell asleep.

CHAPTER 35

New Morning With Kendon
(JUNE - JULY 1982)

I woke up to the love of my life. The boy that I always dreamed about, my knight in black shining armor. I laid in his arms looking at him, smiling in disbelief that he was here. The phone rang and it was Mable. She called to invite us by later for a drink and a little partying.

That night, Kendon and I walked over to Al and Mable's house. Al and Kendon kicked it while Mable and I fixed some sandwiches in the kitchen. This was my first time meeting Al. He seemed pretty cool and laid back. I could tell he loved to party and drink Night Train. He had bottles lined up alongside the wall. I also noticed that Mable was drinking Night Train. I had another shock when I saw that Mable was pregnant. We all sat around and talked.

Later on a couple of buddies stopped by to kick it. We eventually got a Bid Wisk game going. Kendon was quiet around Al's buddies. I noticed that he didn't attach himself so easily and quickly to people. We got pretty high that night. Everybody was yelling and talking plenty crap to each other. I was having a ball. Before the night was over, Mable and I had a private moment. I thanked her again for letting me and Kendon stay in her place. Later, Kendon and I walked home. I asked him, how did he like my friends? He said he thought they were cool. Just a little wild. I said, oh yeah? I was surprised at that response. I thought he'd feel right at home.

The next day was Sunday. We walked up the street since we didn't have transportation. I treated us to breakfast. We sat and talked.
    "You never told me how did the old man handled
     you moving out," Kendon said.
    "Oh, Kendon, it was ugly. I mean real ugly."
    "Did he try to hurt you?" Kendon sounded alarmed.
    "No, he just didn't want me to go. He was crying

and begging me not to go now."
"Well, what about your lifestyle with women, what
  do you plan on doing with that?"
"Let's just say, we can pretend it never happened.
  They are history too. Kendon, you are the only
  man for me and I know that.
"So next week will be a busy week. You're going to
  look for a job and stuff?"
"Yeah, sho', you right." Kendon looked at me.

The little creatures that lived in the house before Kendon and I
cleaned up were slowly disappearing. After a few weeks with
Kendon, I became so attached. I started calling in sick at least once
a week. Then on the days I went to work, I was calling home to
talk with him every chance I got. We would stay on the phone for
hours, talking about nothing. I guess we just wanted to hear each
other breathe.

One morning, before I left for work, Kendon told me that Uncle
Walter was coming to get him so that he could put in some
applications at the meat market where he worked and some other
places. I was so happy, because my boss had started cutting back
my hours. I got home that evening and Kendon was playing music,
smoking on a joint, and dressed to kill. He met me at the door and
kissed me. I was so glad to see him!
        "I got a surprise for you," he said.
        "Oh, Lord, what is it?"
        "Go in the kitchen."

His Uncle and Aunt Myrtle had given us food, linens, towels, and
pots. The refrigerator was filled.
        "Does this mean I have to cook now?" I laughed.
        "Yep. You don't mind, do you?" he asked,
          concerned as if he hurt my feelings.
        "Not for you. I'll do anything for you, boy."
          Kendon came over to me from behind and hugged
          me real tight.

"So how was the application hunt?" I asked.
"Oh, it was cool. We went a couple of places and
they said they will call me if anything opens up."
"Well, Kendon, you're new out here, don't get
discouraged. Just leave it in God's hands, and it will
happen eventually."
"Thank you, baby, you're a good positive woman".

I believed it would happen eventually all right, as soon as he cut off
his press and curl. His hair was longer than mine. It was jet black
and beautiful. It almost reminded me of Desmund's hair.

He was looking handsome in his dark slacks and nice shirt. I had to
buy Kendon some ties. I saw he didn't have any. In due time, I
thought to myself, he will have it together, and will be ready for the
world.

We ate and decided to go kick it over at Al and Mable's. When we
got there, they had already started playing cards. The getting high
was good, but Mable told me that Al had started smoking
Sherman. I was mad and wanted to confront him. She told me
everything was cool, but I knew she was worried. Anyway, the night
went on and a couple of road dogs came through from the days
when I lived with Mable.

Butch (a.k.a. Stupid Ass) came by with Dennis and we sat around
talking shit about nothing. I could tell this didn't rub right with
Kendon because he didn't crack a smile. On the way home Kendon
seemed real distant. Earlier that evening he told me he had to talk
with me.
"Carla, people will only respect you as much as you
respect yourself. I didn't like what I heard tonight."
I tried to excuse the behavior and chalk it up to just
having fun, but Kendon wasn't buying it.
"Men should never feel comfortable calling you
anything other than a lady because that's what you
are. And that

cussing doesn't fit you at all. I've never seen you in
that kind of element."

My mouth flew open. I was shocked and embarrassed. I thought
to myself, this is just street life. What was he talking about? But
then I understood about being a lady. I never had to be a lady
really. I was always the survivor, and my language came with the
territory. Kendon told one of the guys to please not to curse in
front of me. I could have died with embarrassment They looked
at him like he was crazy when he said respect the lady. I know they
got a big kick out of it, especially Mable. I knew they would
probably tease me about it later.

The next day, I went to work and my boss was having a meeting
with everyone. One of the girls had quit and he needed to close up
the Inglewood office. He told me that he was going to have to lay
me off. I couldn't believe it! The timing was all wrong. I got my
last check and left. I came home and told Kendon the bad news.
He said not to worry, because someone would probably be calling
real soon regarding the applications he placed. I felt good about
that. He told me that Aunt Myrtle and Uncle Walter wanted us to
come over for dinner later.

Uncle Walter picked us up, and we had a nice time. Aunt Myrtle
was a talker. She was a 5 foot tall, chubby little woman. Her facial
foundation was so thick she reminded me of a powdery biscuit. I
loved her spirit. She reminded me of Grandma Georgia. She was
very spiritual. She sat there and told Kendon to his face to take
care of me and don't mess my life up. She also told us if we
needed anything don't hesitate to call her.

Within a week, my little pay check began to run out. We didn't
have much money left, just forty dollars. We decided that we
would buy thirty dollars worth of food. We bought bologna,
bread, and sacks of potatoes. As we were coming home from the
store, Mable's landlord was coming in the door of her apartment. I
could have died. What was she doing home at this hour of the day?

Kendon didn't understand.   But I knew that Mable would be hearing from the landlord soon. Mable told me to stay clear of the landlord as much as possible.

Sure enough, the next day Mable called me and told me that Shirley's mother wanted us out of there. I panicked. I told Mable that we had just spent most of our money on a months worth of bologna and had nowhere else to go. Mable told me we had one month to find somewhere else to live now. I didn't want to bother Kendon with this. Everything was going so well.

Finally, Mable said she knew where there were some dirt cheap hotels downtown off of skid row that we could live in. I frowned at the thought. She told me it wasn't that bad. We really didn't have any other choice. Plus she agreed to pay for the first two weeks that we were there. She made me promise not to tell Al or Kendon.

WE HAVE A MONTH TO MOVE
1982

Later that evening, I told Kendon we had to move. He told me not to worry and said he would figure something out. I could see Kendon getting frustrated and tired of our day to day problems. Within that month, Kendon would leave the house late at night "high as a kite".   He was broke, but "high as a kite."   Sometimes he would be over to Mable's getting high. I would find that out a couple days later when I would call Mable. I was so worried about Kendon out in those L.A. streets.

I started feeling like a failure! I kept praying for something to come through for us.   Then we ran out of the bologna and potatoes because Kendon had the munchies more now. We needed food, but Kendon was too prideful and embarrassed to call Uncle Walter to ask him for help. So we starved until something came through. Kendon left one night and said he would be right back. I asked where was he going and he brushed me off and said he was just going to kick it with some friends.   Around 1 a.m. that same morning, I heard him coming in. I got up and he had large cloth sacks filled with change and other things that I couldn't see. But when I looked at his shirt, it had blood all over it. I screamed.

"Kendon, what's wrong?"

"I just had a little run in with the boys tonight."

"What damn boys? Your damn neck is cut, Kendon!"

I was getting hysterical. His neck was cut from one side to the next. I don't know how he made it home alive. I told him we had to get to the hospital immediately. I ran to call Uncle Walter. Uncle Walter told me to make sure he stays awake and he would be over in a few minutes.

Kendon was really mad at me. He kept saying he would be fine and that we didn't have any medical insurance. I told Kendon not to worry about that kind of shit right now.

Uncle Walter was there in less than ten minutes. Walter was driving like a bat out of hell to County General Hospital. I was hoping we wouldn't get stopped by the police for speeding. Kendon rested against my head, trying not to bend his neck and fall asleep.

"Kendon, just stay up a little while longer, we are almost there."

"I'm, tired, baby" he whispered.

"Come on Kendon, man you gotta stay up."

Uncle Walter finally pulled up to the emergency room doors. Kendon was moving real slow now. I didn't know what he was feeling, he never complained or anything.

Uncle Walter told me he was going to park the car and would meet us inside. The blood was now dripping out of the towel that was lightly wrapped around Kendon's neck.

"We need some help," I screamed at the nurse at the desk as we were walking in.

The nurse looked at me and motioned one minute.
"This man's neck is cut, shit, we don't have a
minute."

A man in a green hospital uniform was walking toward me.
"Miss, just let him sit right here and we will be right
with him. He's fine now, he's at the hospital."

I took Kendon to the area that the man pointed to a few steps in
front of me. I went to the front desk to talk to the nurse. I
explained to her what I thought happened and told her that he
needed immediate help, or else he would bleed to death. She asked
for insurance. I told her I left all the information at home. She
tried to calm me down and told me they would be with him soon,
but I would have to fill out some preliminary papers. I stood there
and filled them out as fast as I could. Kendon was struggling
trying to keep awake and his head straight. I would yell at him.
"Kendon, don't fall asleep, here I come."

While I was completing the last document, someone tapped me on
my shoulder .
"Hey girl, you lost?"
I turned around, and it was my Daddy! I couldn't
believe it. I forgot he was a Deputy Sheriff for
County General.
"Hi, Daddy!"
"Hi, Carla. What are you doing here?"
I pointed over at Kendon sitting in the waiting
room.
"My boyfriend got hurt tonight and I'm here with
him."
"You mean your fifty-six year old man."
"No, Daddy, real funny. I have a real twenty year
old boyfriend."
"Oh, that's a nice change. How did he get hurt?"
I knew I had to lie now.
"Well, I'm not quite sure Daddy, but it's not that

bad."

Just as we were talking, he received a page for back-up assistance.
He answered it and rushed out quickly. I was relieved. He told me
to keep in touch and let him meet this boy before we left the
hospital. I just nodded as he left out through the double doors.
Uncle Walter came in as Daddy was leaving.

Moments later the nurses came out with a wheelchair and asked
Kendon to come to the back with them. They didn't let me go
with him, and I was pissed. Uncle Walter took me aside and said he
needed to talk to me.

> "Carla, I have been wanting to say this to you for the
> longest. You need to leave Kendon alone."
> I shook my head no.
> "I told you at the bus station that you are too smart
> of a girl to be with this kind of boy. He will just use
> you and get you into a lot of mess. I'm telling you.
> Watch my words."
> "He is really not like that toward me, Uncle Walter."
> I tried to defend Kendon.
> "I am different to Kendon."
> The nurse interrupted.
> "He's doing fine and the doctors are stitching him up
> right now."

She started asking for insurance information again. Then Uncle
Walter pulled her aside and took care of it. Uncle Walter brought
us home. It was quiet the entire ride. When we got out of the car I
thanked Uncle Walter, and so did Kendon. Kendon went to bed
without saying much. He did say, come here let me hold you. I
laid there wondering what the hell happened to him. I fell asleep in
his arms.

The next day, I called Mable and told her what happened to
Kendon that night, and how he had stolen money from somewhere
and brought it home. She told me that Al thought Kendon had

been stealing money out of their kids' penny banks. She never said anything to me about it before.

"No, Mable, don't tell me that please. Tell me he
hasn't been doing that?"

"Yeah, Carla, I'm afraid so."

I didn't want to believe it, but I could tell that she was serious. I felt so betrayed! I didn't know what to think. Kendon never gave me any impression that he was doing these kinds of things. My friends let him in their house while I was at work, and he was ripping them off. How dare he! I wanted to talk to him about it, but I had other problems.

CHAPTER 36

KENDON AND I MOVE DOWNTOWN
(AUGUST 1982)

The following Monday, Mable and I went downtown to see the place. The hotel was horrible. People were laying all outside the hotel. Beggars, dope dealers, whores, and drug users. It was sickening. I went inside the hotel with Mable, and it seemed a bit better. The cashier was behind these bars accepting registration. I paid the man the money, and he gave me two keys. We went back to Mable's place where Kendon and Al were waiting for us. I still had not talked to Kendon about stealing from Mable and Al. They were sweethearts to let him stay there while I was looking for a hotel. I was so embarrassed to see Uncle Walter come to give us a ride downtown with all of our things.

Uncle Walter dropped us off right in front of the Hayword Hotel. Then he looked at me and shook his head. I gave him a kiss on the cheek and told him thanks. He asked me to call him if I needed anything. Kendon and I went up in the elevator to the third floor. I almost screamed when Kendon opened the door. I thought I saw a big fat rat run across the floor. Kendon said it was my nerves. I told him it was my keen eyesight. The room was small and the window was open to air it out. The only bad thing about that was, the window was outside an alley. What a view! I looked in the bathroom and the toilet looked like it was from the year 1907. We put our bags down and sat on the bed. Kendon looked at me. He could tell I was almost losing it. I was on the edge of screaming. He pulled me to himself and sat me on his right leg.

> "Carla, we are not going to stay in this position long.
> I can't stand this! I don't know about you, but I am
> not used to this type of living."
> "Well, this is all that our money could get us,
> Kendon!"
> "Carla, why did you talk me into moving down here?
> I was fine in Fresno. I ain't never went through no
> shit like this before. Ain't never had to. You

understand me? I had women that saw to that."

I was getting madder, and now I didn't care what came out of my mouth. I raised my head up and looked at him.

> "What the hell do you mean that they saw to it that
> you didn't experience this? Hell, I have always had
> women and men that saw to it that I never would see
> a situation like this either. I have been trying to
> make it for the both of us. I can only do so damn
> much you know? When in the hell are you going to
> do something for us?"
> Tears began to roll out of my eyes but I continued
> to talk.
> "Instead of sounding ungrateful, when are you going
> to do something legal? Stealing from my friends
> that fed both of us and gave both of us money!
> How could you, Kendon?"

I didn't want to address the stealing like this, but it just came out with everything else. Finally he responded.

> "I couldn't help it. I just couldn't help it. We were
> broke, we had eaten up all the bologna, and I just
> couldn't help myself. It was right there in my face.
> Carla, I miss my Momma. I really do." He started
> crying.
> "Carla, I've been thinking ever since you told me we
> only had a month to find a place to live, that maybe
> we need to go back to Fresno for a little while."

I did not want to go to Fresno, but I went along with Kendon to satisfy him. I knew he was taking the adjustment real hard and needed a different environment. He called his mother and asked her to send us two round-trip tickets. She did. She placed them on pick up at the bus station. We were scheduled to come the following week-end.

TRIP TO FRESNO FOR A QUICK BREAK
1982

After we arrived in Fresno, Kendon's mother was standing at the bus depot smiling. She was so refreshing. Her personality was always loving and nice. I didn't tell my mother I was coming down because I knew she really didn't approve of Kendon. She was probably still getting over the fact that I left Brown for Kendon.

We stayed at Kendon's parents' during our three-day visit. Saturday, we woke up and Mrs. Starr had prepared breakfast. We sat and talked with his family. They wanted to hear all about L.A. We talked about how much there is to do in L.A., never a dull moment.

After breakfast Kendon and I took a walk around his neighborhood and went to the local park. Kendon took off his jacket and laid it on the grass for me to sit on. We were away from our poverty and our problems that we left in Los Angeles. The time we spent in Fresno felt so perfect and right. When we returned that evening, it was dinner time. After we ate, everyone went into the living room to watch one of Bruce Lee's last films. Kendon was a black belt. In fact his entire family, except for his mother, were specialists in the martial arts. During one of the commercial breaks, Mrs. Starr asked if we were going to get up in the morning and go to church with her. I was the first to say yes. Kendon looked at me and smiled. He nodded yes as well.

That next morning seemed to give us exactly what we needed. We needed hope. The church service was beautiful and the message was impacting. I always felt good in church. The music and the preacher were great. He spoke on family and the power of having a loving family, and contrasted that with the broken families that many people have been a part of. Then he suggested that those which are a part of God's family had a second chance for love, because we gain the entire family of God. I really identified with what he was saying. My family was so broken, it put Humpty

Dumpty to shame. After service Kendon and I had a long conversation about getting our life together with the Lord and even considering getting into a church to have that foundation and background. I wanted that so much for us to be right with God. It seemed like Kendon wanted that too. I never knew that was a part of him or his family.

It was time to go back to the reality that awaited us in Los Angeles. I saw Kendon's mother place some money in his hand as she was saying good-bye. While on the bus, Kendon asked me if I would consider moving back to Fresno.

> "Hell no, Kendon, not me! There is nothing in
> Fresno for me. Look, this hardship is temporary. I
> will have a job soon. I don't know about you,
> Kendon, but I will have a job real soon."

Kendon squeezed my hand to reassure me that he felt the same way.

> "I am going to get me a job too, Carla. You just
> watch and see."

When we returned from Fresno, we ended up seeing Aunt Myrtle and Uncle Walter. Uncle Walter would check and make sure that we were all right. Kendon didn't like this, because it showed them how irresponsible he was. He told me to stop accepting handouts, and don't let Uncle Walter know that we are in need. I knew it was embarrassing for Kendon, but I was hungry. I did not have pride problems like he did.

> "Why can't we call them Kendon? We need them."
> "We don't need them." Kendon said. I'm tired of
> their drilling and talking about us."
> "Kendon, they love us and are concerned."
> "I don't want to talk about it no more. Stop talking
> about it."

I didn't know what to say then. But I thought to myself, he can starve his ass if he wants to. Let them ask me if I wanted something. I was going to tell them, yeah. Uncle Walter did call to check on us with the downstairs reception, but I honored Kendon's request like a fool. Then we didn't hear from Uncle Walter as often anymore.

One morning Kendon and I did not have one dime, and were both hungry. We had nothing to eat. I couldn't just sit there. I told him I was going outside to walk around and hopefully someone would try to flirt and invite me to breakfast. I told him that I would bring back a doggie bag. He wished me well. I stood outside the hotel and watched the busy streets zoom by with cars and buses. Fifteen minutes later a large garbage truck pulled up, and a heavyset dark-skinned man jumped out.
"Hey, cutie, how are you?"
"Fine, and how are you?" I answered.
"I'm going to get me a little breakfast, would you like
to join me?"
"I don't mind if I do."

He was shocked that I said yes so fast, I almost blew my cover! I was shocked someone asked me out to eat soon as I walked out of the door. I thanked God under my breath.

We went into this little "whole in the wall" breakfast place next to the hotel. We ordered and sat down at one of the tables. I asked the white man behind the counter to cut my ham and egg sandwich in two. I nibbled on that sandwich for ten minutes and said I was so full. The guy was shocked and asked if I was sure.
"You just ate half," he said.
"I know, I get full fast."
He seemed to not believe me, but didn't pressure
me.
"So, little lady, do you have children?"
"No, I don't." I wondered why he asked me that
question.
Maybe he thought I was saving it for them.
"So do you live around here?"
"I work in the neighborhood."

He tried to glance at my clothes without being
noticeable.
"I'm running early for work and that's how you
lucked up with a breakfast partner." He laughed.
"Well, here's my number in case you want to have
breakfast or even dinner with me."

I thanked him for breakfast and scooted out of the booth back to
the room.

Kendon was looking out of the window when I walked back in our
room. I walked over to him and gave him the small brown paper
bag with the sandwich in it. It looked like he had been crying. I
didn't say anything. I looked at his now fading muscular body. I
felt so guilty. He was now looking like a struggling boy. Oh, how I
couldn't wait to get us out of this situation!

We had to find new friends. Because of what Kendon did we
couldn't hang out at Mable's as much anymore. Instead, Kendon
and I befriended the street people who lived downtown. We were
all either trying to get money for room and board, or support a
drug habit. I went with Kendon everywhere, especially at night.
He found some guy that let him sell dope. The streets of
downtown are so scary at night. People everywhere, doing
everything. People in corners of parking lots trying to get high.
People trying to get warm and beating on other people.
Everywhere you turned, there were mothers dragging their kids
around. It was sad to see them in these conditions.

Then one day Kendon got back to the hotel and told me he knew
where we could get free cheese, meat and milk with county
vouchers off of Wall Street. It was a county building around the
corner that he was referring to. We went that evening before 5:00
p.m. to fill out the information and they gave us some temporary
vouchers until ours came in the mail. The place was so sad. The
room was filled with people. I saw little kids and their mothers
barefoot and dirty. I couldn't believe I was in this line with them.

I wondered which wrong road did they take to lead them to this place. I knew the road I took. It hurt me, and I said to myself that I am coming out of this! This poor homeless scene was my daily sight, and my stomach was growing weaker every day.

Before the best came, we experienced the worst of skid row. One night after coming from Mable and Al's house Kendon lost the key to the room. The hotel man would not give us another one because our rent was one week late. We didn't have any money and Kendon kept telling them that his county check should be coming any day now. The man told Kendon once he got his money, he would give him a key to the room so that we could get our things. That night we walked around as much as we could. We knew we could not go back to the room. We didn't know what we would do now. We had spent our last change in bus fare coming from Mable's house.

> "Kendon, why don't you call Uncle Walter and Aunt
> Myrtle and ask to borrow some money until we get
> some."
> "Naw, that's all they want, us to ask for a hand out."
> "Kendon, it's cold out here and we can't walk around
> all night long."
> "I know, baby, let me think of something, okay?"

I wondered what happened. How did we get so far into misery and doom? I couldn't believe what was happening to us.

Kendon ran into some men that he had met on the "row" (as they called it) and asked for some get high. They told him that we should come around the corner to a little get together everyone's having.

Some church people had come out and brought a lot of food for the people that lived on skid road. They left truck loads of food, blankets and other things.

We were hungry and decided to walk around the corner with these crazy looking brothers. One man had his jean was cut off and the other man was walking with no shoes and shirt on. They were stinking, but were acting cool.

"Come, on baby, you want to check it out?"

"Check what out, Kendon? Shit!"

"My homies say they got some happenings around the corner."

"What could be happening around the corner, Kendon?"

"Look, Carla, just come on, shit, and we will find out."

When we got around the corner, there was a little gathering of people standing around a fire. Somebody was playing a radio. I could hear a familiar tune by Natalie Cole, "I'm Catching Hell." My childhood misery song followed me all the way to skid road and not much had changed. I was just older catching hell now.

There were some large aluminum foil containers with ribs, beans and all types of food. They even had plates and napkins around. There had to be a mother in the crowd to keep things so tidy.

I saw a couple of kids laying on a blanket near the curb. It broke my heart to see kids laying on the streets. There were about thirty people on the corner sitting around the curb side talking and smoking. It was the saddest thing I had ever seen in my life. Then I was right there too. Someone was probably looking at me saying how sad also.

I felt so scared knowing that I couldn't go home or anywhere for that matter. Kendon wanted some food so we fixed us a plate.

I blessed it before we ate it. I thanked God for He must have really known we were coming through here tonight. I didn't know where or what we would eat that night. After Kendon mingled and smoked with the brothers, he pointed to a bus stop bench across the street.

"Hey, baby, let's go sit over there."

"Where we going?"

"We ain't going nowhere, I just want you to get off
your feet."

Kendon was still trying to take care of me, even with nothing. I was
so glad it was summer time because the night wasn't freezing.
There was a breeze, but Kendon covered me up in his little jacket.
We sat on that bus stop bench for hours.

"Baby, if you fall asleep, don't worry, I will be right
here. I'm not sleeping tonight, okay?"

"Kendon, I'm sorry about all this."

"Carla, I'm sorry too, but its not your fault, okay.
Baby, don't worry about it. I just need to think, you
go to sleep."

I cuddled up in Kendon's arm as if we were in our twenty-five
dollar a week room. He still made me feel so safe and loved.

It had to have been around 6 a.m. when I woke up because I could
see the break of daylight. Kendon was up looking at the skies,
patting his left leg. There was music still going on from a distance,
you could hear it.

"Hey, baby, I'm right here." Kendon felt me
moving.

"I love you, Kendon."

"I love you too, baby."

"It's going to work out, watch." Kendon tried to
assure me. Kendon saw somebody else he knew and
told me to stay right there.

"No, Kendon, where are you going?"

"Baby, I'll be right back."

The guy seemed as if he knew Kendon. They did the handshake
and buddy hug like brothers do. Then I saw the guy reach into his
pocket and give Kendon some money. Sharon came to mind as I
was sitting there waiting on Kendon to come back. I knew she

would die if she knew I was sitting on a bus stop all night. I didn't want to call her, but I had to call somebody.

When Kendon came back he said we were not going to have to sleep out here another night. I asked him what did that guy give him.
> "He let me hold a twenty spot until I could pay him back."
> "I need to go to the phone booth and call my sister."

Kendon and I walked back to the hotel around the corner to use the phone in the lobby. As we were walking, something came over me. I started getting weak. Then I started getting chills. I told Kendon I felt like I wanted to throw up. We only had two more blocks to walk. I could tell Kendon was feeling embarrassed because he was looking around at who was looking at us.

He slapped my face when he saw me fading in and out, saying, "Come on, Carla, snap out of it. You ain't sick. You were just all right. Baby, what's wrong?" I felt angry toward him, but I could not respond, my body felt too weak. I was too weak. He had to pick me up and carry me the rest of the way to the hotel. I felt like I was dying. I didn't know what was happening.

He took me right to the phone booth. I called my sister collect.
> "Hi, Sharon," I said in a low voice, suffering.
> "Hey, baby girl, what's going on?" She sounded so happy.
> "I'm sick." She got very serious.
> "Where are you, what's happening?"
> "I don't know, but we don't have a place to stay anymore and I need..."
> "Well, hey, you guys can come over here for a month, I'm moving in with Dennis today."

Tears started coming down my cheek. I knew it was a miracle from God. I thanked her and told her we would be there as soon as we could get a ride. She told me that she would pick us up if I needed her to. I told her we needed a ride.

When I hung up the phone, Kendon asked what was up and why was I crying. I told him about the conversation with my sister. He kissed me and hugged me when I told him the good news.

When Sharon walked in the lobby, she started walking fast as soon as she saw me. I knew I wasn't Sharon's blood baby sister, but she loved me as if I was.

"Where are your things?" She didn't speak too
friendly to Kendon.
"There in the room. I can't get them because we owe
a balance still."
"How much?"
"Fifty dollars."

Sharon walked over to the front desk and told the man behind the desk that she wanted to pay the balance so her baby sister could get her things out. He quickly took her money and gave her a key.

"Carla, I will go up and pack everything. You just
rest right there, okay?"
"Thank you."
Kendon went upstairs to pack.
"Now what's going on here?" I started crying.

I told Sharon what had been happening for the last two months. I told her I lost my job and things just went downhill from there.

"What the hell is Kendon doing about work?"
"He's looking, Sharon."
"You don't need to be going through this kind of
shit. You've gone through enough shit. How come
you are just now letting me know about your
situation?"
"You know how pride can be, don't you?"
Kendon came down with our two big suitcases with everything that we owned in them.

CHAPTER 37

MOVE BACK TO SHARON'S APARTMENT
(SEPTEMBER 1982)

Sharon stayed mad at me because I didn't let her know what kind of situation I was in. I didn't realize I had cut off everybody from my life, even those that really cared for me.

Sharon left her phone on so that we could use it and her utilities also. I was so indebted to her. I couldn't pay her. All I could do was shake my head in amazement to see how she was always there for me.

I contacted Ronnie, the girl I made Brown jealous with before I moved away from him. I remembered that she owned a restaurant and figured it would be wise to keep in touch. We really didn't develop an intimate relationship, but I remembered that she was so cool.

She was really understanding when I first called and told her I was out of the life because I was getting together with my school boy love. She teased me, but still said when it was over to call her. I could tell she was busy by the noise of customers in the back.

"What's going on, Ronnie, this is Carla!"
"Is that man gone yet?" she asked, laughing.
"Nope, we are still hanging. I think it's going to work
   out now."

I briefed Ronnie on all the stuff I had been through since the last time she saw me. I told her I was a size three and a weak five.
"Are you on cocaine?"
"No, I can't go into everything right now, but you
   don't have to worry about that habit. I do need your
   help with some food though."
"What about your old man? Can't he buy you some
   food?"
"Come on now, Ronnie."

She figured out that Kendon was not working yet and then started beating up on him, telling me I needed to get rid of the dead weight in my life. I told her I needed about one hundred dollars and I would pay her back once I started working again. I gave her the address where we were living.

Later on that day Ronnie came by. I introduced her to Kendon, and she fired up a joint for us to smoke. We sat in the living room listening to the "Isley Brother's." Ronnie hung out with us for a good while and then she asked me to walk to the store with her. I told Kendon I would be right back. He didn't care, he lit up another joint as we were leaving. As soon as we got outside, Ronnie started fussing at me.

> "What the hell has happened to you? Yo' ass look
> like the pink panther's sister. Your hair looks like
> weeds, and it's just not you! What have you let this
> man do to your life, Carla?"
> "Ronnie, it's not him. Really, it's me! I don't know
> what went wrong, but I am tired of life. I don't
> know what to do anymore!" I felt ashamed.
> Ronnie chilled out, because she saw I was really
> having a tough time.
> "Look, all I know is that you were doing fine and had
> a good job when I first met you," she said. People
> were walking by looking at Ronnie fuss at me.
> "Ronnie, let's drop it for now, I don't want to break
> down out here."

We walked up the street to the liquor store. I bought some chips and a six pack of Old English 800 with part of the money that Ronnie had loaned me.

> "Listen, I really thank you for coming through for me
> girl."
> "It's cool. If I didn't like your little ass I wouldn't be
> here."
> "Well, you are going to see a change in me real soon."

"I hope the first change is getting rid of that nigga upstairs."

Ronnie didn't understand what Kendon meant to me. She didn't realize that he was the only man that stayed in my heart all these years. He was the boy that protected me, and the only man that ever thought anything special about me. I couldn't get rid of him. I didn't trust any other man like I trusted Kendon. The next week I was in the newspaper daily looking for a job. I saw something that jumped off the pages at me.

"I can do that," I yelled.

I saw a listing as a bill collector and circled it with my pen. I thought to myself, I'm sure I can do that. I've never done it, but how difficult could it be, the ad said they would train. I was so excited that I called and set up the appointment.

The next day, when it was time to go to the interview, I was feeling so bad. I still hadn't gained enough weight to properly fit back into my clothes. I had to wear the best thing I could find. Thank God, I didn't lose weight in my feet. I could still put on my pumps and stockings.

I caught the bus to Crenshaw and 43rd Street to a building that read Southern Insurance. I went inside. The receptionist buzzed Mr. Allen. I saw him from the corridors coming down toward the front. He was tall, dark, thin, about 6'3". He appeared to be in his thirties. The interview was not that long. He was impressed with the fact that I went to Sawyer Business College and took shorthand, typing and basic business math. He also said he could use my book-keeping experience from the podiatrist's office. He hired me on the spot.

I stood up, shook his hand firmly, and thanked him for hiring me. I was so happy. The hours were part-time, Monday through Friday. Pay day was weekly. I sat at that bus stop crying and thanking God for His mercy. I could feel the return of the independent Carla. I called Ronnie.

Kendon came in the kitchen that night and kissed me. I turned around from washing dishes and said, "Guess what?"

"What, Carla?"

"I got the job!" I jumped up screaming.

He was trying to calm me down.

"Good, baby, good. I'm so happy for you."

I knew Kendon was happy for me, but at the same time it made him feel a little awkward. I told him that it wasn't a lot of money, but enough to buy food and hopefully pay our rent.

"I'll be making three hundred fifty dollars a month, part-time." He smiled.

I could tell he was high. His eyes were red, and he was wobbling a little bit. He went into the living room and sat on the couch grabbing for the remote.

"Are you hungry, Kendon?"

"Yeah, I'm starving."

I had a surprise. I had cooked some lasagna and cornbread with a tossed salad. I suggested that he go take a shower and I would have dinner ready when he came out.

When he came out of the shower, I had candles on the table and music playing in the background. The lights were dim. He smiled as he walked toward the table. He told me how nice things looked and thanked me for dinner. I pulled out his chair to seat him like they do in the restaurants, and placed a napkin in his lap. We ended up having a lovely dinner and conversation. The shower seemed to have sobered him up a little. We talked about the future we hoped to have together. Kendon talked about his frustration at not being the breadwinner, but how he had made up his mind after tonight that he would set his pride aside, even if he had to work at McDonald's he would.

The day to day duties at the office were very repetitive and easy to manage once I got the swing of things. All of his clients' insurance files were in a cabinet drawer in alphabetical order. He left daily instructions on my desk as to who was late with their premiums and who were new prospects to call. He trained me on how to pursue new prospects through the newspaper. I was excited that I was learning how to bring in new business over the phone. I enjoyed my work, and I did it well. Mr. Allen would always compliment me.

One day when Mr. Allen and I were leaving for the day at the same time, he asked me if I needed a ride home. I wasn't too crazy about the idea, but I accepted. He had already started to get on my nerves because of his flirtatious gestures. He was always looking at me and he stood very close to me when he had to talk to me about the clients. He would put his hands on me when he needed to pass by to move me out of the way.

One day, I said, "Please just say excuse me. You don't have to touch me." He smiled and played it off by saying he didn't mean any harm.

My happiness with my new job was dwindling. Crazy stuff started happening with the pay days, like his checks bouncing. When I would go to the bank, the cashier would say there is no money in this account. He would leave early on Fridays and not return until Tuesday. He would make the check good that next Tuesday, but we had to starve over the week-end if we didn't have any money from the week before. This shit was really getting to me, because Kendon still wasn't bringing in any money.

The end of the month came and there was not enough money to make the rent, which was only two hundred ninety-five dollars. Kendon had taken the little money I made to buy more drugs to sell and smoked up what profit there was. It was backfiring again! I couldn't believe it. We needed two hundred ninety-five dollars for the next month's rent and it wasn't there. I was so depressed. I found myself mad at everybody. Kendon, my boss, and me for being so damn stupid! How come this wasn't working for us? For me!

The next day, Sharon called and said her landlord called her on her job and asked for the rent, because it was late. The landlord didn't know that she wasn't living in the apartment anymore. She threatened to mess up Sharon's TRW/credit. I told Sharon that we were going to have to do something, because we were just a little short.

     "How short are you?"
     "Two hundred ninety-five dollars".
     "Damn! What's been happening, Carla? Kendon
     ain't found a damn job yet?"
     "No, sis, not yet, but he is still looking."
     "The hell he is," she said.

I didn't comment, I was too weak. I told her not to worry, we will get the money. If we didn't we will be out of the place. She told me that she didn't care about the woman reporting to TRW, she just wanted her baby sister to be all right.

     "Thank, you Sharon."

I called Ronnie later and told her of our situation. She laughed and told me to kick that nigga out of my life.

     "I would have taken care of you better than that,
     baby, but you didn't want to give me the time of
     day."
     "Ronnie, this is serious."
     "I'm serious too. You know how much I digged you
     before that loser came into your life. Come over
     here and give me some, and I will give you the rent."

I felt alone again, but I knew somehow, someway it would work itself out.

KENDON'S PROPOSAL FOR PROSTITUTION
(OCTOBER 1982)

Kendon came home that night and told me he knew where he could get the money. I asked how and where? He said he met this woman named Linda Singleton. He told me that he met her through his drug dealings.

"I knew she wanted me but I told her that I was
taken," he said.
"But she informed me anytime I wanted it, she
would pay for it."

My heart dropped and my mouth opened. I couldn't believe my ears.

"For sex?" I asked.
"Yeah, baby, for sex."

I smiled in a crazy way, my lips shaking. I told him I don't think he should even consider doing anything crazy like that. I immediately switched the tables and told him I could get the money from Ronnie, he didn't have to waste his body like that. I told him I would take care of it. Kendon got angry and said no, I will be back in the morning with the money like I said. I started crying and begging him not to do it.

"Please don't do this to me."
He was looking at me so strange.
"So, it's okay for you to do it, but I can't do it with
some hoe that don't mean shit to me? Maybe you
just want to be with your damn woman, hah?"
"No Kendon, that's not it."
"I'm trying to provide the best way I can, and that's
not good enough for you, is it? You must want me
to kick your ass,"

I flashed back quickly to that time he beat that girl outside his home.

"No, Kendon, I don't. Don't talk that way to me."

"Well, get the hell out of my way then."

I continued to beg all the way to the front door. I told Kendon we were committed to each other, and I didn't want another woman with him. I told him I couldn't handle that. He didn't understand. I was blocking the door. Before I knew it he had placed his hand around my neck and slid me up off the ground. I was choking. Then he said, "Why are you trying to stop me from doing the only thing that I know how to do?"

I was trying to say I'm sorry, but I couldn't speak. He saw the tears running down my face and the strain in my voice. Kendon let me down and shook his head as if he had just come out of a trance. He left out the door and slammed it, saying the woman wasn't a big deal and he would be back tomorrow morning. I found myself drained from every inch of my imagination and emotions. I didn't understand the depth of my pain. I knew Kendon was only trying to help us, but I couldn't handle the way he was doing it. All I knew was that it would never be the same again if he went inside another woman in the midst of our commitment. In a weird way, I wanted to keep our relationship right and faithful. The thought of him in bed with another woman tormented me beyond description. It hurt, and I ached. I walked to the corner of our bedroom and fell to my knees. I began crying to God asking Him not to let it happen. My crying soon turned into just moans. My throat was too sore to keep crying as hard as I was. I found myself on that floor in that corner with my knees in my chest, rocking back and forth, still begging Kendon not to do it, as if he was standing right in the same room.

Hours later, I could feel someone nudging my shoulders while I was asleep. It was Kendon. He reached out his hands to me to get up off the floor. He held me in his arms.

"You're home," I cried.
"Yeah, I had to come back. I didn't want to hurt
you. I couldn't do it."

I cried even more, and thanked him over and over again. He pulled me back and wiped my eyes.

> "Carla, I don't ever want to do anything to purposely hurt you. I don't ever want to be the one to hurt you, you understand?"

I nodded yes, trying to bury my head back in his arms where I felt so safe. Kendon continued to talk.

> "We are going to get through this rough time. I swear we are," he whispered.

CHAPTER 38

Ronnie Opens Her Doors For Us
(OCTOBER 1982)

The next day, I called Ronnie and told her what was going on. She offered to clear out one of her supply rooms and let us stay there in the rear of her restaurant. She lived there too. She also warned me that Kendon would not be able to come, unless he had a job lined up or some kind of money to support the rent. The rent was fifty dolllars a week. I told him, and he was sure that his uncle's job would hire him within the next week or two.

That next morning when I arrived at work, Mr. Allen was there waiting for me. He had prepared my last check. He told me he had to leave for a short time to close down his insurance business. I was sad that our money supply would be interrupted again. Kendon was sad, when he learned about my job ending. I decided to take this opportunity to tell him how people look at him when he goes for a job interview. I told him that employers look at black men that have long beautiful pressed and curled hair a certain way. They liked short, clean-cut looking men. I think if you cut your hair, put on some slacks, a shirt and tie, they will see you in a totally different light. He stood there in disbelief. I saw that he didn't want to cut his hair and kind of got an attitude about it. I walked away disappointed. He didn't understand what I was trying to say. Instead, he thought I was trying to control him. I'm going to stop doing his hair, I said to myself.

Kendon started selling Sherman again for some people that gave it to him on consignment. He didn't need any money to get started. That allowed us to give Ronnie her fifty dollars a week. Life in that restaurant was an entirely different experience. The restaurant was filled with customers throughout the day. Ronnie had video machines in front of the place for people to enjoy while they waited for their chicken dinners. She had a take-out only restaurant. One day, as we were talking, I learned how she got the restaurant. Ronnie's Daddy had passed away a few years ago and left the restaurant business to her family. However, all the rest of the family wanted was the profits and not to actually work the restaurant. Ronnie was the only child out of seven that helped her Daddy while he was living from sun-up to sun-down working the business. So now she works day and night to continue to keep the business going. Sometimes I felt sorry for her. I would hear her get up at five and six in the morning to get supplies and prepare to open up by 11 a.m. for the lunch. She specialized in chicken. The place was called Chicken Gardens. And believe me, she sold some chicken. Sometimes, I would keep her company and sit with her throughout the day.

A week went by and Kendon heard nothing from his uncle. I suggested that he go up to Church's Fried Chicken to apply for a position. He didn't want to at first, but Ronnie and I both talked him into going. I was becoming tired of trying to get him and me situated. I began to get real bitter and resentful. I never thought I could have these fed-up feelings that I was having for Kendon. I was tired of him.

One afternoon, Kendon left the restaurant and said he would be back. When he returned, he was different. I looked, and my God, all of his hair was cut into a low natural. He came through the door smiling, all proud and stuff. I was shocked and so was Ronnie.

"Well, how do you like it, baby?" he said,
"It looks so good," I said.
"Just for you," he said.
I smiled and gave him a kiss.
"You are going to see a difference now," I told him.
Kendon said this was the new him for the coming year.

The next morning when Kendon and I got up, he suggested we go up to Church's Fried Chicken on Vernon and Western. I said "okay." We got ready, and by 12 noon we were there. He was excited and so was I. He looked so nice and handsome. We had a good time as we talked and laughed about previous times together in Jr. High. I prayed so hard that he would get this job. We got to Church's and a tall middle-aged man wearing a pin which read "Manager," came to the window.

"May I help you?"
He was so conceited, it was dripping all off his
words. I couldn't stand it.
"Are you hiring?" Kendon asked The guy told him
yes, but they weren't calling people for another week
or two.
"Can we fill out an application?"
He looked at me and smiled, handing Kendon the
applications.

We left there and stopped by other food places to leave applications. It was a nice sunny day. We rode the bus back home, thinking about what we had been through since we were together. Kendon started off by saying, he had never gone through anything like this with any woman in his life.

"I must love you, Carla. You have taught me what it
means to be responsible. Lord knows, I'm trying."
"And you're doing a good job. It's only a matter of
time now."
"Speaking of time. I think it's time to be serious."
I didn't know where Kendon was going now.
"What do you mean, baby?" I said.
"How do you feel about marriage?"
I was speechless.
"I think it's time that we start thinking about
marriage
Carla, because God doesn't like people shacking up."

I thought I would scream, but I didn't. When we get a job, we can save up our money and stop all this partying and get right with God and do it the right way.

"Well, Kendon, I would love to do it the right way! I
think that's great. Boy, my Mother and Daddy are

not going to believe this!"
"My Mother won't believe it, either," Kendon said.
"Where would we get married, In Fresno or Los
  Angeles?"
"Probably in Fresno.   Our parents would kill us both
  if we didn't."
"You're right, they would."

Kendon sounded so different today. It sounded like he had taken a
wake-up pill or something. He even mixed some religion in with
his conversation. That was different. Was it really true? Was he
changing in front of my eyes? I hoped with all my heart it was true.
We kissed and he held me until we got to our stop. We enjoyed the
rest of the evening by relaxing and watching TV until bed time.

The next morning, Ronnie was knocking on the door.
"Hey, Carla! Telephone. Pick up by the stove."
"Okay, thanks," I said.

I dragged myself to the phone. We had a few drinks before going
to bed and boy did I feel them now.
"Hello," I said, wiping the sleep out of my eyes.
"Carla Lee, this is Mark Bates at Church's Fried
  Chicken."
I perked up immediately.
"I'm calling to give you some good news."
"Oh, wonderful."
"We would love to hire you for a position. Are you
  available?" I hesitated.

I thought he was going to tell me that Kendon was hired for a
position, not me. I wanted to be back in an office environment, not
a fast food place. But we needed the money. I said yes, trying to
hide my hurt and disappointment. I couldn't help it, I had to ask.
"What about my brother, Kendon Starr? Is he going
  to be working there also?"
"No, we have enough men here. We are short of

girls."

"Oh," I said. "Well, thank you very much."

"Don't hang up before I'm able to tell you your starting date. Will next Monday be fine?"

"That will be fine."

"Okay, come in at 8 a.m. and speak with Melba, the Assistant Manager, she will get you started."

I dragged myself back to the bed where Kendon was lying. I couldn't tell if he was asleep or his eyes were just closed. I looked at him and rubbed his hair and neck. I didn't know how I would tell him that they hired me and not him. How would he take it? He cut his hair and everything. This was like a slap in the face.

Kendon opened his eyes while I was rubbing his hair.

"Who was that on the phone?"

"Oh, it was Church's Fried Chicken." He jumped up.

"What did they say?" He was so excited.

I tried to sound as mad as possible.

"They said they have enough men and they needed more women and so they hired me." He laid back down.

"But they said they would be hiring men in a couple of months." I felt so bad, I lied.

KENDON STARTS WORKING
January 1983

Later that day, Ronnie came to us and said she had an idea that would probably work for the both of us. She offered Kendon a job working for her starting January 1, 1983. Ronnie said this would pay for our room and board. Though the job didn't provide a lot of extra money, it did pay our necessities. Kendon was cool at first with just knowing that he was keeping a roof over our heads and food in our stomachs. I could tell it gave him a sense of pride. Ronnie would work the day shift, and Kendon would relieve her from 5:00 p.m. to 11:30 p.m. It seemed to work out pretty good. Kendon didn't seem to mind.

After a couple of months Kendon started tripping. He started being very late for work. He knew he had to relieve Ronnie at 5:00, and would show up between 6:00 p.m. and 6:30 p.m. We also discovered that he started back smoking more Sherman than he was selling. He was also becoming paranoid with my relationship with Ronnie. He started accusing us of sleeping around on him, being freaks together behind his back. I didn't know what the hell got into Kendon. He would also go on a "poor me can't find a job" trip and tell me how many whores he had that would give him anything he wanted. I couldn't figure out his mind set from one day to the next.

FEBRUARY 1983

Ronnie eventually told Kendon that they had to talk about his inconsistent commitment to the job. I knew Ronnie was tired of Kendon. She had also noticed that her supplies (i.e., cigarettes, candy, and sodas) were getting smaller & smaller. She told him he was going to have to leave. I didn't know she was going to say that to him. She said I could stay, but he would have to leave. I was surprised on one hand, but then a little relieved on the other. He had to go back to Fresno. He tried to find somewhere in Los Angeles to stay, but even his own family wouldn't let him stay with them. They told him they didn't trust him. Kendon didn't take this too well. He was sure now that Ronnie and I were plotting against him, so we could start messing with each other. I told him that wasn't the case, it was out of my control and maybe for right now. It was the best thing for us. He blew up at me and started telling me about all the stuff he had done for me.

"I came out here for you! I left my mother and
family for you! I left hoes that would work for me

for you! I cut my god damn hair off for you, Carla!
And you can't do nothing for me!"

He started hollering and slobbering on the sides of his mouth. He
scared me!
"I love you, Carla, you hear me? I love you! I don't
know what I'm going to do without you!"

I kept telling him it was only temporary and would only last until I
got on my feet. But he wasn't buying it. He started looking
around the room real weird.
"Carla, Ronnie wants you, I know it. I can tell by the
way she looks at you when you're not looking."

Kendon sounded so crazy while he was describing her. His eyes
were widening because of the Sherman. I tried to calm him.
"No, baby, she doesn't want me. She just can't afford
to take care of both of us. We have to take care of
ourselves."

Damn, it hurt me to see him in this state. I was watching my Jr.
High love leave right in front of my eyes. Maybe I had destroyed
him more by bringing him to L.A. Who knows? Maybe he would
have never experienced what he was experiencing now. I had never
seen him do these kinds of things. I blamed myself for this.

Uncle Walter came by to pick us up and to take Kendon to the bus
stop. We hugged and kissed all the way. I kept assuring him that
we would be seeing each other real soon. "Just watch and see.
Please hang in there, Kendon." Did I really believe what I was
saying? I didn't even know. I just knew I didn't want him leaving
without any hope. On the way back, Uncle Walter began to talk
with me.
"Now Carla, I know you've been through a whole lot.
I know you have really been trying to make this
thing work. But girl, if you get back involved with

that boy, you are crazy. The boy has been crazy
since he was able to walk. I'm telling you, his parents
didn't do right by those kids and they know."

I was crying. My dream man was gone and I felt tired. Uncle
Walter continued to talk with me, but his words sounded far off.
What was Kendon thinking about on the bus, I wondered. Was he
still sad or was it a big front and he too really wanted to get out of
it? When I got back to the restaurant Ronnie was waiting on a
customer. I went directly to my room and straight to bed. I just
wanted to sleep forever.

CHAPTER 39

Reflections — April 1983

Kendon moving back to Fresno was not the end of his presence in Los Angeles. He would call me at least once a week to see how I was coming along with finding us an apartment. His threats kept me walking in fear. Every time the phone would ring my stomach would fill up with butterflies. There were even times when he would get so mad, because there was no progress that he would accuse me of sabotaging our relationship. Then he would threaten to kill me for setting him up for failure because it looked bad to his people in Fresno.

I would remember how he beat that prostitute until her whole face was bloody. I would find myself literally shaking to the point I had to sit down when I was on the phone with him. He told me that I would never get away from him and he would find me one day and get me for what I did to him. I went through that scenario off and on for about two to three months, until one day he just stopped calling.

I kept praying to God to please keep the distance between me and him. I never thought a man that I had so much love for would turn out to be a man I feared.

A few months later, my sister AlmaFaye told me that she heard Kendon had gone back to jail, and would be there for a long time now because the authorities considered him to be unable to function in society. I was so relieved.

I remember coming home from work, laying in my bed looking up at the ceiling into the corner where there was a familiar cross imprint. It was just like the one that was in my bedroom when I was a little girl. The cross always allowed me to feel safe and close to God. I didn't know why I needed him so badly. I could always feel an intense shaking going on inside of me every time I would think about it for any length of time. God, what is it all about? Is

it just about quitting drinking, quitting smoking, and quitting sex?
    "What is it, God, what must happen and how?"

I began to cry softly so that Ronnie couldn't hear me. But I asked God for direction. No answers came right away. Sometimes, I would beg God to let me hear His voice, or see a sign or something. No sign would come and no voice would be heard. But I knew He was there somewhere. I told God that morning, "I am going to do better. I am going to do the right things in life. But please help me. Help me to see right and do the right thing God, please."

I told Ronnie that I had decided to chill out and just kind of lay dead. I told her that I didn't want to go out to the clubs anymore, and I didn't want to get high or party anymore either. She told me that was a good idea. I told her that I needed some spiritual guidance. She said she had the perfect hook-up.
    "What you need to do is experience the gift of
    meditation."
    "What is meditation?" I asked.
    "It's the key to success and your spiritual balance in
    life. It keeps you focused. It keeps you safe from
    manipulators and people that don't need to be in
    your life. It helps you to always be in control."

It was sounding real good and like something that I needed in my life. Lord knows I had enough people in my life that I didn't need.
    "Only if I had this meditation thing going on earlier!
    Then I guess I would not have experienced the shit
    I've been through."
    "Carla, it's very simple. I do it every morning," she
    said.
    "How does it work?" I asked.

She reached underneath the cabinet and handed me a red and white book called "The Key to Human Understanding on How To Keep Your Mind." Ronnie explained that the objective of the book and exercise was to get focused on your inner emotions and feelings.

The exercise was guaranteed to decrease anxiety, confusion, and to give a clear objective thought process. The book also discussed the morals and values of common everyday interactions. It talked about why we hate people for no reason and how we can always help others solve their problems, but lack the ability to solve our own. It talked about how we allow people, world, family, and jobs to manipulate us. And finally, how people truly get what they deserved, no matter how good or how bad life is. The book was accompanied by three tapes, with three levels. I would start off on level 1. Ronnie sounded so excited about the book and told me to try it right now since I was in a place of seeking spiritual balance.

"Go in your room, grab a chair, and place it in the
middle of the room. Take this tape and pop it in
the cassette. Listen to it and follow the instructions.
Turn all lights off before you start the tape and close
the door so there is no light in your room at all."

So, I did what she said. There was a calming, soothing sound for thirty minutes of the exercises. It was pretty damn boring to say the least, but a few things caught my attention. I noticed the philosopher harped on one thing. He emphasized self forgiveness and made clear that people get what they deserve in life. He also talked about abusive mothers and fathers. I began to feel like my mother had no more control over me. In addition, she was getting whatever she deserved in life by being an alcoholic. Forget trying to kiss up to her and make things better. Be myself, and if she can deal with it fine. If not, the hell with it He stressed being free from parental manipulations.

AUGUST 1983

I couldn't believe I had been meditating over a month. I was proud of myself. I thought about my mother more and more. I found myself becoming so furious at her. Then I thought about Kendon and was able to release the guilt of thinking I screwed up his life. He just got what he deserved.

I got a call from Mable one day asking if I needed a job! Her next door neighbor, Shirley, had an attorney friend that was looking for a receptionist. I screamed, "Yes, I need a job!" I interviewed with the attorney and they hired me on recommendation alone. I quit Church's with a one-day notice. Thank God! Things began to look up. I was focused and really feeling good about myself.

I came home after my first week of work and told Ronnie I needed a car. She said she would help me find one and asked what type was I looking for. I told her that my dream car was a Buick Regal, but I would settle for what I can get until I saved up enough for my Buick. We started looking in The Recycler Newspaper and found a gray 1975 Monza. The guy selling the car was Jamaican. When we went by to see the car he served us drinks and made general conversation before we saw the car. He was selling it for four hundred dollars. I paid for it that night and said I would be back for it the next day.

The next morning, Ronnie and I both saw why he got us drunk first. The car needed body work and interior work. But this was my first car. I was glad and grateful. I attributed my good fortune to staying home, being good, and meditating day and night. Nowadays I wasn't complaining about living in the back of a restaurant in a supply room. But patience was needed, like they taught on the meditation tapes.

One Saturday morning, Ronnie and I were watching television. I told her I wanted to do something else in life. She asked what did I want to do. I couldn't single it out then, but I knew it was in the law enforcement area. I had always been interested in legal business. So I went to the store and got the L.A. Times and looked up various school programs. I came across a program called Paralegal Studies. This would make it possible for a person to work closely with an attorney. It sounded challenging and financially rewarding. I told her I wanted to do this. She was happy and told me to call the school to see when the next class was being offered. I called the number in the paper and spoke with a career adviser who gave me the class schedule for the next semester. School officially started in three weeks and orientation was being held now.

PARALEGAL SCHOOL ORIENTATION
September 1983

I went for the orientation the following week. The orientation was so cool. Seeing different people and having that college feeling again made me feel like I was doing something great. I registered. This was it for me! They offered a nine-month condensed night course.

The law firm where I was working said I could move from Receptionist to General Secretary within a month, and I did. I was now typing letters and legal forms. The promotion was exciting.

By this time, I was gaining all my weight back. I grabbed an old pair of one of my favorite jeans. Something was in the pocket. I took it out and saw a phone number written on the back of a matchbook, Tory. I remembered her so vividly! Ronnie and I met her one night at the Bowl of Cherries, and I saw her quite a bit at "The One Club." She would always sit and just watch me dance though I would never pay attention. I thought I had lost her number back then. How in hell did it get in these jeans? I kept staring at it and getting real bad urges to call her. I wondered what she was doing these days. Then I caught myself. No! I told myself, no no no. You are doing so well, Carla, don't even try it. Keep meditating, I told myself.

A couple of weeks had gone by and I still had not called that number. I was too embarrassed to tell Ronnie, because she was being committed to our agreement to not party, look for women, or get back into that crazy scene. It was amazing how Ronnie and I would stay up some nights and talk about having husband and children. Ronnie didn't really have a desire for a man, but she knew it was the right thing in God's eyes. Same here. I knew it was God's way, but my nature kept wanting the opposite. Ronnie and I spent much of our time together after she closed up shop. We would kick it in the back room where she slept. We kept beer in the fridge and music in the back. Ronnie loved to sing. She had a passion for it, but didn't have enough confidence to go all the way and pursue a singing career. Some nights we would sit up and take turns singing to each other. Our favorite singers were Stephanie Mills and Tina Marie. We would play their albums back to back. Through our conversations and singing a bonding was happening. We were buddies forever.

CHAPTER 40

Return To The Familiar Place
(OCTOBER 1983)

One Saturday, I broke down and called Tory. A lady answered and told me that Tory was at church. I felt relieved and disappointed at the same time. I told myself it was not meant to be and this was God's way of not letting me get caught up again in that lifestyle. The thought did not last very long. I didn't want to call her back, but I kept thinking about her.

I won't get caught up again, I would tell myself. I could handle just a phone call! That's not getting back into the life. I can have more than one friend outside of Ronnie! I was convincing myself real good now. The next time I called, she answered.

"Hello, is Tory home?"

"This is Tory speaking."

"This is Carla."

She let out a noise that sounded like a scream.

"Where have you been the last couple of years?"

"I tried to do some things different, but it didn't work out that well. But I'm back on this side of sanity now."

"It's so good to hear your voice."

"The same here," I said.

"So when am I going to see you again lady?"

"When do you want to see me again," I boldly asked.

"Today, right now!"

"Whoa, a woman who knows what she wants and when she wants it." We both laughed.

"Well, give me your address and we will see if we can work that request out."

I wrote down her information and got off the phone. I just sat there like a drug addict who promised not to use again, but got weak and did it anyway.

I convinced myself that I was strong and it wouldn't be anything serious or lasting. Just a friendship, I kept telling myself. There is nothing wrong with a friend. I still didn't tell Ronnie.

I put on a casual shirt, blazer and levis. I didn't want to look too girly or boyish.

When I pulled up in front of her house, my stomach starting tripping. Where in the hell did the butterflies come from, I wondered to myself.

I walked up the long walkway leading to the front door and wondered if she could see me. I was so nervous. I knocked on the door, and a young dark-skinned man appeared.
        "Hi, my name is Carla, and I'm here to see Tory."

He smiled, looked me up and down, welcomed me in and escorted me to the living room. The house was large and beautiful. Several people must live here, I thought to myself.

Then Tory walked out with a big smile on her face. I got up and she came over and hugged me as if we were old schoolmates. I immediately asked her if she wanted to drive to the store with me, I needed some cigarettes. I needed a smoke. This girl really got me nervous now. When we got back, we sat in the car in front of her house.
        "So what's been going on with you for the past couple
        of years?" I said.
        "I finally got out of that relationship with Jeanie.
        Then I started going to church and concentrating on
        living right."
        "That's good. In fact that's where my head is too."
        "I been working in the medical field as a
        Chiropractor's Assistant."
        "Cool. I know where I can come get a massage,
        hah?"
        "I don't know about that. I just do the bookkeeping

and billing."

"I'm in paralegal school trying to get my certificate
from Southland College."

"Are you serious?"

"Yeh, why?"

"That's where I go in the mornings."

"I go there at night."

"No." We both looked at each other in sheer
amazement.

"How long have you been going there?"

"I just started in September."

"Wow, me too."

"You mean to tell me that our paths have been
crossing and we may have been maybe walking
down the same hall?"

"Probably. It seems that way, hah?"

We jumped from one subject to the next, avoiding coming to the
end of the evening.

You can only stay in a car for so long. Before I left, she told me
that her birthday was the following Tuesday. I asked her how old
she was. She told me twenty eight years old. I asked her if I could
take her out for a birthday drink on Tuesday night at the club, if
she still did that. She said that would be nice.

"Okay, I'll pick you up around 8 p.m. and we'll go up
to the Ruby's Room. Okay?"

It was only Sunday and we had two days to wait. She got out of the
car, and I watched her go into the house safely. While driving
home I thought about her beautiful ways. I was in my own world.
When I got home, Ronnie was just closing the restaurant.

"Hey, Ronnie, what's happening?" I was feeling
great.

"Nothing much man, just closing up shop."

"I went by to see this girl I met some time ago."

"A girl?" Ronnie was surprised that I had gone over a

girl's house, because of the vow we both made.

"Oh, so you getting back into the life, hah?"

"Well, not exactly." I kind of got a little lonely and wanted to do something different."

Ronnie did not approve. I could see it all over her face.

"Look, it ain't no big deal, we just talked" I hollered out as I was going toward the back to my room.

"Well, we will see how much it ain't a big deal." Ronnie hollered back, as she followed me to my room.

She looked at me sadly.

"You want to go have a drink at the club tonight, Carla?"

"Now, Ronnie, we said we weren't going out to the clubs anymore, didn't we?"

Then, I thought to myself real quick and changed my mind, because I remembered inviting Tory out for her birthday at the club.

"Well, I guess a drink won't hurt. Plus, we will have each other there to be responsible."

I started wondering had Ronnie been holding up her end or just playing me? Ronnie finished closing down, took a shower, and we were out the door to the club. We walked in like strangers. We hadn't been in the scene for a while. We ordered a drink and sat down at the bar. The crowd was different on Sunday nights. It was more of a conservative crowd; business men and women and a few freak mama's and daddy's. They even had a Sunday night gospel show. I didn't understand this, nor did I agree with it. I felt it was like slapping God in His face with our crap. I told Ronnie, if the owner wants to go to church, then let him but this needs to stop. She agreed it was bad business. We ordered another drink of Hennessy for Ronnie and Gin and Coke for me.

"So tell me about this Tory," Ronnie said.

The music was loud.

"Well, she's cute, nice and just what the doctor

prescribed for me, and I'm going to go after her."
"What?"
"Yep, I've decided to try and hang with her! I've been
thinking. I'm ready now."
Ronnie took a big drink. "What do you mean that
you're ready now? Earlier you said she was a friend.
Now you want to marry her. Where did that come
from?"
"Well, I have my life pretty much together and I can
settle down in a meaningful relationship."
"Does she know you have decided to settle down
with her?" Ronnie said sarcastically.
"No, nigga, but I don't think I'll get a whole lot of
objection from her."
"Well, how old is she?" I didn't want to tell Ronnie
she was damn near twenty-nine years old, but I did.
Her birthday was coming up.
"Ah man, what yo little twenty-year-old ass gonna
do with a twenty-nine year old woman?"

Ronnie laughed, trying to make fun. I tried to convince Ronnie
that I was tired of playing around and wanted someone that I could
be stable and serious with. Something that I could hold on to and
really know that it's mine.

"Man, you better be careful, you know what Roy
Master says about women that are seductive and
sexy. They are controlling and manipulative. You
better check that woman out first. It sounds like she
already has you hooked."
"Ronnie, you or Roy Master don't know what the hell
you're talking about now."

I tried to defend Tory's character, but Ronnie was convinced
through the meditation messages that we can't really trust beauty
and niceness.

"You've been meditating too damn long Ronnie.
Everybody don't manipulate you. I have control over

this situation!"
"How do you know that, Carla?"
"Just watch and see!"

We partied and danced hard after they changed the gospel music
to R&B.

TORY'S BIRTHDAY -- NOVEMBER 1983

Tuesday came so fast. It was Tory's twenty-ninth birthday. I
knocked on the door. The door opened and there she was. She
looked like she stepped out of the pages of a charm book. She had
a beautifully laced ruffled white blouse on with some nice fitted
black slacks. She had pearl studs in her ears and clear polished nails.
She was simply a cutie pie.
"Are you ready?"
"Yes," she said.

The club was quiet that night. There were no more than fifty
people in the house. They played oldies, but goodies. It was
perfect. We stayed at the bar together, and our knees constantly
bumped from the turning stools. A nice slow record came on and I
asked her if I could have this dance. She said yes. The night was
going so very well. It felt like I was in a dream.

After leaving the club I drove Tory home. There was a 76 gas
station next to an alley right before we got to her house so I pulled
in there. I told her what a nice evening I had.
"You are so beautiful, Tory." She blushed.

We sat there for about another hour. I learned about her
background and her lack of relationship with her mother. She and
her sister are the only two in her family, but she always felt her
mother played favorites between them. She seemed real sad when
she was telling me that part. Her story reminded me of mine a
little. I took her hand in mine and rubbed it with my fingers. She

seemed to not mind.

I leaned over my armrest to whisper in her ears.
> "I think you are the most beautiful woman on the
> face of the earth and I feel so lucky to have the
> privilege of being with you tonight."
> "Thank you for celebrating my birthday with me."

Her perfume was intoxicating me, she smelled so good.   I kissed her on her neck and she didn't seem to mind.
> "Your skin is so soft. And your perfume is running
> me crazy."
> "It's my birthday perfume."
> "What's the name of it?"
> "Opium."

She turned me on and I wanted her in my arms to hold and to caress. The damn armrest was in the way.
> "Do you think I could kiss your soft lips before I take
> you to your doorstep?"
> "I think so."

She turned to me with her sexy ways. Her skin even tasted good as if she had candy-flavored body lotion on. Her kiss was soft and sensuous. She pulled back.
> "Okay, that's enough."
> "Why?"
> "Because I want to go home in one piece."
> "I wouldn't tear you apart out here."
> "I mean, mentally in one piece. Your kissing is
> turning me on."
> "What do you think your soft lips are doing to me?"
> "I don't know."
> "I think you do. But I will be a perfect gentlewoman
> and take you home." She smiled, clamping her
> hands together.

I drove the car around the corner in front of her house.
"Thank you again for making my birthday so
special."
"Any time. I mean, you're welcome."

On the way home I felt like a new person. I also felt that I had met
somebody so precious and sweet. She seemed so innocent. My
insides were jumping with anticipation of really getting to know
her. How did I ignore her all those years, I wondered to myself.

From that time on, we started talking to each other everyday, for
hours at a time. We couldn't get off the phone. In all of our
conversations, Tory always wanted to be sure I wasn't still chasing
other women as she always observed me doing in the past. She
would tell me that I was wild and could not be tamed. Each time
she brought it up I would try hard to convince her that I wasn't the
same person. I finally got around to asking her how she felt about
relationships. She changed the subject. She wanted to know who
Ronnie, my roommate, really was to me. I explained how we met,
and how we are really only buddies now.

One evening, Tory told me that she had been thinking about
getting her own place so she could have her privacy. She was upset.
Her sister had started complaining about her missing Sabbath day
services ever since I started coming around. This didn't set too well
with Tory.

One Friday night, Tory asked me if I wanted to go to church with
her that week-end. I told her sure, no problem. That Friday night
I picked her up from work. We went to dinner first. At dinner we
talked about her church, their beliefs and practices. After I heard
everything she had to say I thought it was a little crazy. It had so
many rules. The religion said it was wrong to be on the phone on
Friday's. She couldn't exchange any money, she couldn't do any
work, and she couldn't go places other than to her place of worship.
I laughed because this was ridiculous to me. She also told me,
whatever the pastor says to do the congregation has to trust that he

is hearing from God and do. I asked her to give me an example. Tory told me he had the whole church sleep on the floors of their homes to feel sorry for the homeless people who had no bed to sleep on. I said, "Now look, enough is enough. I ain't sleeping on the damn floor unless I ain't got a bed. That shit is stupid, Tory. That's a control gimmick. Those people downtown don't know you laying on the damn floor for them."

"What is that?" Watch your mouth, Carla!" Tory didn't use profanity.

We arrived at church after a delicious dinner. It was about a fifty-member church, mostly family. It was a storefront church, nothing modern about it at all. It had four walls and hard chairs. I sat in the back and watched. In the pulpit was the Rt. Rev. Wylee, as they called him. They were old women. The musical instruments were to the far left side of the church. I don't know what kind of church this was. It felt strange. It didn't feel like church.

They kept the center clear for shouting space. That's what happened the first hour. Someone got up and said "Praise the Holy Ghost," and the music and shouting started. It was so loud. I said to myself, now the Holy Ghost is fine, but what about Jesus? They have not said one thing about Jesus. I learned about Jesus from Grandma Georgia and Aunt Drena. I know I didn't know much about Jesus, but I expected to hear His name at some point. I didn't even hear them say anything about God.

I sat back and analyzed the whole service. The pastor looked my way and smiled. When he stood for pastoral remarks, he brought it to the church's attention that they had a visitor. He asked me to stand and introduce myself. I felt like I had invaded a private session of an occult. I stood up and made a short comment. Afterwards my head was throbbing because the music was so damn loud. The sermon was short and ineffective. I couldn't remember what he was saying from one word to the next. I had a headache. The headache was so bad tears began to roll down my eyes every time I would try to talk.

A few minutes later, he gave an altar call and a laying-on of hands. Tory suggested I go up there to get my headache prayed for. Then he shouted out "Anybody here in pain, come and let me pray for you." Tory nudged me. I got up and went forward. He took both of his hands and put them over my ears with his face right next to mine. He was speaking so fast in my ear. He touched my head, threw my head back, and said, "You're healed daughter, you're healed." The congregation started going off. They were screaming and shouting. Then he backed up and looked at me. He had this big smile on his face. He asked if it was all gone. I said to myself say yes, Carla, so that this man's face won't be broken and embarrassed. I told him it was all gone. Lying through my teeth. God, please don't strike me down, I prayed under my breath.

After service everyone was embracing me and asking me to come back. The mothers of the church cooked fish dinners and were selling them in the back. I couldn't wait to get out of there. I didn't understand it. I've always loved church, but I wasn't too sure of what I had just experienced.

On the way home, I tried to tell Tory something was wrong at that church. She told me that I didn't know what I was talking about, because I wasn't into church like she was. Then she told me when I decided to commit and get serious I will understand religious things. I laughed and said, when I decide to commit, I know I'll understand, but it won't be at that place. I dropped the subject because I could see how upset it was making her.

Later that night, I was supposed to take Tory over to meet Ronnie. Tory asked me if I thought my roommate would accept her. I told her if she didn't too bad, because I accepted her. When we arrived at the restaurant I remembered that I didn't tell Tory I lived in the back of this place in a stock room. When she found out, she said it didn't matter. Ronnie and her new friend Valerie were in the back listening to music and getting high. The agreement that Ronnie and I made to stop messing with women was blown for sure now. I guess we were fully back into the life again.

Tory and I walked in the door. I introduced Tory, and Ronnie introduced us to Valerie. We had a few drinks together and smoked a couple of joints before going out to the club. Ronnie was in rare form tonight. She sang a song by Stephanie Mills to Tory. Tory smiled and blushed. Valerie asked if I sang. I shook my head no. Ronnie looked at me and said, "She's lying, she does sing." She made me sing "You and I" by Stephanie Mills. After the song went off I said, let's get the hell out of here and go party.

On the way to club, Tory whispered in my ear that she really liked the song I sang. We drank and danced, danced and drank. I had a ball. Tory held my attention and interest. Every time I looked at her she would run her tongue across her lips and wink at me. She flirted with me all the time.

We left the club around 3 a.m. I dropped Ronnie and Valerie off first and then started to take Tory home. Leaving each other was becoming more difficult for both of us. We didn't want to be out of each other's presence. I told her how much I was beginning to care about her. She said that she was there too. I told her of my spiritual struggle with the lifestyle I was living, but that I decided that I would go to hell for this one. I had never felt anything so right and so good. She expressed she felt the same way. I told her I didn't want to go home that night. She was silent. I found a hotel for the night and we stayed there.

The next morning we were up early enough for Tory to sneak back into the house without anyone knowing she was out all night. I told her I would call her later on that day and maybe we could go have lunch.

My relationship with Tory's family, especially her three nieces, grew closer and closer. They began calling me Auntie Carla. Everybody said Tory and I were like sisters. We made sure they never saw us do, or say, anything out of line.

Tory's sister became friendly toward me eventually. Of course, she knew what was going on between Tory and me. One day she told me that she appreciated my feminine appearance, unlike what she had seen in the past. I thought to myself, she just didn't know how boyish I acted away from her house with Tory. At times I felt like Desmund because Tory treated me as if I was a king.

Thanksgiving weekend Tory and I went to a new club that was opening downtown. The place was large and predominately white. The music was cross and mixed with disco and R&B. We didn't stay long, because it wasn't that hot. We decided to leave there and go to our usual club. That night I asked Tory would she be mine. She told me yes. My heart melted with happiness. While partying that night at the club, who did I run into? I saw about three different women I used to mess with. They came up to me and started talking. Tory didn't like this too much, so I introduced them to her as my lover. So now she really didn't need to be mad, I thought to myself. Tory told me that she noticed everywhere we went I would always run into people from my past. I told her it was a busy past, but not an important one. She smiled and rolled her eyes at me.

The next morning Ronnie came in my room to tell me that my mother had called and wanted me to call her back as soon as possible. I called Momma back and she wanted to know if I was coming home for Christmas. I told her that I wasn't sure this year. She pressured me by telling me the kids wanted to see me. I just couldn't imagine being away from Tory. But Momma had never begged me like this before. I did miss my mother. I told Momma that I would let her know in a week or so. She sounded sober and that's when I was the most vulnerable to her, because I would relax and let my guards down.

After hanging up with my mother I got a call from Tory. She sounded excited. I waited for her to calm down to tell me what was this surprise she kept screaming that she had.

"I found my own apartment. The landlord called
   and told me I could move in anytime I wanted to."
"Where is it, baby?"
"Right off of Western and Jefferson."
"Cool, baby. That's great. Congratulations."
"I can't wait to move in."
"I can't either. Now I have somewhere to fall asleep
   after we come home from the clubs late at night."
"That's right. You can fall asleep right in my arms."

When I hung up the phone, I called my sister AlmaFaye to get the
run down on what's happening in Fresno since Momma wanted me
to come down.

"I'm coming home for Christmas, so we can catch up
   then, okay?"
"Are you serious?"
"Yes, I am. I want to know what state of mind
   Momma is in."
"Carla, Momma has changed."
"How so?"
"She worries me so much by the way she is talking
   out of her head nowadays."
"Like how? What does she say?"
"The other day she called me and said somebody
   had been cutting her hair. She said Mr. Calvin and
   her friend Isalee were cutting her hair and giving her
   a rinse, and they turned her hair green."
"What, are you kidding me?"
"No, Carla. I'm serious, but the crazy thing about it,
   when I went over to see Momma, her hair was
   beautifully cut and it was kind of green, as if
   someone had put a color rinse on it."
"Well, why you think Mamma's crazy?"
"Well, she said someone is doing voodoo on her like
   they used to do in Louisiana."
"AlmaFaye, I will be home for Christmas."
"Yeah baby, I will see you then."

I got off the phone and went to my room to lay down. I thought about my mother. I thought about how we never really had a fair chance to know each other, and I was angry about it. My mother was getting worse. She was drinking herself to death, and no one was doing anything about it. Could anybody do anything about it? I prayed to God, I wanted to love my mother and forgive her. I hurt so bad. I had turned against her with my emotions of the past. That stupid meditation exercise I was doing was making my emotions worse. It made me feel condemned to be compassionate. I asked God for help and forgiveness.

I began to go to church with Tory every other weekend to be a part of the family and stay close to her. We would go to the night clubs, after the sun went down on the Sabbath days.

This particular weekend we didn't go out because Tory was moving in her new place, and I was so glad. She had a beautiful two bedroom house. Tory would get up in the mornings and play Shirley Caesar's "No Charge" song and Aretha Franklin's "Amazing Grace". I loved these songs and asked Tory if she would tape them for me. She taped them and made sure I had them the next day. I listened to the songs every time I got in my car. I had to stop listening to them so much because I would began to feel real guilty about my lifestyle. So I would only listen to them on church days. Christmas was coming in a few days and Tory and I agreed to see each other after Christmas because I would be in Fresno.

DECEMBER/CHRISTMAS IN FRESNO 1983

Christmas in Fresno was going to be interesting, I thought to myself as I prepared to catch the bus. I hadn't seen my mother in a while and decided I would surprise her so I didn't call her back that day. It was cold in Fresno. My knees were shivering as soon as I stepped off the bus. I flagged down a cab. The cab driver pulled over to the curb, jumped out to take my bags then opened my door. I was so thankful to get into his warm car.

"Where to?" the Latino driver asked.

"25 E. Touloumne Street, sir."

As we drove through the city toward home I felt an instant sadness and a knot in my throat. The knot would not leave, until I left Fresno. I got out of the cab and there she was in her window smoking like a chimney. She cracked a smile when she saw me. I paid the cab driver and he drove off. I knew Blacky would no longer be greeting me, because he was dead, but I still missed him every time I walked through the gateway where he would meet me. I walked into the house. Momma stood up and hugged me. I hugged her so tight that I didn't want to let go. I told her I missed her, and that I needed this hug from her.

"You're looking good," she complimented me.

"Thanks, Momma."

My sisters and brothers came through the door giving hi-fives and hugs. It was so good to see them again. Being in that house always seemed to pull tears out of me for so many reasons. It always felt like there was a dark feeling that I wasn't ever comfortable with. My brothers and sisters always came in to see what I had brought them from L.A. I brought a couple of things and told them to put them under the tree. The tree was the same old aluminum silver tree with the same decorations of red, blue and green round bulbs. Momma still had that gold and white star that went on top of the tree, and the silver and gold drapings of the paper shingles. I sat down next to Momma, after putting my things away. I couldn't believe how some things just never change in a million years and a day. Momma asked me about Brown and corrected herself.

"You left him for that boy Kendon, didn't you?"

"Yeah, Momma. Why you ask?" I was embarrassed,

"Well, he came by not too long ago. A couple of months ago."

"Oh no, did he Momma? I thought he was still in jail."

"Yep, I talked to him. He didn't say much, just kind

of grinned a lot and said soon as things were fine
ya'll were getting married."

Oh man, I muttered to myself. Momma wasn't too high right
now. She had some things in her cup simmering but she hadn't got
high. I changed the subject.
"So, AlmaFaye coming by today?"
"Yeah, you know we'll play cards this evening, and
everybody will make their way over here soon. And
we don't have to talk about that boy no more if you
don't want to," she smiled. I smiled back. Momma
noticed I changed the subject.

Momma and I made small talk about everything. I purposely hung
around the house and did not go visiting like I usually would to
avoid her ridicule. I was determined this was going to be different.
It's time to learn who Momma is instead of running away.
Momma said she wanted to lay down. It was around 12:30 in the
afternoon. She was cooking turkey and dressing for dinner. She
told me to watch it while she got a little rest. Now that wasn't like
Momma. She was always short for words but never rested in the
middle of the day. I sat there in her chair when she left and looked
outside the window that she stares out of so much. I watched the
cars go by. I saw the planes land. I even watched Mrs. Harrison's
house across the street. The lady I used to work for. I asked about
Mrs. Harrison. Momma yelled back that she had been sick but
she's a lot better now. I didn't ask any more questions. I sat in that
seat and tried to literally feel my mother. I don't know what I
expected, but I longed to feel her insides. I longed to feel her hurts,
pains, fears, and confusions, but mainly her thoughts. She would
never tell me anything but I knew they were there. She was human
just like me, they had to be there. I went to check on Momma. As
I walked in the door, I could see her body jerking.
"Momma are you all right?" I asked.
"Yeah, girl, just a little gas pains in my chest. Don't
worry about me."
Every five seconds she would grab her chest.

"Momma, if I need to call the ambulance you better
tell me."
She sounded very convincing this time.
"No, I ate too much stuff and gave myself gas.
Really baby."
"Momma, remember I used to climb up in your bed
with you a long time ago?"
"Yeah, why?"
"Well, I'm going to climb in this bed with you now
until you begin to feel better, okay?"
"Girl, you too big for that."
"I'm never too big, Momma." She didn't know how
much I needed to be close to her.

I laid next to my mother, scooting right in front of her. I felt the
bed tremble each time she would get a pain. She didn't know but I
was praying to God to please help her. I silently asked God to help
her stop smoking and drinking. I laid there with my face turned to
the wall so she could not see the tears in my eyes. I needed her, and
she needed me. I began to think of ways I could get my mother
out of this dead house and dead city. I thought about going to
school, getting my degree, and a good paying job. Then I could
move my mother out of Fresno to Los Angeles with me. I
whispered to God, after I fully thought about the plan.

"Okay, God? Let me do that for my mother. Just let
me do that," I begged,

Then I heard somebody at the door. I told Momma to keep
resting and I would go check to see who it was. It was my oldest
brother, Gable.

"Hey, baby girl. When you get down here?"
"A few hours ago."
"Where's Momma?"
"She's in the bedroom in pain but she won't admit to
it."
"I'm fine," she yelled out.
Gable and I went to the bedroom and held

Momma.

She must have gotten a pain at the same time, because her hug got tighter and Gable reacted with a groan. Momma got out of the bed and said it was time to get the day going and the party rolling.

We all got together and began to play music. We put on some Marvin Gaye, "Let's Get It On," Thelma Houston's "Don't Leave Me This Way." Momma yelled out, "Now ya'll ain't go be playing that stupid stuff all night, cause I'm going to hear me some Bobbie Blue Bland and B.B. King!" We all had fun laughing and talking with Momma. Molly, Lee, Rhea, and her friends came over. The whole gang was there. Momma began to talk like she always did, and in spite of it, I stayed.

Later on that night, I noticed Momma was drinking two and three half pints of whiskey by herself. While I was in the kitchen cleaning up from the party, I heard Momma in the front room with AlmaFaye cursing and talking. Everybody had just about gone home and the kids were sleep. Mr. Calvin finally came home. I walked in the front room only to see Momma get up out of her seat to grab Mr. Calvin in his chest, because she was mad at him. She slipped and staggered, falling down. She barely missed hitting her head on the edge of the wooden coffee table. I jumped for her. Then Mr. Calvin reached for her and she fell over him.

Momma was belligerent in calling Mr. Calvin all kinds of names. She accused him of screwing everybody in the streets and now coming home to her. But then I saw something I had never seen before. I saw Mr. Calvin talking back to Momma and calling her names too. Then as she was coming up on him again, he grabbed and jerked on her telling her to take her ass to bed. AlmaFaye was just standing there watching. I was so mad at him! He was the whole reason Momma was an alcoholic anyway I felt. But I didn't know what to do. Why was he so cold now? I couldn't understand, I began to cry. I guess Momma was right, maybe he was out with his whores. Momma got up off the couch and went to bed. I was ready to go back to L.A. at that very moment.

CHRISTMAS DAY

The next day I planned on leaving early. It was going to be sad leaving Momma now, knowing what I knew about her more intense drinking and chest pains. Something wasn't right. I could feel it in the air. As I was leaving out the door, I went over to Momma and hugged her. She stood up and looked at me real stern.

"Carla, remember what I have told you in the past?"

I nodded my head yes in respect.

"Baby, get somebody that wants you. Fuck what you
think you want. Okay?" She continued. "We
always want somebody that don't give a damn about
us and then we try to make them want us."

"Yes, Momma. I will always remember that."

"And be the girl at the club that's in the corner at the
table sitting by herself. Don't be all up in every
niggas face, okay?"

"Momma, I have somebody that wants me.
Her name is Tory. She is the most beautiful person
I have ever met."

"Oh, girl, you need to stop that shit and you know
that. You need to find you a man that will love
you."

"Momma, I don't ever want to deal with a man. I've
seen too much of what they do to women."

"Are you coming back to Fresno for New Year's?" she
said, changing the subject.

"I don't know, Momma. I will try." The cab was
blowing his horn.

"Carla, I just don't feel like I got long here. God
knows I'm tired. I told Him I want Him to take me
on home with Him, so hurry back."

"Momma, just wait, I'm going to move you back to
L.A with me."

"Ain't nothing in L.A. for me."
"I'm working hard. I'm going to paralegal school and
  I am staying cool."

The cab blew again. I grabbed my things and said goodbye to the
kids who were already outside. Momma followed me out.
"Bye, Momma, I'll see you soon. Okay?"
"Yeah. For New Year's" she said again.
"I don't know, Momma. We will see, I told you."

I went back to L.A. in a perplexed way, like I always did when I left
Fresno. I spent the entire time on the bus seeing my mother living
with me. I really enjoyed being with my mother this time. It
wasn't anything major as far as our relationship. It was nice. She
talked this time without her cursing me out. She was still herself,
but I guess she was growing out of dogging me out. I don't know
what it was. I was just glad it wasn't like it had been in the past.

I came home to Ronnie filling chicken orders and moving fast. I
ordered a chicken dinner from her while I was walking through the
back door.
"Hey, man, how was the trip?"
I dragged myself up to the counter where she stood.
"My mother was very sad looking Ronnie. She has
  aged. She looks about sixty years old, and she's only
  forty-eight years old. She's drinking herself to
  death."
"Look, man, don't come back here with that guilt
  stuff now. Don't let her suck the life out of you
  again."
I got mad at Ronnie for her stupid response.
"Look, Ronnie, that's the only mother I have! Right
  or wrong I don't give a damn what she does, she is
  still my mother. She needs help. Everybody has a
  right to get help don't they?"
Ronnie came over to me and held me.
"I'm just saying, Carla, I don't mean to be insensitive

but I don't want you to go into another depression,
blaming yourself. Okay?"
"I don't mean to be snappy, but she is the only
mother I got. She wants me to come up there for
New Year's."
"Are you?"
"I don't know, I kind of want to, but I don't know if I
will. She says she don't have long to live."

I went and dropped my bags in the room. I called Tory when I got
situated. She was happy to hear from me. I was happy to hear her
sweet voice over the telephone. We decided we would get together
that evening. I went over to Tory's house every night and ended up
sleeping over until New Year's Eve. It felt so much better than that
supply room. She would cook dinner everyday. She began to spoil
me. Every day when I got home from work, Tory would have bath
water and food ready. At the end of each night we sat up and
talked for hours.

We became great companions and friends to one another, even to
the point we knew what each other was thinking. I told her one
day how happy she would make a man feel, just by the way she
would treat him and being attentive to his every need as she was to
mine. I had decided to spend New Year's Eve with my mother just
because she asked me to. I couldn't deny her, because it was rare
that she asked me to come see her. I promised Tory that I would
be back before New Year's night was over.

CHAPTER 41

NEW YEAR'S DAY - 1984

I arrived in Fresno at 8:00 a.m. New Year's Day. I didn't call Momma to tell her, I just showed up so she would be surprised again. She was in the kitchen this time, not in her normal window position. I came in the house and sneaked up behind her. She thought I was one of the kids, until she turned around.

"Hey, baby! What are you doing here?" Momma was cooking black-eyed peas, collard greens, turkey and chicken, and homemade peach cobbler.

"I thought you wanted me back for New Year's Day."

"Yeah, but you didn't call nobody to let them know you were coming."

"I wanted to surprise you, Momma."

"Well, you certainly did that."

We walked back to the living room and sat down in our favorite places.

"When are you leaving?"

"Later this evening. I have to be in Los Angeles before midnight to be with my love."

Momma looked surprised, but disappointed.

"Girl, you just like to waste money, don't you?"

"No, Momma. You asked me to come for New Year's and I am here."

Momma went to check on her food and my sisters came in screaming. Catherine, the baby was always so dramatic when she saw me. She always acted like I had a million lollipops hanging over my head. I loved her eyebrows, they were so thick! Then Brenda came in. She kind of favored me I thought. She was excited too. The boys were out with their daddy hunting. These kids were turning eight, nine, ten and eleven years old. Momma got mad at Mr. Calvin every time she had to bring his name up. I guess Mr. Calvin was still cheating on Momma and she couldn't handle it.

She threatened to kill him over and over again. Then finally, she said she was leaving him. I asked Momma where was she going? She told me that she was going somewhere, but she just didn't know where. I told her to please just hold on, and I would move her to Los Angeles with me as soon as I get my place. I graduate in September of this year. She smiled and said okay in disbelief.

"For real, Momma, I'm in paralegal school."

"Girl did you ever finish High School?"

"Yes Momma, remember, you and AlmaFaye didn't come like you said you were."

Momma picked up her cigarette and took a big puff.

"Sometimes you can't do what you want to do in life, girl."

I didn't mean to offend Momma, but I was even more hurt that she couldn't remember that I graduated. I looked at her. She was hurting again. I could tell that she cared about her husband regardless of what they had been through. She still cared for him.

"Oh Momma." I hugged her. "It's all right."

"Let's go to the store" Momma said.

We walked around the corner. I had not done this with Momma in over eight years. As we were walking, I remembered when I was younger and Momma and I walked to the store. I would always run fast toward the store, leaving her behind. Then I hid behind the bush on the side of this big house. I was planning to scare Momma when she would come around the corner. When she got close, I would jump out and scare her. Each time she would jump and try to hit me. I would laugh all the way home.

On the way back from the store Momma asked about my Daddy. I told her he was okay.

"I pretty much stay far away from him though. He never got to know, or understand, me."

"Well, he never got to know me either, so don't feel too bad". We laughed.

After we got back to the house, Momma opened one of her beers and offered me one. I refused this time, because I wanted to treasure my sober moments with her. Out of nowhere, Momma brought up church.

"Yeah, girl, I've been thinking about going back to church."

I looked in amazement.

"What?" I smiled.

Oh God, was there this kind of hope for my mother, I thought to myself. She started telling me how her mother raised fourteen children, and they were all baptized in the river near their house.

"Your uncle Junebug baptized all of us. He was the preacher in the family."

"I go to church too, Momma, but I don't quite feel it there."

"Well, when you go to the right one where Jesus touches you, you'll know," she chuckled to herself.

I was so happy Momma said that. I remembered Tory recorded those Aretha Franklin and Shirley Caesar tapes at home. I couldn't wait to get back home and send them to her.

The silence broke when Momma put down her beer and put out her cigarette. I got scared. I didn't know why, but I had never seen her look at me like this.

"I love you, Carla. You are my baby and will always be my baby, you hear me?"

"Yes," I nodded. I was moved by Mamma's words.

"There are so many things in my life that I didn't handle right. If I could just turn back the hands of times I would."

Her eyes were filling with tears.

"I know I hurt you so many times, baby. I didn't want to and I didn't mean to. I know I ran you away from me and your home. I didn't know what

to do. I know that my husband did what you said
he did to you. I did believe you, Carla, but what
could I do? I didn't know."

She cried even more now.

"I had four children by this man. I had no job and
nothing to call my own. I was to afraid too jump up
and start all over again, and I loved him so much.
But I always believed, you baby. I just didn't know
what to do. I'm so sorry I made your life so
miserable as a child. I know I took that away from
you. I should have left you in Phoenix with your
other sisters and brothers," she smirked.
"I guess that's why I drink so much, it helps me deal
with the pain. You may not have had to experienced
the shit you've gone through if I was there for you.
You didn't need to be out there in those streets
selling your body with those grown folks like that.
Baby, I'm sorry."
I was crying now.

My mother finally spoke out of her heart. Oh how I wished I
could take away the pain, regrets and guilt that were clearly taking
her to her death through that bottle. I knew she meant every word
she spoke. We held each other and cried. I told Momma that I
forgave her and all I ever wanted was for her to love me and be
proud of me. After we sat there a little while longer, I had a chance
to talk to Momma about smoking and drinking less. She told me
that she asked God to bring her on home.

"Carla, I'm tired of this cruel world. All I want to
do is see my babies reach a certain age and then go
on home to be with Jesus."
I didn't like to hear my mother talk like that.
"I tell you one thing, if you go anywhere Momma,
He better take me too because I'm getting in the
coffin with you." We both laughed.

This was the best trip I had ever had in my life, and it all started with her telling me she always believed my side of the story and that she really loved me. She brought back so many years in our lives. I told Momma that I was going to come down more often so we can get closer. Momma told me I should just move back. I told Momma that was a little too much for me right now. We laughed. I left that same evening, going back to Los Angeles. I thought about Mamma's words of confession and apology all the way back home. A part of me was in total disbelief that it even happened, but it did. I felt so much hope for me and my Momma.

I returned to L.A. and went directly to Tory's house. I was tired and decided to get in the bed.

"I am very tired, Tory. This trip was a trip." I went
to sleep for a couple of hours.

When I woke up, Tory asked me questions about my trip to Fresno. I told her it was better than ever.

"My mother expressed to me that she wanted to get
back into church."
"For real?" Tory said.
Tory was so happy for me.

I continued Paralegal school Monday through Thursday six to nine o'clock at night. By the time I got home dinner time was ready. I loved Tory so much. She was everything to me and treated me as if I was everything to her.

Before long, I got enough nerve to ask Tory how did she always have so many hundred dollar bills available to do anything she wanted.

"Tory, if you don't mind me asking, where do you
get so much extra money from?"
"No, baby, I don't mind. Me and my co-worker
have this real lucrative scheme going on where we
bring home at least two thousand to three thousand
dollars extra each month depending on the mail.

And I do mean literally, the Mail."
"Well, can I get in?"
"Consider it done."

Tory sat me down and explained the ropes and the trades of this business, and it was easy as pie. No appearances, just show up and pick up your money.

Tory knew my birthday was coming up and asked me what did I want to do. I told her because of my past I wasn't too excited about birthdays.
"Your mother would actually forget sometimes?"
"Yep. And eventually so did I."
"Well, those days are over. Everyone of your birthdays will be special from now on because you are special as long as you are with me."

Tory took me out to Marina Del Rey to a restaurant called Gully's. It was expensive, but so what. It was fun and we had the money to buy anything we wanted. This was the first birthday that I wasn't so drunk I didn't know where I was. We began to live a pretty extravagant life. We had limousine services when we wanted to do special things. There was nothing that we denied ourselves, because we had the money to buy it. I even started sending my mother more money. I had already been sending her money from my job. She had told me that Mr. Calvin stopped giving her an allowance and was spending all of his money on his women and children. So after I started making extra, she got extra.

Everything in my personal life was so exciting. But working at the law firm was getting boring. Then I learned that everyone else in the firm was getting a raise. Not that I needed the money, but it was the principle. I believed I was doing a great job and everybody else got a raise except for me.
That following Monday, I immediately started looking into the L.A. Times Newspapers for another position. I found something that grabbed my attention. It was for a Secretary/ Receptionist and

I called the office. I spoke with a lady named Stacy Prena. I was scheduled for an interview the next day.

I was offered the job on the spot at Cordubra Corporation. I was told I had a beautiful demeanor and pretty smile. She also said my experience was sufficient for the position and she would personally teach me the secretarial side if I needed help. She offered me a better salary plus benefits. It was great. I walked out of there saying thank you GOD! I went back to work the next day and gave my one-week notice.

After I started my new position, Ronnie wanted to take me out to celebrate. Even though I was seeing less and less of Ronnie these days, since I was living with Tory, we still kept in touch.

Life was really looking up with the fast money, new job, school, an exciting relationship with Tory, and an improved relationship with my mother in the makings. I didn't think it could get any better than this. Then I bought my dream car, Buick Regal just like hers. I remembered Sparkle's car and always said when I get a chance, I was going to buy me a Buick Regal too.

I bought a shining gray Buick Regal. I wished I could show everybody I knew. But more importantly, I wanted to show my mother. I would soon get a chance to show her for the Easter holiday that was coming up. I decided I would drive to Fresno.

Tory wanted to go with me, but I didn't think it was the right time. I was still ashamed of how my mother looked for her age. The liquor had really made her look old and rough. I told her that I preferred this time with my mother alone. Instead, I contacted an old associate to hopefully travel with me to Fresno in my new car - Viola, Barbara's sister. I had kept her telephone number over the years in my phone book. Viola would often go to Fresno to visit. I was hoping she was planning on going to Fresno for Easter and we could car pool. I called and she answered. She was so happy to hear from me. As a matter of fact, she was planning on going to

Fresno and didn't mind car pooling with me. Tory didn't like that too much, but I didn't know how to explain to her that I was ashamed of my mother's condition and the way she looked.

EASTER IN FRESNO - 1984

Easter morning came. Viola was so happy to see me. She said, "Girl, what are you doing these days?" I filled her in briefly on my life. She told me how happy she was that I wasn't tied up with Barbara and Bobby anymore. She told me that she use to look at me and cry inside.

"You were no more than twelve or thirteen years old."
"I know, Viola," I said regretfully.
"I always wondered what was my crazy sister doing running the streets with a child like you. Well, thank God those days are over."

It was great and kind of scary. I had never driven such a long distance in my life. But this was cool, and my Regal drove so smoothly. We arrived in Fresno in good time. I dropped her off at her mother's who lived across the street from AlmaFaye, and so I decided to just go over to AlmaFaye's house first. I was excited. I parked the car as close to the house as possible. I was going to be showing off. I walked in the door and quess who walks out from the back room? My mother was coming out of one of the rooms. She didn't look like the woman I had seen only four months ago. She had aged and she was so tiny. Momma came closer to me, looking real weird.

"AlmaFaye is not home right now, but don't I know you from somewhere?"

I could have died. My mother was face to face with me and didn't recognize who I was.

"Momma, it's me, Carla!"
She looked at me again and said, "Damn, sure is you! I know I'm sleepy now, for sure."

It wasn't sleepiness in my mother's eyes. I felt so crushed to see my mother like that. I didn't know what was wrong, but I knew something wasn't right.

"Momma, what's been going on?" She pulled out a
cigarette and lit it.
"Nothing much. I finally left Mr. Calvin. I told you
I was. I left him."
"Oh, Momma, that's good. I'm glad for you."
I didn't know where to go from there. I sat at the
table quiet. She would drift and have a blank look
on her face.
"Momma, I got a new car."
"Oh yeah."
"Yeah, come on and see it."

She got up very slowly. She was almost bent over. What was wrong with my mother? What happened to her? Her eyes were wrinkled. Her hair was almost snow white with gray. She looked about ten years older than the last time I saw her. I took Momma outside and she smiled. I could still see her glow underneath all those burdens and pains. Momma had been through some stuff. Her appearance was totally different. I noticed her not having any teeth. We got back in the house and Momma told me that she had all her teeth pulled.

"They were giving me problems, so I told the dentist
to pull all of the sons of bitches. I got some false
teeth now."

I cringed at the thought. She grabbed her purse and pulled out a jar to show me the dentures. I almost got sick.

"Momma, shouldn't they be somewhere in the
bathroom?"

AlmaFaye walked in the door. I was furious. I jumped up out of my seat and went toward AlmaFaye.

"What the hell is going on with my mother,
AlmaFaye?"

"Carla, we have to talk, so much has happened since
you left the last time. Momma has really been going
down on a daily basis."

I followed AlmaFaye back to her bedroom. Mr. Calvin is still
cheating on Momma real heavy, and she can't handle it. Sometimes
he don't come home, and the woman he is cheating on Momma
with is my next door neighbor. I was giving a party here one night
when Mr. Calvin and Momma came over. Mr. Calvin went to the
store with the woman and never came back. Momma suspected it
then and one day Catherine saw them kissing. Momma hasn't been
the same since. She's not eating, and has been getting sick all the
time with those seizures."
        "Where are the kids?"
        "Well, Edwin is the only one here with Momma all
        the time, when he is not in school. He really is close
        to Momma. He don't let her out of his sight."
        "Damn AlmaFaye, Momma didn't know who I was
        when I walked in the door. Do you hear me?"
        AlmaFaye stood there shaking her head side to side.
        "Momma didn't recognize me. How come?" I
        started crying.
        "How can she destroy herself like this in less than
        four months? Why didn't anyone tell me she was
        deteriorating like this?"
        "Carla, what was you going to do for Momma? I
        can't hardly do nothing for her. You know how
        Momma is and how stubborn she gets."
        "Why don't you put her in an alcoholic hospital?" I
        said.
        "Because Momma ain't gonna go to no goddamn
        alcoholic hospital. She's here with me."

I asked her for a joint and told her I was going out to my car. I
smoked it outside in the car and took a beer with me while I
listened to music.

I drove around Fresno. As I was driving, I could not think of one place that I enjoyed in this city. There was not one street that brought back any damn good memories. I wished that the whole city could just burn down. I saw certain people that I went to school with hanging out near cars in the yard of homes. I saw familiar faces hanging out at the liquor store. There were some faces I had never seen, but they appeared to be caught up in the same riff raff of the streets. Fresno was so small you kind of knew everybody and their mother. I was so tempted to go check out Bobby and Barbara, but I had to fight that feeling. I wanted to just go somewhere and escape.

I made it back to AlmaFaye's house. Momma had gone to bed and AlmaFaye was watching TV. Momma being asleep was not like her at all. She was a hell raiser and a partying woman. She was not making too much fuss these days. I guess she wasn't feeling too well. I went and laid next to her while she slept, and talked to God. I told the Lord that I would change my lifestyle if he would save my mother. I will do anything, Lord. Just save her. I am just now getting to know her. Please save her.

I got up the next day and Momma was up early sitting in the living room, sober. She sounded much better, but still looked the same. She and AlmaFaye were having coffee.

"So I didn't know who you were yesterday, hah?" Momma said.

"Not at first Momma," I said.

"Well, I guess I had enough to drink or either I'm getting old, hah?"

"Yeah. Momma, I brought some tapes down for you because the last time we talked you said you were getting into the church. I brought you Amazing Grace and A Change Is Gonna Come by Aretha Franklin."

She smiled. Momma wasn't the fast talking loud mouth that I left in Fresno months ago. She was very slow speaking and reserved.

Could her heart be that heavy? I didn't know.

Sunday came sooner than ever. Momma was sounding real good to me. We talked and I sang "Amazing Grace" with her that night, and that's what we went to sleep on together.

The next day, Momma asked me to come back down for Mother's Day.

      "We will see, Momma."
      "Come on back, Carla."
      "Momma, we went through this for New Year's
      Day."
      "Come on now, please," she begged.
      "Momma, I have been out here too many times this
      year."
      "Ain't no such thing as being out here too many
      times, this is your home!"
      "We'll see, why don't you let me come out in June."
      "No, I want you here for Mother's Day."
      After arguing with Momma. I told her I would
      come.

I left Fresno, more determined to get my mother out of that city before she killed herself or lost her mind. I picked up Viola and we drove back to Los Angeles. I thought about the promises I had made to God for Him to help my mother. I told Him I would change my life and do better by Him.

After dropping Viola off at her house, I went straight to Tory's house. Tory was cooking. I told her how much I missed her.
      "Carla, you look tired. How are you doing?"
      "Mentally or physically?" I asked.

Tory brought me a drink of Hennessy to the table. I picked up the glass and went into the bedroom and turned on the TV. I fell out before I knew it. Later that night, I got up and went into the living room where Tory was. I sat on the couch, thinking about what I was going to do and how was I going to change my life for the good like I told God. I needed to help my mother badly before it was too late. Tory and I sat up and watched television after the girls went to sleep. I told her I needed to talk with her about something. I cut off the TV.

"I need to move out."

"What do you mean?" Tory asked.

"I mean, I need to move back at Ronnie's place. I can't fully explain it now, but it's something that I agreed to do with God."

"Carla, I understand that you are hurting right now about something, but what about us?"

"I will still call you and come over, but I just need some space to myself."

"What do you mean you will still call me and come over? Does this mean it's over and now we're just friends?"

"Maybe. I just need to go think and then I promise I will be more clear."

"Carla, is there something I can do to help?" she asked.

"No baby, just try to understand right now. That's really all."

Tory could did many things to make my world beautiful, but she couldn't make this decision for me right now. I knew my lifestyle was not pleasing to God. I also knew I told God I would give up my lifestyle to the one person that made me feel important, appreciated and loved. If God would just heal my mother and let her come out here to live with me everything would be fine.

I kept my space from Tory for about a week, with a casual call here and there. I went back into meditating to see if that would strengthen me to stay away from Tory, the clubs, and getting high. I couldn't stop smoking and drinking but everything else I guess was okay.

A couple of weeks went by and I had to see Tory. I missed her so
much and wanted to be in her presence. I had been calling her and
hanging up the phone once she answered. Hearing her voice was
good enough. However, I needed more than just to hear her voice.
I called and invited her to lunch.

"Hello."

"Hi, Carla. How are you doing?"

I could tell in her voice she was happy to hear from
me.

"Do you think we can have lunch today?"

"Sure, if you want to."

"I will pick you up in a couple of hours."

"Okay. I'll see you then."

I hung up the phone and my heart started beating real fast. I was so
nervous. Almost felt like a junkie going back to the dope house for
another hit. Could I really just see her for a moment and then go
back to my corner of the world? I would try. I showered and
dressed. It was Sunday afternoon and all the restaurants would be
packed with church folks. I decided to go to the pier to give us
more time together and talk.

After ordering two marguerites and our main entree, I let Tory
know how good it was to see her and how difficult it has been not
seeing her. She was very quiet and reserved. I thanked her for
giving me the space that I needed to work out my convictions and
direction. She remained silent. Then she finally told me that it
had been hard not seeing me in the evenings and spending time
together.

"Tory, can I plan a trip for you this Mother's Day?"

"I thought you were going to Fresno to visit your
mother."

"Well, I have decided not to do that. Instead I
would like to treat you to an innocent evening away,
if that's okay with you."

She paused and looked very suspicious. "Innocent?
May I ask who will be present?"

"Just you and I."

"Innocent" she repeated.

"Okay, you have my word. I will not do anything
that you will not consent to." I laughed.

"No, seriously, I will not invade your emotions. I just
want to spend a little time with you."

"Well, I guess that won't hurt," she said hesitantly.

We finished our lunch and walked by the water before getting back into the car. I took her home and we said good-bye as friends would do, without any intimate gestures. I thought that was the hardest thing I could ever do. I didn't realize how much I was so intimately attached to her until I chose to refrain from any emotional and physical intimacy. But I did it, and I was glad!

CHAPTER 42

Trip To Catalina Island
(MOTHER'S DAY, MAY 1984)

For the next few weeks I kept tabs on my mother and tried to prepare her for me not coming down. She was still asking me to come, but I tried to let her know I would not be coming this time. It was hard to tell Momma no when she wanted something bad. I was determined this time not to fall weak to her. When I hung up the phone I said I would send Momma something real nice and expensive. I went back to my room and started thinking about Tory as I often did. I wanted to do something for her, something exciting and mysterious. After thinking for a while, I decided to plan a trip to Catalina Island on Mother's Day for Tory.

I told her I was taking her to dinner on the pier out at San Pedro, near Long Beach. She went for it. We arrived there and I parked in the parking lot next to this boat where people were standing in line.

I looked at her and said, "Are you ready?"

"For what, Carla?"

"A little boat ride to Catalina Island."

Tory was so surprised and overjoyed she could not speak. We were on our way.

We boarded the boat and began our trip. We ordered drinks as the woman came around. I was more nervous than anybody on the boat, because I didn't know how to swim. Then I learned quickly that the worst thing I could have done was to take a drink. I got even sicker as the boat felt as if it was rocking up and down and all around. Finally we arrived and I motioned for a driver to take us to the hotel where we had reservations.

The trip was so exciting and fun. We did everything we wanted to do on that little island. I was really doing good during the day as far as keeping my distance and not violating her emotions. But by night time I failed my promise not to touch her. I wanted to make love to her so badly, and when I could not resist any longer she let me make love to her the entire night. I found myself loving her body from head to toe, as if I couldn't get enough.

The days were controllable, but the nights were pointless in terms of maintaining control and refraining from the intimacy that we both wanted so much.

The last morning was Mother's Day, and I thought about my mother. I called her from the hotel room before we checked out, and she was back at her house. I told her I was sorry I didn't make it down. She told me that no one sent her a card, including me. I felt so damn bad. I forgot to mail her package before I left for Catalina. It was home in my room. But that didn't make my mother feel any better. "Momma, I'm sorry. I love you very much." She wanted to get off the phone, and told me to have a good time wherever I was.

When Tory and I got back to Long Beach, I took her home. Then I went to the restaurant to talk to Ronnie. I was sad and depressed, because I disappointed my mother. I walked into the restaurant and Ronnie had a place filled with hungry people.

"Hey, man, help me knock some of these orders out."

"Sure, you gonna pay me if I do?" I was only joking. Within twenty minutes it was empty. Ronnie asked how my weekend went with Tory. I told her it was all right.

"Why the long face then," she asked.

I told her I was hurt about disappointing my mother by not spending Mother's Day with her.

"I have to do something, Ronnie."

"What are you going to do?" She lit a cigarette and passed it to me.

"I don't know, but I want her with me. I don't want her in Fresno anymore. That's it, I need to get my own apartment. I can afford my own place."

"Yeah, with all that damn money you and Tory

collect each month you can afford a couple of
places."

I got excited. How come I had not thought about that before? I
guess we were spending and splurging so much, I never thought to
do something so meaningful with the money. I could have had her
out here much earlier in her own place. Ronnie recommended
that I go grab a newspaper.

Within a few days, I found a perfect apartment and called the
landlord. A middle-aged woman answered the phone and I asked
if I could come see the place. She set up an appointment for the
next day and I was there. It was so cute. It was a one bedroom,
and kind of reminded me of the place my mother and I use to stay
in when I was a little girl. Only difference, this apartment had a
bathroom on the inside, and it was pretty straight. It was perfect!
I asked the woman if I could have it. She told me she had to check
my references and would get back with me by the end of the week.

I would go get her! I left there praying hard. I asked God to please
let me get this place and then I could move my Momma in with
me. Then Momma wouldn't drink and smoke as much. She
wouldn't have the some-timey friends that only hung around her
when she had money to buy drinks. I would buy her new clothes
and help her change her entire image.

By the time the people in Fresno saw her again she would be a
brand new woman. I was so happy. I wouldn't have to worry about
her anymore way down there where I couldn't be near her.

A few days later, the phone rang. It was the landlord. She told me
everything checked out and I could have the place in two weeks.
She had some work to do on the place. I shouted and screamed
thank you God! Oh it was the best news I had all year. I called
Tory, and she was shocked that I was even looking but was
immediately glad for me. She asked if I had any furniture. I told
her I had a couch and that was it. She suggested that I do a house

warming and I would get everything that I needed.

"Cool, that's what I will do," I said.

I went back to my room and was so happy.

Ronnie called out again and said, telephone. I got up to answer it.

"Hello."

"Carla, this is AlmaFaye."

"Hey, what's happening, AlmaFaye?"

"I wanted to call you because Momma has been in
the hospital in intensive care."

"What do you mean? How long has she been there?"

"Well, it's going on a week now. But they said she is
coming home tomorrow."

"What the hell you mean she has been there for a
week, and they said she is going home tomorrow.
Why didn't somebody tell me that she was in the
hospital AlmaFaye? How come no one called me?"

"Well, Carla, they kept saying she was going home
the next day, so it was no need to bother you."

"What happened, why is she in there?"

"She had another seizure and now she has pneumonia.
The doctor kept telling Momma not to drink with
her pills but she would keep on drinking anyway."

"Well, please keep me posted." I hung up the phone.

A few moments later, the phone rang. Again, Ronnie called me
back out. It was AlmaFaye.

"Carla, I just got a phone call from the hospital.
Momma has been rushed back into intensive care."

"What! I'm on my way!"

"Okay, I'm going back up to the hospital right now,"
AlmaFaye said.

Ronnie stood there listening until I got off the
phone.

"I'm going to Fresno, Ronnie."

"Damn man, when?"

"Right now. My mother is in intensive care."

I picked up the phone again to call my sister Sharon at her job. I told her what was happening and asked if she could go with me to Fresno. She said, pick me up. Sharon was always there for me when I needed her.

I picked up Sharon, gassed up, and we were on our way to Fresno. My sister Sharon was a Christian now. She wasn't partying with Mable and the gang anymore. I was mad and bitching all the way to the freeway. She tried to calm me down. We began to hit Friday night freeway traffic, which was bumper to bumper. We were in traffic for the following two hours. By the time we reached Magic Mountain the sun was down. We were finally on a smooth flow with traffic, when all of a sudden the car started slowing down. I put it in D-2, thinking perhaps these steep mountains were giving my Regal a challenge. That helped for a short while. As time passed on, it got darker. All we could see was in front of us, on the sides of us, and tall mountains all around. Then something started happening to the car again. I saw smoke come out from under my hood. I hit the dashboard with my hands.

"I forgot to check the water and oil!" I shouted.

The car was overheating. We were in the middle of the grapevine and there were no gas stations for miles.

"It's time to start praying," Sharon said.

It was 10:10 p.m. and getting late. I didn't feel like praying. I just wanted to go. I needed to get to Fresno now. I was scared for my mother. Sharon said, "Just believe God, Carla, okay? The car is going to start again." Then she said she believed God wanted her to pray right then and there for my mother. She started pleading the blood of Jesus over her life. We prayed for about thirty minutes. Cars were passing us and no one ever stopped. Sharon kept on praying. Every now and then throughout the prayer, Sharon would stop and say, "Now try to start it." The third time she said it the car started up. I began to praise God. She was already praising God. We drove for twenty more minutes and got to a gas station at the bottom of the grapevine. The man looked under the hood and it exploded in smoke

"I don't know how your car got here. It has no water, no oil, and is low on transmission fluid," he said.

The car was hot, but he fixed it and we were on our way.

CHAPTER 43

Trip To Fresno
(JUNE 15, 1984)

Two hours later we made it to Fresno. I went directly to
AlmaFaye's house and ran out leaving Sharon in the car. I walked
in. AlmaFaye was sitting in the living room in front of the TV. She
turned and looked at me, her eyes worn from crying.

"Hi Faye." I knew something was wrong.

"How are you doing?"

"She's gone, Carla," she said without looking up at
me.

"What, Faye?"

"Momma is dead. She died at 10:40 p.m."

It was the same time that my car stopped on us and Sharon was
praying for Momma. I didn't say anything to AlmaFaye. I
couldn't. I turned around and went back outside to meet Sharon.
She was coming near the apartment.

"How's your mother, baby?"

"It's too late. It's too late."

Sharon grabbed me and held me.

"I'm so sorry, sis," Sharon whispered.

We walked back in the house. I went over to
AlmaFaye and hugged her. She held me so tight.

The pain of the reality slipped in and out of my mind. I looked at
AlmaFaye, hoping she would tell me that she was just playing.

"We are not going to the hospital to see Momma,
hah?"

AlmaFaye just shook her head, no.

"AlmaFaye, maybe we should just go there. Maybe
they lied to you."

"Why, Carla? She's dead. Why are we going?"

"She's not! I want to see her. I didn't get to see her,
damn it. It's not fair! You said she was in fucking
intensive care! You didn't say she was dying,

AlmaFaye. You said they were going to let her
come home."
AlmaFaye grabbed me and just held me as I cried
on her shoulder.
"AlmaFaye, I don't understand! What happened?
Tell me!"

AlmaFaye was quiet for a long time. Then she pulled me away from
her and re-positioned herself on the couch so that she was now
facing me.
"When I got off the phone with you earlier this
evening, I went to the hospital when I called you,
and saw her."
AlmaFaye stopped and laughed.
"What's funny?" I asked.
"Momma asked about you and wanted to know if
you were here yet. I told her, no not yet. Carla, I
didn't know you were on your way. She asked for
you as if she knew you were coming. The doctors
needed to give her some more medication and asked
me to leave the room. That's when Momma started
shaking her head no. I could tell she didn't want
me to leave that room. Momma couldn't speak to
me because the tubes were everywhere from her
mouth to her arms. I wish I knew what she was
trying to say. By the time I got back to my house
the nurse was calling me to get back down there
because Momma had suffered a heart attack. When
I got there they told me she had just died."
I started crying again.
"Look Carla, we have to be strong for the kids.
Okay?"
I was crying hard.
"We have to pull ourselves together."
"Where in the hell is Mr. Calvin?"
"He's at home."
"What is he saying about this?"

"He said he didn't know Momma was that bad off."
"It's his fault she died, it's his fault," I screamed.
"Come on, Carla, we can deal with that later. Come
on and let's get ready for bed so you can get some
rest."

Sharon told me that she was going to spend the night over Aunt
LaDonna's house. She hugged me and told me to call her if I
needed anything. I kept waking up in the middle of the night
crying and then crying myself back to sleep. AlmaFaye was right
there next to me.

I woke up the next morning and went in the front room where I
heard AlmaFaye cleaning up. I looked into her eyes and saw that I
was not dreaming the night before. Momma was gone. I needed
to see the kids and see how they were doing. I drove over to Mr.
Calvin's and the kids were not there, they were over to Aunt Doris'
house. I went over there. Calvin Jr. and Edwin were acting like
they were strong, the girls did not. They started to cry when they
saw me. I grabbed them and held them. God it hurt me so much
to see them go through this at such a young age. I knew my time
for crying was out for a long time. There were four children under
me that needed strong hands and arms. I asked them if they
wanted to go with me and they said, " yes." I took them back to
AlmaFaye's with me. There were calls that needed to be made.

I called my job. I told them that my mother had passed away.
They were very sorry and said if there was anything that they could
do, not to hesitate to call. Momma had an insurance policy, but she
had borrowed on it so much that what she had left was going to
take a few weeks to process for financing her funeral. We had to
get money and fast. We suspected the funeral to happen in the
next week. We tried to plan for Saturday, but that wasn't possible.
It had to be on Friday. So there was lots to do with such little time.

AlmaFaye contacted everybody out of town on Mamma's side.
Now I had to go back to Los Angeles to prepare to be in Fresno for

the next week. There was so much to be done. I didn't have a long period of time to dwell on the fact that my mother had died. I knew she had died, but I was so consumed in making preparations and making sure everybody was doing okay and holding up. AlmaFaye and I agreed that our time was after the funeral, after we got this together.

That night AlmaFaye, some friends of hers, and I sat around the table drinking. We got sloppy drunk and started having confession time. We were very drunk, but somehow started talking about getting our lives together for God. I brought up the subject. I told everybody that God had been telling me to be right for years. He kept warning me, but I've been too damn selfish. My sister laughed.

"What, you are giving up, women," she said.
"Yep, you watch."

I took a gulp of Old English 800. I hadn't drank that since gin and coke was introduced into my life.

"As soon as all this is over, you will have a new baby sister."
"Yeah, I like to see the day when you give up women."
"Yeah, I like to see the day you give up dipping snuff too. If it ain't a sin, it should be."

Every person took their turns in talking about their wrongs and the weaknesses that they knew was sin. Then it got real quiet. AlmaFaye started talking about Momma and her crazy ways. She talked about how Momma use to aggravate the hell out of people, including us. We laughed until we were crying.

That night, I slept under AlmaFaye. I crawled up under her like a little sister would. I needed my big sister to be my Momma.

I drove back to L.A. with Sharon that Sunday. We got ready and I told AlmaFaye that I would be back tomorrow. I knew I had money waiting for me in Los Angeles. I knew there were money deals that were suppose to come in over the weekend before this happened.

We arrived in Los Angeles and I dropped Sharon off at home. I thanked her for being there. I knew Ronnie wouldn't comfort me like I needed, and I didn't want to hear about that damn meditation process. I packed some clothes for the next few weeks, ran a couple of errands, and went over to Tory's to spend the night. It was kind of late when I got to her house. I came in with my key, took off my clothes, and got in the bed with her. As soon as I did, she woke up and knew it was me.

"Hi baby." I shook her softly.
"Hi, how are you doing, Carla?"
"I guess I'm doing all right. I feel kind of weird.
Really not sure how I feel."

The tears began to roll out of my eyes. She held me and said, "It's okay, cry, it's okay." I fell asleep in her arms.

Around 3 a.m. I woke up sweating and my eyes were wet with tears. I was crying about Momma in my sleep. I shook Tory and asked her to get up with me to have coffee. She got up and put on the water. "Are you okay?" she asked. I grabbed my cigarette pack and lit a cigarette, I just couldn't sleep.

I had so much on my mind. I needed to talk about some pretty important things. She brought the coffee to the table. I told her that I needed to make a major change in my life once I returned to Los Angeles. I really needed to get out of the life. She looked very sad, but tried to be understanding. I confessed to her that I knew God was calling me to do the right thing and that's to live for Him. I made a vow with him and still have not kept it, but I was going to now. She asked me what kind of vow did I make with God. I told her that I promised Him if he would save my mother I would stop living this sinful lifestyle.

"Tory, I didn't keep my word. So, why should He

keep his?"
"Carla, please don't blame yourself for your mother's
death."
"Why not? Doesn't it make sense?"
"No. It was time for your mother to go. You or
nobody else couldn't stop it. Carla, you have to live
for you, not for your mother."

I was too angry to hear her words no matter how much sense they
made. I was tying my mother's deliverance and happiness to me,
as I had always done. When something went wrong, I blamed me.
Tory didn't say any more. She just sat next to me and softly
rubbed my back. All I knew is that my mother was dead. I began
to feel something I had never felt in my life and that was a total
disconnection from my mother now. The abuse and the name
calling didn't separate me like her death did. I felt part of me was
missing and the voided space was so real. I didn't realize the strong
biological connection between a daughter and a mother. I
apologized to Tory for being so damn confused and crazy.
    "You don't deserve this, Tory. I know you don't."

She told me that I was right in wanting to do right and she should
have that same strong conviction too, but she loved me too much. I
felt the same way.

After a couple of days of tying loose ends at home, with my job,
and the apartment, I hopped on the freeway to go back to Fresno.
I traveled by myself this time. I left around 5:00 in the morning.
It was crisp, but not terribly cold. I enjoyed the peace I experienced
in the car on the way. I took the scenic route. It was a dream drive
filled with peace and evidence of a God-made pathway. I had
never experienced such peace while driving. I began to reflect on
my mother. I tried not to because I didn't want to get too upset
while I was driving. The thoughts of her kept coming to me. I kept
remembering the last time I saw Momma and how she kept asking
me to please come back home for Mother's Day. If I would have
come home, that would have been the last time I saw her instead of

Easter. I got mad at myself.

"How come the hell you just couldn't go back home
like Momma asked you, huh?" I asked myself.
"No one is more important than your mother!"
I could now relate to my mother's words when she
told me.
"If I could just turn back the hands of time on some
of the decisions I made, I would do them
differently. How I understood those words so
much now. I promised to take Momma to dinner
when I was there for Easter, but I got so depressed
about her drinking that I just went for a ride and got
high the rest of the time I was there to avoid the pain
of her condition. I thought about the roses I gave
Viola, which I really bought for Momma, but she
never got them. I was going to buy her some more
once I got to Fresno, but I never got around to it. I
had every opportunity to see her again and I didn't
think it was important this time around. I kept
asking God, why now?"
"Why now Lord? You know I wanted to go get her
and take care of her. I was about to graduate from
paralegal school. I wanted her to be proud of me
and see me do some positive things in life. God, I
wanted so badly to take care of my mother."
I then started talking to my mother. I told her how
sorry I was for letting her down and not being there
for her when she needed me the most.

When I finally got to AlmaFaye's house, she was in the kitchen
writing stuff for the obituary. She told me that just about
everybody on Mamma's side of the family had confirmed except
for her oldest brother JayHue. She also told me that Sadie and
Tarah were in town and were staying over to Aunt Mercy's house. I
asked about Gable. She said he was taking it the worst. She was
real worried about him. I learned that they wouldn't let Tyrone, Jr.
out of prison to attend the funeral. I know that must have hurt. I

asked how the younger kids were doing. AlmaFaye said she hadn't seen them. Mr. Calvin kept them over Aunt Doris' house to be with her kids while he worked.

I sat down with AlmaFaye to complete the order of the funeral services. I gave her Tory's niece's name to add as one of the singers. AlmaFaye said, the viewing of the body would start tonight. I asked her when were we going as a family? She said, tonight. We planned out the entire week of things to do. Tonight we were viewing the body, tomorrow we were shopping for Mamma's clothes, and Friday was the funeral.

AlmaFaye had a new boyfriend. She had broken up with Darnell. She told me that her boyfriend's name was Phil. He came over to give us a ride to the funeral home. This would be the first time I saw Tarah and Sadie in years. I couldn't understand why they weren't with us when we were finalizing Mamma's funeral arrangements.

We walked in the funeral home and it had an eerie silence and stillness about it. I didn't like it. I felt sick. I glanced at the sign-in book and saw several names of Mamma's running buddies. Then my sisters, Tarah and Sadie, embraced us as we walked in. They went in first and AlmaFaye and I followed. We were holding onto our brother Gable, who had arrived as soon as we were walking toward the back. We knew Gable would take it real hard. Gable buckled to his knees when he saw the coffin from a distance. We pulled him up. "Come on, Gable," AlmaFaye said. We escorted him to the coffin.

We stood and looked at her. Mamma's face looked like Momma. Her hair was pressed and curled, and the gray shone like silver. Momma also had on a lot of makeup. She would never wear that much on her face. Her hands were crossed and very wrinkled. Gable reached down in the casket to hug Momma and began to cry uncontrollably. I could not handle seeing my brother so torn up. AlmaFaye and I had to pull Gable away. Then he ran out of the funeral home. AlmaFaye just stood there with a strong expression on her face. She kept complimenting on how well Momma looked. So did the other girls. I remembered Momma telling me during New Year's that she was tired and wanted to be with her Jesus. I told her I would get in the coffin with her. I wanted to do that so bad. I wanted to lay down right next to my mother and hold her. We all went outside together. Tarah and Sadie were leaving with our cousin, Mercy. I asked them to come to AlmaFaye's house tonight.

After we all got back to AlmaFaye's house, I couldn't hold my peace. I asked Sadie and Tarah how come they looked like they were not affected by Mamma's death. Tarah was the first to speak up.

"Carla, you must understand we loved our mother too, but she didn't raise us. She raised you. We lived with our Daddy and his wife."
"We didn't know Momma like you did," Sadie added.

Little did they know, I really didn't know my mother either. I ached to know her and we were just now beginning to have the relationship I always dreamed of having.

I guess I understood what Tarah meant and just chilled from there. We talked about the distance between all of Mamma's children and how it really shouldn't be this way. I brought down tapes and albums.

"Let's have a theme song from this gathering."

Gable was the singer and dancer in the family. Tarah was also a dancing machine along with myself. AlmaFaye didn't dance too much. Sadie mainly just shook her bootie a lot. I put on the album by Tina Turner, "Let's Stay Together." We all got up on our feet, sang the song to each other, and bonded. We hugged and we cried together. We continued bonding with each other the remainder of the evening.

CHAPTER 44

THE FUNERAL SERVICE

The cars pulled up outside the door. Two long stretch limousines. Everybody had to meet at AlmaFaye's house, including Mr. Calvin. Everybody showed up one by one. Gable and his old lady Linda, my brothers and sisters -- Sadie, Tarah, Edwin, Brenda, Catherine and Calvin Jr. When I looked at them, it broke my heart to see them have to face such tragedy so young.

There were so many cars at the church when we arrived. The funeral service was held at the St. Rest Baptist Church where Momma took me to church one night when I was a little girl. That's where Momma and Olivia took a drink out of the bottle before they went in.

I was feeling awfully weak this particular morning. I felt my strength seeping out by the tons. I didn't know if I could make this trip or not. It had been going so well, seeing Momma everyday at the funeral home, but now I knew this was leading to her final resting place. The room was filled with about two hundred and fifty people. I was able to take a glance at people as we walked in. I saw my Daddy with his wife, Daddy and Ms. Estee, Lewis Burton and his wife.

Each one of Mamma's men, including her husband, was there in support of her home going. I thought that was so amazing. It made me feel so much better to see them. I even saw Barbara and Bobby (who I didn't expect to see) and other friends of mine. The soloist from the church was coming to the microphone to sing the first song, which was not on the program.

The music started and it sounded so familiar. I knew that tune. It was so familiar. Then I heard it. It was " I'm Going Up Yonder," one of my favorite songs. I remembered listening to that song on Sundays when I was a child. It touched me in the same way when I was hurting. But it was more special now. You could hear moans throughout the place. Then you heard my Aunty just haul off and scream here and there. I didn't look up for a long while.

Tory's niece was getting up to sing. She sang, "Yes Jesus Loves Me". I had never heard it sung like that. It was so beautiful, and that was my breaking point, I guess, because I was thinking about Momma and myself in conjunction with her life. I knew Jesus was there for me, somehow and someway. He was there for Momma. I began to remember how Momma used to talk about her God, and how she was baptized in the Louisiana River by her brother Junebug, and how God loves her. She would tell me from time to time that she was going back to God. Did you Momma, I asked myself. Did you go back to God before you left here? My heart ached, hoping the answer was yes. The Pastor got up to give the eulogy after several songs were sung. Out the corner of my eyes, I saw Mr. Calvin wiping at his eyes. AlmaFaye was crying, and so were the kids. I couldn't hold back anymore. It was time for someone to comfort us. We all were holding each other. The Pastor made his eulogy short, emphasizing the importance of being ready and right with God. I had to think about my life again.

Then it was time for the parting viewing. The organist started playing "Well Done." The soloist sang softly. They opened the casket and there was Momma. Oh, how beautiful that baby blue satin gown looked on her! How beautiful her hair shone with the streaks of gray! How wonderful she was made up! We had to stand to go around and view the body. Her sisters went first and then the children. My sisters were ahead of me. Each one touched Momma, including Gable. When I got to Momma I didn't want to leave her in that casket. I knew this was the day I would never see her again. My sisters came up to get me and comfort me. We were ushered back into the car to go to the cemetery. I kept my eyes on the car ahead carrying my mother's body that was about to take her to the grave site. The pain was unexplainable and unbearable.

After we arrived, we were escorted to seats that were pre-set in front of an open grave. I kept my head buried in my sister AlmaFaye's arm. The pastor said a few words, after which they dropped the body in the ground. Suddenly I felt the depth of the separation between my mother and me. As long as she was at the funeral home, she was still here with me. It felt as if, as long I could see her everyday and just sit there next to her in that casket she was still with me. She was gone now, and I won't ever be able to see her face on this earth again.

My little sisters and brothers were devastated. I couldn't bare to see them go through so much pain and agony. How could they go through something like this so young, God? Why do they have to experience this kind of trauma at such a young age, I asked Him. It's not fair, and they don't understand. They are not strong enough for this, God. This is cruel for any kid to have to experience. Why, God, why? Couldn't you have waited until they were grown like me? I kept questioning God as if He would stop it and change it back to normal as I watched their tender souls cry out for a mother that would not return. I hurt for them. I could see the longing and the confusion. I felt helpless. I could do nothing for them to take that pain away. It was out of our hands. Afterwards, we were escorted back to the cars to be taken back home. I turned backwards, watching the grave site until I could not see it in my view any longer. I was trying to keep her beautiful picture forever in my mind, trying to remember the glistening gray and the subtle smile on her face.

Most folks did not go to the grave site, but went directly to the reception hall at the church. I met my aunts and cousins from out of town for the first time. We also went around thanking everyone that came. I saw the old people in Mamma's life -- Ersha (the Contractor of the grape fields) and Rosey (the woman who called the foster home on us when we were little kids). My old Sunday School Teacher, who I didn't recognize at all from Mt. Pleasant Baptist Church, was there. I didn't know who this woman was, but she knew who I was. She told me that she use to teach me about the love of Jesus.

Tory and her niece came to the reception with us. I had not spoken with her all day, but I knew she was there. I wasn't ready to talk with her now. She came by to let me know that they were driving to San Francisco today and would be back tomorrow. I nodded and said, "Okay, give me a call." My sisters and I continued to talk and mingle with people for a couple of hours. Then it was time to go home. The day was over. The sympathy remarks and comments were all said and done. "Let's go home, sis," I told AlmaFaye. We asked Mr. Calvin if the kids could come with us. He said yes. Mr. Calvin was hurting and I hurt for him, because I knew he felt bad. I knew he felt alone and hopeless too. All the hell he and Momma went through together. Fifteen years of their lives that had been shared, for better or worse. Their worse started before their better. I could not reach out to him like I wanted to, but I did hug him and tell him, "God bless you." I fought the feelings of compassion that my heart was trying to have for him. I hated it and didn't know why it was there. I felt guilty when I hugged him. I guess the old stigma that was drilled in my mind from Momma was still there. In a very weird way, I felt close to Mr. Calvin, even closer to him than my real Daddy. I couldn't understand it, but I did.

Later on that night we all got together for the last time. Everyone was leaving out the next morning, going back home. Daddy and Ms. Estee came to AlmaFaye's house, and so did others. We played music, talked, and got drunk. Tyrone was the Daddy of three of Mamma's children. The one who allowed me to carry his last name until I was ten. He talked about Momma, saying how whorish and crazy she was. I got mad at him. He told me it was only the truth. But why talk about her like that now? I didn't feel that was nice, nor appropriate. I only wanted to hear good stuff about my mother, even if it had to be squeezed out of the memory of somebody.

    "She had her ways, but that wasn't all of her," I said,
       not able to speak any further.

The night ended and everyone went home. What a long night! I sat in bed looking at the ceiling, feeling kind of numb. I was wishing to myself that this was a dream and I would wake up soon.

The next morning Tory called me and said she and the family were back from San Francisco. I told her that I wanted her to drive back to L.A. with me. She came over. AlmaFaye and I talked one last time and promised that we would stick closer and closer, because we are all we got. I went to Mamma's house and said goodbye to the kids and Mr. Calvin. I wished him well the best way I could in spite of the pain I know he caused my mother as well. I had not been in Mamma's house since Easter 1984. The window was there, but not Momma looking out of it and puffing on her cigarettes with her coffee, Canadian Mist, or V-8 juice sitting on the desk. It pained me. I stayed strong and showed no emotions. I kept telling myself you will have to do that later. Just keep being strong for the kids.

We traveled through the scenic grapevines. The peace I could be assured of each time I drove through. It was peaceful and so quiet. Six hours later, Tory and I made it back to Los Angeles. I dropped her off at home and went in for a minute. I laid on the bed. She fixed me a cocktail and brought it to me. I knew I shouldn't be on her bed, and I had better get the hell out of there if I was going to go. I didn't go, I needed to be with her. I needed to feel her softness next to me.

I got up the next morning and left, going back to the restaurant. I apologized to Tory before I left. Tory was upset. She got mad at me for the first time and accused me of being confused and playing with her emotions. She told me I couldn't keep playing with her emotions. I apologized and told her I wouldn't do it anymore.

After I got back to the restaurant I called the landlord that was holding the apartment for me before Momma died. I let her know I was back in town and could proceed. She told me she still had the place and was saving it just for me. She was very sorry about my mother's death.

The following week I sent out invitations to the housewarming that Tory suggested that I do. Of course Tory volunteered to host it. I received lots of helpful gifts, from my friends. Tory bought me a stereo system, TV, microwave, and a papasana chair. My Daddy helped me bring over an entire bedroom set that was sold at a yard sale. I was surprised at him, but he told me it seemed like I was learning responsibilities.

By the time of my housewarming party my apartment was fully furnished. I felt so guilty that Tory was doing all this for me during my efforts to separate myself from her. She told me that she still loved me, and it really didn't matter if we were together or not. She would still do for me as if we were together.

Getting back into the swing of things with work and school was so hard to do at first. I kept getting mental blocks. Then the worst happened. I showed up for work one day and was fired. I was told the reason was because I wasn't doing a satisfactory job. I couldn't believe it. They couldn't be serious, but they were. I got my last check and went over to Tory's job. I was depressed. I still had money deals and dope deals that would clear a couple of thousand and could easily hold me over until I got another job. I didn't know how to handle this disappointment. I needed to talk to someone. I was feeling alone again and thought about Tory. God knows I didn't want to mess with her emotions and confuse her again. I called her and invited her to lunch. She was willing. As soon as I saw Tory I told her I could not help myself. I tried to stay away from her, and do the right thing. But I came to the conclusion that I needed to see her every now and then if it was okay with her. She asked me to explain exactly what I meant by that. I told her that when I get the urge to love her body, I need you to just give it to me and not reject me. Tory was shaking her head no. Her last words were she would always be there for me, no matter what.

GRADUATE FROM PARALEGAL SCHOOL
SEPTEMBER 1984

Graduation time from my paralegal classes finally came. It was very rewarding for many, but a bitter sweet accomplishment for me. It really didn't hold the value that I wanted it to now that Momma was gone. For a celebration gift, Tory knew I loved Michael Jackson, so she rented a limousine and coordinated with my sister Sharon, and we all went to the concert that weekend. It was awesome. We drank and made a toast in the backseat of the limo and thought we were the baddest dressed women in town.

ENROLL IN SOUTHWEST COLLEGE

Tory and I seriously decided to stop our relationship. We decided to just be friends and go back to college together to work on a degree. I was interested in theater, so I took beginning acting, speech and sociology. Tory took the same classes with me except for Sociology. I wanted to major in sociology and psychology, so one day I could help people who came from hurting backgrounds like myself. I would spend the night sometimes, because I could pick her up to go to school and drop her off at home. Sometimes I went in for a drink and decided I was too tired to go home. We would lay together, but I was still trying to keep my word and not touch her. As we went on, I stopped fooling and lying to myself. I was utterly miserable not being able to love Tory. She was unhappy too. I talked to God and told him, this is too hard for me to bear. I have tried to turn away from this, but I can't. I will have to go to hell because this is one thing that I can't kick. I began to question God.

> "Why, God, is the very thing that makes me feel
> good, wrong? Why God, is it that the only person
> who has ever accepted me for me, I can't have?
> Why, God? Why is this so wrong? It's love. Why is

loving this woman so wrong? She loves me like no
one else has ever loved me. She takes care of me and
does everything I want her to."

I paced my apartment, looking at the door which bore a cross
imprint. I had not noticed that before. I was angry. What do I
do? Just saying no was not working. I began to cry. It's not
working. I wanted to please God so much. I wanted to do right,
but didn't find the power to do it. I had increased my smoking to
three packs of cigarettes a day, just like my mother before she died.

I called Tory and told her this was the last time I am changing my
mind. I told her I am going to have to go to hell with this sin.
Tory was happy again and so was I.

Things started looking up for me. I interviewed at a few firms and
finally accepted a job offer. Our weekdays consisted of work (nine
to five) and school. We had little time to eat, but Tory would make
sure dinner was ready by the time I got home. If we had to take a
plate with us, she would feed me on the way to school in the car. It
was so much fun again. Our classmates began to look at us in
peculiar ways. When I talked to her I said, baby this, or honey that.

At school, we discovered that we were being watched. It was fun.
People tripped, we laughed and went on. We were two gay happy
people once again. The fast money kept rolling in, and we kept
shopping. It was so much fun to not think about how much money
you are spending. We decided to take a trip to Fresno, so we
packed up and drove in Tory's new car. She bought a Dodge
Daytona, cash! It was gold and beautiful. We drove up to Fresno,
bragging and showing off our stuff. Sometimes we would forget
and walk down the school corridors holding hands.

The first house we went to was AlmaFaye's. She was so happy to
see us. Later that evening, we went by my mother's house to see the
kids. Mr. Calvin was there. I had called Mr. Calvin a couple of
times since Momma died just to touch base and say hi. I wanted to

let him know I was thinking of him and my brothers and sisters. He seemed appreciative each time and was concerned about me as well. While I was at the house, Mr. Calvin got his camera out and took pictures of me and Tory. He knew Tory was my woman. He heard Momma talk about my lifestyle, I'm sure. Anyway, I asked him the big question. Could the kids come down to L.A. for Christmas? He said, yes. I knew it was a miracle, because Momma would never let the kids go anywhere. Just like she did me when I was young, unless you caught her on a sho' nuff good day. So I was happy about that and looked forward to the following months. I gave them money and went back to AlmaFaye's for the evening. The next day we would go back to Los Angeles.

CHRISTMAS SHOPPING - 1984

This year was certainly going to be different than any Christmas I ever had. We had thousands of dollars and every credit card you thought you wanted. We spent over six thousand dollars on gifts for her nieces (that came down to visit her for the holidays) and my sisters and brothers. We bought what we wanted and for who we wanted. My sisters and brothers came down this year and I spoiled them with everything I could think of. That was a memorable Christmas for us all. The kids returned home very happy. I even sent a couple of gifts for Mr. Calvin back with them.

CHAPTER 45

HAPPY NEW YEAR'S -1985

I had lots of things on my mind for resolutions. The very issue of resolutions was to get right with God for me. The issue of my lifestyle had been pressuring me endlessly as always. I hated the tugging at my insides. I thought I had effectively buried and smothered it through my constant partying, spending, vacationing, and drinking. So I had another conversation with Tory. I asked her to give me some room. She was pissed.

"Look, take all the damn room you need. I'm finished with this roller coaster ride with you," she said.

This time Tory didn't wait around for me to change my mind and come crawling back when my jones hit me. I had heard through my friend Ronnie that she saw her at the club with somebody else. I couldn't believe it. I wouldn't believe it until I saw it for myself!

The next weekend I went out with Ronnie. And sure enough, Tory was there and with somebody. I couldn't believe my eyes. My heart dropped. She saw me and kept entertaining her date at her table. Then she danced a few dances with her. I couldn't move, I watched her most of the night. Ronnie was playing and teasing me.

"Jody's got your girl and gone."

I told her it was cool with me. She needs somebody that wants her. I ordered drinks until I couldn't drink anymore. Ronnie had to carry me to the car.

The beginning of the year was quietly and solemn for me. I didn't want to celebrate birthdays, Easter, Mother's Day or even think about June 15 (the day My mother died). Instead, on all of those days I got pissy drunk and made sure I fell out.

ENROLL IN SCHOOL
MR. LAWSON INQUIRES ABOUT ME
(SEPTEMBER 1985)

The fall semester had begun, and I was determined to continue on no matter what. I called Tory, after not hearing from her for a couple of months, to see if she was returning for the school year and if she wanted to take some classes together. She politely told me no it would be too painful for her. I said I understood and hung up the phone. The knife of her going on with her life went so deep inside me, but I knew it was for the best.

So I went back to school by myself. I took up Speech II, Sociology, Theater, and English. My teachers remembered me from the last semester, and made me feel real good. In particular, I enjoyed my Sociology and Speech classes. I loved learning about other cultures and people. I had been desiring to return to speech course to break my shyness.

Tory always said I wasn't shy but, I thought I was! My Speech teacher's name was Mr. Lawson.
        "Where is your friend from last semester?" he asked
        me.

I told him that she decided not to come back this semester. I didn't know if he was trying to hit on me or her. I was very leery of men and their inquiries.
        "Was that your sister?" he asked.
        "No sir, she was my lover!"
        "What did you say?" He was shocked!
        "I said, my lover."

It never bothered me to tell him or anyone for that matter. Mr. Lawson was shocked and I could tell he was quite curious about this lover business. As the semester went on he wanted to talk more, so he asked if he could call me. I made it clear to him that I didn't mess around and reluctantly consented to him calling me.

In our first conversation on the phone, he told me that he was a minister, and I was happy with that. I wondered what he wanted to talk about if he was a minister. He then asked me about fulfillment with another woman. I thought he was being some pervert and wanted gory details of our intimacy. I told him it was unexplainable and that he would just have to be a woman to understand. He laughed.

"Carla, I can't even begin to see what a woman can give another woman."

"First of all, Mr. Lawson, a woman knows what another woman needs. She knows her body inside out. She knows where the nerves and spots are. She takes out time to find out. The touch, the patience, nurturing affection and empathy for what we go through."

"Men don't care about finding out what pleases a woman and her needs. In fact, they get offended when you try to tell them about your uniqueness. They think all women are the same and their needs are the same."

"Well, I have to come to my brother's defense, not all men are selfish and inattentive, Carla."

"Bulls----, oops, I'm sorry."

I apologized because I remembered he was a minister.

"All I am trying to say is that Men don't understand what it means to be gentle, patient, and attentive. They are selfish and only desire to get their needs met and the hell if you get yours or not."

I kept slipping with my vulgar tongue, and I tried to catch myself. He laughed again.

"It seems like you have been hurt by men."

"A lot of men," I said.

"Is that why you choose to be with women?"

"Maybe I happen to prefer them over men."

I didn't tell him of the struggle I was having with the conviction in my heart about women. I was too far into my defense and standing my grounds for a woman's affection and fulfillment. He changed the subject quickly and told me that ever since he talked with me in the hallway, the Lord has been laying me on his heart to pray for, especially after he learned of my relationship with Tory.

"Well, thank you for your prayers Mr. Lawson.

That's very kind of you.

"We all need prayers," I told him.

I tried to move beyond the weird unsettling feeling that was coming over me. It felt like I wanted to cry for no reason at all when he talked about prayer.

"I have to go now, but I will see you in class next week."

"Yes, you will, have a good night."

We hung up and boy, my heart was beating so fast.

I was now sitting in the back of the class at school. I would be the first one out of the door, so that I didn't have to talk with Mr. Lawson. I didn't want to be faced with confrontations of my lifestyle.

Even though I dodged him in class I couldn't dodge his calls when he would catch me at home. Now he would call and ask if he could just have a word of prayer with me. How do you tell a man of God no, don't pray for me. It would be like telling God, I don't need You. I would let him pray and I would listen. Each time he would pray for me, my face would be tore up with tears. I tried not to let him know how deeply I was being touched by his prayers.

I spent a lot of time all alone these days. I worked, came home, went to school, and to the liquor store to pick up a pint of Gin and Coke. Sometimes I'd pick up a bag of weed. I would go out to the club to listen to music and dance. My two escapes outside of women, were listening to music and losing myself in dancing. I could dance for three to four hours straight and order more drinks to get my blood running again. This continued week after week. I soon met new friends and new women that wanted to get involved with me. I resisted any kind of commitment to any other woman, but enjoyed the flirtatious passes. I'd rather do that than mess with Tory's mind.

One night while I was at the club, I ran into Tory. She told me she had one thing to tell me. I stepped outside to let her say whatever she wanted to say.

"You could have simply been honest about not
   wanting to be with me."
"What are you talking about?"
"If you are trying to get your life together with God,
   what are you doing out at clubs all the time?"
"Tory, I come out for a drink, or to dance for relief."
"Yeah, right, I see you in these girls' faces too.
"Tory, they're coming to me if you notice."
"Look, I just wanted you to know. I'm not a fool,
   though I may look like one."

I tried to explain that I was being honest. I was not involved with anyone and still in love with her. I was just out having a good time.

"Well, if you're not here with nobody else, then let
   me come home with you tonight."
"Tory, please, don't even try that."
"See, I knew it, you must have something to hide."
"No I don't."
"Well, how come I can't just come over? I can't drive
   all the way home."
"Fine, Tory, if you need to sleep over, you can but
   that's it."

She came over to spend the night. Tory's behavior had changed, from this low keyed caring woman, to this feisty pushy person. She was smoking a lot of cigarettes too.

The next morning I was awakened by the phone. The voice on the other end said, hi Carla.

"Hi, how are you?"

I recognized that Mr. Lawson, minister man. He said, "The Lord put you on my heart and I wanted to know if I can pray with you this morning?"

"Yeah, please do that for me. I need prayer real bad," I said.

He prayed for me in a special way. He covered every ground concerning me, my lifestyle and my future. I had never heard a prayer like this. It brought tears to my eyes. I felt so much better after he prayed too.

Before he got off the phone he invited me to his church.

"One of these fourth Sundays you ought to come visit my church on youth day."

"I will one day, Mr. Lawson. I don't want to make you a promise, but one day I will."

I got off the phone and Tory turned over and asked who I was talking to. I told her Mr. Lawson, my school teacher. She remembered him from last semester.

"Is he a preacher?"

"Yeah, and he's been preaching to me every time he gets a chance."

"He knows about you and me."

After a couple of weeks of him calling me because as he says, "the Lord placed me on his heart," he became a pest. I made the mistake of telling him one day that I knew God wasn't pleased with my lifestyle and that I just didn't know how to give it up. From that moment on, I regretted that I told him. That's all he would talk about. He would pray so much on the phone with me. I didn't mind it, but I got kind of weird feelings when he began to start binding up spirits and loosing stuff. He would holler out the spirit of bondage, the spirit of fear, the spirit of lust, the spirit of homosexuality, the spirit of anger, and the spirit of bitterness. Sometimes when he would finish praying, I could feel the depth of his sincerity in wanting me free from all that had me bound and to know his Jesus. Before Mr. Lawson got off the phone, he said he had something to ask me. I told him to go ahead.

"Will you go out to get a bite to eat with me one evening?"

"I don't know about that," I told him.

"It will be harmless," he defended.

"Just to change atmosphere and to get to know each other."

"Like where?" I asked.

"Maybe out to Santa Monica."

Hum, I thought to myself, "I guess it will be all right."

"I promise I am a perfect gentleman."

"Alright, we will see. If not, I'm turning you in to the school board." We laughed.

From that night with Tory, she started getting real pushy. She continued to refuse to believe that I was struggling with trying to get out of the life. Especially, after she would catch me always in some woman's face at the club. So, she would show up at my door step anytime she felt like it and would come in with her key that she still had. She no longer had any respect for me wanting to "change," as I would call it. As the weeks went by, I still found myself hurting for the presence of my mother and mourning her death. It seemed like Tory would always call or show up during those dark times. I was drinking more and more, to the point I had to have a drink by a certain time of day. Then the cigarettes were increasing like a chain. I felt just like my mother. I woke up many mornings with the same cigarette I fell asleep with still between my fingers. My health started failing me. I felt myself deteriorating and getting mentally and emotionally worse. I started experiencing severe chest pains, to the point I had to go to emergency room at least twice a month, then it increased even more. Each time would scare the living hell out of me. It felt like I was having a heart attack. Eventually doctors placed a seventy-two-hour heart monitor on me. It was designed to curtail my chain smoking. Instead I smoked more than the three packs a day that I was gradually surpassing. The fear gripped me, and I thought many times that I would die. The findings of the medical heart report were serious. My doctor told me that he was not going to beat around the bush. I was in critical condition. My pressure was low. My emotional state was chaotic. He warned me that if I didn't stop smoking, I would surely die.

"You mean cut down, right?" I asked the doctor.
"No, I mean stop! It's killing you."

I had to call Tory after that report. I didn't know where else to run. She came over with dinner that she had prepared. She knew I was scared and needed a friend. She spent the night and held me. That night turned into many more nights with Tory. I was right back in my guilty and confused state of mind.

It appeared that each weekend that I would allow Tory to stay, Mr. Lawson would call that next morning. The times she didn't spend the night, he wouldn't call. It was almost like he was spying on my house. Of course when he called, he wanted to pray. I would sit straight up in the bed and listen to him as he prayed for me while Tory laid next to me. The last time he called he reminded me about going to get a bite to eat. I tried to give him a hard time about it, but he held me to my word.

"Look, Carla, I enjoy talking with you and you are a nice person. I just wanted to treat you to dinner if that was all right."
I hesitated and reluctantly said, fine.
"When do you want to do it?"
"Next Friday," he said.
"That soon," I blurted out.

I woke up Tory. I placed my finger up to my mouth to ask her to not say anything. He asked if we could pray before getting off the phone. I hung up the phone and grabbed a cigarette. Tory asked who I was speaking with, grabbing for her robe.

"You remember Mr. Lawson in our speech class, don't you?" I said.

"Yeah, the black man with the Jheri Curl that was praying for you the last time I was here."

"Right."

I was nervous for some reason. I didn't want to tell her he invited me to dinner, because I didn't want her to get the wrong idea.

"Does he like you?" she asked.

"Hell nah, he probably wants me to be one of those saved girls."

Tory was silent and went to the bathroom to get dressed.

That entire week leading up to that Friday was filled with anxiety. I didn't know what to do or expect. I couldn't wait until it came and went. I asked myself all week, why did I say yes to this crazy invitation.

I asked myself a thousand questions of what to do. Do I put on heels or loafers? Should I dress like my studdish ways with my blazer, dress shirt, slacks and loafers? This was the most nervous evening I had spent trying to get ready that I can ever remember. I didn't know if I should wear a dress or pants. I didn't know if I would put on make up or go natural, put on lipstick or lip gloss. I didn't know what to do! I paced the floors and became so frustrated. I had not been out with a guy in so long, I wasn't even sure how to act. I cried. I got frustrated and grabbed my white Levi jeans and a pullover red sweater with black semi heels. I thought it would not send a mixed message of any kind. I waited for him to knock at the door.

When he finally got there, I rushed out to meet him at the door. He said hello, and I said, hi.

"I'm very hungry. Let's just go."

He said okay, turned around and went back downstairs to the car. He opened my door, and it made me feel so awkward. I thought to myself, I did that kind of stuff for my woman and how dare he insult me that way! But I just got into the car without looking at him! When I finally decided to look his way, he looked nice and casual, and smelled very good. I didn't tell him that. He drove us to the Seafood House in Santa Monica. The place was nice and I had fun.

We talked about each other's likes and dislikes. He enjoyed singing, preaching, reading, and church. I learned that he was working on an album, one of his dreams. He came a medium size family with two loving parents, as he puts it. I envied that. He asked me things about myself, but never brought up my lifestyle, as he had agreed. I didn't even want to talk about my family, at least not now. I decided to skip mine and kept asking questions about his.

Finally, he got around to asking me again to come to his church on Youth Sunday. I told him I'm coming one day, really. Mr. Lawson was a pleasant man to be with if I had to say so myself. I found him to be very sincere and without ulterior motives. I had not met a man like that before. He was almost attractive to me, but I made sure I would curse that thought every time it tried to surface. I told him he was my guardian angel sent by God to prick my conscience, and I appreciate him and his prayers for me. He was appreciative of my words. He asked me what type of hobbies I had. I told him, I loved to dance, sing, play Bid Wisk, and shoot pool.

"Pool?" he asked.

"Yeah, can you shoot?"

"Well, not anymore. I used to."

"Oh, church people don't shoot pool?" I asked him.

"Well, I just haven't had time to lately."

I laughed and said, "Yeah, right."

It was getting late and about time to go. Mr. Lawson paid the check and escorted me back to the car. When we pulled up to the apartment, he got out to open my door. I felt so weird. I felt like a punk for some strange reason. I even felt embarrassingly vulnerable somehow. I was subject to the reality of myself as a woman being in this man's presence who smelled so good and looked good too. I certainly didn't tell him every time I thought about it. He kindly walked me upstairs to the door and turned back around to go to his car.

"Thank you and see you at school next week."
"Remember to study for your test and have your
   speech prepared." I laughed.
"I will and I won't even expect any special treatment."

I went in and my butterflies finally settled to the point that I didn't have a log in my throat anymore. The night was so great. I made up in my mind that I would never go out with him again. He was nice, but I had to fight too many thoughts and feelings as I sat in that good-smelling man's presence. Then I thought about the special man he had been to me. All he ever wanted to do was pray for me. The thought brought tears to my eyes. We had many conversations about salvation and his relationship with Jesus. He once said to me before he prayed, that being saved is not about going to church. It was about a relationship with the man Jesus Christ. I thought about that. I got up, got me a drink and went to sleep.

Mr. Lawson and I went on many more casual outings back to back, which continued to make me very nervous, yet closer to God in a weird way. He suggested that I call him by his first name, Melvin, when we were away from school.

"You can call me Mr. Lawson on campus and
   Melvin off campus, okay?"
"Sure, and you can call me Carla at school and
   Ms. Carla out of school." We laughed.
I started enjoying the refreshing conversations of how much Jesus

loved me. When I was out of Mr. Lawson's sight, my struggle with my gay lifestyle really was tormenting me. I was always thinking of God and really wanting to please him. The pressure was getting so unbearable. To make matters even more complicated, I also noticed an attraction growing toward Mr. Lawson that I didn't know what to do with. Of course, I knew I could never tell him. He was so nice and caring. The best I could do with those thoughts is pray to God that if he ever changed me to be a normal woman, to give me a man just like Mr. Lawson, if not Mr. Lawson himself.

The last time I saw Mr. Lawson during that school year, I noticed I had reverted back to my normal, distant, serious demeanor, as if to turn him away from approaching me and inviting me to dinner and lunch. It didn't work, because before he let out class before the Christmas break, he had one last invitation for the year. He asked me to think about coming to church for Youth Sunday on Christmas. He told me I would love it. I told him I would think about it, but not to be disappointed if the next time he saw me was after Christmas break. He smiled and said, "You know you are in my prayers always." Lord knows I knew that without any doubts.

A couple of weeks after school was out I had an aching desire to party and get sloppy drunk. I called Ronnie and asked her if she and her lover wanted to go partying with me. She said they would meet me at the club. I called Tory and asked her if she wanted to go. She said yes. I told her that Ronnie would pick her up and we would all meet at the club. It only made sense, because Ronnie lived closer to Tory than I did. After arriving at the club that night, I found myself looking out at the crowd and drinking on my Margarita. The music was the same, loud and drowning you out to the point you could not hear yourself think. The people were still the same (wild, loose, drunk, high, and out of their minds). The drinks were still rotating a hundred miles an hour. But still, something was significantly different. I still drank as much as I did before, and was still maintaining my chain smoking. Ronnie, Valerie, and Tory had arrived and took seats downstairs in a corner. I couldn't even sit with them for some reason. I just was not feeling my usual self. I went to the table and spoke to them, then I told Ronnie and them that I was going to walk upstairs for a moment to the pool table and would be back. I walked up the stairs and stood near the ramp which overlooked all of the Ruby's Room.

The smoke was rising to the top of the ceiling. The screams from the crowd were rising also. The special effect lights were racing up and down the walls. I saw a darkness over the club that I had never seen before. I heard a soft voice saying to me, "You are in the den of the pit of hell, Daughter, it's time to come home."

The most grotesque feeling came over me. I knew without a shadow of a doubt that was the Spirit of God speaking to me. I felt like I wanted to throw up. I knew I had to leave. I had to go away from this place right now. No matter how drunk I was, the voice was clear! But, I had to tell Ronnie, even though I wasn't sure if I could stand being in there a second longer. Ronnie was coming my way, thank God.

"Man, I got to go. I'm getting sick," I told her.
I turned and left.
I heard her hollering, "That's what you get for
drinking with no food on your stomach."

She started laughing at me. I didn't care what she had to say. It wasn't food! It was sickening as hell. And I saw myself in the midst of it. I ran to my car and started it up. I drove off fast. I went down Crenshaw Blvd. like a "bat out of hell." I was drunk. I ran up the stairs to my door with tears running down my face. In a weird way felt like I was running from someone or something. I went straight to my bedroom and fell on the bed.

"God, please take it away. I want to change, but you
have to change me. God, I can't change myself.
You have to do it. God, I can't. Please save me, !
from myself! I'm so tired of this confusion," I
screamed.

Those were the only words I could utter out of my soul. That night

I cried for hours. Finally, catching my breath, I thought about my Momma and how I wished I could hear her voice. But Momma was gone. I couldn't call her anymore. I got angry, because I needed her so badly.

> I found myself screaming at her "How come you're
> not here? And why in the hell did you leave me now?"
> My voice quieted.
> "Momma I need you so much," I whispered.

Suddenly, I felt my bed shaking. I noticed that nothing else was shaking in the room. It shook for about seven seconds. I looked around the room, and nothing else was moving. Then Mr. Lawson popped in my mind, and I grabbed the phone. Melvin answered the phone, he was asleep. I told him I knew it was time for me to change, and I was ready.

> "I want to be what God wants me to be, but I can't
> do it on my own. I need some kind of help."
> He told me God never required that I change
> myself, but that I submit my life to Him and He
> would do the changing. I listened intently.
> "Carla, I am here and will be here for you. Okay?"
> "Yes," I said.

He then said, "But Jesus is always at hand. As you get to know Him you will know that you are never alone." I was crying harder.

> "Okay." My voice was still trembling.
> "Carla, Jesus suffered for you that you might be
> saved from your sins and darkness. He has been
> drawing you to himself believe it or not all this
> time."

Then, he said "Let's have a word of prayer." After the prayer, I thanked him and told him that he would see me tomorrow morning at his church. The next day was Christmas. Mr. Lawson let me know that he was preaching tomorrow. He gave me the name and address and I wrote it down. I told him how thankful I was that he hung in there with me and never gave up on me.

"It was a joy watching God draw his Daughter to himself,
he told me.
"One day you will be doing the same thing I've done for
you. Carla, believe it or not, there are so many young ladies
out there just like you. You are not along."
I thought to myself, it felt like I had been along all these
years, but maybe not.

I hung up the phone and looked to the ceiling where the cross was imprinted in the corner of my room, and I thanked God for always being with me and sending me a true friend in Mr. Lawson. I smiled at the fact that I would be in church the next morning at the New Hope Baptist Church to hear my professor preach. I looked at the clock and realized I had only three hours to sleep before I would have to get for church.

CHAPTER 46

A New Day - Christmas Sunday
(DECEMBER 1985)

The next morning the sun was shining through my window. I woke
up with a smile on my face. I had not slept so peaceful for as long
as I could remember. Today was going to be a great day! I knew
it. I couldn't explain it. I guess if I had to give it a name I would
call it leaps and bounds of joy, and great expectations. I was
looking forward to being in the house of God. I tried to get
dressed, and my phone was ringing. I knew it was probably Tory
or Ronnie, but I couldn't answer it. I was on my way to God's
house. I made up in my mind that I wasn't going to let nothing
interrupt or stop me anymore, I was on my way to God's house.

As I drove the streets I turned on the radio station and they were
playing Gospel Music. I heard a woman singing the last part of
"Amazing Grace." Then I began to sing it to myself like I heard
Aretha Franklin sing it, and I heard Grandma Georgia who used to
baby-sit me. I made my way directly to 5900 S. Central to New
Hope Baptist Church. As I walked through the doors I was met by
a smiling usher who showed me to an available row near the front. I
saw Rev. Lawson sitting in the pulpit. He acknowledged my
presence by a subtle nod. The feeling of being in that place was
awesome. It felt like a real church. It felt like God was there.
After the announcements the choir got up to sing.

As I sat there the words that the young woman was singing were
awesome. It was called "I Will Wear A Crown." She had to be
about twenty-one years old and her voice was simply beautiful.
Her face was bright and soft. She reminded me of an Angel. As I
watched her I could tell this song was real to her. She sang with
such conviction. Someone yelled out "Sing, Thely," I guess that was
her name. The song moved me. By now, chills raced through my
body. Emotions erupted inside me. Trying hard to fight back
tears, I was a running faucet whose pipes were about to explode.
The words she sang went to the depths of my soul. She kept saying

when it's all over she would wear a crown. I said to myself, "I guess life's troubles, heartaches, pain, and injustices, are over."

After she finished, the congregation was caught up "in the spirit" and some were softly crying to themselves, waving their hands in the air. Rev. Lawson stood and made his way to the podium. Despite his controlled demeanor, you could tell he was also moved. Rev. Lawson was always dressed smart. This morning he was draped in a dark navy suit with a matching tie. His shoes were dark and shining. And he proved to be just as dynamic preaching the Gospel as he was in his speech class. He opened with a powerful prayer.

After the prayer, I looked at him and smiled. This is the man I thought was trying to flirt with me. Little did I know this man was on an assignment from heaven to see about my soul. And now here I sit in his church about to hear him preach God's Word. I couldn't believe it.

The room filled with Amens and Hallelujahs as he spoke with power. He talked about what Christ had given us in life. He asked us what shall we give such a gracious Christ who has given His life that we might be saved eternally? His sermon was powerful. There were times his words pricked my very soul to tears as he talked about the undying love of Christ and the forgiveness of our sins. How Christ identifies with our pain, but now we can find healing and salvation through His blood. The message was not long, but direct and clear. God came to save the world for their sins through sending his son Jesus Christ! And Christ came to set free, forgive, and feed his people with truth in the inward parts of their beings. Then without warning, Mr. Lawson extended the altar call to accept Christ as your personal savior and have a personal relationship with Him. I remembered he told me last night on the phone what the difference was between having a relationship with Jesus and being a Sunday church goer. I wanted this relationship so bad. I wanted to know Him. I was scared.

People started responding to the call by coming down the aisle. The choir was singing "Come To Jesus While You Still Have Time." The congregation was clapping and praising God as people came forth. Young people, middle-aged people, and old people were coming down. Every now and then Rev. Lawson's eyes would catch mine looking. I was sitting there, tears rolling down my face. For some reason my legs felt like lead. I wanted to get up and run, but I felt paralyzed. The butterflies in my stomach were heavy. Then I got scared. Questions were flooding my mind. Would God really forgive me? Could He really make the pain and hurt go away? Could He really forget all the wrong and sin I've done? Could He change my lifestyle into what He wanted me to be? Then the hardest question. Could He clean me white as snow as the preacher was saying? I felt so dirty. I tried a million times to get myself right.

Then I heard a soft voice saying "Come to me." I knew it was God. I knew it! I got up out of my seat, making my way toward the altar. When I got to the end, Rev. Lawson met me, and I fell in his arms. He stopped the altar call long enough to tell the congregation that I was one of his students that he had been praying for, for some time. They clapped and praised God! One of the altar workers ushered me to the side where the others were standing and gave me some tissue to wipe my face. Rev. Lawson continued with the altar call. More people were coming up. I made it! I made it! I kept telling myself, I made it. I couldn't describe the feeling I felt as I stood there. It was a special place where I stood. I guess I would have to describe it in one word. Safe! I felt safe for the first time in my entire life. Just like the childhood game of "Hide and Seek." I got to the base in time and I was now safe. No more hiding and looking over my shoulders! I was on base and I was safe. Nothing could turn me around. The fast money couldn't lure me back, the guilt and shame that kept me bound to my lifestyle of lesbianism had lost its powerful grip. God was calling me, and it was strong. He was calling me to live for and with him. I felt as if I had been running in a race all my life, and as I arrived at the finish line I discovered I had not lost the race, but rather I had ran right into the arms of the winner who had run the race for me. Jesus Christ! I knew it was different this time.

Then Rev. Lawson came over and hugged me real tight. He continued the altar call for others to come and many others came. After he shook hands with everyone that came down, he asked each person for any comments. When he got to me he gave me the microphone. I nervously thanked God for His mercy and for waiting on me to come to Him. I thanked God for not closing His door. He asked if I had a prayer request. I asked him to pray that I would stop smoking three packs of cigarettes a day, and that I would have the right desires in my life. He knew exactly what I meant! I thanked God again and gave him the microphone back. I was saved from all of it.

When he walked to the next person, stages of my life flashed in front of me. How as a child, I was abandoned many times by my mother into the hands of strangers in many cases. I thought about the many sexual violations and rapes that seemed to never stop. The disappointments and deceptions about my Daddy, and then the rejection of my Daddy once I met him. But God still loved me. I thought about trying to lose my pain in drinking, smoking, and sex, and not being able to destroy the pain that lurked over my head daily. The wishes and yearning for love that never seemed to be fulfilled. But God still loved me. Life was one uncertain road after another, filled with a tug-of-war of experiences. But that day, I felt so safe. I felt I was in the arms of God forever!.

Rev. Lawson was waiting in the hallway when I walked out of the counseling room. He had a great big smile on his face.
"Carla, I just want to congratulate you again for
making the most important decision you will
ever make in life"
"Mr. Lawson, I mean Rev. Lawson, thank you for
doing what God sent you into my life to do.
Save me, through your words."

I didn't want to start crying again, but I did. He hugged me and told me he would be checking on me. I nodded and thanked him for not giving up on me and doing only what God assigned him to do for my life.

Almost every step I made, going to the car, I was interrupted by members greeting me with hugs and smiles. One of the young ladies in the choir gave me a big hug and said "Welcome to the new family. My name is Judy. If you need anything, please let us know."

This was indeed the best day of my life. As I drove I thought about my family in Fresno, and then I thought about how proud my mother would have been to see my life turning in another direction. I knew inside somehow, someway, she would be so proud of me. Then I thought, well since I never got the chance to physically bring her home with me, I will spiritually bring her home in my heart. Knowing she will always be with me, smiling at me.

I noticed I had been in such deep thought and excitement that I went the wrong way on Central Avenue. Instead of going north, I went south. I didn't care, because for the first time since I could remember, no one was waiting for me -- not Tory, not Ronnie, or any other woman. I felt free to do whatever I wanted to do.

I turned right at the next intersection, which was Imperial Highway, heading east toward the airport. There were a few families on the top of the hill. A little white poodle running from a smile child caught my attention. The child seemed so happy with her little dog. Not far from the child were two adults sitting on a blanket, looking up toward the airport. I never noticed this place before. The adults were watching the planes take off. Then I realized there were other adults watching the planes take off too.

I decided to pull over. As soon as I made the right turn there was a parking space. I got out of the car. The weather was beautiful. I stood at the bottom of the hill right near a ramp. Music was playing loudly from one of the families at the top of the hill. I could tell they were playing the same station I had on in the car. I could hear the radio announcer saying the call letters, 102.3 KJLH. I felt a longing to play with that little girl and her dog. They brought back precious memories of Blacky.

The planes seemed to be flying so close, almost close enough to touch. Fresno was the last place I watched planes take off. I didn't know Los Angeles had a special place where you could actually come and watch them take off too. It was so cool.

I wanted to walk up the hillside to watch at least one plane take off. Before I knew it I was making my way up the walkway, holding onto the metal rail. Suddenly, I felt a sharp pain, like a cut on my finger. I discovered I had grabbed hold of a loose fence wire, that was wrapped around the rail. It hurt so bad I wanted to cuss, but I remembered how good I felt coming from God's House. And plus, I knew the scar would eventually heal, just like all the others.

Perspectives

D̲r. C̲lyde O̲den, J̲r.
President and Chief Executive Officer
WATTS Health Foundation, Inc. — Los Angeles, California
Senior Pastor
Holy Trinity A.M.E. Church — Long Beach, California

It is rare to have a front row seat in which one can view the drama of a person's life, and then read about it in a book. My views come from observing the life of Candace Cole over the last fifteen years, which in terms of the accounts in SCARs, is much later in her life and yet it is this later view that gives such a powerful perspective about redemption, reclamation, reconciliation and liberation.

I met Candace Cole at a point in which she was searching for a safe place in which to express the messages God was placing in her heart. She had felt a call on her life to preach the Gospel of Jesus Christ, but her previous church did *not* believe in woman preachers. At that point, she didn't say she definitely wanted to preach, but she knew she had something to say and her soul needed a safe place to say it. She joined Ward African Methodist Episcopal Church in Los Angeles, and at that time I was teaching a class for new members.

Fast forward to several years later, when Sister Candace Cole began her official journey to become *Reverend* Candace Cole. By then she had written several plays, and her spirit was soaring and she wanted to do more and say more about the redemptive and liberating power of Jesus Christ. It was at that time she shared with me her first version of SCARS. Rev. Cole had the courage to put on paper what she could not voice from the pulpit — a life of ups and downs, a life of pain and sufferings, and a life of experiences that made this man cry, when I grasp the depths of her life's journey.

You should know that after reading SCARS and discussing that first draft with Rev. Cole I encouraged her NOT to publish the book. It had little to do with the contents per se. I knew the postscript of the story and it was important for the reader to know that the book would not be a tragic story, but actually a story of triumph. However, if the subsequent victories were not revealed, the price of the journey Rev. Cole took would be *under-* appreciated by most readers. But Rev. Cole insisted that her story had to be told.

As God would have it, SCARS was being revised and refined, and other messages that had been imprinted in Rev. Cole's spirit were also being written, performed and published. Rev. Cole's plays were tremendous successes here in Southern California. And her books, <u>Daughter There Is More To You Than Meets The Eye</u> and <u>Lamentations of a Child</u>, have been wonderfully received, by persons inside and outside of the Church. The timing is now right for SCARS to emerge.

The journey of Rev. Cole is more than pain and pathos -- it is more than tribulation and tales of woes. It is ultimately a story of triumph and liberation. The courage to tell her story allows for other women and men to tell their stories and to understand that their *"Scars"* do not have to be the end of their stories. Life is often cruel, and has its twists and turns and disappointments. Yet God, through the power of the Holy Spirit, can not only heal, but also restore.

In an interesting way, Jabez, the biblical character found in 1st Chronicles, Chapter 4 has his story of "scars" told in just three verses. Verse 9 and 10 in that chapter and verse 55 of 1st Chronicles, Chapter 2. Jabez was born and his mother cursed the occasion of his birth by the name she gave him -- Jabez, "Because I bore *him* in pain." 1st Chronicles 9 (New King James version). Yet the Bible says that despite his scars and the curse of his name given to him by his mother, Jabez "was more honorable than his brothers ... Jabez had his own SCARS, and overcame.

Rev. Candace Cole overcame -- **that is the power of the story.**

Perspectives

Wendy Wise

What can I say about Candace Yvette Cole, my best friend. Candace has played a stupendous part in showing me how to deal with my issues as I walked closely with her during the writings of Scars. I experienced her pains, her shames, her regrets, her joys and still her hopes. Consequently, I too was faced with my dark past, which I tried so desperately to bury and forget. I learned courage to face my past through my relationship with Candace.

Out of all the underserved pain she has endured through her childhood I am most amazed at her strong will to love those that came short of loving her. That is one of the strongest virtues that she has, not holding grudges toward anyone. Candace is one of the most dedicated persons I know. Whatever task she finds herself involved with she does it with passion and the utmost of intergrity. Over the years I've learned to understand, accept, love, and appreciate this selfless woman. I have watched the countless sacrifices that she has made for others, even when it meant coming up short for herself at times. She displays so much humility that you'll say "what an ego".

Who is Candace Yvette Cole? She is a child of God, on a mission to help the helpless. She walks in her calling, unapoletigically.

I am honored and elated to have such a wonderful and sophisticated friend in my life.

Perspectives

Sheila Miller

*Our doubts are traitors, and makes us loose the good we oft might
win by fearing an attempt ... William Shakespeare*

I had the opportunity of meeting Candace Cole several years ago. I can
remember the impact of our first meeting. I was mesmerized by this small
woman, who exuded great strength.

During the years of our friendship we have shared many things. However, it
was not until she approached me with her desire to assist her with editing of
her book did I understand the depth of our friendship. When I read the
draft of Scars I was overwhelmed with sorrow. I could not believe that anyone
could experience such grave degradation and pain. After reading just a few
pages of the draft I can remember offering Candace every excuse possible for
not assisting her with the finalization. Although I rallied her courage to go
forward with this project, secretly I pondered how she could reveal to the
world her dark past. Both Candace and I were raised in small country like
settings. We were bought up by the old traditions that says "what goes on in
this house stays in this house." In pursuit of her healing, she chose to defy
those teachings and eventually moved forward with her book. I am so glad
that she did because her defiance not only meant deliverance for her, but we
all benefited from this courageous act to overcome the doubts.

About The Author

Candace Cole travels throughout the U.S. and Europe touching lives in conferences, revivals, workshops, retreats, in inner-city schools, juvenile facilities, group homes and on college campuses. She carries the message "there is abundant life after abuse." Her passion is found in her commitment to encourage both adult and children survivors of abuse.

Candace is an anointed vessel. Ordained by God to minister the gospel through the arts. Candace Cole is President/Founder of CCTP (Candace Cole Theatrical Production) as well as an acclaimed Playwright, and Producer. She is an award winning creator of theatrical musicals known throughout Southern California such as: "Busline 210", "My Child, My Child", "The Anointing", and "Where Shall My Shame Go?"

Academically, Candace is a graduate of MTI Theological School of Ministry, where she obtained her Bachelor's Degree. She is currently enrolled in Fuller Seminar pursuing a Master's of Divinity degree (M.Div), with a concentration in Counseling/Psychology.

Candace is no stranger to our Los Angeles Community as the Director and CEO of The Dare to Dream Scholarship Society Incorporated (a non-profit corporation). DTDSS is designed to assist "at-risk" students in achieving their academic and artistic goals.

Candace has served at her home church, as part of the teaching staff at Faithful Central Bible Church, ministering in the New Members Department. She also facilitates Women's Discipleship classes. She is a vessel of honor with the pen of a ready writer. A beacon of hope to men, women and children everywhere.

For additional information on having Candace Cole as a keynote speaker for your conferences, seminars, workshops or school assemblies, please call us or visit our website at:

www.candacecole.com

For those who wish to write letters to Candace Cole, please include a self-addressed stamped envelope and keep in mind that due to the large volume of letters we receive, we will not be able to answer every letter. But we sincerely thank you for your support.

Engagements & Events

If you are interested in more information regarding speaking engagements, workshops, or theatrical productions write or call us at:

Candace Cole Enterprises
ccpprod@Aol.com
(310) 821-8147

Order Form

Milligan Books
1425 West Manchester, Suite B,
Los Angeles, California 90047
(323) 750-3592

Mail Check or Money Order to:
Milligan Books

Name _____ Date _____

Address _____

City_____ State _____ Zip Code_____

Day telephone _____

Evening telephone_____

Book title _____

Number of books ordered ___ Total cost .... $ _____

Sales Taxes (CA Add 8%)   .... $ _____

Shipping & Handling $4.50per book......................$ _____

Total Amount Due... $ _____

_ Check   _ Money Order   Other Cards _____

_ Visa   _ Master Card   Expiration Date _____

Credit Card No. _____

Driver's License No. _____

Signature   Date